COME
ALONG
100

COME ALONG 100

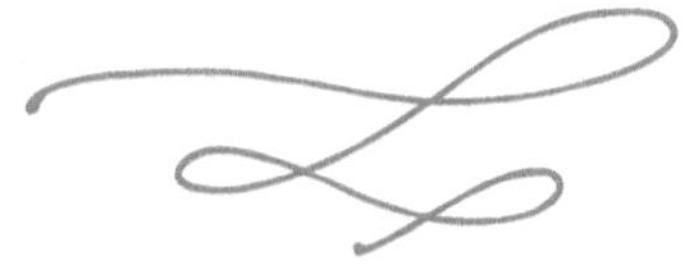

RUTH HERTZOG

ISBN 978-0-9898893-3-9

This book is a work of fiction. Names, characters, businesses, places, events, locales, and incidents are either the products of the author's imagination or used in a fictitious manner. Any resemblance to actual persons, living or dead, is purely coincidental.

Cover photos: top left, photo of young boy © Africa Studio / Adobe Stock; top right, photo of corn field © Fawkes Creative / Shutterstock.com; bottom photo of farm © John / Adobe Stock.

Book design by Cecile Kaufman.

CHAPTER ONE

Market Day

The brisk evening air had the feel of winter's first chill. The sharp breezes spurred members of the Heydt family to complete their daily assigned farm chores. Del, a ten-year-old blessed with a discerning mind, thought each day held the same boring routine. Not so today, although all her tasks would be completed by nightfall. She considered words like "definite," and "always," should be stricken from the spoken language. Circumstances forced a change of heart, of mind, and of plans.

This Wednesday was different from the rest of the week. Father left early in the morning, traveling to Philadelphia with Grandfather's sweet creamery butter, fresh eggs, poultry, and produce from neighboring farms. This had been Cecil's job, Grandfather's trusted employee, but he was injured in an accident and unable to work. Grandfather never operated a truck and considered himself too old to drive such newfangled contraptions that could not respond to his command like a team of horses. But a trip to Philly with body wagon or sleigh required more than one day. Stiffened with arthritis, Grandfather made arrangements for his son-in-law, Del's father, to make the market trip. For the time being Father was going to the big city using the train three miles away. Father had already completed two trips.

This day was also different when Fritz, a mutt with a head the size and distinct markings of a St. Bernard and a body like that of an over-sized German Shepherd, did not meet Del and Bill, her twin brother, at the dirt lane that marked the entrance to the Heydt homestead, also known as the "Y" farm. Del finished her task of throwing chopped cobs of corn to the pigs. She was always entertained by their greedy feeding. The noisy pigs would drop a half eaten cob of corn to grab the next cob that fell close by. They jostled and shoved one another for position at the feeding trough, yet quickly left all to chase an unwanted chicken from their pen with snapping mouths and loud grunts.

Del made long backward glances to the small open door on the barnbridge. The small door was cut into one of two large sliding barn-doors opening to the threshing floor. She kept a close watch on Fritz, so he wouldn't rush onto the threshing floor, which was off limits to him. Father would not allow Fritz or anyone else to enter that upper floor of the barn while work was being done, or any other time for safety reasons. No one, absolutely no one, was allowed on that heavy planked floor during chore times or any other time for fear of some-one falling through a trap door cut into the threshing floor, which was opened only to push forkfuls of straw to drop onto the cement floor below where it would be spread among the stalls and provide clean bedding for the animals. Father warned, "You look around carefully whenever you are there. Make sure you see the large metal ring used to lift the trap door laying on the floor. Then it is safe for you to be there." Father made sure all understood his directive.

Two weeks passed since Father shifted standard work routines when he traveled to Philly. "William," Father had said, "you are old enough to handle more responsibility. You help Tilghman with some heavier barn work. That means cleaning the stanchions, feeding and bedding for the cattle, and securing the barn for the night. Do you think you can handle that?"

"Sure can," Bill had replied.

Del was a little disappointed with Bill's eager response.

"Adelaide," Father turned and placed his hand on her shoulder, "I know you and William work very well together. I don't especially like breaking up a good team. I wouldn't do that to a trained team of horses, but then horses aren't people. Changes come and go as we grow older. Show Carol some of the lighter chores you handle. Teach her how to safely shell corn for the chickens. Make sure she lets the cob of corn to fall free into the hopper before turning the wheel to shell it. You'll still tend the pigs and help Gloria with some of her henhouse work. You will be on call to help your mother in the house whenever she needs you. Benj will be here on Wednesdays, and he'll see to it that you have chopped corn for the pigs. When it comes to slopping mash for the pigs see to it that you make the buckets only as full as you can handle. I think you can do that."

Del merely nodded her head.

She could visualize her father's clear blue eyes. She thought of her father's stern yet tender gaze as a chilled blast of air caused her to shiver. Oh well, she thought, this change is another one of those growing pains Uncle Sam was always teasing her about. Del liked her Uncle Sam and remembered his words. "How about those growing pains. I see you probably had some since I last was here. You are up to here now." He would measure her height and Bill's against his body. She remembered his repeated words. "Small hurts are soon outgrown and forgotten, its those that come later in life cause the greater hurts and problems." She did wonder about small and greater hurts.

Del felt the chore changes didn't seem so small as she went skipping down the lane that separated the house and yard from the barn. Benj was standing by the open front woodshed, its shape similar to shelters for horse and carriage, like those standing by the side of the hotel in town or the ones across the street from her church in the next village. The woodshed was the only building on the property that faced west and looked out upon all farm activity as it stood by the stonewall at the lower end of a closed-in barnyard. A watering trough fed by a spring stood along the inside wall. It's overflow fell into the small stream that flowed behind the woodshed and under a plank bridge marking the entrance to the Heydt homestead. The stream continued its flow, tumbling over rocks marking the edge of the front yard underneath cooling shade trees and a weeping willow tree.

Benj was waiting for Del. He made a large sweeping motion with his arm to bring her his way. No call necessary, he knew she'd come. Fritz ran ahead to where Benj was waiting and lay down in front of his feet. "*Schmarta hund* [Smart dog]," Benj would say when Fritz chose to stay close by. "Fritz beat ya here. He knows my job won't change. I found me a new buddy." Benj was amused. "*Seinah wee lung oss sell gade* [See how long that will last]." Del had grown up hearing adults speak the Pennsylvania Dutch language with English mixed in. The folks of Benj's generation spoke this unique dialect among their age group instead of English.

Fritz was called the half-breed. The twins were four years old when Grandfather brought the abandoned pup along home from the big city. They immediately accepted the pup and Fritz became a favorite pet and bodyguard. Fritz lay near Benj, who was not one to fuss with a dog or even bother to pet an animal. He was a talker. And talk to the children he did all the time. Fritz did not respond to his talk, or the occasional blast of colder air. Each gust just made Fritz open his mournful eyes and move them slowly from side to side as if the cold air was a nuisance. Del knew Fritz wanted nothing more than to be with both Bill and Del.

"Hello, birthday girl!" Benj always greeted Del in this manner. The woodshed was next to a huge rock that pressed against a tall oak, its roots nourished by the stream by the dirt lane that opened to the Y farm. The sturdy oak provided ample shade over the woodshed all day long, only allowing the late afternoon sun as it was sinking in the western sky. Benj's home was located at the outermost end of the east lane where it met the newly built cement pike that passed through the heart of the rural community.

"Hi," Del responded, though not too happily, despite her Mama's reminder to treat Benj kindly.

"Well, looky here! Do we have another Fritz? One unhappy like the other. Ya must get used to the new changes. Ya wait and see." Benj stepped aside. "Ya have a little time, do ya?" he asked with raised eyebrows.

"Some. I guess that is until Mama calls."

"Sure don't want to keep ya from helping yer mom. Ya may go as soon as she calls."

"Good," Del thought, "he won't start a long story."

Benj stepped inside the woodshed and proceeded to split a few more pieces of wood. He wanted to talk all right. He knew she would wait. It seemed he always needed time to consider which story he was going to repeat. Del sometimes grew weary of hearing his oft-repeated tales.

She talked softly to Fritz while stroking his head. Fritz looked at her with those soulful dark eyes, only to close them again. He would not be comforted. "I get no greeting at all?" Del said as she roughed his coat. "You didn't meet us after school today. Why is that? You're always waiting at the cement pike for Bill and I."

Benj stepped outside, pointing a finger at Fritz saying, "*Sez veilleicht mei schuld. Geb eehm vennich mehner szeidt* [It's maybe my fault. Give him a little more time]." Benj stood quietly as he looked at Fritz. "*Es vot aulrecht* [It will get all alright]."

"Fritz never forgets to meet us." Del paused, waiting for a better explanation. She could tell none was forthcoming. "Fritz had better forget his pouting. It won't change things. That's what Mama says."

"*Du bischt recht* [You are right]," Benj agreed. He went back to splitting wood and Del was left with her thoughts. Change all right, nothing is the same. Del thought again about her father's Philadelphia travels. He said the trip was a long and tedious one. He understood why Grandfather claimed the travel day was too long and hard with his arthritis.

Benj made sure he was there each Wednesday to be a handyman around the house while Father was gone. 'Just some things a woman and children can't do,' is how he explained his presence. This elderly man came as close as anyone Del ever knew as being permanently set in every way. He certainly did not fit the pattern of change happening all around. His mannerisms had a calming effect. Slow and steady was his gait. The only emotion he ever showed was in his stories. He carried his coarsely boned body cautiously, his shoulders stooped forward as though they were too heavy to lift. His dress never changed. Summer or winter his outer clothes were always the same. She thought about the stories he repeated again and again. Could he not see she forced herself to remain interested in a story she heard before? His gestures, from the onset, sometimes told her which story would be repeated one more time. For sure, yesterday, today, and tomorrow Benj will be the same.

"I must keep yer brother busy." Benj interrupted her thoughts. He took great care to hang the axe between two spikes driven into the side beam of the shed. "Now there is a *schusslich* [energetic] one." He spoke as he stepped outside. "Can't have him wait for the next armload of wood. Gotta be ready."

Del looked at Benj and smiled. She knew what he was up to. He was teasing her about Ollie, her younger brother, a very impatient and hurried fellow who never had a quiet moment. Sometimes too quick and anxious to be of real help, Mama would say.

"Fritz could help Ollie, like he always helped Bill and me. But he won't. Come, Fritz, you can carry this piece of wood for Ollie, you aren't doing anything right now."

Fritz made no effort to get up. "Okay Fritz, if you no longer want to do as I say, or meet me at the cement pike, I will have to call Dewey." Del looked about to see if the neighbors' cat was nearby. "No cat around. I'll have to draw some nice cats for me to play with." Del picked up a sturdy stick and began to outline cats in the loose gritty dirt that collected in the lane. "Oh, look at these pretty kitty cats. Here kitty, kitty!"

That was more than Fritz would allow. He got up, cocked his head, and looked at the drawing with disgust. Then Fritz sat down in front of Del, his back to the drawings. He sent the dirt flying with a swish of his tail.

"So much for that. I knew you could move." Del rubbed his head vigorously. "No more kitty cats. You will always be my favorite pet." She lifted a floppy ear and whispered softly, "I know, I miss Bill too."

"*Dough vil ich auver* [Here I will wonder]." Fritz's antics brought surprised laughter from Benj. He gasped as tobacco juice dribbled into his throat and produced a mix of laughter and coughing. Shaking his head and throwing his chew, he came over to touch the dog's head ever so lightly. "Ya know, he comes to meet me every day. He's smart enough to know 'bout the time I come. Smart dog, he knows what time ya come home from school. I used to think he'd hear the school bell ring, then head out the lane. Not so. Saw yesterday he'd start 'fore that bell rings." Benj stepped inside the woodshed and reached for the hatchet to split kindling.

So, Del thought, Fritz was with Benj when he could have met them. She looked at Benj hoping he would explain just why it was that Fritz did not meet them today. Benj showed no sign of that as he made kindling to start a quick fire in the morning. "Ollie and Carol are supposed to gather bark chips," Del reminded Benj.

Benj chuckled, "*Ich waise* [I know]. I want to see how long it'll take him to let me know 'bout that. It'll be all right, ya can use the splintered wood anytime." He paused. "*Dough kummed ah* [Here he comes]."

Ollie came running and dropped his baseball glove and ball on the elm stump that remained by the walkway to the house. He ran into the shed, loaded his arms full of wood, saying, "You are mean to me, there's plenty of wood in the house to start a fire." He left while calling to Carol, the youngest of the family to open and hold the door for him to enter.

"Now there is an interesting fella. I'll watch him as he grows up. Figered he would have more to say 'bout me splitting wood to keep him busy. Can't have him catch me watching him."

Del knew he was teasing Ollie. She had a glimpse of his deep-set, devilish green eyes hidden under bushy brows on his heavy boned forehead. He glanced toward the house to see if Ollie was on his way back.

Del knew she would have to wait for his story since it seemed he could never talk and work at the same time.

Ollie came dashing back as he let the screen door fly; it closed with a bang as he hurried over to the shed. "For gosh sakes, will you never stop splitting wood for me to carry? It's not that cold yet. You'd have me carrying wood until tomorrow morning! The big box in the porch is already half full from the extra I carried in."

"Next time, perhaps ya will tell me when the wood chest is full. *Ich kann soo ebbis net rieche* [I can't smell such a thing]." Benj spoke in a most innocent tone.

"Huh, you know all right. You know exactly how much wood it takes to fill the chests. I heard Bill and Del say you always knew when enough wood was split. They never had to tell you when to stop."

"So ya know that," Benj said with a tinge of surprise.

Ollie couldn't maintain his displeasure any longer. He smiled ever so faintly, turned quickly and ran across the lane to the elm stump where he grabbed his baseball glove and ball. He proceeded to throw the ball against the gable end of the yellow stucco house. He caught it as it bounced back.

Benj watched Ollie run off. Once Ollie was out of hearing distance Benj said. "See, I told ya he'd have something to say." Benj made a slight wave of his hand as he looked toward Del. "Why ya laughing?"

"Ollie knows you were teasing him."

"That so," was his only comment. "Now what ya thinking?"

"Oh Ollie. He is playing ball every chance he gets. Throwing the ball against the house wall and catching it. Good way to play all by yourself."

"Yep, I know. Take Ollie, a complicated little fella. More *geduldich* [patient] than I thought." Benj paused, placed a finger alongside his face as if to think things through. "He's not the usual little boy, ya know. Yep, he'll be a fine young man. Ya wait and see."

"How can you tell?"

"There are things I can tell 'bout people. But I won't be 'round to say I told ya so. You'll see and remember old Benj told ya so," He paused for a long moment. "Ya haven't forgot already, have ya? It won't be long 'fore we'll have ourselves that big day. Yep, only once in a lifetime that Easter Sunday and our birthdays fall on the same day. Mark my words, ya will not celebrate yer birthday ever again on Easter Sunday no matter how old ya get to be. March twenty-four and Easter Sunday only once in a lifetime, it won't happen for everyone. We'll be among the few, me, you, 'n Bill. Yep, 1940, that's the year, long way off, we will celebrate Easter Sunday and our birthday on the same day." Benj paused. "I keep this paper in my pocket. Yep, here it is." With shaky hands he unfolded a piece of yellowed celluloid protecting a newspaper clipping from which he read, "In 1582 Easter fell on March 24 and one other time in 1799, after that it will happen in 1940. *Bin en older mann. Vil huffa ich kanns mache. Du bischt yunn, kannscht mache* [I'm an old man. Will hope I can make it. You are young and can make it]. No Easter Sunday again on March 24 until the year 2391."

Del wasn't anxious to hear his oft-repeated story. "Why do you tease people?" she said, hoping to change the subject.

"So, ya can tell that too," he answered quickly. "Like I told ya, Ollie is complicated, but he's good-natured. He could have said something long 'fore he did. Perhaps he will be something like yer father. Never could figger him out. *Sell iss waahr* [That is true]. Why every time I think I know Elwood Heydt, he's fixing to trick me again." A faint smile crossed his face as he sat on the chopping block. "Woodie is tricky alright."

"He's tricky?" Del was suddenly interested.

"Does that please ya, birthday girl?" Benj shifted his position, stretched his legs, crossing them at his ankles. "Ya see, I like knowing a man's character. Not just knowing a face. Once ya know, really know a man, ya know what to expect he will do in a predicament." With pointed finger and great emphasis he stated, "That's the way I like to know a man!"

"What's a predicament?"

"Never ya mind! Yer is much too young to know 'bout predicaments."

"Oh shucks," thought Del.

"Now take yer father, there's a man I can't always figger. He takes *sposch* [pleasure] in knowing he has me guessing. Yep, he surprises me." He raised his forefinger and placed a shaky finger to his temple. "*Fersthay* [Understand]! Woodie never made fun of me to other folk. Nor does he belittle me in any way. *Ses schpassich* [It's unusual] yet laughable. What happens is just between Woodie and me. No one else hears about it. No sir! Woodie is just plain interesting. Not anything like other folk around here."

Del stood back, straightened her posture and settled to a likely long story. Fritz seemed to sense her thoughts. He stretched, plopped down and rested his head on his paws. Del was curious about his remark about her father and the locals.

Benj interrupted her thoughts. "Now take the day ya was born. I remember it well, 'twas like yesterday. Yep, time flies by so quickly."

Good heavens, Del thought. He'll get into the same story again and she would be obliged to listen.

"Now yer father, there is a tricky feller." Benj raised a finger and cocked his head.

"The start to this story is different," Del thought with a glimmer of hope.

"What ya thinking *Gebottsdaag maedel* [Birthday girl]?" He caught her changed expression.

"Nothing, nothing at all." The chilly breeze caused her to shiver.

"Ya know, twas on my sixtieth birthday ya was born."

Del nodded her head in acknowledgement.

"What a beautiful day that was. *Wunderbar* [Wonderful]. *Unser Gott* [Our God] gave me a start to a whole new year that day. *Friehyaahr* [Springtime] is good fer birthdays. Like Oaschter [Easter], there's the promise of new life. The earth tells the whole story. Winter wheat sowed that's a healthy dark green in spring gives higher yields. *Des hawe ich schund oft mols gesehne* [This have I already oftentimes seen]. Yep, best to sow wheat in the fall. Trees blossom, flowers bud and bloom. Nothing more need be said. *Ess schenescht zeit fum yaar* [The prettiest time of the year]."

"That's what my grandfather always says," Del interrupted.

"Twas a grand day alright." Benj ignored Del as he settled into the story. "'Specially when I learned ya was born on my day." He paused as he walked into the woodshed to check whether the hatchet and axe had been properly placed.

Del wondered about that too. Benj always checked and double-checked that every little detail was completed.

"Nothin' like wasting time huntin' for a tool ya fergit to put away," Benj murmured.

He sure is exact, Del thought as she watched, guessing he needed time to ponder a different continuation to his story.

"Uh, uh," coming back he was fumbling for the right words. He placed his foot onto the chopping block and rested an elbow on his knee. "Yep, I was working that mid-woch [mid-week], worked only the half day. Had to be home with Ann that afternoon. Didn't see the widder go in the lane that day. Always 'bout four in the afternoon, couple times a week she leaves with her *millich kessel* [milk kettle]. See her again early the next morning for that day's fresh milk. Sam was still living that time. Doesn't need as much milk now-a-days." Benj paused. "Ah, ah but this particular morning she was carrying a basket covered with a cloth, no kettle handle hanging from her hand."

"Bet she had chocolate cookies." Del interjected.

"So, ya like her cookies?"

"Sure do. Dark chocolate cookies, big round ones. Mama doesn't make that kind."

"Ya was not here to eat them that time. Now *luss mich sehne* [let me see]. Ach yah [Ah yes], the next mornin' she was on her way afore day-break. I knew something was happening 'cause she was making trips in the lane more often than usual. Being a *midfrau* [midwife] well, *sel saaged en lott* [that says a lot]. I can't ask Becky who she is helping. Folks know they can trust her to keep things to herself. Ya know they call me the wunnerfitz."

Del nodded her head and smiled. She knew that meant an inquisitive person.

"Must say, I like to know what's going on in the neighborhood." Benj cleared his throat. "My Ann was a little better the next day. Said she never saw Becky that day. We can see when Becky enters this lane. She lives across the street from me, ya know. Becky was so good to Ann and me. She many a time brought some hot soup and cooked for us when Ann wasn't in shape to do anything in the house and I had a full day's work." He paused, looking in the direction of his home. "Well, the week passed and I heard nothing. The next week I expected Becky was spending the greater part of each day with yer parents. 'Course could have been someplace else. This lane is a shortcut to a couple other places. *Ennich ha so wauszs* [Anyhow so it was]. After that, *mei wunnerfitz hut mich kabloughed* [my curiosity had me bothered]. I knew Woodie would come by my place on his return from the creamery. He always delivered his milk regular time each morning. Heard the horses and wagon come down the street, still dirt that time. Had to put on good speed to make the sharp turn and get up the steep incline as ya left the street to enter this lane." He pointed to the lane by the huge oak. It was a hard pull for a team of horses.

Del could envision the team making a run to pull the wagon while turning onto the steep grade as it left the road, now a cement highway, to enter this east lane.

"Woodie saw I was waiting fer him, standin' by my wooden pump. 'Whoa,' he called, pulled hard on the reins." Benj went through the motions as if he were handling the team himself, pulling back hard, as one must do, halting a team after using extra force for the climb and an immediate stop by Benj's home. Benj paused and turned to look around. "'Course the team came to a stop." He stopped for another long thoughtful pause before continuing.

"'*Un wie is dah Benj heit* [And how is Benj today]?' yer father asked. *Oh, Ich bin aulrecht* [Oh, I am all right]. Fine and dandy, wish I could say the same fer my Ann. I have been wonderin' if you have something new to tell me."

"How is Ann?" yer father said.

"*Es vaht nimmi besser* [It won't get any better]. 'Not what I like to hear,' says he. 'We can keep her some days at our house if need be. My wife needs to be at home with the children. I've been wanting to tell ya that. Never saw ya around whenever I come through. Must tell ya, *ess hutt geh bubbled*."

Del knew that meant a baby was born. She saw a tear roll from Benj's eye.

"Eh, I knew Becky was spending many hours in this lane." He pointed his forefinger to the lane in front of him. He paused briefly. "*Bin secgzich now* [I'm sixty now]. Was it born anytime close to my day? I need to know first thing if'n there is another Easter birthday to celebrate. '*Ich dank soo* [I think so],' yer father said with a nod of his head. 'Becky said she thinks your day is the twenty-fourth.' Well well, I said, never knew of another to be born on my day. *Saage mir waas wauszs* [Tell me what it is]. 'We have a little girl,' said he. 'We named her Adelaide. That was my mother's name.' That so, I said. Good to hear. Never had a little girl myself. Is everybody alright? Come to think 'bout it, never did see the doctor go in or out the lane. But he coulda come in the lane by Straub's house." He pointed to the lane that came into the homestead beyond the barn and sawmill a piece and then turned to the right.

Del could visualize the lane that broke off to the right beyond the sawmill area. A huge boulder stood in the middle of the lane and forced one to choose the lane that bore to the right or left. A footpath behind the rock led to a path beyond the Printz property and continued through the forest to the village of New Jerusalem. A single lane immediately behind the rock followed stone fences and met Forgedale Road. The east lane entrance from the new cement pike passed through the Heydt homestead separating the house on the right and the barn on the left traveling from east to west and continuing to that immense rock. The right lane below the huge rock was the North Entrance, sometimes referred to as the Pioneer Trail, and met Bieber Creek Road. Looking at the positioning of the three entrances to the Heydt property the letter Y could be recognized from an overhead view from the east lane and became known as the Y farm. 'Suited so well," Aunt Eva would say, 'since the letter Y is also the middle letter of the Heydt name.' Del's thoughts ended abruptly as she again heard Benj say something about a girl being born on his birthday. She was about to interrupt and ask, but what about Bill?

Benj did not hesitate. He was eager to get the story told. "I asked how my birthday girl was doing, also yer mama. Yer father said, 'Everyone is fine. We had Becky come in and tend to the housework and the children. Come in and see our little Adelaide sometime.'" Benj nodded, recalling that day. "That will I do. Need to meet my birthday girl. I have someone to celebrate with me when that day comes *yaahrer fun nah* [years from now]." Benj sighed.

Del knew he was thinking about his deceased wife. He lived all by himself in that house close to the new pike with a high terrace that lifted his house above street level. Benj looked down upon Becky's house across the street. A total of eight steps from the street in front of his house to the top of the terrace, two more steps to the walk and another step onto a small front porch, only large enough to protect a seldom-used front door. Del knew, for she had counted that first set of steps a number of times as she walked by on her way to and from school. The mailbox was stuck into the terrace to a height the mailman could reach. Benj lifted his cap and brushed a hand across his shiny, bald head. Del observed its bony appearance and wondered if all heads were like that after the loss of hair.

"What ya thinking, girl?" Benj spoke quickly.

Del just shook her head, unsettled that he caught her thinking.

"Well, another couple of days came and went 'fore I waited for yer pa to come down the street. He rushed the team up the sharp grade and once again called 'Whoa' as he pulled hard on the reins. The screechy wheels came to a full stop. I was ready to ask when it would suit fer me to visit. Never got the chance. Woodie greeted me and said, 'Now that the snows are gone and spring is fully in the air, come in and see our baby boy. We have been waiting fer ya. He is growing like a weed.' Now Woodie, what's going on here?" Benj's face reddened some as he recounted the story. "Ya told me ya had a little girl, born on my day. That's what you said! Ya had a baby girl. Ya named her Adelaide. Yer father looked shocked," Benj stopped to think a bit. His face lit up. "Come to think of it, I bet Becky knew." He was speaking softly, barely audible. "Yep, she surely knew!" Del wondered what he was saying about Becky as he straightened up as best he could and looked at Del and said, "Yer father asked me if I remembered fer sure. I said, *Bin ich sure* [Am I sure]?! Sure, I know what ya said. He looked so *verhuddelt* [confused] he didn't say anything for a few minutes. 'Benj, now ya have me wondering,' he said. 'How could I make such a mistake?' *Ah hut stutched* [He did hesitate]. He looked like he was really shocked that I would even mention a *glae maedel* [little girl]. How could I be wrong? He sure looked puzzled as he sat there with the reins hanging loosely from his hands. I looked him straight in the eye. He never let on he was teasing me. Not one bit. Then he slowly said, 'Now Benj, ya really have me guessing. I really don't know what to think. I must be losing my mind. Surely a man knows what is born to him. *Des iss an arriech ding* [This is an awful thing]. Are ya sure that's what I said? Can't believe I could be so wrong. A man shouldn't make that kind of mistake. Don't want to steer ya wrong. I will have to hurry home and see fer myself what was given to us on yer birthday. Ya come over and see fer yerself whether we have a boy or a girl.' I told yer father it wouldn't take me long to know if a girl or boy was born on my day. I'd take a peep in the *windel* [diaper] and I'd know fer sure."

Goodness gracious! Del was embarrassed. She felt herself blush all over. She turned her back and looked toward the house hoping he would not notice her discomfort. At the same time she was aware Benj displayed more emotion than she ever saw before. He slipped into the Pennsylvania Dutch language more often too. She was suddenly aware that she was not hearing all he was saying.

"*Sell g'saagt* [that said], Woodie whipped up the team and hurried in the lane so fast the *schtaab iss gfloge* [the dust flew]. He needed to leave in a hurry so I wouldn't catch him laughing. He surely was laughing all the way home." Benj was quiet as he fumbled to grab his Red

Man tobacco from a back pocket. He compressed a small amount of tobacco in the cup of his palm, turning it over several times before placing it in his mouth.

Del became impatient as she began to pat Fritz's head thinking he, too, wanted to hear more.

Finally, Benj spoke. "I'm sure yer father was grinning from ear to ear," Benj laughed at the memory while shaking his head. "Yer father knew I would come. Becky too, was ready to sit with Ann. She was waiting fer me to ask her help. I told her I had to see if'n a girl or boy was born on my day. Woodie is teasing me. Must see fer myself what was born on my day. Becky wasn't 'bout to tell me anything. Becky is like that." He paused.

Del knew Becky maintained complete privacy of all she did as a healer for people in the neighborhood.

"After dark I took my *lutzer* [lantern] and walked in the lane. Yer father was expecting me all right. 'Our neighbor is here,' he called to yer mama. Yep, Woodie's smile was so wide I could see his gold tooth." He laid a finger on his right cheek.

Del knew the gold tooth was not visible unless her father laughed heartily.

"Yer mama greeted me and asked if I would prefer some cider or coffee to drink. She said, 'The cider in the pitcher is good and cold. A little on the hard side. The first barrel turned hard early. We'll let it set for vinegar. Come help yourself to all you need.' I told yer mama *sie saage sel gebts ess allerbescht Essich* [they say that gives the very best vinegar] when it turns early. Yer mama didn't agree. '*Ess wot zu schtarick. Es nei fass hut zu fiel brandewei drin. Haava sez aul de weg wee mahs gleiche* [It gets too strong. The new barrel was tossed with quite a bit of whiskey inside, it depends on how one likes it].' I told yer parents, first I want to see this birthday child. Ya can pour some of that cider. I want to see your bundle."

Del pictured the pitcher used for cider. It always stood on the white baking table. There were dancing couples painted in formal black and red all around the pitcher. It was one of the gifts Mama received by purchasing items from the Keystone Products Co. Six glasses and a tray completed the set.

"Woodie called, *'kum dough how* [come here].' I walked to where Woodie was seated on the rocker. 'Come look, and see if ya can tell,' yer father said." Benj shook a finger, "I said it won't take me long to tell. I will peep into the *windel* [diaper]."

"Goodness he said it again," Del thought and blushed once more.

"I walked closer. There between the rocking chair in the corner and the couch was a good-sized *wesch kareb* [washbasket]. I couldn't believe my eyes. There were two babies laying side by side in the basket. *Tzway, tzway* [Two, two]!" He waved two fingers, shaking his head and smiling—something Del didn't often see. His teeth had severe tobacco stains and were all yellowed. *"Zwilling! Kann des net glaawe* [Twins! I cannot believe this]! And Becky never said a word. She kept the news of twins to herself." He shook his head slowly and thoughtfully. "Townsfolk didn't know either, *sel hed ich gheert* [that I would have heard]."

"Yer daddy said, *'Ess glae maedel waar erscht* [the little girl was first], that's why I first told ya we had a girl.' He laughed and handed me two packs of tobacco. I held ya quite awhile, ya never fussed. Yer mama took ya and Woodie gave me the boy. Yer mama said, 'We named him William. Woodie had a brother named so and my father's name is William.'" Benj paused. "I could tell this was the boy when I held him. He was a little heavier, had a larger hand, fit it around my little finger." Benj smiled ever so pleasantly. "So twins was born on my birthday. *Es bescht gebottsdaag im leweslang* [The best birthday in my lifetime]! Yep, yer father is a tricky feller, but I like him. Best neighbor I ever had." Benj paused. "Yer daddy never lied to me, mind ya. He just didn't tell me the whole story the first time. There is something about him that's special. He does things that, well, ya can remember them and laugh and enjoy the memory."

"I hear Mama calling." Del interrupted.

"Run along, birthday girl," Benj waved her off.

Del wondered what else he was remembering; as she skipped across the lane she turned back. "Will you stay for supper? It will be nearly dark when Father comes home." Benj nodded his head, indicating he would.

Fritz headed for the garden ahead of Del as she walked across the stretch of lawn between the lane and the house and onto the large porch that extended the entire front of the house. She took the two steps at the side entrance in one long stride. A few skips and a jump and she was seated on the porch wall at the closed end. Twisting her body to avoid being pricked by thorns, she slipped between the rose trellis and the corner spouting and jumped to the ground. She ran down the terraced lawn and reached the garden by the shortest route. Fritz was already there, and so was Mama.

"I don't like your jumping off that wall." Mama said.

"I won't hurt myself."

"It's not only that. I planted some lily bulbs there for next spring. If you keep pounding the earth at that same spot, it sure won't help their growth."

"Did you have to? Oh well, I'll just jump farther out and not land there. How else am I going to get here from the other side of the house?"

Mama laughed. "Walk around the porch like everyone else does."

Del said no more as she glanced over the garden with large areas of bleak brown. Most everything was harvested. Plants were cleared in preparation for the first killing frost. Some endive remained; it would be given a protective covering against the cold air. Baskets of turnips were setting in the path to be carried into the ground cellar for winter's use. The teas and herbs were being readied to carry to the attic floor to dry. Chew cherries were scattered on the bare ground; a job for Carol to gather. Del remembered that was her first garden task when she was younger.

Along the north side the currant bushes were gray and bare awaiting winter's rest. A couple of stray onions were shooting here and there. Del stood under the lilac bush that still held its leathery green leaves. She wondered if they ever changed to fall colors, as was the case with most leaves. On the other corner stood the frail-looking quince tree, it produced enough fruit to make the quince jelly everyone enjoyed. She observed its twisted trunk, all gnarled and knotted with loose bark that peeled off like scales. On the upper corner stood an early apple tree, stripped bare of its leaves, and beyond that was the strawberry patch. That work still needed to be completed, the runners needed to be trimmed both now and again in the spring. Straw would be placed to protect the plants throughout the winter months.

"Have you finished your work?" Mama asked.

"Yes, long already. It was good you called."

"You're not that anxious to work?" Mama smiled as she straightened up to look at Del.

"It's not that." Del said hesitantly. "Benj, he likes to finish a story he starts . . ."

"You mustn't be impatient with Benj."

"I wasn't." Del was quick to answer. "Fritz and I listened to his story." Fritz tilted his nose upwards as if sniffing the breeze to show he was attentive.

"Come come, Fritz." Mama laughed. "I bet you slept through it all."

"Not this time. Benj got rather excited and loud at times. His story was different."

"Oh, how is that?"

"Well . . . the story, his favorite about us sharing a birthday, but he made it different."

"What did he say?" Mama said it mildly, but looked intently at Del.

"He said father is a tricky fellow. He isn't, is he?"

Mama smiled broadly. "I wouldn't say that. Everyone sees a person differently. While he says your Father tricks him, it means he is teasing him."

"How could it happen that way when Bill and I were born?"

"What do you mean?"

"He said Father tricked him. He told him a girl was born on his day and later he told him a boy was born on his sixtieth birthday. After he came to visit he discovered twins were born on his birthday."

Mama hesitated, then laughed softly. "Yes, it happened that way. We explained we thought he couldn't stand the shock of hearing twins were born on his birthday, that's why we did what we did."

"Then Father did play a trick on him, like Benj said."

"Oh, I suppose you could call it that. Benj doesn't let anyone forget every time he adds another year about that birthday on Easter Sunday if he lives long enough." She pointed to some rolls of paper on the ground. "You may carry these rolls of spearmint tea up to the attic. Get your apron before you come back. Take this roll of parsley with you too."

Del was underway immediately. She entered the back door, having grabbed the parsley and spearmint Mama had wrapped in brown paper to place on the attic floor for drying. Immediately before her was the stairway to the second floor. She took two steps at a time until she reached the hallway; turning left, she entered her parents' bedroom. At the farthest end was the stairway to the attic. As she approached she knew Mama had made numerous trips already. The air was heavy with the fragrance of drying teas and herbs. She tread two narrow steps on the bedroom floor to the attic door. A lift-latch handle opened the door as it swung to the inside on the attic landing; moving cautiously she climbed the steps slowly, the shallow depth supported only the front of her foot. The stairway itself was narrow. Approaching the top, she spotted the area to place teas. Two full steps before the top she bent over and got down on her knees to slide the rolled paper in place under the eaves where it rested against the broad stonewall that met the roof on the house. She opened the first roll and spread the parsley evenly across the paper and then repeated the process for the spearmint. Crawling back to stand up she took the steps sideways, aware of grooves worn into the wood from many years of wear, the white paint gone except for the ends where no one stepped.

Back in her parents' large bedroom she walked by a window, a large bureau and another window all along the front of the house. Ori and Carol shared the room immediately in front of her. Their room had a window on the front of the house as well as another on the north side looking down on the garden. She passed by her bedroom when she remembered to get her apron hanging on the clothes tree in her bedroom, the smallest room in the house. Its one window also looked down on the garden. A single iron bed and a chest of drawers was all the small room accommodated. She slipped into her gingham apron, one that Mama had made, and down the stairs she flew, rushing and jumping, taking two steps at a time. She grabbed a sweater hanging on a hook in the wall behind the stairs door, then out on the little stoop and down the terrace to the garden.

"I wish you wouldn't rush the stairs like you do. You could fall and break your neck."

Del looked at her mama wondering how she knew.

"I can hear from all the noise you create. I see you remembered the apron. Over here I have some *Katza graut* [catnip]. Take those two newspaper rolls first. I am tired of chasing Dewey from the garden."

"Is Dewey here? I was looking for him earlier."

"He makes his appearance every day. I just now chased him again. He's here, especially when I am working in the garden. I don't appreciate his rolling around in my catnip tea."

"Can't say I blame him. Who wants to spend all day in a fenced-in yard with hedges so thick and high you can't see to anywhere. Only when I am upstairs can I see over that hedge. Sometimes on a warm evening I see Mrs. Straub sitting on the side porch swing with Dewey on her lap."

"I don't think the fence or the hedges bother that cat at all. Cats can get through the tiniest of places. If it's petting he wants, Orphelia has more time than I do."

"Maybe they don't have any catnip in their garden."

Mama shook her head. "There is plenty of catnip over there for him to roll around in. I don't need any of his cat hair on the attic floor. There, I think that's enough for this winter's belly aches."

"Fritz chases him away. Fritz keeps all the other cats on the property close to the barn. Father calls them his mousers."

"All farmers like barnyard cats. I think Fritz knows that much."

"I know. Grandfather calls his outside cats mousers too. They stop the mice that would make a home in his big red barn and the granary. Silky keeps the creamery free of mice."

"Silky is the fattest and biggest cat I ever saw. Your uncle Homer is surprised that cat is quick enough to pounce on prey. He believes Silky lays down and suffocates his catch." Mama smiled. "Your grandfather and uncle also give Silky licks of cream. But Silky is not on the creamery floor when they are separating all cream from the milk. Silky gets penned in your grandfather's creamery office then."

She pointed to more paper rolls. "Next there is *solwei* [sage]. I think I have enough for this winter's sore throats. Last of all there is *Gwendel tae* [thyme]. Be careful on those attic steps."

"Don't worry, Mama. I take those steps sideways coming down."

"Good. Then you may carry these filled baskets of turnips around to the other side near the cellar entrance. Perhaps Benj can lift the cellar doors for you after you unlock them from the inside."

"I can push the doors open with my arms above my shoulders."

"That's alright, but I'd rather you ask whoever is around to help you. Those wooden doors are heavy to lay open once you have them upright. This parsley I am cutting now I will take along when I go in. I'll cut it fine for keeping this evening after all else is finished. While you're inside get yourself a decent sweater or jacket to wear. I don't know why you insist on wearing Gloria's old rag."

"Ori doesn't care."

"It's not good enough for wear anymore. Next time I get my hands on it, into the rag bag it goes. Which reminds me, I had better get my bag of rags ready. And send them along with Benj. It's time for the ragman to make his rounds once more before winter sets in. There's a job for you, when you aren't busy—you can snip all the buttons off the worn out clothing in the box on the attic floor. That sweater will find its way there too."

A period of silence passed as Del carried everything to the garden's edge. Once the baskets of turnips were at the top of the terrace, half the job was done.

"When you finish that, you may set the table for supper. Remember to set a place for Benj. I will ask him to stay for a warm meal on my way to the barn."

"I already did."

"Did what?"

"Invited him to supper."

"I wish you would make yourself clear and finish your statement the first time." Mama spoke sternly. Softening her voice, "I am glad you did. It'll make him feel welcome. I will mention it all the same. Remember to get the *schmier kase und lott warick* [cottage cheese and apple butter]. Put them on the table along with the vinegar cruet. Then if you have time enough, you can go along with Fritz and Carol to collect bark chips. Just get them started. We need to get that work habit started. "

Fritz sprang to his feet, wagging his tail hearing his name.

"You never give up, do you Fritz?" Mama spoke to the loyal dog. "You are both guardian and playmate for Adelaide and William and you can be the same for Carol and Oliver. You know their tasks as well as anyone."

Mama placed another stem of cut tea on the paper. "There, I guess that will keep you busy for a while. I will tend to the kitchen fire, then head for the barn."

"All night," Del muttered, though she was willing to do her portion of work.

"What did you say?"

"I said, all right."

Mama smiled as she peered at Del over the top of her black-rimmed glasses. Her dark eyes appeared to match the black frame. "It won't take as long as you think. It'll be done in a jiffy once you get started."

"You heard that, Fritz," Del said after Mama was gone. "Mama means it. You can have fun with Carol and Ollie, too."

Fritz groaned and left her side, turned the corner at the front porch and sat there. The last glimmer of sun cast a long shadow of Fritz that extended beyond the house and under the weeping willow tree.

"I see your shadow, Fritz," Del called. "You needn't hide. It won't work. We'll have to find some other playtime. You heard I will show Carol how to do her first chore. You'll be with me." Fritz was up and quickly by her side ready to go. Del rested her hand on his back. "Not now yet. I have to finish this job first. You're a good buddy." She stroked him gently. "You're much better than Taw-taw. You know what everyone thinks of Ori's pet duck. He is one piece of ill-tempered fowl, at least that's how Grandfather describes him. Sometimes he says an ornery cuss. I don't know what he means by that, it can't be anything nice."

Del carried the baskets of turnips to the other side of the house. She wanted to get to the ground cellar while there was enough light to shine through the small window in front of a metal grate in the darkest section of the cellar. Fritz chose to wait by the porch steps. Del brought the last basket to the entrance and was surprised to see the double doors to the cellar lay open. Someone must have gone inside and removed the bar from the brackets that held the doors closed. Perhaps Mama had removed the bar. The doors were quite heavy and took all her strength to lift the wooden door with both arms upright and high enough to take one step and then another until she had climbed enough steps to rest the heavier door on the cement base and do the same for the second and lighter door to rest on the cement base on the other side. That it was already done was a big help.

Del grabbed one basket and scooted down the steps, counting as she went. Eight, she counted out loud, as she walked to the raised cement platform along the front wall and placed a basket of turnips there. On tiptoes she walked past the swing board to look at the pastries. "Sure enough," she thought to herself, "Benj was here and helped himself to a piece of funny cake." That probably happened early in the afternoon. He surely knew beforehand there would be cellar delivery for her this evening. Del remembered too, that once in a great while Mama was a bit annoyed when she wanted to offer pastry to guests and found that a piece had already been cut. Yet at the same time she was pleased to know Benj enjoyed baked goods no longer available at his house. Besides, she'd say, 'We tell him to make himself at home. He earns whatever he eats. It gives him something to do plus he keeps the place neat and orderly. And where else can he get as much first-hand information as that which happens around here.'

After several more trips the cellar work was done. Del lifted the lighter-weight half door standing on the top step, held the door with arms lifted over her head as she stepped slowly and carefully one step at a time until the door came to rest. Father always cautioned her not to drop the door. She gave the heavier half door with the round metal ring a tremendous pull and gently lowered it, taking the steps slowly and carefully while holding the half-door above her head until it came to rest. In the darkening cellar light she reached for the wooden two by four and slid it into the brackets that locked the doors. She made her way up the steps that opened to the kitchen. Her thoughts were still with Benj, wondering why Mama always asked the children to treat him kindly. She never said that about anyone else.

Del ran back to the garden and grabbed two more bundles of tea— the maximum her apron was able to carry. She moved quickly to the attic, spreading the paper rolls next to those already opened to dry. "There," she said, pleased with her job as she stood on the top step and looked around for a minute. The center of the attic held the meat cabinet her Uncle Sam built. It had screened doors for ventilation and stood empty now. Sides of bacon and cured hams hung there during the winter months. The odor of cured meats would drown the aroma of drying teas and herbs once winter butchering was done and the large cabinet would again be filled with smoked and salted meats.

She couldn't resist going to the other end of the attic, its two small windows begging her to look about. She held the curtain aside for a clearer view. The winter's cold allowed frost to form on the wide stone sill like a soft layer of fallen snow. The small metal window frames, opening like a door to the inside would rust and stain the curtains year after year. Making new curtains was a spring house-cleaning project for Mama each year. Del was always interested in observing what could be seen both near and far from a higher point of view. Night was creeping in fast. The Blue Mountains in the distance were no longer visible. Over the top of the apple tree she could see the Edgar Losch dwelling, one of two families that lived in the north lane from the huge boulder to Bieber Creek Road where it met the Pioneer Trail. The Losch house was home to little Ernie, frail and suffering from tuberculosis. Mr. Losch came by every other day for milk from one cow. Dr. Schlicher ordered it that way. He selected the only Ayrshire in the barn to fill that need. Father didn't mind the extra work involved in keeping that milk separate as long as it helped bring about a child's return to good health. The next house further into the lane belonged to the Straubs. No children there. Del heard Mr. Straub was a retired schoolteacher. Mrs. Straub took in sewing. A fine seamstress, her clothes were always attractive.

Del gently replaced the curtain, being careful not to touch the window frame, knowing how fragile the rusted metal was. Mama would handle those windows very carefully. The lift-latch closing never held securely. A strong wind caused it to rattle and unhook the latch. Winter winds could play havoc in the attic. The rattle alone was enough to cause a sleepless night. Mama always secured the two windows using bent nails. The nail point was hammered partially into the window's wood trim and then bent over the metal frame at several precise places. Mama did not want anyone to tamper with her makeshift holds.

Del scooted over to the other window. The row of cherry trees did not hamper her view from that window. She saw the home of Jonathan and Adeline Conrad. They were up in years and no longer kept cattle but had a pig or two and some chickens, just enough to remain self-sufficient. Father farmed their small acreage. She looked down into their barnyard and saw Jonathan walking with his cane; he crossed the yard and entered the barn closing the door behind him. He had a black horse he'd hitch up to his well-kept buggy to travel to church or Sunday School. He wore a wide brimmed hat and kept a long white beard. He reminded Del of the Amish men in the area although he was not Amish. Del never heard him speak a word of English, only the Pennsylvania Dutch dialect.

Del often entered their house, seeing only the barest necessities when Mama asked her to deliver the dough cutter for Adeline to use. A day or two later Mama would send her there to retrieve the same item. Del never knew how Mama knew when to send her there to deliver or retrieve something.

She came back to the steps and pondered the only window on the side of the stairs. It was inconvenient to get to. She would have to push hard on tiptoe to see anything at all, as the chimney came alongside the uppermost step. On sudden impulse, she stretched and stood on tiptoe while leaning forward to look around to the barnyard below. She caught a glimpse of Bill under the barn overshoot. She heard the train whistle in the valley three miles away. That meant Father would be arriving at the station; it sent her side-stepping down the stairs. Had there been any problem on the tracks one would not only hear one long whistle but also four short repeated whistles. Del thought taking the train to Philadelphia would be exciting, as Father always had something interesting to talk about. She hoped to make the trip with him some day even though Father warned her that his going there was a temporary thing. She made a second trip to the attic as quickly as she could. She stood on the small back porch and called for Fritz, knowing he was somewhere near the garden. Fritz came running as both entered the kitchen. Carol, the youngest, was seated on the couch.

"Are you finished?" Carol asked Del.

"With the garden work, I am. We still have to collect bark chips for Mama. I also need to check the pots on the stove to make sure there is enough broth so nothing burns." Releasing a sigh, she said, "My, but that pot roast smells good. Did you hear the train whistle? Father will soon be home. Get your sweater, put it on. We need to find Ollie to help you. This will be your chore every evening." Del paused. "Mama needs bark chips or kindling every morning to start a fire in the kitchen stove. When there isn't enough bark or wood chips to pick up at the sawmill Benj will make splinters for you. Come along, Carol."

"You go first. Fritz won't follow me," Carol pouted. She was disappointed that the dog wasn't as attached to her as to Del and her twin brother.

"Fritz will follow anyone going outside, especially when no one is left inside." Del advised Carol. "Come along."

Benj was seated by the pump under the grape arbor. Fritz ran to Benj and sat tight against his legs. Benj stroked the dog's head. *"Schmarta hund* [Smart dog]," Benj laughed.

"I know what that's all about. He really doesn't want to help with the kindling any more," Del acknowledged.

"Ya is right." Benj slowly pushed Fritz's body, directing him toward Del and Carol.

"I can see Ollie standing by the feed entry door. He knows he needs to help. Come on Fritz, let's go. Only a half-basket full is needed today." Ollie joined them as they passed by the barn.

"Fritz won't come with me," Carol lamented.

"You aren't any more eager to do this than Fritz is. You need a change of attitude," Del said. "Ollie isn't complaining."

Del's hand rested on Fritz as she walked beside him. Ollie followed on the other side. Del encouraged Carol to do the same once they were underway.

"Fritz won't stay with me," Carol continued her complaints.

"You need to get used to doing this. Ollie isn't fussing," Del figured Carol's real problem was getting into the habit of doing chores. As the youngest, she had been spared work until she was old enough to handle some responsibilities.

"What's the use?" Ollie said, "I know this is for me and Carol to do. It's better than the things I was doing." Ollie was next in line behind Del and Bill. He was two years younger than the twins and already accustomed to farm work.

"Only time I see you doing anything is carry armloads of wood or throwing that ball against the house. That's having it pretty good," Del responded.

"Huh, Benj is teasing me all the time. He always asks me how many mice I see in the granary. He has me looking all around before I scoop any oats, wheat or barley to feed the animals. Same at the corncribs. I hear people say rats burrow holes under the cribs and eat corn all winter long. It's not funny, I can see you laughing," Ollie protested as he looked at Del.

"That's why father has all those mousers. You know that," Del explained.

The three reached the sawmill area. "Ollie already knows this routine," Del gestured to the ground strewn with bark chips and sawdust.

"Must I do it all?" Carol was not pleased.

"Hush your grumbling. Ollie is here to help. You will learn. Fritz, you stay. I will be back to help carry the basket." Del turned and slowly walked back as she looked for Bill. While walking by the feed entry door, she didn't see him. She entered the walkway and passed the wooden water pump and trough. Benj was still seated there.

"Those two doin' alright?" Benj inquired.

Del nodded, "Ollie knows what to do. I'll go back after I have the table set for supper."

Del hurried into the house. She returned a short time later. Beyond the barnbridge stood an implement shed with corncribs attached on both sides. Del didn't see anyone. The next building facing east was the henhouse, where she thought she might see Ori. Attached to the one-story henhouse was the feedhouse, two stories high. On the other side was the pigsty, completing the long building. Entries to the henhouse and the pigsty were through the feedhouse. Across the lane from the pigsty and outdoor pigpen was their small orchard. Recently planted sour cherry trees lined the lane behind a stone fence. Apple trees filled the center. Next were a couple of spindly-looking pear trees and an apricot tree that blossomed beautifully each spring, setting between the house and Mama's washhouse. The washhouse had a built-in furnace that held two large cast iron kettles to heat water for laundry and was equipped for butchering, rendering lard, making apple butter and home-made soap. Next to the lane was the small milkhouse. A few English walnut trees were on the lane's edge and a row of chestnut trees arched over a portion of the lane to the sawmill. Father warned the children never to pick fallen chestnut burrs, which stuck firmly to your hands with burrs sharp as fine needles. You couldn't free a burr from one hand with the other hand.

Fritz was digging in a pile of sawdust searching for mice or rats as Del approached. She was not going to tell Carol why Fritz was digging so feverishly in the pile. Rodents, even groundhogs, prepared secure and warm nesting places for the cold winter months. What better place than a pile of sawdust? Fritz was covered with the gritty sawdust when he came running to answer Del's call. She hoped Ollie would not mention it at this time.

"Did you see the sawdust fly?" Carol asked as she petted Fritz.

"Fritz would like for you to dig from the opposite end."

"Should I do that?" Carol answered giggling.

"No, never do that! You'll get sawdust in your eyes and that is very painful. Mama would have to place a flax seed in the corner of your eye to remove that speck of dirt. You sure don't want to experience that. Keep your distance when Fritz is digging. Bill and I would make noises like we were digging. You can pretend too, but never get sawdust on yourself because it's very itchy. Fritz likes getting sawdust all over himself. You just wait, you'll see how he shakes his body to get rid of it. We need to get back. I didn't see Ori yet. Her work should be complete by now unless her duck is giving her problems again." She pointed to Carol and Ollie, "You carry the basket Carol, Ollie can take the other side." Once in the lane Del walked slowly with them. "Grandfather should see me now," Del thought. "'The skippiest child I ever saw', is what he often said."

"I want to walk with Fritz. Do I have to carry the basket all the way?" Carol complained.

"Fritz carries the basket too. Ollie knows that. I will show you. I'll take your handle and Fritz will carry Ollie's side. Come on, Fritz, show Carol how it's done." The woven rounded bottom bushel basket with wood handles had open areas below the rim on both sides where Grandfather affixed rope handles for Fritz to carry.

"Let me, let me." Carol was anxious to work with Fritz.

Ollie ran ahead. "You stay right here." Del called. "Fritz will carry only so long. There are three of you. You need to learn to share turns with Fritz. I will not help you many more times."

"Good dog." Del praised Fritz. "He likes if you encourage him." Fritz continued even though the basket was uneven and tilting away from him. Carol could hardly refrain from giggling.

"Good work, Fritz," Del said as she dropped a hand on his back. Ollie took a brief turn. "That's it," Ollie said. " I am running home. There are enough of you to finish."

Impatient Ollie, Del thought, although she too was anxious to get back. Without hesitating she took the place of Carol. It was Carol's turn for relief.

"You know Grandfather always enjoys seeing Fritz carry this basket of wood chips. He designed these rope handles just for Fritz. Plus he always has a treat in his pocket for Fritz," Del said to Carol.

Fritz was nudging Carol. "Why does he do that?" she inquired.

"He's ready to carry the basket now. Give him your handle and you take mine. He's a big show-off." Del skipped on ahead. "I'll hold the porch door open."

Darkness had fallen. Del, Carol, Benj, Fritz, and Ollie were inside awaiting the rest of the family. Ori stepped into the closed porch with Taw-Taw perched on her shoulder. She carefully placed the bucket of eggs she collected on the big and heavy safe. She then placed her duck in a tall cardboard carton too narrow for that duck to spread his wings and escape. She cleaned the eggs with a soft, dampened cloth. She weighed them small, medium or large on the aluminum scale Grandfather had given to her. Ori was assigned the daily henhouse duty, which meant gathering the eggs, cleaning and filling the chickens' water hoppers, and measuring the proper amount of laying mash for each feeder. Kernels of corn were scattered close to a short ramp entry enticing the chickens to enter their house for the night. Del's job was to set a small bucket inside a larger bucket of shelled corn in the feedhouse to scatter outside in the morning, coaxing the chickens to jump outside to the ground. Taw-taw, Ori's pet duck, would be her last work. A special pen inside the feedhouse was built for that duck, where he was housed every night. Father would not have any surprise attacks by night visitors to the Y farm.

Benj eyed Taw-taw through the windows above the sink as he moved to the rocking chair. Benj never fussed or bothered with Taw-taw, thinking ducks were food, not pets. Taw-taw likewise maintained a comfortable distance from Benj.

"Did ya see that duck watching me while he was perched on her shoulder?" Benj said after they were gone. "I didn't take my eyes off him neither. He knows I can out-stare him."

Del smiled. The twins wondered why Taw-taw never bothered Benj. "I told him I ate tougher ducks than him; he knew what I meant," Benj had growled.

The twins knew there was more to it than that to make Taw-taw steer clear of Benj.

"Yer father should be home soon, train was on time." Benj said quietly as he pulled his watch from his pocket and looked at the time. The watch was attached with binder twine to his jacket buttonhole, and he slipped it back into his watch pocket. *"Bis seller zeit isses dunkel* [By that time it's dark]." Benj gazed through the window to the western sky.

Del moved quickly as she dipped some warm water from the stove's water tank into a basin. She reached for a towel, tossed it over her shoulder and proceeded to wash her hands before the evening meal. Ori stepped into the kitchen, washed her hands and began straightening up as was her custom. She could make herself look busy when she really wasn't accomplishing anything.

Bill came into the house, removed his overall coat and hung it up in the porch closet. He entered the kitchen, stood by the sink and began to wash up. Fritz pressed hard against his legs. Bill struggled to stand still. "Go to the bench, Fritz, I will sit there when I finish." Fritz moved slowly to the bench in front of the rear window and waited impatiently for Bill.

Benj shook his head and said, "I swear, I don't know how that dog understands everything ya say."

Mama came in. She left her milk bonnet and heavy muslin apron in the washhouse where the milk pails and sieves were washed and then returned to the milkhouse ready for the twice-daily milking. She checked the fires and placed the pots to cover half of the front burners. She wanted all the food ready to serve when Father arrived.

"Ahs vennich schpode [He's a little late]," Mama said as she looked at Benj. He nodded his head in agreement. *"Bin froh von ah nimmi fatt geh*

muss [I am glad when he no longer must go away]. That will be a welcome change," Mama said.

Ori looked at the mantle clock with music notes and a singing bluebird painted on the lower half of the glass door. "I don't know why Father takes that old horse to the station. I wouldn't trust her to bring me home. He should be home by now. Why, I really puff when I walk up that steep hill. Must be a problem for an old horse. He should get rid of her."

"Ori wouldn't puff when climbing that hill if she weren't so chubby," Del thought, but like the rest of the family, spared Ori their frank observations.

"Til knows better'n anyone else what Doll can do. He's cared for her all these years." Benj's remarks were a bit surprising.

"You are exactly right," Mama responded. "Go look where Tilghman is." Her gaze was directed at Bill.

Bill was back almost immediately. "He is sitting out there under the arbor. He's waiting until Doll comes home so he can give her a drink and stable her for the night."

"Not everyone takes such good care of a horse as Tilghman does. He's learned from my father, and he's well-known for his knowledge of horses," Mama commented.

"Is that what horse sense is?" Ollie asked.

Mama chuckled and said, "No, Oliver, but your grandfather has that in abundance too."

"I can't see why we don't eat. I'm hungry," Ori stated.

"We will wait for your father," Mama announced in a calm tone. The other children cast skeptical eyes at Ori.

"Train on time. Heard the whistle. Yer father is late," muttered Benj.

CHAPTER TWO

Something Mysterious in the Barn

Subdued noises were accented in the kitchen as talk was nil. The usual clanging of stove lids was muted as Mama lifted them to check the fires again and again. Setting and resetting the tea kettle, and then the pot containing the evening meal, she kept herself busy which told Del she was concerned. Taking a heavy breath she stepped back and rested crossed arms on her bosom. Del heard the creaking sound of the rocking chair as Benj moved slowly back and forth. Ollie shuffled his feet, and Mama didn't notice. On other occasions she would admonish him for his habit of scuffing the tops of his shoes.

"Father is really late compared to other trips," Bill spoke slowly and cautiously. The clock striking the hour filled the whole room like a gong. Carol counted the six strikes out loud, but no one complimented her accurate count. It seemed like a full ten minutes passed without comments from anyone. Even Ori tired of pretending to be busy. The knife and fork drawer needed no more straightening. She rearranged the Bible, Sears Roebuck and Montgomery Ward catalogs, the Farmer's Almanac and the daily Reading Times newspaper beside the radio on the cabinet at the far end of the kitchen. Del found it most surprising that Mama tolerated her constant pretenses of useful work.

No one bothered to turn on the regular evening radio broadcasts. It was cold outside, and Til now sat in the enclosed porch in father's desk chair. All could hear the springs creak when he stood up. He stepped into the kitchen and stared at the clock. He had the faintest smile on taut lips. Del figured he did not want to show how concerned he was. Til, at fifteen was a happy-go-lucky, easy-going person. "Maybe I should go outside and wait for Father," Til said to Mama.

"You won't be warm enough. You had better stay inside," Mama said as she turned to look at Til, "You can meet Doll and your father just as quickly from where you are." Til turned back and again the springs creaked in Father's desk chair. Del looked at the mantel clock and its beautifully painted bluebird on the glass door. The upper clear glass displayed a face with Roman numerals and dark delicate hands proudly showing the proper time of day. The mantel clock stood on a triangular shelf in the corner above the rocking chair where Benj was seated. The clock was a treasure from Father's mother's kitchen. One of Father's favorite phrases was, "Time is music to the ears." Del glanced at the painted bluebird and considered the sound of hoofs and a wagon would indeed be music to her ears.

"Why don't some of us eat?" Ori asked impatiently.

"You heard me earlier. We'll wait until everybody is here," Mama replied with a warning note in her voice.

"Father should know better than use Doll to make the trip home, it's just plain too steep a climb for an old horse," groaned Ori.

"How would you like it if anyone said that about your old duck!" Ollie argued. "In fact, who but you would care if he'd croak?"

"I agree with Ollie," Del announced with a giggle.

"Now now that's enough," Mama said.

"*Ya, sel saagich au* [Yes, that I say also]. No one takes better care of a horse than Til. If'n Woodie thought Doll couldn't make the trip, he wouldn't take her. It's the same with Billy, yer father," Benj pointed at Mama, "He's just as particular with his horses."

Mama nodded as she slid the kettle once more to a lower heat. She lifted the stove lid, opened the wood chest, grabbed two pieces of split wood and carefully laid them on the fire. "That should do for awhile," she said softly to herself. She sat down on the wood chest with folded hands in front of her.

The clock struck the half hour. Bill softly stroked Fritz's head, to calm both himself and the dog. It was extremely quiet in the kitchen now. The tick-tock of the clock appeared slower than its usual measured time. This added to the uneasiness of wondering what may have happened to cause Father to be late.

"Still say it's that old horse. I hope this is the last time he takes her. He'll have learned his lesson." Ori refused to stay quiet.

Mama said sharply, "I don't want to hear any more of this! You don't blame anything on something you don't know for sure."

"I still think we should eat!" Ori stopped speaking as Benj placed a finger on his lips, closed his eyes in disgust and shook his head.

"We waited this long, we'll just . . ." Mama never finished speaking.

"They're here!" Til shouted, sticking his head through the open kitchen door, and hurriedly turned around to greet Father and Doll.

Del's eyes filled with tears. She reached into her apron pocket for a hankie, turned and quickly slipped into the side room. She didn't want anyone to see her tears. Bill and Fritz ran outside to meet Father.

Benj was the first to say something. "*Sisz gude aus ah doh isz, yuscht wennich schpode* [It is good that he is here, just little late]."

"We know he didn't miss the train," Ollie hurriedly added. Del was taken aback. She had never given thought to Father missing the train.

Benj got up. "*Ich schaffe mich selwart aus um weig* [I'll work myself out of the way]." He left the rocker and seated himself next to Carol on the couch. However, Carol got up and seated herself on the empty rocking chair and began an awkward rocking movement, much to Benj's bemusement. She was at that age where she wanted everyone to think she was older than she was.

Del knew Til was relieved his horse brought Father home. He'd talk to his precious Doll and lead her to the trough for fresh water and then on to her stall with fresh hay and bedding. After supper he'd go out to the barn and curry her. Bill helped Father with the harness and wagon. Mama started to slice home-baked bread, for soon everyone would sit down to eat.

Til burst into the kitchen with a very concerned look on his usually cheerful face. Bill followed, with a puzzled look. Fritz came immediately behind Bill, his tail pinched between his hind legs like he had been reprimanded.

"Mama, Father wants you to come out to the wagon. He wants to talk to you," Til said. Bill nodded silently in agreement.

Mama froze. She looked at the boys most seriously. Del never before saw such bewilderment on Mama's face. "Is your father all right?" she quickly inquired.

"I think so," said both boys in unison.

Before Til could say anything more Mama was on her way out without a wrap. The children looked at each other dumbfounded. Benj was fidgety while everyone else was mouse quiet. *"Des nemmed en ayewich-kite* [This takes forever]," he murmured.

The moments dragged on. "Do you know what's happening?" Del whispered to Bill.

"No, nothing," Bill shook his head slowly. "I wasn't at the wagon yet when I heard father tell Til to go back in the house and stay there and tell Mama to come out."

Del's mind darted from one worried thought to another. The fact that Til said Father was all right was of little comfort.

After long minutes, Mama stepped inside and quickly walked to Benj and softly said, "We need you outside."

Benj showed surprise such as Del never saw. Without waiting for an answer Mama headed for the closet in the side room, grabbed a sweater, and put it on while walking to the rocker as Carol was still moving slowly back and forth. Mama grabbed the fancy shawl that was draped across the back of the rocker. The many shades of gray with an intricate design always fascinated Del. No one was allowed to use it. So why did Mama grab that shawl?

"The rest of you stay right here unless we call you," Mama ordered. On her way back, she looked at Benj now standing by the sink. Mama nodded her head. He stepped immediately behind her and followed her out the door.

"Well, I declare," Del said loudly. "Never thought Benj could move that fast."

No one said a word. Del thought about what could possibly be happening outside. Mama was always so very particular with that shawl she grabbed. It was a treasured heirloom from Mama's father's great-great-grandmother's loom. To grab it so hurriedly had Del suspecting something had happened to Father after all. Til moved onto the enclosed porch. Father's desk chair springs creaked.

"One of these days I'll remember to oil those springs," Bill spoke softly.

"And me the attic door," Del remarked. "Are you sure Father is all right?" She pressed Bill for information.

"Seemed okay to me," he replied.

"Horse okay?" Ori asked sharply.

"You ask Til. She sure seemed all right—just as happy as always to see Til," Bill stated.

"Sure she's all right. There's nothing wrong with her," Til said as he stepped in from the porch.

"Is that all you have to say? Didn't you see any more than that?" begged Del.

"No Del, and the rest of you, there is nothing more to say." Til shrugged his shoulders. "I wasn't near the wagon. I went to unhitch Doll like I always do. She was already snorting and blowing, you know how she does when she sees me. She was bobbing her head up and down; there's nothing wrong with my horse," Til emphasized as he looked straight at Ori. "She sure was glad to be home." He paused as all eyes were focused on him. Then came a bold announcement. "And there is nothing wrong with Father either. I saw him come down off the wagon, same as he always does."

"Come, Carol," Ori said, "sit on my lap and I'll rock you." Carol obliged as she let Ori settle into the rocker and climbed on her lap.

"What do you suppose could be happening?" Ollie questioned his oldest brother.

"Beats me. Perhaps Father has something in the wagon he doesn't want us to see," Til spoke softly.

"Christmas presents!" Carol chimed happily.

"Fraid not!" Bill stated flatly. "It's too early for Christmas presents." Fritz lay by his feet with sad eyes. It seemed he too needed to ponder on the unusual activity.

Everyone turned abruptly as Benj opened the porch door and stepped into the kitchen. "Til, ya can take care of Doll." As Til moved, Benj caught his right arm and whispered something into his ear. Til nodded his head and went on his way. "Bill, ya come with me." Bill spun around on his heels as he grabbed his coat to follow. Benj stood in the doorway a moment longer and looked at each one individually. He said nothing, then turned and led the way for Bill to follow. Fritz was about to follow as well. *"Da hundt bleibt doh* [The dog stays here]." Benj made a hand movement backing Fritz away from the door. Fritz understood that. He moved under the table, head down and tail pinched.

"That means we all stay here," Del said as Ollie got up and headed for the porch.

"I'm only going for a fresh drink of water," Ollie said. He stopped by the bucket on the white table, grabbed the dipper and headed for the outside. Grabbing the long handled dipper was unnecessary since there was the tin cup or half coconut shell always available by the pump.

"Be sure that's all you do," Del admonished him.

Ollie's glanced at Del. "No one said we must all stay inside," he retorted as he left. He came back almost immediately and made his way into the kitchen.

"It wasn't worth going out, now was it?" Del smiled at Ollie.

He said nothing, pretending he heard nothing at all. He laid the dipper down alongside the small but heavy milk pail used to provide the household with fresh drinking water. He sat on the wood chest, folded his arms in disgust and then dropped them hard against his body. Del figured someone out there told him to go back inside.

Mama was first to come back. Everyone looked to her for answers. She spoke not a word, but moved about with a definite purpose. First she went into the side room, opened the stairway door and up the steps she went. Del listened carefully to know where her steps would carry her. She returned carrying a well-worn thin blanket, a tattered old quilt, and a comforter that had served a better day. She dropped them on a chair in the porch. She walked back into the side room. Del could hear her open a cabinet door. It closed, another door opened; it creaked like the closet door. Mama returned to the kitchen carrying an old sheet Del herself had placed on top of an empty lard can only yesterday to tear up for strips.

Mama said, "When Benj and the boys come in, you can eat. It is late enough for Carol and the rest of you. Adelaide, you slice bread. Be careful. Gloria, place hot food on the table. Leave some in the pots and set it aside, enough to stay warm for the rest of us."

Mama was gone as quickly as she had entered.

"See we can eat," Carol said eagerly.

"Carol and I will eat," Ori replied. "It's soon bedtime for her." She got a plate, cut some meat and prepared plates for the two of them. Del sliced some bread and buttered two slices for her sisters.

"I want to know what Father brought home," Carol admitted. "I don't want to go to bed."

"You can stay up as you sometimes do. I will have you ready for bed before you fall asleep," Ori assured Carol.

"Why do you say Father brought something home? We don't know that," Ollie questioned.

Del was thinking. The bedding that Mama carried out had her perplexed. She observed the same puzzled look on Ori's face. "What are you thinking?" Del asked.

"What I am thinking doesn't matter to anyone but me," Ori replied in a tone of superiority.

The door opened once more. Bill entered.

"I thought Benj would come back with you," said Del.

"He walked out the lane. Suppose he's going home. It's late enough already," Bill said as he sat down at the table.

"You mean toward his house?" Del was surprised. "It's dark outside." "You know a lantern is always handy. Mama said we could eat if we want to," Bill spoke soothingly.

"You really don't know what's going on out there. Do you?" Del could read Bill's puzzled face.

"I don't know any more than you." He answered with that same furrowed brow Del saw earlier that evening. "Whatever is going on is happening in the top of the barn. I am not allowed up there."

"You were out there! Didn't you see or hear anything?" Ollie wondered.

"Told you, not a thing," Bill replied.

"Does Til know more?" Del questioned Bill some more.

"Til doesn't know any more than I. He is busy with Doll. He was told the same as me," said Bill

"What were you told?" Ollie was quick to ask.

"'Tend to your business,' Benj told me, 'then go inside.'"

"Father is okay?" Del emphasized "is."

"He is alright," Bill nodded his head.

"It must be a wild animal we need to tame," Ollie decided.

Bill looked at Ollie skeptically but said nothing. He turned to Del. "I am sure Father is all right." Bill spoke with confidence.

"You know Mama was here and took bedding with her. . . . I really wonder about that. And that shawl from her Aunt Lizzie. . . . no one is allowed to use it."

Bill looked at Del and said, "I know, I saw it too." He patted his knee and Fritz immediately placed his head there as Bill stroked him tenderly.

Silence filled the room as everyone was puzzled about these strange events. Til entered the closed porch. The upwards roll of Father's desktop could be heard. Til was probably placing Father's market paperwork inside. Del heard the rolltop desk close. The springs of the comfortable chair squeaked and Del knew he had seated himself there again, as he rocked back and forth.

"I'll go out there and find out what's happening." Ollie was already halfway there.

"It won't do any good," Del reached out to stop him. He twisted his body to prevent Del from touching him as he opened the door to the porch. Just as quickly he returned with a downcast face.

"Told you so." Del knew her brother well.

Ollie plopped himself down on the wood chest looking more disgusted this time.

Del recalled Benj's comment about Ollie. He was so right. She turned to look at Ollie and studied him. Ollie was impatient and inquisitive; it was interesting to watch how he dealt with things.

Benj entered the porch and came directly into the kitchen to everyone's surprise. Why did he come back? Benj's actions told the children he was going to stay awhile longer as he prepared to wash up as he would those times he stayed for supper. Under ordinary circumstances he would be home at this time of night. "Why did he come back?" Bill whispered.

Benj tossed his cap on the hooks behind the door, exposing his shiny dome. Del smiled as she thought about his appearance. Seeing him wearing a cap one would think he had a head full of bushy, unkempt hair. All one saw was thick unruly hair around the base of his head. Coupled with his straggly brows, untrimmed and overgrown, they formed a natural shield shading his deep-set green eyes.

He he passed the teakettle to Ori—which meant she should fill it with warm water from the tank at the stove. Ori obliged without a word. She drew water from the tank, filled the teakettle, and placed it where it would get even warmer. She poured more water into the tank for later use.

"Ya can put supper on the table now." He pointed to the table with the wave of his hand.

Both girls looked at him to make sure they heard correctly.

"Go ahead, *sez allrecht* [it's all right]. They said to give ya a few minutes. They'll be here by the time ya have food on the table."

That was all it took for everyone to get busy. Bill grabbed the water pitcher and went out to the pump for fresh water. He returned with both Mama and Father. Til came in from the porch and stood in line behind his father waiting his turn to wash up. Mama handed the basin to Father. He poured the used water away, rinsed the basin with cold water, came over to the teakettle and poured water for himself. Mama dried her arms and hands thoroughly. She asked Carol to get a clean towel for her father. Carol was pleased to help; she moved to the cabinet next to the couch, opened the door, grabbed a towel and took it over to Mama. Mama tossed the towel onto Father's shoulder. She poked at the fire with the stove lid lifter and added another piece of wood to the fire. Father finished drying his hands and hung the towel on the rack behind the wood chest. Til was there, ready to follow. He finished by returning the washbasin to a nail in the wall where it hung behind the stove.

It was then Father turned to his family. "No greeting?" He smiled with open arms. Carol was the first to run for a hug. All other greetings were more casual. "That's better. I know you are wondering about things. Your mother and I will tell you as much as we can after we eat supper. It's getting late. By the time we've eaten it will be bedtime for some of you. And then, I suppose there is schoolwork that needs to be done for tomorrow. Maybe some of you found time to do your work?"

There was no time for response from the children as Mama announced, *"Huck deich* [Seat yourselves]."

Father took his place at the far end of the table. The three boys were seated on the long bench located between the table and the western wall in front of a deep window seat that held the parsley wrapped inside newspaper for Mama to cut up for drying. "Do I have to smell all that parsley?" Ollie fussed. He was the one family member who disliked most seasonings, especially onions and parsley.

"Pederli dud der nix [Parsley does ya nothing]," Benj said as he seated himself opposite from Father. Del and Ori were seated across from the boys. Mama shared the same side closest to the stove with Carol. Fritz, as usual, was under the table. He was a footrest for Ollie and a

scavenger for both Bill and Del seated across the table from each other. Heads were bowed and grace was offered in unison.

"God is great, God is good.

And we thank him for our food.

By His hand we all are fed;

Thank you Lord, for daily bread. Amen."

The meal was eaten in an atmosphere of relief as Father talked about his day in Philadelphia. He mentioned the people he saw. He talked about the things said. One firm was interested in purchasing more butter if it was available. There were stockpiles of fruits and produce at the huge warehouses on the riverfront. Most of the goods were being shipped to cities near by. He described the giant posters at the Philadelphia station about the coming election. Father saw the stationmaster at Lyon Station, who was back to his old self again after a bout with the grippe. He hadn't missed a day's work for fifteen years. The doctor told him he needed to be careful this coming winter, if he hopes to have another fifteen years with no illness.

Father looked to Til. "I met the veterinarian at the train station. He said he saw Doll when he stopped by to visit with Sam. He said he could tell your Doll is one horse that is well taken care of. I told him you are responsible for her care. He said you are doing a fine job."

Til looked very pleased with the praise.

"No horse for miles around gets more attention," Father chuckled.

"Except," Benj interjected, "perhaps Billy Henry's. There's a real horseman. Every hour his creamery business allows, he is over in the horse barn currying Dick or Harry. Ya must take after yer grandfather," Benj pointed a finger at Til.

"Sam's shop is a gathering place for the neighborhood and anybody else that passes through," observed Mama.

"You're so right, Loll. More news there than you can read in the newspaper," Father laughed.

"I think men are bigger gossips than women," Mama smiled. "Is Octavia all right? Is she over her bronchitis?"

"Sam assured me your cousin is okay."

"Talkin' about politics," Benj continued, "won't be long fer the big political rally on the corner uptown. Levi tells me that German band will play again. Better the band than those political speeches. It's all hogwash anyway."

Mama ate quickly and got up. Del tried hard not to show how very watchful she was of Mama's every move. Mama poured some milk into a small saucepan. Next she poured hot water over catnip tea. She lifted the stove lid, set it aside, and reached for the toasting wire. She placed a piece of bread between the wire holder and held it over a low fire until it was very dark, actually black before turning it over to blacken the other side. She reached for the butter still on the table and buttered one side, laying the blackened toast on a cutting board to cut into small squares. By now Del knew what her mama was doing. Blackened toast with warm milk and catnip tea meant that someone had a bellyache. Del always felt much better after Mama's old-fashioned remedy. As for the catnip tea Del could always do without that. "Who in the world is sick? Do we have a sick tramp in the barn?" Del thought.

When everyone finished Del and Ori cleared the table of used dishes and leftover food. Mama poured coffee for Father and Benj.

"Help yourselves to dessert. I have other things to do," Mama said softly. Mama and Father usually lingered over a cup of coffee and some-times a second cup was poured. They enjoyed this quiet time after an evening meal, but tonight was not a typical evening.

Mama looked at all the children and gave directions. "Adelaide and William, you take care of the dishes. Get Oliver to help you. Gloria, take care of Carol, it's near her bedtime. Keep some boiled cabbage and meat warming on the stove a while longer." Del grabbed the tea-kettle and poured some hot water to do the dishes. "Put more water in the stove's tank for me," Mama gestured while she continued her preparations. "Oliver make yourself handy. You are next in line to clear the table and help with the dishes."

Ollie said nothing and showed no emotion, but he had to be as dis-appointed as the rest of the children that there was no explanation for Father's delay. Del watched Mama pour hot water into a basin from the teakettle and set the basin on her largest tray. Next she placed a bar of homemade soap and washcloth wrapped inside a towel on the tray. She stuck her finger in the warming milk, testing the temperature. She covered the pan of milk with a clean tea towel, got a small spoon and the old tin cup for tea.

Father, too, was watching her. "Soon ready?" he spoke softly.

"Right now," Mama answered.

"Children, it's late. I will talk to you in the morning before you go to school and tell you more about my day." Father turned to leave.

Mama lifted a few items off of the tray to make carrying easier for Father. Not much was said amongst the children as Benj left the table and returned to the rocking chair. Del washed dishes while Ori put food to warm on the stove.

Bill grabbed a tea towel and threw it to Ollie, "Try your hand at that." He grabbed a second towel for himself and said with a smile, "I will help you tonight. From what I hear you are taking my place in the kitchen."

Ollie accepted the challenge with nary a word. Fritz left his place by the bench, moved over to Benj and sat against his legs.

"*Doch wil ich awwer* [Here will I wonder]. Huh," Benj mused, "now you come to me like I belong." He stroked the dog's head and commenced to talk inaudibly to Fritz. As Del moved to the table to collect the last of the dishes she caught a few of his words. "*Druwwel auschaft* [Trouble brought on]." He rubbed the dog's head roughly. It appeared Fritz had fully accepted Benj as family. Surely that couldn't bring any trouble. She didn't mind sharing Fritz with Benj, and was quite sure Bill would accept that as well. Fritz already spent a lot of the day with Benj while they attended school. "Bet that's why Fritz didn't meet them that day—he was somewhere with Benj," Del supposed.

The kitchen work was completed in quiet efficiency. Ori kept the kettle of food only half way on the heated stove lid to keep it warm. Ori began preparing Carol for bed. "Must I?"

"For now, yes, Carol." Ori replied.

"I want to be here when Father comes back," Carol protested.

"Father told us nothing more will be said this evening," Ori said as she undid Carol's pigtails that were tied up in a loop. She placed the red ribbons on the window seat behind the couch. She brushed Carol's hair with slow easy strokes. Her widow's peak was noticeable as her hair was brushed back. That made her Mama's child since she had a similar hairline, only Carol's hair was a soft brown and Mama's hair was very dark. Ori checked the water, put some in a basin and told Carol to follow her upstairs. Carol was fussing.

"Don't you fret. I need to do this now. You may come down in your nightgown later. Better you go with me, else I might have to carry you to bed. I still have some reading for school tomorrow and it is already later than it should be."

After they left, Ollie looked at Benj as he seated himself at the table with his schoolbook and tablet. "You can tell us what's happening in the barn. You were out there." All the children looked at Benj.

"That yer 'rithmetic book?" Benj pointed to it. "Ya work at that. That's all I have to say." He looked around the room. "The rest of ya had better get yer work done. Ya heard what yer father said. It may get too late fer him to tell ya anything more tonight."

When Mama returned she looked at Benj and smiled. She was pleased about something. She made another two pieces of toast as dark as before and warmed more milk while she stepped into the side room. Del heard a cabinet door open, then that of a small tin can pried open. Mama returned, and Del spotted the folded parchment paper as she laid it on the tray. She knew exactly what that meant. The folded parchment held worm powder that Mama kept in a small square red tin container. It was precisely then Del figured for sure Father brought a person home. One dose of that brown powder kept in neatly folded white parchment would cleanse the intestinal system. Mama tested the warmth of the milk, picked up the pan and headed for the outdoors.

"What did Mama get in the other room?" Ollie asked.

"Worm powder," Del answered with immense satisfaction at her powers of observation and deduction.

"Worm powder!" Til exclaimed. A reaction of this sort was most unusual from him. "Are you sure?" Til was indeed as curious as were the rest of the children.

"That's what I said. I know where mama keeps that stuff. I saw her get it once when she showed Aunt Lillie what Dr. Schlicher's worm powder looked like. She even gave her one dose to take along."

"Why on earth would she take worm powder out to the barn?" Bill thought out loud.

"For someone sick," Til answered slowly and softly.

Ori returned with Carol, looked around, and asked, "Now, what is going on?"

"Mama came back. She took more toast and milk with her. Del says she took worm powder along." Ollie spoke without taking his eyes off his tablet.

"Who believes that!" Ori scoffed.

"I do, I saw it," Del replied.

No one spoke for quite a spell. Benj looked at Til. "Are ya making guesses about what is going on out there?"

"I have no idea," Til replied. "I thought maybe Father had a sick animal that he was being very careful with. But worm powder! That's not used on animals."

"Why else would Mama make burned toast and warm milk? She makes all of us eat that if we have a bellyache or something," Del said with conviction.

"Maybe it's a sick tramp Father took pity on," Til paused. "He might need worm powder."

"Could be." Bill mulled over that information. "That isn't so bad that we couldn't know about it." Bill paused: "But I didn't seen anyone in the wagon." Bill turned his gaze on Benj.

"Don't ya look at me, *gsaadah nix* [tell ya nothing]."

"It could be Clint. Early autumn he heads for Florida and spends the winter there. Maybe he's hurt and Father brought him along home. He sleeps in the barn when he passes through. I bet that's who it is," Til said confidently.

"Father wouldn't have to explain anything. We already know all there is to know about his cousin Clint," Ori snorted. "Come on Carol, we'll go to bed. I'll grab my library book and read some before I go to sleep."

"Your light isn't bright enough for you to read up there. Mama says you will ruin your eyes," Del reminded Ori.

"I won't be reading that long. I am tired too," yawned Ori.

"Surely more of ya have studying to do," Benj said.

"You are never here when we do our lessons," Ollie was quick to answer.

"That's where ya is wrong. I come and sit on the front porch and wait 'til all the lessons is done, then yer parents and I chat awhile."

"Really!" Del was most surprised.

"Yep, sometimes Becky, sometimes Ed and Hester. I never hear yer going over and over the same lesson," Benj turned to Del

"I don't study much. I know everything by heart," Del admitted.

"*Un wie is sel* [And how is that]?"

"I hear the older grades recite their work. After eight people recite the same poem, give the same book reports and spell the same words, I know it all by heart. I pick the most interesting things I hear from the others and teacher always says, 'Very good.' Besides that, I hear Ori and Til go over their lessons and poems."

"Does the teacher know this?" Benj asked.

"He should. He sits there with his eyes closed when someone is reciting a poem. He knows immediately when you make a mistake. He himself must have everything memorized. He must know we can do the same," Del giggled.

There was no response as both parents returned. They signaled to Benj; he got up and headed for the door. Before the porch door closed, Del heard, "*Isses recht mitt deer* [Is it alright with you]?" Father questioned as they headed outside.

Benj nodded his head. "*Ses nootwennich. Mah duhna wos mir kenna. Sehne eich mariye* [It's necessary. We do what we can. See you tomorrow.]"

After all kitchen work was completed, Bill stepped outside carrying the dishwater to the drain in the washhouse. Returning, he whispered softly to Del, "Benj is walking in the lane with a lantern. Someone else is with him too."

"Who else?"

"Don't know."

Her parents returned. Del noticed not one dish was returned. Mama carefully folded the shawl over her arm and laid it on the couch.

"Maybe we should check after a couple of hours," Mama looked at Father. He nodded his head in agreement.

Mama immediately set out to put the leftover foods away. Whoever it was that Ori set the pot of warm food aside for was not going to need it. Del wondered who that could have been but refrained from asking.

The children waited to hear if Father had anything more to say. Del's mind was busy trying to put two and two together.

Father looked at them and said, "It is late. Get a good night's sleep. Everything is alright for now."

The clock struck ten. That meant it was time for everyone to occupy the second floor. Del made her way slowly up the stairs, taking one step at a time. She turned at the top of the stairs and walked the strip of carpeted floor in her parents' room and onto the linoleum flooring in her room. She quickly turned and decided to go to Mama's bedroom window, which provided a view to the barn area. She saw a bent figure standing beside another tall figure in the darkened area close to the barn. "Could Grandfather be here this late? Can't be Grandfather, how would he get here? Was food kept warm for him? Just who is that other person?" and other questions raced through her mind.

She moved quietly and quickly to her bedroom. In no time at all she was under the covers, determined to lay awake and think about all the unusual happenings. She said her prayers by rote. Del remembered Father's concerned face as he looked at Benj and cautiously asked, "Is it all right with you?" and Benj's answer. Del's mind swirled with questions. "Was Benj staying the night? Bill said he saw Benj walking toward his home earlier but he came back after that. What was necessary? It couldn't be Father's cousin, who is a tramp," Del thought. "He stays in the barn by himself and gets large helpings of whatever Mama prepares for us. He never needs covers, either." Del planned to check if all the knives were sharpened in the morning, because Clint always did that to repay them. Then she would know for sure. She thought about a hobo's life and drifted off to sleep.

CHAPTER THREE

Distractions at School

Mama's heavy footsteps on the bedroom floor awakened Del. She immediately remembered the night before and sat up abruptly.

"Good morning. Are you awake already?" Mama greeted Del as she moved around her bed for the last time, straightening the patchwork quilt so that it covered the bed evenly. "Fix your bed, then come down and help me with breakfast. Ed is doing your morning work, Gloria's too except for collecting the eggs."

Del moved quickly as she dressed for school wondering why their neighbor, Ed, was here this weekday morning. He usually stopped by after a day's work for milk, as did other neighbors. "Was he one of the people she saw last night by the barn?" she pondered.

Her gingham apron, hanging on the clothes tree, was all Del needed to help with the morning breakfast. Mama taught her to pin the apron pattern onto fabric and cut the material. Del was fearful of making a cutting mistake even though Mama had looked over the pattern pieces and gave her approval. She pulled the apron ties firmly around her waist and tied it in back as she headed down the stairs.

The morning was the usual routine. The parsley, untouched from last evening, heavily scented the kitchen. Ollie was sure to fuss about that. Til and Bill were already up and out in the barn along with Father completing their morning chores before heading off to school. Carol, who usually slept until breakfast call, came down just ahead of Ori and slumped down on the couch. Ori moved about slowly. You never hurried her—she had her own pace and a fixed routine. She reached for her plaid jacket that hung on the wall behind the stairs door and headed outdoors. Ori liked the colors and the fit when Mama's Aunt Lizzie brought the hand-me-down along from her home in Boyertown. Although Mama said the jacket did not have any warmth to it, Ori wanted it anyway. "Red is my favorite color, it has lots of red." Mama decided to keep the peace, then busied herself designing and making a flannel lining to fit the garment. Ori wore it spring and fall for a couple of years. Now it was faded and worn through at the cuffs and collar.

Mama muttered after Ori passed through the kitchen. "That jacket will disappear one day."

"I don't think Ori will like that."

"Like it or not, its got to go after this season. I'll let her wear it for the outside work this fall. It's worn so thin it surely can't keep her warm."

"I saw her put a sweater on underneath that jacket. She says Taw-Taw likes the jacket as much as she does."

Mama smiled with a faint "hmm" but said no more.

Ori's morning responsibility was to take care of the chickens. She would prop open the small doors for the chickens to jump to the outside and peck at shelled corn scattered about on the ground. Next she collected the eggs, added fresh water to the water hoppers and supplied laying mash to fill the slender troughs throughout the henhouse. A piece of board with small strips affixed across it made a ladder to allow all poultry to enter the henhouse for food and water and select a nest to lay their eggs during the day. Of course, her precious Taw-Taw needed to be released from his coop. However, this morning she was especially slow getting anything done since Ed did most of her morning work.

"She didn't braid my hair." Carol sat up after Ori left to do her morning work.

"There's time for that when Gloria gets back. You are up earlier than you need be," said Mama. "Adelaide, set the table. Get the biggest fry pan and put it on the front burner. Slice bread, not too thick. Quarter the boiled small potatoes for frying. I will add lard and place them in the pan when I get back."

Mama prepared a mixture of cocoa, sugar, some water and a pinch of salt in a kettle and set it aside. Del knew fresh milk would be added some time later. Mama put on her bonnet, her bright pink sweater, and headed for the outside. Del knew she would not do any milking since she was wearing her bright pink sweater, a gift from her Aunt Kate last Christmas. Mama did return as expected with a tall pitcher of fresh milk.

"I see you set a place for Benj. Good. He'll be having breakfast with us."

"I thought so. It's the first time he's here for breakfast," Del spoke freely. "Why did he come back last night? Bill saw him head for home. Was he here all night?"

Mama hesitated, then finally said, "Not all night." Del sensed Mama did not wish to say any more as she decided to talk about schoolwork.

"Last night Benj wondered why I never study at home. I don't think he believes me—I remember things from hearing them repeated again and again."

"Oh?" Mama seemed surprised. "I think he does. He knows you are a bright girl." Mama paused again. "I don't want you to tell anyone about Benj spending the night in the barn. You are not to talk about anything pertaining to last evening. Nor that your father was late coming home."

"Oh, I won't. Do I have to go to school today?"

"You want perfect attendance again this year. You will go the same as all the rest. Concentrate on your school topics today. There would be more questions asked if one or all of you didn't go to school. Your teacher would be here in a jiffy, and this very day for sure. He'd want to know what was happening. It's just today and tomorrow, then there is Saturday."

"Is this a predicament?"

Mama laughed. "I know where you get that word from. Benj refers to everything as a predicament."

The door opened slowly, and in came Becky. "Woodie said I should stop by and say hello. Is there something I can do for you?"

"Come on in, Becky. Adelaide, why don't you go and throw some corn to the pigs this morning, not too much since they also get corn every evening. Take Carol with you."

"But my hair isn't braided. I am not dressed to go out. Must I?" Carol questioned.

"You may go along just as you are. You'll be taken care of later."

"Come along, Carol." Del immediately knew her mother needed to be obeyed without any questions. She grabbed a sweater that fit like a coat around Carol. She took her hand and moved slowly to the outside. Along the walkway Carol complained some more.

Del sighed, "I could let you sit here by the bench under the grape arbor if I could trust you not to go back inside while Becky is here." They entered the dirt lane that separated the house from the barn-yard and passed by the side of the barn. "Might as well see what Bill is doing," Del paused, "or Til."

Carol half-ran alongside to keep up with her sister. "I can't walk so fast."

"Sorry, we can move slower. I forget you're too little to keep up with me when I'm in a hurry."

Del tossed some scrawny cobs of corn into the pigpen. She started the last crate of scrub corn. The pigs made short work of the scraps thrown to them. Carol seemed to enjoy the hogs pushing and shoving to get at the tasty corn. Del saw Mama and Becky walk out of the house. She watched Becky walk in that slow, shuffling movement of hers, which she considered equivalent to a slow waltz, while Mama grabbed Becky's milk kettle. Del knew it was ok to return to the kitchen.

Breakfast was mostly quiet yet disrupted with members of family com-ing in and going out. Everyone was told to help themselves with choices on the table. Ollie was the first one in. "I'll get my food and sit outside under the grape arbor to eat. That parsley smell will surely make me sick."

Mama said, "You'll survive, Oliver. I'll take care of that before you come home for dinner."

Ollie left with a bowl of cornflakes as his brothers came in laughing, their morning chores completed.

Del asked why Fritz wasn't with Bill. He spoke softly. "He decided to stay in the middle of the lane, he can watch everything from there." Del could picture Fritz's guarding position, wondering what the dog thought of last evening's events.

Mama asked if everyone had enough to eat. A simple nodding of heads ensued. She bid the children good day with, "Mind your manners, don't mention anything about last night or that your father was late coming home. You hear me," she said firmly as she prepared more of the same food taken to the barn last night.

As the children gathered for their walk to school, Fritz was nowhere to be seen.

"Well, I'll be," Bill said as he whistled for Fritz. "He was here a bit ago." Fritz came running from the back of the barn. "What have you been up to?" Bill asked impatiently. "We never have to call you when it's time to go to school."

The twins walked out the east lane with Fritz between them along with their siblings. They took advantage of this time to share thoughts and discuss ideas.

"There's a person in the barn," Del remarked quietly.

"Don't think so," Bill shook his head.

Del was convinced she was right.

"How do you figure that?" Til questioned.

"I don't think Father would keep a person in the barn," Bill concluded.

"Clint stays in the barn," Ollie chimed in.

"It's not Clint. I know that much," Til said. "It's no secret when he is here."

"I've been thinking. I read that a lamb is very tender and needs the same care as a person, if something happened to a mama sheep," Ollie concluded.

"Surely a lamb wouldn't be fed human food!" Del paused as she looked at Ollie. "I think it's a man." Del straightened her shoulders as she looked at the others.

"Nothing so far makes any sense," Bill said. "I go along with Til's idea that Father doesn't have a sick tramp in the barn. Whatever it is, Father doesn't want us to go near. He told us this morning to do our work with the cattle, but don't go up to the threshold until he wants us there. He also told us not to talk about this in school today. He did say that he's getting a truck. That is exciting news."

"I didn't know anything about a truck," Del exclaimed. "Why does Father want a truck?"

"I'm sure Ori knows. She won't admit to anything. I saw Father speak to her after she got the eggs." Bill concluded.

Til walked slowly to hear what Bill and Del were talking about. His long legs usually took him to school much faster than his younger siblings. He listened without entering into the conversation. Ori followed at a good distance. The duck slowed her walk as he strutted alongside. Taw-Taw only followed to the beginning of Benj's yard. Ori would pick him up and turn him back toward the homestead, while Fritz waited until the twins walked down the cement pike a couple hundred yards. Upon their turn onto Funk's Lane that led to the one-room schoolhouse, the dog also turned and headed for home. If Taw-Taw had not made it back by that time, Fritz surely hurried that duck along.

As Del entered Funk's Lane, Mae, Ori's classmate, was waiting at the lane where her father dropped her off. "Ori is on her way," Del announced.

"I already see her," Mae answered.

"How can you be sure it's a him?" Bill asked quietly.

"I heard Benj say, *'Ah dutt zhimlich gute* [He does rather well].'"

"I heard that too," Til chimed in. "We had better forget about the whole matter right now. The Shultz boys are coming, so we can't say much more."

Del and Bill nodded their heads in agreement. Del started skipping as she always did and entered the school grounds with a promise to herself. She would forget about last night's happenings. She would meet her desk buddy, Emma, on the school grounds. She was usually there when Del arrived. Joe, Em's brother, greeted Del and said that Em was sick and at home. Del would not be tempted to tell Em about events Mama warned her not to talk about. It would be an easy day for her.

The school bell sounded. Mr. Strunk was still placing the rope on the holding hooks that stilled the bell as each child got in line to greet their teacher 'good morning', and immediately proceed to their assigned seats. A wide aisle down the center of the room separated the girls from the boys. Boys sat on the right and girls on the left. A one-step platform ran along the front of the room. Blackboards occupied the front wall and maps were rolled up above them. Teacher's desk was centered on the front of the one-step platform. Two rows of double desks ran along both sides of the center aisle. Narrow aisles ran between the double-seat desks. All students stood beside their desks and school started with a Bible reading, a prayer, then singing songs and reciting the Pledge of Allegiance.

Del sat alone at her desk. She looked over the library books on the deep window seat during the first recess time. She found a book about fish, trout in particular; she had never heard a book report on trout from the older grades. She grabbed the book as Mr. Strunk headed to the vestibule to ring the bell, signaling with one ring that recess time was spent. Returning, he walked over to the window seat and asked, "Are you taking that book home?"

"Maybe." Del was surprised he noticed.

"That book is a little too easy for you, but of course you may read it. The more challenging books are back there on the third window seat."

"I never heard a book report on it. That's why I picked it up. Is it a boy's book?"

Mr. Strunk studied Del for a moment; she was beginning to feel uneasy. "No, it's not just a boy's book, it's for anyone to read. As I said, the books on the back window seat are more for your age group. I don't think you heard book reports on those either. All those books are new. You'll have to read them if you want to know what's between the covers."

With that said he turned on his heel to check if all the children were accounted for. Del knew the full number would be thirty-four students—sixteen girls and eighteen boys when there was full attendance.

It was a quick run home for dinner. Mama wanted to hear about the morning session. She first looked to Til.

"Tilghman, what say you?"

"No one said anything about yesterday."

"Is that so for all of you?" Mama looked around the table. "That sounds a little too easy. Are you sure you had no problem?"

"Em would have asked me about the Philly trip, but she is absent today. I have no one to talk to," Del said.

"Good, everything seems to be alright," Mama commented.

"We got new library books," Del announced.

"No we did not!" Ori interrupted emphatically.

"Oh yes, we did. Teacher told me we got new books on the rear window seat that I should read."

"When could you have talked to him?" Ori wanted to know.

"You and Mae always go off by yourselves at recess. I stayed inside and looked at the new books."

"You always have to know everything first."

"Now now, girls. I know library books are exchanged from time to time with the other township schools. It doesn't happen often enough," Mama said with a reproving tone.

Ollie was quiet throughout the dinner hour.

"Everything okay with you?" Mama asked Oliver.

Ollie shrugged his shoulders, tossed his hands up, and said. "There is nothing to say, so I said nothing. I was the pitcher today when we played Round Town. Til said I did pretty good."

"You keep your mind on pitching ball. You'll be alright." Mama seemed pleased as she checked the stove; she slowed the fires by tilting all the lids and assessed the water tank level. Del thought she was just doing things to appear busy and not encourage questions.

Fritz was out in the lane waiting for the children as they headed back to school for the afternoon session. The dog didn't go all the way. He turned back as they approached Benj's yard, which he sometimes did when Benj was not at home. The heavy wooden door was shut. Benj had to be somewhere on the homestead, as well as Father. Neither of them had come by for dinner.

Del's wondering about things did not cease. Perhaps the barn was empty now. But Mama still prepared food for someone. Del asked Bill what he thought. Bill simply shrugged his shoulders.

"You didn't say anything to anybody, did you?" Del inquired as she gazed at Bill.

"I said nothing, nothing at all. Lester thought I was much too quiet. I assured him I was feeling just fine."

"Good for you," Del said as Bill joined his brothers rushing to meet the Shultz boys. Del was left to her own thoughts. All the boys met and turned into the school lane. Wilbur and Amanda Shultz were the parents of five boys. There was no mistaking who was first born, for Amanda named her children in alphabetical order. Del skipped by herself on the sandy surface of Funk's Lane. Del and her siblings were among the few families living close enough to the one-room schoolhouse to run home for dinner. On rainy days Del sometimes felt envious of those who carried a lunch box or bag.

During the late afternoon period, Mr. Strunk chose to sit on the vacant half of Del's double desk seat. This was an embarrassing situation, because it usually meant one needed additional help or close watching, or even worse, disciplining. Del tried to appear engrossed in her work, but to no avail. Mr. Strunk laughed quietly as he pointed to her open book turned the wrong way. Del could feel herself getting quite red as she turned her book to its reading position. She shyly glanced about to see if anyone else had noticed. She knew everyone was aware of where Teacher was at all times. She was doubly cross with herself for not concentrating on her geography lesson in the earlier period. She could not answer the question the other class members had missed. Mr. Strunk usually depended on her to have a correct answer. The whole episode kept her from concentrating on anything else the remainder of the day.

At long last the day was in. All the children lined up. The front rows first, in single file, to take Mr. Strunk's hand and bid him 'good day'. Del gave him her hand, but decided not to look into his face. She hated herself enough already. The idea that the entire school thought she needed some kind of supervision was a feeling she was not accustomed to bear.

He shook her hand and laughed a bit. "Your mind wasn't on the work today. I suppose tomorrow you'll do better."

"Oh yes, I will." That said, she avoided looking at his face and instead focused on the shock of bristly gray hairs that covered his head. Dropping her eyes she noticed Mr. Strunk's gray eyes studying her. She rushed outside and waited for Bill.

"What in the world did you do that Teacher had to sit with you? Did you tell him what we weren't supposed to talk about?"

"I said absolutely nothing. He said I was daydreaming, simply because I couldn't answer that one stupid geography question."

Til, who sat in the very last seat, was always the first one out, and he opened the heavy outside door and set the prop. He was tall for his age and needed the biggest desk to sit comfortably. He waited for Del and Bill. "Should I stay with you, and explain to Mama that no one said anything to make Teacher ask if something was bothering us?"

"There is nothing wrong, I told him. I didn't say a thing."

"I know that. Mr. Strunk said as much."

"What do you mean?" Del asked.

"He told me he didn't think you sitting alone today would cause you to daydream and not concentrate on the work and lesson to be reviewed. He laughed at that."

"Why would he think that is funny?" Del questioned. " I don't know why he had to tell this to you."

"You okay then?" Til wondered.

"Sure I'm all right," Del assured him. "Still don't know why . . ."

"I'll tell you later." Til started his long stride.

"Tell me why Teacher chose to sit with you." Bill spoke softly as the twins headed up the hill to the dirt lane.

"How should I know? I sure wasn't talking too much. He could have been tired and decided to sit where there was an empty seat."

"He never does that. He has his own desk chair in front of us all. Or else he will sit in the last seat at the center aisle where he can watch everything that is happening." Bill knew there had to be something more to cause Mr. Strunk to be seated next to his sister.

Del was not going to admit that her opened book was upside down. "Who knows?" was her only response.

They entered the east lane. Fritz was there waiting for them, wagging his tail wildly as they greeted him in their usual fashion. Del skipping, one hand resting on Fritz's back, Bill on the other side taking long strides, also keeping one hand on the dog's large head. Benj was waiting by the woodshed.

"And how was yer school day? Did ya learn anything new?" Benj dropped the axe and looked squarely at the twins, studying their faces intently. Del observed how his green eyes opened wider than usual as he peered from one to the other.

"Everything go all right for ya?" He straightened up as best he could and waited for a reply.

Bill spoke. "Sure, no one had a problem. Ori doesn't say anything to anybody. Til and the Shultz boys only talk about horses and farming. Raymond had the sniffles and stayed well to his side of the desk while Ollie has his mind on playing ball all the time."

"And me," Del interrupted. "I didn't have a partner all day. Em is sick. Who could I talk to?"

"Well now, that's just dandy. Good to hear. Just one more day."

The twins looked at each other, pleased that Benj seemed to be satisfied, and made their way to the house for whatever snack Mama would have on the table.

"There's some of dem dark chocolate cookies on the table. I beat ya to them. Must say, dem is the best," he called after, with the wave of his right arm. The chocolate cookies said it all. Del immediately knew Becky had been back at the homestead sometime this day.

Mama was waiting as the children gathered. Ori of course would be a little later. Her pet was at his usual place under the plank bridge covering a running spring near the entrance of the farm. Taw-Taw would be there at the end of the school day. Ori never appreciated that. He would be wet when she came home. She had to wait for the feathers to dry before she allowed him to perch on her shoulder. If Taw-Taw spent time in the creek then there was no holding Taw-Taw the entire evening.

"How did you all do this afternoon?" Mama asked.

"Just fine," the children said in unison.

"Mr. Strunk told me he would stop by sometime this week and ask Father if he can get milk since his cow is about to stand dry," Til volunteered to Del's surprise because Til had not said anything about their teacher wanting milk at noon-time. Til continued, "I told him we had one cow that is about to calf and told him the Ayrshire, Daisy, was milked separately and saved for little Ernie. He sure was surprised at that and wondered how long this was the case."

"So no one told him his great-grandchild gets milk from only one cow," Mama smiled.

Mr. Strunk made regular visits to help Ernie with his schoolwork, so he could stay with his class once he was strong enough to come back to school. Del thought it was good of him to do so but Benj thought differently. 'Amos Strunk would not do that for a child outside his family. *Blut laafed dicher oss wasser* [Blood runs thicker than water],' he had said when he learned about the special teaching.

"Will he ever be all right again?" Bill asked, interrupting Del's thoughts. "I haven't seen Ernie at all this year."

Mama replied, "Of course you haven't seen Ernie. Tuberculosis is quite contagious. That's why he is isolated. We hope the richer milk from Daisy will help him get well."

"I was in the barn when Dr. Schlicher came in to look at the cows. He picked Daisy right away," Bill offered.

"The doctor must know something about cows. Your grandfather knew immediately when we brought her home. The richer milk said it all." Mama was pleased that her father recognized the richer Ayrshire cream after operating a creamery business for many years.

Fritz was by Del's side as she finished pouring slop for the pigs. He came from the barnbank where he could watch most everything that was happening. She patted him gently as they walked slowly back and forth, to and fro, placing all buckets and tools in their proper places and securing latches. "Yes, Fritz, you and I will be just like before, and Bill too, when whatever is going on around here is settled. I'll race you to the walk." Fritz obliged. The shadows of dusk were fast approaching as the sun slid behind the hill. It was time to go inside and set the table.

Mama was busy mashing a large pot of potatoes. "You better set the table right away. Get a clean tablecloth. We can eat very shortly."

"Was Bill in to tell you they are finished outside?" Del asked.

"No, Benj was," Mama nodded her head in the direction of the rocking chair where Benj was seated.

Del said no more as she washed her arms up to her elbows. She was pivoting about as she was preparing the table rather hurriedly.

"We have an army girl," Benj laughed. "She turns around on her heel like a soldier."

"I suppose she learns that from her school teacher. He can turn around on his heel so quickly, he sometimes almost loses his balance," Mama added.

"How do you know that?" Del asked.

"He was my school teacher too."

Del would have had more questions about that except Father and the boys entered the kitchen at that particular time.

"*Huck deich* [Seat yourself]," was all Mama had to say. The clock struck once. It was half past the hour of six.

The meal conversation was a mixture of questions Father kept asking, attempting to make it seem like just another school day. "Will your partner be back in school tomorrow?" he asked Del.

"Don't know for sure. She hardly ever misses school, but with it being Friday tomorrow, I'll probably have the desk to myself again."

"You shared your desk with Teacher today," Ori announced.

"It will be good for Amos to come by for milk until his cow is fresh again. It will give Tamara a chance to visit." Del was happy Mama changed the subject.

"No one needs an excuse to stop by here," Bill observed. "It seems everybody comes here one time or another and any time they please."

"True enough," Mama said. "But Mrs. Strunk is a bit more formal than most folks around here. She doesn't want to infringe on anyone's personal time. I always tell her I can cook and bake and do my work even though she is visiting. Talk doesn't require the use of my hands. She knows what it is like to be busy. She raised a large family. Her children are all grown and on their own. Only now she has a day to herself."

"Del shared her desk with teacher today," Ori chimed in once more.

"So that's what's wrong," Benj looked at Del. "Ya was much too quiet this evening."

Til responded. "She didn't misbehave." Del was grateful for her older brother's defense.

Del was glad her mother had other things on her mind as she watched her rise from the table and prepare a tray with food. Mama placed mashed potatoes in a cereal bowl with plenty of gravy. She buttered bread and poured warm milk in the old tin cup that had been used last night. And tea—*sallwei* [sage] leaves were brewed.

"*Bischt ready* [Are you ready]?" Father asked Mama.

"Yes, we can always come back for more if need be."

With that Del's parents were off to the outside.

"Absolutely another person," Del whispered to Bill as they gathered the leftover food and dishes. Bill tilted his head slightly, but Del couldn't tell whether he agreed or not.

"So ya didn't misbehave," Benj couldn't wait to hear more about the school episode.

Del turned and looked at Benj. "No, I didn't. And I don't know why teacher chose to share my desk."

"*Ich dank doo duscht. Mir finnis ouse* [I think you do. We'll find it out]."

"Just like I'll find out what's out there in the barn. It is a person! Isn't it?"

"Now, now. Don't trick me here. Ya will find out soon enough." Benj sat back in the rocking chair and picked up the newspaper, making sure there would be no further conversation.

Mama returned, looking extremely pleased. She scooped some more mashed potatoes into the bowl and heated the gravy until it was quite hot. She took a cup and poured gravy into it. Once more she headed out to the barn.

"A person is in the barn. I am convinced of that." Del announced as she looked around the room. Her siblings did not appear convinced.

Benj paused for a long moment, while he stroked Fritz's large brown and white head ever so gently. "Ya will get nothing from me. Tomorrow. . . . can't wait fer tomorrow to talk about all this. And ya know how I like to talk. Fret not, it'll be a surprise, pleasant I hope. *Ich wil ennicher so huffa* [I will certainly hope so]."

Mama and Father came inside. With a few whispered words to Benj they gathered fresh cups of coffee and moved to the parlor. Del wanted very much to listen to the conversation between her parents and Benj. Unfortunately the noise of dishes being washed and the dried ones being stacked covered their words.

Til grabbed a schoolbook from the windowsill and made his way upstairs. One by one the others climbed the stairs. Del put the last dish away and checked the bread supply for the morning. She slowly moved past the table and to the stairs. Once alone in her room she looked through her only window and saw nothing in the darkened night except for bits of light here and there. She tried to clear her mind of all the jumbled ideas and speculations. She closed her eyes and said her prayer automatically. But, as it is with all farm folk, once tucked beneath the covers fatigue took its toll and she was fast asleep.

CHAPTER FOUR

A Shocking Story

Friday morning Del stepped into the kitchen and Mama handed the scrap dish to her. "Here, take care of this. The ground is soaked, heavy rain fell during the night. Wear your rubber footwear. When you pass the barn tell your father I want two extra quarts of milk to make custards and rice pudding. When you come back, my flour and sugar containers need filling."

Del entered the porch and prepared for the outdoors. The sun, mostly hidden behind fractured gray clouds, allowed a bit of warmth to the morning air that predicted the coming of colder days. Fritz met Del at the base of the pump. "Did you have your drink of water this morning? I suppose so—you are not waiting at the trough," Del remarked to the dog. She hurried to the pigpen and lifted the pan high enough to drop scraps into their pen. The pigs' squeals brought Benj to the barnbridge door. Surely he was with whoever was inside. She called to him, "Are you going to see Father?"

"*Ich conn. Fa waz* [I can. For what]?"

"Mama wants two extra quarts of milk today."

Benj nodded his head and headed toward the feed entry on the side of the barn.

"Is it going to give what Benj calls a flatcher[1] today?" Del asked as she returned to the kitchen.

"Can't say. Depends whether or not I have leftover pie dough when I finish making the pieces I want." Mama would roll out the extra pie dough, and fit it to a pie tin. She would add sugar, flour, butter, milk, cinnamon and bake until lightly brown on top. It was known as *Schlapp kucha* [Milk cake]. Setting the table Del wondered if Em would be in school. She took the flour can and headed for the attic, stepping lightly across Mama's strip carpet covering the bedroom floor. She reached the two steps to the lift-latch handle, which rattled as she opened the attic door. She tread the creaking attic steps, taking them carefully. She stood in front of two large canisters containing baking supplies. She grabbed the wooden handle with metal sides fastened onto a rounded dome lid on a large aluminum container that could hold fifty pounds of flour. A metal scoop was kept inside. She filled the flour can quickly. The time would come when she couldn't reach deep enough to fill the large scoop with flour. Someone would have to tilt the container for her to reach the flour. She replaced the lid and carried the flour can to the kitchen, placing it on the baking table. She removed the lid to the sugar can and again headed back upstairs. She filled the can and replaced the wooden handle with aluminum sides soldered to the lid of the sugar container, and again took the narrow attic steps sideways. She closed the door carefully behind her, letting the metal latch to slip quietly into place.

"How many times are you running up and down this morning?" Ori said sleepily.

"Can't carry flour and sugar at the same time on those narrow steps. Time for you to get up anyway." Del moved quickly downstairs.

"Is Gloria up?" Mama asked as Del entered the kitchen.

---

1   Flatcher is Benj's nickname for the Milk Cake

"She's awake," Del spoke softly.

"Look if we have enough cornflakes here for everybody. You may as well get the other box from the pantry." Mama spoke hurriedly. Del entered the side room as Benj stepped into the kitchen and placed an empty dish on the sink. Del took her time while paying attention to their soft-spoken words.

"*Alles gesse* [All eaten]," Benj said as Del returned with a large box of cornflakes. Mama immediately grabbed a round tray and placed a small glass of milk plus a slice of jelly bread on the tray. "*Dem des* [Take this]."

Benj left as the boys entered the kitchen after completing their morning barn chores. Ori entered the kitchen at the same time. Del was convinced a person was staying in the barn. Why should that be so secret?

Mama instructed, "Get yourselves ready for school. I want to get an early start with the baking this morning."

"I still have to feed the chickens and Taw-Taw," protested Ori.

Mama hastily replied, "I think Benj took care of that for you. Bring Carol down."

Ori left and returned with Carol rubbing her eyes and still in her nightie. "Sit down and eat, I will take care of Carol later," Mama commanded. Ori joined her siblings around the table as they ate breakfast quietly. As they filed out to walk to school, Mama called, "Adelaide, come back. My lard crock needs filling. You'll have enough time. You won't be late for school."

"I'll wait for you," Bill said as Del ran back into the house.

She moved the large-sized dark brown crock forward and grabbed the knob handle, gently laying it on the baking table, knowing the lid held a fine crack. Del opened the cellar door and snapped the light switch and descended the stairs to a cement floor. The screened pastry cabinet stood immediately in front of her. She took a high step to enter the other half of a divided cellar. First was the potato bin, a rectangular wooden box that stood on four square wooden legs. Baskets of potatoes were underneath the bin. Father would sell those at market or give to friends and relatives. She walked by the two medium-sized crocks that contained fermenting shredded cabbages for sauerkraut; one job Del did not appreciate. Mama would shred the cabbages, salt the layers and then the stomping would begin. She could feel the fatigue in her arms as she remembered the continuous pounding with a heavy wooden club. She thought about butchering time, when the latest batch of sauerkraut was put to the test. Pigs were butchered the first day and a good meal of fresh pork and sauerkraut satisfied the appetites for all the help.

Barrels of cider were on the ledge to her right. Late apples in crates already half empty filled the ledge along the inside wall. She pushed one crate of cabbages aside as it was placed in front of the lard cans. The same cans were used year after year. She dipped a large and heavy metal spoon into the lard and counted out one, two, three, saying seven much louder as that spoonful filled the crock to the rim. She replaced the lid to the lard can, pressing it down firmly all around. She made her way to the steps. Mama was waiting at the open door to receive the filled crock and spoon.

The twins and Fritz hurried along the lane heading for school.

"How are you feeling?" Bill asked.

"I don't ever want another day like yesterday." The memory of the Teacher sitting at her desk still caused agony. Del looked directly at Bill.

"I can't believe Ollie didn't say something. He can't keep anything to himself. He always wants to be the first one to spill news, even if he isn't supposed to reveal it. He can't contain himself. He will say something. You know that," Del explained to Bill.

"I know what you are saying. He hasn't said a word about the truck, either. You would think he couldn't keep that news to himself," Bill concluded.

"I think there's a sick boy in the barn. I hope we get the full story tonight. I don't understand why this is so secret."

"Ditto. I mean about getting the full story," Bill agreed.

Del giggled. "You said ditto. Only Father uses that word."

Bill smiled. "Why are you so sure it's a boy in the barn?"

Del held up two fingers. "Two reasons. I heard Mama tell Benj when he came in for more food that we should see improvement soon. Someone must be sick or something like that. Then, I saw some used clothing going out there, and it was boy's clothes."

"You could be way wrong." Bill said thoughtfully. "We'll see. I just don't think Father would let anyone stay in the barn other than Clint, and I know it isn't Clint!"

The day at school was even worse than the day before. Del couldn't focus on school lessons as she thought about who was in the barn. Spelling class went badly. The entire school was aware of it. Del had looked over the list of words in her homework assignment and felt there was no need to concentrate on any of them to make sure she would spell them correctly. She was now standing in the third position, no longer in her usual spot as head of the class. This was mortifying.

Mr. Strunk caught the changes in the Heydt children. Til's happy-go-lucky demeanor and laughter was diminished. Ollie was always restless and fidgeting, and even that was worse today. Mr. Strunk tapped him on the shoulder more than once. Ollie knew what that meant, but sighed deeply during the first session. Mr. Strunk stopped by his desk after recess and inquired whether or not he was feeling well.

"Oh sure, I'm okay," was all Ollie said. He did sit up, trying to appear at ease. Ori was the only sibling who appeared the same as always. Never outgoing, she held a somber attitude no matter what the circumstance. Whether joy or sorrow she contained her feelings, or just plain didn't care. But for one exception: if something happened to her pet duck, her squawking was as loud as the duck's.

Mr. Strunk said not a word to Del as she took his hand upon Friday's closing. It seemed he looked long and hard at her trying to see the reason she was distracted. She passed through the door, and her tense body relaxed as she leaned against the rough plastered exterior schoolhouse wall taking a long deep breath. "Thank goodness," she said softly to herself.

"What is wrong with you?" Bill asked as he walked over to her. "All day I have been thinking about the changes up town."

"What do you mean 'changes up town'?" Del was interested.

"You know, Grandfather is considering selling his creamery business. I don't know much more. He is helping Father to buy a truck."

If Father isn't going to Philly much longer, why buy a truck?" Del questioned.

"I hear you talk about a truck." Til joined the twins.

"Why is Grandfather helping Father buy a truck?" Del asked.

Til shrugged, "Just know Grandfather doesn't want another truck, but he is helping Father to buy one. Father has his reasons."

"Why would Father get a truck?" Del questioned.

"The Hoylers were here last week and told Father about a need for deliveries of livestock, especially calves and young pigs. He needs animals to process for his shop. He sometimes asks us for poultry too," Til said and then he and Bill hurried to catch up to the Shultz boys.

Del continued alone along the dirt lane until she met the cement pike, then walked the hill to where Fritz was waiting.

"Good boy, Fritz," Del greeted him. She looked back. "You can see all the boys are talking about something. I bet Til is talking about horses or the new truck Father is going to get. Who cares anyway?"

Til and Bill caught up to Del and Til said, "Teacher said he would probably come by for milk sometime this evening. He wants to see Daisy. He wants to know what Dr. Sam saw since he suggested Daisy's milk to help Ernie get better."

Ollie raced up to join his siblings. "Well I'll be. I can't believe Ori is home before us. She has Taw-Taw already. How did she manage that?" Ollie said as they approached the woodshed and saw Taw-Taw pecking at corn kernels.

Til said, "Mae and Ori were first out the door at dismissal time. Mae must have known her father was waiting by the falter[2] just beyond the schoolyard to pick her up. Ori rode along. They must have dropped her off at our lane."

———————————

2 Falter is the entrance to a field.

"I will ask why she was first to leave," Ollie concluded.

Del shook her head. "I'm not going to ask at all. She always makes me ask a million questions." Del remembered how Mama became annoyed with Ori's tidbits of information slowly revealed over many questions.

"It's Ori's way of making herself feel important, is the way Mama's Aunt Kate explains it," Til offered.

Taw-Taw was finishing the shelled corn Ori scattered. She oft-times kept a small dish with just a handful of corn hidden somewhere in the woodshed for easy access after school, ready to give her duck a treat— her way of keeping her duck from going into the creek. Of course that only worked sometimes. That duck had a mind of his own and did his own thing regardless of how often Ori thought she had a trained duck. Fritz had his own issues with the duck. He didn't like his squawks. Fritz would show his teeth and the duck would keep a safe distance between them. Ori complained about Fritz's scare tactics. Both Del and Bill would reply innocently, "You know Fritz is only smiling." They both knew that Fritz would do that duck no harm. The twins entered the house filled with the aroma of freshly baked goods.

Del scanned the table and then the stove-top to see if there was an over-baked pie or burned cake of some kind. "No samples?" Del asked her mother as she headed for the stairs to change clothes.

"None so far, everything went well. Good draft to control the oven temperature. You can have a piece of custard pie when you come down."

"Oh boy!" Bill exclaimed as he headed up stairs.

Del already dreaded washing all the pie tins and baking dishes added to the regular supper dishes and Ollie's reactions when drying them. She looked down on the garden from her bedroom window to a large section of bare ground that had been littered with chew cherries across the garden and under the bordering currant bushes earlier that day. Picking them was time-consuming chore. It probably took Carol and someone else most of the day to pick so large an area. Del expected to hear grumbling from Carol. At the same time, that suggested the possibility of delicious chew cherry pies. Del also expected Mama sent someone up to Grandfather with his favorite freshly-baked pie.

"Adelaide, what's taking you so long?" Mama called.

Del rushed down the stairs. "I was looking over the garden and saw chew cherries were gathered. I believe Carol did some garden work."

"Yes, she helped. She is tired. I think you had better do your outside work without her."

Del didn't tell Mama that Carol was too young to be good help. "Where is she?"

"I sent her with Gloria and told her to watch all that Gloria does."

"She already knows most of what Ori does every evening."

"I know. I don't want her to fall asleep before we eat," said Mama.

Benj was in the woodshed as Del walked by the pump, his foot propped on the large block of wood for splitting, his elbow rested on his knee. It appeared he was engrossed in serious thought. She waved her hand but he didn't notice. Going down the lane she saw Ori struggling with Taw-Taw. Del immediately knew where Benj's interest lay. Ori shooed Taw-Taw away from the trough overflow that fell into the shallow creek below and added to the stream flowing by. Taw-Taw quickly skedaddled under the boarded gate, into the barnyard pen, and flew into the cattle's watering trough. A difficult situation! He could swim back and forth and keep Ori from reaching him. Father forbade the children to enter the barnyard when work was being done in the barn. You never knew when an animal would be released into that pen. An animal could escape through an open gate, or worse, attack a person.

"You are going to get real wet in the cattle's water trough," Ori scolded her duck, and vowed if he'd stay in that trough any longer she would not bother with him the rest of the evening, leaving him to fend off the creatures of the night. Ori remembered, as did Del, that Father shot one of the largest raccoons anybody ever saw. Father had it mounted and it covered the full length on the top of Father's large roll-top desk. Del knew Taw-Taw would not be controlled by Ori or anyone else as he flew from the trough, skidded on the stream below, then half-ran, half-flew along the creek bed. There he awkwardly lifted himself on the air currents and, gliding unsteadily, he landed on a lower branch of the willow tree. Taw-Taw had great difficulty settling on the flimsy branch. Ori walked over to retrieve him. He lunged to a higher branch closer to the trunk. He managed to settle there even though the willow branch swayed under his weight. "Okay. Stay there! 'Least you can dry your feathers up there." Ori stomped back to the henhouse.

Del looked back and was aware of Benj's amused expression.

"*Ah hucked net dot wann ich doh binn* [He doesn't sit there while I'm here]. I'll get him down. I have the old hay rake handy." He pointed to an old wooden rake with missing teeth hanging from a side beam in the woodshed. "I use that to reach a branch and shake and shake until that duck flies out or falls down." Benj was laughing. "*Saage nix* [Say nothing]."

"I can't believe Ori puts up with that duck. She is up in arms about everything else right away. Mama offered to clip Taw-Taw's wing feathers. Ori won't allow that even though that would keep him grounded."

"*Ich kanns auh net glaawe* [I can't believe it either]." Benj commented.

Del continued, "One of these days Mama will fix that bird without telling her. At least that way he can't fly into a tree anymore. What's more, he will never land on someone's back and flap his wings. He scares the living daylights out of people. Who ever heard of a duck beating up on people with his wings for no reason at all? And to think, she gave him a special treat today after school. He'll never be a trained duck."

"*Sel con ich fixah* [I can fix that]."

"You better not," Del warned.

"*Fa waas net* [Why not]?"

"Don't know, just better not," Del replied. She went on her way to prepare slop for the pigs and throw chopped cobs of corn into their pen. Fritz stood in the lane not knowing which way to go when he decided to move near Carol, as she was seated on one of the steps to the feedhouse entry.

"You can't watch what Ori is doing from there," Del observed.

"No place for me to sit inside," Carol replied.

"True enough. You can watch me mix the mash for the pigs even though you saw this before."

Fritz got up and moved closer to the bottom of the barnbank.

Benj walked up behind Del. "Duck still in the tree?" she asked him. "*Nay* [No]."

Del stared at Benj. "You don't know where he is!" "*Graad naw net. Schaffe michselwert doh.* [Not right now. Work here for myself]. That door is open." He pointed to the smaller door cut into the big sliding door that opened to the threshing floor.

"Fritz and I will stand guard," Del offered and immediately asked. "Why is the door open?"

Fritz got up and sat by Benj.

"*Schmarta hund. Mehner licht* [Smart dog. More light]," Benj answered.

The top of the barn was off limits for Fritz, too. She figured Fritz was waiting to see who would come to enter or close the barndoor. "You stay and guard the place if you must," Del said to Fritz with a wave of her hand.

"What about me?" Carol said. "Can I go in? I am tired of waiting for Ori."

"Sure. I'll take you there. I know you are tired. Mama said you picked chew cherries today."

"Hey, hey. Not so fast there," Benj said. "Carol and I picked a big section clean."

"I thought that was a lot of work for one little person."

"*Mei boukel saage ma aus ich gscheft hab* [My back tells me that I have worked]."

"Come, Carol, I will carry you. Benj can tell Ori I took you in to Mama."

After taking Carol to the house Del came back and entered the feed-house. She grabbed the handle to a tall bucket of freshly chopped corn and dragged it along the floor as far as the door. She placed some into a smaller pail and stepped outside. The noisy grunting and squealing started immediately, until enough corn fell to quiet the pigs. Fritz moved closer to Benj who was seated yonder on a rail piece used to close the falter; from there he could look directly through the open door. Del was really tempted to sneak over to the barnbridge and perhaps see what Benj could see from where he sat.

She stood quietly by the little door entrances for the chickens as she closed them for the night and waited there. She heard movement in the top of the barn. Father was probably forking straw from the loft onto the barn floor for bedding. Then the trap door would be opened and the straw pushed to the opening, allowing it to fall on the cement stable floor below. The hay was pushed to the end of the hall landing above the stairs. With a little push the hay tumbled down the stairs onto the feed entry floor. There Til and Bill would place it by forkfuls into the mangers for the cattle to munch on throughout the evening.

Del had grown accustomed to doing her work automatically. Caught up in her thoughts she rushed into the feedhouse, making sure she had emptied the tall bucket of chopped corn. "I should have known better," she thought, "no need to look. The pigs would have let me know otherwise." She scooped a mixture of mash into the feed buckets and set them on the express wagon that had been altered to move the buckets to the feeding troughs. The wagon bed extended over small wheels to accommodate buckets of slop and water. She checked the milk cans containing the slop that came from the tank located on the backside of the creamery. Fortunately, they weren't too full for her to handle. She tipped the can and allowed the liquid to spill into the buckets. She ran back to the feedhouse for her paddle and thoroughly stirred the bubbling mash as it mixed with the liquid. She pulled the wagon closer to the lip of the feeding trough. The squealing and shoving of the pigs for position started all over again. Del turned to grab a bucket and there was Benj behind her. "You're going to help me pour this?"

"Yep."

The mash was poured into metal sloping troughs. It ran down the trough faster than the larger pigs could gobble it up. The smaller pigs found their place along the second trough filled from the overflow of the first larger trough. Benj rested his right arm on the fence post as he looked once more toward the top of the barn. Del pulled her wagon and empty buckets back to the feedhouse. "I still have to rinse these buckets and paddle, put them away, and check on Ori. She may need more water to fill the chicken hoppers."

"Ya all finished then." Benj said as he stayed close by.

"With the pigs I am, just waiting for Ori to close the henhouse and secure this feedhouse door." Del checked her remaining chores. "You know Ori can't carry a bucket of eggs and lock this door at the same time."

"Did ya see that bird?"

"No, I did not."

"Not in the henhouse with Ori?" asked Benj.

"No. He's surely slopping in the creek again or still in that willow tree."

"*Ah's nett* [He's not there]. Better take a look and see where that critter is hiding. Can't trust him ya know. Ya better look in the henhouse once more, maybe Ori found him. Should have kept my eye on him."

Del turned without another word. She went back into the feedhouse, trudged over to the henhouse door and stuck her head inside. "Is anyone in here?" she called.

"I'm here, don't turn the knob." Ori called from the interior.

"Is Taw-Taw with you?"

"I have a nasty cluck here. She won't let me reach for her egg. I'll have to place a glass egg under her. Can you get one for me?"

"I'll get one and lay it inside the door." Del stepped carefully passed the brooder to the ledge in the feedhouse corner and grabbed an opaque glass egg. She then opened the door a crack and placed the fake egg on the henhouse floor. "Is Taw-Taw in there with you?"

"What does it look like?" came the sarcastic reply.

"Just wondered." Del was already closing the door as Ori answered loudly. "He is not here. When would I have time to go looking for him. Take Carol back to the house."

"Carol is with Mama," Del called out.

"That duck is not with Ori," Del said to Benj as she returned.

"Aye aye. *Ich wunner waz au gade, veil tzu ruhich* [I wonder what goes on. Much too quiet]."

"He doesn't have to be up to something, does he? He is usually squabbling or strutting around somewhere."

"Now Del, ya know that duck as good as me. *Ach izs yuscht graad schlect* [He is just plain naughty]."

"I know. You can't take him for granted. He knows it's time to find a place to spend the night. That door is still open," Del said as she pointed toward the barn.

"What ya thinking now?" Benj said as he slowly walked toward the barnbridge.

"Fritz is unsettled, too. He doesn't know where he wants to stay and watch everything. Maybe Taw-Taw has him upset."

"*Denk net* [I don't think so]," Benj replied.

Benj moved closer to the open threshold door. Del was tempted to ask if he could see anything and thought the better of it. Benj tossed his tobacco chew into the field. Del grew impatient. She needed to help Mama before long. She wanted to secure all the doors, but had to wait for Ori to finish her chores in the henhouse. She felt Benj was waiting for both of them to finish the outside work so he could step onto the threshold floor, and probably Fritz too.

Just then it happened. Taw-Taw came flying from a tree in the orchard across the lane and landed on the center of the barnbridge.

"Feller, ya need yer wings clipped fer sure. Ya is headed fer trouble," Benj spoke harshly, yet with controlled intensity, trying not to alarm that duck; he moved as quickly as he could toward Taw-Taw hoping to stop that critter before it got to the open threshold door.

"Ya walk up on the other side and see if'n we can head him in another direction." Benj motioned to Del which way to go. Taw-Taw, seeing them approach, started scampering for all he was worth toward the opened door as a means of escape. Fritz came running up the center of the barnbridge, and before anyone could stop him that duck landed inside. Fritz was right on Taw-Taw's tail and then onto the threshing floor. Del and Benj were close behind. "Trap door could be open, ya stay back," Benj spoke, all out of breath.

Del saw the wagon on the threshing floor, and in it, a pair of large, frightened eyes staring directly at her as a small hand pulled a blanket over to cover them. Fritz hit the floor planks hard as he caught that duck in his mouth. Fritz turned as Taw-Taw flapped one free wing and trotted all the way to the bottom of the bank barnbridge before Fritz dropped him.

Benj motioned to Del for her to follow Fritz. Taw-Taw squawked and flapped his wings furiously, raising the loose gritty dirt. The evening breeze blew the fine granules directly into her face. Del turned to protect her eyes and sneezed hard three times. The touch of a hand on her shoulder caused her to jump as she turned toward Benj and noticed he had closed the door behind him. Taw-Taw wasn't all the worse for his encounter with Fritz, but plenty of downy feathers floated on the breeze as the duck squawked for all he was worth and spun around in circles.

"Is that the way an angry duck acts?" Del started laughing as she looked at Benj. Her laughter stopped abruptly as she saw Ori standing in the feedhouse doorway. She must have heard the wild squawking.

"Well, Fritz. Good boy. We can close up. Lock everything up tight and head for the house." Del said.

"*Ya, geh yuscht* [Yes, just go]," Benj pointed toward the house.

Ori furiously stomped over. "See, like I always knew, if I hadn't come out when I did, Fritz would have killed my Taw-Taw. He would have eaten him alive." Taw-Taw stopped spinning and Ori quickly picked her duck up. Just as quickly she put him down and pressed on his back holding him in place. "If I hadn't been here that monster would have eaten him for sure. Just look, feathers all over the place. I am going to tell Father about this. I knew long already that dog is waiting for a chance to get rid of my Taw-Taw."

Del retorted, "As if Fritz would do anything like that. He's a good dog. He has all the chances in the world to get rid of your duck. He could get rid of that duck while we are in school. Even bury the remains and you would never know where to look for him. Your duck is all wet because he was in the watering trough before that. When he is in the cattle trough one of the cows could easily make mince meat of him."

"That's what you think. It's your dog that needs to learn a lesson or two." Ori's face reddened with anger.

"He saw it, too." Del pointed to Benj. "As if Fritz could be mean. He is a smart dog. He knows how to behave. He is not stupid like another pet I know. You can't train your duck to do anything. You can call his name and he won't come; if I call Fritz, he will come.

"You don't know anything. Taw-Taw is a good duck." Ori was smoothing his feathers while trying to get him settled. "I'll tell Mama what Fritz did to my duck."

"Go ahead. If you'd let Mama clip those wing feathers maybe, just maybe you could tame him." Del paused. "But I doubt it. Your stupid duck flew into the barn and probably half scared to death whoever is in there."

"How can you say that, he scared my Taw-Taw half to death." Ori stopped arguing as she realized Del had seen something. "But who's in the barn?"

"*Sel is genunk. Sez alles alrecht* [That is enough. Everything is all right]. End this. No damage done." Benj put an end to the dispute.

Del looked at Ori, "Would you like another burlap bag so you can hold and dry your duck?"

"*Geh yuscht, Ich geb aucht druff* [Just go, I'll take care of it]," Benj said with firmness in his voice.

Del walked slowly with Fritz by her side until she got as far as the grape arbor. She sat there; she needed time to ponder. "You know, Fritz. It's a little boy for sure. I saw his big black eyes. You were protecting him."

Ori passed by with the larger wooden egg bucket three quarters full. Ori held her duck securely tucked under her arm with a burlap bag wrapped around him. She had a second burlap bag draped across her shoulder. He had to be quite wet. Del got up and secured the hen-house. She checked the small henhouse door entrances once more and made sure the propped entrance ladders held securely.

"I'll go inside with ya," Benj said as he joined her.

"Everything all right up there?" Del asked.

Benj nodded his head. Del understood he did not want to talk.

Ori was in the closed porch weighing eggs on her egg scale and placing them in the double egg crate Grandfather always supplied. Taw-Taw had quieted and was resting on a dry burlap bag in an open box where Ori could quickly lay a hand on him.

Benj, Fritz, and Del entered and she stopped to take a closer look at that bird. Taw-Taw shifted uneasily in a worn butter box once used for shipping twelve pounds of Grandfather's sweet creamery butter. There was plenty of burlap there to absorb wetness. A wet burlap bag lay on the floor.

"I'll tie your dog if he ever touches Taw-Taw again," Ori warned.

"You'll do no such thing. You have some sort of problem with your stupid duck every evening."

"Girls, girls," Mama spoke as she entered with her milk bonnet in hand and immediately moved to wash her face, neck and hands thoroughly up to the elbows. Mama spoke softly to Del, barely above a whisper. "I hear you were in the barn."

Del walked into the kitchen to prepare the table for supper without commenting on Mama's statement. She opened the cellar door, took the butter dish and the jar of homemade strawberry jelly off the shelf and placed them on the table. Next down the cellar stairs she went, returning with a loaf of homemade bread.

"How much bread do I still have down there?" Mama asked.

"One more loaf. Are you going to bake bread on Saturday?"

"I have to. There won't be enough to last until Tuesday."

"*My schuldt dank ich* [My fault, I think]," Benj muttered sheepishly.

"*Nay ses net* [No it's not]," Mama was quick to respond. "*Bok net uft uf da Somschdaag. Awwer ses nootwennich* [Don't often bake on Saturday. But it's necessary]. The children are older and eat more. Plus I am carrying a lot of bread out to the barn. This isn't the first time I need to bake bread more than once a week. *Druvvel dich net* [Don't trouble yourself]."

"I hear you were in the barn," Mama said again, yet with a particular sternness that Del knew would require an answer. She looked at Benj and wondered if he told Mama what happened. Del was bewildered not knowing what to say.

"Well," Mama questioned. "Don't you have anything to say?"

"Not really. I was barely at the open door. I didn't see much. You should have seen how Fritz caught Taw-Taw in his mouth and he didn't hurt that bird one bit," Del decided it was safe to say that.

Mama wasn't satisfied. "You can talk. Gloria is outside trying to dry that duck some more. What did you see?" Mama pressed Del for an answer.

"Goodness! I knew for sure this morning that a boy was here."

"Ah hah, told ya that mind was thinking," Benj commented.

"What made you think that?" Mama demanded.

"The food you took out to the barn was for a person. Everything you did said the same thing. He looked scared. I saw his hand pulling covers over his head."

"Just like her to figger on things," Benj chimed in.

A silence before Mama said anything more. "Hmm. You will not be as surprised as some of the others."

"Anybody can put two and two together and figure it out. Why did Father bring him home?"

"Finish setting the table. Your Father will tell you all when he comes in and that should be shortly," Mama ordered. Del moved quickly to complete the table settings.

Father, Til, Bill, and Ollie came in, standing in line to wash up before supper. Ori was immediately behind them, placing her duck in the tall narrow carton in the porch. Everyone gathered around the table and dishes were passed briskly. As plates were filled an extreme quiet set in.

"*Siz auver rooich, soo isses von maa blendi tzu essa henn* [It's very quiet, so it is when we have plenty to eat]," Benj spoke with a great deal of satisfaction.

Del thought he seemed pleased to be a part of the family activities from day to day. Perhaps he was lonely and wanted to be part of a family. Mama said over and over again, 'Treat the man kindly.' Sometimes she added, 'He had enough heartache to last a lifetime'. Del had long wanted to know just what Mama meant. She was always told she needed to wait until she was older. "How old is old enough?" she thought as her attention turned to her father.

"Children, I will tell you what happened when I went to Philadelphia." Father's face displayed a look of concern and determination Del had never before seen. Father's eyes focused from one to another before continuing. Del put her fork down wanting to be sure she would not miss anything Father was going to share, as did her siblings. Benj sat back and slowly took a sip of water.

"When I got to the Philly market I was told an abandoned child was hanging around in the alley, always looking for something to eat. The market folk tried many times to get rid of him. The market manager had just come around the corner looking for 'the stray,' as they called him. I thought he was talking about a dog or cat. 'No, no,' he said, 'This is a boy who hangs around here for, well, on and off at first, but steady for a couple of weeks now. Something has to happen now that nights are getting cold. He will freeze to death, if he doesn't starve first. He doesn't talk. We offered to help him find his parents. We walked some blocks around here, asking people about lost children. No one seemed to know anything and no one has come looking. We throw some rags or used burlap into the alley for covering at night but we don't want to make things too comfortable for him because we don't want him hanging around. Don't want an outbreak of a disease around our market place- that's bad for business.' Father paused and took a long drink of water.

The children looked at each other in shock, trying to imagine a situation like Father described. Del distractedly realized that Ollie was scuffing his shoes. Mama called him the shoe butcher, especially at such times that his shoes needed to be polished to look half decent for Sunday wear.

Father shook his head. "I told them you can't stand by and watch a child starve or freeze to death. Can you? Mr. Foose said, 'That's exactly why we want him out of here.'" Father looked at his family. "I just couldn't let it go at that. I had questions. Did you report this to the police, I asked. 'Yes we did, and they said they would see what they could do, but there are many abandoned children already. Places we asked are full and would not take another in, especially this one,' they said. When they saw my concern they said I should wait, they would catch him and then I could see for myself why. It wasn't long before I heard a commotion. Father shook his head again with a look of disbelief on his serious face. "Two men came forward with a bundle in burlap and placed it in my arms. It didn't weigh much, but I could feel trembling and hear whimpering. 'There,' they said and started to laugh, 'we don't want him. No one wants him!'" Father stopped, overcome with sudden anger. Del saw tears in his eyes, too. The whole family's attention hung on every word. "It was then he moved and the burlap fell away. Skin and bone was all I saw on a very young boy. I knew I was looking at starvation. For them to let this happen and do nothing to help really bothered me. That's just not the Christian way. The market manager saw my concern. 'You have a farm,' he said. 'You raise your own food. Surely you can feed one more.'"

Father rubbed his eyes and looked at Mama and Benj, who were quiet and also watching the children's reactions. The children were silent, each absorbing the somber thought of being abandoned and starving.

"A lot of thoughts went through my mind," Father continued. "What would my family say? I have a full house already. What would the townspeople say?" Father paused. "We already have a busybody up town and she can make a heap of trouble from all sorts of false accusations and cause strife between neighbors and families. We've had problems with her before."

Mama nodded. "Food and shelter are not problems. It is all the other things that could cause big problems," she said.

Father looked at Mama, and softly said, "I know, I know. It's weighed on me, too." Father paused. "I saw his sunken eyes and the hollows in his neck and I could not release him. I held on to him more tightly.

I could not bear the guilt of letting one of God's children die. So I said, Yes, if you are sure no one wants him, I will see to it that he gets enough to eat and has a warm place to sleep. But, if someone comes looking for this child, you let me know and I will bring him back to his family. I still can't believe the market people would help this boy! People do such harsh things in desperate times," Father murmured. He paused and laid his hands on the table. He looked around at the silent children before him. "I put the boy in the wagon with me and drove to the train station. He cried and slept all the way to Lyons—I could not comfort him. When we reached Lyons, I hitched Doll to the wagon. On my way home, close to the top of the hill, he became sick. I stopped, and when Ilifted him off the wagon, he tried to run away. Because he was very weak, I was able to easily catch him and bundle him up in a blanket. So now you know the reason I was late. What questions do you have?"

After a long pause, Til was first to speak. "We can't let someone starve to death. Sure we'll feed him."

"I'm glad you feel that way. It's the Christian thing to do." Father looked pleased. The other children nodded their heads in agreement.

Mama looked at Del. "Now tell me what you think?"

"What happened to his parents? Will he go along to Philly every week to look for them? What is his name and how old is he?"

"Whoa, hold yer horses. Told yer that mind gets busy," Benj said as he looked at Del's parents.

"Adelaide is a lot like my sister. She asks a lot of questions." Father seemed amused.

"We can't answer all your questions," Mama spoke gently. "We'll have to wait and see how things develop."

"Why didn't you bring him into the house right away?" Bill asked. "Why keep him in the barn?"

Father replied, "We couldn't be sure he wasn't carrying a contagious disease. Maybe TB, like our neighbors have with Ernest. Becky examined him and thinks he's healthy except for not getting enough good food and shelter. Up to now she has found no problems that your mother's cooking cannot take care of. It's a good thing we have Becky."

"Bringing a child this age to a new home could cause numerous problems," Mama said as Benj nodded his head in agreement.

"What kind of problems?" Bill asked.

"I said I would take him, so I did," Father said with conviction as he looked at Mama. "I want you all to help in any way you can."

"Sure will," Til announced with a serious look on his face. Bill and Del nodded in agreement.

"Yes, I guess. But what problems . . . " Bill stopped for a moment, his furrowed brow indicating deep thought.

"Well, if he runs away every chance he gets, don't ask me to run after him. All we need is another little boy around here." Ori managed to sound petulant and disappointed at the same time.

"Gloria, that's enough!" Mama said and for once Ori sat up and looked like she had been slapped.

Father brought the conversation back to the boy from Philadelphia. "I want to know what the rest of you think about a new member to our family?"

"Can I play pitch and catch with him?" asked Ollie.

"That's a good possibility," Mama admitted. "He could be your age, or maybe a bit younger."

Ollie was thrilled at the prospect of a playmate.

"We'll do what we think is best for that boy and for us," Mama stated softly.

"*Soo dank ich* [I think so too]," Benj agreed.

The room was quiet. It seemed everyone was mulling over this news.

"Where is he going to sleep when you bring him into the house? Is he alone out there?" Ollie asked with increased interest.

"We never leave him alone. We need to find room for him here now that we are sure he's healthy. You and William already share a double bed. Tilghman has a room with a single bed. Perhaps we can fit a double bed in his room or better yet another single bed. Tilghman will lose some space." Del could tell Mama had given this situation some serious thought.

"*Ich kon sel seztler* [I can settle that]. I have two beds I don't use. *Aye schtupp recht waarem* [One room is real warm]. The stove pipe from the coal parlor heater goes through the room above. It was Samuel's room, and good size too. When we had real cold winters we would all gather in his room to sleep." Benj thought a moment. "It might be good if he stayed with me." Another pause. "Guess maybe better fer us all. *Luss de leit sage wos sie wolla* [Let the people say what they will]. I can handle it. I'm an old man. What can they say to hurt me?" Benj looked at Father and Mama; that pair of piercing green eyes held such a steady gaze it actually caused Del to shiver.

"My goodness, Benj, that is most kind of you. I never considered your place. For the time being I think it best we keep him here with us until we talk to the doctor, the schoolteacher and more of our friends. Becky said she would help with anything we might need. She knows this could cause trouble. We'll have to see." Mama spoke slowly and thoughtfully.

Del was confused. What on earth could be so difficult to feed and house another person—who could object to that? The other question in the back of her mind and which she wanted an answer to was: "Who is Samuel?"

"I think we will have him sleep on the couch here in the kitchen until we figure out sleeping arrangements upstairs." Father pointed a hand toward Benj. "We'll get together, Becky included, and discuss all the possibilities." Father always had a positive attitude. He suddenly sat up straight. "We are going to bring this boy in tonight yet. I was thinking we would wait until morning for all of you to meet him. Loll, what do you think about that?" Father looked to Mama and she nodded her head in assent. Father then turned his eyes to Benj for approval.

"*Recht mit meir* [Right with me]. People will talk, that's fer sure. No stories about this from me."

"There will be plenty of gossip," Mama murmured.

"Good to be around when people find out. We will know what kind of neighbors we have in *dem gleena schteddl* [this small town]," Benj concluded.

"Benj," Father said, "you have been very helpful from the start. We could not have managed without you and our good neighbors. I think we'll adopt you as a grandfather. You make yourself at home here."

"*Ya glaenna kinskinner hawe ich net kott* [Yes, I have not had little grandchildren]. The tongues in this town and the next will be flapping. This time, I will be playing Woodie's game." He raised his forefinger and tapped his head.

Mama told the girls, "You may clear the table. Leave dessert dishes. We will take food out for him as we always have and we'll all have dessert together."

The girls cleared dishes and leftovers. Del started to wash dishes. There were so many this evening with extra baking bowls and tins from Mama's baking. Her mind dwelt on all the revelations she heard. She was anxious to meet the boy Father brought along home. Mama prepared a tray for him while Father waited. As Del turned to collect more dirty dishes she noticed a glow of satisfaction on Benj's face. He appeared to be filled with pride and contentment at the same time.

Mama smiled. "Let's go. Tilghman, you and William carry the warm food; we'll see how he takes to meeting you. Then we'll bring him along in. Your Grandfather is in the barn right now. I'll bring something for him too. Gloria, put your duck away for the night."

"May I go along?" Ollie couldn't stand not seeing firsthand what his brothers were going to see.

"Yes, Oliver, if you wish. You boys can meet him at the same time."

"Hey, not so fast." Mama caught Ollie's arm as he raced by. "You carry this chew cherry pie for your Grandfather. Be careful how you handle it. Take your time."

Ori made her way into the porch. Taw-Taw was squabbling as she laid the carton on its side. When Taw-Taw moved slowly forward, Ori pressed her hand down on him so he could not get away.

"You needn't squawk at me," Ollie said to the duck as he followed Til.

"I won't dirty your feathers either," Bill said as he passed by.

Mama gathered her milk bonnet and apron in the porch to make her way to the milkhouse before following the boys.

"Come, precious," Ori said as she doubled a dry burlap bag and laid it across her shoulder. She placed a hand firmly on the duck's back and forced him to rest on her shoulder, her elbow protruding like a protective weapon. "I'll take you outside where you will find peace and quiet," Ori said as she left the closed porch.

"Alone is where that duck should be all the time. That way no one would ever have a problem," Del said quietly.

"*Geb aucht* [Be careful]! Ya don't want her to hear that," Benj said.

"She didn't," Del replied.

"Guess ya want to tell others about Taw-Taw when they come back," Benj mused.

"Can't wait," Del answered quickly. "Wonder how much they know about the whole incident. Maybe they know all about it already. Father was out there. Ori sure won't say a thing unless she can make others believe it was Fritz who caused the whole ruckus."

Benj patted his lap inviting Carol to sit with him on the rocking chair. *Schockle dich* [Rock you]."

Carol obliged.

"Is that boy afraid of Fritz?" Del asked.

"Did ya ever know Fritz not to sniff things out and make friends with anybody who needed a friend? Fritz stayed with whoever spent the night in the barn. Our lad got used to the dog right away. He knows Fritz is a good dog."

"But," Del looked at Benj and said, "The commotion could have frightened him. Surely he never saw that duck before."

Mama returned. "Everything is going all right. I'm sure he knew other children were around. Accepted them like he was expecting them."

Ori returned. "Grandfather is leaving. Ed will take him home."

"So," Del thought, "Perhaps Grandfather stood in the shadow of the barn that first night with their neighbor, Ed. How did he come that first night? How did Ed know to fetch Grandfather that first night?" Del was curious to know.

Fritz was the first to enter from outdoors. Look how he struts, Del thought. He feels like he is introducing someone new. Ollie was next, and his eyes were open wide. Del couldn't tell if he was pleased or just plain shocked. Mama was all smiles and observing closely as each one entered. Then came Bill, with an expression Del could not read. He touched Fritz briefly as he passed and took his seat on the bench behind the table.

"Where are the rest? Mama asked Bill.

"Getting a drink of water, showing him how the pump works," he answered calmly.

At last Father came in . . . carrying . . . goodness gracious . . . a Black boy! Father seated him on the couch. Til followed emotionless. The Black boy's eyes cast about the unfamiliar room and new faces. Fritz was the only one besides Father, Mama and Benj who did not show the slightest degree of shock or surprise on their faces. Del wondered how the boys reacted when they first laid eyes on him in the barn. She knew for sure it must have been a surprise for them. Del could hardly wait to ask Bill what he thought when he first saw this Black child.

Benj moved from the rocker and sat on the couch beside the new boy. He placed his arm around his shoulders. "These children live here," he said in his best English, pointing at the children. "Ya will have lots of company and friends. Don't be afraid."

"He has a brown head!" Carol said, loud and clear.

Mama quickly said, "Don't laugh," before her older siblings could giggle. "Carol never saw a Black person before. She noticed a difference and that's okay." There was a quiet moment after Mama spoke.

"We told him there would be cake and milk in the house," Ollie stated.

Mama looked to all the girls. "We do have *Sees Kucha* [Sweet cake]. But I think custard will do just fine for him," Mama nodded her head toward the new guest.

Without another word, Del left to retrieve the cake to dunk.

"Well, children, what do you think?" Father waited for Del's return. There was no response for a spell.

"I thought he was dirty. I only saw his hand and his eyes." Del was immediately embarrassed after she said that.

Mama chuckled.

"You hear that! Del did sneak into the barn when she wasn't supposed to," Ori said with an accusing tone.

"No! I did not. It was your dumb duck that flew in where he wasn't supposed to be. If it hadn't been for Fritz, who knows what would have happened!" Del protested.

"You mean Fritz was chasing my pet. No wonder he went in the barn, he was all wet and flustered."

"Now girls, enough of that. We'll settle that Taw-Taw episode later," Mama promised.

"I know she did something on purpose," Ori added.

Benj softly tapped Ori on the head and motioned with a finger on his whiskered upper lip for her to be quiet. She obeyed, much to Del's surprise.

Conversation was nil around the table. Carol was quick to make sure she would be seated next to Mama. Benj seated the boy next to himself at the lower end of the table. Mama kept some mashed potatoes and gravy warmed in case he wanted more food. "So far, you've eaten everything we have given you, right?" Mama said with a great deal of satisfaction as she looked at the little boy, who was so shy he wouldn't look at anyone.

Benj merely nodded his head.

Del carried the dessert plates to the table. All hands reached for a plate. Benj pulled a plate with a piece of custard in front of the little boy. He handed him a fork and motioned to others around the table to eat and not stare at the new child who appeared ill-at-ease and kept his head down with chin pressed to his neck. His full face was not easily seen.

"*Luss ihn leenich un net wache soo hatt* [Let him alone, don't watch so hard]. He needs to eat without feeling out of place. *Ah con ich waiss* [He can, I know]." Father spoke in the dialect to the children. The setting was awkward indeed. The children ate quietly while the new lad was motionless.

Father finally spoke. "Now children, I know this is not the first time you've seen a Black person, except for Carol. He is just like you. Once care and food help him get strong and healthy, we'll find out what we can about him. For now let us enjoy our dessert."

Everyone was still seated when they heard a knock on the door. "Teacher!" Til said suddenly, quite embarrassed. "I forgot to tell you he is coming tonight."

Benj was ready to pick the Black boy up. *"Ich nemme ihn in de anner schtubb* [I'll take him in the other room]."

"No, we'll leave him right here. We are not going to hide from anybody," Father said as he walked to the door.

"Come in, come and have dessert and coffee with us," Father said as he greeted Mr. Strunk.

"I didn't mean to come before your supper was finished," said the children's teacher.

"We had a little delay before we started dessert. Come in and join us," Father added.

"I thank you. That will be good. I do have a few things I want to discuss with you."

Father took the lead and Mr. Strunk followed through the closed porch and into the kitchen.

"Some coffee, and how about a piece of custard?" Mama offered.

"I thank you. You are most kind. I didn't intend to intrude. Coffee sounds good."

"Boys squeeze together and let Gloria join you on the bench. Here is a seat for you, Amos, " Mama directed.

Mr. Strunk walked farther into the kitchen, his hand ready to pull the chair back and seat himself when he spotted the new child at the table. He immediately strained to stand erect. The shock on his face was something to behold. His face turned white, then red. He fumbled for words, but none were forthcoming. His body shook as he tried his utmost to compose himself. Father got up, took hold of his arm to steady him.

Mr. Strunk moved back. "I . . . I already had my meal before I came," he said in an almost inaudible voice. "Woodie." He took a deep breath. His body was shaking. "Woodie, what have you done?" His words were garbled like he had a swollen tongue. "What have you done?" His hair stood on end like that of an angry cat, and his face turned to white again. "What have you done? I can't believe my eyes." His body shook.

Del never saw anyone so unhinged, especially so her teacher. His disciplined stature was blown to the winds. She felt sorry for him.

Father pushed a chair behind him and helped him to sit down. "Believe it. Yes, I have a new boy at the table. I surely didn't mean to shock you. I will tell you briefly how this came about. The children can give you the rest of the story in school. They just learned the details before you came. As you know I have been going to Philadelphia for a few weeks. To make a long story short, I took pity on a homeless child and brought him along home. You can still see he was not getting regular food for a while. He looks much better than the day I brought him home. Thank goodness for the neighbors. All were very helpful, especially Becky."

Mr. Strunk was beginning to calm down a bit. His face once fire red, now was very pale.

"But, but a Black person in this town! This could spell trouble. Old Benj . . . What say you? Am I the last to know?" Mr. Strunk paused. "Who else knows?" Mr. Strunk's unsteady voice forced words out.

"Becky knows. Billy Henry knows, our neighbor Ed knows," Father added.

"Yes, yes, yes I . . . I passed them as I was coming in the lane. What do you intend to do with him?" Mr. Strunk gained some control as he got up and strained to stand erect.

"Here's your coffee, sit down." Mama pointed to the chair he had just vacated. It appeared Mr. Strunk never heard her.

"What are you doing? Are you going to keep him? Have you considered the trouble you may be in? Where are his real parents?"

"Whoa there. Enough said. Same as I do with every child here. Take care of him. Send him to school," Father said calmly.

"Surely, you don't mean MY school!" The teacher said nervously as he pointed to himself with a shaky hand.

"Of course, all the children in this Township must go to school. I didn't mean for you to find out about our boy this way. I want Dr. Schlicher to see him first and get an idea how old he is and what his health is like. There's much that needs to be done before any schooling can begin."

"My, my school is, well, it can be over-full once we find out if children are moving into the Printz home. I hear it may be up for sale. Stimmel's school is already overcrowded. The same could happen to my school." Mr. Strunk stressed the word "my".

"You sure you don't want a cup of coffee?" Mama pointed again to the empty chair and the coffee she placed on the table.

He sat down. His hand was shaking, rattling the cup and saucer. He set them on the table, stuttering as he spoke. "Yes, yes," he muttered, "I was going to ask about your children, but now I understand."

Mama moved the coffee cup closer to Mr. Strunk.

"Talk about completing a sentence!" Del thought. "Teacher is really rattled." She heard Father speak as she looked around the table.

"First thing we need to know is: did this child have any schooling? He has not told us anything about himself. You tutor Ernest. Maybe we need to start with tutoring before going to a classroom."

"I think we, well, I need to think about this some more," Mr. Strunk said weakly.

"*Ah, hut gegucked halver dotd odder recht grunk* [He had looked half dead or very sick]," Benj told Mr. Strunk. "*Da Woodie hut ihm schpaared vun verhungerer* [Woodie has him saved from starvation]."

"I . . . I must get back home. Tammie will wonder what, what took me so long."

"You don't have to go on our account. However I will go along and get milk for you. Unless you wanted fresh milk in the morning."

"Tamara wants the milk so I will take, take it along tonight."

Father held on to Mr. Strunk's arm as they left the kitchen together. Mr. Strunk still seemed shaken as he moved on unsteady legs. He did not say goodnight to the family as he left.

"That, my friend," Benj tapped the boy's arm, *"Des izs da Schule mayschter doh* [This is the schoolteacher here]. You will be going to his school."

Mama walked over, sat beside the little boy and repeated in English what Benj had said in the dialect. Mama added, "I will call you child until you can tell me your real name. I know you are old enough to know your name. We will find room upstairs for you, but tonight you'll sleep on the couch here in the kitchen, where it's nice and warm. You won't be alone. Fritz will be here and one of us. You needn't be afraid. I hope you'll like it here." Mama stroked his arm as she talked. "Do you have anything to say? Anything that you would like to tell us?"

"I like to live here," Carol said quickly.

Everyone broke out with smiles and laughter. Even the new child hung his head but kept a straight face.

"Can you tell us your name?" Mama asked. She then started with, "Alvin, Allen, Albert, Alfred, Austin, Abraham. Are any of those your name?"

There was no response.

Looking around the table, Mama said, "Let's finish our work. Tomorrow will be here before we are ready." Mama looked directly at the quiet boy. "You will remain indoors until we find decent shoes and clothes for you. Then you can run around outside with all the other children."

"He only has one shoe. Why?" Ollie asked.

"He lost the other shoe. We'll take care of that."

Father and Mr. Strunk were still outside, and Del could hear their voices, but not their words. Mama looked like she was tempted to know what was being said out there. She looked to Benj and said, "I guess I better stay here and wait. Depends on what is said, I will be more abrupt with a reply. I know that doesn't work. Woodie is probably telling him the whole story."

Ori carried a sleepy Carol to bed. Til also climbed the stairs. Del was surprised he didn't stay around any longer. Mama told the rest of the children to get themselves to bed as well. "Get a good night's sleep," she said. "Tomorrow will be a big day."

Del waited her turn to take the stairs and then prepared for bed. Both Mr. Strunk and the Black boy were foremost on her mind. She felt sympathy for both the new boy and her teacher in different ways. Del half smiled. Her mind was in a state of wonderment as she drifted off to sleep.

CHAPTER FIVE

A Name Is Decided

SATURDAY MORNING, Del straightened the bed covers and dressed to go downstairs. The boy from Philadelphia lay in a relaxed position on the couch. Benj was seated on the rocker.

"Good morning, you two," said Del.

Nothing more than a nod of Benj's head. He pointed to the simmering pot of oatmeal, "Might need more milk."

She added milk and began stirring with a large wooden spoon.

"Nothin' to say this morning?"

"I said good morning. Did you sleep good, him too?"

"*Es whar allrecht* [It was alright]."

"I will never forget our teacher's face. When words came he was stammering and I think he actually bit his tongue." Del pointed to the little boy. "What do you think he will do?"

"*Du huscht gute gwacht. Ahr muss des vennich iwwerdenke. Artlich gute gwacht.* [You have good watched. He must think over this a little. Very good watched]." Benj moved his head from side to side.

"Just hope he doesn't have it in for us from now on."

"Vee weescht do soo eppes [How know you such something]?"

"I hear people talk. Mama says he sometimes didn't like a student and everybody knew it. Were you here all night?"

Benj looked at Del for a time while shaking his head no. "I went home after ya all went to bed. Came back very early and stayed with our feller here."

"I see he is wearing a pair of Ollie's pajamas."

"That whose they are. Fit pretty good."

Del persisted, "Was Mr. Strunk very angry, or what? Never saw anyone react like that."

"Bung, verzaant allebeed veilleicht. Kann sei. Ah hut ebbes geich en schwatz [Afraid, angry, both maybe. Could be he has something against a Black person]."

"How long did he and Father talk last night?"

"Net lang [Not long]. Yer Father had other things to do. Closed the barn for the night."

Del wasn't satisfied with Benj's answer. "Bet Father explained more to Mr. Strunk than what he told us."

"Did ya sleep good?"

"Do you know what Father said to our teacher?"

"Did ya sleep good?" Benj just looked at Del.

Del smiled. "All right." Del paused. "How many are up this morning? I know I'm later than usual. Must get busy and do my morning work. Where is everybody?"

"Ya is not the last. The girls and Til are still in bed."

"Til usually isn't in bed at this hour of the morning. He isn't sick, is he?"

"Nay, ahr iss net grunk [No, he is not sick]. He took a turn to stay with our boy here and yer papa said he could have the pleasure of sleeping late. Bill is out there taking Til's place."

"I was surprised Til went upstairs before me. Didn't think he would have anyone else take care of Doll first thing in the morning. Does Bill know all that Til does?"

"Ahr iss lang genunk um helfe fa wisse waas au gehed [He is long enough at helping to know what goes on]."

"I wonder what Doll thought when Til wasn't there for her this morning."

"*Du sedscht besser wisse* [You should know better]. He went out to the barn 'fore he went to bed."

Del walked into the porch, saw the stable doors were open and the cows were in the barnyard gathered around the watering trough, which meant barn chores were finished and the family would gather for breakfast. She returned to the kitchen and slid the coffee pot over direct heat on the stove, and moved the oatmeal kettle forward to allow more heat. She grabbed the large metal spoon and stirred the oatmeal thoroughly.

"*Fa waaz sel* [For what that]?" Benj pointed at the heavy metal spoon.

"It stirs better. Oatmeal sticks to that wooden spoon," Del said as she again walked into the porch to see what was happening outside.

"*Waas huscht gsehne* [What did ya see]?"

"I wanted to see how many are coming in. I saw Mama going into the milkhouse. Didn't see Bill or Fritz. I know one thing, when Til comes down he will hardly take time to eat, he will have to see if Doll is all right before he does anything else."

"*Bischt denkich recht* [I think you are right]."

Mama was first to enter. She asked if the young boy had washed his face and hands.

Benj shook his head.

Mama brought a basin with warm water over to the chair in front of Benj. "*Nay geh yuscht. Ich geb ocht druff* [No just go. I'll take care of this]."

"*Des doh machs laywa g'warde* [This here makes living worthwhile]," Benj pointed to the little boy.

Mama seemed especially pleased. "He may eat in his pajamas. I will look for better fitting clothes after breakfast."

Father and the boys came in as Til came down the stairs. Fritz stayed in the porch, which was the rule when his paws were wet.

"You get enough sleep?" Mama asked Til.

"Yes, I could have gotten up earlier, I was laying awake for about ten minutes. Thought I'd wait until breakfast is ready."

"It's oatmeal this morning," Mama said. "We'll get breakfast over with as quickly as we can, in case Dr. Schlicher comes by. It rained after I went to bed, two hours after midnight I still heard the rain."

"*Ma greige en ganz woch rege* [We'll get a whole week of rain]," Benj said with certainty.

"I wonder what Teacher is going to say on Monday morning," Til said with a serious face. "He sure was surprised. I thought he was going to faint. I wonder what he is going to do?"

"Tilghman, I wonder too," Mama said as she helped to set the breakfast table. "We'll find out soon enough. He must accept the child in school because it's the law."

"He has time to figure this out for himself. I think he will come around to doing the right thing," Father said upon entering the kitchen.

Mama gave Father a long look. "I hope you are right. I don't feel so sure he is willing to accept another student. He can say he has full house already, he has thirty-seven students with the Goho's three children. The school board tries to limit all township schoolhouses to forty students each. This is one of the smaller schoolhouses in the township. We may have more children before long if someone takes the Printz farm." Mama was mulling things over while talking.

Benj merely nodded his head while looking at Mama.

"Something needs to be done there. Taxes are delinquent. Nothing happening there since the enumeration was taken," Father said.

"We can't go there and cut any of those beautiful white peonies along the picket fence every summer like we used to," Del mused.

"No, Adelaide, that's out of the question. It is surely the most fragrant peony I ever found. One bouquet of that peony fills the room with a wonderful fragrance. We may not be farming that land much longer, depending who the buyer is," Mama added.

"*Da Edgar is noch net kumme fa sei millich* [Edgar has not yet come for his milk]," Father said.

"*Viellicht iss ahr om waarde fa da dokder* [Perhaps he is also waiting for the doctor]," Mama answered.

"He is a little later this morning. We had heavy rain last night and more is predicted," Father changed the subject.

"He sure doesn't want to come when it rains if he doesn't have to," Til added. "Everyone knows he doesn't like to dirty his machine."

"Oliver, you use too much sugar on your oatmeal," Mama admonished.

"That's the only way oatmeal is good." Ollie was the fussy child when it came to food.

"Here, take some warm milk, dilute some of that sweetness," Mama ordered.

Father spoke, "I asked the neighbor to send the doctor our way next time he sees Ernest. He said he would." Father changed the subject again. He too was famous for using heaps of sugar on his oatmeal and in his coffee.

Mama asked Father if Edgar asked why we wanted the doctor to stop here and he shook his head no.

Those trips from Lyon Station where the doctor has his office to the rural community of New Jerusalem were usually made on Saturdays or early Monday mornings, if unsuitable weather interfered with Saturday rounds.

One could not miss Dr. Schlicher's coming. The fancy Chrysler he drove was sure to alert every living thing that the doctor was in the area. He sometimes leaned on the horn to announce his coming, which wasn't necessary. The motor itself could be heard in that quiet rural setting. Regular visits to the Losch house made passing the Y Farm a short-cut to the cement highway where Becky lived, and he always stopped there. Becky told him about people she had visited and the particular problems she dealt with. Where and when a baby was due and whether there were any particular concerns she might have about any folks on the hill. New Jerusalem, in the center of Rockland Township, was the highest point in the township.

Father also heard lots of news in the township. His relationship with the Boyers, who were the proprietors of the hotel at the upper end of town, and with Grandfather's creamery across the street from the hotel on the inside corner of a right angle turn, these were two good sources of information about the rural community. Father knew most all residents of the township. As Father was the township tax collector in addition to farming and operating a small sawmill, these activities brought a steady flow of people to their farm. Plenty of gossip was heard. Residents made a visit to the Y farm at least once a year to pay their school, road, and county taxes. Del heard her parents say that school and road taxes could be paid with pocket change. Father also spent time at township schoolhouses on Saturdays close to the tax deadline, making it easy for residents to pay taxes close to their homes. He made monthly visits to both the Road Board and the School Board meetings, making settlement with the Boards on the monies collected. He also visited the County Courthouse in the city for settlement of county taxes.

There was a soft tap on the door. Becky opened the door and stuck her head inside. "Come on in," Mama called. Becky was prepared for the fine drizzle. *"Sez aa newwelich* [It is foggy]." She set her big black umbrella by the door in the porch and proceeded to undo her boots, the kind that men wore. Becky needed this kind of footwear to travel through rain and heavy snows attending to her healer duties. Del once heard the doctor say, 'I wish all communities had a Becky looking after them. It would make my job a lot easier.'

"You needn't bother about your boots. Leave them on your feet, keep your feet warm."

"Thank you, nevertheless I will do as Fritz does. I don't want privileges he doesn't have. I'm more comfortable without them anyway." Fritz thumped his tail on the porch floor as if he agreed with Becky.

"We're waiting for the doctor. You are welcome to coffee and cake."

"I didn't come to eat. I passed Amos in the lane with a milk jar as I was going home last evening. Does he know anything?" Becky asked as she looked intently at the little boy sitting on the couch.

"Sure does," Mama paused, then added, "What a big shock for him. Didn't know what to expect for awhile."

"Amos came because he was concerned about the children's behavior at school." Father looked around the room from one to another.

Del hoped no one saw her surprise. Becky was more involved than she expected. Becky passed Mr. Strunk last night coming in our lane while all the rest of us were having supper. Del thought, "How much time did she spend in the barn in the past couple of days? Becky might have seen that duck incident. She might have been in the barn when they brought him in the house." This was something she needed to ask Bill.

"*Sie iss um danke* [She is at thinking]."

Del became aware that Benj was pointing a finger at her.

"You didn't hear, I told you to fetch an A.P. cake. It's alright, William is getting it. What are you thinking about?" Mama asked.

"Nothing really."

"There is no such thing as nothing. Your mind was busy," Mama stated assuredly.

"I want to know what the doctor has to say, if he is coming today."

"Do you know for sure Dr. Sam is coming?" Becky asked.

"Not really, Woodie told Edgar to have the doctor stop here if he visited there," Mama responded.

"I rather think Monday since this day is predicted to have heavy rains. It looks like it, too. Skies are gray all over," Becky added. "Everyone knows the concerns Dr. Schlicher has for his fancy machine."

"It feels like rain, I can tell. *Mei gnoche losse mich wisse lang vannenaus* [My bones let me know long in advance]," Benj acknowledged.

"I tell people all the time, keep your children's feet dry. It'll save them a lot of aches and pains later in life. That goes for ourselves, too." Becky pointed to Mama, Father and Benj.

"My mother was poor, but she always made sure we had rubbers or boots to keep our feet warm and dry," Father admitted.

"*Dood ah now gschwetze* [Does he now talk]?" Becky asked.

"*Nay, noch net* [No, not yet]," Benj quickly responded.

"Hmm," was all she said.

Del was relieved that Becky was helping from the beginning. Becky moved toward the boy from Philadelphia and brushed the top of his head with her hand. "Bet you like being in a nice warm house. Can you tell us something about yourself?" Becky placed her hand under his chin and lifted his head. "There, that's better. You have a nice face. It needs some filling out."

"Boys, now that we have eaten I think we will go back to the barn and do the regular morning work. We waited long enough. We can hear the doctor's machine come in the lane. I want to be ready when someone comes to deliver my truck, or pick me up to fetch it." Father stood and stretched.

"Can I come along?" both Til and Bill said simultaneously.

"We'll see how things work out," Father replied.

Ori opened the stair door and stepped into the kitchen. "Carol still asleep?" Mama asked.

"She stirred a little. I moved quietly."

Just then the door opened and Edgar Losch stepped into the porch; he touched Fritz and leaning over the dog he briefly looked up to say, "I have the milk. Thanks, Woodie. Ernest is doing better. Doctor is taking more time between visits. I will settle with you at the end of the month as always."

"That's quite all right. Tell the missus and Ernest we said hello. Watch out for the rains and stay dry."

"That's not going to be easy with what they predict. I'll try all the same." That said, the door closed and Edgar was on his way.

"*Ich dank ahr hut des kindt net scayna* [I think he has this child not seen,]" Benj was quick to say as all the adults let out their held breath.

The door opened once more. It was Mr. Losch again. "I had to make sure I saw what I thought I saw. There IS someone different sitting back there. Is Susanna down from the coal regions? Yes, it must be so. I can't believe my eyes." Mr. Losch stepped into the kitchen. Looking at Becky he said. "What do you call this? He's just a little boy. Can't be of much help. *Ah gooked bedauerlich* [He looks pathetic]. Ernest looks better than that."

Becky shook her head, "I don't need . . . "

Father interrupted Becky. "I brought him home from Philadelphia. I had to save him—he was a lost or abandoned child there. You can see for yourself he is far too skinny," Father spoke emphatically.

Edgar turned his attention to Father. "What do you mean, save him?"

"Edgar, you would have done the same thing. You wouldn't leave a young boy in an alley, grabbing whatever he could find to eat out with no protection from the cold, but for burlap bags that are never good for warmth." Father looked directly at Edgar. "Would you leave someone like that to starve or freeze to death?" Father paused, holding his gaze at Edgar before he spoke again. "I did the Christian thing to do."

"*Kann senna oss ah hilf havve mus* [Can see that he must have help.] I don't know about a Black child, though. What are you going to do with him? Is that why you want to see the doctor? I . . . I don't know how the neighbors are going to . . . *Well, sez kan onner schwatz doh im dem nochberschaft. Un ordlich weit doh ruhm. Mir hen genunk Druwwel kott* [Well, there is no other Black person here in this neighborhood. And rather far here around. We have enough trouble.]"

"Wait a minute," Father said. "Just as I said. He is a human being. He deserves a chance to grow up."

Mr. Losch stood there, dumbfounded. His eyes circled the room as he looked at everyone; he pushed his cap back, exposing his deep temples while scratching the top of his head. "Are you in on this?" He pointed to Becky. "Am I the last to know?"

"No, you are among the first. I brought him home from Philadelphia on Wednesday. Amos Strunk knows. He was here last evening. And those you see here."

"What did Amos say?"

"Same as you. He was surprised. I want to get this boy out in the neighborhood. I don't want a lot of rumors flying around before they see him and know why he is here."

"*Fa sel vid duo da dokder sehne* [For that you will want to see the doctor,]" Edgar said thoughtfully.

"My father also knows," Mama added.

"I don't know, Woodie. I won't make any trouble for you. But as you surely know there are some people in this town who won't take this lightly and others who will not accept what you say as truth."

Father had a serious look on his face. "I thought about that a lot. If I can help my relatives in these hard times, I can feed one more mouth. The Philly market folks say he has been hanging around on and off for weeks."

"*Waas denksch du daweah* [What think you about this?]" Edgar looked at Becky.

"*Ses besser oses wohr. Ahr wohr halwer dodt. Ahr wohr aarmseelich.* [It's better than it was. He was half dead. He was pitiful.]"

"Do you think he's all right, no particular disease?" Edgar asked anxiously.

"If you call starvation a disease, that he had. Needs more nourishment for sure. Bones are strong, no bumps. Woodie saved him."

Everyone looked shocked.

"Yes indeed." Becky said it with certainty, and then continued. "Woodie did what Jesus taught us all to do—to do unto others as you would have them do unto you."

Del never heard those words said that way before.

"I must get home to the missus. She'll wonder what has taken this long. As I said, I won't make any trouble for you. *Gudae dawg* [Good day]."

Father grabbed his flannel-lined overall coat and followed Edgar outside.

The family was quiet for a spell, except for Mama. She fussed a bit with the fires in the stove. "If I didn't know any better, I would say this wood is as damp as the outside." She poked at the pieces and turned them over to create more heat.

"Now there is somebody else that knows. People will talk about this for sure," Ori said.

"Talking is good. It's when they start whispering we could be in for lots of trouble," Becky said thoughtfully. "I guess we might as well give up on Dr. Sam and his flash of lightning."

"Flash of lightning, that's funny," Til said. All the children laughed.

"Did you ever see anything else so bright red with lots of shiny metal streak by so quickly?"

Til's face was all smiles. "I never heard his machine called that. That bright red Chrysler, with black fenders and running board, and yellow spoke wheels has plenty of shiny metal. It is a flash of lightning!"

Mother laughed. "Tilghman looks over that motor car thoroughly every time it's here."

"I just hope I'm here when he comes. I want to hear what the doctor thinks about him." Del turned her gaze to the Black child. "How can he tell how old he is? Whether he is healthy or just plain real skinny?"

"I hear Adelaide is one to ask a lot of questions. Being inquisitive is the only way one learns," Becky said with humor.

Father returned. "Everything all right?" Mama questioned. Father merely nodded his head.

"Boys, let's head for the barn. It will soon be dinnertime and we haven't accomplished anything. Gloria, are you going out with us? Put your galoshes on. Be mindful of your duck; if anybody comes, see to it that you pen him up in plenty of time," Father advised as he walked out of the house.

"I really think you should leave him in his pen, else you may be running around in pouring down rain when its time to put him in his coop," Mama advised.

"I know that much, Mama. That's why he isn't on the loose right now," Ori asserted.

Becky sat next to the Black child. Del could tell she was someone he knew. Taking his hand, she rubbed her hands over his. "His hands are strong but need more flesh over the bones before he can do much of anything. His hair is a mess. Some trimming was done, more needs to be done."

"I'm thinking all the boys are ready for haircuts," Mama said. "Tell Ed to bring his *Gscharr* [barber tools] along, see if he can do more work." She looked to the rescued child. "Not enough light in the barn and no chair to do a decent job."

"So," Del thought, "Ed was in the barn. He trimmed that head of hair already. How many people know about his rescue?"

Becky sat back smiling. "I see you are surprised, Adelaide." Becky looked at Mama. "May I tell?"

Mama smiled, nodding her head indicating yes, as she left the room to look for clothes for the little boy.

"Adelaide, Ed knows, his wife Hester too. Living next door to me they saw Benj come over to my place carrying a lantern Wednesday night. That doesn't happen unless there is a problem of some kind. They saw me leave with Benj. Never did see either one of us come back since both of us stayed the night. *Erschta ding mariyetts ve ich daheem waar, sie hen wissa wolla waz au gehd. Denksht du net* [First thing in the morning when I came home they wanted to know what was happening. Think you not]?" Becky glanced at Benj.

"*Sie wara glei doh* [They were soon here]." Benj acknowledged with the nod of his head.

Mama returned with clothes, including two pairs of socks. She helped the child make a fist. Becky helped also. Mama had a good pair of Ollie's socks and proceeded to place the foot portion around the boy's fist to find the proper size.

"These will not fit, too small," Mama said. Next she tried a pair of Bill's socks. "*Grosse feese* [Big feet]," Mama said. "*Des gebt en grosse mann* [This gives a big man]. Need this larger pair of socks. Plenty of room." Mama put them on his feet. Mama looked at Del. "This won't take long. I'll let you know when you can come back."

Del made her way into the parlor where she relaxed to think things over. Her thoughts rested on the coal regions and Susanna. Why did Edgar think the little boy came from there? Del knew Susanna was Becky's granddaughter who she never met. Susanna never came to visit Becky as much as Del knew. It was the same with Becky's daughter Rachael. But why did Ed mention Susanna? Del remembered hearing Becky say if she could no longer be alone, a great-grandchild would come and stay with her. She was not going to leave the town where she was born, grew up, and raised her family; this was where she was going to die no matter what. Del knew very little about Becky's family. Del could not comprehend why Mr. Losch thought Susanna was here. What could he mean about trouble enough?

"Okay now," Mama called. Del returned and saw the young boy in regular clothes. What a big difference! He was wearing a shirt and sweater that belonged to Ollie. Looked plenty big, although the sleeves were too short. The much-too-big bib overalls he was wearing had the leg bottoms turned over several times. He would surely grow into them sometime and make a better fit. Father had gone through the worn shoe box and retrieved a pair of low shoes for Sunday wear.

"Well, now, that doesn't look too bad," Becky said, as Mama stood back and took a good long look.

"It's good enough for right now and around here. The shoes have too much room inside but won't hurt his feet and he's not going anywhere until we have something that looks and fits better. At least he has something solid on his feet."

Becky tucked and positioned the bib overalls properly. "You never wore anything like this before. *Dade mei lewe druff wedde* [Would bet my life on that]."

The boy looked pleased even though the clothes hung on his body.

Til was back and looked at him with some surprise. "He sure looks different. More like a farmer now."

"*Ahr kon audlich gute choomper* [He can pretty good jump]," Til laughed as he left for the barn.

"How does Til know he can jump?"

"Tilghman tried that last night in the barn when they were there to bring him in. He helped him across the barn floor to the door, from there he was carried in, so they tell me." Mama continued. "I have hand me downs from our Allentown folks. No farmer's clothes there. He'll need Sunday clothes too. I will look through those later."

Del heard Carol moving about upstairs. She decided now was the time to clean the upstairs. She cleaned her room and the boys' rooms, plus the hallway. She saw her library book and decided to get some reading done, but her mind was not cooperating; after reading a chapter she didn't remember what she read. She gave up and walked from one upstairs window to the next, taking in the view on three sides.

She looked into the barnyard pen. The cows were outside drinking the fresh spring water in the long cement trough. There was Daisy, the red and white Ayrshire. She stood out from all the rest. Del returned to the window in her room. Looking across the fields, she saw Edgar removing the swing that hung from the ceiling on their porch. It was nice to swing slowly back and forth on a hot summer evening. Del had not been there since Ernie could not have any visitors. Del avoided the greenish colored pane in the middle of the lower row in the top half of a six over six window. She was annoyed that the painter had broken the middle window pane and replaced it with an old greenish pane that distorted the view. Looking through other panes she saw the Conrad's house no longer obstructed by leaves on trees. The row of sour cherry trees were all bare of foliage. Conrad's red tin barn roof gleamed from the rains. Ori came upstairs to do her cleaning. "Where are you?" she called.

"In my room. You could see if you'd look," Del replied

"You should go down."

"Why?"

"Mama wants you."

"For what?"

"Don't know."

Del ran down the stairs just as Til and Bill entered the kitchen at the same time.

"Adelaide, I was going to send you out to fetch the boys, but they are here now," Mama said.

Til walked over to where Benj and the boy were seated. "Those aren't our clothes but they look pretty good on him."

"He looks a little better; take him along, see what happens. Keep him with you. Don't let him alone. Bring him in if you see he tires."

"Can you get on your feet?" Til gave him his hand. Bill stood close by and lent support to the boy.

"*Ich geh mit* [I go along]." Benj also got up.

Til smiled at the little boy. He waited a bit, then looking at him said, "Come on, you can do it."

Sure enough, the Black child used Til's hands to pull himself up and stood erect as a pinched smile crossed his face. He did exactly as Til had said. He hopped on his right leg. His left foot scraped the floor and dragged a bit. Bill held on to the other side of him. It appeared they all but carried him.

Del was shocked. She hadn't realized he couldn't walk. Father did carry him in, and Benj always helped him move the short space from the couch to the table, which didn't require walking.

Becky asked Mama, "Did you see that? That left foot is more relaxed already. Still scraping and sliding on the floor. *Ich wil ihm vidder gute begucke. Won ahr erscht schpringa kon siss nix letz. Siss oll im kopp* [I will carefully look him over again. I'm sure he can walk. If he first could run nothing is wrong. It's all in the head]. I want to hear what Dr. Sam thinks. I think I shall head for home. Maybe I can still beat the heavy rains."

"Are you sure you won't stay a while longer? Have dinner with us," Mama said.

Now, Laura, you know that much—I never wear out my welcome. Never stay anywhere at mealtime unless circumstances are such that I am needed."

"You most certainly earn all that is offered. What would we have done without you these last couple of days? I will have a bigger meal at suppertime."

"You folks will be busy doing all sorts of odds and ends a Saturday brings. I don't want to hold you up."

Mama was insistent, "You aren't keeping us from doing the things that need to be done. You heard Woodie say a truck will arrive sometime today. One of these days he'll have to build a garage for both his vehicles. At any rate we'll have two machines to keep in the dry."

"I'll stay a bit, but I'll not eat. I really want to watch that boy when they come in to eat, if you don't mind." Becky settled back in her chair.

"'Course not. You are most welcome to stay as long as you wish."

"I just think he is able to walk. *Yusght bong aus ahr tzsrick gay muss* [Just afraid that he must go back]."

"I hope that truck comes before it rains this afternoon," Mama said.

"That's the only talk that goes on around here," Ori said as she entered the kitchen. "It's just a truck, for goodness sake."

"How many trucks did you see already?" Becky asked.

"There are plenty of trucks in the city; they make all kinds of deliveries."

"Yes, I know you get to the city once in a while. You are fortunate. Many of your friends never leave this area."

"Father's truck will be different, from what I hear. Not like those you usually see," Del answered.

"How do you know anything like that?" queried Ori.

"If you would listen to what Bill and Til say instead of trailing behind, you would hear what the boys are talking about."

Ori wasn't interested; she left to clean the parlor, and Del soon heard the sound of the hand sweeper in the front room.

Mama took care of Carol. She washed her hands and sat her at the table and placed a small dish of oatmeal in front of her. "You can redd up[3] upstairs." Mama looked at Del. "Check all the bedrooms, let mine alone. I will take care of that myself."

"Already did that. I have a book I should read."

Mama wants private conversation with Becky, Del thought as she climbed the stairs. "Whose beds get stripped this week?" she called back downstairs.

"The boys' rooms."

Del completed that chore and had read three chapters when she heard engine noise. She quickly ran to the window in her parents' room, looking down onto the lane. Sure enough, the truck was being delivered. The menfolk came from all directions. Del could see everyone except the new boy. Everyone moved in such a hurry they must

---

3 Term for straighten or clean up.

have left him behind. Del expected he was with Til in the horse stable. Then along came Benj. He had that boy and of all things, he was seated on her small flat wagon she used to complete her every day chores.

"Well, I'll be," she thought to herself. "Everyone must have run off to see the truck and left him behind. Benj would not abandon him. My wagon sure comes in handy! I wonder who thought of that?" She watched as all were walking to and fro around the truck. A man with a black leather cap was talking to Father while showing all the operating features. Ollie took a high step while holding on to the open door and seated himself behind the steering wheel. Til and Bill stood by as one side of the hood was lifted to take a look at the motor. Father seemed happier than she saw him for a while. Benj dropped the pull handle on the wagon and it fell to the ground. He said something to the boy. Benj looked into the cab where Ollie was seated and had taken charge. He was busy pointing to various places within the cab. Ollie appeared pleased as he moved over and invited Benj to seat himself also. Benj declined. Del decided to go down and join the gang after she saw Mama and Becky join the onlookers.

"Ori won't let me go out." Carol complained as Del reached the kitchen.

"Here, let me get something for you to wear. You can go along with me. Everybody else is out there. Wait until you see the green truck. I didn't know it would have yellow spoke wheels just like Dr. Schlicher's car."

"Is it a green I like?"

"You tell me if it's a green you like. Here, let's go." Once outside, Del helped to place Carol on the running board and helped Ollie struggle to pull her onto the seat beside him. He pulled her across his body and slid behind the steering wheel once more.

The man with the leather cap left. Del saw him walk beyond the woodshed. He stopped briefly. He was talking to someone and motioning with his hands. Shortly after that she saw Ed and Hester approaching—the neighbors living next door to Becky. Ed was a silk mill employee who was laid off quite frequently. He and Hester spent many hours at the Heydt house along with Benj and Becky. They surely heard and saw the delivery of the truck and were inquisitive enough to come by and see. Ed took his place with the men as they were looking at the motor and discussing all sort of mechanical things. After the excitement subsided, Mama and Becky turned toward the house, and Hester headed home by herself.

"Come, Carol, we'll go in as well." Del reached for Carol, gently helped to lift her over Ollie and let her down. "I think that's all we'll hear the rest of this weekend. I am tired of it already. What more can they see or say?"

"I can see you are not interested in motor cars," Becky observed.

"Adelaide, you may as well set the table when you go in," Mama said. "We will follow. They can gawk at their truck the rest of the day. Good thing all the talk will take place outside. It was the same when we got the Studebaker, and especially when that heavy Auburn motor arrived to run the sawmill. I couldn't make head or tail out of anything they said. I don't know motor parts or what they are talking about half the time. Same when Isaac comes, they really get into mechanic talk. Wait until he hears we have a truck."

Benj came in too. "*Ich bleib wu es waerme es. Sez now verdolt feicht* [I'll stay where it is warm. It's now very damp]." The rocking chair creaked as he sat down. "*Feichtdichkeit in dem schockelschtul* [Dampness in this rocking chair]. Sounds like my bones," he muttered.

Del went about setting the table.

When Mama cam in she said, "We can make a few sandwiches with the leftover ham. Some fried sausages are here. Woodie likes those. One or two can have the leftover boiled cabbage. I'll heat that. Gloria likes it heated up again and again."

"For me it's best the very first time," Del chimed in.

"Leave the apple pie downstairs. Instead bring some folly walder[4] apples along for peeling. Here, take this dish. Whatever small cake you see you can bring along. Not my high-layer cake. I want to save that for

---

4 Folly Walder apples were exceptionally large, round, green-yellow apples with a tart flavor and soft texture. Generally eaten raw.

tomorrow if company comes. Get the jelly as well. I'll make cocoa if someone wants it."

Del returned with apples set on top of the cake saver. "Not all the apples. Still half as many there."

She ran down the cellar steps again and brought the remainder of the things Mama requested. "Where is the boy now? I saw him on my flat wagon. Did the man in the leather cap say anything about him? Where did he go? I saw him talk to Ed and Hester. How will he get home?"

"The other delivery man never came in the lane. He didn't know if he could turn around in here. He stayed by Ed's place."

"*Huscht duh en baddich deller fa des kindt* [Do you have a special plate for the boy]?" Becky asked.

"I used the heavy pewter plate and tin cup most of the times. Sometimes I used the pewter cup. Pewter holds heat longer." Mama smiled and looked to Del, "Use those pewter pieces and place them on the table, but not before he is here and sees them placed."

Del gladly obliged.

"See now!" Benj raised a finger. "Look who wants to play a trick."

"Not me! Mama said so," Del protested.

"*Verschteh nix. Bothered mich net* [Understand nothing. Bothers me not]." Benj walked into the porch. "I will see to it that our boy comes in. He's been out there long enough."

"Tell them all to come in and get a bite. The men talked long enough," Mama advised Benj.

Ollie was the first one in. He held the porch door open and looked back. Becky got up and walked into the porch. "*Ich wil sehne wie viel aus de buwe des kindt helfe muss* [I want see how much the boys must help this child].

Til and Bill flanked the little boy, one on either side of him. "He seems to come along quite easily. The boys manage quite well."

"I forgot to ask Ed if he has time to trim his hair some more. The boys need hair cuts too," Mama sighed.

"I'm sure he will do it, Loll. You should have seen Hester when she first saw the lad. Her face drew white. Thought I'd have to tend to her," Becky recalled.

"I hear she doesn't like to be around sick people. I wasn't out there when she and Ed first saw him. I know Hester is very squeamish. This boy sure looked sick."

"We appreciate Ed's help," Mama said. "People call him inquisitive sometimes. Maybe so. But he's a very kind and considerate person. The men are on their way in. Enough talk for now."

One by one the boys and men washed their hands and took their place at the table. Mama took the basin over to Benj. Becky leaned over, took the boy's hands to help him. She placed his hands in the water and he did the rest. Bill stood by and held a towel for him. He completed the job.

"Good job," Becky said.

Del realized this wasn't the first time Becky helped him.

Mama stood by the stove with her arms crossed and watched the process. *"Ah muss des aul lanne* [He must this all learn]."

"Ya gewiss [Yes sure]," Benj said softly.

"Ah hutt sel sehne. Ah wase aus sel sie deller is. [He has seen that. He knows that is his plate]," Becky said as Del got the pewter plate and cup and set it on the table. "See what kind of effort he makes to sit there."

With Benj's help the boy pulled himself up; holding onto a chair top he fell rather heavily onto the seat. A soft sigh of relief made it clear that everyone watched his progress, trying not being too obvious.

"Schteel sin tsu handich [Chairs are too handy]," Becky said skeptically.

Ed stuck his head in the door to say. "It's been a busy day, we are going to spend the rest of the day with our son."

Good-byes were said and the door closed behind Ed.

"That can't be so easy, either. Their only child staying with the grandparents so the two can work to make ends meet," Becky commented.

Benj placed his hand on top of the Black child's head. *"Mer misse ihm ess bede lanne* [We must learn him to pray]." Benj seemed to take a lot of interest in the young Black boy. Becky consented to have a cup of cocoa while the others ate. She set it on the table while she remained seated on the couch. The clanging of coffee cups and milk glasses followed as a crumb cake was cut and served. Mama began to peel and quarter apples. She placed the quarters on a separate plate. Mama told Til first to help himself to dessert. Til, of course, chose a piece of cake. Bill was next. Mama knew Bill would choose peeled apple. Mama passed the plates until they reached Benj and the little boy. "He can choose the dessert he prefers. If he really doesn't want freshly peeled apple quarters he may choose a piece of cake." Mama was pleased he was happy with fresh apples. Benj chose cake.

Ori braided Carol's hair and then her own dark hair in one long pigtail, finally getting around to what should have been done in the earlier morning hours. Mama was annoyed whenever Ori ignored regular schedules and chose her own time, but she allowed it. Del would not get away with behavior like that.

"While all of us are here," Father spoke, "we need to give this young fellow a name until he is willing to tell us his name. Think about it for a minute, then tell me what you suggest."

"I know! Forrest is a good name. The only Forrest I know is Isaac's neighbor. He's a real nice guy."

"Good, Tilghman. That's a start."

"I know a name, Dewey! I like that cat. Only he won't stay." Carol was pleased with her suggestion.

"I don't think we want to call him Dewey. It's a nice name, Carol. But we will never know who we are calling, this boy or the cat." Father kept a most serious expression, which was enough for the family to know not to start any silly laughter. "Think of a name no one else shares."

Dewey visits my garden too, Carol." Becky added. "I usually stop and pet him awhile. I think he likes that."

Del watched Becky while giving thought to Dewey. Meanwhile Becky had positioned herself to examine the boy's lame leg. She moved her hand back and forth feeling every muscle and bone in the leg, bending the knee, moving the ankle carefully. It seemed she knew where and how every muscle and bone should move.

"Is that all the suggestions?" Father looked around the table. "I should think you children have more ideas."

"We don't have an Austin in school. I like Felix—that would really be different. The book I am reading has a man named Felix. That's an interesting name."

"Adelaide, we can consider those. Now we have Forrest, Austin and Felix."

"Dewey too."

"Yes, Carol, we have Dewey too. Anyone else have a suggestion? Benj, how about you?"

"Woodie, *Sel duhnich ich net* [That I won't do]. Whatever ya decide is all right with me."

Becky stood up. "Now I am going home, while you decide on a name. *Ich blieb datt ess everrish fum daag* [I'll stay there the rest of the day]."

"Thanks for coming, Becky. Do you have a name for this boy?"

"I am with Benj here. Not for me to say. I will give him my own name anyway."

Del knew what that was all about. Becky kept a log of the people she ministered to. Anyone could read her ledger and not know who she was referring to. She had her own code name for each individual.

"Come anytime, Becky! Bye Becky!" the children called out.

Fritz came back after Becky closed the door. Father said, "Surely there are more ideas here for names. Maybe he'll tell us his true name. In the meantime we shall decide on one for him."

"I thought of one," Ori piped up loud and clear.

"Okay Gloria, let's hear it."

"How about Phillip? That would suit since he comes from the city of Philadelphia. We can just call him Phil. No one in school has that name either," Ori concluded triumphantly.

"Well there, that really sounds good. What about you, Loll? What do you think about that?" Father asked.

"Sounds good to me," Mama agreed.

"Do we all agree?" All heads were nodding as Father looked around the table and room. "I think for the time being we have that settled. From now on we shall call him Phillip."

Father got up, put his hands on the Black boy's shoulders. "You are Phillip, unless you tell us your name now." Father waited.

There was no reaction from Phillip.

"*Becky gsaat ahr kon lawfa. Sez nix letz* [Becky says he can walk. There's nothing wrong]." Father continued speaking in the Dutch dialect. "For some reason he chooses to limp and drag one foot. Becky thinks he wants to stay here. We need to assure him he has a home with us. Who knows what happened to this little boy? Maybe he's trying to tell us he won't run away. Or maybe he is trying to fool us into thinking he can't run and will run away first chance he gets, but she really doubts that."

"I feel quite sure that's not the case. He likes to eat," Mama said in English.

Benj pushed a chair back a bit and nodded his head, acknowledging his agreement with what was said.

"Benj, Loll and I talked some more about where this child will sleep. We certainly appreciate your offer to take him along to your house."

Benj just nodded his head.

"We sure appreciate your support," Father said. "We feel it would be best for this youngster to grow up with our children. We'll make room for him here."

"It will be inconvenient for him to sleep at your house and be with us the rest of the time," Mama spoke thoughtfully.

"*Sez aul recht, fei mit mir* [It's all right, fine with me]," Benj assured all. "Thought of that myself. If he would come to my house, he would have slept in Samuel's bed. The name Samuel is painted on the headboard. *Sel hawwe ich selvatt g'duu* [That have I myself done]."

"I know you are very good at painting fine art work and lettering. Ann showed me your settee and chairs. Beautiful painting, your own design," Mama confirmed.

"Tilghman has a larger room and a double bed all to himself. We will move his bed into Adelaide's room. We will take the twin beds from the room that Bill and Ollie share and put them in Tilghman's room. Adelaide's single iron bed will go in the boys' room. All we need is another single bed. How does that suit everybody?" Mama asked.

"Suits me just fine, I can really stretch out in a big double bed," Del was first to agree.

"Ollie will share a room with Tilghman. I hope you don't mind sharing again," Mama looked at Til.

"No, I'll still have my own bed, just have to get used to somebody else in the room with me."

"Good enough, Tilghman." Father was pleased.

"*Ich schoff mich hame* [I'll work myself home]. "If you need a single bed, I have that too." Benj stood up.

"Your own bed will wonder what happened to you." Mama smiled as she looked at Benj.

"*Sayn dich mariah* [See you tomorrow]." Benj picked up his lantern in the porch. He had brought one with him after Wednesday's activities, not knowing how long he would stay. Fritz followed him to the door. Benj spoke to Fritz as he was leaving, too softly for Del to hear.

Father stood and spoke. "I think it's good that Becky and Benj decided to go home this early. They won't get caught in the rain that will surely come. I'm surprised it held off this long. I am going out and park the truck under the sawmill roof. There's room enough to get most of the truck in the dry."

"I'll go with you," Til said.

"You can probably help me clear some space, should I need more."

Before Father and Til were back the skies opened up. It poured and poured rain some more. Mama said she knew the men were in the dry but may not have rain gear to bring them back. Bill offered to walk back with rain apparel for Father and Til.

"We'll wait a while, the rains could slow."

Del got a jigsaw puzzle and asked Carol to sit by the table in the side room and help find pieces to fit. Carol, with her knees on the bench, leaned on the table and found border pieces. Bill helped Phillip to the side room in case he wanted to help Carol. In short time Father and Til returned; the heavy rain had slowed to a drizzle. Bill and Ollie joined Father and Til as they returned to the barn.

A quiet evening was spent around the table. There were no guests or visitors. "This is how its going to be," Father said to Phillip. "This is your new family. Maybe we will find your family. But I will never make you leave."

Del thought Phillip understood what Father was saying, though he remained expressionless.

Til offered to take a turn staying with Phillip that night. Father agreed and said he would come down later and stay with him until morning.

Del moved to the closet and got her newest sweater to wear.

"Where are you going with that?" Mama asked.

"I am not going outside. I will head upstairs. I need to read my library book, I didn't get very far yet. It's too cool and damp to sit on my bed without wearing something to keep me warm."

"I don't want you to wear it too often before Christmas."

"I know, Mama." How she disliked the sweater. All the teasing that was sure to come every time she wore it. She disliked it for its 'granny' style. She was not pleased with the deep rust color but was happy it had two pockets. It was a birthday gift she had received earlier in the year from her mother's Aunt Kate. Come Christmastime she and all her brothers and sisters knew exactly what they would be receiving. To think that she was to wear a hat and gloves, sometimes a scarf as well, all the very same color caused her to shudder. The sweater was belted as well, and long enough to extend over her hips. Gosh, it could be a long coat for Carol. She shivered as she slipped into the sweater.

"Goodness, are you that cold? I hope you are not catching a cold."

"No, Mama. I don't feel like I'm catching a cold."

Del brought the belt forward, slipping it through the bone buckle as she rounded the table and headed for the upstairs. Mama cut all buttons off clothes, and saved all buckles from items that were worn beyond saving and ready for the rag bag. She kept things in different-sized jars on a low shelf in her bedroom closet. All white buttons in one jar, colored in another. Del looked at herself in the large mirror attached to the bureau in her parents' bedroom. There was no mirror in her room. She pulled the belt tighter, then loosened it again to see which way she preferred to wear it. Aunt Kate always managed to ask how one liked the sweater after wearing it a few times. Del could honestly say she appreciated the large pockets on each side, which were handy to carry a hankie. She might suggest that all her sweaters have pockets in the future, but she knew not to make that kind of request. Aunt Kate received leftover portions or skeins of yarn from a relative who lived in the city and worked in a factory across the street from her house. The leftover yarns could be had by anyone who desired to make use of them. It depended on the amount of yarn she had in the same color as to the size and extra pieces Aunt Kate would add. What a mess of this ugly color she must have had! The color would have been more suitable for a boy.

All the sweater designs and colors were different for the children. Mama once remarked, "How can you use a different stitch for each piece?" Aunt Kate answered then that it depends a lot on the weight of the yarn. Some stitches just didn't look nice on different yarn weights. Besides, once she made a style and pattern, she didn't want to repeat it for the next piece. That was boring for an expert knitter like her. Del would have liked to tell Aunt Kate that one year she especially liked the medium blue outfit, best of all she ever had. The hat had fit her perfectly and was quite becoming. Deep enough to cover her ears on those very cold wintry days. A rather large pom-pom of white yarn, with a few darker blue yarns in the center, placed perfectly over her right ear. Del wore that hat all winter long. Her classmates also liked it. She wore the hat again the following two winters even though it no longer matched her new sweater. Mama somehow allowed it. The third winter her hat showed pitiful signs of wear. The yarns were stretched and pilled. It really begged for replacement. Then came the day her hat could not be found. "You have a new cap to wear," was all Mama said.

Del wondered if Aunt Kate already knew about Phillip. She had always been kind and helpful for as long as Del knew her. Aunt Kate was a lot like Becky—each very supportive in their own way. Del opened the top drawer in her chest. It was not very deep and could only hold small things. Her little cedar box held that white ribbon she won last spring at field day exercises. She was allowed to enter, though a grade too early. It was her first year to compete in picture study and poetry and she won blue ribbons in both. Next was her birthstone ring Mama brought along from the city. Ori received one at the same time. All her school papers lay flat on the bottom of the drawer. Her perfect attendance papers with gold seals indicating the year. Her passing to each higher grade, and the certificate with gold seals for completing the number of books to read. She felt a little guilty about that. She did not read them all. She relied on her memory of what other students reported at book report time. Last of all was the gold piece Mama had given to her to keep. She arranged the items neatly and closed the drawer. Up to now she hadn't done anything in the way of straightening her room. She didn't have time earlier, even though she told Mama differently. The white-painted deep window seat would be first. Even today it felt wet. She took her cloth and dried it. She knew it wouldn't last. During the winter months she oft-times had a thin covering of sparkling frost resting on the window seat. That side of the house was exposed to the cold north winds that could add a covering of ice on the outside windowpane for weeks at a time. She used her dampened cloth and dusted the woodwork around the small panes. They, too, were damp to the touch. Most of the white paint was gone on the bottom strip of the small-paned window where the moisture rested. Time for a touch-up again come spring. Next, she dusted her clothes tree. She returned the unused hangers to the closet. Mama had Uncle Sam design a closet between Ori's bedroom and her own. The addition of a closet for both bedrooms was quite modern for that day. She retrieved the dust mop from the hall and moved slowly over blue and white print linoleum flooring. "All finished," she said out loud to herself. She took the mop and cloth downstairs and stepped outside on the little stoop. She shook both mop and cloth thoroughly and replaced them behind the door, ready for the next use. She decided to go back downstairs. Mama was fixing the fire. Bread was baking in the oven.

"Are you still having trouble with the wood fire?"

"No, I had a few pieces of pine; those always burn slowly and hold the heat, but it's hard on the stove pipes and chimney. Pine creates soot that sticks to the chimney and can cause a chimney fire." She placed the chopped pieces of wood ever-so-gently as she returned the stove lids. "Many a house received fire damage due to a burning chimney. My father is particular, he never burns any wood other than birch in his house. No soot in the chimney and a good fragrance in the house." Mama placed bread on the table as she prepared food for the evening meal. "Go down in the cellar and fetch a pan full of potatoes, and get some endive. Cover the endive again. I don't suppose we'll get company tonight. Amos and Lizzie usually go to the movies on Saturday nights. Lizzie doesn't want to miss adding a piece to her collection of Depression glass. She wants a complete set. Most will probably stay home with this rainy weather."

"Why did father get a truck?" Del thought this was a perfect time to find out what her parents had planned.

"Your father wants to use his truck for business purposes. If it works out all right he can earn a little extra money. Sure would help. That's all you need to know about it."

CHAPTER SIX

The Explosion

Del arose to calmer and cooler skies on Sunday morning. The ground lay wet as the morning sun peeped between heavy gray clouds slow to move on. Del descended the stairs quietly; upon entering the kitchen Mama spoke, "Be sure to dress warm enough for Sunday school, there's no church today. You'll need to walk home. It feels like colder air is here to stay. I started the table setting, you may finish it. Once the morning chores are completed your father will take you to Sunday school."

Del counted the plates out loud. "Where is Til? His glasses case is lying on the cabinet. He always keeps it by his bed. First thing he reaches for every morning." The round lenses with a thin black wire frame set him apart from most other school children.

"He was down two hours early," Mama said. "He relieved Benj from staying with Phillip, said he was awake. He is out in the barn. I am going out to see how far the menfolk are. Benj did your chores."

Sabbath day or not, barn chores and milking were done the same time each day.

"Is Phillip out there too?" Del asked.

"Yes. Out there with the boys," Mama said as she was leaving. Del's thoughts rested on how the neighboring town folk would react once they saw a Black child playing, eating and my-oh-my yes, traveling with them in Father's tan with black trim Studebaker. The car had four doors, a running board, and an affixed metal plate with ridges on the driver's side to scrape grit from the soles of shoes before stepping inside. The passenger side had a rubberized strip with grooves along the full length of the running board for the same purpose. What will people say when they see a Black child on board? Del remembered the shock and disbelief from some, especially Mr. Strunk. Of course her relatives living in larger towns or cities might not make a fuss. They lived with different cultures. They also appreciated the produce always available every time they visited and were grateful for the advantages they had. Compared to city residents without relatives or friends living on a farm, they could help with planting, weeding, pruning, and harvesting fresh fruits and vegetables, and receive food and produce in exchange for their efforts.

Most all families in New Jerusalem were farmers, or offspring of farm families. Retired farmers settled for a home in the village, leaving the outlying farm to the next generation. Others were self-employed or held a manufacturing job while maintaining enough acreage for gardening, housing a few chickens for a continuous supply of eggs, roosters to fatten, and a pigsty to provide fresh meat for the household. Larger acreages kept a cow or two and horses. The farmer making a living off the farm had more acreage, more animals, and larger barns. Self-sufficiency was taught and established early on. Country children were directly involved in all activities from planting to harvesting to canning and preserving meat and produce to consume throughout the year.

Aside from the small village, the surrounding areas were dotted with farms of various sizes. Forty acres was considered sizable. Sixty- to one-hundred acre farms were a prize. Father's farm was the largest acreage located within the heart of the community. Her mind's eye followed the cement pike all the way to the upper end of town as she considered all the individuals living in the fourteen houses along the way. She had counted them many times as she walked to the upper end of town for a needed item from Drumheller's store. On the left side of a right-angle turn stood the New Jerusalem Hotel. Levi and Martha Boyer were the proprietors. Father made his home with Levi and Martha when he was a teenager. They were a second set of parents for Father and they in turn considered him a son. Prohibition forced the Boyers to seek other means of income. The hotel had eight bedrooms, a large kitchen with built-in fireplace, and dining room. They lodged wards of the county to make ends meet. Levi accepted a job as Warden for the Berks County Prison System, which recognized the need for a place for people who were unable to work to live in a home-like atmosphere. The hotel was home to an epileptic suffering with seizures, a blind man, and three other men with difficulties. The county provided funds for care of them. Martha was very busy providing their meals and doing laundry and cleaning. The hotel was open daily, selling large pretzels for a penny plus candy, soda, ice cream and tobacco items. At the Saturday evening hoe-downs hot dogs were served.

On the inside corner of the right angle turn stood Grandfather's creamery. Thick stone walls kept the creamery building cool inside summer through winter. A right-angle turn from the cement pike took one to a single-lane entrance where, under a roofed unloading dock, farmers placed their filled milk cans. The same dirt lane made another right-angle turn that separated the creamery from a red frame with white trim horse stable. The stable housed Grandfather's two well-kept horses. That same lane circled to the back of the creamery where farmers would stop, pick up their emptied milk cans, and refill their cans with slop, the liquid left after the cream had been separated from the milk. It was held in a cement trough that stood on a solidly built cement base. Farmers would mix the slop with mash for their pigs. Nothing was wasted.

Behind the horse stable stood a tall, unpainted frame icehouse, which provided ice for the creamery and the hotel year round. The ice was cut from a dam behind the hotel during the bitter cold winter months. The blocks of ice were placed one on top of another, stacked very high. Plenty of sawdust was used to keep the ice blocks separated. The icehouse door was never opened, except to remove blocks of ice. The tall icehouse stood close to the falter opening to the acreage of Grandfather's farm, whereon stood one of the larger red barns in the Township, with a center track close to the roof and a large hook that could lift large amounts of hay or straw at one time and drop the load onto the loft or a side bin for storage. Beyond the overshoot stood the cattle pen with a watering trough along the bottom end of the barnyard which was supplied with spring water that kept the trough filled to overflowing, causing it to spill into a deep gutter that lay between the barnyard and the newly built cement highway.

A machine repair garage, an orchard, a chestnut grove and large vegetable garden, a shoe repair shop, and a wheelwright completed the businesses in the village. People operating the various businesses were Pennsylvania Dutch folk, speaking the dialect fluently. English was mandated in the schools, however some first-graders starting school were unable to converse in English. The High German language was spoken in the area churches. Recently the churches began to alternate one week German language and the next week English. Mama always spoke German when repeating the Lord's prayer or singing the Matins and hymns. Except for a noted few, neighbors looked out for one another while respecting privacy, and whatever their station or circumstance were willing to help one another while striving for self-reliance.

Del suddenly remembered the words of Mr. Losch. "I won't make any trouble." She never before gave thought to the fact that she had heard of individuals here and there whose attitudes and talk were accepted with a grain of salt. She heard of people being troublemakers. Father's saying was, "There is every kind of individual under the sun in each and every town. Things are not always as people wish them to be." Del grabbed the smaller pail and walked out to the pump for fresh water. She saw Benj and Phillip by the barnbridge. Bill and Til stopped to help Phillip and he hopped along between them. Del called, "Work all done?"

Bill nodded his head. They entered the house and helped one another wash up. Father and Benj, along with Mama, followed. Ori was last to enter the house; she removed her shoes and left them in the porch and headed upstairs, as did all the boys. Til grabbed his glasses case.

Ori brought Carol half-dressed to the table.

"Did you take care of your duck? It's Sunday, we may be getting company sometime today," Mama said.

"Taw-Taw is all right."

"Does that mean he is cooped?" Del asked.

"I said he is all right!" Ori snapped unhappily.

Breakfast was consumed with little conversation. Phillip pointed to food he desired, and Benj was pleased to help him. "*Mei bu* [My boy]," he said several times.

"Everybody ready?" Father asked. "Tilghman, you may bring the car down to the walk for me." Til grinned and ran outside.

"Don't talk about Phillip today. However, if anyone asks if your father brought a child along home from Philadelphia, you say yes. Say what you will about his condition, but don't tell anyone we kept him in the barn for a couple of days. People will think we are mistreating this child. You hear now!" Mama admonished.

The children merely nodded their heads in agreement, except Ollie.

"I won't tell anybody. They won't hear me say he slept in the barn." Ollie said while pointing a finger towards Phillip.

Ori, in her good Sunday clothes, held Carol as she finished combing her hair. She placed a hankie in her pocket with a coin tied in one corner for her offering. Mama also handed coins to the boys; as Del tied her coin in a corner of her hankie, she stuck it in the pocket of her granny sweater. This would be the first time her Sunday School classmates would see her new sweater. The Studebaker approached as Ori placed a bonnet on Carol's head. The machine came to a stop by the walkway. Father was there as Til took the lead and all piled into the machine while the motor was running. As Del walked around the back of the machine she noticed that Father had his foot on the brake, for the tail light was lit; it had the name 'Studebaker' in the round piece of red glass. "Now, you know I won't fetch you," Father was saying as Del climbed onto the back seat. "Boys, you help your Grandfather, take care of his horse and buggy. Get the horse and buggy for him after the service and if he has no other passengers he may bring one or two of you along home."

There was no talk about Phillip at church, neither before nor after the service. After bidding good day to the Pastor the congregation gathered in small groups to greet fellow parishioners and exchange news. Til stood by Grandfather's horse as Mama's uncle and his wife, Jeremiah and Kate Barto, climbed into Grandfather's buggy. All the Heydts and the Shultz boys collected as a group and started the walk home. Carol and Elton, the youngest Shultz boy, needed to be carried from time to time. Once the group reached the Heist place, all crossed to the opposite side of the street. Always, but always, three large police dogs would run back and forth behind a high wire fence and bark savagely, scaring the group, especially Carol and Elton. Til carried Carol on his back while Abraham took charge of Elton. However, this day someone was seated on the porch and the dogs lay by his side.

They reached the Shultz place at the bottom of the hill. Amanda stood by the gate as she greeted the children. She reached for Elton telling Abraham he should make his youngest brother do more walking.

Til put Carol down and told her she could walk the rest of the way. The children started the uphill climb and passed the Conrad place; halfway up the hill near the entrance to Funk's school lane they heard a horse and buggy behind them. They knew it had to be Mr. Losch, returning from the Sunday service. He would stop at the white-plastered home of Jonathan and Adeline Conrad. The Conrads slowly and cautiously stepped down from the buggy and entered their own home just above the Shultz place. The children heard the horse and buggy turn onto Bieber Creek Road behind them. They saw several of their neighbors clustered in the middle of the street ahead. It was quite apparent the neighbors did not want to share whatever was going on. They hushed, then watched until the children were beyond hearing distance when their chatter continued.

Ori looked back. "They sure didn't want us to hear anything. Wonders me why?"

Fritz heard the children. He met them in the lane just before the little red barn that once housed a cow or two and a team of horses. The well-kept structure, a part of Benj's many stories, stood empty beyond a fenced-in yard separating house from barnyard on his tidy property. The barn rendered a hollow echo as one passed by. An old well-worn wooden wheelbarrow with high sideboards and a rusted iron-rimmed wheel stood underneath the overshoot. The overshoot was a haven for pigeon roosting. In the past, barn swallows built nests on the open beams. Since the barn was empty of livestock, the swallows migrated to other barns. Benj missed them. He mentioned more than once that he liked to watch their acrobatic moves.

"You know, I didn't see Becky in that group," Ori spoke again.

"What about Ed and Hester?" Ollie questioned.

"I don't think Becky is at home. Maybe she is at our place and we know where Ed and Hester go every Sunday," Bill added.

"You better believe Becky is not at home. She would have stopped that gossiping long already," Til announced.

"I bet that dumb boy ran away and the whole town saw him. That's what those people are talking about." Ori continued, "I bet I'm right. Now what am I going to do? No one will talk to me anymore. You see how they turned their backs on us already." Ori kicked at a small stone in the lane and sent it flying.

"I will talk to you," Carol said softly.

"Just wait, we'll know what happened when we get home," Til said as he hastened his pace.

"I don't believe he ran away," Bill commented.

"He can't even walk. His shoes don't fit that good," Ollie assured all.

"Fritz came to meet us. He would not have come if Phillip ran away," Til said. "They'd take Fritz along to find him."

"Good thinking. I believe you are right," Del agreed.

Ori admonished Carol. "Watch where you tread. I am the one to clean your shoes. See to it that you follow me. Don't step in any muddy spots."

"Benj must have been home but left in a hurry because he didn't prop the door to the shed behind the pump," Del offered.

"Perhaps he is at our house. He will know what happened," Ollie said.

"No Ollie, he props it open with a crowbar. He keeps the shed door open should a hobo come along seeking shelter. They know his place is always available. He leaves an old comforter inside," Del replied.

"Benj is out there looking for that boy!" Ori announced angrily.

Del passed over the plank bridge and by the woodshed she turned to look back and make sure Benj wasn't seated on the chopping block inside. But he wouldn't be there on a Sunday. All followed single file on the narrow walkway into the house. Benj was seated on the rocker and Phillip was by his side on the couch. Fritz immediately chose to lay on the floor in front of the rocking chair.

"See Ori, everything is all right." Til said mildly.

She made no reply. She had Carol sit on the couch next to Phillip while she removed her shoes and set them aside. "I'll get your regular shoes when I come down." Ori left to change her Sunday dress.

"Where in the world is everybody?" Del turned to Benj. "Do you know what is going on? What are all the neighbors talking in the street?"

"I have no answers for ya, birthday girl," Benj said.

Del continued, "Something happened this morning, not so?"

"*Ve weescht du* [How you know]?" Benj was curious to know Del's source of knowledge.

"Til told you all the neighbors were out in the street." Del pointed in the direction of the highway. "They are busy talking about something."

"They hushed as we passed by," Bill added as he seated himself on the bench.

"Where in the world are Mama and Father?" Ollie asked.

Benj looked up, gazed straight ahead but said nary a word. A full minute later he said, "I tell ya this is a real puzzle. But if we keep quiet, we are going to find out who did it."

"What happened? Where is Becky? Where is Mama?" Del peppered Benj with questions.

"What could cause such a commotion, especially on a Sunday?" Even Ori was curious as she returned to the kitchen with weekday shoes for Carol.

"Will tell ya no more. Just the same as *Ya, ich wais net fiel* [Yes, I know not much]."

Til recognized the sound of the Studebaker coming in the lane. The boys got up.

"*Bleibed alle ebber dough* [Stay everybody here]," Benj ordered.

The children did not question Benj. They sat in silence waiting for Father to enter. When he finally did, Ollie was the first one to blurt out, "What is going on? Where is Mama?"

Father gestured calm down with his hands. "Your mother and I took Becky to Marty Reifinger's place. Sallie was starting a fire this morning. She held a match to the wood and then, boom, an explosion. The stove lid lifted, hit the ceiling, and then hit her upper left arm. From what I saw she has quite a gash. She's lucky she wasn't hit on the head. It's just good she was starting a fire and the stove lid wasn't hot yet, or she'd have a nasty burn too. Your mother can tell you more when she comes in. She was there helping Becky," Father concluded.

Mama entered the house without her apron. "You need to help yourselves with whatever you find for dinner. There is a platter of cold beef in the springhouse. Fetch that," she said as she looked to Ollie. "The rest of you get some bread to make sandwiches for yourselves. Sallie will be all right. She is quite shook up. I saw today why Dr. Schlicher says every town should have a Becky. The way she cleaned that arm, stitched and bandaged it like she was a doctor was something to see. She will probably stay the rest of the day to make sure everything is all right. It's a good thing Dr. Schlicher didn't come yesterday. Becky wants him there, first thing tomorrow morning." Mama paused as if she was trying to remember something and then said, "Oh yes, Benj, will you check Becky's house, make sure everything is all right? She left in such a hurry she is quite sure the fire will burn down and die. Tomorrow, if she is home, she will go along with the doctor."

Benj nodded his head with closed eyes. *"Ich geh graad naw* [I go right now]."

"Come back and eat something," Mama called to Benj as he left the kitchen.

"How will the doctor know to come tomorrow?" Ollie said half out of breath as he set the covered platter of meat on the table.

"Becky has her way of sending word to his office. She always finds someone who is going his way or is willing to make the special trip to notify him. Your father has been her messenger many a time."

"You mean he will come tomorrow for sure? Then Becky won't be here when he looks at Phillip. I won't be here either." Del was disappointed.

"I think she will. They'll probably tend to Sallie first. That will give her time to mention why we want him to stop here."

"That means he will come here before he sees Ernie. He will be coming from that direction." Del pointed in the direction of Becky's house. She thought to herself, "I'll surely miss the doctor's visit. If he goes to the Reifinger's first, then here, and to Losch's last." Del wondered why Mama wasn't wearing an apron. She could have taken it off to go away. If so, it would be draped over a chair or laying about somewhere in the kitchen. Father lifted his hand to quiet the children.

"Benj had gone home this morning. It's a good thing he did. He came back all out of breath. One of the Reifinger neighbors came running to fetch Becky. Benj immediately came to us and we drove Becky back to the Reifingers." Father looked at the children wih a very serious expression. "Children, Benj and I have been sawing firewood, as you know from the slaps I get trimming the logs for nice pieces of lumber. I haven't delivered any firewood this fall and Sallie's husband didn't order firewood. No one can say I laced wood with *pulfer* [gunpowder] to prevent theft. Right now it seems gunpowder caused the explosion. There may be a lot of talk in school tomorrow, especially from those who live nearby. Let others do the talking." Father's voice was quite firm. "This goes for all of you. We have not delivered any firewood to anyone this season." Father looked around to make sure everyone understood.

The children milled about in the kitchen and chatted about this news. Phillip helped himself to the table using chair backs for support as Til hovered nearby.

Benj came back from Becky's home. "*Nix letz* [Nothing wrong]," he said to Father. He seated himself beside Phillip and gave him a good strong hug. "Woodie, *gute oss ken holtz fer kawf'd huscht* [good you haven't sold wood yet]" he said looking at Father.

Father and Mama both nodded in agreement. Father laid a hand on Phillip's shoulder as he said to Benj, "*Ma nemme dich mit wann de zeit cummed* [We'll take you along when the time comes]. I bet you will like truck rides." Phillip did not react to the English sentence. "*Sella weg sehne de leit waz maa hen* [That way, the people see the living situation] one family at a time."

Father turned to the children again. "With the Reifinger incident people will have plenty to talk about. We can take more time to let people know about Phillip. The people that already know about Phillip won't start any wild rumors. Your teacher is going to help you tell the story about Phillip. You can say whatever you will about Phillip. *Vil ennichhau so huffa* [Will anyhow so hope] that most people would make a decision exactly like the one I made."

"Maybe yes, maybe no," Mama wasn't so sure.

Del thought about the rural farm area. Some folks were indeed isolated. Some farm homes were surrounded by woodlands. Rough dirt lanes entering homesteads ofttimes were the long way around fields or through forest. A neighbor was not so very far away if one considered the narrow walking or riding paths through wooded forest and along fencerows. Neighbors chatted where fences met. Del was suddenly aware that she needed to pay attention to what Mama was saying.

"Martin is not a thief. People lace wood with *pulfer* [gunpowder] when they suspect someone is stealing ready split wood to burn. The thief gets a little scare when the stove lids lift a little from exploding gunpowder. This today was more than a little powder. Someone meant to do harm. Martin and Sallie do not deserve such treatment. Remember this: Keep your eyes and ears open and your mouth shut." Mama was quite stern as she raised a forefinger and pointed to the children.

Del felt there was more to this than was said. Since it was freshly sawn firewood maybe people would think it was stolen from their sawmill. But it was too early to come to that sort of conclusion.

"If you would like something more than your sandwich, there's some icicle radishes that go good with a sandwich. I don't have time to heat anything right now," Mama spoke hurriedly.

Phillip helped himself fairly well as Mama watched. Del knew that look on her face. She was as convinced as Becky that Phillip didn't have a real injury to his foot, but like Becky, didn't know why he would pretend to be lame.

"I still have my arithmetic problems to do. May as well do it right now," Til spoke quietly, then loudly announced, "Isaac's Hudson!" Til recognized the sound of any motor car that came over the plank bridge.

Del watched as Father and the boys went out to greet his sister, Eva, and her husband. Benj took charge of Phillip. The girls were left to clean up. When Del stepped outside and shook the tablecloth, everyone was at the new truck Father acquired the day before. Eva walked around the vehicle once and then to the milkhouse with a milk kettle in her hand. Then over to the washhouse with old newspapers to burn or small pieces of soap to add to the next making of soap after all the butchering was done. Eva almost ran to the house. Mama met her there. "Is everyone--" Mama raised her hand to stop her talk. "My apron is soaking in water. I'll explain that. We had a serious accident at a neighbor's place, but everything is all right here."

Mama and Eva entered the closed porch. Mama showed Eva all the potted plants she had brought in before the first killing frost. There were her geranium slips, which would fill next year's flowerbeds. The deep window seats were the ideal place to keep plants thriving over the winter months. Eva stepped into the kitchen and greeted Benj. She stopped short and said nothing for a bit but simply looked and looked some more at Phillip as if she couldn't believe her eyes. Her stare caused Phillip to squirm. Eva turned to Mama," Woodie told me I would see a new child inside. *Ah guckt oss ah net doh khared* [He looks out of place here]."

"*Ah iz doh* [He is here]," Mama said. "Eva, this is Phillip."

"Hello, Phillip. *Ah gooked aarmseelich* [He looks pitiful]. Wait until Isaac sees him." Eva studied both Mama and Phillip.

"*Besser oss ahr wohr* [Better than he was]." Benj patted Phillip's shoulder in a fatherly gesture. Phillip remained still and silent.

"Benj here has been a good helper. He and Phillip get along quite well. We needed someone to stay with him that first night and Benj was right there," Mama informed Eva.

"I suppose Brother is telling Isaac the whole story," Eva said, looking to Mama to provide her with all details.

Mama quickly recounted the Philadelphia story, then told Eva about the accident. "About this morning and the apron: You remember where we always picked wild strawberries? The Reifingers live close by there."

Eva nodded. "What happened?"

"To make a long story short, Sallie started the fire this morning, and they think someone placed *pulfer* in a piece of wood, a good amount, too. The stove lid hit the ceiling and then coming back down the lid hit Sallie on the arm. Big gash," Mama said, spreading her fingers to the dimension of the wound. "We took Becky there. She did an excellent job stitching the arm and bandaging it. Becky will be staying the day."

Eva, Benj and Mama talked a bit more about the firewood incident and how neighbors would help them out.

"There sure is a lot going on here! Eva exclaimed. She turned to Del and her sisters who were washing and putting away the dinner dishes. "And how are you girls?" Eva asked as they worked. Carol was placing the knives and forks in the drawer.

"I will need help with my crocheting. I had to take it apart several times already," Ori said glumly.

"Try to do it right the first time, Gloria. The more you work with the thread the harder it is to handle."

"I know, I am finding that out."

"How about you, Adelaide?" Eva asked.

"I am okay. There will be a lot to talk at school tomorrow. Em, my friend, lives two houses above the Reifingers. I know she will talk about that all day."

"Carol, what do you have to say?"

"Those big police dogs didn't bark at us today."

"It's the house halfway home from church, they have police dogs that carry on when the children walk by," Mama chuckled. "The man of the house must have been at home today—that's the only reason the dogs didn't bark."

"How was your morning?" Mama asked Eva.

"We stopped by the orchard. I talked with Estelle while Isaac and Wolfgang toured the orchard. That man is sure proud of his trees. Of course, he works hard. Estelle had her health problems this year but is grateful things are nearly back to normal for their busiest time of the year. She can tend to customers while the men spend all day in the orchard. But she sits down every chance she gets." Eva leaned in and spoke quietly to Mama. "I need to tell my sister beforehand about this boy you found. We can't spring this surprise on her," Eva said with a worried look on her face.

Del remembered a past Easter when Father's relatives came to visit. Eva showed up in a sheer pale orange dress with a matching three quarter length jacket. Her outfit was accented with satin trim. This satin trimmed the V-neck line of her dress. A narrow satin strip ran down the center of the jacket sleeves. She completed her Easter outfit with the same orange satin material banding her brimmed straw hat with a huge yellow satin cloth flower on the right side. She always dressed attractively. It was one of the fringe benefits where she worked. She could purchase leftover materials at a discounted price. Small pieces could be had for the taking. Being a good seamstress, she usually made her own clothes. Del always took notice of her outfits.

Lillie and Sam, Father's older sister and brother-in-law were already seated in the kitchen that Easter day. Lillie near threw a fit as Eva walked in the door and removed her hat. "You bobbed your hair!" Lillie screamed, and sprang to her feet so fast the chair tilted over. She jumped up and down a couple of times shrieking so loudly it stunned everyone, thinking something awful had happened. "My God, Eva! You bobbed your hair! You bobbed your hair!" she said again. "You see too many movies. That beautiful crop of hair! How could you do this? What do you think Mother would say, bless her soul, were she here? Never thought I'd see the day my baby sister would go Hollywood and bob her hair." Lillie was so upset her whole body shook.

Eva stood in the doorway and gave her sister a long look. "Now sis, get hold of yourself. No one else carries on like you. Isaac's mother is a whole generation older than you and she said my new hairdo is very becoming. Yes, she went shopping and bought this speckled ivory barrette I am wearing. She said it was an early birthday gift."

Only then did Del notice the barrette that pulled her hair softly across the upper right portion of her forehead. It was similar to the way Del combed her hair and pinned it back with a smaller barrette. Eva's rich reddish brown hair was longer on the sides and shorter in back—it looked quite nice. Del was equally surprised at Mama's reaction as she always wore her hair in an old-fashioned style pulled tightly back in a bun exposing her full round face.

"I like it. I bet it feels comfortable, although I don't know if I would like my hair hanging loose around my head. I'd have to get used to that. It seems when my hair loosens up, I have to redo it. If I don't, I'll have a mild headache," Mama admitted.

Eva smiled as she looked at Lillie and firmly stated, "If you had to sit and sew in a factory where it is stifling hot, with no air moving at all and you dare not stop because the foreman is watching all the time—you would make yourself as comfortable as possible. There are times it is difficult to breathe. I sweat and my hair is all wet by the time I go home. I wash it and it doesn't dry till morning on those warm humid nights. This is so easy." She pushed her hand through her hair. "I will never again wear a bun."

For a brief moment Lillie accepted the fact that it must be cooler and easier to keep. "I remember how overheated we were when we worked in the Acorn Glove factory. I was a thirteen year old girl." But then she countered with, "Just think about your birthday time. It gets bitter cold come January. You'll catch all sorts of colds. A hat won't keep you warm. You'll see. As for me I am going to keep my hair exactly the way I have been wearing it since I was thirteen years old."

"Adelaide, fetch some of the apples we keep in the washhouse. Pick the nicer ones," Mama ordered.

As she fetched the apples, Del thought about her Aunt Lillie's hairdo which was different from any other lady she ever saw. Her hair had some natural curl. She parted her hair down the middle from the front to the back of her head. She braided and twisted her long hair into a large round bun on each side of her head, positioned over her ears. Her hair was the same rich reddish brown color as Eva's. Del returned with a dish full of apples from storage.

"Here are some drops," Mama said. "It's really a good eating apple but doesn't last long. Becky says they always called it the banana apple, mostly for its deep yellow peel. They're from that very tall tree."

Eva began peeling apples and held the peeled quarters on the point of her knife just like Mama did to offer to the children. She pointed an apple section toward Phillip, and he accepted it and immediately took a bite. "*Ah weass waz mah dood mit sel* [He knows what to do with that]." Eva smiled at him.

"We know nothing about his circumstances. Was he abandoned or lost? Does he have any family? Depending on those answers, we could be in a great deal of trouble," Mama paused. "You came at a good time. We'll wait until Isaac and Woodie come in and see if we can shift some beds around and make room for Phillip to sleep upstairs with the boys. Everyone around here can then get a good night's rest." Mama smiled at Phillip.

"Phillip, as you say, is a good name for him, since you found him in Philadelphia," Eva stated.

"It was sort of Gloria's suggestion," Mama said.

"It wasn't sort of, I gave him the name Phillip," Ori stated as she stepped in from the front room.

"Is Carol with you?" Mama asked. Ori nodded her head.

"This is the piece I've been working on. I finally managed that last crochet stitch you showed me."

"You work with that a while longer before I show you another stitch. You need to make all the stitches alike."

"I think it will look better once I get to threads I didn't undo," Ori said in a matter of fact tone.

"Adelaide, go fetch an apron for me. One of the nicer starched ones."

Del hurried upstairs and pulled a fine blue print apron from the drawer.

"What are you going to do about school?" Eva asked as Del returned.

"The teacher already knows." Mama spoke while adjusting her apron. "I feel undressed if I'm not wearing an apron. I hope Amos will agree to tutor him after we know he's got the necessary vaccines. He already tutors his grandson with TB, even though that is a place he should stay away from. He has his own health to consider, plus all the children he is around all week long. No one makes an issue about that. I suppose no one wants to start any trouble. Not many except for close neighbors know about this since that boy never started school. Amos goes there most every Saturday. I don't know if the health board even knows. The health board is here soon enough if there is an outbreak of measles or chicken pox. They attach a quarantine sign on the house immediately. We need the doctor to make sure Phillip doesn't suffer an illness or disease before we do much of anything. We don't want to get into any trouble with the authorities. Becky believes there is nothing wrong with Phillip that food and warmth won't take care of."

"You should be concerned for your own children with that TB case. In the borough where I live, patients with tuberculosis are isolated. The whole neighborhood would know. Your doctor should report this." Eva, like everyone else, feared TB, which could be fatal or lead to a lifetime of poor health.

"I think Dr. Schlicher considers that boy completely isolated. Then too, there's a relative on the school board." Mama narrowed her eyes as she contemplated that.

"I know how it is with rural folk. We were raised in a rural community. I know this wouldn't pass in Emmaus," warned Eva. "You said Becky is helping you. I know she is a good person, but didn't she have enough of this kind of trouble?"

Mama looked around the room. "Adelaide, see if you can find something to do."

Del knew what that meant. She decided this was a good time to finish her library book. She moved into the parlor and got comfortable on the sofa. The well-worn book, loosely bound, had a musty odor. The hard cover had damaged corners and inside the cover were names of people she didn't know. She began reading but did not remember what she had read. She tried again, no success. She was unable to concentrate. The question of Becky's 'same kind of trouble' consumed her mind. She wanted to hear the conversation in the kitchen but knew she needed to stay away. She counted how many people knew about a Black boy living in this house. First, her teacher Amos Strunk had the most memorable reaction. Benj, Becky, and Grandfather were involved from the beginning. Probably Grandfather's sister, Mama's Aunt Lizzie had been told. Other relatives, Jeremiah and Kate Barto, who had the shoe repair shop probably knew. Father's best friends Levi and Martha Boyer. Edgar Losch saw Phillip before he had his name. Ed and Hester knew. What about Edgar Losch? He worked at Hoch's feed and grain mill where he would see many farmers in the area. He was a member of their church council.

Her thoughts turned to Sally Reifinger and she wondered if Sally was in pain. Del remembered the intense pain she endured when she was filling jelly jars with piping hot quince jelly and some spilled on her hand. It was the most extreme pain she ever felt. She glanced at her left hand, it had healed nicely. She remembered how Mr. Strunk would look over the entire classroom with fierce, scrutinizing eyes. He didn't miss any little thing. He had asked how she burned her hand, which she tried to keep hidden. Why should he know she was hurrying to finish a job Mama had asked her to do.

Del sat up and stared out the window. More people than she knew could be talking about Phillip. Father told Mr. Strunk the children would talk at school about the addition to their family. She suddenly remembered to add the names of Isaac and Eva Hetrick to her list.

Eva worked in a pajama factory and was laid off more often than not. This depression left many folks with little or no work. Isaac, being very handy, had a way of finding work for himself when laid off for extended periods of time. Isaac was a jack-of-all-trades, from painter to tinsmith and roof repair, plus auto mechanic, clock repair, or whatever needed to be done. His tinkering helped him become an excellent mechanic. He repaired anything from small items to farm machinery. Any apparatus with moving parts sparked his interest. He managed to make ends meet. He helped Father set up the sawmill along with Uncle Sam, who was a carpenter by trade. They also helped to build a roof over the mill.

Del walked to the window that looked out toward the barn. She saw the men slowly making their way to the house. She wanted to hear what Isaac had to say once he saw Phillip and returned to the kitchen. She heard Mama say, "Come in, Isaac, I know Woodie must have told you about our new child."

Del wondered if Isaac even heard her Mama speak. He stood alongside Father like a statue, his eyes studying the room and especially Phillip.

"Find a seat." Father motioned toward a seat by the table.

"Hello, Phillip," Isaac paused a moment, "and the rest of you." Turning again toward Phillip, he smiled and said, "You have come to a good place. You will be given the best of care."

"Stay for supper, two extra people are no bother at all. I already told Eva we could use your help rearranging our upstairs." Mama said.

Isaac smiled, "Woodie said the same thing." He nodded his head. "Sure we'll help you out. Woodie wants to give me a ride in his new truck."

"The truck comes in handy already." Father seemed pleased.

"We need to get this done now. Monday will be a very busy day if Dr. Schlicher can leave his office . . . " Mama was focused on the doctor's examination of Phillip.

Father interrupted, "You will be here tomorrow?" He nodded his head toward Isaac.

"*Ya, erschta ding* [Yes, first thing]. Both of us laid off. Eva's boss said give him two weeks. He keeps saying he is waiting for a new order that was promised. I sometimes think he says that even though he knows there is none coming. I just finished putting new tubes in a radio for a fellow down the street and fixed a cuckoo clock for someone in Allentown."

"I don't like to hear the usual 'no work today', but I am glad for your help," Father said. "Isaac, this is a good time to fetch that bed at the hotel. We'll take Phillip along; there's enough room to seat him between us. He will have his first truck ride. I know Martha and Levi want to meet him. Tilghman, come along but you will ride on the back. Once there, you need to stay with Phillip while Isaac and I get the bed."

"This is a good time for all of you to do your school work. You have been distracted enough already. Carol and Phillip, you spend your time with Adelaide or Gloria," Mama suggested.

The boys scattered. "Not with me," Ori stated, "I want to do my arithmetic. I don't want Carol talking to me all the time."

"Come Carol and Phillip," Del said, "Grab two coloring books and come with me. I will try a few chapters in my library book." Del knew Mama wanted some time alone with Eva and Benj. Del took Carol's hand and headed for the parlor. Benj helped Phillip hop into the parlor and take a chair at the table. She positioned herself so she could hear the kitchen conversation as she quietly helped Carol and Phillip choose colors and told them to stay within the lines.

"Have you heard from anyone what people are saying?" Eva asked.

"Not so far. One good thing about this explosion, it gives people something really important to talk about. Maybe Phillip will not be so shocking an impact. I suppose it will give some talk once the whole town knows. Easiest way out of this situation is that his family comes forward to claim him. I almost wish for that. But since no one seemed to care about him, we may just as well consider him part of our family. I am more concerned about this situation than Woodie is," Mama admitted.

"Our mother said Woodie is like his father. He would give a stranger the shirt off his back if need be and suffer the cold himself," Eva said.

"It is good to be generous and kind, but this is unusual. What will people think?" Mama shared her concerns.

"Since we can't have any children, Isaac and I considered raising a child from a relative's large family. But it would be unfair if one child of that family had more than the other children. There would be resentment among the siblings. And to adopt a child without knowing family background . . . well, we discussed it, then just dropped the idea altogether. I can certainly appreciate Woodie's decision; kindness comes first, the consequences come later."

The children heard the truck returning. They came from all directions to the kitchen, except Ori. Til and Isaac came into the kitchen carrying bed rails and went directly upstairs. They were back as Father helped Phillip inside.

Phillip appeared to be very pleased. Father spoke in the dialect. "*Sie hut naa allebade vennich eis crème gewwe* [She gave them all a little ice cream]."

"*Huscht sel sehne* [Did you see that]?" Benj spoke as he noticed Phillip appeared to be intently listening every time the dialect was spoken.

"*Ya, fer hoftich* [Yes, for sure]," Eva said.

Father ordered, "Boys, let's get the rest of this bed inside. Tilghman, you help me with the heavier piece. William, you help Isaac. We'll bring the springs and mattress inside when the rooms are rearranged and the beds are set up."

Mama and Eva headed upstairs to supervise as the men left the kitchen. Del, Carol, Phillip, and Benj remained in the kitchen.

"I may as well get the table ready for supper," Del said, "Mama will want a clean tablecloth." Del walked into the side room, opened a drawer to the buffet and started to leaf through its contents. When she came back Benj was holding the door wide open for the men to pass through.

Father and Til came through the door followed by Bill and Isaac. There was lots of activity upstairs. Del heard Mama call Gloria to hold Del's bedroom door open; it had a tendency to close all by itself. Del figured Ori was willing to help without back talk because she would not want her Aunt Eva to see her disagreeable nature. It was Del's bed they moved first. Til's double bed would surely be their next move. She was already picturing the little walking space left for her to move about in the new layout. She looked at Benj and exclaimed, "I've never heard so much activity on the second floor! It sounds like dancing is going on up there."

He smiled and nodded his head. "When the ladies are housecleaning upstairs and moving furniture back and forth, we menfolk say, *Ess dunnered* [It thunders]! Do ya think we'll have rain?" Benj laughed as he tapped Phillip's shoulder, who quietly observed all the activity.

Both smiled when they saw the men carry a mattress upstairs. "*Du schlofed gute dienacht* [Ya sleep good tonight]." It appeared Phillip knew what Benj was saying.

Ori came down the back stairway, saying nothing as she passed through the kitchen to start her chores. Taw-Taw would be no problem. He was cooped up all day and would remain so. Ollie was told to help William with the barn work. Tilghman could start the milking. Del had the table set, ready for supper; she peeped into the oven from time to time. Her favorite meal was in the oven. A medium size crock with the last liver pudding was heating there. There were mashed potatoes in two separate containers. Mashed potatoes, liver pudding and cut up raw onions on top with buttered bread—Del considered this meal especially satisfying. She could hardly wait for suppertime as she hurried to complete her outside work. Benj and Phillip were busy staying out of everyone's way.

When the upstairs work was finished the adults returned downstairs. Mama smiled. "Thank you," she looked to Isaac and Eva. "We accomplished a lot in a short time."

Father and Isaac immediately left to do the barn work. "The boys are out there already. Tilghman may have milked a cow or two by now. He looks ahead, he knows what needs to be done," Mama called to them.

Del returned to the kitchen after completing her chores.

"You finished?" Mama said.

Del nodded yes. "I am going upstairs to look at all the changes as soon as I finish washing up." Del looked into the boys' rooms first. Next she opened her door, slowly. There was less walking space than she thought. She closed the door. It just managed to get past the bed post. She headed down the back stairs. Soon all returned from their chores and were ready for supper.

There was a lot of small talk around the table when the meal was served. Phillip depended on Benj to fill his plate. Del thought he was shyer than usual with the presence of her uncle and aunt.

"*Ich glaabt ah iz arig schtolz ah hutt en bet fa schlofe drin* [I believe he is very proud he has a bed to sleep in]," Father said, looking at Phillip while all nodded in agreement.

After everyone finished the main course, a two-layer spice cake with raisins was placed on the table. Eva and Isaac, plus Mama and Father, ate their cake and then proceeded to carry their coffee with them into the parlor. "You children clean up," Mama said as she motioned for Benj to follow. Del knew that meant her parents wanted privacy with their guests.

Benj followed, saying he would stay only until the boys helped Phillip upstairs, then he would go home.

Isaac replied, "No need to walk home. I'll take you along in the Hudson."

Phillip assisted while seated at the table by collecting and stacking dishes for Ollie to carry over to Ori for washing. Carol stood on a chair to rinse the washed dishes and Bill and Del dried and placed items in the cabinets. After a spell Father came into the kitchen and said it was time for children to go to bed. "Tomorrow is a school day and you need to rest." Father looked at Til and said, "You and Bill help Phillip upstairs."

Father stayed to observe as Til motioned to Phillip, "Come on, Phillip, let's make our way upstairs. Tonight you will sleep in a bed instead of the couch."

"I had better go ahead of you since we will be sharing my room," Bill said. Everyone watched what Phillip would do. Impatient Ollie gave Phillip a slight nudge in the direction of the stairway where Til was waiting.

"Just grab his arm and have him follow you as best he can. See what he does," Mama said as she stepped into the kitchen.

Phillip moved in his usual fashion, holding onto something to help himself forward as he hopped along the table and onto the landing in front of the opened door to the stairway where Til was waiting. She could hear the rather noisy movement on the stairs. She could hear a chuckle and knew Til was pleased about something. Til was certainly strong enough to help Phillip move from one step to another. He could have slung Phillip over his shoulder and carry him up the stairs. Del guessed Phillip used the railing to boost himself just as he used the chairs.

Tomorrow, school began again. "I will miss the doctor's visit," she thought. How she wished she could be there. Maybe Dr. Schlicher could guess Phillip's age. Mama said he could be small for his age if he never had enough to eat, but she suspected he had care early in life or wouldn't have survived til then. "Oh well," Del thought, "I need to wait for some answers." She slipped under her covers stretched across the larger bed. It took so much space it was against the side wall. She heard voices from the parlor below but couldn't hear all that was said. The ceiling register over the parlor stove was close to her bedroom door but the floor register was still closed at this time of year. She heard the laughter and the voices of the adults downstairs. She drifted off to sleep wondering what the next day would bring.

CHAPTER SEVEN

The Doctor's Examination

As Del entered the kitchen, she decided to fill the water bucket with fresh water for this morning's use. Ori was out earlier than usual, for Taw-Taw was strutting about as Del pumped fresh water. What a day this will be! She would listen to Em's story about the Reifingers at school. Then she would tell Em all about Phillip and how he came to live with her family. She would simply say, "We have a Black boy living with us." Em surely would scream. Carrying the bucket of water to the kitchen, Mama took the bucket from her hand and set it on the white table.

"I didn't expect you this early. I will tend to the fire." Mama detailed her needs. "You set the table. Then go upstairs and get the flannel materials I have in the bottom drawer of the big bureau in my bedroom. You know where I keep materials. Just get the flannels. I will start to make clothes for Phillip. Come to think of it, while you are there, get the white feedbag materials I have bleached, lay them on my bed, then bring the flannels down. While I have the sewing machine open I may take time and sew bags for the summer sausages; we will need them when butchering time is here."

"Do I get to lay the pattern pieces?" Del asked.

"That depends when I have the time and whether you are available. Depends on how the day goes. I may not get around to any sewing. At any rate, I will have the materials handy."

"Why does Phillip share a room with Bill?" questioned Del. "He and Ollie are more the same size. At least it seems that way. He is wearing some of Ollie's clothes."

"Oliver is a bit too young to share a bedroom with someone who may need help."

"I'm not the only one up early. I saw Taw-Taw is strutting around already. Ori must be out there somewhere," Del said.

"No, she isn't. Benj let him out. He'll pick him up again. He wanted to show Phillip how to handle that duck. Taw-Taw sure did plenty of squawking. Phillip watched it all."

"Is he walking any differently? Becky is sure there's nothing wrong with his legs. Here she comes now."

"Come on in!" Mama called to Becky.

"Good morning, Adelaide. You're up early this morning."

Mama replied, "You know her. She wants to be here when the doctor comes. How is Sallie doing?"

"I think quite well, considering the circumstances. The arm is still very swollen and sore, but it hasn't gotten any worse. It is a clean wound. That doesn't say infection couldn't set in. I was there very early this morning. I didn't change the dressing. I want Dr. Sam to look at her wound carefully; he may dress it for the day. He can do a better job than I and give her something more powerful for pain."

"You were up early too, if you saw Sallie this morning," Mama motioned for Becky to sit down.

"I'm always up early. I go to bed with the chickens and I'm up before the first rooster crows."

Del's thoughts turned to the doctor. He always laid his cigar on an outside window ledge before entering the house. He wore a distinguished-looking hat. He would push it up to rub his forehead as he studied someone seriously. A deep bass voice, one any church choir would appreciate. She remembered Grandfather's description of the doctor: "*Ah hutt an rotlich gsichtsfareb. Sei schprooch fie Englisch* [He has a ruddy face color. He speaks fine English]." He certainly was nothing remotely close to *Pennsilfaanisch Deitschscher leit* [Pennsylvania Dutch people]. Dr. Sam wasn't from the area when he moved here to practice medicine. Yet he often acknowledged he liked the area and the people. Del heard him say that among them a word or handshake was as good as gold. They were, above all, a trustworthy people. This gave Del pride in her heritage. She was so engrossed in her thoughts she wasn't paying attention to the conversation her mother and Becky were having until she heard the name Phillip.

"I thought that would catch your attention." Becky said. "What in the world were you thinking about?"

"Don't forget those materials," Mama reminded Del. "Be careful how you lift them, not all the pieces are full." Del immediately headed around the corner and up the stairs two at a time.

"Take those steps decently, no need to rush," Mama admonished.

"Okay," Del spoke softly as she slowed and took one step at a time while practicing an erect posture. On rainy days, when the children couldn't go outside to play at recess time, Mr. Strunk would keep order by suggesting competitive things to do. He had the students walk the center aisle while balancing a book on top of their head, practicing good posture.

Del thought of Becky's arched brow over the right eye as she tread the stairs much slower than usual. Her right eye was noticeably larger than the left eye. She didn't see Becky as regularly or as close up as she had these last few days. What she first remembered about Becky's features was the large dark mole centered on her left cheek. Del peeked into Ori's bedroom. The door stood slightly ajar as she made her way to the large bureau along the front wall of the house that filled the space between two windows bearing lace curtains that Mama had made. It appeared both girls were still asleep, for all was mouse-quiet. She stood in front of the big mirror and observed herself for a moment. She was disappointed with the color of her own eyes. Thank goodness they were both the same size, but they weren't blue like Father's eyes that seemed to shower tenderness, nor the rich dark brown like Mama's that blazed at times with unyielding harshness. One immediately knew when Mama meant business. Mama's Aunt Lizzie said Del's eyes were a hazel color. "You have the wrong name, girl," she sometimes said. Bill's eyes were a blue/gray hue, not near the clear blue eyes like Father's. There were rare moments when Bill's eyes were as cold and rigid as a slab of pale gray granite. Just as suddenly it was gone, and a gentle tenderness came shining through.

Del stood in front of the large bureau. A small, very dark blue glass in the shape of a coal bucket with a metal handle sat on the bureau and contained small odds and ends. A large mirror tilting forward allowed Del to see into the blue glass bucket. Pins, buttons, clasps, small items for immediate repair were always handy. Getting down on her knees, she reached for the metal handles to pull on the drawer. Goodness, it was heavy. The drawer creaked and scraped as she grunted trying to open it far enough to carefully root through the materials and select the pieces Mama wanted.

"Must you make all that noise so early in the morning?" Ori said sleepily. "You'll awaken Carol."

"Can't help it. This drawer is so heavy I can hardly move it. It's this deep bottom drawer." Del grunted, "It would be easier if it weren't so heavy. What's more I don't think I can close it. It's time to get up anyway. Taw-Taw is waiting for you."

"It's not full daylight yet."

"Quiet, you're the one to waken Carol," Del said as she leafed through materials. There was the blue checked material, a dress she wore. A red flowered print for Ori. An all-color stripe Mama made for herself. The feedbag material was stacked neatly on one side of the drawer. She placed them on the quilt on the bed immediately behind her. She dug deeper and found the flannels. Two plaid flannels, one brown, the other red, and another a soft light mix of blue plaid. She laid them on the bed as well. She gave the drawer a shove and grunted; she couldn't budge it at all. "Goodness, I can't close this drawer. It's stuck," Del said softly to herself.

"If you would take the time and start the drawer evenly on both ends, you could close it." Ori managed to sound superior and exasperated at the same time.

Del shrugged, "Well, I can't do it that way. I can't reach both ends to lift and push at the same time."

"Huh, you're simply not doing it right."

"Okay, why don't you try? I have the materials Mama wants." Just then Del heard a noise; a machine was approaching for sure! Sometimes the doctor would honk the horn, but not this early in the morning. No announcement was necessary. He was expected. Del quickly stacked the materials as she slid her arms under the bleached white feedbag materials that Mama had saved. She tried again to lift the drawer to close it. It was stuck. The drawer was tilted down and forward and she couldn't lift it. I need to tell Mama I can't close the drawer. Del followed Ori into the hall and said "I see you are as nosy as me to hear what the doctor has to say."

"You are the nosy one. You're dressed for school."

"I was up early. Got my work done," Del said with great satisfaction.

"I need to get Carol up, then I'll collect and grade the eggs."

"Is that duck anywhere near this morning?" the doctor asked Del's father as he stepped down off the running board of his fancy car.

Til carefully looked over the doctor's car while the adults talked. He knew all the features on that machine, down to the two big round headlights mounted on an arched rod in front of the radiator. Dr. Schlicher called it his fifteen-hundred-dollar thrill.

Father said, "We kept him in his pen this morning. That duck is always in his pen if we know anyone is coming."

"Then I suppose I can safely walk and not have eyes in back of my head!" Dr. Schlicher laughed. "I sure don't need any surprises this morning, but I hear there is one already."

"You are talking about the explosion."

The doctor nodded his head.

"I have one more surprise for you; come along inside and see."

"Are your children sick?" the doctor asked.

"My family is fine. I have a new fellow for you to examine."

"Woodie!" The doctor stopped briefly. "Don't tell me another baby and I knew nothing about it!"

"Not that. Wait till you see."

Dr. Schlicher followed his normal procedure. He held his hands under the spout as Father pumped for water. He shook them dry and carefully laid his cigar on the outside window ledge as he followed Father inside. Del looked through the porch window at the highly polished motorcar with whitewall tires and wheels with yellow spokes. Del thought the spokes should be the same color as his car. It had a black canvas roof and a polished handle on the back, which, when lifted opened to a rumble seat for extra passengers. Dr. Sam, as Becky called him, looked at Ori as she left her egg bucket in the porch.

"Gloria still has those rosy cheeks, a picture of health. What kind of surprise could you have for me today? I see Adelaide is growing nicely." He patted her on the head as he was walking by. He stopped to take a good long look at her. "She appears to be in good health, a little thinner than need be. That will change as she grows older. Is one of the others sick?"

"No, I told you, all my children are fine. I have a new boy I want you to look at," Father said.

"I don't under. . . ."

Father interrupted before Dr. Schlicher could finish his sentence. "I brought a young boy along home from Philadelphia. He was left to fend for himself. See what you think," Father said as they entered the kitchen.

The doctor first greeted Becky, "You're riding with me to the Reifingers. I promise I will take it easy over the worst ruts." He smiled and the other adults laughed.

"I know you will. You are more concerned about your motorcar than you are about my old bones." Becky spoke most sternly while smiling at the same time.

"Hello, Laura. You look well. It appears everyone is an early riser this morning," the doctor commented.

Benj headed as quickly as he could into the house as Del held the open door. He wanted to hear the doctor's conclusions as much as she did. It wasn't long before Bill and the dog entered. Bill told Fritz to stay in the porch.

The doctor made his way to the sink; there he had full view of the large kitchen. "Well, well . . . What do we have here?" The doctor backed up a step, pushed his hat back and stood against the sink studying the situation. He then moved forward and looked squarely at Phillip. His stunned face told it all. He pushed his hat back a bit farther. He looked at Father, then Mama, and again at Father. He looked back at Father and shook his head. "Did Billy bring him along home?" He looked at Father. Del knew he was talking about her Grandfather.

"No. I did. I saw his pitiful condition, he needed help," Father said quietly.

"This entire family should stay away from that city." The doctor looked again at Father and Mama. "So . . . that's your surprise. Hmmm." He cupped his chin with his hand. "This is my first Black patient."

"Does that make a difference?" Father asked. Del thought Father was deliberately keeping a mild tone to his voice.

"No. We are all the same flesh and blood. The skin color is different, and that could make a big heap of trouble around here. I shouldn't have to tell you this," he said as he turned to squarely face Father.

"I know. I am asking a lot of my family and perhaps the neighborhood. But it's not Christian to leave a child starving and out in the cold. I did not consider skin color at the time. He is a human being in need of care, but I thought about that plenty on the way home."

"What say you?" the doctor pointed to Becky.

"I deal as best I can, with any and all situations at hand. I make no judgments, other than this child is much better off with this family than trying to live on his own."

Father mentioned that the market people contacted the police about the boy and they wouldn't even bother checking with orphanages to take care of the little boy. There were too many such cases already. "So . . . here he is," Father concluded.

"Woodie, Woodie," the doctor shook his head. "There is no other like you. You are truly a Christian person, and so is your wife," he said looking at Mama.

"Will you look after him like you do for the rest of my children?" Father asked.

"Yes, I will examine the lad and treat him if necessary. I may ask you not to bring him to my office, not right now anyway. Depending on who would be in the office we could have the start of a second civil war over one small boy."

"*Eppes as erscht iwwerblosses muss* [Something that must first blow over]," muttered Benj.

The doctor looked at Benj. "Now there is some Dutch I understand, but you lost me with what was said."

"It can have several meanings. Benj means people have to get used to knowing he is here. Then slowly accept the fact," Mama was quick to make Benj's statement clear.

Father sighed and said, "Everyone expects trouble. But there were no slaveholders in our area. Our cemeteries hold Union soldiers. My grandfather was a Civil War veteran. This is God's child. And we will treat him as family."

Dr. Schlicher looked at all around the room. He nodded his head, and seemed to accept what Father said.

"I take it Edgar doesn't know about this. Does anybody know besides the neighbors that are here?" the doctor asked.

"Well, you see Becky and Benj, but Edgar indeed does know. He saw the boy when he last fetched milk."

"Well then, the missus doesn't know. She would have told me."

"Edgar said he wouldn't tell anybody. The schoolteacher also knows."

The doctor walked over to the couch, pulled a chair up close and dropped his satchel on the table. That startled Phillip. "Sorry, little fellow, I won't hurt you," the doctor said as he sat down directly in front of Phillip. His pushed his hat further back, giving the appearance that this was a very serious situation, as he looked at the child. Benj seated himself on the wood chest so he could clearly see what was happening.

"Becky, what do you think of his health?" the doctor asked without taking his eyes off of Phillip.

"I examined him thoroughly a number of times from head to toe and formed my own opinions. I want to see how you find the lad. How old do you think he is? How is his health? The lame left leg has me wondering what the problem is."

Del thought Becky would have said more had she been alone with the doctor.

"He was quite sick when Woodie brought him home. That is understandable. There may be much more to this," Mama added gesturing towards Phillip's lame leg.

"*Ich glaab au aus ah laafe kann* [I believe too, that he can walk]," Benj chimed in.

Dr. Schlicher nodded his head. Del didn't know whether he understood Benj or not. He commenced to examine the boy's eyes. Next he asked Mama for a tablespoon. He used the holding end as a tongue depressor and forced Phillip to open his mouth. Phillip made no fuss, only sank back deeper into the couch. The doctor said quietly, "His six year molar is decayed. It may be beyond saving. The other side is okay. His tonsils are larger than need be but its not an immediate problem, its something I can do in my office if necessary." He felt the sides of his neck, picked up his arms, dropped one and ran his hands along the bone and muscle structure. Then he did the same with the other arm. The doctor put his hands on his rib cage. Phillip was ticklish as he wriggled, with a giggle he could not hold back. The doctor sat back momentarily and laughed with him. "Found your funny bone. I think we'll let you rest a bit."

The doctor looked at Father and said, "This may not go the way you hope. I suppose you are aware of this."

Father nodded his head. "Yes. I know."

"People will believe exactly what they want to believe. You know your neighbors better than I but there's a troublesome gossip in town. She may spread many untruths. Of course I could be wrong."

"You are not wrong," Benj said to the doctor.

The doctor and Becky moved aside to compare observations and ideas. Mama quietly served bowls of hot oatmeal to the boys. She motioned to Benj to be seated at the table. He shook his head—he was in no hurry to eat. He paid full attention to Phillip's examination.

"Adelaide, find a seat and eat."

"How about a cup of coffee and some cake?" Mama was already filling a cup to set before the doctor at the far end of the table. She also handed an empty cup to Benj, inviting him to help himself to coffee and cake.

"I never say no to your offer, but I'll just have coffee for now." Doctor Schlicher slid the chair he was seated on closer to Phillip.

"You boys had better get yourselves ready for school as soon as you finish breakfast," Mama directed. Ollie, never fond of oatmeal, ate a bit and headed upstairs to dress for school. "I don't know where Gloria is, she better get herself in here. She needs to eat." Mama was concerned.

"She was outside when I came in," Til offered.

"Go out, look for her." Before Til could move, Ollie came flying down the stairs, ran by everyone and hurried to the outside.

"That one sure can move," the doctor said after Ollie brushed by his chair.

Mama almost laughed. "Tilghman, go see why Oliver is in such a rush and tell Gloria to come in. I don't know what's keeping her."

It wasn't long until Til, along with both Ollie and Ori, entered the house. "There you are! Mama grabbed Ollie's arm to stop him from going deeper into the kitchen while she pointed to Gloria to eat. "Don't bother with Carol. I'll take care of her when she gets up." Mother handed Ori a dish of hot oatmeal.

Ori never gave a reason for her delay. Something caused Ori to spend all that time outside. Del knew she couldn't be that disinterested in what was happening inside with the doctor's visit. Del, too, needed to get ready for school. Taking two steps at a time, she reached her bedroom and hung her apron on the clothes tree. Del passed Ori coming up the stairs as she was on her way down. "We'll wait for you if you hurry."

"I won't be long. I'll eat a piece of cake on the way."

"I intend to do the same thing." Del replied.

Del entered the kitchen as Becky was describing Phillip's initial condition on that first Wednesday night. She hurriedly cut two pieces of a funny cake that stood on Mama's baking table next to the wood chest.

Bill stepped into the porch. Fritz was still lying there. "Rough morning for you, Fritz. You can walk with us. By the time you hurry back, I suppose you can go into the house. I wish you could tell me what else is going to be said," he whispered into a lifted ear.

The boys left. Del rushed to join Bill, with Fritz trotting alongside. As Del left the house, she heard the question of vaccination come up. Her parents wanted to know whether or not Phillip was vaccinated for smallpox. They hadn't seen a scar on his upper arm when they bathed him. Del could still see her scar.

Ori was last out the door with a piece of funny cake in her hand.

"Did you hear any more about a vaccination?" Del asked as Ori ran to catch up.

"I saw they had taken the shirt off of Phillip as I was leaving, that's all."

"What about a vaccination?"

"Never heard anything about a vaccination."

"How could you not have heard it since you were right there?"

"I told you what I know. They took his shirt off."

"They probably didn't want to undress him in front of us all," Del concluded.

"Well, I'll be. This doesn't often happen. We are all together this morning to walk to school," Til chuckled.

"Taw-Taw isn't here," Ollie said. "Ori finally reached him and put him in his pen. She won't tell you about it." It was a standing rule that the duck was penned when company was expected or visiting. Ollie jumped up and down. He could no longer contain himself. He was excited to be the one to tell the news. "I know, he flew and landed on the roof of the doctor's car. I saw it from my upstairs window."

"Okay, Ollie. You don't have to preach it to everybody!" Ori was not happy the cause of her absence was known.

"I just hope he didn't leave a trademark on top," Til said as he and Bill laughed.

"Maybe she had to wash something off." Bill forced a sober face.

"Not that I saw," Ollie eagerly said. "She couldn't reach him. He kept moving from one side to the other. I ran out and stood on one side so she could reach him." Ollie grinned as he pointed to Ori.

"I nearly had him before you got there!" Ori snapped.

"I bet Father told you to keep him in his pen until the doctor left and you didn't listen. That's why you don't want to talk about it!" Bill laughed again.

"I sure hope he didn't leave any marks on that fancy machine. The doctor is particular about it. You can bet your bottom dollar, he doesn't want duck poop on his car!" Til announced, trying unsuccessfully to control his laugh.

All but Ori were laughing with Til.

"Not funny. Not funny at all!" Ori snapped. "The top of his machine is clean. I brushed some loose dirt off. That's all," Ori said hurriedly, loudly defending her duck.

"That better be all," Til said as he continued to speak. "If the doctor takes his time on the way back to the Reifingers he can steer around the worst holes. Where lanes are really rough, he doesn't drive those at all. Someone will meet him and take him the rest of the way," Til spoke seriously.

"How do you know that?" Ollie asked. "He drives our lane every time he comes."

"Our lane is okay. Sawdust serves a good purpose. I was at the creamery once when the doctor parked his car there and rode into the holler with Grandfather's horse and wagon. Both Dick and Harry are trained. No need to tuck the line when I take them to the blacksmith shop. All I say is 'Gee' or 'Haw'."

"See Ollie, we learn a lot by listening and asking questions. I didn't know that myself," Del acknowledged.

They reached the cement pike and all dispersed in the usual manner. Mae was waiting for Ori. The Shultz boys were waiting for Del's brothers.

Del went skipping by herself and thought about the kind of trouble Dr. Sam warned Father about. Del was still considering that conversation as she met Em.

"Hi Del." Em was quite excited. "Have I got something to tell you!"

"I expect you do. I heard about the explosion. But you must know a great deal more."

"Sure do," Em exclaimed. "It was early Sunday morning, not all of us were up yet. I heard a very loud pop. Ma and Pa ran out of the house to see what happened. They heard Sallie screaming and crying. She was afraid to go back into her house. She was covered with blood. Ma said she couldn't see where all the blood was coming from. Ma thought the stove exploded. Sallie thought another piece of wood would catch fire and explode. She didn't want Martin to go back inside else he would be hurt. But he did after he pumped a bucket full of water to pour on the fire. My pa got Sallie to go inside. And Maggie across the street, you know she can't stand the sight of blood, she took off and headed across the fields for Becky. She yelled as she ran, 'I will get Becky for you!' All of us had to stay home. Ma said, 'I don't know if what we find is fit for you children to see.' Besides, she looked at me and said, 'You didn't feel well enough to go to school for two days, so you stay right where you are. Mind me!' Later Pa came home and he said it was not as bad as he thought for so loud an explosion. He expected much worse. 'Sallie's arm is hurt and Becky is there to take care of her,' Pa said, and he also said Martin declared, 'Never again will I have her start fire in the morning. It's something I always do. People will think I did this to my wife.' Pa said he was in tears over the whole incident. Pa said he hadn't been feeling well the day before, though he was up and about. So Sallie said this particular Sunday morning he should lay awhile longer and she would start a fire to warm the house and make a good breakfast for him. He told Pa he feels guilty about the explosion. Pa told him no one on earth would believe such a thing and certainly not Sallie."

"How did they stop the bleeding?" Del asked.

"I don't know." Em paused. "Ma grabbed something, I don't know what and wrapped it tight around Sallie's arm. Pa went outside when

Becky came. First thing Becky wanted was warm water. Pa said they went across the street to Maggie's house for it. Of course she was no longer there. She ran all the way to Becky's and was so winded she needed to rest there before heading home. Martin and Sallie got all upset when Pa decided to start a fire to warm their house, especially Sallie. Pa looked over the wood carefully and it was fit to burn. The neighbors examined the remaining wood and they found no more gunpowder. Someone used a large amount in one piece of wood. Such excitement in the neighborhood we haven't had since Mickey killed Bright Eyes."

"Who in the world are Mickey and Bright Eyes?" Del was intrigued.

"Didn't I tell you? It happened this past summer, I guess that's why . . . Well, anyway. Mickey is a big German police dog the Schwoyers always have tied. He slipped his collar and killed the neighbor's cat. The Schwoyers and the Mutters don't talk to each other today yet. Bright Eyes was always taunting that dog. That cat knew exactly how close he could get to the doghouse and the dog not reach him. Well, one time it didn't work."

"I never heard that."

"Well, it's true. Pa said both men were standing next to each other, asking Martin what they could do to help. Pa said it looks like the men could get along. He thought it had to be the women who remained so stubborn. Pa said, 'One only has to make the first move and all could be settled.' Don't you think?"

"I suppose so," Del said.

"I feel sorry for Sallie. She is such a generous person, always willing to help. She always gives us some of her wild strawberry jelly. She always said the berries are here and it's a shame to let them go to waste."

"I know that's true," Del said. "Mama and my Aunt Eva used to pick wild strawberries there. Sallie stayed with us when we were real small and Mama had a funeral to attend. Mama's older sister was buried that day. Who could do such a nasty thing?"

"No idea. It was some time later when Ma came home. She helped Becky with the bandaging and talked to Sallie while Becky did the stitching. Becky had brought her own remedies along with her. She had something she washed on the arm to deaden the pain. It was a deep green color. Ma heard talk of Becky before. She says Becky is a NATU-RAL," Em put extra emphasis on the last word.

"What do you mean, a 'natural'? I never heard that."

"Ma believes Becky is as good as any doctor. She heard Becky knows all there is to know about birthing a baby. She said she would trust her to birth her own baby after seeing her work with Sallie."

The bell rang. It was time for everyone to scamper to their seats.

"You all had enough time to talk about the flying stove lid. Let's forget about that and start our school day." Teacher had a most stern look on his face. Del figured he heard many different versions from the children who came from that direction. The regular opening exercises were concluded but Del's mind was back at her house.

The morning passed rather quickly. Del was pleased with herself; in spite of all the distractions, she managed to have a normal first half of the school day. She ran and skipped all the way home for dinner. Bill joined her at the cement pike and asked she talked about Phillip.

"Nothing, nothing at all. Everyone is talking about the explosion." Del was disappointed. "It's just like Father and Mama predicted. I wonder what else happened at home this morning."

"I didn't tell anybody the doctor was at our place when we left for school. Did you?" Bill looked at Del.

"No." Del paused. "If it wasn't the Reifinger story, then it was the story about the Schwoyers and the Mutters and their fight over a dog and a cat."

"That's news to me."

"Well, its silly, that's all. It happened this past summer some time."

"Any big surprises birthday boy and birthday girl?" Benj said as they approached the woodshed.

"The talk was all about Martin and Sallie," Bill spoke.

"And you, birthday girl. Was yer friend there?"

"Yes, she was."

"Tell me. Do they think Martin stole the wood?" Benj asked.

"I heard nothing about that. I don't think Em even knows Mama was there."

"That so? Run along, your mama has goodies on the table," Benj waved them along.

As the twins walked to the house, Bill turned back to look at Benj. "That's funny."

"What's so funny?" Del asked Bill as they entered the walkway.

"He hardly ever calls me birthday boy. I can't remember when he last said that."

"You aren't always around to listen to his stories. I've heard him say 'birthday twins' a number of times already."

Mama stood in front of the stove, poking at the wood as she lifted the round front lid on the stove.

"Where in the world is Phillip now? What did the doctor say about his leg?" Del would have continued with questions except Mama raised her hands to stop the onslaught.

"You do ask a lot of questions! I am glad you remembered to call him by name. I hear 'boy' too many times. Everything went pretty much as expected. Your father took Phillip with him. The doctor's pretty sure he will forget his limp if we pay it no never mind," Mama said.

"And where are they now?"

Mama pointed in the direction of town. "He took him along to the creamery. They should be back before long. Your father wants to be here when Isaac and Eva return from their visit to the orchard."

"Father drove up the cement pike with Phillip!" Del was stunned.

"Yes, he did," Mama said casually.

"How many people bother to look around when a horse and wagon pass by?" Til added.

Mama shook her head, "Your father used the truck. People will look when they hear a truck go by."

"Everyone looks, even if you walk the street," Del replied.

"We're not hiding him," Mama said. She asked how the morning went. "What was said?" Mama inquired as she set a platter of baked omelet on the table plus cold ham leftover from the weekend. "You should be telling your friends about Phillip, the sooner the better."

"Mae and I talked to Beatrice Schwoyer," said Ori. "She said her mother was glad to ride along with you, when you took Becky to the Reifinger place."

"Em didn't say that. She said Maggie had to rest awhile at Becky's place before she started back," Del remarked.

Mama stopped her work. "See, that's how different stories get started. Yet both are correct. Maggie was winded. She stayed at Becky's house while Becky came for us to take her to the Reifinger's. Maggie rode along with us." A plate full of the thickest, dark chocolate cookies Del ever saw was placed on the table as Mama spoke.

"When did Becky have time to make these? She always has big round cookies, but these are different." Bill picked one up.

"Almost like a piece of cake," Ori said after her first bite.

"Becky called them brown bars. She said her granddaughter Susanna's husband came by on Saturday and brought a few for her to try, plus the recipe," Mama said as she set a pitcher full of chilled milk on the table. "I think Becky decided to try the recipe immediately."

"I really wonder how Phillip likes being in the creamery with Grandfather." Til spoke most soberly, not showing any semblance of a smile. That was as serious as Del's big brother would get.

"I didn't know Phillip would stay with Grandfather. What can he do there?" Del was surprised. "No one will see him there. I can't see anything when I step inside. There's only one big light bulb hanging from the ceiling," Del complained.

"There's enough light to see what my Father needs to see . . . ." Benj came in before Mama finished speaking and motioned for Fritz to follow him to the rocking chair. Bill seemed as surprised as Del that Fritz followed Benj's command. Benj was a good one to judge the time needed to complete a particular job, and he probably thought it was time for her father to be back. He wanted to see and hear firsthand all that would be said.

"What do you think of them cookies?" Benj asked, as he started a slow rocking movement. Fritz lay down in front of his feet. "That widder sure can bake. It doesn't wonder me any more why her Sam weighed three hundred pounds. That coffin was heavy to carry. We needed two extra men to handle it properly."

Mama just looked at Benj, then said, "You children had better get back to school as soon as you can. I will clean up," Mama directed.

"I was hoping Father would be here before we go back," Bill said.

Benj said, "*Ich dank da Billy muss ihm uff weise wie da blatz gschafft* [I think Billy must show him how the place works]."

Mama smiled. "You could be right, my father is extremely proud of his creamery. You have a good lesson this afternoon," she ordered the children.

"Never did hear that before about Becky's man," Bill said as they passed by the huge oak.

"Nor me," Ori said as all agreed.

"I wonder why we never see Rachael or Susanna or hear that they come to visit Becky. I need to ask Mama about that." Del paused. "Becky says her people come from the coal region."

"Yes sure, you always have to know everything, that doesn't bother me one bit. Who cares who Rachael is," Ori said sullenly as she started walking at a slower pace.

"You know. Rachael is Becky's only child and Susanna her grand-child, Mama told me that."

There was no further comment from Ori.

Bill said quietly to Del, "What bothers me is that the whole town may know today about Phillip and we didn't tell anyone."

"We didn't have a chance. Everyone is talking about the explosion. That's all anyone is interested in," protested Del. Fritz walked with the twins but not all that enthusiastically.

"Alright Fritz," Bill said. "You're concerned because Phillip isn't home. He will come back. You head back to Benj as soon as we reach his red barn."

That said, Fritz was suddenly more alert and bounced about in circles. He ran ahead, stopped by the barn and waited there.

Til looked back at the twins, twisting his body so hard he almost lost his balance, with a look of utter disbelief. "Well, what do you think of that? Old Benj is right. Fritz understands talk."

"Fritz knows because we often run races with him, and we always tell him go to the red barn. We don't want him running onto the highway," Bill explained.

Del started her skipping as Til and Bill joined two of the Shultz boys. The afternoon was long and slow. Her thoughts returned to Susanna's husband visiting Becky. Why didn't Rachael and Susanna visit? The Sunday accident was all talked out but there was no chance to mention the news at her house.

When dismissal time came everyone rushed to get home. Fritz met them at the entrance of the east lane like always. The truck was parked in the lane beside the cherry trees. Benj stood by the woodshed as Bill asked, "Where is Phillip?"

Benj said nothing, just tilted his head towards the washhouse. "Just go in. There's a surprise for you."

Ed was in the washhouse. "I wanted to finish before you came home. I would be too, if I hadn't cut Woodie's hair first and trimmed Carol's before starting on this head of hair." Ed pointed to Phillip sitting in the chair. "I never cut a hair like this. What do you think? I'll do no more today. Working these clippers, my hand is beginning to cramp. I will leave my bag here and come back tomorrow for the rest of you."

"Big difference," Til said as they admired Phillip's haircut.

"He looks like a handsome young man—right Phillip?" asked Ed as he showed Phillip his reflection in a mirror.

Everyone, including Phillip, nodded their heads in agreement.

"No work?" Bill asked, as he watched Ed place his barber tools in order to carry home.

"No work," Ed affirmed sadly. "The silk mill will be closed all week. I went in this morning, turned around and came home. The foreman could have let us know on Friday there would be no work today."

Mama was busy in the kitchen. The children scattered upstairs to change into work clothes. Del heard a machine coming in the lane. It was Isaac and Eva, who stayed long enough to say their goodbyes. They were going to be back tomorrow morning to work in Wolfgang's orchard again. They had apples to deliver to the Allentown relatives. They left a dish full of various drops[5] for the family to enjoy. Isaac came over to Phillip and complimented him on the nice haircut as Isaac took Phillip's hand and, with a shake and jolly laughter, he added: "Now you look like a stylish young man. Bet you like the haircut." Isaac looked to Eva. "Don't you think so?" Eva agreed. Phillip shyly smiled but said nothing.

---

5 A drop refers to produce that fell from the tree. In this case, apples that dropped from the tree.

CHAPTER EIGHT

No One Is Listening

Tuesday morning Del was determined to tell Em all the news at her home. Bill agreed that something needed to be said as they walked the lane with Fritz. Til kept pace with them. "Mr. Strunk wants us to say something, anything."

"I know, Til, Father told us the same thing. But how?" Del asked.

"I think we should start by saying a hungry boy was hiding in the alley where Father delivers butter," Bill said thoughtfully.

"What then, Bill?" Del wasn't sure this approach could work.

"Someone will ask why would a boy hide in an alley?" Bill responded.

"It will be fine," Til sounded more confident as he added, "Teacher will help us, he said so."

This day Em rambled on and on with new speculation about the firewood explosion. Del, hoping to change the conversation, said, "My father went to Philadelphia last Wednesday and he . . ."

"I know that story, you want to go along. Well, you can't. You can't miss school for something like that." Em was completely absorbed by the explosion and speculation in her neighborhood and not one bit interested in anything Del wanted to talk about.

Em was upset when Mr. Strunk told her enough was said about her neighbors. She needed to pay attention to her schoolwork. Del tried to concentrate but while re-reading the history lesson she was aware of the younger classes reading the poems they had to memorize over the coming weekend. She remembered them all and recognized when one word was mispronounced or a line skipped. Even Teacher almost nodded off, except to hear something incorrect, which sparked his attention. "How boring it must be to teach the same things over and over again," she thought. She remembered the pleasure that showed on his face when he managed to reach one student who seemed to have a difficult time with a particular subject. After all the years of teaching he still found satisfaction in what he was doing.

She noticed Mr. Strunk looked at her as he glanced over the room. She turned a page in her book and pretended to read. Her mind drifted again. She wondered about the discussion she overheard between the doctor and her father, especially about a busybody up-town, who delighted in spreading all kinds of vicious gossip. Father wanted to get his story told before false rumors would spread throughout the town.

"Adelaide. Adelaide, are you ready with the reading of your next poem?" the teacher called out.

"Sure am." She arose abruptly and stepped forward, blushing as she walked briskly to join her classmates on the one step platform facing all the other students.

Mr. Strunk pointed to her first. "Adelaide, you have the first reading."

"I know it by heart," Del announced.

Mr. Strunk looked from side to side, then said, "All right I'll give you full credit for the recitation if you do it correctly."

"A poem by Walt Whitman, O Captain! My Captain!" Del started and then completed the recitation.

"Good enough," Mr. Strunk confirmed.

As she returned to her seat, she remembered a poem she learned in third grade titled "Twenty Froggies" by George Cooper. She still liked that poem and recited it silently to herself to make the morning go faster.

At the midday mark, Del, as usual, skipped and ran all the way to the lane, where Fritz was waiting, feeling guilty that nothing was said about Phillip. Bill wasn't far behind. They joined up, with Ollie running to catch them, just beyond the small red barn. Til was always first out of the door to get home and greet Doll, his mostly black horse with white hairs above the hoofs. She was probably at home since Father now had a truck to deliver the morning milk. Ori, who could never be hurried, trailed on behind. When she picked up her pace, she ran awkwardly. People said Ori was knock-kneed.

"Tis the usual order," Benj observed as they approached the large boulder by the woodshed. A mud puddle covered the space between the woodshed and circled the front of the big rock, which made it impossible to lean against the rock and not mess his shoes.

"Will have to fix this sometime," Benj stared at the muddy patch. "I must ask Woodie what he would like for me to place there. Maybe I should let it fer that duck. *Ich kendt ihn nei schmeisse* [I could throw him in]. He'd dirty himself to last fer days to come."

Del heard a faint rumble of laughter coming from Benj. "*Saag maah, wie iss da fommidawg gange* [Tell me, how did the forenoon go]?"

"The normal routine," Bill replied. "I see Father is back. Is he in the house?"

"*Ich glaabt ah iss. Geh yuscht nei. Noch kannscht duh sehne.* [I believe he is. Go just in. Then can you see]." He motioned with an open hand to the house. Fritz ran alongside of Bill.

"Well?" Benj fixed his attention to Del.

"Well what?" Del turned, looking back at Benj.

"*Wie worrs bie deir* [How was it with you]? Don't ya have anything to say?"

"You know already. Bill told you as much."

"Yer right about Bill's day. How was yer day?"

"Same. The whole school has the same lessons. Did the doctor say anything new about Phillip yesterday?"

Benj changed the subject. "I'll lay a few pieces of slabs over that mud puddle. I have them here already." He pointed to a few slabs, pieces of bark cut from a log, propped against the chopping block. "*Sie kummt now* [She comes now]," he said tilting his head to Ori.

"She better not let that duck out. Did Isaac and Eva come? Are they working in the orchard, like they said?"

"*Ya sin doh. Nemmed yuscht dah halb daag* [Yes, they're here. Takes just the half day]."

"I suppose Phillip went along to the creamery again. He gets truck rides the rest of us don't get," Del lamented.

Benj replied, "*Du gehscht fa lanne, ah dut net* [You go to learn, he does not]."

Del just smiled as she headed indoors. Looking back, she said. "You coming inside?" He shook his head no. Benj sure is the *wunnerfitz*, she mused, just like herself. Right now he was mindful of his post. He wanted to see what Ori was going to do about her duck.

Mama, Father, and Phillip were seated around the table. Phillip looked pleased. Still shy, he turned his eyes downward to avoid contact beyond the briefest exchange of glances with the children.

"Did he talk yet? Where is Carol?" Del asked as she turned her eyes to Mama.

"Carol is sleeping on the davenport. She was up early showing Isaac how fast she can run," Mama said as she placed snacks on the table. Del saw her favorite: Cottage cheese with fresh fruit. A kettle of peeled apples was heating on the stove. That meant some canning would be done.

"Applesauce," Del said with satisfaction as she lifted the lid. "Are you canning some?"

"I'll do some canning today. I'd rather make applesauce than dry *snitz* [slices]."

"Does Phillip help Grandfather in the creamery?" Del asked her Father.

"Of course, he appears to like it. Sure didn't see anything like that before," Father replied.

Ori came in and Benj followed her.

"Now that everybody is here, does the school know about Phillip?" Mama waited for an answer.

"Told you, I won't tell anyone," Ori stated.

The other children glumly shook their heads no.

"None of you has said anything about Phillip. We can't let that continue. It will be harder to tell your friends tomorrow than it is today," Father advised. He paused, then continued. "You say something, just anything; Mr. Strunk will help you."

The children left for school with little conversation. "One of us has to say something," Til advised.

"Told you, not me." Ori was definite.

The afternoon session was uneventful. Del couldn't find the proper time to bring up the news. Em did make one remark when she saw Del standing in the second position in her spelling class. "How come you're in second place? You're always in the first position."

"It happens once in a while. It's funny Joe didn't tell you that happened last week."

"He doesn't talk about things like that. My parents sometimes ask if he was in school," Em said with a grin.

The school day ended. Del could tell Mr. Strunk was disappointed. He expected someone would mention the Black child from the big city. That would spark intense interest. He may have said something to Til. Del noticed her brother and Mr. Strunk left to fetch fresh water for the school down at the Stahler house. Their place was located just below the school ground on the other side of the lane. This was usually a job for two older boys, not the teacher.

Benj was not around as the children and Fritz neared the homestead. When she entered the house, Father was speaking to the boys.

"As soon as you boys have changed clothes we will start our evening work." As Father finished the sentence Ori walked in and Benj trailed her with Phillip leaning heavily on his arm. Benj looked at Ollie and pointed to the wood chest. "There is enough wood split for you to take care of."

"I know. I saw that," Ollie replied.

"How did everything go at the creamery? How many people saw Phillip? What did everyone say?"

Father put up his hands, "Whoa there, Adelaide, not so fast. Isaac arrived after you left for school; by the time we got there, all the early birds had already been there and gone. We took time to show Phillip just what happens to the milk we take there. He likes to be around your grandfather and seems interested in the creamery operation. You know your grandfather. He's proud to own the creamery making the sweetest butter around and proud of his big city sales. And Billy," Father laughed as he looked at Mama, "You know your father doesn't like to speak English, so he explained everything to Phillip in Dutch. *'Ach muss de schprooch lanne* [He must learn the language]' is what he said. That's all Phillip hears at the creamery." Father, Mama and Benj all laughed and the rest joined in as well. Phillip shyly smiled.

"Well, I'm not going to speak to him in Dutch. You usually speak to me in English."

"That's okay, Gloria. I'm sure he knows English." Father looked directly at Phillip. "I think he knows all the English he needs—once he is ready to talk. Adelaide, you will show Phillip what you do with the slop I bring along back."

Del nodded as she left the kitchen.

"Teacher must be crazy, why does he let you recite a poem ahead of time?" Ori asked as she followed Del.

"Why should I stand up front and read the poem when I already know it by heart?" Del retorted.

"You think you're smart," Ori said snappily.

"You could do the same thing. When you hear eight people read or recite a poem, you already know the half of it."

"Well, you shouldn't do that. Next thing you know we will have to memorize more poems than one a month. I hate doing poems. Mae says the same." With that said, Ori disappeared into her room. Del paid her no never mind. She thought of the phrase Benj often used. 'Goes in one ear and out the other.' She expected he never let remarks bother him any longer than that.

When Del returned to the kitchen Til was seated at the table eating freshly peeled pears. It seemed Mama couldn't peel them fast enough. Benj reached in and took a quarter and Father helped himself too. Til stuck a peeled quarter on a fork and held it in front of Phillip. He took it and ate it handily.

"Don't give him any more. He should have eaten enough pears by now," Mama cautioned. "He'll have to leave room for supper. Isaac and Eva are coming back. We'll wait for them."

"I have to go out to the barn. Doll will wonder what took this long. I only stopped in to say hello and blow in her ear," Til laughed. "That makes her wiggle her ears."

"Take Phillip along. He needs exercise to keep his muscles and bones strong. He can learn a lot from you, Tilghman," Father said.

Til looked pleased with the compliment as he washed his hands and got ready to return to his evening chores. Phillip turned his body, leaning toward Til's direction as if he was ready to get up and go along. *"Ah hut uns verschtanne* [He has us understood]," Benj and Father looked at each other at the same time. Mama quickly wiped Phillip's hands with a wet cloth. "Just be careful with his shoes, they aren't the best fit."

"The waache isz naegscht zum haus [The wagon is next to house]," Benj called out.

"I will use it if I need to," Til said as he looked at Phillip. "Come along with me."

Del saw the faintest look of pleasure on Phillip's face.

Til turned, took a long stride back toward the table and extended a crooked elbow for Phillip to grab. That was sufficient support for him to hop alongside.

"Better than dragging the foot," Mama said softly. *"Hilf ihn net soo viel. Ah muss selwerd mit mache* [Don't help him so much. He must help himself along]." Mama was determined to have him walk on his own, and soon. Father was more patient and easy-going.

"Won't we hear anything about the trip uptown?" Del asked as she headed outside to do her chores.

"There isn't anything more to say, Adelaide. I took him along. I don't think anyone saw him," Father said as he stood up.

Benj had seated himself outside by the pump, observing if all went well with the boys as Del walked by. "Did you see if Taw-Taw is around?"

"Net doh danowed [Not here this evening]." Benj got up and walked with Del.

"I never did hear what happened on Monday morning after we left for school." Now was her chance to get crucial details of the doctor's visit.

"Ya didn't miss much, just the regular check-up everybody gets."

"Did they find a vaccination, or must he have one?"

"*Net uff da aarem.* [Not on the arm]. He has a scar, but we still need the vaccination paper before he goes to school."

"Even if he was vaccinated and can show the scar?"

"Nope, ya need the papers. That's the law. Then there is the thing about a paper that ya was born. Not so when my young ones were born. Papers for vaccination *net node vennich* [not necessary]. Birth certificate *soo waahr nix* [there was nothing]. A big problem now. Ya need proof ya is born. Looking at a person and seeing *Aus levendich* [he's alive] isn't proof enough nowadays. Just as ya need proof ya is vaccinated and ready fer school. What is this world coming to? The government will soon want to know how many visits are made to the outhouse." Benj was amused as he said that. "*Un aa wie lung aus ess nemmed* [And also how long it takes]." Benj lifted his cap and waved it a bit while he used his left hand to stroke his smooth crown. Laughing heartily, he continued. "*Soo ebbes vil ich huffa gebbs net* [Something I hope won't happen]."

"I expect the Hudson will soon be here," Del said. "In that case I better get busy and do my work. Mama will need me in the house."

Fritz was not around as Del headed toward the feedhouse. She paused and looked about to see if he was nearby. She found her bucket already filled and a second bucket was half full with chopped corn for the pigs. That's something Benj must have done this afternoon. She tossed the corn one half cob at a time into the pigpen as she pondered on Benj's young ones. She had just started to carry the full bucket with broken cobs of corn when Carol appeared by her side.

"I thought you were sleeping. Heard you showed Isaac how fast you can run. Did you help Mama with the pears? I saw another basket half full is setting there."

"I handed pears to Mama to peel, that's what made me tired."

"Are you going to help me?"

"Mama said I should go out and get some fresh air and watch what you are doing."

"In that case you can throw some corn into the pigpen, not all at one place. Throw high enough to get it over the fence. Never, never reach through the board fence for the pigs to grab the corn. They will bite your hand. You hear me now. You don't want to lose any fingers. You throw the corn as far into the pen as you can while I make their mash and slop." Del proceeded to the feedhouse and dragged a bucket of corn in front of Carol. She threw the first few cobs into the pen and left Carol to continue. She scooped mash into two separate buckets and took them outside to the barrel that held the daily slop from the creamery. "I wonder if we should wait," she said to herself. "Father said Phillip needed to see what we did with the slop. Guess not. I am here now and want to get this done. There will be plenty of time for him to see this later."

Carol called, "I can't hear what you are saying. These pigs are noisy."

"No matter, I talk to myself sometimes. Just remember what I told you. You throw the corn as far as you can over the fence to drop inside. Don't forget that." Del spoke sternly to make the strongest impression on her little sister.

Ori entered the feedhouse on her way to the henhouse. Her smaller wooden bucket already held shelled corn to be scattered throughout the henhouse. Benj must have shelled the corn. He sure helped to get the evening chores done in less time. Carol walked over to Del after the corn was thrown and watched her mix the mash. Next thing Del knew Benj was by her elbow as she pulled the small-wheeled wagon close to the trough just outside the wire fence attached to the board fence all around the pen. Del fit the metal slide to the trough. As soon as the pigs heard that, they left the unfinished corn in favor of the mash.

Del turned to Benj. "Where is Phillip?"

"*Ahr iss mit de bouva im shire, ess melke um watcha* [He is with the boys in the barn watching the milking]."

"Wonder if he ever saw that before."

"*Ahr huts har're kenna* [He could hear it]." Benj gestured to Phillip's initial place in the barn.

"I suppose so. Milk buckets and sieves clanging plus animal noises would be heard from the floor below. He might have been frightened."

"*Ach waar wennich baung* [He was little fearful]. Another reason to have someone stay with him."

"I'll wait for Ori to finish and make sure all the doors are closed before I go in."

"*Geh yuscht nigh. Ich gebt ach druff* [Go just in. I'll take care of this]." Benj motioned her along with the wave of his hand.

"Come along, Carol. Take my hand and skip along with me. I'll take my time. Mama said you are tired. Come along, we'll do it together." Carol made an effort and was doing fairly well. "You're doing good! Isn't this fun?" Del said to encourage Carol's efforts.

Tomorrow it would be one week since Phillip arrived on the farm. No one knew at school. "I just have to tell Em about Phillip tomorrow," Del thought to herself.

Del heard the Hudson coming in the lane. Del and Carol waited by the walkway to greet Aunt Eva and Uncle Isaac. Isaac drove into the lane far enough to make an easier turnaround. Mama came out to meet Eva while Isaac headed for the barn and Eva walked the lane with Mama, Carol, and Del.

"Did you get your smokehouse apples?" Mama asked.

"I have two bushels for Lillie that she'll get tomorrow. I'll help her make applesauce. She also dries *snitz* [slices]. Isaac will come over tomorrow. He'll bring Sam along. Together they can work on a body for Woodie's truck. I'll get apples for myself later this week."

"Then we won't see you tomorrow." Mama sounded disappointed; she liked Eva's company.

"No, just Isaac. I will be helping Sis tomorrow. I'll have all day to figure out how to tell her about Phillip. I have to break it to her a little at a time."

"She won't be opposed to what we have done?" Mama questioned.

"No, it's not that. You just can't spring this kind of surprise on her. You remember how she reacted to my bobbed hair."

Mama nodded and laughed. "That is unforgettable."

Once she thinks it over, she'll be all right," Eva reassured Mama.

"How did you do in school today, Adelaide?" Eva turned to Del.

"Everything was okay. I recited my poem for the month ahead of time. We were only to read it aloud today."

"What do the school children know about Phillip?" Eva peered down on Del.

"Teacher knows but no one else does."

"Are they not to say anything?" Eva looked at Mama.

"No, the children are free to tell. But all the talk is about poor Sallie and the explosion. Are you and Isaac staying for supper? I have already prepared for two more."

"I think you can talk Isaac into staying," Eva laughed. "Isaac tells me Benj is a regular."

Mama nodded. "Yes, he is. He earns his keep. He was helping out on and off, especially when he knew Woodie would be away. It gave him something to do. Since last Wednesday, well, he's at home here. Though it was on the threshold floor we really needed Benj's help those first few days. He seemed all right with that!"

Eva raised her eyebrows and appeared shocked. Mama nodded, and then continued talking.

"Phillip seems to like Benj. Woodie and I don't have the time to look after him twenty-four hours a day."

"Why do some people say old Benj?" Del thought this was the perfect time to get an answer.

"Where do you hear that?" Mama asked.

"From people around here."

"Don't ask him to tell you. He doesn't want to talk about it. He had a son by the same name. They referred to the son as young Benj and, so he became old Benj."

"I heard him say it was Samuel's bed he offered for us to use." Del probed for more details.

"True. Forget it for now. We'll talk about that some other time." Mama thought it best to change the subject. "Tell me Eva, how are things at the orchard?

"Wolfgang is really aging. His hair has thinned and it's all white now. It was kind of a shock when I first saw him. I'm not sure he'll continue the orchard for more than a couple years. Your new boy, I can't believe it. *So aarmseelich* [So pitiful] first I saw him. He looks better already. It's amazing what enough good food and care will do, and how a young life springs back so quickly. He'll be running around in no time."

Mama looked pleased to hear that.

Del set the table while this conversation took place. Ori came in and walked over to the couch where Carol was laying all stretched out. "Is she okay?"

"She's okay. Just tired. She'll be fine after she eats something warm," Mama said.

The menfolk all came in at the same time. Even Phillip stood in line next to Benj, ready to wash his hands.

"*Ah hutt sel g'lannt* [He has learned that]," Eva smiled. "*Dood ah aa baida* [Does he also pray]?"

"*Noch net* [Not yet]."

One by one the boys were seated at their usual places. Phillip sat aside of Benj. Mama talked to Eva in Dutch about Phillip, noting that he needed to walk correctly. "I don't want him to ruin a good pair of shoes. It's too bad we haven't found a good fit in our used box." Mama looked at Phillip over her glasses.

"I haven't heard what the school children said when you told them your story about Phillip."

Isaac turned his eyes first to Til and then Del.

Til shook his head. "Nothing."

Del shook her head too.

"No one wants to hear anything else except talk about the explosion," Bill said.

Eva offered to help with the dishes after supper. Mama said it wasn't necessary. But she insisted all the same. She washed and Del and Ollie dried dishes. Even Ori was more helpful. She put the dishes away as fast as they were dried. Mama, Father, Isaac, Eva, and Benj talked about all the events of the past days in Dutch. Small bits of information could be gleaned from the conversation. Mama mentioned that Phillip was vaccinated sometime. He was taken care of sometime in his life. They still had no idea why he was staying near the market.

Mama was careful with what she said, even though she spoke in the dialect. "The doctor said all his bones are correctly formed. The malnutrition was a short span of time and should not have lasting harm. That was a relief to hear. Becky is sure he is alright. The foot is perfectly formed, there's no need to limp. We hope he'll trust us to tell us who he is. That way we can obtain a birth certificate."

"Jeremiah came to the creamery while I was there," Father said, switching to English. "He looked at the lad. He believes he has a pair of shoes that will fit Phillip for now. It's a pair of cowboy boots, like new. He found no one to wear them as yet. Jer will take a proper measurement of his feet and then see what's what. He thought Saturday would be good for a visit to the shop."

"*Falleicht vot sye lauffess besser von ah shue hut oss fitta* [Perhaps his walking will be better if he has shoes that fit]."

"*Ya, Benj des kanned graught so sye* [Yes Benj, this can exactly be so]," Isaac agreed.

Del would have liked to hear more conversation, but it was time to turn in.

CHAPTER NINE

The Story Is Told

Dᴇʟ ᴇɴᴛᴇʀᴇᴅ ᴛʜᴇ kitchen, humming a tune.

"My goodness," Mama said, "What makes you so chipper this morning?"

"I couldn't fall asleep last night thinking how I would tell Em about Phillip. But now I know what I am going to say."

"Good," Mama said. "The story must come out. We'll have eggs this morning. Last evening Gloria had an unhappy cluck hiding eggs on a nest of straw she made in a corner on the cement floor. Gloria saw eggs in that nest. The hen pecked at her hand every time she reached for an egg, which may have caused fine cracks in the eggs," Mama said, "and some were damaged beyond use." She checked each egg before adding it to a frying pan.

Eggs were seldom prepared for breakfast on school days. "Couldn't have been that many eggs under one cluck." She laughed. "Ori probably used her bucket with eggs already gathered to chase a hen off a nest. I saw that already! Or Taw-Taw could have been the real problem. He may have landed on eggs as Ori was gathering them or did damage to eggs a hen laid somewhere else." Del held back her smile. "We'll hear more about this sometime."

"I'm not so sure. If no one was around to see what happened, Gloria will never say anything different," Mama replied.

Del set the table with plates and utensils, salt, pepper, butter, and bread. "Where is Phillip this morning?"

"He is with the boys."

"Isn't it too early to get him up? Benj too, where is he?"

"All those questions. Will you ever break that habit?" Mama chided. "We don't expect Phillip to do any work right away but we are not going to treat him like he is someone special. Farm life seems new to him. He will watch and learn while he is getting stronger. We still need proper clothes for him, especially shoes. We'll see where he can help with chores."

Benj and Phillip were the first to come in. Til had brought Phillip as far as the door.

Del noticed that Benj had a smile of satisfaction on his face. He helped Phillip wash his hands and spoke to him in his fractured English, "Told ya, eggs this morning."

Phillip nodded his head shyly.

Ori entered the kitchen in her work clothes. Benj lifted his hand to stop Ori. "Chickens all taken care of. Ya can get ready fer school. The duck stays in the coop fer this morning."

Ori showed no emotion whatsoever. Mama's face was another matter, as she was very curious to know what was going on.

Til led the way to school. Once outside, he said, "We have to talk about Phillip today. Teacher told me this has gone long enough."

"I'm never going to say we have a Black boy at home," Ori stated. "My pet has to be penned up all the time just because of him."

"What happened in the henhouse this morning?" Del asked.

"None of your business," Ori muttered.

"Something happened with her duck. I heard the commotion from the barn. Benj and Phillip know what happened. Benj won't tell us. Maybe Phillip will tell us once he talks," Bill explained.

That's okay, Taw-Taw's old enough to croak anyway," Ollie said emphatically.

"Huh, you don't know anything." Ori was unhappy about something.

At the schoolhouse, Ori met Mae, and the boys waited for the Shultz boys as Del met Em outside. "Lets go inside," Del said as she moved toward the door.

"I promised the boys to pitch ball until Ollie and Benny joined them," Em replied, shaking her head.

"They aren't far behind. I'll go inside. You can meet me there," Del said.

Inside, Del saw two new girls and a boy standing by the huge round coal heater located in the section of the building behind the classroom that extended the length of the vestibule wall, providing an area for shelves to hold lunch boxes and coat hooks. "Hello. I stand here sometimes to warm up on cold winter days."

"It is warm here. We had a potbelly stove in the middle of the room at our old school. This stove is much bigger," said the older of the two girls. The bell rang and school was in session.

After opening exercises Mr. Strunk introduced the new students. He asked them to remain standing. "We have Anabel, Maria, and Gordon Goho. They will be attending this school for the remainder of this year."

The morning session ran smoothly, and a fifteen minute recess time was called. Del stood by the center window and waited for Em to join her, as this was their usual gathering place when they stayed indoors. "You're not going out?" Em asked.

"No, let's talk," Del said as she was looking at the assortment of books on the deep window seat. "I want to tell you about something new at our house," Del said as she cleared her throat.

Em interrupted, "You have a new truck. Your father can haul things. I don't care about a truck. Heard it all from Joe already. He talks about it all the time."

"You said Joe doesn't talk about anything at home."

"Well, that truck is different," Em sighed.

"My father took the truck to Philly today. He will be home earlier now," Del announced.

"You won't get that train ride now," Em observed.

"No train ride for me," Del said sadly. "My father said it wasn't a passenger train. He used the freight car to go back and forth, and he always said the train ride would be exhausting with all the loading and unloading, plus getting up very early in the morning," Del explained.

"You mean a box car!" Em was appalled.

"I suppose."

"Who would want to go there anyway?" Em questioned.

"Lots of things to see in Philadelphia."

"I'm not interested in seeing a city. My grandmother lives in Reading. Not much to see."

"That's because you go there all the time!" Del was quick to say.

"Oh, I must tell you. Sallie's arm is healing. Ma says Becky comes by every other day for a spell and goes home again. Ma thinks she does some cooking and cleaning up. Men aren't good at doing those things." Em whispered, "We better stop talking! He looked over our way twice already." Em turned her eyes toward their teacher.

"So? We're allowed to talk at recess time," Del said softly.

"Are you girls having a serious conversation?" Mr. Strunk came over to the middle window where the girls stood.

Em and Del looked at each other. Em finally spoke. "We were discussing firewood at . . . Well, at the next door neighbors. Pa says we shouldn't talk about it anymore."

"I thought your discussion was about another matter. I am sorry. You talk about anything you wish." Mr. Strunk walked away.

"We should have gone outside," Em said with an 'I told you so' tone.

"I never got to tell you what I really wanted to say," Del said plaintively.

"It's the truck."

"No, its not. I'll have to tell you about it later."

"You know something about Martin and Sallie that I don't know?"

"No, Em, that talk is finished."

"What is it?" Em insisted.

"Can't tell you now, Em."

"Why not?"

"Too long a story, this afternoon I'll have more time."

Del couldn't think of an easy way to say 'Father brought a Black boy along home last Wednesday' to her friend. She worked quietly during the second morning session. She was determined to get all her arithmetic problems finished. She even made an effort to write smaller. Mr. Strunk told her several times she was using too much paper. He examined each tablet carefully before issuing another. A lengthy multiplication problem when completed formed a diagonal across the page and left the opposite corners blank. "Fill in those corners with smaller problems," he encouraged all students. All were told of the importance to make good use of the school supplies the taxpayers provided.

Del headed home for lunch, skipping slowly most of the way. She joined Bill as they headed up the cement pike. "Did you mention Phillip to any of your friends?" Del said resignedly.

"I talked about the Chevrolet truck. Lester asked me if I rode in it already. I told him Father took us for a ride out our lane and back again."

"I didn't know you boys had a ride!"

"Yep, he even told Til he was sure he could drive it," Bill said and changed the subject. "Teacher and Til have something planned. They talked again at recess time.

"Ya sure are busy chattering. Hear something new?" Benj asked as they walked by the woodshed.

"Nothing to say," Bill said as the children moved on.

Til was in the house eating an apple and holding another in his hand—which was probably for Doll—as Del and Bill approached.

"What is Teacher up to?" Bill asked.

"Wait till this afternoon," Til said as he bit into his apple. Til stopped talking as Mama and Benj walked into the kitchen.

"You children did alright this morning?" Mama questioned. There was no answer.

"Father took the truck today again," Ollie said.

"That's right. We have it to use," Mama commented.

"Not a truck anywhere except for our truck and Grandfather's old wrecked truck," Til stated.

Mama was amused at Til's detailed knowledge of all vehicles in the neighborhood.

"Em's father has a machine. He takes them to the city most every other weekend."

"Yes, I know, Del," Mama said. "Does Emma realize how lucky she is? There isn't another person in that section of the township with a motor car, not that I can think of right now."

"I bet everyone will be sticking their heads out their homes to see our truck."

"You are probably right, William. Wait until they hear we are going to get a telephone. The telephone company has to string a line from the corner up town to here." Mama shared this news with a big smile.

"Goodness gracious! When did all this happen? Mae's father has a telephone!" Ori exclaimed as she stepped into the kitchen with Taw-Taw.

"Get that bird out of here," Mama ordered. "You know better, the porch is as far as he can go."

"I know that, just heard about the telephone," Ori retorted.

Benj stood back as he entered the kitchen and watched Ori trudge back into the porch with the duck pressed firmly to her shoulder. "*Ich wunner woo sie augfange wille* [I wonder where they will start]."

"They will have to follow the street to your place and then come in our lane," Ollie volunteered.

"*Bischt recht.* [You right]," Benj acknowledged.

"I can call Mae on the telephone," Ori said as she re-entered the kitchen, having placed her duck in his escape-proof box.

"Mae's father has a business, and his phone is meant for business purposes only. That's why it is out in the packinghouse where he spends most of his time. I'm sure he doesn't want his girls using the phone to call friends. The upper end of town has a few telephones. Good thing that vicious gossip doesn't have a telephone," Mama said, barely audible to Benj. "And good we don't have a troublemaker at this lower end." Mama paused and said in a louder voice, "The telephone should come in very handy, especially if someone needs a doctor in a hurry like this past Sunday, but it's for business only, Gloria."

"Grandfather has a business. He doesn't have a telephone," Ollie interjected.

"Oliver, you should know your grandfather won't get a telephone. He says he is too old to learn these new fangled contraptions that cost money—as he refers to anything he didn't grow up with. His business served him well all these years without a phone. He isn't going to be in business much longer. The way things are is good enough for him." Mama was most emphatic.

"Adelaide, I don't hear anything from you; did you say anything to Emma?"

"No, she thinks all I want to talk about is the truck," Del said sadly.

Thankfully Ori changed the subject. "Did Phillip go along to Philly today already? He gets to ride the truck before me."

"No, Ed took Phillip up to the creamery with our milk and left him there with your grandfather. He will spend the day with your grandfather."

"Harry and Dick will get to know Phillip. Grandfather visits them several times a day." Til spoke with conviction.

"My father will teach him all there is to know about horses," Mama concurred. "Get yourselves going or you will miss out on play time."

Back at the schoolhouse, Em was playing Round Town ball with the boys. She could throw the ball as well as any boy. She always won the girl's field day contest for throwing the ball farther than any other girl at school. For that reason alone the boys chose her to be a part of their team.

Del made her way to the rear of the schoolhouse. She wandered along the stone fence separating the forest from the school ground, hoping to find new birch shoots. She found some to strip and chew but the best was all gone. Birch bark was most tender in the spring of the year. A buzzing sound caused her to suddenly stand still. She saw a hornet's nest hanging between two large stones in the fence. She back-tracked ever so carefully, stepping onto the school ground as the bell rang. Teacher needed to be told about that nest.

As the afternoon classes were underway Del noticed Mr. Strunk glancing at the clock more often. She turned her head, looking to the back row where Til was seated, who showed no indication that some-thing was planned.

Em whispered, "Can you tell me now?"

"Okay then. We have something new and different in our house." Del decided a guessing game would be the best way to break the news.

"You told me already. Your daddy has a truck."

"True. But besides that. We had this before we got the truck. Father brought this along home last Wednesday."

"So, what is it?" Em was getting frustrated.

Del whispered, "I'll give you one more hint. It's alive and comes from Philadelphia."

"Huh, that can't be so special. You have lots of animals," scoffed Em.

Del just grinned and returned to her lesson.

As the afternoon period drew close to day's end, Mr. Strunk spoke. "School is over, but you are not dismissed. We will use these last min-utes to share something with all of you. Right now we are going to tell you what some pupils have known for a spell."

A hush came over the entire room.

"Tilghman, would you please come up front and stand beside me."

Til was out of his seat and shyly took his place beside Mr. Strunk. Del glanced around the entire room. All students were looking about with eyes open wide and puzzled expressions. Ori was pale—which was strange because she usually was complimented for her rosy cheeks.

"Tilghman and his brothers and sisters have an interesting story to share with you. Mr. Heydt brought someone along home on his trip to Philadelphia this past Wednesday. The children didn't learn who came along from the big city until Friday after school." He looked at his students. "I ask all of Tilghman's sisters and brothers to come up front to share their story with us."

Ollie was the first to make a move. Em nudged Del; she got up and followed. Bill and Ori were immediately behind her.

The teacher cleared his throat. "First of all, I will tell you that Mr. Elwood Heydt heard the business people he dealt with talking about a poor boy they thought to be homeless. He hung around their shops, ate scraps of food and wore rags for clothing."

A pronounced "ahhh" came from the class.

"Mr. Heydt asked them 'Is this really so?' They told Mr. Heydt they pitied this unfortunate child but at the same time they didn't want him hanging around the market. They thought he was homeless. The police couldn't help, saying all orphanages were full already. Mr. Heydt was told that he'd been there for weeks and the market people were afraid they would find him dead one morning."

Del noted the silence in the classroom as Mr. Strunk looked around the room.

"This child ate the food the shop keepers threw away. Not fit to eat, nor nearly enough for a growing child to maintain a healthy body. Do you have enough to eat?"

Mr. Strunk raised his hand and nodded his head in the affirmative as all the children followed his lead.

"Well, Mr. Heydt didn't like what he heard. He decided his family could save a child from starvation and give him a warm place to sleep. That's what is needed for a normal life." Again raising his hand Mr. Strunk asked, "How many of you would help a starving child with no place to call home, and give him a place to sleep and food to eat?"

'Oohhs' and 'ahhhs' were heard as a few school children raised their hands.

"Mr. Heydt took him along home?" blurted out one of the younger pupils.

"Yes. He did. How about you and your family? Would you do the same for a helpless child?"

The children looked puzzled. A few half-raised their hands.

Mr. Strunk again raised his hand and nodded his head. "Of course you would."

A few more children raised hands.

"You wouldn't want a child to starve to death, would you?"

There was a fast mumbled 'no', while others shook their heads.

"There you have it. Said and done. We would all do the same thing."

Del observed many of her classmates seemed genuinely surprised that a child could live like that with no place to call home.

"You may ask questions of the Heydt children or perhaps they would like to add to their story."

Ori immediately stated, "We named him Phillip, because he came from Philadelphia. I was the one to give him that name."

Del's jaw dropped. This was a shocking surprise since Ori had previously announced she was not going to say anything! Del heard real pride in Ori's voice as she spoke.

"Is he too little to come to this school?" was the first question asked by the children.

Mr. Strunk looked at the Heydt children and said, "No, he is of school age. He needs to get healthy first."

It was then Til spoke. "We knew something unusual happened. When Father came home last Wednesday, he was late. It was dark and we didn't see Phillip in the wagon. My parents kept him apart from us in the barn threshold in that wagon until Friday evening. That's when we met Phillip."

"I guessed it had to be a person because of the things my parents were taking out to the barn." Del stopped abruptly. She suddenly remembered Mama had warned them not to tell anyone Phillip was first sheltered in the barn.

"You kept him in the barn?" Benny Shultz stuttered.

Del continued, "Father has a cousin who is a tramp and comes by twice every year and sleeps in the barn on his way to Florida where it is warm."

"That's who I thought it was, cousin Clint," Ollie mentioned. Some of the children laughed.

"We had a tramp sleep in our barn, too," another student said.

"That's a good way to help someone in need." Mr. Strunk seemed pleased. "This boy will probably be here long enough for you to know him."

A new third grader was brave enough to ask, *"Wil des buwele cum doh haah zu des schul* (Will this boy come here to this school]?"

"Clara, you know better. In this building you will speak English," the teacher reprimanded her. "Then I will answer your question."

"Will the boy come to this school?" Clara said very slowly.

"That's much better. When the time comes; we'll have to wait and see. Mr. Heydt will ask every time he goes to the city whether anyone is looking for a lost boy. If so, he will return him to his family." Mr. Strunk looked around. "Tilghman said they didn't meet the homeless boy until Friday after school. Is there anything else you'd like to say?"

Del looked at her siblings and said, "Father told us the market folks hoped someone would take him along so he wouldn't freeze to death on their property."

Del could hear the audible murmur of "Oh, no," in the classroom.

She continued, "Father said the boy was crying and sobbing so badly he was shaking all over when he held him in his arms. Father said he did the Christian thing to rescue him. You know what? He covered himself with burlap bags and lay in cellar entrances to stay warm at night. You know burlap can't keep anyone warm."

"Is he still in the barn?" another student asked.

"Oh no. He slept in the house since Friday night already. He sure likes to eat," Ollie added.

"No wonder, if he had nothing but scraps to eat," Em commented.

The teacher clapped his hands. "Dismissal time is upon us. You can talk about this tomorrow. Right now its time to line up and bid you a good day."

Upon that request all the children took their place on two sides of the center aisle, shook the teacher's hand, and left the schoolhouse. Em was waiting for Del outside. "Why didn't you tell me?" she demanded.

"I told you, you weren't interested in anything except that stove explosion. I'll tell you more tomorrow, okay?"

"Guess so." Em said dejectedly.

Joe was waiting by the corner of the building for Em on the first of three large oblong flat rocks used as steps to drop to the lower side of the playground and onto the lane. Del skipped by herself in the lane going home. She felt like a heavy burden was lifted as she hummed the tune 'Take Me Back to Renfro Valley', a favorite song of her father's. Ori and Mae had their usual slow walk discussing something. The Shultz boys and her brothers were walking the lane together. Til was probably asked a lot of questions, for he was walking slower than his normal stride. On the way home, Del entered the cement pike all alone. She moved slowly, waiting for the others to catch up. Til was the first to catch up to her. Del turned, seeing Bill. "Come on, hurry up. Fritz is waiting for you. He's dancing around in circles."

"You're a good buddy, Fritzy boy." The twins greeted their dog, petting him as he wedged in between them.

Bill remarked, "I couldn't believe Teacher. I wonder why he changed his mind about him coming to school. Someone must have talked to him."

"I figure Father told him everything about that first night." Del paused.

"Oh my!" Del put her hand to her mouth. "No one mentioned Phillip is a Black child."

The other children looked startled.

"You're right, no one said that," Bill acknowledged.

"Teacher could have said something," Del added.

"We can't blame him. Any one of us could have mentioned it," Til remarked.

"But wait until they hear that!" Del's relief turned into worry.

"Mama said we were not to tell anyone we kept him in the barn," Ollie said nervously.

"It came out so quickly," Til said, "it's just the way it happened."

"I won't tell her we said he stayed in the barn," Bill said.

"I said it too." Del recalled.

Fritz walked quietly between the twins. He sensed the twins were troubled.

Benj was at his regular spot under the woodshed as Del and Bill approached.

"And how was this day?" Benj looked to Bill first.

"It was okay," Bill replied. "Everybody knows about Phillip now."

"*Whar whor es blappermaul* [Who was the chatterbox]?"

"Don't look at me," Del responded. "It was Teacher's idea to tell everyone."

"That so?" Benj looked to Bill once more.

"That's right, you should talk to Til. He can tell you more."

Benj appeared puzzled as he followed the children. "Yer Mama has some of those good smokehouse apples."

"Why in the world do they call them smokehouse apples? It's a dumb name," Bill said almost in disgust.

"*Froge mich net* [Ask me not]. All I know is, it's a good apple for apple-sauce or *snitz* [slices]."

"Did Isaac and Eva go home already?"

"*Ya, sie cumma widder mariye. Allebeit hen ken arewet allewile* [Yes, they come again tomorrow. Both have no work right now]. This time helping here, not the orchard. Wolfgang needed help today. *Sie kenne glae bissel verdiene* [They can little something earn]. They took more apples along for yer family in Allentown. Tomorrow they build a body for the truck. *Mus des watcha* [Must watch this]."

"The truck has a body already," Del responded.

"Yep, but not high enough fer yer Father," Benj said.

"That's why Uncle Sam is coming along tomorrow," Bill said.

"*Sel hawe ich net gwisst. Cummed de Lillie mit?* [That I have not known. Comes Lillie along]?" Benj was interested in all the comings and goings at the Heydt farm.

"Probably not. She will be busy taking care of all those apples for her crew. Sam can figure out how much and what kind of materials are needed," Bill answered.

"*Geh yuscht nigh* [Go just in]."

Til and Ollie had filled Mama in on the eventful close to the school day when Del and Bill entered the kitchen.

"So the story is told," Mama said.

Del merely nodded her head. She couldn't tell if Mama was pleased or not.

"It's just as well, this way they all know at the same time," Mama paused, and then asked, "How did the children react when they heard we have a Black child living with us?"

The children looked at one another sheepishly. It was Ollie who finally said, "No one said he's a Black person."

Mama was stunned. "How come none of you said that?"

"I never thought about that," Til said.

Bill said he didn't either.

"Don't look at me," Ori pointed to herself. "Del and the others did all the talking."

"Who was it that said his name is Phillip?" Til was quick to respond.

Everyone pointed to Ori. Mama nodded.

"I will have to tell Em tomorrow first thing," Del said with a serious expression on her face.

"Do that." Mama continued, "It's better that you tell her than if she hears it from someone else."

"Ollie surely you must have said something," Mama was certain.

"I said something. Where is Phillip? He isn't with Grandfather all this time, is he?"

"He's at the creamery until your father comes back. He will take him to Uncle Jeremiah's shoe repair shop as he may have a second-hand pair of shoes he can fix for Phillip to wear."

"That'll be something, when he has a pair of shoes that fit his feet," Del said.

"You can be sure the shoes will be a correct fit. The cowboy boots were too narrow. Making a new pair of shoes will take a while longer," Mama spoke softly.

"Benj said Eva and Isaac were helping at the orchard," Ori changed the subject.

"Yes, Estelle needs a break, she needs to take care of herself. In a way it's good Eva and Isaac have these days with no work. They can earn something and help a man out at the same time. Tomorrow they want to start looking at the truck and build another body for it," Mama concluded.

"Benj said something like that. I didn't know Father wanted something different," Del said.

"Your Father wants a taller body with a roof and screened sides."

"What for?" Del was very curious.

"You wait and see."

"I hear the truck." Bill and Ollie were immediately on their way out.

"Better change your clothes and get your chores done," Mama ordered.

Del rushed up the stairs. She wanted to be around once Father came inside to talk about the day at school.

CHAPTER TEN

News Travels Fast

THURSDAY MORNING WAS a typical day. Outside work completed, Del and Ori were going to the house when Isaac and Sam arrived and headed toward the sawmill to begin work on the truck. Mama fixed the fires while telling Ori she needed to awaken Carol. Del prepared the table for breakfast. Mama went outside with her milk pitcher.

The children were glad the entire school now knew about Phillip, but the whole truth still needed to be told. Would Phillip be accepted? Del knew what it felt like to be looked down upon. She and her siblings heard the titters from city children, when twice a year they spent time in the city with their cousins. They were embarrassed but silent when their cousins' friends made snide remarks about their Pennsylvania Dutch accents and homemade clothes. Del was baffled that the accent was mocked even though their cousins were part of the same culture but no longer spoke the language.

Could that be a problem within Becky's family? After all, Mama once said Rachael had the privilege of going to nursing school in the city and became a nurse. Did Rachael feel superior to those she left behind in the country? Rachael never visited her mother, a person everyone looked up to and appreciated for her help and many kindnesses. Why not visit her mother?

Mama returned with a full pitcher of milk at the same time Ori entered the kitchen with Carol, who was fully dressed. Father and Del's brothers came in for breakfast and took their places at the table. Benj and Phillip were still outside.

Father said, "It's not good to keep Phillip's skin color a secret. Tell your friends Phillip is a Black boy and continue with the rest of the story." Father looked around the room. "They'll no doubt ask you a lot of questions. Answer them honestly. Keep the facts straight. That's always the best way to handle things. Perhaps your teacher will tell the school the whole story. The sooner everyone knows the better." Father looked at Mama. "I think things will work out just fine." "What are we supposed to do? Just announce Phillip is a colored boy? I am not going to be the one to tell them anything." Ori said emphatically.

"That's all right, Gloria. You let one of the others be the first to mention it. Tell your friends to stop by and meet Phillip." Benj and Phillip entered as Father was speaking. "Children do not have built in prejudices. That comes from their elders. What say you?" Father looked to all the family.

"*Sez hatt fa ouse szu figgere* [It's hard to figure out]." Benj added his comment as he and Phillip took their places after a fast washing of their hands.

"You children mind your manners," Mama cautioned as the children prepared for school. Fritz was first outside. Mama followed and admonished them, "Don't you tell children we kept Phillip in the barn a couple of days. I don't want people to think we were mistreating him—we had to wait until we knew he didn't have any contagious illnesses that could have spread to you. You hear now."

The children looked from one to another and started walking to school. There was no comment from anyone.

"Who is going to tell Mama they already know we kept Phillip in the barn?" Ollie whispered as he looked back.

"Don't worry Ollie, you aren't alone," Bill said softly.

Till didn't want to dwell on that worry. "I think Phillip is going along to the creamery this morning, something he can do until he starts school. Grandfather likes a young person to do the running back and forth with his paperwork. It saves a lot of walking for him. That's all I do whenever I am there. No hard work at all. Just a lot of walking back and forth," Til said.

"But Phillip can't walk by himself. How can he help Grandfather?" Del exclaimed.

"There is plenty to hold onto or lean against in the creamery. He can go anywhere Grandfather points to."

"I wish I knew as much about the creamery as you do, Til. I only get to step inside the door once in a while," Del admitted.

"Grandfather doesn't want more people inside than absolutely necessary. He needs to keep the place very clean. He never has people step in farther than the doorway unless it's someone to help operate the equipment," Til offered.

"I'd really like to have a closer look at his stand-up desk with all those compartments. Some close with a drop lid and a key." Del hoped to explore and take note of items the many compartments held.

As usual, the Shultz boys were waiting to greet the Heydts. Mae fell in line next to Ori. Del went on skipping slowly, walking a few steps before skipping again, pondering how she would reveal the full truth about Phillip. Del was sure Ori would be the first one to tattle and tell Mama that the school children already knew about the barn stay. Del was glad she was not the first to say it. Del heard the truck approaching the cement pike; looking back she could not see who was seated in the cab.

Em was waiting at the very edge of the school grounds by the boulder alongside the persimmon tree. In the fall its branches hung low enough sometimes for a taller child to grab a branch and get a foothold to climb atop the smooth boulder that marked the boundary line on the school property. Of course any attempt to scale the rock was only made when Mr. Strunk was inside. Behind the rock was an open pasture where cattle grazed. A small forest clearing for first base on the left side sat before that huge rock.

Em surprised Del by blurting out, "For God's sake, he's a Black boy! I wouldn't want a Black person living in my house. I surely wouldn't tell that to anyone either. But, you could have told me!" Em softened her tone.

"I was going to tell you!" Del paused. "Who told you?"

"Does it matter?"

"Yes. How did you know?" Del insisted.

"My Pa stopped for eggs on the corner on his way home from work—it's his week to work the night shift. He always stops at the corner creamery when Ma needs eggs. Right there inside the creamery he was being shown how to weigh eggs."

"You mean grade eggs."

"Whatever."

"What did your father say?"

Em looked puzzled. "He just said that could be the last time he would get his eggs from Billy Henry. Pa thought it terrible that he had a Black child working for him. A slave! Pa said he thought the war settled things and that he always had a lot of respect for that man. Ma said we should support our local neighbors and that Pa appreciated that special he got there. Pa looked at Ma, then said he would think about it."

"It won't matter all that much. My grandfather can sell those eggs other places. He takes eggs to Philly."

"Who is your grandfather?"

"My grandfather operates the creamery. Billy Henry. That's who. And Phillip is not his slave."

Em looked surprised, and then frowned. "We told Pa and Ma you had a new boy living with you from Philadelphia. That's when Pa asked Joe if he knew anything about this boy. Joe just said that he would have starved this winter for sure. I told Pa your father pitied him and brought him along home, that's all. Pa asked if he was named Phillip. Joe said yes. Pa thought this boy was a slave, and he couldn't believe such a thing could happen here. My Pa said, 'It's a real kindness they're doing for the boy'. My Ma said it's no surprise that your Pa would do something like this, because he gave my grandma food and firewood when my grandpa died." Em concluded.

Before Del could reply to all this information the bell rang and the morning session began.

At recess time, neither girl left their shared desk, except for a quick run to the outhouse. A chill blowing wind kept most of the students inside playing games.

"What are you thinking?" Del looked at Em.

"I don't know what to think," Em replied.

"Your father might bring a child like that home, too. There are lots of poor children in Reading."

"No, he wouldn't either." Em retorted. "We don't have a farm like you. Besides we don't know anybody who is starving."

"My father says times are hard. Some people send their children out to work at relatives' farms in exchange for food and shelter. My father grew up that way because his father died when he was only three years old. He says he knows what its like to be really poor. "

The girls were unusually quiet during the second morning session. Each one tended to the work before them. When dinnertime came Del left quickly. She walked slowly over the uneven playground. Once in the lane she picked up her pace, but she didn't start skipping until she neared the cement pike. Bill was waiting for her by the east lane. Fritz greeted them at the boundary line.

"Does Em know the truth now?" Bill asked.

"Em and I talked about it. I explained why I hadn't told her before."

"Was she angry?"

"Don't think so. It's okay, I guess. What did the boys say?"

"We formed a circle outside, some knew from Joe that Phillip is a Black child. His father told them."

"Em said the same. How do the boys feel about that?"

"They asked a lot of questions. Til and I answered some. You should have seen Ollie, he was all excited. Told them everything he knew." Bill laughed, "He was so very proud to share the story."

"So now all the boys know," Del said.

"Except for the little ones who stayed inside," Bill corrected Del. "We'll see," Bill laughed. "Benny wanted his questions heard, but stuttered so badly, he finally sang his sentences and you know what, he didn't stutter. He wants to see Phillip because he's never seen a Black person. Til told him to come anytime. I think he'll be up today yet," Bill said smiling while shaking his head.

"He better ask his parents first." Del said and then sighed. "Em said she wouldn't want one living in her house; I think she has to think about that awhile. Her ma and pa think our father is kind, especially to people who need help." Del repeated the story about Em's grandmother receiving help from their father.

"Ya would walk right by, and never say hello," Benj teased as they walked by the woodshed.

Both turned and smiled. "Fritz didn't tell us you were there," Bill said.

"*Ya da hund iss schuldich. Sie wissa alles nah* [Yes, the dog is blamed. They know everything now]?"

Del and Bill nodded affirmatively. Del said, "Pretty much so. I didn't have to tell Em Phillip is a Black child.

Benj grunted and said, "Her father saw Phillip at the creamery and musta put two and two together. *Wie hen de kinner des gnumme* [How did the children take this]?"

"The boys had a lot to say," Bill replied. "Benny especially wants to come and see him. He never saw a colored boy."

"*Vielleicht isses besser gonach aus ich gemaindt hob* [Perhaps it went better than I had thought]," Benj half said to himself.

"I only talked about it with Em. She sees plenty of colored folk," Del said.

"Oh, that so?" Benj waited.

"She said she wouldn't want one living in her house. But I really think she wouldn't let a person starve," Del said in defense of her friend.

Benj waved his hand, motioning them to go inside.

Father was back from delivering the morning milk. Benj and Phillip lingered out at the water pump. Mama greeted both Del and Bill. Ollie was already there and Ori was close behind. "Now, that you are all here, how did this morning go?" Mama asked.

Ori wailed out, "Mae says our father is a slave driver, that's what!"

"She surely got that from somebody else. Did she say who says that?" Mama took a quick look at Father.

"No," Ori said as she plopped herself on her regular seat at the table.

"How did she know?" Bill asked.

"How should I know?" Ori retorted.

"Is she still your friend?" Mama asked quietly.

"Sure, and I'm glad. I was afraid it would make a difference."

"Em knew more about Phillip before I got to school," Del spoke up.

"How did that happen?" Father asked.

"Her pa gets his eggs at the creamery, he saw Phillip there."

"From what I hear all the boys were interested," Father seemed pleased.

"We told them Phillip surely would have starved this winter. I think most all would do what we did," Bill commented.

"Why are those two sitting outside?" Ollie asked, pointing to Benj and Phillip.

Mama said as she waved to them to come in, "We didn't know what you might be telling us, and didn't want Phillip to hear any bad reactions."

After their dinner meal, Ollie asked, "Is it all right if Benny comes this evening after school to see Phillip?"

"Of course, we are not going to keep anyone away," Mama said. "Tell him first he needs to tell his parents where he is going. I'm sure he has evening chores to do."

"I will tell Benny he can come today!" Ollie was excited to be in charge of the first visitor.

Del stopped to watch Ori pick her duck up and take him back to the feedhouse. The coop was inside and once the henhouse doors were secured she'd let him roam around inside the henhouse. Ori caught up to Del and Bill, which was unusual as she preferred to walk by herself at a slower speed. Ollie was half running as he tried to keep pace with Til and his long legs.

There was very little discussion as Fritz pranced along between the twins. Becky was out by her mailbox as they left the dirt lane. She called out to them "*Ain ich ebber, ausgelosse iwwer des nei kindt* [Anybody unruly over this new child]?"

"There's lots of talk going on right now." Ori said peevishly.

"What say you two?" Becky looked at the twins.

"They want to see him, that's all," Bill said.

"Lots of them seemed to already know," Del chimed in.

"*Sel laut zimmlich recht* [That sounds fairly right]," was Becky's only response.

After school the three Shultz boys—Abe, Benny, and Carl—had permission to follow the boys home and meet Phillip. Til and Abe took the lead. Bill and the other two followed, walking the school lane together. Del was left to skip by herself. She arrived at the east lane before the others.

"You might as well walk with me," she said to Fritz, "all those boys are coming this way because they want to meet Phillip. We'll walk slowly. Bill can catch up to us if he wants to."

"What's all this?" Benj said as he came out to the plank bridge. "Much too noisy today."

"You'll see soon enough," Del replied. "The ABC boys are all coming to see Phillip. I hope he's around."

"*Hinner naus* [out back]," Benj said as he pointed in the direction of the sawmill, at the same time the group of boys appeared. He took a step back as they went by. Del noticed he looked the boys over very carefully.

"I know you want to see Phillip," Til said to Abe, "but I must say hello to Doll first; you can come with me." He smiled broadly as he headed for her stable with Abe. Til's love for horses, especially Doll, was well-known. Benny and Carl continued walking with Bill. Fritz decided to accompany Bill and the boys.

"The Shultz boys?" Mama spoke as Del entered the porch and announced that all three brothers were there to meet Phillip. Mama was busy watering her potted plants on the deep window seats in the closed porch.

"The boys told you Benny was really eager to come. I suppose they all decided to come," Del said.

"I wonder if they'll stay for a snack. Maybe I better put more food on the table," Mama said. "Fetch some apples, pick the nicer ones. Put them in the fruit bowl on the table."

When Del came back from the cellar, Ori was talking to Mama. "I don't know why the whole school didn't come at the same time. Some said they would come soon. Even Joe said he would come. All the boys want to meet Phillip."

Frank and Archie Howard came into the lane as Del was pumping water. "Is the boy inside?" they asked.

"No. Go back to the sawmill, all the menfolk are there." Del was surprised to see them, as they stayed at the schoolhouse over the lunch break and couldn't have told their parents they would be delayed returning from school.

"I don't see the duck. Is he around?" Archie quickly asked.

"It's safe. He's in his pen," Del said reassuringly.

"Did you hear that?" Del asked Mama as she entered the kitchen. "The Howards came as I was pumping water, they asked if that duck was around somewhere. They never visit here but they knew about that duck. Where is Ori?"

"Right now she is upstairs," Mama replied.

"The Gohos also asked me about that duck. Maybe that's the reason they walk the longer way around instead of taking the short-cut through here to get to school."

"What are you saying about my duck?" Ori asked defiantly as she walked into the kitchen.

"Everyone asks where your duck is as soon as they are in the lane. Stories about your duck must get around," Del announced.

"You blame everything on my Taw-Taw. Those girls never used this lane. Only Gordon did a few times," Ori was quick to say.

"Enough, girls," Mama said in a tone that held a warning to it.

Ori left to take care of her chores.

"I suppose Isaac and Sam are still here. Did they say anything about Lillie and whether she was told about Phillip?" Del asked.

"Sam didn't say and I didn't ask. I suppose she knows. She and Eva will be here tomorrow. If Eva spends enough time here I will ask her to make her cheese custard. It's baking day for me anyway."

"Do you think she'll help at the orchard again?" Del wondered.

"If she wants more apples, yes, maybe. You better change and get your work done," Mama advised.

Del took Carol along to help with her after-school work. Ori arrived carrying her two wooden buckets with metal rims, one stacked inside the other. "Here, Carol, you may take this smaller bucket and help me gather the eggs," Ori instructed Carol.

"Go ahead, Carol, you help with the henhouse work. I can finish this work by myself."

"I picked the rest of the chew cherries today and helped Mama pull winter radishes. How much more must I do?" Carol lamented.

"I think you will have done enough for today after you help Ori. There weren't many chew cherries left to pick. The winter radishes are fast work; I know, I used to do that work. I saw the wood chip basket isn't hanging on the spike in the woodshed. Bill or somebody else is taking care of that tonight. They are all back at the sawmill anyway with all the fellows wanting to meet Phillip."

Father walked towards the house with Phillip hanging onto his arm. He was half carried, just allowing one foot to touch the ground.

"I hope walking will be better before long," Del said.

Father nodded and looked at Phillip. "Jer thinks he can fix a pair of shoes for him. We'll see what he comes up with."

"I can't wait until you have a pair of shoes all your own. Then you can walk like the rest of us. What a big difference that will be for you," Del said to Phillip.

There was no comment from Phillip.

"Sure you can walk," Father said to Phillip, "you only need to tell yourself you can. Come on, you can help with the barn work. Your shoes are good enough as long as you stay in the feed entry area. Tilghman will help you."

"Ollie walked past me still wearing his school clothes. Where are all the other boys?" Del asked her father as he slowly moved with Phillip towards the barn.

"Isaac will drop all the boys off at their homes since he is ready to leave." Father laughed, "The boys didn't have to be asked twice. That car was full. They piled into the back of that Hudson so fast Isaac didn't have time to change his mind. Three of the boys sat in the back and Sam held Benny on his lap in the front seat. The smaller of the Howard boys sat on a lap on the back seat. I don't know if any of them ever rode in a car before. Surely not a Hudson. Isaac was chuckling all the while."

Del walked with her father and Phillip until they entered the feed entry door. Del stopped by the henhouse door to see if Ori was still there.

"Here," Ori said, "you can carry one bucket of eggs."

"I may as well wait and lock everything up, then I'll follow with your bucket of eggs."

The supper conversation was all about the schoolboys' visit. Ollie commented about the way Benny took great interest in Phillip, to the point of actually staring at him. "He introduced himself to Phillip saying, 'I am Benny, I would like to touch you.'" Ollie touched his own face to describe the action.

Father looked pleased. "I think Phillip was happy to see other boys." Father looked at Mama. "Loll, how are we doing on clothes for Phillip?"

"I haven't had time to start on clothes, but I have some materials ready," Mama replied. "Tomorrow, if Eva and Lillie come, I will ask

Lillie if she wouldn't mind working on shirts for Phillip. She is so quick and efficient at sewing, and she will need something to do. I think Oliver is something like her when it comes to needing something to do. We have to keep her busy or she'll work on our nerves just pacing back and forth."

"We'll get *dah yung* [the youngster] all taken care of before long," Father continued. "I don't think Dr. Sam is going to stay away for very long."

"*Geb ihm ebbes stu do* [Give him something to do]," Benj said while nodding towards Phillip.

"I know what," Ori said as she pulled open the knife and fork drawer, "Sit him here. He can put those things away when Ollie has them dried."

Til helped Phillip get there, while Ollie grabbed a chair for him.

"Good idea. Look at that. I believe he is eager to help," Til said cheerfully.

"*Ich gay heem, leig mich uff mei ohr* [I'll go home, lay myself on my ear]. Will be here very early tomorrow," Benj said as he stood up.

"You don't have to be here so early," Father said. "Isaac likes to help with the milking. We won't get started on our project right away."

"*Woodie sedscht besser wisse aus sel, Gute Nacht* [Woodie should better know than that. Good night]."

There was a chorus of good-nights from the children and parents as Benj departed.

"How was the rest of the school day?" Father asked the children.

Bill was slow and deliberate. "I was surprised how everyone was so interested. I think all the others from school will come to see Phillip sometime."

"Oliver, your turn, I bet you can hardly wait, " Father said with a grin.

Ollie literally jumped up to speak. "So many things happened all at once. Raymond said maybe he would come with his father on Saturday or Sunday. He sure would like to see someone who was starving. He saw Black people before but he never talked to one or saw one close enough to touch. He can't believe there are people who would let a person starve. I am glad I don't have to be careful with what I say. It's going to be much easier to talk about anything now."

Father laughed, "I am glad the day went well for you. Your teacher did us a big favor and I think Raymond is a very kind boy. He will grow up to be a fine young man." Father smiled as he pushed his chair back. "I see Carol is half asleep. I think all of us need to turn in."

Ori was first to help Carol to her feet, and they made their way upstairs. The rest followed one by one.

CHAPTER ELEVEN

The Relatives Help on the Farm

Friday morning Del awakened to the sound of the Hudson coming over the plank bridge. She hurried to the window in her parents' bedroom, leaned forward standing on tiptoes with her forearms pressed onto the window seat, and watched the Hudson pull to a stop by the barnbank. She saw her Uncle Sam step down off of the running board. He was a most handsome man, and considerate, patient, and kind. His facial features were perfectly balanced, affording him a distinguished appearance so very different from Isaac, stepping down from the driver's side, who had roughly-cast facial features with heavy protruding cheek bones and deep-set eyes. However, his soft brown eyes sparkled with laughter and gentleness, and his open smile revealed his pleasant personality.

Sam opened the back passenger door and out stepped Lillie in her lilac print dress, a shawl held over her arm. Presently bare-headed, her abundant auburn hair framed her full face nicely. She stood by the machine and waited for Eva to join her from the other side. They placed their folded shawls on the back seat of the Hudson and headed for the barn, walking single file until they reached the feed entry door and disappeared inside.

Del walked back to her bedroom upon hearing her brothers moving about. She really wanted to be around the first time Aunt Lillie would see Phillip, so she hurried to get downstairs. Mama was slicing whole boiled potatoes into the largest fry pan she had as Del entered the kitchen.

"Here," Mama said. "Get the other two fry pans. I will need them later. Then finish these potatoes while I cut onions." Del went on her knees to open the door to the wooden cabinet with the white enameled top and black striped border. She lifted the pans onto the enamel top. "You will have a lot of work this morning. My flour and sugar containers need filling again. Wear a sweater, it's rather cool in the attic. My lard container needs filling as well." Mama continued with her instructions for Del, "You needn't bother with any outside work, just check to make sure it's done."

"How many boys are up?" Del asked.

"Only Tilghman and Oliver. Of course, Tilghman needs to see Doll every morning as soon as he is up. In that he is exactly like my father. He greets his horses before he unlocks the creamery. Tilghman will be back to help William bring Phillip down the stairs." Mama sliced onions while she spoke and Del's eyes began to burn and tear.

Del finished the potatoes, grabbed the flour and sugar crocks, and headed upstairs. She heard Til's voice as he entered the house. "Are they ready to come down?" he was asking Mama as Del approached the attic door, which creaked as it swung open to the inside. "Still didn't oil those hinges.," Del thought to herself. "I must remember to do that sometime." She hurried up the flight of stairs to the attic and began shivering. She carried the filled flour container to the kitchen baking table. Taking the same stairs a second time she could hear the boys helping Phillip on the stairway to the kitchen. She returned with the sugar and grabbed the large brown crock for lard. Upon returning to the kitchen she encountered Bill.

"Good morning, Bill. I heard you were awake. Where is Mama?" Del looked at Bill as he was slow to answer. "She went out for milk."

"You know, I can't wait to see Lillie's face when she comes in."

"She was told, it won't be so bad. You stay with him." Bill looked toward the couch where Phillip was seated, still in his stocking feet.

"Phillip," Del said as she turned to him. "We'll have plenty of company today. You will meet my father's older sister. You already met the others coming today."

Phillip just looked at Del, and if he had any thoughts about meeting more family, he kept them to himself.

Mama stepped into the kitchen. " I told the boys to come in and eat as soon as they could and get ready for school. We have enough help out there. You children eat first. I can clear those dishes. The rest of us will eat later."

Del remarked, "I want to see how Lillie . . . "

"That's enough," Mama said curtly. "She has been told. She knows what to expect."

The boys came in. "Good," Mama said. "Eat, get yourselves ready for school."

"Lillie is letting Doll eat oats cupped in her hands." Til looked especially pleased.

"Better check on Gloria. It's time she gets up. She needs to take care of Carol." Mama motioned for Del to leave the kitchen. "I won't have time to fuss with Carol this morning."

Del ran up the stairs and dashed over to Ori's room. "Oh, I see you are up." Ori was standing in the doorway. "Breakfast is ready. You needn't bother with any outside work. Get dressed for school. Bring Carol down too. Mama won't have time for Carol. Our company is here."

"I heard you up here earlier. You always have to make a lot of noise."

Ori woke up in an irritable mood, which Del accepted as normal for the start of her day. Ori mumbled something as Del headed down the back stairway from her parents' bedroom. The boys and Benj entered as Del returned to the kitchen. Benj immediately walked over to Phillip, sat beside him and put his arm around Phillip's shoulder.

"*Mei bu* [My boy]," Benj said as he hugged Phillip. "Will take you along outside and we'll watch what the men are doing. They'll be busy today."

"You children, eat now, the rest of us will eat later. I will pour a little cocoa for Phillip," Mama looked at Benj.

Benj nodded his head, "*Aah bleibed mit mere* [He stays with me]."

Don't forget my lard crock needs filling too," Mama turned to Del

"I already did that, plus all the other containers!" Del protested.

"You must have run up and down the stairs again." Mama wasn't pleased.

"She hurried because she wanted to be around the first time Aunt Lillie sees Phillip," Ollie said without taking his eyes off of Phillip.

"You have nothing to say. You are as *wunnerfitzich* [inquisitive] as she," Mama chastised Ollie.

Lillie had an exuberant and expressive personality and her outbursts, whether good or bad, were always remembered. Her initial reaction usually resulted in throaty and unsteady utterances. Her double chin would quiver, and her whole body seemed to struggle to control her physical movements. Her arms flew all about. Seeing Phillip would surely trigger a memorable reaction. Aunt Eva was supposed to take care of preparing Lillie to meet Phillip but that was no guarantee as to Lillie's reaction.

The porch door opened. "Yoo hoo, everybody," Lillie said placidly as she looked around the kitchen at all the expectant faces. "Everyone is up early." Without hesitating, Lillie continued. "You needn't worry, Laura. I'm not going to get all excited. Eva told me the whole story. I know my brother would give someone the shirt off his back. After my father died we really had hard times. There were times we had nothing to eat other than hard bread spread with lard. Woodie knows what it's like to go hungry." Her gaze rested on Phillip.

Eva walked by Phillip and sat on a chair at the far end of the kitchen. "He filled out some already since I last saw him."

"How can anyone be thinner than that?" Lillie remarked with shock.

"Rest assured. *Ah waar. Ah gooked ennicher nimmi grunk* [He was. Anyway he no longer looks sick]," Eva stated firmly.

"Believe me, he was in terrible shape when Woodie brought him home," Mama murmured to Lillie.

"I suppose that's why you kept him in the barn," Lillie pondered.

"We had no choice but to quarantine him until we thought he was free of diseases. Well, at any rate, in those first few days he was never alone. Phillip didn't seem to mind the scent of all the hay and straw stored on that floor." Mama chuckled. "He won't suffer from hay fever."

"What can we help you with today?" Eva smiled. "You know Sis needs something to do. I will keep myself useful as well."

"I didn't know what you had in mind. I thought you may want to help your friends at the orchard," Mama said.

"Not this time," Eva replied, "but I do want more apples. My neighbor wants a half bushel more."

Mama nodded. "Friday is baking day for me, so there's plenty to do. We will talk about that after breakfast. Right now lets catch up with the news. How are the Allentown folks?" Mama seemed eager for gossip.

"Sam's boss is doing the best he can. They are completing a row of houses on Tenth Street. Unless he has enough buyers he may not start the next block. Of course, he is willing to repair houses to buy or rent, just so he can continue to keep his workmen. He gives the whole crew equal time. Sam usually has two or three days a week, once in a while less than that. We can't complain, this way everybody earns a little something." Lillie continued with her news. She hadn't finished her recital about her family as Ori and Carol stepped into the kitchen.

"Carol, you are going to be the image of your mother," Lillie stated. "Laura, do you have a picture of yourself at that age for comparison?"

"No. I have none that show the widow's peak. That's what people notice. We'll see when she grows up," Mama replied.

"Will you be around to help me with my crocheting?" Ori asked Eva.

"I expect I will," Eva said with a smile.

"I sure need help again," Ori said glumly.

"Look at those shoes!" Lillie said somewhat rattled, as she looked at the shoes setting beside Phillip. "Where do they come from?"

Mama replied, "I know they don't match. That's the best we have for now. We got the makeshift pair from our old shoe box. My Uncle Jeremiah will take care of shoes for him, even if he has to make a pair. He is working on a decent pair of weekday shoes right now. Then Phillip can run around with the boys."

"That should improve his walking," Eva added.

The boys, dressed in their school clothes, gathered books and homework. Ollie rushed around picking up his scattered paperwork as Benj placed the shoes on the floor in front of Phillip.

"*Cum mit mir. Misse de schuh erscht uff duh* [Come with me. Must the shoes do first]." He lifted Phillip's foot and without another word, Phillip held the shoe tongue firmly in place while Benj did the lacing. "I wouldn't wear those shoes," Ollie said while rushing about.

"You hush Oliver, they're the best we have right now. I think Phillip is happy he has something he can get around in. You could place your schoolwork in your school bag as soon as you finish it. That would make life a lot easier for you," Mama reprimanded Ollie as she gave him an over-the-top-of-her-glasses look.

Lillie stood up and followed the children to the door, to check that all were properly dressed as they left for school. "Wear a sweater or something with a little warmth today. Forecast calls for cooler temperatures and blowing winds later this morning and the rest of the day."

Bill made a motion for Fritz to follow. "Lillie sure looks out for all of us," Bill said as they entered the lane. "Did you see she got a sweater for Phillip before we left?"

Til chuckled, "She means well. Maybe she's a little overbearing with us in the way she fusses with coats and scarves to make sure everyone is warm enough. Father says he can't blame her because she saw enough illness and death as a child."

Walking to school, Del remembered hearing about the hard days from Father and Lillie's childhoods and about three brothers who died at a very young age.

"Mama is pleased. She likes the way Phillip is ready to lend a helping hand," Bill commented.

"He is changing a lot," Ollie said, nodding his head.

"I can't wait for him to talk. To say good morning or ask for something he wants to eat without pointing," Bill said.

"It will come, it will come, Bill. Like Becky says, all we need is patience," Del assured Bill.

"He could tell us how he feels about being here," Ori spoke up.

"To walk without help would be nice. The sooner the better," Bill said. Til nodded his head in agreement.

"Don't blame you boys. I wouldn't want to be bothered with half carrying him along everywhere I go," Ori said.

"Doesn't bother me, Ori," Til said mildly.

Del felt optimistic as she skipped alongside of Fritz. "Did you see how Phillip took Benj's hand this morning? He isn't dragging that foot all the time either, he lifts it off the floor enough so the shoe doesn't always scrape." She turned to the dog. "Did you see that Fritz? He'll soon walk on his own."

"If you wouldn't watch everything so closely, he might do better," Ori criticized.

"That's not true." Del turned to look back at Ori.

"I see Mae is waiting. Go join her," Til advised Ori. Del assumed Til didn't want to hear any more back-and-forth squabbling between his sisters.

The first half-day of class time passed quickly. Mr. Strunk was making up for time spent earlier on non-academic matters.

Del smiled as she entered the kitchen. Sam was seated in the rocking chair. He beckoned to her. "Come here, girl, let me measure you."

He stood up straight and tall, and with an outstretched arm said, "We'll see if you still fit beneath my arm."

Del stood by his side as he said, "Still room for more growth, I won't be doing this many more times. You will soon have to stand alongside so I can measure you from my shoulder."

"You may have to do that with William already," Mama said. "He is beginning to stretch tall."

"What say you to that, young lady?" Sam asked.

"Nothing at all," Del shrugged her shoulders. "Boys usually are taller than girls."

"I don't think he'll be as tall as Tilghman," Sam mused. "Of course Tilghman was always taller than boys his same age. Tilghman has the bone structure of his grandfather. I believe he is going to be broad-shouldered."

Del was surprised at Sam's observation. She never thought about the size of bones, especially her brothers' shoulders. She was ready to ask about Ollie's bone structure when Mama opened the oven door with her cake lifter in hand and reached into the oven. Out came shoo-fly pies, one after another; five in all.

"Now that really smells good," Sam observed.

"Who's sewing?" Ori asked as she looked at fabric pieces laid on the couch.

"Your Aunt Lillie," Mama replied as she put the next items the oven. "She likes to sew and I have a lot that needs to be done. Phillip will need winter clothes and some for right now. I hope you have your duck cooped up." Mama looked to Ori.

"I checked on him. He thought I came to let him out. Where is everybody?"

"Sam, you tell the girls where everybody is," Mama suggested.

"Your father took the truck and headed to town with Phillip. Carol went along too. Phillip stayed in New Jerusalem with your grandfather. Your father came back and decided to go to Hoch's feed mill. Carol went along for a second truck ride. Fritz will always occupy an empty seat. Now Ed and Benj are working on the new body for the truck. I showed them what needs to be done, then came in for a break. It will take a while before they need me. I saw Isaac and Eva leave for the orchard for apples. If they don't come back, I won't have a way home. How do you like that? Bet you didn't know I could tell you that much," Sam laughed.

"They'll be back," Mama assured Sam. "But nevertheless we'd find room for you and Lillie."

"Yes, and I know where," Sam teased. "The same place you keep my wife's cousin."

"Clint refuses anything better than the barn," Mama responded with a smile.

Everyone was laughing as Lillie opened the stairs door, showing nearly-completed bib overalls she altered. She said, "I thought bib overalls that fit would help him feel welcome. I need to measure for length before I hem these. Do you have buttons for a shirt? And material for one pocket. Where is he? I also need to measure him for proper sleeve length."

"All that! Take a break and rest awhile," Mama said. "I have both colored and white button jars in the clothes closet in my bedroom, on the floor at the front end."

Del saw the brown plaid material that she had taken from the heavy bureau drawer was now a shirt. Lillie and Mama discussed finishing another shirt. Lillie asked if Mama had odds and ends of material she could use for facing on cuffs and collar, maybe even the button bands. Nothing went to waste, and Mama routinely used different material for hidden parts of clothing.

"Adelaide, you run upstairs and fetch that plain blue flannel," Mama commanded. Turning to Lillie, she continued, "That piece isn't big enough to make anything else. It should do for facing."

Del returned with the material and Lillie headed upstairs again.

"Stay awhile," Mama repeated. "The others will soon be here for something to eat. "What you have already done in one morning would take me the whole day."

"The trick is to sit down and not be interrupted," Lillie said.

"That's when things are done quickly. I sure appreciate all you are doing." Mama said gratefully.

"Did you inspect everything out there?" Sam said as the boys came in for the midday meal. "Come here, William. I have already measured Adelaide. Now its your turn."

Bill obliged. "Sure enough," Sam exclaimed. "You will have to stand alongside of me. Laura, you cut back on his food until Adelaide catches up." Sam chuckled as he again seated himself.

"Sit down and eat," Mama said to the children. "Then get yourselves back to school. The shoo-fly pie is still warm. Cut one if you like."

"I like when it's warm," Til said.

"Me too!" Ollie added, as the pie was placed on the table.

Mama asked if anything more was said about Phillip at school; the children reported they heard nothing.

The adult conversation turned to future plans. Mama asked, "Have you thought about Thanksgiving this year? We hope to get all the corn taken care of and perhaps butcher a pig or two before then. Can we count on all your family this year?"

Sam nodded, "We are the usual thirteen in all."

Laura, you have one more already," Lillie cautioned. "If this gets to be too many for you, just say so. Heavens to Betsy, how are we going to seat everybody? You can depend on the same things we bring every year. I will make my two large crocks of potato filling ready to stick in the oven."

"Lets go," Til announced to the children.

"Yes, it's time you head back," Mama agreed.

Bill whistled for Fritz once they were outside. "You know Fritz isn't here. He went along to Hoch's feed mill," Til reminded Bill.

"You're right," Bill said sheepishly, "Fritz will also go in hiding when all of Lillie's grandchildren come. Those six children are the noisiest bunch you ever heard."

Til smiled. "I know we have to keep them off the threshold floor. Father is always concerned about that. We prop those doors so they can't get inside. They hold their noses just walking by the cattle pen."

"Pigsty is worse," Del added, they all agreed. Nothing smelled worse than the pigpen on a hot day.

The return home at the end of the school day was routine. Fritz was waiting. A pile of wood was split. Benj, Phillip, and Sam were seated under the grape arbor by the pump.

"Is the truck body all finished?" Bill asked as he kept Fritz by his side.

"Go take a look. It's parked on the other side of the barnbridge," Sam answered. "Mighty fine looking body, if I say so myself. It's exactly what your father needs to haul calves to the abattoir in the city. Still needs to be painted. Ed says he will take care of that."

Bill and Del turned their heads and looked at each other upon hearing the news of how the truck would be used.

"I believe I let the cat out of the bag," Sam said apologetically.

"*Sez aulrecht. Es hut mich gewunnert os sie net davor gfrogt hen* [It's alright. It had me wondering that they had not asked before]," Benj said with a wave of his hand.

"You probably wouldn't say anything, even if we did ask," Bill quickly replied.

"*Sel maagscht waahr sei* [That may be true]," Benj chuckled.

"I must tell Woodie I didn't mean to spoil his surprise. I think you two are the first to know." Sam looked at Benj, who nodded.

"Now you have a secret to keep," Sam said conspiratorially.

The twins returned to the farmhouse, where the other children were assembled.

"You have less work," Mama said as she looked at the boys. "Lillie wants to try her hand at milking. The men will be doing some barn work too. Help out where needed."

Sam shook his head. "I don't think my wife will have enough energy to finish one cow. You better not dismiss the boys too soon."

"She milked before," Bill said, recalling a previous milking time.

"Yes, William, but its been awhile. She grew up on a farm and used to do lots of milking. Same as your Father; he was hired out to work on a neighbor's farm."

"Did you live on a farm?" Del asked Sam.

"Sure did, Adelaide. When you are as many boys as we were in one family and only one farm to hand down, that means we had to find other means to make a living. I learned carpentering from my grandfather."

Ori came inside. "You were out there awhile. Is my wife still milking?" Sam asked.

Ori shrugged, "Don't know. I stayed in the feedhouse and cleaned the eggs there. I could talk to my precious Taw-Taw for awhile. Poor

Taw-Taw is cooped all that time when we are cooking apple butter, husking corn, or butchering."

Lillie stepped in the door. "How did it go?" Sam asked.

Lillie slowly shook her head and sighed, "My fingers aren't as flexible as they used to be. I never realized stiffness in my hands before this, but I got it done. For me it was always easier than some of the other farm work. It's cleaner than forking hay. I didn't like getting itchy all over from hay dirt."

Del left to see if all her evening chores had been completed. They were, so she checked all the doors and made sure they were closed and secured for the night. She returned, washed her hands, and helped Mama place additional boards in the table.

"You expect the doctor tomorrow?" asked Lillie.

"Probably," Mama replied. "He'll want to see Sallie's arm. He also needs to check Phillip's arm, because his vaccination didn't grow[6]."

Suppertime was a typical Pennsylvania Dutch meal of dried green beans and ham in thickened ham broth. It wasn't one of Father's favorite meals, but the guests and children enjoyed it. Benj was seated next to Phillip and took complete charge of placing food on his plate. The guests noted how comfortably the two interacted with each other. Benj looked at them and said, *"Des is mei kindt* [This is my child]."

"I can tell," Eva smiled, and Isaac nodded in agreement, saying, "No doubt about that."

"Maybe the person he most trusts is an elderly man," Lillie pondered.

"That's the way it is since he is here. He likes Billy Henry too," Father said.

"Sett net soo sigh, en alda mann widder aafange fa eens uff tsu bringa [Should not so be, an older man again starting to bring up one]," Benj said. "It makes life worth living again."

Father mentioned that Grandfather was going to retire. That meant no more Philly trips. "I plan to start a hauling business for our local

6 The smallpox vaccine of the time created a pustule at the injection site that could grow to about the size of a dime before healing and scarring the skin.

farmers. I'll take their produce and needed items to and from Reading," he announced.

Everyone was excited about this idea.

"How can you make deliveries both ways?" Til asked.

"I hope to collect calves and livestock to deliver to the abattoir," Father answered. "After that I will hose off my truck body and pick up items local merchants and neighbors have on order for pick-up; whatever else they need or want, I will find for them. There is a need to receive goods from the city on a regular basis. I will be making the trip at least once a week. I will have place for two people to ride along and attend to their business in the city. What do you children have to say to that?"

"Ya have something to say. Out with it," Benj said looking at Del.

"But if you don't go to Philadelphia, how will we ever find out if Phillip has relatives there?" Del asked as all eyes turned to Phillip.

Father nodded. "I understand your concern. The market people in Philly know how to get in touch with me if they receive any inquiries."

Before Father could finish Benj chimed in, "*Bis sella tzeit is ah ol mei* [By that time is he all mine]."

"That's all one really needs is somebody to care. Phillip knows in Benj he has a good buddy," Isaac acknowledged. " If Phillip's family is looking for him, they'll find him well taken care of here."

Everyone agreed with Isaac's assessment. Talk continued about the possibilities of Father's new business ideas as the adults carried coffee to the parlor while the children were left with the clean up.

CHAPTER TWELVE

A Civil War History Lesson

Awakening to winds rumbling on the tin roof overhead, Del thought, "Its Saturday, no school today." The bedroom was cool and damp. Del looked down on the garden from her window. Sure enough, rain fell during the night, as the garden lay wet with water setting between emptied rows—and she slept through it all. She remembered that Dr. Schlicher was expected this day.

Ori walked by her bedroom. "Goodness, you are up early," Del said. "You want to be here when the doctor arrives."

"I don't care if he is coming," Ori answered.

"One can guess that much."

"There you go mumbling to yourself again, I don't hear the half of what you are saying," Ori said as she moved on.

Del entered the kitchen and realized she was the one who was later than usual.

"Ya must have slept pretty good." Benj said, while rocking back and forth.

"I did. Never heard when all the company left last night. Sometimes I hear the machine leave. Didn't hear the rain either. Where are my brothers?"

Benj replied, "*De buwe sin imm scheier* [The boys are in the barn]. I stayed until they were finished. *Im hoidenn* [in the hayloft] I watched from the *dreschdenn* [threshing floor] *ossez ken dummheadea gebt* [that no foolishness happens]."

Mama came in, her milk bonnet in hand, which usually was kept in the milkhouse. Becky followed her into the house.

"I have the coffee pot setting aside to stay warm. Should be just right to drink," Mama said as she tossed her bonnet on a chair in the closed porch. "Would you like coffee?" Mama asked.

"Not this morning," Becky replied. "I know Dr. Sam will soon be here. His red machine entered Bieber Creek Road as I was crossing the street."

"You can see that from your place?" Del interrupted.

"Now Del, think about it. I can look out any window on the lower side of my house and see anything that comes up the pike. I'm close to the crest of the hill. I sometimes watch for his machine. I happened to be outside this morning, I heard and saw his flash of lightning turn onto the road below me."

"Woodie and the boys are on their way in," Mama said. "Gloria must put her duck in his coop or in the feedhouse," Mama spoke in definitive terms.

"Yes," Del said as she recalled the doctor's last visit. "I wonder if Dr. Sam discovered Taw-Taw was on the roof of his machine the last time he was here and Ori couldn't reach her duck."

"What!?" Becky exclaimed.

"That isn't the worst. Taw-Taw may have left a mark up there. Ori won't admit to anything but Ollie saw it happen from his bedroom window. He rushed down the stairs and past us like he wasn't interested in the doctor's examination of Phillip to help Ori get Taw-Taw off the car roof."

"Oliver did come down the steps like a house on fire," Becky remembered.

"He hurried to help Ori," Del confirmed as Mama, Becky and Benj laughed. Becky reached for her hankie and dried her eyes.

"Ori was angry when she heard Ollie tell us all about it," Del spoke softly.

"Could have been much worse. I suppose Gloria will never tell anyone what really happened," Mama concluded. "Good that duck didn't leave anything there that Gloria needed to wash off."

"Oh no!" Becky laughed so hard her belly shook. "I can picture it all. Maybe that duck taught her a lesson." Becky's robust laughter gradually reduced to a giggle. "I'm not bothered or fearful of that duck, because I have far too much skirt flowing around my legs, so he can do me no harm." Becky, true to form, turned serious. "I didn't see your boy for a whole week now," she said calmly.

Benj just beamed as Mama started talking. "He's gotten used to the name Phillip. He's learned to eat more slowly and help himself, and he has adopted some of our ways, like washing hands before we eat. He was taken care of sometime in his life and properly taught. William says there is nothing like watching him get under the covers and tucking them tight around his neck, which isn't surprising considering what he went through. I hope we can handle any problems," Mama paused, "as they come along."

Benj nodded his head.

"You saved a life. Nothing more important than that," Becky said firmly. "Dr. Sam would agree. We discussed it some. And we know he has a vaccination mark."

"Yes, at least we think its one," Mama agreed.

"He will be vaccinated this morning," Becky spoke with certainty. Then he'll have the paper of proof for school. It surely won't grow if the mark we see is good.

"The doctor sees Sallie during the week?" Mama questioned.

"*Freih mittwoch* [Early midweek]."

"Not every day? I heard Dr. Schlicher came every day," Mama questioned.

"*Net recht. Yuscht tzway mols de woch* [Not right. Just two times a week]," Becky corrected her.

The door opened and in stepped Ori and Ollie along with Bill and Fritz.

"The doctor is on his way. I could see Edgar walk toward his machine when I was standing at the top of the barnbridge," Bill informed the group.

"Everyone is coming in. Teacher is out with Father right now. He'll pick his milk up after he sees Ernie. Father said it would be waiting for him in the milkhouse. He paid it already," Ollie spoke excitedly. "He's wearing high buckled galoshes, his pants tucked inside and carrying a big black umbrella. He never comes to school like that."

"He is there long before you get to school, so you don't see him dressed for all kinds of weather," Mama said.

"Father told him he could stop in on his way back and find out what else we have learned," Ollie stopped abruptly.

"Well . . ." Mama waited, "Is he going to do that?"

"Don't know. He didn't say," Ollie said slowly.

"It would be better for him to stop here before he sees Ernest," Mama concluded. "One time he visited a family that had a case of scarlatina before he stopped here and my baby picked up the illness. He apologized for that and paid for the doctor."

Del was about to ask which of them had scarlatina when the door opened. Til led, Phillip following closely while having a firm grip on Til's extended elbow. He moved carefully, sliding his left foot on the floor surface. Once far enough into the kitchen, Phillip shyly moved himself by holding onto chair backs and proceeded to seat himself next to Benj.

"*Mei bu* [My boy]," Benj boasted proudly.

Becky sat erect as her eyes moved from Benj to Mama, then back to Benj and then Phillip. "*Kann des schier net glaawe. Des isz ennanner kal. De shue net ausgewore. Wem sie shue sin sie? Des kindt laafed glae bissel* [I can't hardly believe this. This is another person. The shoes aren't worn out. Whose shoes are they? This child walks a little]."

"Jer fixed these for the time being, they come from our shoe collection."

"I wish he would lift that foot a little more. *Ah muss mit mache* [He must get along]," Mama sounded hopeful.

"Those shoes would look worse if I didn't lift him across the wet spots. He hops most of the way," Til explained with a smile.

"He doesn't look the same. I expected change. But this, goodness gracious! *Scheer net glavve* [Hardly not believe]." Becky was impressed.

"How is Sallie doing?" Mama sought to change the conversation.

"I think just fine, considering the wound. It is healing nicely now, and she has some movement. Still black and blue from top to bottom, and quite painful. The neighbors are good to her. Maggie Schwoyer and Elda Mutter are speaking again and each takes turns helping out. That rift is healed, thank goodness."

"Yes indeed, something good came out of this. No word of a guilty party?" Mama asked.

"No . . ." Becky thought a moment. "I think Martin has suspicions, but he doesn't say anything."

All became quiet as the sound of a motor came within hearing. Del walked to the window in the closed porch. Father stood by as the machine came to a stop. She saw Dr. Sam step down off the running board. He stood there momentarily as he waited for Edgar to close the door on the other side and walk around the motorcar to match strides with Dr. Schlicher. Both looked around briefly and proceeded toward the house. Dr. Sam followed his usual procedure, laying his lit cigar on the outside window ledge. He turned back, held his hands under the spout while Father pumped water. Dr. Sam shook them dry. Edgar Losch followed the doctor's ritual, spoke briefly to Father and followed. Del returned to her place in the kitchen. Fritz left his place under the table by Bill's feet and moved over to the couch where Benj and Phillip were seated.

"It's alright, Fritz, no bodyguard needed," Bill said as Benj touched the dog's head lightly.

"So. . . . they call you Phillip." Dr. Sam stood back, and looked straight at the little boy. He lifted his black leather medicine case and carefully placed it on the deep window seat. Edgar Losch stood by the sink alongside Father. A long moment passed. "Rebecca Funk, what do you think?" Dr. Sam asked.

"Well, if there were other Black boys in the area, I'd say they switched boys."

Dr. Schlicher pushed his hat back and turned to look at Edgar. "Sure would be nice if your son could recover as quickly. Your son's healing is a slower process, but we will get there."

"That's good to hear. I go along with Becky. Looks like a switch was made." Edgar agreed. "Didn't see him since that first time. I shouldn't step in this house *aver ess wunnerfitz bloughed mich* [but my inquisitiveness bothered me]."

"No need to be concerned about Phillip's health. He was just plain neglected and undernourished," Becky added.

"I saw what I wanted to see. I will go home," Edgar said as he walked out the kitchen. "Need to tell the Missus about this boy."

"Stand up, Phillip." Dr. Sam made motion with both hands for Phillip to stand. He was slow to respond but did manage to stand up. Dr. Sam grabbed a chair and seated himself in front of Phillip; he looked him over carefully, then he bent down on one knee and pushed Phillip's left foot correctly and solidly on the floor. "I will hold this foot. You lift it for me." No effort was made. "Someone come here and show him what I want him to do."

Ollie was right there, happy to volunteer.

Dr. Sam did the same to Ollie. "Pick up your foot." Ollie struggled a bit, but did so with some release of pressure.

"Good, Oliver. Fair amount of strength for a boy your age." Ollie was pleased.

"Alright Phillip, we'll try it again. Now, lift your foot!"

Phillip's face showed confusion and some distress as Dr. Sam released some pressure.

"Come now, see if you are as strong as Oliver. That's good, bring your heel up." Dr. Sam tapped on his heel. "Wiggle if you must."

Benj had his hands ready to support Phillip.

"Bring your foot up." Phillip was trying. There was movement as he brought the heel up a bit.

"I knew you could do it. Let's take those shoes off. Are they a good fit?" Dr. Sam looked at Mama.

"It's not the best fit. But they won't hurt his feet. He has enough room in each shoe," Mama explained.

"Let's try it again, this time without the shoes," the doctor ordered. Benj helped Phillip take his shoes off.

Dr. Sam proceeded to pull the socks off. He compared both feet as he held them side by side.

"You say he ran away that first night you brought him home, Woodie?"

"Sure did," Father confirmed.

The doctor used his hands to rub and knead and turn one foot every other which way, and then the other. He held the two feet side-by-side again and pronounced his diagnosis. "Good news. One foot is like the other. Do you understand me?"

He looked directly at Phillip while shaking his forefinger. "You have two good feet. If you can walk on one foot you can walk on the other. You must have gained, hmm. . . . How many pounds, Becky?"

"If I didn't know better I would say five, six pounds for sure. Ten pounds is more than a child should gain in so short a time. The gaunt look is all but gone, but I still see hollows in the neck area. *Doht engel nimmi doh. Ah hut lewe* [The Angel of Death is no longer here. He has life]," Becky said quietly.

The doctor eyed Phillip carefully. "I believe he'll grow tall. He has good bone structure. The ribs need covering. All in good time." He turned and asked the children to leave.

Mama just waved her hands saying, "Go."

The children knew what that meant and scattered in different directions. Til, of course, headed outdoors, followed by Bill. Ori went upstairs, it was past time to get Carol up. Del found things to do in the parlor. Ollie followed Del into the side room and sat on a chair he pulled close to the kitchen entrance. He wanted to make sure he could hear sounds that came from the far end of the kitchen. "You're not going to hear much," Del told him.

"I'll sit here anyway."

"Suit yourself."

"Breakfast will be real late."

"You'll survive Ollie. I'm hungry too. You should have joined your brothers."

Ollie strained to listen for a moment, and then sighed, "I think I will."

Del took her shoes off and stretched out on the davenport. She rested briefly but then decided to run upstairs, taking the back stairway. She grabbed her library book to do some serious reading. It would soon be time to return the book and she hadn't really gotten around to finishing it. Though she started several times, too many other things kept her from concentrating. This time she wanted to give a report on a book she had never heard presented by another student. A full hour passed and it was a little past nine when Del looked at the large shiny alarm clock on her mother's bureau. She heard noises downstairs that told her people were moving about. She placed a marker in her book and felt satisfied with the chapter she read. "I think its safe to go down, I'll check for sure," she said to Ori as she moved to the window and glanced down. "Yep, Dr. Sam is helping Becky into his machine."

"I'm glad," Ori said. "I'm tired of waiting."

"I'm hungry," Carol said.

The girls headed for the downstairs. The boys also returned to the house.

"Finish setting the table, please," Mama said as Del entered the kitchen. "I'll take time to make a big breakfast. We'll eat fruit and cottage cheese as a snack at dinnertime. And some cut pastries as well. That should hold us until suppertime. The men will be busy with outside work."

Del looked to see if Phillip had gotten a vaccination. His long sleeves covered his arms. "Was he vaccinated and which arm has the patch?"

"Phillip may tell you which arm you should not touch."

"Where did the doctor vaccinate you?" Del looked at Phillip.

Phillip made no comment. He turned his head slightly to his upper left arm.

"I take it we are not to touch your left arm. Is that right?"

After a long moment Phillip looked to his upper left arm once more.

"You can do better than that," Mama said to Phillip. Turning to the other children she said, "Don't grab his left arm."

"Is the doctor coming next Saturday again?" Ollie asked as Mama was breaking eggs into a large dish for scrambling. Thin slices of ham filled the large oval baking pan that was placed in the oven while large fry pans contained scrambled eggs. Ollie displayed his impatience, breathing heavily as he waited for an answer.

Mama finally spoke. "Not likely, unless something turns up. Dr. Sam was satisfied with things the way they are progressing."

"*Sez awwe ruhich* [It's really quiet]. Nothing ya twins have to say?" Benj asked.

Bill and Del looked at each other. Del thought Bill was thinking the same as she.

Del burst out "What did the doctor think? How long before we know if he was or wasn't vaccinated before?"

"There, I knew questions would come," Mama said.

"You might as well answer them for her. She won't give up. She'll ask again," Ori said sarcastically.

Mama just shook her head in annoyance. "You can take your seats and butter bread for yourselves; it won't be long until the eggs will be ready. I am not going to take time to make toast, so don't ask. It's late enough."

The boys took their seats on the bench. Carol pushed a chair closer to the table and seated herself. Benj patiently remained seated on the rocking chair, waiting for Phillip to make a move.

"You didn't answer my question," Del reminded Mama and Benj.

"Yer father or yer mother may tell ya what is what," Benj said as Father entered from the closed porch. He had gone to his desk where he kept a log of daily expenses and activities.

Mama looked at Father and he responded, "Table prayer first."

Heads were bowed and thanks were offered.

"Yes, Phillip got a new vaccination. You already know that Dr. Sam thinks the scar we found is from a previous vaccination. We'll know for sure before long. If it grows, then he didn't have one before. If not, then we know he's had it. Becky will let the doctor know what happens, so he doesn't have to stop here for awhile."

"He might stop before then, just fer cake or pie. Yer mama always has something on hand. Funny cakes went along with Becky and Dr. Sam," Benj mentioned.

"I made that batch only yesterday and already we are down to two."

"No wonder it took so long for us to eat," Ori said grumpily.

"All the eating done around here is what keeps me poor," Father added with a smile

"*Nay gor net, des isz mich un ol de onner leit oss du fiedersch sin schuldich* (No surely not, this is me and all the other people you feed are at fault]," Benj said.

"Woodie is good to people. He grew up poor. He had relatives who had enough but made no attempt to help his widowed mother. As long as we can, we freely give," Mama said.

Father nodded. "Levi and Martha treated me alright when I boarded with them, more than they needed to. It's just the Christian way to treat people," Father added.

A new routine was getting established after each meal. Phillip collected used dishes and stacked them on the table. It was something he could do leaning against the table for support. He looked happy to be helping. Del and Ollie carried the stacked dishes to the sink to wash them. Benj told Phillip to dry the dishes and gave him a dishtowel. Benj helped to seat Phillip on the wood chest for that task. Phillip dried the smaller, unbreakable pieces and set the dried pieces aside on the white baking table.

"That's alright, ya can dry and set them here. *Mei hond isz tsu schidlich fa es gscharr weg tsu do* [My hand is too shaky to put the dishes away]."

"*Huck dich* [Seat yourselves]. Gloria has time to put them away," Mama ordered.

The sound of a motorcar was heard.

"I think we have company," Ori said.

"I know we have company—that horn is Isaac's Hudson," Ollie said as the Hudson was coming to a stop.

"I can see the Hudson now!" Ollie stretched his body to look beyond the kitchen door and through the double windows in the porch.

"You finish the dishes before you go anywhere," Mama warned Ollie. "Isaac said he might come today. We'll see if Sam came along to put finishing touches on the truck body."

"If Ed sees them come, bet he will be here too. He said he had some leftover green paint he would bring along to paint the new woodwork," Ollie stated.

"Oliver, where did you hear that?" Mama asked.

"Last time he was here. He helped to chop corn and shock it. He left his chopper here. Father wants to chop more corn today, if it doesn't rain. Ed said he would come in today," Ollie explained.

"A couple of men can chop a lot of corn," Mama said as Til returned to see if Phillip was ready to go out. "Isaac is here and Sam too," Til said.

"You take Phillip along. He can sit in the truck if he tires. Adelaide and I will finish the work here."

Ollie was happy to hear that. He replaced a dish he had already picked up to dry. "Remember, if you are hungry mid-afternoon, come in for some fruit. You boys take the wagon Adelaide always uses for her work and seat Phillip on that. Bring pumpkins along in, the ones that are easy to get. Be careful with Phillip, no rough-housing!"

"Do you think they'll remember all that?" Del asked as she watched the boys leave.

Mama smiled, "The men will be there to watch. Pumpkins are plentiful this year. We'll take the nicest ones to sell at the creamery Monday morning. My father sold all the extras we had last year," Mama stated.

"*Ich geh mit. Ich conn acht gewwe* [I'll go along. I can give care]," Benj offered.

As soon as the girls finished the dishes, Ori told Carol to go along with her to the henhouse.

"Put a warm sweater on her," Mama ordered.

"I'm going to see if Taw-Taw has enough water."

"You may as well collect the eggs. Your father and Ed cleaned the henhouse floor and placed clean straw in the feedhouse for you. Spread it evenly across the cement floor." Mama also told Ori to clean the water hoppers and metal feeding troughs, plus check the laying boxes and add straw where needed. "That will keep you busy for a while. Good time to show Carol the extras that come along every few weeks. Have her help you where she can with the extra work. Don't let your duck roam," Mama emphasized.

"I know that much, you don't have to tell me," Ori retorted.

Del grabbed her weekday sweater and decided to walk to the sawmill to see the changes to the truck body. She wore her ankle-high rubbers over her shoes to protect them from the mud. She met Bill and Ollie pulling her flat wagon loaded with pumpkins. "Where did you leave Phillip?" she asked as she walked by.

"He is sitting with Benj at the sawmill."

"Leave my wagon right here, I will take those pumpkins to the feedhouse after I look at the new truck body."

"Unload the wagon and bring it back. We'll need it for Phillip," Bill called to her as they trotted off.

Del continued until she spotted parts of the original truck body lying by the side of the truck, pushed partly under the sawmill roof. She thought one piece could be a shelter for baby chicks. She wondered what Father was going to do with it. She studied the new body on the truck. The sides were rebuilt much higher and there was a roof now. The new body was fully enclosed with fencing wire.

Bill joined Del at the sawmill. "I'm going to walk back as far as the big rock. Are you coming along?" Del asked.

"I will as far as the cornfield. I want to see what the men are doing. Uncles Isaac and Sam must be there since they aren't working on the truck. It's been a while since I walked to the rock myself. It's not a clear day. We won't be able to see far in all directions. Not into *Ledde Dahl* [Clay Valley]." Bill said.

Del was amused that Bill used the Dutch name for the area.

"I like the view from the big boulder. I can see the New Jerusalem church from there on a dreary day. If it weren't for the forest behind the Printz home, I think we could see far and wide full circle," Del commented. They turned as they heard voices and walked along a stone fence surrounding a cornfield.

Benj and Phillip had moved to the falter and were seated on a low wagon that had been lifted and stabilized on rocks for both to sit comfortably and watch the chopping of corn stalks. The men gathered cut stalks and bundled them with binder twine, then collected those bundles and stacked them in an upright position to form a shock of corn to dry. Completed shocks dotted the field. Fritz was romping to and fro and it was easy to spot all the pumpkins in the field as the stalks were cleared.

She neared the huge boulder with its unusual high rounded dome, a smaller rock pushed hard against the large one, leaving a space where gritty dry mold and small varied-colored granules gathered loosely in a crevice deep enough to allow seeds to sprout there. Fine granules covered the rock and looked like they could roll down on the north side, though that was not possible. Del stood there and looked at the abandoned house and barn at the Printz farm. She saw the footpath behind the rock where it met the Pioneer Trail turning onto Bieber Creek Road, and then continued to the village of Stony Point. It was this same trail that the Gohos could use as a shortcut past her home to get to Funk's School.

"Good you are back," Mama said. "Where were you so long?"

"I walked to the big rock and looked all around. Then I watched the fellows in the cornfield pick pumpkins that were easy to get. I got three others along the stone fence. I brought them along in with those Bill and Ollie picked up earlier. They are in front of the feedhouse. I took the wagon back for Benj."

"You may walk back there again. I put some apples and a few pears in one of the egg buckets. Take this out to the men. Ask if they want something more substantial. Find out if Sam and Isaac are staying for supper. I doubt it since it's Saturday. However if they are staying to help with the evening chores, they may as well eat before heading home."

Before Del was underway Til stuck his head in the door. "How many pumpkins do you want?"

"Not any," Mama said. " I have all I need for now."

Del grabbed her rubber footwear and ran after Til. "Do you want any fruit? I have apples or pears."

Til grabbed two apples and put one in his coat pocket. That was probably intended for Doll.

Benj and Phillip were in the lane. Phillip sat on Del's small wagon. Del held her bucket toward them. Phillip reached in and grabbed a pear. Benj waved his hand, indicating he didn't want any. He looked at Phillip and then grabbed an apple for Phillip as well. Del continued her walk to the area where the men were working. She approached Isaac, "Have some fruit. Are you and Sam staying for supper?" Del asked.

"No, not today. We will be going home very shortly. We want to get home before dark," Isaac replied.

"Remember to take pumpkins along for yourselves. There are plenty here this year. Take some along for your relatives too. "

Isaac helped himself to fruit. Del moved on to her father and Bill. "Here is fruit for you." Bill took a pear and laid an apple by some chopped stalks.

Father smiled as he also took an apple. "Growing boys need to eat," he said as he watched Bill move back to the corn stalks.

"How long will you stay out here?" Del asked her father.

"We'll be in to start our barn work shortly. Folks may have plans for this evening. Besides, I feel a fine drizzle now and then. You had better get yourself, Benj, and Phillip into the dry. Have them go along in with you."

"I will do that right now." Del returned to Benj and Phillip. "Father says you two should go inside. It's getting too damp to be outside."

"Will soon be where it is warmer," Benj said. "*Feichdichkait isz net gute fa en alda mann's gnoche* [Dampness isn't good for an old man's bones]."

Del, Benj and Phillip returned to the house. "The men are not staying for supper. They want to get home. I told them they can take extra pumpkins," Del reported to Mama.

"Good thing. There are plenty of neck pumpkins[7] out there, more than I can use.

"Funny, some years we just have enough to go around and the next year we have so many we don't know where to go with them all," Del remarked.

"It depends on the rain and sunshine at the right times." Mama said.

Sunday was spent quietly. The children attended Sunday school; Father drove them there and picked them up because it was raining. The younger children had to sit on their older siblings laps for the short drive. Sunday was a day with only the necessary everyday barn work done to feed and care for the animals. It was a restful day. Except for Benj, no visitors or neighbors made an appearance. Mama did a bit of hand mending and paged through the Montgomery Ward and Sears Roebuck catalogs. Father sat at his rolltop desk making note of income and expenses for the past week and updated his tax collector books.

Monday morning turned out to be a different story. The heavy outside door was closed when the Heydt children arrived at school. Em was waiting outside for Del with a worried and angry look on her face. Mae, Ori, Del's brothers and the Shulz boys were all dumbfounded as they stood outside the school. No one could imagine why the door was closed on a school day.

"Why did you take that colored boy to Sunday school and church?" Em whispered in Del's ear.

"Phillip stayed at home. We didn't have church service, only Sunday school because our Pastor only comes every other Sunday," Del whispered, and then asked, "Why isn't anyone playing outside?"

"Teacher is angry," she whispered. "You took that colored boy to church! For heaven's sake why?"

"I told you, Em, we didn't have church, only Sunday school and Phillip didn't go with us!"

"You took him to church. That's what! Don't tell me different."

---

7 Similar to a butternut squash, but with a longer, curved "neck." Used for pumpkin pie filling.

"For the last time, Em. I tell you, Phillip never went along with us. He doesn't have Sunday clothes yet."

"He has clothes, you said so. You took him along to church," Em insisted.

"None that are suitable for church. You are saying things that aren't so," Del argued.

Em pulled Del close as the door opened and Mr. Strunk bid them a good morning; they entered a quiet room with earlier arrivals already seated. Del and the others quietly took their seats.

Mr. Strunk stood by the door as he counted those gathered inside. The most unusual situation Del ever encountered was right before her eyes. All the other students, every last one, were seated with heads bowed to open books. The room was so quiet Del could hear the turning of a single page. She couldn't understand why Em had been outside when her brother Joe was seated inside.

Mr. Strunk cleared his throat and said, "We need to settle something here and now. I will ring the bell in a few minutes and school will be in session. First I want to ask the Heydt children about what happened at church yesterday."

Dumbfounded, Del and her siblings looked at each other. Del decided to speak. "We didn't have church, only Sunday school. Phillip stayed at home."

Mr. Strunk's face turned red. "Tilghman, is this true?"

"Yes, its true. Phillip hasn't been anywhere but our place and the creamery."

"Yes, yes, I should have known better. I know when you have church—it's opposite from my Sunday schedule," the teacher said, half to himself.

Mr. Strunk walked to the vestibule and rang the bell. "School is now in session," he announced. "Please rise and take your neighbor's hand on each side of you and say good morning before we recite the Pledge of Allegiance in unison. Remain standing for one song this morning: 'My Country tis of Thee.' You will all sing." Mr. Strunk then opened the Bible and read a selected portion pf scripture. "You all know the

Ten Commandments." He read them slowly, then said, "I don't want to hear falsehoods or lies from any one of you. I will only hear decent language from all. We will respect all people. I remind you, all people!" Mr. Strunk looked around the classroom, gently closed the Bible and laid it aside. "We will pray the Lord's prayer, heads bowed and eyes closed."

Del wondered what this was all about.

"Before we get started I have history questions for you. Write them down. One. Why did we have the Civil War? Two. Where did it take place? Three. What changed after that war?" Mr. Strunk paced around the room, observing all the children. "You will read Civil War history until you can answer these questions. We will now follow our regular morning session." Mr. Strunk spoke firmly.

Del glanced over the students; there was more good behavior that morning than any time she ever experienced. Even at recess time play was subdued, not nearly the boisterous yelling and screaming as usual. When the second period ended children going home for dinner departed quietly. Del wondered what everyone was thinking as they walked the lane.

Fritz greeted the twins eagerly as they met. Del and Bill talked about the unusual start of the school day, baffled about where Em heard that false story and why she believed it as they walked in the lane with Fritz.

"Good boy Fritz, you always stay the same," Bill said as he stroked the dog's head gently. "I wonder what happened for Teacher to become so upset."

"Lies, that's what. What else was said this morning, I don't know. Em insisted we took Phillip to church." Del was puzzled. "I told her that wasn't true. She didn't believe me."

"Someone lied about Phillip and our teacher thought it was true," Bill said slowly.

Benj, standing in the woodshed, greeted them as they walked over the plank bridge.

"How was the morning?"

"Oh, alright," Bill said very slowly.

"*Ich denk net* [I think not]," Benj said knowingly.

"Who told you anything different?" Del inquired.

"Del, ya is not the only two coming home at noontime."

"What did Til or Ollie say?" Bill asked.

"*Da maeschter isz base* [The teacher is angry]."

Bill shrugged his shoulders. "Teacher was different. I think he scared some students. Everyone was quiet this morning," Bill answered as they headed into the house.

Phillip was not in the kitchen with Mama. Del asked where he might be.

"He and Carol are with Father on the truck, they went to the bank."

"And Fritz didn't go along?" Bill asked.

"Your Father wants to stop at a number of places. He didn't want to leave the dog alone in the truck—depending on who or what Fritz would see, he might not stay in the truck," Mama explained.

"Why are all of you so quiet?" Mama questioned. "You usually have plenty to say."

"I knew he would make trouble. I just knew it."

"What are you saying Gloria?" Mama asked with a worried look.

"I don't know why we have to do all that reading and writing by tomorrow. I didn't say anything wrong. I don't even talk about Phillip. If it were for me . . ."

"That's enough, Gloria. Tilghman, tell me what happened?" Mama demanded.

He shrugged "I don't know. Don't know who said something our teacher didn't like. Whatever it was, it happened before we arrived at school this morning."

"Does anyone know what the problem is?" Mama scanned the children and settled on Del, "Adelaide, how about you?"

"Em asked me why we took Phillip to church yesterday but I told her more than once he hasn't ever been to our church."

Mama pondered what she said.

Ollie added. "Teacher knew someone wasn't telling the truth when he realized he knows the Sundays we do or don't have church."

"Someone is telling a tall tale. Your teacher doesn't like to hear lies," Mama concluded.

"We told him Phillip stayed at home. He asked Til if that was true," Bill chimed in.

Til nodded his head agreeing with Del, and the rest of the children joined in. The children were very subdued during their meal as Mama pondered the situation.

She finally spoke decisively, "When you go back to school, don't talk about Phillip or anything happening around here. I am sure your teacher has good reason for doing what he did." Mama muttered half to herself. "Must be somebody outside of the Stony Point area. That village knows when church occurs. We aren't the only family that attend that church and have children going to Funk's school."

At the end of the school day, Del and her siblings walked by Benj and Phillip. Benj was busy splitting wood while Phillip handed him smaller pieces from the filled wheelbarrow sitting close by. Benj stopped and pulled a watch from his pocket and stared at it. He rubbed his head. "Something is wrong here, my watch and I can't both be wrong. Teacher musta kept the children a little longer today. Wonder what Fritz is thinking? What do you think kept them?" Benj asked Phillip.

Phillip shook his head no.

Benj looked at Del and said, "Phillip knows your schedule." He looked approvingly at Phillip. "Ya need a cap. *Muss vennich rhum gookka* [Must look around a little]." Benj finally turned his attention fully to Del and Ollie, who was hurrying by. "What kept ya late at school?"

"Everybody stayed after school," Ollie said as he continued walking.

"Did everybody misbehave?"

"No." Ollie kept moving toward the house.

"We had a Civil War lecture to listen to. We must read and write a story about it for tomorrow. That's all," Bill said to Benj as he walked by.

Del, who had waited with Benj and Phillip till Bill caught up, turned to leave. "We have our chores to do, and lost some time already staying late," she said.

"So that's why Ollie was in such a hurry, to get his work done so he can write his story."

"Other way around," Del said hurriedly, "some of us must read in our history books plus read material Mr. Strunk handed out before dismissal and write a story from all that. By the time Ollie carries the wood and does the rest of his work it'll be near dark. I must go."

"Phillip can set the table fer ya. That should help some."

"Thanks," Del moved quickly. She heard him continue talking with Phillip, and thought, "He has a new audience in Phillip now." She smiled.

"How come all of you were a little late?" Mama asked as Ollie dropped an armful of wood.

"Del can tell you. Extra stuff to read. Wish I could throw that book away. The classes below me don't have to do any writing," he complained as he dashed out for another armful of wood.

"What say you?" Mama asked Del as she, Ori and Til entered the house.

"All the classes except those below the third grade have to do some reading and writing before tomorrow. Ollie has less to read and write than the rest of us."

"I don't know why I have to read three chapters and write a story about that and all by tomorrow morning. Why does Teacher have to take it out on us? I'm not going to count my words either." Ori complained.

"Two hundred words for my class. He may count my words. I won't," Ollie said after dumping another armload of split wood.

"I believe the talk this morning came from Stiller's corner," Til said to Mama as he entered the kitchen. "Those children are always at school before us. They were the ones inside."

"That could be. We have some rough characters back there," Mama was quick to acknowledge. "Never should have had this prohibition thing in the first place. Children, we'll help you with your chores so you can get your homework done. I'll take care of the cleanup tonight."

At the supper table Father was fully informed of the unusual school day. He and Mama exchanged a couple of long looks but didn't say anything other than encouraging words. The evening was quiet and long. Del sat at the table in the side room with Bill to share their reading material. Mama did the kitchen duty as promised and she took care of Carol as well. Til and Ori worked at the kitchen table together as they also shared some extra reading. Benj, Phillip, and Carol quietly worked on a puzzle. Ollie spent his time in the parlor and did his work on the library table. Father's desk chair creaked; he worked at his desk to bring his ledger up to date.

Benj went home about nine o'clock and Father walked with him. Mama moved to the rocking chair, keeping watch over Phillip and Carol seated on the couch. Del could hear the rocker creaking on the floorboards. Ollie was the first to get up. "All finished, good enough. I am going to bed."

Father returned from walking Benj home and there was discussion between Del's parents, held at a whisper. Del finished writing and sat quietly waiting for Bill to finish his report. Del heard a book close loudly. When she heard two pairs of feet she knew that had to be Ori that finished, and she was taking Carol upstairs. Bill finished his report and sat quietly with Del, not wanting to disturb Til by walking through the kitchen. It wasn't long after that the twins heard Til get up with a sigh. They followed him upstairs, and Del was instantly asleep as soon as her head landed on her pillow.

CHAPTER THIRTEEN

The School Receives an Education

TUESDAY MORNING Del was passing by her parent's bedroom window when she saw Mr. Strunk enter the barn with an empty two quart jar for milk and almost immediately reappeared with Father. A short discussion ensued and her father returned to the barn. Del went downstairs to do her breakfast chores wondering what Mr. Strunk could want at this early hour when he should be getting the schoolhouse ready for the day.

Benj entered the kitchen as Del yawned and got the table ready for breakfast. She swished the tablecloth across the table and straightened it all around as Bill and Phillip came down the stairs. It only took one of her brothers to help Phillip down the stairs now. "Good morning, you two," she said.

Phillip seated himself on the couch. Bill stepped into the porch, grabbed his work shoes and sat there to put them on. Del stood by the opened door to the porch.

"I saw our teacher stop by this morning carrying his milk jar. He talked to Father and left his milk jar here," Bill's voice was just above a whisper.

"I saw it too," Del spoke softly.

"Do you think he will pick his milk up after school?"

"Told you what I saw," Bill said as he finished lacing his shoes.

Benj seated himself on the rocking chair, reaching for Phillip's shoes resting on the floor beside the rocker. "What are my birthday people talking about this morning?" he asked.

Del stretched and yawned again.

"Still sleepy," Benj said.

His observation caused Del to yawn once more. "I have to get to my chores."

"Yer morning work is finished, that fer Gloria too, except fer her duck."

"Goodness, that is nice of you, you must have been here very early."

"Twas early to bed, early to rise, ya know the rest."

Phillip stood up without being told and placed the dishes Del had set out on the table. Benj looked immensely pleased. Since there was no outside work, Del returned upstairs to change into her clothes for school. Ori was up and about but Carol was still fast asleep.

"Mama will have to take care of Carol this morning, I won't have time for her. She wouldn't go to sleep last night. I was trying to finish that dumb story and read some in my library book." Ori sounded unhappy.

"You were told not to read in your room at night. Besides, didn't you do your writing on the kitchen table?" Del reminded Ori.

"I finished it upstairs. You and Bill were always saying something to each other. Who can work when the two of you are around? I was doing more writing than reading anyway."

"You could have said something. Besides, you could have gone to my room, it has a ceiling light."

"Well, I didn't. Why does it matter to you? I get my work done."

"Benj did your outside work. All but your duck. You may have time for Carol after all."

Both girls headed down the stairway. As they entered the kitchen Benj pointed a finger at Ori, "All ya gotta do is let Taw-Taw out. I will not be responsible fer that duck."

Ori turned and headed back upstairs without any comment.

The boys came in with Mama. They were especially quiet, quite unlike their usual comments or discussion about something after their morning chores. Even Benj looked around the room wondering why no small talk.

"*Zin ma oll griddlich da mariye* [Are we all cranky this morning]?"

Mama smiled. "The boys have a lot on their minds, as do I. How about that?" Mama looked to both Bill and Til, expecting an answer.

The boys responded with a nod. "We'll find out soon enough, I suppose," Til said.

"As soon as we get to school," Bill agreed.

Ori returned with Carol who was still quite sleepy. "You lay on the couch awhile. You can slip behind Phillip and go back to sleep. Next time you go to sleep when I tell you to."

Mama looked at Ori and raised an eyebrow, then scanned all the children. "Eat your breakfast and head for school. Phillip may walk with you. Did you all finish your paperwork?"

"Don't look at me," Ollie said. "I did my paper. I counted my 200 words."

"Who said they weren't going to count words?" Del teased Ollie.

"Changed my mind," Ollie retorted.

"Who said we had to count our words?" Ori inquired.

"Teacher said two hundred words," Ollie said with certainty.

"I didn't hear anything like that!" Ori exclaimed.

"Raymond asked how much we should write and Teacher said, "Two hundred words should do it.""

Mama smiled. "Two hundred words has always been his answer if anyone asks. You will learn not to ask."

"I'm glad Raymond asked," Ollie spoke up. " I was tired of writing."

Mama sent Phillip along with the children on their walk to school. "Have him walk as much as he can on his own. Be there for him if he needs help. Benj will follow. He'll know what to do," Mama spoke softly to the boys. "He needs to use those legs more."

Del, Fritz, Bill, Phillip, and Til spread across the entire width of the lane. It was only after they were en-route that Bill mentioned Mr. Strunk had visited early this morning carrying his milk jar, and that he left the jar in the milkhouse to pick up later. Ollie had been in the lead; but he drifted back to hear what the conversation was all about. Fritz moved impatiently in and out among the children. "Fritz has a problem this morning," Til laughed. Benj was following at a slower pace pulling the low flat wagon behind him. Ori, minus her duck, trailed him.

"Fritz, you have Benj and Phillip to walk back to the farm with you." Del continued talking, addressing Phillip this time. "Phillip, Fritz is restless, as you can see because he wants us to run. Once you can walk faster and have shoes that fit properly you can run with us. How would you like that?" Del looked at Phillip.

Phillip nodded his head.

"Del is right," Til added. "You are walking better all the time."

"Make believe we have to run. What would you do then?" Ollie questioned.

Phillip hung his head.

"Okay Phillip, that day will come. This is as far as you go, Fritz," Til said looking at the dog. Turning back to Phillip, he said "Fritz has been trained never to go beyond this place. There across the street is where Becky lives." Til pointed to her house across the cement pike. Phillip opened his eyes wide—he knew who Becky was. He gazed at her house as if he expected to see her walk out and wave to them.

"This is where Benj lives." Del pointed to Phillip's left to see Benj's house and property. Phillip turned his head to look at that house and barn as they walked by and then back to Benj. Benj just nodded.

Ollie tapped on Phillip's arm while pointing to the schoolhouse. "See that building way over there with a bell tower on the roof? That's our schoolhouse." Ollie wasn't interested in any response from Phillip as he kept pace with his brothers entering the cement pike.

Benj stood by Phillip as Ori complained about her duck not getting his needed exercise as they reached the last pine tree that stood on the corner of Benj's property. "Fritz gets to go anywhere and everywhere."

None of Ori's siblings wanted to debate the problems with her duck and remained silent after her remark. Benj tapped Phillip on the shoulder, as he pointed to Fritz waiting for the children to enter the school lane.

Mae was waiting as Ori hurried to meet her. Before Del entered Funk's Lane her father's truck motor could be heard. She looked back. She saw Benj and her father help Phillip onto the truck seat. Fritz jumped on board also. She turned and ran to the schoolyard. Em was playing ball with the boys as Del walked by. The dirt lane was used to complete a makeshift ball field. First base was a small cleared area on the forest's edge. A diagonal line to second base was below the boulder and close to the lane. Third base was a diagonal line across the dirt lane to an electric pole in front of a stonewall bordering a field. Home plate was across the lane and up a terraced rise to the school grounds. Del reached over to touch the rock as Em passed the ball to another and joined Del.

"You didn't have to stop playing your game. Not much time left for play after I get here."

"Playing ball was something to do until you came."

"We had a slower walk this morning," Del informed Em.

"We were the first ones here. Pa dropped us off at the bridge. Teacher was unlocking the door as we came up the side steps."

"I bet he was surprised," Del quickly added.

"He told us the building was still cold. He was going to start a fire. He said we could come inside if we wanted to. It was only the two of us," Em stated.

Del didn't mention that the teacher had stopped at her farm first.

"Tell me, what was it that made Teacher so angry yesterday?" Del asked Em.

"Can't say. Did you take you-know-who to Sunday school?" Em asked once more.

"No, for the last time. Mama stayed at home with Phillip. He needs Sunday shoes and clothes first. And he still needs help to walk."

"You mean he's a cripple?"

"No, nothing like that. Doctor says there's nothing wrong with his feet. Just like he'll talk once he gets over his shyness."

"He doesn't talk! Why? For goodness sake!"

"Don't know for sure. He sure hears a lot of our Dutch dialect, especially from the older folk in my house. I bet he never heard that before. He likes to be with my grandfather, and he never speaks English."

The bell rang and school was in session. At morning recess time a man driving a Whippet went by. Twas most unusual to have any machine go by, especially that of the Justice of the Peace, or Squire, as he was referred to more often. Mr. Strunk hurried out to make sure all the children were on the school grounds.

Going home for lunch the boys talked about the Whippet going down the lane while school was in session. Benj was seated under the arbor as the children arrived. Phillip wasn't with him. "I suppose Grandfather has a helper today," Bill said as he walked by.

"Yep," was all Benj said.

"A man of few words, how unusual," Del said as she had slowed to hear Benj's remarks.

Benj just grinned.

After the afternoon session was dismissed, Bill was out of breath as he ran up the hill. "Good boy, Fritz, you waited for me. Hi Phillip, you were waiting too. How did you get here? I thought you'd be at the creamery longer than this."

Phillip pointed to Benj's house.

"Did Fritz let you know when it was time to leave?" Bill asked.

After a few seconds, Phillip nodded his head.

"What did he do?" Bill didn't give up as he hooked onto Phillip's arm and waited for Til to join them. Til trotted up after an extended chat with Abe, who was usually in a hurry to get home.

Phillip was quiet for a long moment, then finally said, "Bark."

Everyone laughed.

Phillip looked away and Til changed the subject, turning to his brother and sister. "I think Teacher is working on some kind of assignment for all of us."

"How can that be? He didn't even look at any of the papers we turned in, they just laid on his desk." Bill sounded discouraged.

"It's something he talked to Father about this morning. I don't know what it was he wanted. I overheard a little of what Father said to Mama as I came out through the feed entry door this morning. It was something concerning Phillip, I don't know what."

Benj stood by the woodshed with the wagon handy.

"*Sez ebbes letz* [There's something wrong]," Benj said as Ollie carried an armload of wood into the house while still in his school clothes.

"He doesn't dirty his clothes all that much with one armload of wood. I bet he selected clean pieces," Del reasoned.

Ollie said nothing while munching on cookies and milk. He finished his snack so hurriedly a milk line was noticeable across his upper lip.

"Oliver, how was your school day?" Mama asked. "You usually have something to say."

"Okay." Ollie ran upstairs and changed his clothes. He then dashed outside and returned carrying an armful of split wood. "This is my last load of wood. I am going out to the barn to see what the others are doing."

"I am sure they'll find something for you to do. No going into the top of the barn."

"I know that. I won't go there," Ollie told Mama hurriedly as he raced out.

"Benj thinks there is something wrong with Ollie. He says he is too quiet," Del said as soon as Ollie left the kitchen.

"We'll find out soon enough," Mama countered. "That's right. I didn't hear any school reports from any of you. Adelaide, how was the day?"

"Teacher looked over the reports during recess time. He returned some of the written papers. Em wasn't too happy with what he wrote on her paper."

"What did he write?" Mama asked.

"Not sure. Em just said 'I couldn't think of anything more to write.'"

"Ollie got his paper back. Teacher was chuckling when he returned it. He said something very quietly to him. Ollie folded it over and over again and stuck it in his pocket. He won't talk about it or tell us the grade he got. Not even if it was good or bad," Ori said.

"Any more of you get your work back?" Mama asked.

"Not that I know of. It was mostly the younger classes who got their reports," Del answered.

"You may as well get your outside work done. It gets dark earlier each day," Mama told Del.

Ori and Carol were outside. Del was surprised to see both were coming down the lane with bark chips and no Fritz. Mr. Straub was with them; he headed toward the barn. "Every time I see that basket, here of late someone else is carrying it," she thought. They left the basket set in front of the feedhouse as they entered the it. Del heard them shelling corn as she pulled the flat wagon over to the rain barrel to finish mixing mash for the pigs. Del remembered Benj saying he had shelled corn for Ori as she passed the feedhouse. Opening the door she yelled, "Benj said he shelled corn for you, so look around. You will find it somewhere."

"Don't you worry about me. I know what I am doing," Ori answered curtly.

"Do as you wish," Del replied with a sigh.

Del went back to her work. She saw Mr. Straub step out of the feed entry door and Father was with him, followed by Benj and Phillip. Phillip was holding the small wooden bucket of eggs with just a few inside. He sat on the feed entry step as he waited for Benj to pull the flat wagon over to him.

"You sure do surprise me! Is everybody switching jobs around here?" Del said as she walked over to Benj at the wagon and smiled at Phillip.

"*Ah muss alles lanne* [He must everything learn]," Benj said. "*Des isz oll nie* [This is all new]."

Del finished her work. She rinsed her buckets and paddle, set them upside down inside the feedhouse and carried enough water in a bucket to set outside the henhouse door for Ori to fill the hoppers with fresh water.

Mr. Straub greeted her and said. "Adelaide, we don't see much of you. You and Bill have grown quite a bit. How old are you now?"

She said, "We will be eleven years old come spring."

Mr. Straub laughed. "When you're young, you can't wait to be that one year older. When you are old like me, the next birthday is here much too soon. I must go. Say hello to your Mama for me."

"I'm hungry," Carol said to Del as she opened the feedhouse door. "Ori said you should take me in."

Mama wasn't around in the kitchen. "I'll get some warm water, you need to wash up," Del advised.

"Just my hands?"

Del shook her head, "No, all the way up to your elbows. I don't know where Mama is, but she'll be back soon. You can rest on the couch once you've cleaned up."

"I believe you are finished for the day," Del said as Benj and Phillip entered.

"*Yep sin faddich* [Yes we finished]. We worked hard today. How about that Phillip?"

Phillip agreed by shyly nodding his head.

"All done?" Mama asked as she opened the back door and stepped into the kitchen.

Del shook her head no. "Carol is ready for supper. I brought her in. I need to go back to see if Ori is finished. I need to close everything up for the night."

Til and Ori entered with Ollie immediately behind them.

"Bill and Fritz are checking everything," Til said to Del as he took his seat on the bench.

"Then I don't have to go out anymore," Del was happy to say.

Bill stepped inside and Fritz with him. "Mama, Father is out by the pump, he wants to talk to you."

Mama was on her way before Bill finished speaking. Fritz sat near the table where Bill always sat. In short time, Mama and Father entered the kitchen. Mama looked very pleased. "I have a new dish for you Phillip, it's a beef pot pie. You liked my chicken pot pie, but then again I haven't made anything you didn't like so far," she smiled at Phillip. Everyone took their places at the table. Mama placed a large bowl on the table and the children said their supper prayer.

"Why was Mr. Straub here? Did he want to see Phillip?" Del asked.

"You answered your own question," Father said. "Yes. He was here to see Phillip. Tomorrow we will take Phillip there to visit so the Missus can see him."

"A lot of people want to meet Phillip," Ollie said. "The boys at school are going to stop in on Friday after school."

"You mean the same boys are coming again," Ori challenged.

"I didn't say the same boys, I said the boys. Maybe some the same, maybe not," Ollie said.

"I thought more children would have come to meet him by now," Bill commented.

"We may need to take him where everyone can meet him," Father said thoughtfully.

"We could take him to school and Teacher could say this boy will be a new student," Del suggested.

Mama said. "That's a good idea, Adelaide."

"*Vielleicht dade sel shaffe* [Maybe that would work]," Benj gave Del a nod of his head.

"I will talk to your teacher, this may make what he has in mind a lot easier." Father sounded confident.

Del surmised something was discussed with Mr. Strunk that her parents were not sharing. What did her teacher have in mind?

Father looked at the children and asked, "Tell me how did the written reports go? You needed extra time to get them done."

There was no immediate answer. "Anybody?" Father said.

"I didn't get my paper back. Em got hers, she wasn't pleased." Del said.

Mama turned to Ollie, "Did you get your paper? Did you get a good mark?" Mama asked.

Ollie shrugged, "Yes, but I never looked, I stuck it in my desk. I was busy doing my arithmetic problems."

Del could tell from the narrowing of Mama's eyes that she was suspicious about something, but Mama didn't press Ollie for more information.

Father changed the subject as they ate. "Ed isn't working again. He's thinking of doing something else. Something he can still do, if he gets called back to work at the silk mill," Father concluded.

The evening was quiet. Benj decided it was time to go home. "*Sehne eich mariyettz* [See you tomorrow]," he said as he picked up his lantern, struck a match, and replaced the glass covering the flame. He went on his way.

Mama and Father made their way into the side room, each carrying a cup of coffee, and took a seat in the semi-darkness. Del heard enough of their conversation to have a new question to answer—was Father going to Philadelphia soon? She wondered about that as she completed the kitchen chores to be ready for tomorrow's breakfast.

Ori and Carol made their way upstairs. The boys did homework at the kitchen table and Del decided to stop speculating and finish her library book. She went upstairs. She thought about what it was that Ollie wasn't admitting. She saw him fold his written report over and over again and stick it in his pocket, not in his desk. She remembered her own embarrassing denials recently. She did some reading, said her prayers, and soon found sound sleep.

Wednesday morning Mr. Strunk left the barn as Del looked down upon the barn activities from her parents' bedroom window.

"Goodness, not again this morning!" Del thought.

Upon entering the kitchen Del asked, "Our teacher was here again this morning. He never comes for milk everyday. What's going on?"

"Never you mind," Mama said, as she headed for the back door.

Del realized Mama wouldn't offer any explanation. Mama spent little time in the kitchen while the children helped themselves to cereal and cake.

Del entered the school grounds and Em greeted her. They ran inside as the bell rang and school was in session.

"We are a few minutes later this morning. I had a little difficulty getting the room warm enough for school to begin," Mr. Strunk advised.

He had the remainder of the written reports with notes on them. Judging from the expressions of students as he handed them out, most contained comments that didn't produce smiles.

He turned to face the classroom and said, "This is not a written assignment, but I want you to know the origins of your families. Indians inhabited this region before our forefathers came to this country. We know that, do we not? We find Indian arrowheads and tomahawks along creeks and in plowed fields. Ask your parents where your family's ancestors lived before coming to this country. All of us are descendants of immigrants. You need to understand your ancestors came to this country of their own free will, while people in Africa were forced to come to this country and sold as slaves. Even children were taken from their parents, placed on ships and sold to work as slaves."

The first recess was called. Del looked at Em and asked where her parents came from.

"What do you mean?" Em asked.

"You heard what our teacher said. Did your family come from France or Germany or someplace else? My ancestors came across the ocean a ship named Brothers that came to Philadelphia. You aren't related to Indian tribes that lived here, are you? You may not have come from the same place as my family or else your family would speak Pennsylvania Dutch too. You certainly aren't old order Amish. They speak Dutch like we do but go to their own schools and churches."

"How do you know all that?" Em wondered as she shook her head at this amount of information.

"Because my family and relatives talk about the past generations."

"Who cares? I still think Teacher is angry with us," Em said.

"Don't you want to know where you came from? My grandfather often tells us he learned the creamery business from his parents and his grandparents in the old country. He likes to tell us that generations before him were always in the creamery and farming business. Whether or not it's something Grandfather told us many times before, Mama makes us listen to what he has to say."

The girls became quiet as Mr. Strunk looked their way.

When Del, Bill and Fritz arrived home for the noon meal they were surprised to see Benj seated under the grape arbor wearing a blue work shirt that looked new. He also wore a jacket, part of a suit, and a dark gray button-front sweater, hanging open. It was the kind of sweater Father wore on cold winter days under a coat.

"Well, I see ya is *im recht odder* [in right order]," Benj chuckled. He waved them along, "Ya go inside, yer Mama is waiting."

"Something is wrong here. He doesn't want to talk to us," Del spoke softly to Bill as they continued their walk to the house.

"I should have asked him about his clothes. He wears clothes like that on Sundays only," Bill whispered to Del.

"That wouldn't be very nice. I noticed that myself."

As soon as the children were inside Father said, "If you could tell the school children anything about Phillip, what would you tell them? You'll have a chance to do that today. Mr. Strunk will tell you when. I tell you this now so you won't be surprised. Think about what you are going to tell your friends."

"Anything?" Ollie asked.

Father simply nodded his head in the affirmative as he shifted the conversation in a different direction. The children all looked at each other, wondering what was in store that afternoon. Father didn't notice. He talked about the situations with some of their friends and neighbors, including the difficulties Ed and Hester were facing since both might be unemployed before long.

The children left for the afternoon session discussing whether the announcement at their dinner break had something to do with what Mr. Strunk and Father talked about the past two mornings. Til asked Ollie what he was going to say.

Ollie was deep in thought, walking more slowly than his normal pace but becoming more animated as he considered what he was going to say. "I will tell them he was too weak too walk. Not at all." Ollie made hand movements. "We had to carry him. I'll tell them he was vaccinated." Ollie tapped his upper left arm with his finger. "So he can come to school. Don't know what else to say."

Ollie became more excited about the prospect of sharing what he knew. Til noticed and said, "Calm down Ollie. You'll be alright. No need to worry." Til hoped to calm some of Ollie's pent-up energy.

"He behaves like someone else we know," Del spoke softly to Bill as her thoughts rested on her Aunt Lillie and her bursts of excitable energy.

"I know, I see it too," Bill's whispered with a nod of his head.

Del entered the school grounds pondering what she was going to say to the classroom. Just then the school door opened wide and Del saw Mr. Strunk reach for the bell. It rang twice. Twas all that was needed to get the children inside. Mr. Strunk stood by his desk and waited for all to be seated.

"We will begin the afternoon session as always. But class times and discussion time will be shortened."

The children were surprised and looked around at each other.

Mr. Strunk started with the first graders. Del found it hard to concentrate on her arithmetic problems. Thank goodness she didn't have spelling class, now that she had regained her first position. Del glanced at the clock, looking forward to recess time.

Then came the surprise announcement from Mr. Strunk. "We will not have recess time this afternoon."

There was a soft groan from the students. The teacher ignored the reaction. "We will continue with our class sessions. Different arrangements are made for the remainder of our day."

"Now what is going on?" Em whispered.

"I really don't know," Del cautiously whispered back.

After the lower grades had their class periods and returned to their seats, Mr. Strunk spoke. "I have arranged for you to hear the whole truth from the Heydt family about adding another member to their household. Listen carefully. You are free to ask questions. When you go home, repeat only what you heard here. I will punish any student that spreads falsehoods. You will hear why Mr. Heydt decided to provide a home for this child."

"You know what is happening!" Em whispered.

Del shook her head. Her mind swirled with thoughts. Del was sure the early morning visits had something to do with today's plan. She guessed that was why her teacher was late preparing the schoolroom for students to arrive. What did he plan to do? Soon a motorcar could be heard—it was the family's Studebaker.

Attention was quickly diverted to what Mr. Strunk was saying. "Yes, we have a surprise for you," Mr. Strunk said as he walked to the door and looked through the small window in the top half of the inside door to the vestibule.

Del could hear all sorts of murmured comments from the children. Mr. Strunk opened the door and the room quieted. Del had never before noticed that those door hinges creaked. All heads turned to the entrance. In through the narrow vestibule stepped Father and Benj supporting Phillip between them. Del heard the gasps, as Becky followed Mama holding onto Carol's hand.

"Phillip is here!" Ollie was really shocked, his whole body quivering. "I didn't know Phillip was coming to school," he exclaimed loud enough for everyone to hear.

Hearing Ollie, Mr. Strunk smiled. He greeted the visitors kindly and asked two older boys to get the folding chairs behind the big round furnace on the girls' side of the building and place them in the center aisle.

"No wonder Benj was dressed in his best clothes," Del thought. Phillip was wearing the new shirt Lillie had made for him. Mama must have found time to place the buttons and finish the buttonholes. It fit nicely.

Til moved over, which gave Phillip enough room to be seated at Til's desk. Phillip sat with his back to Til, his legs dangling from the side of the older boy's seat toward the center aisle.

Mama, Father, Becky, and Benj sat in a row across the center aisle. The room was hushed. Mr. Strunk walked over to Phillip. "I met you before but I didn't introduce myself. I am Amos Strunk, the school-teacher here. Phillip, let us shake hands." Phillip stuck his hand out to Mr. Strunk's hand.

"Phillip. Hello and welcome to this school and to the neighborhood. These are the friends you will meet once you start school." Mr. Strunk, turned to the students and said, "I want to introduce our guests. This is Benjamin Fronheiser. He lives by the lane to the Heydt farm. He's been a great source of help to that family at this particular time. Next, we have Elwood and Laura Heydt, the parents to Ori, Til, Bill, Del, and Ollie here in school. There is yet one more, Carol, who is too young to attend school." Mr. Strunk walked over to Becky and stood behind her. "Here is Rebecca Funk. I suppose most of you know her as Becky, an asset to the neighborhood."

"I never saw her before," Em whispered to Del.

Mr. Strunk continued. "Rebecca and her late husband donated the land this schoolhouse stands on. We are grateful for their generosity."

The teacher walked to face the adults seated in the classroom. "Mr. Heydt, can you tell us your story about how you brought Phillip home?"

Father stood up and told the story Del heard several times before. Some minor details were new. The children were very attentive. They sighed and groaned when Father explained the awful conditions Phillip endured and how the market people treated him. "Being homeless, hungry, and helpless, the fear and desperation this little boy faced alone is more than any of us want to endure. It took a great deal of courage to survive. I could see this poor child needed help. What would you do?"

"I sure wouldn't let him starve," Benny burst out, without stuttering.

"That's exactly what my father said," Til proudly exclaimed.

The teacher nodded his head. "Mr. Heydt did a very good job of describing what conditions were like. He couldn't walk away and do nothing. I can vouch for that. I saw Phillip on Friday evening. He does look much better now."

The Heydt children all nodded in agreement.

The class was quiet until a second grader asked, "Did he look like something the cat dragged in like Mama always says?"

Everyone, children and adults laughed as Mr. Strunk struggled to keep a sober face.

Mr. Strunk called on Ollie to speak. Ollie obliged. He walked over and stiffly stood aside Phillip. "The first time I saw him was a Friday night after supper. We didn't know what to expect for a whole TWO days." Ollie put a great deal of emphasis on the two days while raising two fingers on his right hand. "We call him Phillip because my father found him in Philadelphia. Boy! I sure was surprised when I saw him. He looked real scared."

"Good, Oliver. Bill, do you have anything to say?" Mr. Strunk inquired.

"Yes, he looks much better now," Bill replied. Del knew he preferred fewer words to more when speaking.

"What was the first thing you saw that was different?" Mr. Strunk pointed to Bill again.

"He wasn't white like me, and he was very skinny."

"Did he look terrible because his skin and hair were dark?" Teacher asked.

"No. He looked different because his pants were torn and his knee bones stuck out. Never saw such a bony leg."

"Were you afraid of him when you first saw him?" Mr. Strunk asked Til.

"No," Til paused. "Phillip here, he was so skinny. No one should look like that, like my father said."

Ollie interrupted, turning and looking at Becky said, "She said he looked like death was knocking at the door."

A few children snickered at that remark.

A look from Mr. Strunk silenced them and he said, "Continue, Oliver. I never heard that before."

"He's filled out a bit now. He eats everything Mama makes. I think he likes living with us. I sure like him. Maybe he can play ball with me when he can walk better." Ollie looked at Phillip and Phillip shyly smiled.

"Maude," Mr. Strunk called on an eighth grader, "You seem interested. Do you have any questions?"

She stood up, "Why did you keep that colored boy in the barn?"

Mr. Strunk sharply corrected her. "Phillip is of the Black race and everyone here will use his name. Most importantly, he is a human being no different from the rest of us."

Father said, "I can answer that question. You know how families are quarantined when someone has a contagious illness. We didn't know if Phillip had any health issues that could make the others sick. With Becky's expert help we nursed him on the wagon in our barn until we were satisfied he didn't have any diseases like TB or diphtheria."

The children murmured approvingly—everyone knew someone who had died from those feared diseases, and many had gone through a quarantine too.

Maude walked over to Phillip and held out her hand. "Hello, I am Maude. Welcome to our school." Phillip shook her hand and gave her a small smile before dropping his head.

Del concluded Mr. Strunk chose her first because of her friendly nature. He was sure she would be kind to a stranger. Her curly blond hair bounced as she walked back to her desk.

Del studied Phillip. When he first arrived in their house, he appeared bewildered and frightened in his new surroundings. However, over the course of a few days he had lost that look. Here in this new place, his initial reserve had already diminished, and he was willing to meet new people. "Maybe its because we're all children," she mused to herself.

"We'll take this row by row. Introduce yourself as you take his hand." Mr. Strunk instructed the students. "How about this row of boys over by the window? Line up." The younger ones moved quickly. They appeared as shy as Phillip. Grade four seemed eager to meet him. Some asked a question or two. Phillip did not respond, but Til was right there to answer questions. As more children came forward Phillip offered his hand more easily. Mr. Strunk looked at the clock. "Time is running short. We'll have to move more quickly. I know there must be questions you want answered. We'll see if we have time for a few questions after everyone said hello to our guests."

A hand went up. "Yes Lottie, your question?"

"Are you going to take him back when he is alright again?"

"Good question. That's something I can't answer at this time." Father was still standing up front. "We don't know anything about Phillip's family or what happened to bring him to the situation I found him in. It will depend on what we can learn and what Phillip wants. For as long as he is with us, he is one of my family."

"Yes, Harold. You have a question."

"Did he cry a lot?"

Father shook his head, "No. I think he was too weak to cry." Father answered.

"Yes, Eugene."

"Can't you take him to a place for poor people?"

"Those places, we were told, are over-full already with orphaned or abandoned children, and it isn't right, but many won't take children like him." The older children understood the unspoken words in Father's statement and nodded. "We're giving him everything, and more, than he would get in an institution, and we're happy to do it." Father looked around the room.

"If he is better now, I would take him back," Eugene said.

There was a hushed, mixed response of "Oh"s and "No" from the other children.

"I can't do that. Back to where? We don't know where he came from. A cold dirt alley is no place to call home. It's not Christian."

"Martha, your question?"

"Did you treat him like an animal when he was in the barn?"

Father looked at Mama. "You answer that."

"Of course not," she said. "There was plenty of bedding to keep him warm and someone was constantly with him from the first night on. Becky, Benj, my father, who many of you know runs the creamery uptown, or one of us was always with him. We cared for him there until we were confident his only problems were lack of food and shelter. She paused, then continued, "Phillip slept most of the time, he must have been exhausted from his time on his own."

Becky nodded her head as Mama talked about Phillip's first days. The last row of girls lined up to greet Phillip. Em was in line. Her question was, "Why can't he walk? Is he a cripple?"

"He is not a cripple. His bones are strong. But the experiences he endured just aren't healed overnight. Time is a good healer, and that plus continued care are all he needs," Becky explained.

Del liked the way Becky stated things. No one questioned her judgment.

Til spoke again "He is walking a little. At first he didn't walk at all. Two of us had to assist him. He is doing much better now."

"Maxine, last question."

"Are you sure he would have died?"

Mr. Strunk looked to Becky, and said, "I will ask Becky if she can answer that."

"Yes, I saw this boy when Woodie first brought him home. Benj here," she pointed to Benj, "came to my house that night and said I should come along with him. I knew it had to be something serious for him to fetch me after dark. I carried my own lantern because Benj told me he wasn't going home that night. I really expected something awful happened in the Heydt family. When I saw Phillip, I was very troubled. I couldn't be sure he would be alive come morning. Goes to show what a little care, food, warmth and sleep can do. And sleep he sure did after he had some food in his belly. It was gratifying to see. I have watched him since then," Becky said as she slowly walked over to Phillip and placed her hand on his shoulder. You could tell Phillip knew and liked her. "He has strong bones. He is going to be fine. And yes, he will walk when the time is right."

Phillip and Becky gazed at each other, and she gave him a little pinch on the tip of his nose, provoking him to laugh. The whole classroom laughed again.

"I think we have used all our time. You may ask the Heydt children questions tomorrow. Let's show our appreciation to these people for coming to our school and presenting us with the facts about this entire situation." The school broke into cheering and applause. Phillip buried his face in his hands.

As the children lined up for dismissal to say goodbye, one of the girls asked Mama if Benj was the grandfather to the Heydt children.

Mama said, "Yes and no. We gave Benj the role of grandfather. He spends a lot of time with us and especially with Phillip."

Del saw that sparked a surprising reaction from Benj. He blinked rapidly to hold back tears. In his broken English he stated, "He is like a son to me. I lost two, ya know. Now I have another. If he doesn't have a last name I will give him mine." Benj declared.

That statement brought tears to Del's eyes.

Em put her arm around Del's shoulder. "What's the matter?"

"It's okay. I'm all right."

"I know something is wrong,"

"I'll tell you later." Del dried her eyes one more time.

Becky tapped Mr. Strunk on the arm and whispered to him. He looked at her and nodded his head.

"I have something I want to share with your students." Everyone watched as Becky stepped into the vestibule and returned with a long rectangular basket, not very deep, its contents covered with a cloth. The scent of her chocolate cookies filled the room.

"School is dismissed," Mr. Strunk smiled and was amused as the children hurriedly bid him good day and quickly passed on to Becky. Her uncovered basket held enough large chocolate cookies for everyone. She handed a cookie to each one. The thank-you was hardly said before the first bite of cookie was in each mouth.

The evening meal was a simple one with lots of chatter. The children talked about the school day, and Phillip nodded and smiled but remained silent.

Mama looked around the table and focused on Phillip. "Phillip, you saw many children; they are just like you. Everyone wants to know more about you. You will be an interesting person to have around once you are willing to talk."

Phillip responded. "I'm okay."

Everyone laughed and smiled and congratulated Phillip as he finally spoke. Phillip said once more, "I'm okay."

"Phillip what did you think about that school?" Father looked directly at him.

Phillip raised his hand while pointing one finger.

"I suppose you mean one room for all. All the schools are like that here."

"Do you want to go to school here?" Mama asked.

Phillip dropped his head.

Mama and Father looked at each other, and then at the children. "Let's leave it at that for now. Phillip, anytime you want to talk some more, you just go ahead," Father said.

"Is he ever going back to Philly again?" Ori asked, tilting her head in Phillip's direction.

"*Sel wissa ma net* [That know we not]," Benj said.

"Not ever?" Ori asked again.

Father rebuked her in Dutch. "Gloria, this is not the time to talk about things like that. He is just beginning to feel at home; see how relaxed he is. We want him be at home with us. What you are asking is not helpful."

Del felt no sympathy for Ori. After that there was very little small talk. Ollie was ready to dry dishes as soon as Del washed them. Phillip was right there, placing dried dishes on the enameled baking table. Ori and Mama cleared the food. Father, Mama, and Benj each had a cup of coffee sitting before them. They would linger downstairs awhile longer. Del was sure the afternoon would be discussed after the children had retired for the night. Del knew it was time for her to call it a day. Once alone in her bedroom, Del thought about Benj and his lost two children. She pondered how to get some answers about that until sleep took command.

CHAPTER FOURTEEN

Corn Husking Starts

"We isz da dawg gange [How did the day go]?" Benj stood by the woodshed and waited as the twins drew near.

"What did Til say?"

"Ach, ya know. Til only says okay. His horse is more important than my *wunnerfitz* [curiosity]."

"Teacher kept us busy all day," Bill responded. "At recess times, there were lots of questions. Everyone was wondering about all kinds of things."

As soon as Del stepped inside Mama pointed to the scrap dish. Late pears were canned. She headed outdoors to the pigpen. She emptied the scrap dish and the peelings were gone immediately. She threw unfilled cobs of corn to the pigs as Phillip and Benj came around the far corner of the pen with more buckets full of scrawny cobs. Phillip was seated awkwardly between the buckets, hauled on the same wagon Del used. "Goodness, but we have a lot of those scrawny cobs this year. I need to get more crates for the scrubs and stack them along the back wall in the feedhouse," Del said as she greeted Phillip.

"Look in there, the crates all ready fer ya," Benj replied. Benj and Phillip prepared buckets with the mash mixture and moved containers to store scrub cobs of corn.

"Good. I'll start cleaning the inside corner right away," she said, glad to have their help.

"*Fa waz denksch du oss mere es welschkanngrutze im kareb galust hen* [Why do you think we left the scrawny cobs of corn in baskets]?" Benj questioned and gestured to Phillip. "We'll do the cleaning there."

"I never do this job until the husking is complete, when all of us are out there collecting the scraps and bringing the damaged pumpkins in to the pigs. Who decided to pick scraps up before we really get underway?"

"*Niemand* [No one]. We cut the scrawny stalks along the fencerows, I toss 'em aside—easy to pick up and throw in the pigpen, fodder and all. I strip the full ears of corn, throw them in the *kareb* [basket]. Can't ruin dem shoes that way if'n we stay in the lane. *Missah ihn recht lanne* [Must teach him right]. Will clean the areas when huskers finish a shock of corn. *Sel is fa unz tsu do. Ah konz bicke du* [That is for us to do. He can do the bending]. Ed's busy with his hand-chopper. He's here days while ya is in *de schul* [the school]. Woodie and I do the binding and shocking. Phillip does the watching." Benj laughed.

Del laughed too, "Good we save all these dented buckets that can't hold water. Can't use them for anything else."

"*Mer yusa wasewwer hendich isz* [We use whatever is handy]. We'll make one more trip while ya finish de corner. After that, let's get something warm to put in our bellies. How about that Phillip?"

Phillip just smiled.

Del thought about husking time, soon to begin. Neighbors from the area would see Phillip, many for the first time. Womenfolk who spent all their time at home would be among the first to see him. Husking was one time each year they could meet and earn a little spending money. Menfolk also came out to help. Huskers arrive early in the morning prepared to work until dusk, with lunches packed and dressed warmly for the day. Sometimes they rode to the fields ready for husking on a body wagon drawn by a team of horses.

Men would undo the shocks and lay them on the ground. The huskers sat on the fallen shocks to husk each cob of corn individually with a hand-held husker. They tossed the corn on a pile or into a bushel basket, then moved on to the next fallen shock of corn. The baskets of husked corn were picked up and emptied into a body wagon, and a team of horses pulled the filled wagons to the corncribs. Men used large grain shovels to toss the cobs onto metal chutes to slide and fall into the cribs. It was lots of work for a short period of time, and every farmer appreciated the help of neighbors.

Friday morning the children were eating breakfast when Father stepped into the kitchen. He informed Phillip he was sending him to the creamery with Ed. "He's the man who cut your hair. I need to stay, because I expect Isaac and Sam to arrive before long. You may stay with Grandfather if he needs help. If not, Ed will bring you along home. Okay?" Father paused, and Phillip nodded yes. "Good. Finish your breakfast. Ed likes to drive my new truck." Father smiled. "I suppose you like truck rides too."

"*Mer schicke da hund mitt* [We'll send the dog along]. Fritz won't care who the driver is. He is a regular *rutch* [street] traveler," Benj added.

"I would gladly go along to the creamery instead of going to school," Ollie stated.

"I believe you, Oliver. Phillip might say the same in days to come," Mama half smiled as she looked at Phillip.

"Oliver, don't forget to bring your written report home. The others did. I want to see what kind of grade you got," Mama added.

Ollie remained quiet as he finished his breakfast.

The morning session moved slowly. Del passed time by thinking about Grandfather's creamery. Someone named Mr. Gehris would buy Grandfather's business, and he was very interested in Grandfather's butter process. He came to observe the workings of the creamery operation until the sale was completed. She considered the dreary day, with the sun only peeping behind gray clouds now and then. Dreary weather always seemed to dull all ambition for Del—especially so when it came to schoolwork.

Father sent word with Ed and Benj to tell the town that should Saturday be a nice day it would be the day for corn husking to begin. Father knew the women appreciated starting late in the week for the first day of husking, especially avoiding Monday, which was laundry day. One day or even the half-day would be good for workers to become accustomed to working in the open air. There would be long days to follow in the weeks ahead.

Helpers arrived quite early on Saturday morning. The two old maid Frye girls were the first to arrive. They managed for themselves by maintaining a large garden and helping out in the neighborhood. Ed and his wife, Hester, never had factory work on Saturdays and were experienced huskers. Adeline and Jonathan Conrad, the elderly neighbors below the farm, helped only on nice weather days like today. Isaac and Sam came on days they had no work. Sometimes Eva and Lillie came along. Father kept a list of people who helped to make payments based on their time. Even though it was hard work, everyone enjoyed the opportunity to spend time with neighbors they didn't see regularly.

Grandfather loaned Father his wagon and horses during husking times. Father farmed Grandfather's fields, harvested the crops, and prepared the land for winter's rest. His fields around the creamery were the next to be husked. Grandfather came by late afternoons with whoever drove in the direction of the fields and stayed until dusk. He would take his team and wagon home to give proper attention to his horses each night.

The family gathered for Saturday morning breakfast, even though the helpers were arriving. Father and the older boys, Til and Bill, had already been out. Til and Bill came in for breakfast.

"I helped in the fields already," Ori said. "It's hard work. I'll only do it again if I must."

"What did you do?"

"It wasn't easy, Del, I wore farmers gloves and filled the bushel baskets with corn for Ed to dump into the wagon."

"I think that would be one of the easier jobs."

"You try it. Moving from one shock to another picking up corn is backbreaking work. We didn't have baskets for everybody, so I had to pick the husked corn laying on fodder and toss it in one of those big round bushel baskets or fill a bucket and carry it to the nearest wagon."

"I know what you are saying," Mama said. "I used to do that too. It is back-breaking work."

"Is that why Grandfather is so bent? He can't stand up straight," Ollie asked.

"He's arthritic from hard work all those years and the traveling back and forth. It was a two day trip to give his horses a rest," Mama gazed off in the distance as she spoke. Del imagined she was picturing being a little girl again as she recalled those times.

"I drive him to the barbershop every Saturday for a shave, sometimes a haircut too. He's too stiff to get into the Studebaker so he stands on the running board. I make sure the door is closed and locked, and he pushes his upper body through the open window and holds on as best he can. Never had a problem," Til said proudly.

Del was dumbfounded. Grandfather standing on the running board, leaning in through the window! "You're not old enough to drive! Did you know that, Mama?" Del asked.

"Yes Adelaide, my father is as stubborn as he is stiff. There's no other way to get him to the barbershop. His hand is unsteady, and he can't handle a straight razor anymore. I'm so glad he lets us take him to the barbershop every Saturday by whatever means. How he manages to climb onto his buggy to go to church, I don't understand." Mama added more wood to the fire. "Adelaide, scramble some eggs. The fry pan is ready."

"See that, Phillip! Del is cooking. We gonna eat what she makes," Benj pointed to Del.

Phillip turned to Benj with a serious look of concern on his face.

"Mama teaches us all to make the easier things," Del reassured him. "Ollie is next in line. Mama will teach him too. He is already doing dishes. It won't be long before he will be helping with some cooking."

Mama said, "I'll teach you to cook, too, Phillip."

He shyly smiled and nodded agreement.

"You can take my place," Ollie said.

"*Schaft net vee sel* [Works not like that]," Benj said as he placed toast on Phillip's plate.

"That's right," Del said as she turned the scrambled eggs. "I know one thing. Phillip will be a better cook than you, Ollie. He eats everything. Onions and parsley don't bother him."

Ollie looked at Phillip as he shrugged his shoulders. "I can't stand their taste or smell."

"*Fa deel vun de leit issaz airscht mole oss se gwisst hen oss en schwatz doh isz* [For some of the people it's the first time they know we have a Black person here]." Benj commented with a serious look on his face.

"Everything seems alright with the workers so far," Til said with not a care in the world.

"*Wunz sez des net glicher es mehned nix. Es gelt mehned viela meg* [If they don't like it means nothing. Money means a lot more]," Benj nodded his head.

"The smaller wagon is here," Til said. "Father brought Grandfather's larger wagon in earlier, unloaded it and said we should take both wagons back to the fields. It will take longer to fill both wagons."

"I ride the big wagon," Ollie said as they all left the kitchen at the same time.

Benj looked at Phillip. "He rides the big wagon. That's what we'll do. Stay on the wagon and get rides all day long, same as Fritz."

"Don't forget your heavy work gloves. You'll need them. See if you can find another pair for Phillip." Mama motioned for them to be on their way. "Don't keep Phillip out too long. He isn't used to being out in the cooler air and riding on a bumpy wagon all day."

"*Sel gehed fa mich au. Ich kann es kalt luft neemie soo lung schtende* [That goes for me too. I can not stand the cold air so long]," Benj admitted.

At dinnertime Benj was snoozing in the rocker and Phillip was asleep on the couch as Del helped Mama with meal preparations. Both awakened as Bill stepped into the kitchen.

"Aha, caught you napping. Both of you!" Bill laughed.

"*Sez ollrecht waarde yuscht bis du alt bischt* [It's alright, wait just until you are old]. How are things going with the husking?" Benj asked Bill as he sat down to eat.

Soo huddlich. Ken zeit fa schwetze [So hurried. No time to talk]." Bill paused, looked at Benj. "*Es gade gute* [It goes good]. A good group out there. We might be able to start the larger field on Monday."

Del realized that she and her siblings regularly spoke the dialect to their elders, but usually spoke English to each other.

"William, finish your dinner, then check on the huskers. I'd like to know how long they are staying. Did they bring a lunch if they are staying the full day?" Mama had cold beef sandwiches spread with fresh ground horseradish Lillie had sent along for Isaac and Sam as well as Ed and Father. Father and Ed especially enjoyed those. The aroma of horseradish filled the kitchen.

"*Sel isz schtarick* [That is strong]," Benj exclaimed.

Mama nodded. "Don't need to spread much of this on your sandwich. Some years the radishes are stronger than others."

The boys left with the sandwiches. Phillip wrinkled his nose. Benj laughed and then sneezed, and Phillip started to laugh.

"Adelaide, you go fetch that bag Sam left in the porch. Be careful, it has another small jar of horseradish."

"What is all this stuff in the bag?" Del asked as she lugged the bag into the kitchen.

"Some clothes the Allentowners sent along. Maybe I can find something for Phillip. Maybe a little something for Sunday wear. Children's shoes! These could fit someone." Mama looked pleased as she rummaged through the bag and took it upstairs.

"Adelaide, change to some warmer clothes. Get your old shoes," Mama commanded as she returned to the kitchen. "I will send you out to Jonathan and Adeline; they came this morning but will go home mid-afternoon. Give them these sandwiches. If they don't want to take time to eat, they can take them along home. I wrapped them well. Adeline will be tired, she won't need to prepare much this evening."

Mama filled an earthenware barrel-shaped crock with narrow blue stripes circling the top and wider stripes near the bottom with several gallons of warm blue mint tea. The crock had a spout located at the very bottom of the container.

"You have the right thing in mind," Father said as he entered the kitchen. "I came in for a drink. Tilghman is coming in with the team and wagon.

"Adelaide, offer the helpers tea. If you hear anything about problems with Phillip being here, fetch me. I will take care of things." Mama looked intently at Del to make sure she understood.

Father carried the heavy crock with the tea and set it on the flat wagon. "Now take your time and watch where you pull the wagon. Keep the crock as level as you can," Father cautioned Del.

"Hello, Hester," Del said as she approached the first husker, "I have some warm blue mint tea for you. Help yourself to a drink."

"Yes, I sure will. Being out in the air all day makes me thirsty." She took a sip of tea. "Phillip has been around. I hear he moves about better."

"Did you see him walk?"

"No. He's on the wagon, pushing corn up front under the seat making room for another basketful. He looks much, much better."

Del approached the next two women seated on a shock, who said, "We heard you brought a Black child to Sunday school and church."

Del shook her head and said, "No, Phillip wasn't there."

The two women regarded her and said, "Oh, we must have heard it wrong then," and took a drink of tea.

Del decided she had better move onto Adeline and Jonathan.

Adeline greeted her, "Well, Adelaide, it's good to see you. How are you?"

"I'm good—I have sandwiches and cake for you."

Adeline looked at Jonathan and said, "I don't think we should be eating while the others are working."

"Mama said you could take this along home if you want. They are well wrapped."

"We can do that. Tell your folks we say thank you. Tell Phillip he is one lucky fellow. I think he really likes our Blackie."

"Does he see Blackie?" Del was surprised.

"Of course, Benj comes for our eggs. He pulls that boy on the wagon. He says one word—horse." Adeline laughed.

"I didn't know Phillip and Benj came to your place to collect eggs. Benj never said a word."

"You ask Phillip about Blackie. Benj takes him to the stable to visit him. We always had a Blackie. The first was a stallion named Blackie. Then a mare—we named her Blackie too. This might be our last Blackie. We showed Phillip the painting hanging in our parlor of our first Blackie. Benj did the painting." Adeline paused. "You look surprised!"

Del nodded, "I am. I heard Benj painted furniture and that it looks very nice. But I didn't know he painted pictures too."

"You come down, you have to see this painting."

"Oh, I will."

The next workers greeted Del, "Hello, Adelaide. We saw the fellow the Shultz boys are all excited about. We said hello."

"Did Phillip talk?"

"No, but he smiled. Benj is so proud of that boy. Of course he can't replace his own. That barn accident was something awful. It's good to see Benj has interest in living again."

Del really wanted to ask about the barn accident, but didn't have the time. She moved quickly, mulling over the mention of a barn accident. She did her work in the feedhouse, and even shelled extra corn for Sunday morning. She set some corn by the henhouse entrance for Ori's use, plus some water by the henhouse door.

Saturday was a long day. The hardiest huskers left as the sun was sinking. It was dark by the time everyone completed their regular daily chores and went inside for suppertime.

When everyone was seated, Father said, "This was a good day. A couple more days like this and we can get to Billy's fields before the end of the month. Then the Boyers—their smaller acreage shouldn't take long at all. The small fields we can take care of ourselves."

Benj said, "Phillip here is going to be a good farmer. He learns fast. He's my boy."

"I don't hear much conversation," Father said, looking around the table.

"I am tired," Ollie said, "I'm going to bed after I eat my supper." He did look very tired and Mama told him he could go to bed without helping in the kitchen.

"Oh boy! I will!" he said enthusiastically.

"All of you will sleep good tonight." Mama smiled as she looked at Phillip. "How about you Phillip? Are you tired too?"

"I'm tired." Even in their weary state, everyone noticed that he spoke again.

"Remember you all have a paper to write by Monday. Did some of you do your writing already?" Mama asked.

"I didn't have time," Ori said as she turned to get Carol.

"*Ich schaffe mich heem un lege mich uff's ohr. Marriye isz ennanner daag* [I'll work myself home and lay me on my ear. Tomorrow is another day]." Benj got up to leave. "*Gute schlofleis da nacht* [Good sleeping this night]." He hugged Phillip and lifted his hand as the boys headed upstairs.

Del was finally alone with her parents, but she did not have the courage to ask what had happened that Benj lost two boys.

"You are unusually quiet," Mama said. "Something bothering you?"

"No. Adeline told me Benj painted a picture of their Blackie that hangs in the parlor."

"Yes. I know Benj is an artist. Something else bothers you. I know it. Did someone say something nasty?"

"Well, two ladies said they heard we took Phillip to church. They have neighbors that go to our church. I told them it wasn't so."

"Hmm. Maybe that's where the rumor started." Mama murmured. "We are finished here. You must be as tired as all the rest."

Del nodded, "Yes, I'll go to bed too."

"You looked puzzled . . . are you sure no one said anything that you don't want to tell us?"

"Nothing, nothing was said about Phillip, except one lady said he did wonders for Benj because he is willing to live again."

"She said more, didn't she?" Mama searched Del's face.

"Well, yes, Benj said that day in school he lost two, and this lady said something about a barn accident. I know it had to be young Benj and Samuel."

"I know you didn't miss what Benj said. Now you heard more," Mama said. "Did you talk to anyone about this?"

"No, I didn't get to ask anyone about it."

"I think we should wait until you are a little older." Mama looked at Father as he spoke.

"We will tell you the whole story when the time is right," Father said slowly after some consideration.

Though tired, it took a long time before Del could fall asleep. She pictured the red barn at the end of the lane. Did it burn down? It didn't look brand new. Then there was Adeline's news about Blackie and Benj and Phillip's visits there. Del drifted off to sleep with questions whirling around in her head.

Sunday, as always, was not a workday—although the animals needed the same attention seven days a week. Among the children, Til had a heavier work load, as did Bill. Til could manage a cow, sometimes two in the morning. Bill did the feeding and bedding, with Ollie stepping in to help. The morning chores for Ori and Del remained the same.

The family came in to wash-up, put on their Sunday clothes and manage a hasty breakfast. Father took the children to worship services in his Studebaker on rainy or very cold days, but today he drove because Phillip was going to Sunday school. The used clothing from Allentown yielded suitable clothes and shoes for Phillip to wear. Phillip was very surprised when he was given a coin to place in his pocket for the offering. He had to make sure it was there, checking his pocket time and again. He watched as Mama tied a coin in one corner of a handkerchief for the girls to carry. Benj broke into laughter as he explained to Phillip in broken English what needed to be done with the coin. "Ya watch de boys."

Phillip appeared to enjoy riding for the first time in the Studebaker. Father lingered until Grandfather arrived so he could take Grandfather's horse and buggy to the shelter. Til usually did this for Grandfather, but today Til and Bill would be in charge of Phillip. As they approached the church entrance, some folks stopped and glared. The children entered the building and took their places among their age group, minding their father's instructions: "Do not make a fuss of any kind. Best behavior—all of you."

Ollie followed the boys as they helped Phillip to the front right corner of the room where the younger children gathered. The stares and sudden quiet were hard to ignore.

At last the church bell rang signaling the start of the regular opening service. There was the normal noisy chatter and whispers as the offering was received. All age groups dispersed to their particular section of the building for that day's instruction. But the class for Ollie and Phillip was without an instructor. That instructor was observed walking out of the church.

Jonas, the superintendent, realized he needed a replacement teacher for that class as the children gathered around him chattering about what happened. He directed Ollie's class to follow Ori's class to the pastor's study where they always met. But when Ori's teacher saw Ollie's class following her group, she left through a back door without saying a word. Confused children milled about.

The Squire was the adult Sunday school teacher. Speaking as loudly as his shaky voice allowed, he proclaimed, "Any class that does not have an instructor is welcome to join mine."

Del's class took their usual place facing the back corner wall beside the stairway that led to the basement level. Their backs were turned to all this activity. Del could hear chairs shifting as classes reorganized. She wondered where Ollie and Phillip were. She was dying to sneak a peek at what was happening behind her.

After the lesson period, everyone faced forward for the closing worship. Del turned her chair. She saw Ori. She also saw Ollie seated with his class. But no Phillip or Til. Augustus announced the closing hymn, gave the blessing and benediction. There was next to no chatter as children dispersed. The customary handshakes and hearty good-byes were fewer. As she left the church building, there was Phillip standing with Grandfather and Bill while Til retrieved Grandfather's horse and buggy from the shelter. It wasn't long before Ori appeared with Carol by her side.

Til pulled on the reins and called "Whoa." Stepping down, Til reached for wooden steps with a chain affixed to retrieve them and placed them where Grandfather was able to climb aboard. Grandfather moved a package wrapped in newspaper from the seat. Phillip would ride home with him. The boys helped Phillip climb on board. "*Blatz fa noch eens* [Place for another one]."

"How about Carol, we always have to carry her partway," Til suggested.

"*Gute genunck* [Good enough]," Grandfather said.

The Heydt children watched Grandfather's well-groomed horse and buggy pull away. Jonathan and Adeline Conrad pulled away at the same time. Walking home, the class disruption was the only topic of conversation. Ori was really upset that she had to listen to the Squire talk about Elijah. Ollie was so animated in his descriptions of what happened that he circled the group numerous times. No one talked about the two teachers who left rather than teach a class that included Phillip.

"What's the matter with you?" Ori finally spoke. "You always have plenty to say."

"Just thinking," Del said softly. "Will we take Phillip with us again?"

"Sure hope not!" Ori said loud and clear. "My teacher left when she saw Ollie's class was joining us. All because Phillip was with Ollie," Ori concluded.

"I am more concerned about Phillip. How does he feel about all that happened?" Del said.

"I was going to my class and saw what was happening," Til heard the conversation and slowed his pace. "I took Phillip along to my class. I knew Mr. Straub wouldn't care if I had Phillip with me."

Grandfather was waiting for them as the children approached their farm lane. *"Hab gwisst oses net lang nemmed fa heem tzs laafe* [It doesn't take long to walk home]."

Grandfather made no other comment, which was most unusual since he was known to speak his mind loud and clear in any and all circumstances. *"Ich dem de zwee da ganza weg. Yaddis vun eich kann laafe wie schtarick oss ich faah.* [I will take these two all the way. Each of you can walk as fast as I drive]." Grandfather lifted the reins, there was no need to call on his horse to move as his horse responded as soon as the harness lines shifted.

"Grandfather was not pleased. You can be sure of that," Til said with certainty and Bill nodded in agreement.

The twins followed the buggy quietly going in the lane to their home. Grandfather pulled up by the walkway to the house where the children rejoined him. *"Ich gey heem. Wann es millich gerischt isz ich kanns mit nemme.* [I go home. If the milk is ready I can take it along]."

Father and Benj walked outside to meet the group. Father lifted Carol and Phillip off the buggy and Benj let Phillip lean against him. He patted Phillip's shoulder. Til told Father that Grandfather wanted to take the morning milk along.

"Help me lift the cans. I know that will give him an early start," Father pointed to Til and Bill to help.

Grandfather handed his package to Father.

Mama came out and called to Grandfather, "Come and stay for dinner," and as expected he shook his head no. Mama was frustrated by his consistent refusals, knowing he was not going to have a hot meal that day.

Ollie couldn't wait to speak, "Guess what! You won't believe this. I sat with the ADULT"—Ollie stressed the word—"Men's Bible Class today and he didn't sit with me." He pointed to Phillip. "Til came for him."

Mama had a look Del didn't like. "What happened, Til?"

"My teacher walked out instead of holding class," Ori said, interrupting Til.

"I took Phillip with me when I saw the looks on some faces. Mr. Straub welcomed us. He knew something was happening."

"*Da Billy hut nix gsaat. Fer waaz* [Billy said nothing. For why]?" Benj uttered slowly and thoughtfully.

Mama and Father looked stunned that Grandfather didn't say a word about the Sunday service.

"I asked him if attendance was good as I lifted the milk cans into his buggy. He never said a word," Father said. "Just nodded his head. He will have something to say. This isn't finished," Father said.

"You're right. He has to think about this." Mama paused. "You boys still have your Sunday clothes on. Go change."

"I thought Grandfather would tell you what happened. He saw it all," Bill said.

Everyone walked into the house. Father brought the package to Phillip, now settled on the couch. He squatted down and unwrapped a pair of shoes. "These are second-hand shoes, but I'm sure they will be a proper fit. Uncle Jer took that outline of your feet."

Phillip looked very pleased as he put on the shoes. Father had him stand and pressed his hand on the tops, the sides and front of the shoes. "I think these shoes fit your feet very well. Now you can run with the boys and go wherever they go."

"Now tell me what happened." Mama turned to Ori and Del as the boys left for the barn and took Phillip with them wearing his new work shoes.

"My teacher was there but left when she saw Phillip. I don't like her anyway. She dresses like an old maid. I had to sit with the old men's Bible class," Ori complained.

"Don't look at me!" Del spoke. "Bill and I sit in the corner and our chairs are turned to face the wall. I couldn't see what was happening. I could hear some people leaving but I couldn't see who."

"I will tell you, Mama," sighed Ori. "For sure I won't have any friends anymore. It's just good Mae doesn't go to my Sunday school. Might as well stay home after this. I don't like Sunday school anyway."

Mama looked at Benj, "I think we'll just have to wait until my father is ready to talk."

Benj just nodded his head in agreement.

Mama prepared the noon meal; she had much on her mind because she hummed some of her favorite church hymns. She always did that when she was thinking long and hard about something. Benj was also in deep enough thought to let the boys and Father look after Phillip. He had to be reminded to praise Phillip for the fine figure he cut with his new shoes. Del set the table without being told. She fetched bread to slice and placed butter on the table.

"I'm sure he was too angry to talk about it." Mama was talking softly to herself. "Another reason he had to go home right away."

Father overheard Mama. "We should have taken Phillip to church for the first time when the pastor was there. He would have straightened things out then and there." Father concluded.

"We never asked Phillip how he liked going to Sunday school," Mama turned to the little boy.

"Well, Laura, I guess we should do that. Phillip, what did you think of our church? I guess its much smaller than churches in the city." Father paused. "I hope you liked being with the children today."

"I'm not sure. . . ." Mama was cut short.

"I saw a horse," Phillip quietly said.

Mama laughed. "Just like all boys. The horse and buggy is more interesting than anything else. That's right, Phillip. I think you saw more than one horse in the shelters too."

Phillip just nodded his head.

Mama cocked her head and asked, "How many horses did you see?"

Del realized this was a test to see if Phillip knew numbers.

The little boy held up 2 fingers.

"Two horses—were those Grandfather's horse and Blackie?" she asked.

Phillip gave a big smile that meant yes and Benj patted him on the back.

"*Ah isz ennicher net bung veigh geil. Sel isz gute* [He is anyhow not afraid of horses. That is good]," Benj was pleased to say.

Mama said in Dutch, "And he knows some counting. I hope he'll tell us more about his life sometime soon."

"We have to think about what we will do next week." Father was back to serious thought.

"At least if someone at school tells me tomorrow that we took him along to Sunday school I can tell them it's true," Del said with certainty.

"How do the shoes feel, Phillip? You had time to try them out," Mama said.

"*Gucke besser os mei* [Look better than mine]," Benj chimed in.

Phillip just looked at his shoes.

"*Nah bischt en bauer's bu* [Now you are a farmer's boy]," Benj announced to Phillip.

Del watched Mama, who turned to Father and said with a worried tone, "You know how that goes when my father thinks about something for a whole week."

"I know," Father said.

"Ya have me interested enough fer next week. *Geh selvert mit fa des ob wachta* [Go along myself to watch this]," Benj said.

Father laughed. "People may be more shocked by your appearance, thinking you turned Lutheran after all these years in the Reformed church."

"Do the shoes feel all right?" Mama asked Phillip once more.

"Okay." This was becoming Phillip's standard one word answer.

Becky arrived, and Mama invited her into the parlor. "You children can play games. Make a puzzle or two. Or finish school reports if you haven't done so. Get an easier jigsaw puzzle, something Phillip can help Carol with," she instructed Ollie.

Father made his way into the front room. He motioned for Benj to follow.

"I don't expect we'll have any company. Everyone worked hard yesterday, they need to rest up for the coming week of corn husking," Mama said as she waited for Benj to follow Father.

Del went to her room to look over her written report. She found it hard to concentrate. She was still stunned that some of the Sunday school teachers walked out when they saw Phillip. It slowly dawned on her that some people attended church, but didn't really follow the teachings.

Monday morning had a light covering of white on the fields, the first frost of the season. Once the sun was up, the fields would dry out and huskers would appear. The women helpers would arrive later that morning. They would do their weekly laundry before full daylight, and hang the laundry on their clotheslines to dry until they came back. Father had an early start doing the morning work before any huskers arrived. Ed was there early to help.

Del was in the kitchen when Benj arrived, later than usual. Phillip reached for his work shoes when he saw Benj. *"Ich kon ihn mit nemme. Ah muss lanne* [I can take him along. He must learn]."

"Yes, here on the farm the day starts before daylight. He seems pleased to wear bib overalls like the boys wear," Mama smiled pleasantly.

"Besser mach unser weg draus, sehne waz fa druwwle oss ich mache kann. Da Phillip aa [Better make our way out, see what kind of trouble I can make. Phillip also]," Benj said.

"The kind of trouble you make is the welcome kind," Mama said softly.

"Ma duhnah waz ma kenna [We do what we can]," Benj said as they left the kitchen.

Mama was concerned with how the school children would react after Sunday's incident. "See to it that you don't start any fight. Don't make any angry comments. Defend only that which you know is the truth. Hear me now!"

The children solemnly nodded their heads.

"Be on your way," Mama said. "Take Phillip along outside with you. Ed will pick him up. He's leaving for the creamery soon."

"Are you worried about what will happen in school today?" Del looked to both Bill and Til as they helped Phillip walk with them.

"The Squire lives a few houses above our teacher's place. I bet he talked to him yesterday," Til seemed sure.

The truck motor could be heard as the children approached the end of the lane. Fritz danced about in a circle and waited for Ed to stop and open the passenger door to allow Phillip and Fritz to get on board. Til helped Phillip climb onto the truck seat and Fritz didn't need any assistance as he easily leapt to the running board and then the seat.

"Here comes the Whippet! Where is the Squire going on a Monday morning?" Til was most surprised. "Last week one day and today again."

"I don't know why all of you are so worried about the Squire. I'm not," Ori interjected.

Ollie teased Ori, "He's here to keep the peace. He needs to see if Taw-Taw is on the prowl."

"Stop it, Ollie! My duck is well-behaved. He wouldn't hurt anybody."

"Yeah, I know different," Ollie retorted as he started his run down the pike to meet the Shultz boys. Til also moved faster.

Bill, for a change, walked the pike with Del and of course Ori took her time, as Mae was not waiting for her. This was the first chance Del had to ask Bill what he knew about Benj's two sons.

"Only what I heard him say that day in school. I have been thinking about that too. Did you ask Mama?"

"She wouldn't tell me anything. Father said they would tell me when I am older. It was some kind of barn accident," Del replied.

"How do you know that?" Bill stared.

"One of the huskers said something about a barn accident. She said Phillip did wonders for Benj. Have you ever been inside his red barn?"

"No, never," Bill responded.

"Maybe that's why its never used. Not that I ever saw anyway," Del pondered.

"I've been waiting for you." Em said as Del reached the school grounds. "I know you took that boy to church and Sunday school yesterday, don't say it isn't so."

"You're only half right. We took him along to Sunday school, there was no church. We will have church and Sunday school next week."

"Are you going to take him along again?" Em asked.

"Why not?" Del was puzzled why Phillip's attendance was such a big concern to Em.

"Well I know some people won't go to your church anymore and that man with that car who goes to your church was visiting people yesterday. I saw him drive by this morning while waiting for you.

"So, what does that tell you? He's allowed to drive anytime he wants," Del impatiently commented.

"We saw that car at your grandfather's place coming home from the city yesterday."

Del did wonder about that, but decided not to mention that this was an interesting bit of news.

"Well," Em said. "What about that?"

"I don't know anything about that. The Squire may visit and go wherever he wants. Sunday is a visiting day," Del said.

"Pa says he only visits someone if there is trouble," Em assured Del.

"Grandfather isn't in any kind of trouble. He is selling his creamery business, and that takes some legal papers." Del was glad she thought of that.

"Not on a Sunday," Em said.

"Then, I don't know." Del had Mama's comments in mind.

The morning bell rang and school was in session. Nothing was said about church. At the dinner break, Mama was waiting for them to report on the morning happenings. Del could tell she didn't like hearing that there was very little talk about Sunday.

"Em said the Squire's Whippet was parked at Grandfather's house when they came home from the city yesterday," Del informed Mama.

"His Whippet went down the pike as we were going to school," Til announced. "He must have important business somewhere. He doesn't drive more than absolutely necessary. People know he's a real penny-pincher."

Mama listened, but didn't say a word other than "Hmm."

"*Gute fa uns uff tsz waaremer* [Good for us to warm up]," Benj shivered as he entered the kitchen.

"Where is Phillip?" Ollie asked.

"Ya didn't see Fritz, now did ya? *Sin glei doh. Allebeed uhf da waache fa nie tsz bringe.* [They soon here. Both on the wagon brought in]."

"What about the shoes?" Ollie asked.

"He is wearing them," Mama said.

"I wouldn't wear those shoes!" Ollie emphasized.

"There is nothing wrong with those shoes, they fit his feet well."

"Yes, there is! One shoe has eyes for the laces and the other has hooks."

"Finish your meal and get back to school," Mama didn't want to hear any more from Ollie.

When the children arrived Mr. Strunk was playing Round Town ball with the children. This rarely happened. He played each position except batter. He appointed a smaller child who wouldn't usually have a chance to play in his place. Del immediately guessed he wanted to hear what the children were talking about during the dinner hour. The afternoon sped by. Mr. Strunk was in full command. At recess time, Mr. Strunk was out on the playground participating in a game of Farmer in the Dell.

Walking home at the end of the school day Del reached the lane. Fritz wasn't there. Surely he was staying with all the wagons going back and forth. Del waited for her brothers.

Til commented, "You can count the times teacher plays games with us. I bet he didn't want anyone to talk about what happened yesterday."

"He probably heard things at dinnertime when we weren't there," Bill speculated.

"Good thinking, Bill," Del said.

"How did the afternoon go?" Mama immediately asked as the children entered the kitchen. "Was there any talk about Sunday?

"No one had time to talk about anything during classes. At recess times and dinner time, Teacher was outside playing games with everybody!" Til said.

That raised Mama's eyebrows. "No time for idle talk," is all she said.

CHAPTER FIFTEEN

Reports and Reactions

Tuesday morning Del awakened to the sound of a motor. "The Hudson," she said softly to herself. Her uncles and aunts were expected this day. She ran to the window in Mama's room, stood on tiptoe, stretched to lean onto the deep window seat and looked where the machine parked. Isaac and Eva, as well as Sam and Lillie, emerged from Isaac's dark blue Hudson. Del hurriedly washed and dressed. She ran down the stairs to enter the kitchen.

"You better awaken Gloria and Carol," Mama immediately said as Del opened the stairs door. "Tell Gloria to get up, dress for school and take care of Carol. We have plenty of help this morning to take care of your chores. It's too early to work in the fields. Change into your school clothes while you are upstairs."

Del ran back to Ori's bedroom. "Oh, you are awake," she said as she saw Ori sitting up in bed. "Get Carol up too. You won't have any outside work this morning."

"Oh, stop your blabbering." Ori said grumpily.

Del shrugged, changed into her school clothes and entered the kitchen a second time behind Ori and Carol.

"I see you have Carol with you. You have time to take care of her this morning," Mama said to Ori. "Carol can have breakfast now or with the adults later." Mama lifted the round stove lids and the divider and set them aside. She placed the cast iron griddle pan over the fire, which could make three griddle cakes at one time. Some of her last canned sausages were heating in the oven. Del placed molasses and butter on the table and the sugar bowl. Father always sprinkled sugar on his buttered griddle cakes.

Mama checked that all children had their written homework as Father and the relatives entered. Del heard the "yoohoos"—Lillie's usual greeting.

"It's going to be a nice day," Father said as he sat down. He wanted continuous dry and not very cold days until the corn was harvested and in the cribs.

Lillie greeted each child personally as they finished breakfast.

"Feels warm and smells so good in here," Sam said as he seated himself next to Benj. "I think I will spend my time in the kitchen today."

Mama smiled. "I will find something for you to do. Everyone here needs to earn their keep."

"If that's the case, I will follow the menfolk. There I know what I am doing. I will take this young man along." Sam brushed Phillip's hair with his hand. "He can tell me if I am doing a good job or not. Will you do that for me?" Sam asked Phillip.

Phillip pushed deeper into the couch as he looked at Sam. Finally he nodded his head yes.

"That boy shows a lot of improvement. Next thing you know, he will be running around like all the rest." Lillie sounded pleased.

The children left for school. Lillie, as always, stood by the door and checked each one for proper dress while asking if they had enough to eat. Ollie, most impatient, tried to squirm his way through between his siblings. That didn't work. Lillie grabbed his arm and checked his clothes as she did all others. "I know how boys think. You're all right," she said as she released him.

Local husking help was arriving as the children entered the lane. Fritz walked with the children. "No wagon ready for you to ride along right now. We'll see if you are free at dinnertime," Bill said to him.

"I bet the folks are discussing the Sunday school situation right now around the breakfast table. Why do you think so little was said about Sunday school yesterday from Em or anyone else? Em got it wrong again." Del asked Bill.

"I know Mama wonders about that too," Bill agreed. "All I know is Father is going to the creamery this morning," Bill stated.

"Uptown is where Father will find out what is going on," Til said softly.

"You may be right. Em told me the Squire's machine was at Grandfather's place on Sunday. We saw him drive by on our way to school yesterday. Do you think the Squire drove to the parsonage to talk to the pastor? I bet he did." Del shared her thoughts out loud.

"We'll have to wait to know what's happening," Bill said slowly.

All was quiet for a moment when Ori, walking faster without her duck, declared, "I don't know why you are talking about something that doesn't bother me one bit. Maybe I won't go to Sunday school and church anymore."

"You know better than that. Mama wouldn't let you skip church." Del scoffed and her brothers agreed.

Del entered the building as Em looked at her returned homework paper. Del saw her own papers lying on her desk. She picked them up, folded them in half and placed them in her geography book.

"Aren't you going to look what Teacher wrote on your papers?" Em asked.

"I will when I go home."

"Don't you want to see it?" Em questioned once more.

"Yes, when I go home. Teacher said he wouldn't grade them. So it doesn't matter."

"Let me see it. I will tell you if he wrote anything on your paper."

The rope was pulled and the bell rang one time. "Later," Del said as now school was in session. She was glad for that.

At recess time Em again brought up the fact that the Squire's machine was stopped at Del's Grandfather's house that past Sunday afternoon when her family drove by.

"Pa says that man doesn't go anywhere unless there is some trouble or problem that needs to be settled."

"You said that before. I know my Grandfather isn't in any kind of trouble. You are surely hearing rumors but you won't tell me who is saying what. Something good or bad?"

Em gave Del a long look, and then turned and took her seat.

"You okay?" Del said as she took her seat beside Em. There was no response.

The morning moved quickly. Del noticed that Mr. Strunk asked Til to help him carry fresh water at recess time. "Teacher is up to something," she thought. He was probably asking Til to tell him about Sunday school. Del could hardly wait for the walk home at noontime.

As soon as the children reached the pike Del was ready to ask Til what Teacher wanted to talk about but Ori was the first to ask. She wasn't dawdling behind this day.

Til got over his surprise at Ori's unusual curiosity and replied, "All he wanted to know is what I saw and heard on Sunday. That was it."

"What did he say?"

"He said what I did was good."

Before Til could say any more Ori complained, "I don't know why he always asks you. I am the oldest. I could have told him what he wanted to know. My Sunday school teacher walked out."

"He knows you," Til interrupted. "You would have probably told him, 'none of your business.'" Til chuckled at that scenario. "Besides it's the boys that carry water and that's his best chance to ask questions."

Del was glad Til said that to Ori, although he generally did not speak unkindly to anyone.

"What did he want to know?" Bill asked tactfully.

"He wondered how I felt about the whole situation. How Phillip dealt with what happened and was he mistreated. Then Teacher said, 'I believe Phillip felt he was welcome here at my school. Did he seem alright about Sunday?'"

"I don't think Phillip understood what was happening, I told Teacher. I knew Mr. Straub would be alright."

"Teacher will come by for milk this evening after the barn work is completed. He wants to talk about things with Father. He doesn't want to see another nasty outcome." Til looked troubled. "I'd like to know what he is talking about."

"I knew everything was much too quiet," Del said. "Em is the only one that said anything at all about Sunday and that, not much."

"What did she say?" Ollie was quick to ask.

"She said we took Phillip to Sunday school and church. I told her she was only half right. Em asked if we were going to take him along next week again. Then she said she knew people who would never come to our church again."

"What did you say?" Til asked.

"Nothing. Mama told us not to say anything mean. I don't know who those people are."

"*Oll zammer heit* [All together today]," Benj said as they approached the woodshed.

Til laughed as he continued his stride toward the house. He didn't take his usual detour to visit Doll since she was hitched to a wagon in the fields.

"Something go wrong?" Benj eyed them.

"Nothing wrong. We just happen to be together, that's all," Bill replied.

"*Denk ich waise besser* [Think I know better]." Benj frowned.

Mama was packing a lunch as the children entered the kitchen. Mama held a basket with food. "Here, Adelaide, before you do anything take this basket out to Adeline, she is in the field beyond the sawmill; follow the stone fence and you will see her. Give her this basket. Jonathan didn't come with her this morning, she is worried about him.

She wouldn't explain so I sent Benj out to tell Becky. Come back right away. You need to eat and go back to school."

Del found Adeline husking corn close to the stone fence while Phillip was seated on a flat rock and, of all things, Fritz lay between them. Del ran her hand across the dog's head.

"Here Adeline, Mama packed this for you to take along home."

"Your folks are most kind. I sure appreciate this."

Del looked at Phillip. "Its nice of you to keep company with Adeline. I don't know about you sitting on that rock, you could catch a cold."

"I told him the same thing," Adeline said.

Del ran past the sour cherry trees and looking back one last time, she saw Benj pulling Phillip and walking next to Adeline as she carried the basket. Del ran the walkway as Mama told her not to waste any time. She noticed Isaac's Hudson was no longer parked at its morning spot.

"Sit down and eat," Mama said. She pointed to a piece of paper that lay on the table. "Look at that."

Del picked it up. "It's Ollie's paper! I saw him fold it over and over again and shove it into his pocket. Teacher was laughing when he returned it to Ollie."

Mama said, "He lost it when he dressed this morning, I suppose. I know why your teacher was laughing when he returned it. I want to hear what Ollie says when he sees it laying on the table. Fold it up again see what Oliver does when he sees it."

The boys came in. Ollie was last. Mama stood by the stove, arms folded with a crafty look on her face. Ollie grabbed the paper and stuck it in his pocket.

"What do you have there?" Mama said.

"A piece of trash. I'll throw it on the fire before I leave for school."

"I know what you have there. No wonder Mr. Strunk was laughing. You ended your writing with an unfinished sentence. Yes, even an unfinished word." Mama shook her head. "I caught you in a lie. Lies always catch up, one way or another. You should know that by now."

Ollie looked embarrassed and hung his head.

"Did you finish the load of corn?" Mama asked the boys, changing the subject to lighten the serious mood.

The boys shook their heads as they removed their old work coats and washed their hands to enjoy a cup of hot cocoa.

"Do you know what is happening down there?" Bill asked Del as he pointed to the Conrad place.

She shrugged, "Not much. Mama sent Becky to their place to check on Jonathan. Did you hear anything?"

"Nothing at all," Bill said. "I was busy. You saw Adeline. It can't be much of a problem. They never did help husk every day." Bill tried to ease Del's concern.

After school, Del entered the upstairs and found Lillie seated at the sewing machine. "I didn't know you were here. I thought you were still visiting Grandfather."

"You know now." Lillie said without looking up. "Your Mama has a lot of sewing that needs to be done before winter sets in. Brother needs sleeves shortened on his new dress shirt. That requires a lot of work. He won't have to wear those arm bands, which can become a real nuisance. Phillip also needs a Sunday shirt. Tilghman needs flannel shirts. I already made bags for summer sausages at butchering time from those bleached white feedbags. Always lots to do."

"Goodness, I didn't know Mama had that much sewing to do. She does her mending and sewing when we are in school. She just finished a new plaid dress for Carol's birthday present."

Del stepped outside to look around. She saw Mr. Straub and Til bringing the last wagon in. Fritz was on board. Bill and Ollie were placing hay among the cattle stalls as the milking was completed. Isaac and Sam stood by the pigpen as Del walked over to them.

"I am looking at some good pork chops and bacon coming our way this winter," Isaac smiled as he spoke. "Nothing like fresh sausage and scrapple on cold winter mornings."

Once inside everyone washed up for supper. Benj and Phillip headed to their usual places—the corner rocking chair and couch. Del got the extra boards for the table. Benj helped her pull the table apart to place the extra boards properly while he explained the process to Phillip. Phillip helped to spread the tablecloth when Del threw it across the table. He seemed eager to do his part.

Del looked squarely at Phillip. "Did you see our neighbors, Adeline and Jonathan. Are they alright? Some day I hope you'll talk to me."

Phillip gave a faint smile but said nothing.

Mama walked to the stove and opened the oven door, pulled the roasting pan forward, and lifted the lid. "Good," she said. "The meat is falling away from the bone. We can eat as soon as everybody is here. Get the apple butter and cottage cheese. I see you already have bread and butter on the table. Tell Lillie to come down. There isn't enough light to work up there this late."

Benj and Phillip sat as the others came to the table one by one. Carol stood by her chair waiting for someone to place the carpeted wood block on her chair to boost her seat high enough to sit at the table. Sam, Isaac, and Eva came in. Father followed, the boys were last.

Del asked her Aunt Eva, "Where were you all day?"

"Today I worked in the far corner of the big field. I saw raccoons—don't always see them during the day, and squirrels, and a groundhog hole. It was a good day to spend outside. I'll sleep good tonight."

"Probably in the machine going home!" Isaac interjected.

Father waited for all the family and the guests to settle around the table. He offered a prayer of thanks for continued guidance and blessings.

Everyone had questions about the Conrads. Mama raised her hand, "Adeline said that Jonathan wasn't feeling well and maybe she should have stayed at home, but the day was nice and she could earn a little something." Mama paused. "We all know you need a little money to get by."

"Money," Phillip spoke clearly, taking everyone by surprise. "No money, cops, no money." He trembled.

"You're a good boy, Phillip. Don't worry about money. We will look after you," Father said as Benj laid his arm across Phillip's shoulder.

"Something happened," Til said, nodding towards Phillip as Benj tried to console him.

"Yes, Tilghman," Father spoke. "There's more to this I am sure." He changed the topic of conversation. "Becky is staying with the Conrads tonight. We'll know more tomorrow."

Phillip had calmed down and listened intently to every word Father said.

"What was wrong with Jonathan?" Bill asked his father.

"Jonathan fell and hit his head on a chair. He has quite a bump and a powerful headache, which can be understood. It's good Adeline came up this morning, or we wouldn't have known to get help. Jonathan didn't want Adeline to tell anyone about his fall, but she was much too worried to keep this to herself."

"I suppose that's where *gelt* [money] plays a part." Mama didn't want to upset Phillip again with the English word." *Vielleicht kenna sie net en Dokder bezaahle* [Maybe they can't pay a doctor]."

"*Soo haav ich gedanked* [So have I thought]." Benj placed his hand on Phillip's shoulder. "*Mei bu* [My boy]."

"I packed a basket of food for them today. I'll send some things tomorrow." Mama said to Father.

After the long workday, the Allentown and Emmaus folk decided they would not stay and chat awhile after supper. Lillie told Mama the things that she had started which she would be back to complete tomorrow. She was still talking as they walked out of the house as Father and Mama followed them to the car. Cleanup was well underway when they returned. Mama stepped in to help finish the kitchen work.

She looked around at her children. "It's been a long day, get yourselves to bed."

"*Sel gehd fa mich aa* [That goes for me too]," Benj said as he stood up.

"*Ich geh mitt* [I go along]," Father said.

Benj waved a hand indicating it was not necessary.

"*Ya gewiss. Ich wille schur mache oss du daheem kummscht* [Yes sure. I will make sure you get home]," Father insisted.

Benj gave Phillip a hug. Phillip had calmed down after his surprising outburst during supper. Father and Benj left. One by one the children got ready for bed.

The next morning Becky stood outside the house talking with Benj, her milk kettle in hand, as Del stepped into the kitchen. Benj pointed toward the barn. He was probably telling Becky where her parents were. Til was probably out there too, since he was always the first one up after Father and Mama every morning.

"Becky is here. I wonder if Dr. Schlicher came by last night," Del said as soon as Bill and Phillip opened the stairs door and entered the kitchen."

"We'll see," was Bill's only comment. "Let's get your shoes on," Bill said to Phillip. "I'll take you along out. The workers will soon be here. Seems like another nice day. Sun is up." Bill talked as he tied his own work shoes. Bill laced one shoe for Phillip while Phillip worked the hooks on the other second-hand shoe. Bill tightened the laces. "All ready. Lets go."

Del watched the boys as they walked toward the barn. Bill paused and said something to Becky as they met. Becky bent down and cupped Phillip's face up to her's and spoke directly to him. Phillip hooked onto her arm. Mama left the cow stable, and Father wasn't far behind. Benj joined them and placed his arm around Phillip's shoulder.

Ori entered the kitchen. "Where is everybody this morning?"

"Everyone is outside already. Becky is here too."

"Do I have all my chores to do?" Ori asked as Mama walked into the kitchen.

Mama nodded yes.

"What about Adeline and Jonathan? Did the doctor see him last night?" Del asked.

"Becky said Dr. Sam left some medicine and said he would be back in two days. Becky will keep a close watch on Jonathan."

Satisfied, Del headed outside for her morning chores.

Once morning chores were done, the family returned for breakfast. Mama had cereal, cold meats, and cake for dunking on the table.

Father liked cold sliced meats for breakfast with cake and coffee. Mama had a kettle full of hot cocoa and the coffee pot was perking also.

"Del, go look what kind of cake I have in the cellar. AP cakes[8] should be there. Bring two along up and tell me what else is there. I hope I have enough until baking day."

"Enough there," Del said as she returned. "Another AP and that single layer chocolate cake."

"That's right. I forgot about that." Mama said.

The children were soon on their way to school. Bill whistled for Fritz. The dog came running from the corncrib where the wagon stood ready to go to the fields.

"You can go with us, Fritzy boy. You'll hear when the horses are hitched to the wagon. You won't miss a ride." Bill ruffed the dog vigorously.

As usual, Em was waiting for Del at the school grounds. "We got here early. People were going by our place with a spring-wagon and said we could sit on the back and ride along as far as the bridge. They are going to your place today to husk corn. They finished their own husking. Did you see them?"

"No one arrived on a wagon that I saw. But the more huskers, the sooner the harvesting is done."

"My granny said she always liked to help the farmers at harvest time. She lives in the city now and is too old to do that kind of work now."

Noontime came and Del kept up with the boys as they hurried along.

"What do you think about Phillip's reaction to hearing the word 'money'?" Del asked.

"Something bad happened and there wasn't any money—that's my guess," Bill said and Til nodded his head.

"I suppose you're right," Del admitted. "But what would money have to do with anything?"

---

8 AP cakes or apiece cakes are plain single layer cakes typically baked in a pie tin and served as a breakfast pastry. Many PA Dutch people dunk this cake into milk or coffee.

When the children arrived at the farm, there was no one in the house; Mama had food on the table for everyone to help themselves to dinner. Til made a sandwich and left as he downed the last bite. Ori too, came in, ate quickly and was on her way out with a quarter peeled apple in her hand for Taw-Taw. Del and Bill sat down to eat sandwiches. Carol entered through the back door.

"Just look at your shoes. Take them off."

"Mama is in the strawberry patch spreading the straw between the rows. I was helping."

"Good, but you should have been more careful of where you stepped."

"Mama said to go inside, someone would help me," Carol said.

"I suppose that is going to be me. You wouldn't know if Adeline is here or not?" Del asked.

"Mama and me went there. Uncle Isaac is here," Carol said.

"That's good. I'll set your shoes in the porch. What do you want to eat?" Del asked.

"Mama said to wait."

"Well then, you wait. We'll do what Mama says."

Mama entered by the back door. "The strawberry patch is finally all ready for the winter. Should have done that weeks ago."

"I helped!" Carol said eagerly.

"Yes, Carol, you helped. William, you go find your father and tell him and our relatives to come in to eat something before you go back to school."

"Where is Phillip?"

"Phillip and Benj were in early and ate. I packed a lunch for them to take down to the neighbors." Mama smiled at Del. "Phillip was eager to go. There is something special there that has sparked his interest and concern. Must be more than that horse. Get yourselves back to school, if you want any play time at all."

The afternoon dragged on for Del. She moved quickly to take Mr. Strunk's hand at dismissal time. Del and the Goho girls walked along the lane. Anabel and Maria shyly acknowledged Benj standing by the woodshed. Benj immediately told them he knew their mama and grandparents quite well. Ori was in the kitchen when Del entered. On the table were Becky's dark chocolate cookies. "If Becky had time to bake then she didn't spend all her time at Conrads," Del thought.

Ollie hurried with an armful of wood. He let the wood fall into the wood chest, brushed off his sleeve. He grabbed a cookie, took two bites, laid it on the table and made his way upstairs to change clothes without a word.

Mama came in and washed her hands. She turned and looked at Del and Ori. "Benj did most all your evening work."

"Did Isaac go home already?" Del asked, hoping for an answer.

"Yes. He expects to hear from his brother tonight or tomorrow sometime."

"I didn't know he had a brother!"

"Yes, and he won't have to wait until Thanksgiving to see him. It so happens he will be coming to Allentown this week." Mama said.

"What's he like?"

"I really don't know. I never met Isaac's brother."

"Is he a farmer?"

"Not that I know, but he was raised on a farm same as Isaac."

Del said no more, but she was puzzled at this mention of a brother. Why would he show up in their lives now?

The table conversation covered the husking progress, Phillip and the neighbors. Then Father announced, "Your grandfather is closing the creamery the last week of November."

"No more cutting ice for the creamery anymore? That's the hardest work I ever did—cutting ice off a frozen dam," Til looked hopefully to Father.

Mama said to Father, " But there's still a need for ice in the creamery and the hotel."

"I hear tell an ice man will be coming through here regularly with cakes of ice," Father replied.

"Whoever heard of cakes of ice?" Ori exclaimed.

"Never you mind, Gloria. It's really blocks of ice. City people have deliveries all summer long for their iceboxes. With the new highway we have access to many more things," Father explained.

"You will probably have to cut ice this year once more. Don't you think?" Mama looked at Father.

"We'll see. From what I hear, there's an ice route now but they haven't come out this far. Sure would be a lot easier if that should happen." Father turned to Mama. "We could get an ice box then. No running outside to the spring house every time we want something cold."

Mama looked at Father and half smiled. "That would be good, but isn't our lane out of their way?"

"*Sie ghenna wu sie verkaafe kenne* [They'll go where they can sell]." Father said and Til chuckled.

Del thought cutting ice must have been hard work if Til made that comment. He was a hard worker and never complained about any chore.

It was well past the supper hour and the Allentown helpers were gone when Becky and Phillip came through the door.

"You had supper Phillip?"

Mama looked to Becky after Phillip didn't answer.

"Tell her Phillip. Tell her right away what you had," Becky encouraged.

Phillip, as usual, didn't answer.

"You had chicken and . . ." Becky prodded Phillip.

Again no reply. "Corn bread." Becky concluded. "Yes, Adeline cooked a good meal. I haven't had corn bread for a long time. Warm and oh so . . . good," Becky said.

"So you both had your fill."

Becky nodded her head. "Tomorrow we'll go down again. Its time for that streak of lightning to come by."

"Do you want me to drive you down to Conrad's place tomorrow?"

"No, Woodie."

"What about Phillip?" Mama asked.

"He should probably go along in the morning. Dr. Sam could check him there," Becky said. "Well, I'll be on my way. *Gute nacht* [Good night]."

"Thanks for the cookies. *Gute nacht* Becky!"

"*Gey selvert hame* [Go myself home]." Benj accompanied Becky leaving the house.

Del pondered many thoughts as she headed upstairs. She took her schoolwork and graded papers along. She unfolded her returned paper and placed it carefully in her top drawer. She wondered what Grandfather would do once he closed his creamery. Jonathan seemed to be improving, or at least Becky didn't say he was worse off. Del sighed, said her prayers silently and drifted off to sleep.

CHAPTER SIXTEEN

A Visitor Arrives

Saturday morning Del awakened to the roar of a motorcycle. She ran to the window in her parents' bedroom expecting to see Isaac. Much to her surprise, not one but two motorcycles were side by side in the lane. Isaac and who else? She watched as the two men undid the chin straps to the black leather caps, removed the goggles, and hung them on the handle bars. She leaned harder into the hinged window seat that when lifted, revealed a metal box that was fire-safe. The men pushed their motorcycles under the open-front woodshed and propped them there. Her father leaned on an open Dutch barn door to the cow stable. He looked happy to greet them as he reached down and unlatched the lower half-door. Father walked the full length of the overshoot to greet both men. The barn swallows, being disturbed, put on an agitated performance, flying rapidly by while swooping down over anyone close by. Isaac and his friend seemed to enjoy their swooping antics as they met Father in the lane. Father welcomed both with a handshake amidst laughter from all three.

Del rushed back to her bedroom and prepared to meet this new day. She entered the kitchen realizing she would be confined to household duties all day. Layer cake pans, bread pans, and regular pie tins were on the white table. The husking activity prevented Mama from getting all her Friday baking done. Mama came in momentarily and told Del what was expected of her. She just nodded as Mama continued, "I expect Lillie will do more sewing today. Clean your own room, and you and Gloria split up the cleaning of the boys' rooms.

Del asked, "Who is with Isaac?"

Mama replied. "That is Ira, Isaac's twin brother. But they don't look alike."

Isaac's brother was taller and heavier with straight graying hair parted on the side. Del wanted to meet him, but Mama had her mind on kitchen chores.

"Take care of the fires. Keep a good heat. Get the long griddle pan and put it over the fire after you set the stove lids and divider aside. I'll be back as soon as the milk buckets are washed."

Del walked out to the pump and filled the small shiny milk pail with fresh water. Once outside she saw Til, Benj, and her parents talking to Isaac and his brother. Til smiled as he walked away from the group and headed over to the woodshed to examine the motorcycles with scrutinizing eyes. She knew Til would give a detailed description of all the parts.

Bill and Phillip stepped out from the feed entry door and slowly moved toward the group. Bill was most anxious to look at the motorcycles. Phillip wasn't interested, he just wanted to join Benj. Bill ran to the woodshed where he joined Til. She watched them point to areas of interest on the motorcycles.

"Good morning," Del called, as she stood on the walkway. It appeared no one heard her.

Ollie came rushing by so fast he pushed Del aside. "Come look at the motorcycles," he yelled, "two of them are here!"

"What took you so long?" Ori asked as Del returned to the kitchen.

"I wasn't gone long at all. I just looked to see who was here. Ollie came racing out, had I been on the walkway he would have run me over," Del replied with a grin.

"He didn't hear anything I said," Ori remarked. "He didn't even take time to tie his shoes. If he breaks his neck, not my fault."

Mama came back. "Here, Adelaide, you take this overall jacket out to Oliver. I don't want him catching a cold. The men will help finish the morning chores, then come in for breakfast. They said they had a bite before they left this morning. I'm afraid Ira got up pretty early. Had to come in from . . ." Mama paused, "A long way. Good I decided on griddle cakes this morning, I can always make more."

Del grabbed Ollie's coat. "Wear something to go outside," Mama advised.

Del wrapped Ollie's jacket around herself as best she cold.

"Here is another twin," Isaac introduced Del to Ira. "We are different enough. Bigger difference here," Isaac pointed to Bill.

"I didn't know this," Ira said. "So you and Bill are twins. Tell me who is the boss?"

"I don't know," Del had never been asked a question like that.

"Isaac never told you?" Ira questioned. Del shook her head. "First-born is always the boss."

"That's me! I was born before him," Del pointed to Bill. "Benj knows that story."

"*Gonz letz. Sechzich yaahr davohr. Ich waise viel mehner, bin boss* [Altogether wrong. Sixty years before. I know much more, I'm boss]." Benj laughed and all the adults joined him. Benj never let anyone forget he and the twins shared a birthday.

"You went out without a sweater anyway," Mama observed as Del returned.

"I wasn't out long. Ira sure looks different. Not anything like Isaac that I could tell."

"Isaac says he looks like his mother, and his brother Ira is the image of the father. I never met the parents but Eva says its true."

"How comes Isaac's brother is here now? I heard Eva say Isaac's family always get together once a year and that's between Thanksgiving and Christmas in New York. Does Ira live in New York too?" Del asked.

"He is here now." Mama was abrupt. Then she asked, "How is the bacon? I want it nice and crisp."

"I turned it once. Looks okay to me."

"This is the last I have left from last winter's butchering. I bet Ira didn't get this kind of country breakfast for awhile." Mama retrieved the fry pan with bacon from the oven and set it on the stove next to the griddle pan. "Fetch two crumb cakes, it's all I have for dunking this morning. We need to do more baking today after breakfast. I have bread dough rising already. I don't know if we are going to have company tomorrow or not but I don't want to be caught empty-handed."

When Del returned, Mama commanded, "You look, Adelaide, have they loaded the milk cans on the truck?"

Del stepped outside to check. She saw Becky approaching the homestead. She waited to walk into the house with Becky.

"Hello, Adelaide, it's a little cool to be without a wrap this morning, don't you think?"

"I'm going in with you. Did you hear those motorcycles this morning, parked there in the woodshed?"

Becky turned to look back as Del pointed in that direction. "So that's what I heard! They sure make a racket."

"Did they awaken you?"

"No, I always get up very early."

"Uncle Isaac and his twin brother are here. They arrived on those motorcycles. First time I ever saw his brother and they are not at all alike."

"Where is Phillip?" Becky inquired.

"Somewhere with the boys," Del replied.

"I'm sure your brothers were right up front examining those noise makers as closely as they could, that's how boys are. Was Phillip with them?" Becky wondered.

"Bill and Phillip came from the barn in a big hurry. Bill left Phillip with Benj. It seems Phillip wasn't interested in motorcycles."

"I suppose he saw lots of motorcycles, coming from the big city," Becky concluded as she headed for the walkway. Becky watched as

Benj walked over toward the feed entry with Phillip. "He walks better all the time. Don't you think?" Becky inquired.

"Yes, Becky, he doesn't drag that foot like he used to."

"I want to take him along with me this morning after he has breakfast to meet Dr. Sam at the Conrads." Becky spoke thoughtfully.

"Come along in. Mama is inside making breakfast for everybody."

"Good morning, Becky. How are things at the Conrads?" Mama greeted Becky.

"Can't say much for sure yet. Jonathan is holding his own, so it seems. I saw Phillip is up this morning. Did he eat? I want to take him along to the Conrads. Dr. Sam can see the progress he is making. I already told him the vaccination didn't grow."

"Phillip should eat first. I could send a basket with a hot breakfast along for you and the Conrads. Someone can take the two of you there. I know it's not far, but Phillip moves very slowly, the food would get cold."

"I don't move as fast as I used to. Why are you giggling?" Becky pointed at Del.

"Just thinking, Isaac could take you there on his motorcycle and Ira could take Phillip on his. That would be quick and fun at the same time."

"It wouldn't be fun at all. You will know I'm crazy in the head if you ever see me on a motorcycle."

Mama laughed, "Adelaide, take my big pitcher and fetch milk. Your father knows I need to do a lot of baking today."

Del overheard a portion of her mother's conversation with Becky as she entered the porch with a pitcher full of milk.

"It's good Phillip won't be here when we talk to Ira."

"Everyone is coming in," Del said as she walked into the kitchen. Del's curiosity was boundless. What were they going to talk to Ira about?

"Good. Your breakfast is ready to go." Looking at Becky, Mama said, "You tell us when we need to fetch him." She continued, "I need to ask

Adeline what makes Phillip so concerned about them, especially with Jonathan. What do you think, Becky?"

"I don't know," Becky answered.

"From what Woodie says, he really wanted to go home with Adeline. It can't be about that horse even if they say it's the first word he said to them. When we mentioned the word money, Phillip became emotional. No money, cops. I can't quite figure why a child should say that," Mama concluded.

"I don't think we should lay that aside. Especially police? No money to buy what? Buy food, pay a debt? There is something more there that isn't said . . ." Becky pointed a finger as she spoke.

All the menfolk gradually walked into the kitchen and washed up. "Phillip, would you like to go along with Becky to see how Jonathan and Adeline are doing this morning?" Mama spoke as Phillip sat at the table and looked at Becky. "Tilghman can drive the two of you there. You want to do that?"

Phillip looked at Becky and finally nodded his head.

"Good, Phillip." Becky was pleased.

The door opened and the Hetrick brothers stepped inside. Isaac introduced his brother.

Father looked at Til. "Take Becky and Phillip down to the Conrads now."

Til extended his arm toward Phillip. Becky picked up the basket Mama had prepared and followed them out the kitchen.

"Don't waste any time. Come back and take the milk to the creamery. My father likes the milk as early as possible," Mama admonished Til.

Til just nodded his head as he left and Mama commented how very helpful he was.

"Tilghman is good size for his age," Ira remarked.

"He followed his father around the live long day as soon as he could walk. He learned to handle and take care of horses very early. He walked a team to the blacksmith shop when he was only eight years old. I didn't like that at all, although Woodie said he did the same at that age." Mama spoke with pride. "We're waiting to see if William and Oliver will be as tall."

Ira replied, "I will say, my boys, growing up in the city, are more advanced in schoolwork and academics than I was at their age. But I feel I learned more about the basics in life by growing up on a farm. In the country neighbors look out for one another. Not so much in the city, except for relatives." He grinned. "Farming is hard work but so very rewarding. You get tired of husking corn but you finish the job and the same work won't be back for another year. I never regretted I grew up on a farm."

Del realized she needed to get her upstairs work done and be back to help with the dishes. She heard a lot of hearty laughter coming from the downstairs as she moved about upstairs. Del finished the boys' rooms and decided to tidy up Mama's room at the same time. Her room was the last one to clean. When she returned to the kitchen Mama had prepared more bread dough and placed it in the baking pans to rise. Ollie was told to keep enough wood on hand, as he came in with another armful. Del's next job was to grease pie tins with lard that would be lined with pie dough. High cake pans were made ready as well. Mama entertained herself with reciting poetry she learned as a schoolgirl and singing her favorite songs and hymns while she did her baking. Del knew Mama wasn't interested in any conversation.

Just then, there was the sound of a machine coming down the lane. It stopped by the walk. It was Sam, of all people. No wonder Mama was certain Lillie was coming, and Eva was with them. Mama was expecting them, otherwise the breakfast food would have been cleared. Del had never seen that machine before—it was a 1922 Chevrolet motor machine. It couldn't seat more than four adults comfortably.

"Yoohoo!" Lillie called as she got out of the car.

It wasn't long before Til was back from the creamery to examine that machine front to back. Del asked Mama if she could go out and hear the things Til would say about Sam's machine. Til looked at the round window in the back, along with three windows on each side. It had wire wheels with fenders spaced quite high over the tires and a high windshield with a short roof extending over it. Tail lights were fastened to the rear fender, and a glass hood ornament showed if the radiator held enough water. Sam, Lillie, and Eva only accepted a cup of coffee and a piece of cake, saying they had breakfast before they left home this morning.

"Did you bring a camera along?" Mama asked Eva.

"Sure, I brought our camera along. Left it in the machine."

The adults scattered to their different chores while Mama continued her baking lineup in the kitchen.

Mid-afternoon Del was sent out to the fields hauling the large crock on her flat wagon with warm tea for the workers. She took deep breaths of fresh air in the nice fall afternoon.

Father, Ira, and Isaac were husking a shock of corn in an area a good distance from their fellow huskers. Father and Ed were usually the two doing the wagon runs.

Del pulled the flat wagon to the falter and called the nearest huskers to stop by for a warm drink. Father called from afar and said they would walk to her parked wagon. Del reflected on Father's work crew. Usually there were four people to a shock, so why was it just her father with Ira and Isaac? Maybe there isn't a fourth person available? It was a strange arrangement since husking was done row by row.

Mama's baking was winding down. Del saw the results of the busy day. All those pie tins she greased now needed to be washed. Del measured the molasses for shoo-fly pies and the ingredients for a double batch of AP cakes. Mama said they stayed fresh longer than other pastries. Del mixed the batter for a favorite chocolate layer cake. Finished loaves of bread cooled on the window sills. The pie shells she sprinkled with coconut for custards were still warm. Pumpkin custards with cinnamon sprinkled on top were ready to carry down to the swing board that held the week's baking. Til stuck his head in the door. "Anything to eat? he asked.

"The pumpkin custards are ready but the AP cake would be easier for you to handle."

Til said, "Isaac and his brother are leaving soon. They want your box camera. Ira said photographs would show his boys the kind of work being done on the farm."

"Take ours, and Eva's camera is on the back seat of Sam's car, too. Tell all the workers, especially those who weren't here before, to take a pumpkin or two along. We will never use them all." Mama paused. "No place for pumpkins on a motorcycle."

After supper the evening was spent quietly—everyone relaxed after a full day of work. Mama remained seated to enjoy that extra cup of coffee with Benj and Father. Del was tired, having spent all day helping Mama and running back and forth among the corn huskers. Mama checked the last pans of bread, "Give them five minutes more," she said quietly.

Mama asked Father about Ira and how he spent the day. "He was busy trying his hand at all the different tasks. From shoveling corn, loading the wagon, handling the team, yes, and husking corn. He spent a little time helping with the barn chores this morning. He'll come again before too much longer," Father hesitated, "if he can manage the time."

"If he doesn't come again, we can take care of things, not so?" Mama questioned.

"Suppose so," Father added.

"I should have had more film. Luckily Eva brought her camera," Mama said.

The last baking was lifted from the oven and set on the white enamel table to cool. Two batches of bread in one day meant that Mama wouldn't have to bake again before Friday.

Benj arose from his chair, walked over to Phillip, and patted his shoulder. "I'll see ya in the morning." He lifted his hand in a wave, indicating good night.

"Til, you walk with Benj." Mama said.

"*Ich hab en lutze* [I have a lantern]."

"Tilghman, you walk along," Mama said firmly. "Benj, you get a good night's rest."

"Tomorrow will be an easier day. We need to get up a little earlier, since we are all going to Sunday school and church," Father announced as Til and Benj were leaving.

"Some of us have to walk or Father has to make two trips," Bill said thinking about the size of the family.

"That's taken care of. No one has to walk. Time to make ready for bed. We all had a full day." Father sent the children up the stairs. "I'll wait for Tilghman to come back."

Once snuggled comfortably in her bed. Del considered the idea of going to church as a group. For Sunday school only one parent or the other went, not both of them. She remembered Benj saying he wanted to see what would happen when Phillip attended church for the first time. If tomorrow was anything like last week, it would sure be interesting.

CHAPTER SEVENTEEN

A Better Sunday

Mama seemed uneasy as she bustled about unnecessarily, humming a tune. She was dressed in her Sunday best. All she needed to do was remove her apron and place her hat before leaving for church. Phillip, seated on the couch, was dressed in a shirt Aunt Lillie made and pants altered to fit that Bill had outgrown. The Studebaker was parked by the walkway. Del knew they couldn't all fit in the car at one time. "What were these arrangements they mentioned?" she wondered.

Benj came in. He was dressed similarly to the day he came to school with Phillip. He seated himself on the rocker next to Phillip and gently patted the boy's hand. "Found two hats fer ya. See if any fit." He tried one hat and then the other. "Well, watcha think?"

Phillip pointed at the dark blue newsboy cap. "I like that," he said very solemnly.

"Then you wear it!" Benj said, putting it on his head. "That's settled, now to see what happens this week," Mama spoke seriously after she glanced at Phillip wearing his new cap.

"I heard the Squire was busy driving around every day," Til added with a serious look instead of his usual cheerful demeanor.

"It should be better than last week. The news is out," Mama said.

"*Ich vil eppes aagfange* [I will start something]. Will go to my church, and visit some graves. Lots for my family and Becky's are side by side." Benj patted Phillip's hand.

Del immediately realized that Benj's boys would be buried there. She had to walk over to that cemetery and look for the Fronheiser plot.

Father and the boys walked into the kitchen.

"All finished in the barn?" Mama asked quickly.

"Everything is done, thanks to Ed. Now he's off to visit his son and the in-laws."

Ed's son lived with his grandparents in the next village, who had the means to feed and clothe him. Ed's work was scant and Hester's stocking mill had more lay-off days than work days, here of late. They weren't the only family in the area that made such difficult choices.

Grandfather drove by the house, maneuvered his buggy in the turn-around and then stopped by the walk and waited there. Mama went out to greet him. She came back to give instructions to Del and her siblings. "Just stand by Phillip and make sure he is alright. Mind me now! Adelaide and Tilghman, you ride with your Grandfather."

Til quickly stood up still chewing his last bite of cake as they left to board the buggy. Grandfather began chatting before the horse began to move. He made small talk about his dog Brownie, a bearded fox terrier. Grandfather always had the same breed of dog as his walking companion. He talked about how he found Fritz in Philadelphia on one of his market trips. "I may have kept Fritz, except Brownie was just a couple of weeks old at the time and Fritz, well, his breed was too big a dog for me to keep." He spoke the dialect all the while except for a word now and then in broken English, which surprised Del. Surely he knew both she and Til could speak and understood all he would say in Dutch. She wondered if he spoke to Phillip in the Pennsylvania Dutch dialect when they were alone. She smiled thinking how that would shock some people if Phillip knew the dialect. "Cement pike hard on horse shoes," Grandfather said as he pulled to the roadside when it was wide enough for his horse to walk on the dirt shoulder. Grandfather spared his horses any unnecessary hardship. It was not easy for a horse to walk on the new cement road. The metal shoes could cause a horse to slip.

Grandfather made note of the various properties they passed. Where lightning had struck a barn and it burned down. Where a bull crippled a man by pinning him against the stonewall in the outside cattle pen. Where a severe windstorm lifted a house roof. Where four generations lived on the same farm. Where the great-grandparents called home and raised ten children. The buggy crossed Bieber Creek as they approached the church. Grandfather drove as close to the church as he could. He pulled on the reins and called "Whoa." The buggy stood still. Til jumped down and placed the steps that Grandfather had designed and helped him make the descent to the ground.

They stood under a leafless tree until Til came back after taking the horse and buggy across the dirt road, where a long row of shelters stood. Til drove into a shelter, stepped down, took the line and loosely attached it to a metal ring fastened to a bar in the front portion of the shed. It was then the Studebaker approached the church. The whole family would be together now. Father and Bill helped Phillip, while Til took charge of the Studebaker and parked it where a few other cars stood.

Del heard Father say to Phillip, "You try your very best to walk, Phillip. We want these people to see how much you have improved since they last saw you."

Mr. Losch was the usher. He greeted the family and the Pastor extended his hand to each one. *"Mer bleiwe menanner wann blatz huscht* [We'll stay together if you have place]," Grandfather suggested.

"Ganz roi karichesitz [Whole row church pew]," replied Edgar.

"Gute genunk [Good enough]," Grandfather spoke softly.

Til was the first to come down the center aisle and step into an empty pew. Everyone filed in and Grandfather sat at the other end, filling the entire pew. Regular parishioners took their usual places in the church. It was was unusually quiet, Del thought. Normally there was a low murmur of aminated conversations before the service began, but today she only heard the sounds of whispering folk.

Del could tell when the Squire arrived, because the shaky voice said it all. "*Sitz mich selwert* [Seat myself]," he said. He seated himself in a pew in the middle of the church. That was most unusual. The Squire always sat close to the front as he was hard of hearing. Today he deliberately chose a different pew further back.

Mr. Losch's ushering duties picked up as worship time was minutes away. People were filling pews further front. Mr. Reifinger and two boys she never saw before were seated in front of Del. Em would be sure to tell her tomorrow about the visitors next door at her neighbors, the Reifingers.

The church bell rang, signaling time for worship to begin. The pastor came in and greeted everyone, pleased with a good attendance. He said he was happy to greet a new member in the Heydt family. "We welcome him," he said. He made a few community announcements and worship began as he announced the opening hymn. The organ roared to life to play the tune for the first hymn as the hymnals only contained the lyrics and not the music. The choir walked in singing the first stanza of the opening hymn without organ accompaniment, and took their place on the choir loft. Their neighbor Jonathan, usually a faithful choir member, was not there this day. Adeline, too, was absent. Del gave Jonathan a prayerful thought, hoping things would turn out alright as the pastor mentioned them in the prayer in the opening greeting.

Del heard the pastor say, "Today I will stray from the written text. I will tell you about an act of kindness that has taken place in our neighborhood a few weeks ago. Yes, you need to know about a decision one person made to show Christian compassion and kindness to someone who desperately needed help." The pastor paused. "Mr. Heydt could have looked the other way."

Del looked at people she could see without drawing Mama's attention. She noticed the Squire, his chin resting on his chest, his long white beard pushed forward, she couldn't tell whether he was dozing or in deep thought. There were the Reinhards and Abraham and Orphelia Straub, always a very distinguished looking couple. Del heard the word Philadelphia and gave the pastor her full attention.

"Have you ever encountered a situation that required a decision with a moments notice? Not enough time to pray and sleep on it first, as we sometimes do. No time to wait for tomorrow. Have you ever felt the need to help someone but chose to go the other way and your conscience bothered you later? I could have, I should have, those excuses that follow are something we all experienced."

Someone had a coughing spell and Del could hear shuffling of feet and the snap of a pocket book. The coughing was subdued, but not stopped as Del heard a person behind her walk up the aisle and out of the church.

"Now what did he say?" Del wondered.

The pastor asked Father, Mama, and Phillip to stand and be acknowledged. "Let's take this a little further. A starving child, dressed in rags was placed in his arms. Mr. Heydt heard the market men in Philadelphia encourage him to abandon the child."

Sighs, exclamations of 'no' and 'oh my', is what Del heard all around her.

The pastor continued, "You saw this child as you entered the church. Phillip is his name, and he is much better now. Mr. Heydt made an extraordinary decision based not on what people will say and think, but on saving the life of a child. I commend him for responding first as a Christian. I hope we are beyond prejudices, especially when it comes to children in need of our help. We are a Christian congregation and community. We need to respond as our Christ would do. You now know the full story. Think about that and what you would really do if you were in the same situation."

The pastor then proceeded to read the lessons and promised a shorter sermon. Del again scanned the area she could see without turning her head. The Squire was now holding his head in an upright position.

Finally the last hymn was announced. The pastor then admonished all: "For this community—no more talk of falsehoods, you heard the facts. We will not allow and will not listen to any talk that repeats false-hoods. We will not condemn an act of kindness, we will celebrate it. Keep that in mind when you speak and when you act."

That put Del's mind to thinking. That's what the Squire must have been doing, telling people all about Phillip before any false rumors would start. Grandfather must have helped too. He probably told people as they came to the creamery and met Phillip.

Grandfather's wide smile told Del he was extremely pleased with the service, for he said, *"Ich denk ma hen ebbes gelannt* [I think we have something learned]." Father and Mama seemed pleased as well.

Del was puzzled. What did Grandfather learn? Who could she ask to explain what they meant? Del was engrossed in her own thoughts as the first parishioners greeted the pastor and members of her family. She was shocked to see one Sunday school teacher step behind the pastor to avoid shaking hands with the family as she made her way into the room for Sunday school. Del stayed with her family as some parishioners took time to say a word or two of encouragement. Some congratulated Father on his "leap of faith," as Del heard someone say, and other parishioners shook hands with the pastor, acknowledged the Heydt family, and smiled at Phillip.

For Sunday school, her teacher spoke before taking attendance. "I think we need to tell Adelaide and William, their father has done a very kind thing. I will allow a few minutes after the lesson for you to comment or ask the twins what it was like to welcome a stranger into their home."

Del's mind wandered during the lesson as she considered what her classmates would ask. After the closing prayer on the bottom of the lesson page, Miss Lydia announced free time for a few questions.

The first one was, "Why was that boy in the barn?"

She replied, "Father didn't know if Phillip had any disease we could get. He didn't want any of us to become sick."

The boys gathered around Bill. Their main question was, "How can you tell if he is going to stay or maybe run away again?"

The teacher gently responded, "Pretend you are that child. Which would you prefer? Warm clothes and food to eat, plus a house to sleep in or none of that. I think we would all be ready to accept whatever a stranger would offer."

After the closing hymn and dismissal their teacher beckoned Del and Bill to stay behind and said, "Did your neighbor Becky help you those first few days?" Del and Bill nodded their heads. "Who else helped?"

"Becky, Ed and Hester, and my grandfather for sure," Bill replied.

Their teacher leaned forward and whispered, "What about Benj?"

"Benj stayed in the barn that first night," Del said as Bill again nodded his head.

"Benj was there most of the time," Bill said.

Their teacher stood back and shook her head. "This could almost be a miracle," she murmured, and let them go.

Del and Bill ran as Til brought Grandfather's horse and buggy up to the church and stopped under the same tree. Once Del and Til climbed aboard the buggy Grandfather smiled. He obviously liked how this church service turned out. Grandfather stopped at the lane and dropped Del and Til off to walk the rest of the way home.

Del turned to Til as they walked, "What did you think about today?"

"It was good the way it turned out. The Squire's car put on more miles this past week than it does in a half year. He was all over the place."

"Where did you hear that?"

"From the neighbors," Til said as he headed for the barn.

There was much conversation in the kitchen as Del joined the rest of the family.

Mama looked at Del. "Fetch my high chocolate cake. We'll have that for dessert."

Del went to the cellar swing board and grabbed the aluminum cake saver with indented green painted leaves and rose-colored buds decorating the cover.

After the noon meal, the Shultz boys came with their Parcheesi board. The boys, including Phillip, participated in the game in the side room. Phillip seemed to enjoy the game although he didn't talk. There was a game of dominoes on the same table. Ori insisted on playing ball and jacks on the kitchen table with her friend Mae. A jigsaw puzzle was set up on a folding table where Del and Carol spent their time.

Mama made popcorn balls for the children. She stuck each on pointed sticks that Benj had whittled, and everyone enjoyed them as fast as Mama made them. Their company dispersed around chore time.

Benj and Phillip joined the men with the evening animal caretaking. Del and Ori had their own duties. Del was pleasantly surprised to see Taw-Taw had a piece of binder twine wrapped around one leg and was tied to a chicken coop. She smiled as she thought, "Pretty clever. That duck isn't strong enough to drag that wooden coop. This most certainly was not Ori's idea." She opened the henhouse door and called loud enough for Ori to hear. "Corn and water here! I'm going in now. Carol can come along."

"You tied my Taw-Taw! Untie him and bring that coop in here," Del heard Ori yell back.

"Can't do that. I didn't tie Taw-Taw. Pretty clever though!" Del laughed.

"Sure you did it, no one else was here. He wasn't tied when I first came out. I can't even loosen the knot."

"I can pick him up coop and all and put him in the feedhouse for you."

No answer was forthcoming. Del decided to pick the duck up, set him on the coop and place him inside knowing Ori could have more than one bucket full of eggs to carry. Much to Del's surprise that duck didn't make a sound. She looked at the knotted twine. She never saw knots like that, and twine was difficult enough with regular square knots.

Once in the kitchen she asked Mama, "Who tied Taw-Taw to a chicken coop?"

Mama laughed. "I don't know, but that could solve a lot of problems. We'd always know where he is."

"Ori thinks I did it, but I didn't." Del hesitated, than said, "Mama, my teacher wanted to know who helped those first couple of nights in the barn. She asked if Benj was there."

"Did you tell her that Benj stayed in the barn with Phillip?"

Del nodded her head. "She said to herself something about a miracle. What did she mean?"

Mama looked at Del with bemusement. "Oh, that's an interesting thought," and turned back to the stove.

Benj came in. "Everyone in soon. "

"Who tied Taw-Taw to the coop with binder twine?" Del asked quietly. She didn't want Ori to walk in on this conversation.

"May as well tell ya." Benj spoke very softly in the dialect. "It was Ed's idea. I think that duck pinched him. He got a piece of binder twine and knotted it good. Ed did it and hurried home before anyone knew he was here. Now don't you tell her."

"Oh, I won't. She thinks I did it. I'll let her believe that." Del was amused. "I don't often get something on her."

"Yep, another trickster in the making." Benj seemed satisfied with his judgment.

Del shrugged her shoulders and laughed.

Ori was really upset when she came in and immediately declared, "Del tied my duck to a chicken coop. I had to ask Father to cut the twine with his pocketknife. He said no one would be able to undo those knots. Look at her, she isn't sorry she did it."

Del just rolled her eyes and shook her head. "That duck was tied to the coop when I came out. All I did was carry him, coop and all, inside. I did a big favor for you. You don't know how hard it was to hold your duck and carry that coop sideways to get through the open door."

"I'll get even with you for this."

"Forget it, Gloria, your duck is safe, that's all that counts. Adelaide didn't do it. Finish your work," Mama sharply said.

Benj sat in the rocking chair holding an opened newspaper high enough to hide his face. Mama turned her back to Ori and tried to hide a smile.

Supper was eaten quietly. Phillip did his part. "I can help," he said as the girls cleared the dishes. He placed the dried dishes on the white baking table.

"We had a good day, I think," Father said.

Ori pointed an accusatory finger at Del, "Why won't you punish Del for what she did to my duck? I know she did it."

"Gloria, those knots were made by someone who knows how to make difficult knots. I couldn't undo them," Father said.

"Sure, she was the only one out there. She did it," Ori insisted.

"Unless you saw Adelaide tie your duck you can't really say she did it," Father spoke mildly.

"If'n we wait long enough someone will ask questions about the duck. *"Noh wisse mah whar schuldich iss* [Then we know who is guilty]." Benj remarked.

"She did it," Ori insisted.

"Gloria, enough said, I'll tell you one last time. Del didn't do it. Benj is right, we'll find out sometime," Mama had a warning tone in her voice.

Father laid his hands on the table and looked at Phillip. "What did you think about being with us in church and Sunday school? Did you like being out among a lot of people?"

All eyes were looking at Phillip. He waited briefly. "It was okay," he said, then added, "I like my hat!"

Everyone laughed and agreed Phillip looked very handsome wearing the hat.

"Well that makes this day worthwhile," Father said, with great pleasure. Mama had a satisfied look as she smiled.

"Someone is coming up the walk," Ori said as she returned to her egg crate in the porch. Mama called, "Come on in, Becky. I'm glad you came, we have a lot to tell you."

"I know some already. You aren't the first I've talked to." Becky walked over to Phillip. "It's good to know everything went well," Becky said as she smiled at him. "I won't stay long, just wanted to hear if all the *nochberschaft* [neighborhood] behaved like good Christian people."

"Come, Becky, you too, Benj, let's find more comfortable seats," Mama beckoned to the grownups. All four made their way into the parlor. As they walked out the kitchen, Del heard Becky say, *"Da Sam sed des heere* [My Sam should hear this]."

Del pondered what Becky meant when she said Sam should hear this. "Why Sam?" Del wondered. "Did Becky have a similar situation? Who will tell me?" Del was annoyed that she now had a new set of questions without answers.

CHAPTER EIGHTEEN

A Surprise Encounter

Monday morning Mama spoke, "I don't know what will be said or asked in school today. Don't take part in any argument concerning church. Remain calm no matter what is said, and speak the truth. Your teacher will step in if anyone gets unruly. You hear me now," Mama said very sternly.

"What do you suppose Em will say this morning?" Bill spoke softly to Del as they were walking side-by-side.

"I don't know who tells her what is going on in our church that isn't so. I thought all went rather well, don't you think so?"

"Goes to show what the truth will do. Bill looked relieved as he continued. You should ask Em who tells her things that aren't so," he stated flatly.

"I do ask. She won't say. Guess I can ask again, but she probably won't tell me."

"Wish I knew what happened in that barn," Del pointed to the red barn on Benj's property. "His two boys died in a barn accident from the little I hear."

"You asked that before. Where do you hear talk like that?" Bill questioned. "It could have been another barn somewhere."

"I know that," Del was quick to respond. "I heard some talk from the huskers about the good we are doing for Benj since the death of his boys and the mention of a barn accident.

The Shultz boys were waiting along with Mae at Funk's Lane. All the boys scampered ahead. Ori quickened her pace to meet her friend. Del looked back and saw the Gohos were catching up; she waited to walk with the girls and Gordon ran by to catch up to the boys.

Halfway to the school they could see Em looking in their direction.

Em moved towards Del and the Goho girls, and with a wide-open wave of her arm she called, "Hurry up!"

"Come, run along with me. It isn't far anymore," Del said as the two girls joined her.

They reached Em and everyone made their way to the schoolhouse door.

"I have a lot to tell you." Em said excitedly.

"I thought you might." Del expected church and Sunday school talk.

"Spike won't be coming to our school anymore."

"Are you sure?" Del was completely surprised. "How do you know that?"

"I tell you, his whole family moved to a place near the city. We saw a truck with boards up the sides protecting the house furnishings. The Reifingers must know something about it. The truck stopped there. Pa says something fishy is going on."

"Why does he say that?" Del asked.

"How should I know?" Em responded.

"Your parents visit Martin and Sallie every day, didn't they say anything?"

"Pa can't be nosey and ask, that wouldn't be polite Pa says."

"Then we won't see Eugene in school anymore."

"No, that's for sure. But wait till I tell you this—Martin and Sallie had company yesterday and Pa thinks something fishy is going on there too."

"What are you talking about?" Del asked, although at the same time she was not going to reveal that she herself knew the Reifingers had company. Del pondered the fact that the truck moving Spike's family stopped at the Reifinger residence. "Why should Em's father think there was something strange about that," she thought as she and Em sat at their desk.

The bell rang and school was in session. After attendance was taken Mr. Strunk announced that Eugene would not be attending school that day. At recess time all kinds of rumors were flying around about the Huber family. Del heard it said they were sloppy, mischievous, picked-on, hard-working, and didn't mingle with people in their neighborhood. Del didn't know what to believe about all that was said about them. Their residence was the last house on a dead end lane off the center of Stiller's Corner where three lanes turned off on a sharp right angle turn. A sign posted at the entrance said 'No Outlet.' Talk was the sign was stolen from a city street. All three lanes narrowed to become forest paths; it was these paths that inspired the name Stiller's Corner. They led to well-hidden distilleries. Everyone avoided these paths unless someone was there to usher you the rest of the way. It was rumored there were men with guns back there, and that kept people from going there.

At recess time Del asked Em, "How come you haven't told me first thing that we took Phillip along with us to church and Sunday school yesterday? You were always saying so when it wasn't true. We took Phillip along with us yesterday."

"Don't you know Teacher will not allow anyone to talk about that boy? He calls it gossip."

"Well!" Del said. She was really surprised. "No wonder no one talks about our church or Sunday school activities today."

The dinner hour arrived. Del entered the lane and wondered how many huskers arrived this day. Fritz was there to meet the twins. The children reached home.

"What are the children saying?" Mama asked.

"No one said anything!" Of all things, Ori was first to speak up.

"What now?" Mama was quick to ask.

"No one cares about anything we do." Ori was annoyed. "I was ready to tell them too."

"The Hubers moved to the city outskirts somewhere," Til announced as he took a seat on the bench. "Joe said a truck moved lots of furniture, he saw it go. Our teacher said Eugene would be absent this day."

Mama raised her eyebrows, taking in that news.

"Just because Eugene is absent today, you cannot say his family is moving," Mama said. "Your teacher said he would be absent this day. That's all."

"Em told me no one at school is allowed to talk about him." Del glanced at Phillip, who didn't seem to be interested in the conversation.

"I asked Em who told her not to talk about yesterday. Em just looked at our teacher."

Mama just shook her head. After their meal she shooed the children out the door. "Off to school now. Mind your manners." Mama hurried them along.

As Del arrived for the afternoon session she mustered enough courage to question Em again. "Who was it that told you we took Phillip to church when we didn't?" Del wanted answers.

"I won't tell you! Did people walk out?" Em said snappily.

"I won't tell you anything either."

"I don't know. You have to live there and see that colored boy everyday." Em appeared frustrated.

"Emma! He's a little boy. You do whatever your parents ask of you, don't you?"

"Don't call me Emma! Only when Ma is angry with me does she call me Emma."

"Okay, I won't."

"Does he have clothes now?" Em asked impatiently.

"Yes, he's always had clothes! He also has a good pair of shoes now."

Em turned and said no more as the bell rang and the afternoon session began.

The rest of the school day was routine, in fact, at times boring. Del's mind drifted again and again.

"What's on your mind now?" Em asked at afternoon recess time.

"Many things. Who is husking today. Our telephone. Father's last trip to Philadelphia this week. Grandfather's creamery operation shutting down." Del ticked off the list on her fingers.

"Why are you getting the telephone anyway?" Em asked.

"Father says it would help him to have a telephone. It would help Becky a great deal, especially if she needs to talk to a doctor."

"How will it help your father?" Em asked.

"I don't know," Del thought a bit. "I really don't know."

"You don't want to tell me," Em said as the bell rang for the second afternoon session.

After dismissal Del hurried along with the Goho sisters. The girls continued walking home while Gordon followed Til into field to visit Doll, hitched to the wagon.

Del hoped to do her chores and still have time to talk to some of the huskers. She hurriedly ate a snack and changed clothes. It wasn't long before Mama and Carol entered the kitchen.

"Where is everybody?" Del asked.

"Outside. I know you'll ask so I'll tell you—Adeline was here until two this afternoon and when she went home, Becky and Phillip went with her."

"They didn't walk, did they?"

"Yes, Phillip is doing better all the time. He can walk when you go slow enough. They took the wagon along in case he would need it. Benj will bring Phillip back before chore time. Your father took the crock with warm peppermint tea along back on an empty wagon. He'll place it by the falter on that large flat rock. You know where I mean. Go find the huskers and tell them the tea is warm, and to help themselves. Tell Benj to come in, he's been out there long enough. He should take a break before he goes for Phillip."

Del went skipping out the lane. Husking was well under way on the Printz farm fields. She spotted Hester and told her where warm tea was located.

Hester replied, "Come along with me. I intend to do some snooping, before I go home. I hear there is a bit of activity on this vacant property."

"What do you mean?" Del asked.

"There's some activity at the house I hear," Hester explained.

Del pondered that for a moment and then asked, "Do you know where Benj is?"

Hester shook her head. "You know, Ed and I are so relieved since he spends time with your family everyday. Then there is Becky, all alone too. It's a shame. Becky has Rachael, but she's not close by."

Del interrupted. "I know, Rachael is Becky's daughter, but I never see her here."

Hester looked frustrated. "No, and you never will!" she said abruptly. "Rachael washed her hands of this whole village years ago. Stubborn child, the only family Becky has, and it's like having no relative at all," Hester said with a degree of sadness.

Del was speechless.

Hester looked at Del. "It's true!" Hester sighed. "I must place some blame on myself, young and headstrong, sure I knew everything, when I knew nothing at all." Hester sighed again. "Rachael never visits her mother and I think that's awful. From what I hear she's another Becky, an excellent caregiver. She resembles her too, and is well-respected for her nursing work."

Del was very surprised that Hester, an adult, talked to her this way. She decided to learn as much as she could. "She has Susanna too." Del prompted as she remembered those brown bar cookies.

"That was and IS the big problem!" Hester said firmly. "But it's over now, can't change things." They approached the abandoned Printz farmhouse. "Look, look there, a broken window pane under the porch. That's not good for any house. Well, I'm leaving, I saw what I wanted to see."

"I know Mama is looking for me. I need to head back too."

Running home so she wouldn't be reprimanded for spending too much time with Hester, Del stopped when she saw Benj leaning against a fence post near the pigpen, his right hand cupping his right eye.

"Oh, my goodness, what's the problem!" Del was scared. "Did you hurt your eye?"

"*Ess brennt. Ses eppes nie fgloge.* [It burns. Tis something flew in]," Benj groaned as he stood still, his body resting against the post. "*Ess wassered. Kon net uff mache.* [It waters. Can't open it]."

"Come with me, we'll go in to Mama, she'll know what to do." Del took his hand and started a slow walk to the house. Del pointed out the steps and the narrow walkway.

"*Ich kon noch sehne* [I can still see]," Benj dryly said, still cupping one eye.

As Del entered the kitchen with Benj in tow, Mama sprang into action. Mama helped him to a seat by the window and asked him to open that eye if he could.

"The eye is watering and quite red. Is it sawdust?" Mama asked.

"*Nay ses net* [No its not]."

"I suspect it's a bug. Lay back, rest awhile, we'll see if the tears flush it out," Mama said as they led him to the couch.

"*Schaerfe gschtoche* [Sharp sting]," Benj said as he lay down.

"It's good the eye is tearing, sometimes the tiniest of insects can have a very irritating fluid." Mama seemed to think the problem would resolve itself.

After a few minutes, Benj said, "*Es vot besser, Ich kon geh* [It gets better, I can go]."

Mama emphatically shook her head no. "Adelaide, you'll have to go down to the Conrads and bring Phillip home on the wagon. We can't have Benj go there like this. Gloria may finish your work. She won't like that, but she'll have to help out like it or not."

"*Ich geh* [I go]," Benj raised a hand in protest.

"*Ney duscht net* [No you do not]." Mama looked to Del and motioned for her to go immediately.

"I'll take the cement pike. The wagon is easier to pull on it."

"Whatever way you want, just go. Don't waste time talking."

Del ran out the dirt lane and down the street partway, but walked the rest of the way because she didn't want to be out of breath when she got there. She entered the gated walkway and passed by the front porch to the side porch entrance. Del suddenly stopped; there was woman coming towards her on the walkway, from the red barn behind her. A gingham bonnet hid her face as she drew near the side porch but Del could tell from her walk that this was a much younger woman than Adeline.

"Who are you? Why are you here?" the strange woman demanded.

Del was so shocked by the loud angry outburst she couldn't speak.

"Why are you here? Who are you? Answer me!"

"I-I-I came for Phillip." Del stammered and pointed to the wagon propped on the porch.

"Who are you?"

"I am Del-- Adelaide." She answered weakly, pointing to herself. "I'm here for Phillip." Del realized she was looking at Becky's daughter, Rachael. Even in her shock, she could see the family resemblance.

"You shouldn't be here. Why did you come?"

"Benj hurt his eye so Mama told me to fetch Phillip." She said again and pointed to the wagon with a pounding heart.

Rachael's angry face peered at her. "You stay right there. Don't move!" She shook a finger warning her to wait.

Del waited as Rachael opened the porch door and stepped inside. She took several deep breaths to steady herself. She remembered Mr. Strunk's shakiness, and now understood how he felt. It took forever before the door opened again and Phillip limped out. Del could not see anyone else behind him in the kitchen. Whoever opened the door stood behind it. Del quickly moved toward Phillip, still trembling while reaching to bring the wagon forward.

"I can walk," Phillip said quietly.

Del reached for the wagon's rope handle and grabbed a firm hold onto Phillip's arm. She said softly to Phillip, "Okay, let's see how you do. If necessary, I can pull the wagon on the street."

Phillip obliged, grabbing hold of her arm. They slowly reached the gate. The door opened behind them and there was Rachael once more, standing in the doorway. "Don't you ever tell anybody you saw me, not anyone!" she spoke harshly. "Tell no one about this!" She quickly closed the door.

Del mutely nodded her head and turned back to Phillip. "Come, Phillip, Mama is waiting for us. Benj is waiting, too. He just couldn't come tonight." They reached the cement highway. Del cleared her throat. "Sit down, I can pull you on the wagon."

"No, I want to walk."

"OK, Phillip. Let's go."

Phillip grasped her arm firmly as he did with her brothers. Del pulled the empty wagon with her free hand.

"I was scared. I never saw that woman before. Did they tell you not to talk?"

"Yes, no talk about her."

"Are you scared?"

There was no response other than Phillip shaking his head no.

"You must remember, Phillip. We can't talk about this. I don't know how I will explain this to Mama," Del said as they made their way up hill. "Why did she yell at me? What did I do? Adeline and Jonathan always treat me nice. We can't just say nothing. What will we say?"

"Talk about Blackie."

"Good, Phillip. You can talk about Blackie, that will be alright. Did you curry Blackie today?"

Phillip smiled and said, "Yes, I petted the horse."

"I suppose you did." Del paused, and murmured, "As for me, what can I say?"

There was no more talk until they met Funk's Lane, when Del spoke. "Here, you sit on the wagon, I will pull you partway up the hill to give you some rest."

Del strained to pull the wagon with his additional weight. "That was Rachael," Del thought, "But maybe Susanna looks like Becky too. I wonder, did I see Susanna and not Rachael?"

Fritz was waiting for them at the lane. Phillip was pleased and said, "Good dog."

Fritz bounced around for attention. "Yes, Fritz, you are a good dog," Del said distractedly. She turned and looked Phillip straight in the eyes. "You and I will have to talk about this sometime later, but only you and I. You can tell me what happened inside, and maybe why that woman was angry."

"Like me." Phillip pointed to himself.

"Of course, Phillip, I know Adeline likes you, she is a nice lady. That goes for Jonathan, too. I know they both like you. But why should that other lady become so angry?"

"*Alfatt tsz sich selwert um schwetze* [Always to yourself talking]," Benj said as he stood in the twilight by the woodshed. "Been waiting fer ya."

Del was startled and realized she should not be talking. "What did he hear?" she thought. To Benj she said, "I was trying to get Phillip to talk."

"*Sel glaawe ich net* [That I don't believe]."

"Fritz came to meet us, did you sent him to the lane?"

"Del, ya know better than that. Fritz sniffs the air. He knows where everybody is."

"Is your eye alright again?"

"Yer Mama used her eye dropper and special solution a couple of times. Still sore, but better. Go in," Benj waved his hand as he followed, still covering his eye.

"Is my work all done? Should I go out and check?" Del asked Mama as she entered the kitchen.

Mama frowned. "What took so long?" she scolded. "Go out and check for sure, Benj would have returned sooner than you, even with his eye problem. You are pale. You rushed too much, I suppose. Did Adeline talk to you? Did you see Jonathan?"

Mama was the one to ask a lot of questions.

"I didn't see either of them. Phillip came out."

Mama looked at both of them, but she didn't have time to say anything more as Del quickly left to check on her outside chores making sure all closures were secured for the night. She was grateful to get away from Mama and her questions.

"It never fails, you have to talk and talk to people whenever you go anywhere just so you get out of your regular work," Ori greeted Del with criticisms.

Del expected this reaction from Ori. "I am here, doing what I can." Del checked all doors and latches and then she checked all doors a second time to stall for time before returning to Mama's questions. If only she could erase thoughts from her mind like the eraser clears the writing on slate blackboards, never to be seen again. She entered the house following Father, who was usually the last to enter.

Supper was served with little conversation; it seemed everyone was weary from the day's work. Ollie was the first to say he was tired. He was going upstairs to read a little before going to bed. Benj got up to also go home.

"William, you walk home with Benj," Mama said.

"*Net nootwennich* [Not necessary]."

"Yes Benj. Your eye isn't clear. *Nah isses doonkel* [Now its dark]. After a good sleep, most or all of the redness should be gone."

Benj accepted Mama's directive, with a wave of his hand he motioned for Bill to follow.

Ori told Carol to get ready for bed. "When I take her up, I won't come down anymore," Ori said as they made their way upstairs.

Del was surprised that Ori didn't complain more about doing some of Del's chores.

"I'm going up too. I bet Ollie is already asleep," Til said as he made his way to the stairs.

"Take Phillip with you up to his room, that's all. We'll see if he has himself tucked in by the time William gets back. He needs to do things by himself and understand that he has help at the same time."

Del was quietly edging to the stairs when Mama stopped her and gave Del a very searching look. "You said you didn't see Adeline or Jonathan." Mama had a question in that statement.

Del simply nodded her head.

"Did Phillip give you a big problem?"

"He walked very slow on the cement pike and he was also on the wagon—it was slow going, not easy to pull the wagon uphill. He's talking a bit more and that's good." Del desperately tried to change the subject.

Mama had a look that alternated between quizzical and skeptical. "Hmm. Are you sure you are feeling alright? Your color hasn't come back, although it's a little better."

Del just nodded her head and backed towards the stairway.

Mama finally relented and said, "I can see you are tired. Go to bed."

Del sat on her bed and sighed several times. It seemed a long time passed before she drifted off to sleep.

CHAPTER NINETEEN

The Cover-Up

Del awoke hearing footsteps on her parents' bedroom floor. Yesterday's strange encounter immediately came to mind. She lay and stretched for a few minutes, not at all eager to get up. If Mama asked, how was she going to explain last evening's delay? She needed time to think. She needed a satisfactory answer to keep Mama from prying for a better explanation. Why such anger from Rachael? What did Benj know about Rachael and the Conrads?

"Are you going to lay there all day?" Ori said sharply as she walked by a second time. "It's time to get up. You should be downstairs long already. I will have to do your work again and it's a school day."

"I will get up as soon as the bathroom is clear," Del replied.

"Well it is, all the boys are down."

Del got up but took her time to head downstairs. Once there, she set the table for breakfast. Benj was seated on the rocking chair. Mama was probably out with her milk kettle.

"How is your eye this morning?" Del walked over to take a closer look.

"Didn't fall out. *Glae bissel weh noch. Es vot ollrecht. Waz huts gewwe letscht owed* [Little bit sore yet. It gets alright. What happened last evening]?"

"Nothing much. I talk too much, that's what everyone will say."

"That's what Gloria will say. How with you?" Benj added.

"Hester and I walked up to the Printz house because she wanted to look at the place. I ran back to finish my work when I saw you had a problem and my wagon still wasn't here to feed the pigs. What happened to your eye? Was it a bug or something else? Then because of that . . ."

"Wait a minute. You talk faster than I can think." Benj lifted a hand. *"Ses ebbes nigh gfloge. Besser nau. Waz huts gewwe letscht owed* [Something flew in. Better now. What happened last evening]?"

"You know. I needed to fetch Phillip to get my wagon. Who fed the pigs?"

"Mannsleit [Menfolk]."

"Good thing I took the cement pike. Phillip and I walked out to the street and halfway up the hill. You know Phillip did better than I thought he could do. He didn't lean much on me for support."

"Hut sehne aus ah mit mache muss. Waz noch [He saw that he must make his way along. What then]?"

"Are the boys up?" Del asked to change the subject.

Benj nodded his head, indicating yes.

"I'll do my morning work. Don't want to hear more of Ori's complaints." Del ran out to avoid any more questions from Benj. She passed Mama on the walkway and continued running, calling behind her. "Benj's eye is better. Table all set." Mama turned and watched as Del hurried by.

Del was deep in thought as she headed for the house. She walked by Ori carrying her wooden bucket with eggs and held the door for her as she entered the closed porch.

"You don't have to be nice to me now just because I did your work last evening."

"That's not why I held the door. You don't appreciate anything."

"That's right, I don't appreciate your tying my duck."

"That's enough, Gloria, for the last time Adelaide did not tie your duck," Mama said sharply to Ori.

Del stepped into the kitchen. Mama made a large pot of hot cocoa. "That smells so good, may I have some right now?"

"Get the dipper and a cup, help yourself." Del got a cup and filled it with cocoa and handed it to Benj.

"*Fa dich* [For you]," Benj said.

The boys and Father were nearing the porch when they saw first huskers arrive. Father turned around to greet them and tell them which field to walk to. Breakfast was the usual hurried chatter as the boys one-by-one rushed upstairs to change into their school clothes. Ori helped Carol with some final touches although Carol had learned to do most of her morning routine for herself. Del felt self-conscious as she realized Mama was keeping a close eye on her.

"We should get a lot done today," Father said as he returned. "I can hardly believe tomorrow will be my last trip to Philly. It may be a long time before I go there again," Father said with mixed feelings. "It wasn't so bad going by truck."

"Last time I visited Philly was the Sesquicentennial," Benj stated. "Lots of people went on a special train ride." Benj paused. "Nice day."

Father nodded and looked at the children, "Have a good day in school."

"Be mindful and do your work," Mama said with folded arms.

On the way to school, Bill was first to speak. "We wondered why you were late yesterday. Did Adeline need some kind of help? You had to be aware of the time. Father asked me if I knew anything."

"What did you say?" Del asked.

"What could I say, I knew absolutely nothing," Bill was quick to answer.

"It's the best answer I can give."

"Did you see Jonathan?" Bill asked.

"No."

"It was Mama who came out and told Father you weren't back. Everyone knows something happened, so why did you stay as long as you did?" Bill asked impatiently.

"I thought I answered a lot of questions last night."

"Everyone could see you were upset about something. Father saw you coming up the street but said to wait until morning to ask you what happened."

Del stubbornly said, "There's absolutely nothing to say."

Bill appeared puzzled, but said no more as they reached the end of the lane. Del was glad she didn't have to fend off any more probing questions from Bill. She looked back and saw the Gohos hurrying to catch up. She waited for them.

As Del took her seat she saw there was a new face in the room. The usual opening exercise followed. Attendance was taken and Mr. Strunk introduced their new student, "Ephrim Kurtz will be attending school here. Eugene Huber will not be back since he is now attending another school. School is now in session."

The house was empty as the school children arrived home for dinner. They barely had time to take off their coats before Mama and Becky came in together. "I have something for you," Becky said as she approached Del. She set a small gray box on the table. "Adelaide, this is for you. Adeline wants you to have this to keep."

Mama looked pleased. "Open it, see what it is."

"I know what it is. I used to play with this. It's Adeline's dolly tea set, it was hers when she was little."

"Yes, she wants to be sure it you have it. This is the right place for it," Becky said pleasantly.

"Tell her I said thanks. I will tell her myself when I see her. I think it's small enough to place in the top drawer of my dresser, box and all; that's where I will keep it."

"I think that's a good idea," Becky said as she turned around to leave. "I will pick the milk up this evening."

"See you then, Becky," Mama said.

At the end of the school day Fritz met Del at the lane and they waited for Bill.

"The wagons are probably in for unloading, or else Fritz wouldn't be here," Del said as Bill approached.

"Gee, look at that, those are the telephone company workers. Look at that long pole laying on the ground." One of the workmen stood guard making sure the children passed at a safe distance.

After a change of clothes Del was outside taking charge of her evening chores. Two men steadily shoveled corn from the larger wagon onto a metal shoot for it to slide smoothly into the corncrib.

Benj was seated on the rocking chair and Phillip had already set most of the table when Del returned. "You are a good help, Phillip, I sure appreciate that. I suppose you will be doing more outside work as you grow stronger."

"He was helping out already." Mama looked at Phillip and smiled. Phillip smiled back at her.

"Was Adeline here today? I wanted to thank her for the gift, but I didn't see her."

"She didn't come today," Mama said. "You know, she could have brought that tea set up most anytime or given it to you one of the times you were there."

Del offered no comment, instead she asked, "How is Jonathan?" to set thought to another matter.

"He must be getting better, or else Becky would have said something. Do you have anything you want to tell me about last evening?"

"Nothing much. I walked with Hester to the Printz property and knew it was getting late, so I ran home. Then I saw him," Del pointed to Benj, "with that eye problem. I brought him along inside for you to help him."

"I know that. What happened next?" Mama asked quickly.

"You know, you sent me to fetch Phillip. I was told to stay outside and wait for him. So I did."

"What was the problem that took all that time?" Mama pressed.

"I don't know."

Mama turned to look at Phillip. Phillip just looked back at her without saying anything. Del felt uneasy in the silence until Mama finally spoke in answer to Del's question.

"Becky said she was pleased with Jonathan's improvement. She visits everyday. Was Becky there when you came for Phillip?" Mama asked.

Del did not need to answer as the menfolk entered the kitchen. Ori and Carol were with them.

Del woke the next morning when she heard Father speaking in lowered tones to Mama that he needed to get an early start for Philly. She thought about the creamery. She realized she was never going to make that trip to Philadelphia. Then the startling meeting at her neighbor's place was on her mind. Del was sure it was Rachael who she surprised on the walkway. How did she get there? She didn't see a car anywhere. Del dismissed her thoughts and got up as soon as she heard the washroom was clear. The boys were also up earlier than usual. There was plenty of work for them this day.

"Good morning," Mama said as Del stepped into the kitchen. "I think we will have another nice day. The telephone company decided where poles will be placed. The line will be strung after that." Mama continued talking half to herself.

Del remembered her Father saying that it would be handy for Becky and their neighbors to be near a telephone, and how it would help him establish his own trucking business.

Del asked what her father was going to haul.

"For right now, anything and everything. He will pick up calves and deliver them to the city abattoir, other livestock as well. He already goes to the County Courthouse at settlement time for quite a few of the township residents to pay their county taxes, get dog licenses, or file liens on property taxes, which fortunately doesn't often happen. People might ask if there is place for them to ride along. He will pick up items neighbors want. There are other options to consider. We will no longer have to wait for days for a scavenger to come. Your father can haul any carcass the very same day to the fertilizer plant. We'll let people know your Father can make regular visits to Reading."

Mama switched topics, "Can you tell me now why you were late coming back from the Conrads? You surely could have come home before you did, even if you did talk a bit."

Del felt a blush coming so she turned away and said, "It took a while for Phillip to come outside. That's all."

Mama said, "There has to be more to this than you tell us. Becky is there sometime every day, was she there at the time?"

"I didn't see anybody except Phillip because the door opened just enough for him to step outside. We headed for home right away and Phillip decided he would walk."

Mama paused. "Adeline could have given you that tea set anytime. Something isn't right," Mama again said softly to herself. "Benj will visit there today to collect their eggs. I want to hear what he has to say. He is much too quiet about this. I think he knows something."

"What is the matter with Ed? Hester said he wasn't feeling well. Is he alright?"

"I think it is stress. That can bring on a good headache. He heard rumors that the silk mill will close for good. He needs to find another job, but no one is hiring. He can keep himself busy here as always something to do, but we can't afford to pay him much, not enough to get by." She grabbed her coat. "Take care of your outside work. I will see if all the milking is going alright."

Mama and Del left together. Mama entered the milkhouse where all milking equipment was kept. Del threw scrawny cobs of corn into the pigpen.

Ori walked over to Del. "Why did you get that tea set? I'm the oldest and it should be mine!" Ori demanded.

"Go away, I have work to do. I don't want to hear your silly talk," Del said as she walked away.

"You see to it that you get everything!" Ori yelled as she left. "Goodness, she is jealous," Del thought, "but she has many things I don't have. Aunt Eva and Mama's Aunt Lizzie give her hooks, needles and threads for fancy embroidery and crocheting. Aunt Eva helps her practice on different stitches. They gave her a booklet to teach her new stitches.

Del dropped her thoughts when she saw Taw-Taw squeezing himself through the little henhouse door, slipping off the small chicken ladder and falling. He dangled there, a thin rope twisted around his neck, not nearly long enough for Taw-Taw's webbed feet to reach the ground. That duck would surely hang himself! Del ran back, picked him up, and with a firm hold made sure he was all right. "You sure are some tough bird but that piece of rope would have finished you!" Taw-Taw resisted as Del tried to shove him back inside through the small open door. She could not leave him alone. Ollie stepped out from the feed entry door and recognized the problem.

"Drop him, let him hang. Let Ori find him." Ollie was laughing as he entered through the feedhouse door. It wasn't long before the rope was released. She carried the duck inside, holding his beak so he couldn't give her a painful nip. Ollie helped her get a coop. They set it in the feedhouse with enough food and water he could reach by sticking his head between the spokes that held the top and bottom of the coop together.

"We can leave Taw-Taw there. What did Ori have him tied to?" Del asked Ollie.

"That old dented, leaky aluminum bucket"

"That old bucket! She should know better! He can easily drag that bucket. It's not heavy like a milk bucket."

"Maybe she is trying to kill him so she can blame that on someone else, probably you," Ollie laughed as he took off running toward the house.

While Del could almost agree with Ollie's remark, she was not going to mention this to anyone.

The children finished breakfast and left as a group. Del decided to make conversation. "Is Mama concerned that Grandfather needs to find something to do when he no longer runs the creamery?"

"No need to worry," Til reassured her and the others. "Grandfather will make the walk from his home same as always."

"Yes, he will look after his horses every day," Bill stated.

"I know what else he has to check on every day," Til was smiling.

"What is that?" Ori asked.

"You know, he will check on his wine-making inside his creamery building," Til laughed.

Recess time conversation turned to the new student. "Have you talked to Ephrim?" Del asked Em.

"No, goodness no. I can't just go over there and talk to him. You wouldn't either."

"I guess I could if he's walking to school with us," Del replied. "I think you like him," she said in a teasing tone.

"Shut up," Em said as she blushed.

"Today is the last time Father will be going to Philly. He's glad because he says a busy weekend is coming up."

"What so different this weekend?"

"There's a political rally at the hotel this Friday night, plus Saturday afternoon and evening. The German band will be there. Benj has been talking about this for days already. He says he'd rather hear the band than the political speeches, and says he knows who he will vote for, no speeches necessary. He talks about our governor whenever he talks politics, he likes that man."

"I don't know who you are talking about," Em said.

"Election day is in November; on a Tuesday, I think," Del admitted. "Father wants the cornfields husked and cleared before then. We could have snow before then. After the harvest Levi and Martha will host an everybody sale, like they do every spring and fall.

"What do you mean? I never heard of that," Em said with real curiosity.

"The hotel is in the center of the township. Everybody is welcome to bring things there for sale. Levi and Martha wait until the farmers have their crops harvested and stored for the winter to set a date."

"I never heard about such things."

"That's because your family doesn't farm."

The children were in the kitchen eating their noontime meal when Ori stormed in.

"Where is Benj? Why did he put Taw-Taw in a coop? I left Taw-Taw in the henhouse," Ori demanded angrily.

"I don't know what you are talking about," Mama said.

"Someone does. I know where I left him," Ori was adamant.

Del and Ollie glanced at each other and silently agreed not to disclose anything.

"I can't help you there," Mama continued.

"Someone always has it in for me and Taw-Taw," Ori would not let up.

"It will come out in the wash," Ollie said, and everyone broke out in laughter.

"Its not funny," Ori protested.

"Get yourselves back to school," Mama said.

"I bet Benj will be asking a lot of questions at the Conrads. Don't you think?" Bill asked the twins and Til walked along the lane.

"He may have some answers," Til agreed.

Del wondered why everyone was bothered with her delayed return from the Conrads the previous day.

The afternoon went well. Del managed to concentrate on the work assigned for her class.

When she entered the kitchen she saw a pair of brand new shoes resting on brown paper by the couch. Del figured these were for Phillip as she went upstairs. Del expected Benj and Phillip would still be at the Conrads, but she saw Benj out by the barnyard. Mama walked down the lane holding Carol's hand.

"Where had they been?" Del asked herself because she was surprised that Mama would be away from the house at this time of day. Mama had something tucked under her arm, her worn sweater pulled over to cover it. Isaac handled a full wagon of husked corn, coming down the lane at the same time. Fritz was on board, as well as Phillip. They pulled to a stop behind another wagon already being emptied. One crib was already filled and another three-quarters full. Del walked to the top of the barnbank—she could see more clearly from there where any husking was still taking place. Workers were finishing the larger field. Father will be pleased once he returns home, she thought. Del greeted Mama and Carol and asked where they had been.

"We visited Orphelia this afternoon for a short time. It's been a long time since I talked to her."

Del pondered why would Mama visit Mrs. Straub on a weekday. They entered the house and Del pointed to the shoes by the couch.

"Did Phillip see them? Who brought them here?" Del asked they entered the kitchen and Mama stepped into the side room. Del heard the squeak of a latch to a cabinet door.

"Uncle Jer stopped by today and dropped them off. You take your wagon and gather the pumpkins if you have time. Bring all the pumpkins to the falter, so it's easier to pick up there," Mama directed.

Del did her work and some of Ori's work as well. Why would Mama visit Orphelia on a weekday? The only thing that came to mind was that the Straubs had a better view of the Conrad house. This thought concerned Del quite a bit. Del grabbed the rope handle to the wagon and headed out the lane to gather pumpkins scattered here and there.

"How are you this fine day?" Hester called as Del returned to the falter, her wagon overloaded with pumpkins. Del placed them on the rock by the falter while she looked over the field behind her.

"I'm okay, I'm looking for the last of the pumpkins in this field. I need to pick the corn scraps up after that."

Hester volunteered, "I can take a little time to help you. From here I see only four more. It won't take long at all."

Del and Hester passed Eva coming in the lane. "Hello to both of you," Eva greeted them.

Just then they heard the truck coming in the lane. Father leaned on the horn, letting everyone know he arrived.

"It sure is good to see that man coming through that barn threshold door," Hester said as they all saw Benj at that door. "It's good to see he got over his vow never to step onto a threshold floor again."

That sparked Del's interest. "What do you mean?"

"It's over now. Ed saw it happen. Your dog was with Benj. He nudged him, like telling him it was time to leave and walk down that barnbridge. Fritz stayed with him, kept nudging him until Benj and that dog reached the woodshed."

"When did that happen?" Del asked.

"Never you mind," Hester said as they approached the fence to the pigpen. There was no time to ask more questions as they approached Del's father and the group thronged around him.

Everyone asked questions about Father's last trip and talked with one another at the same time. Del half-listened as she recalled the day Fritz did not meet them after school like he usually did. Benj said it was maybe his fault. Fritz wouldn't leave the barn. The threshold was not forbidden for Benj to enter like it was for her and her siblings. Del thought, "Benj says Fritz is one smart dog." Just because she and her siblings were not allowed on the threshing floor, maybe Fritz, wanted to keep Benj off that floor too.

Del thought about the mysterious object Mama had tucked under her sweater. "Was it the box camera?" Del decided to look first chance she had to see if Mama's box camera had been moved. It was kept on a shelf in the built-in cabinet in the side room. "Did Mama take pictures of people husking corn or maybe Phillip seated on the wagon? Maybe Aunt Eva was taking pictures out in the field," she thought. Del passed by the pigpen. The pigs bit into broken pumpkin pieces. Chunks of orange pumpkin with juice and seeds were dripping from their mouths.

Ori and Carol were in the closed porch cleaning and grading eggs as Del entered the kitchen. Phillip already set the table. Father, Mama and Benj were talking in the Dutch dialect. That conversation ended immediately as Del walked in.

"Get yourselves ready for supper," Mama called out to Ori and Carol.

"I don't know how Mr. Gehris will mark the butter from his creamery. My father had a wooden mold of a sheaf of wheat imprinted onto every pound of butter he sold. No one else had a mark like that. Everyone always knew when they had my father's product," Mama proudly said.

Father stated, "Let's sit down and enjoy our supper, and I will tell you about my trip."

Ollie ate so fast Mama cautioned him to slow down, saying, "We have all evening time."

Father started his story describing the new equipment at the Gehris Butter and Cheese Company. "It's all very shiny and there's a large separator and long metal bins for cheese making." He talked about the new truck and the motor, noisy enough to cause a headache after so long a ride.

"But what about the place where you found Phillip?" Ollie could not contain his curiosity about what those market people said when Father told them he would no longer be coming their way.

"Yes Oliver, I will get to that."

Del watched Phillip closely as Father talked about the market where he was found. Phillip showed some interest.

"Our last stop, as always was the place I found Phillip. I talked to them briefly, and they asked about you, Phillip," Father pointed to Phillip. "I told them you were doing fine and that we were very pleased with your improving health. I asked them if they knew anymore about your circumstances but they did not. They asked where I live and how to get to my farm should anyone come looking for you. I told them all they need to do is come along Route 100 and follow that route until they see the most splendid countryside they ever saw, lush green pastures and farms dotted here and there among rolling hills and valleys, with forests and winding streams. That's when, I said, you start looking for narrow roads that turn to the left; there are several to choose from."

Del nodded, remembering that those roads were old Indian footpaths over hills with many turns. She could see huge boulders and rock-studded fields that were good pasture for grazing cattle. She visualized the fields that were bordered with large rocks and stones picked off freshly plowed fields year after year. She saw the small villages and scattered homes, the church steeples and one-room schoolhouses. She shook herself out of her reverie to hear her father recounting, "When you are near New Jerusalem, just say my name and people will tell you where I live."

"Do you think they will ever come?" Bill asked.

Father shook his head and said, "I don't know," and tilted his head in Phillip's direction. "I think the market folk are curious about Pennsylvania Dutch farm life. Phillip, you grew up in the city, but you are becoming a farm boy, just the same. Do you like our way of life?"

"I like it. I want to stay here," Phillip said shyly, but quickly.

Benj put his arm around Phillip. "Same as ya, Phillip, I stay here too. This is my second home."

Father asked, "Do I hear any questions from anyone?"

Til asked if the merchants were interested in the cheese the Gehris creamery would make.

"I don't know. Your grandfather didn't want to invest time and money to make cheese or even to modernize! That's the new word. Milk will now be sold in different grades." Father laughed. "No such thing as slop for the pigs anymore. Different grades of milk can be had at a cheaper price than whole milk. You can buy all cream grades down to skim milk. Whoever heard of such a thing? The Philly grocery stores are getting many more items to sell. Variety stores, they call them. They will sell most items needed in a household."

It was quiet while everyone absorbed all the news about different milk grades and types of milk, and about these variety stores.

Til was the first to speak. "I can hardly believe such changes. No wonder Grandfather says butter will not be butter anymore. I didn't know what he meant by that."

"Tell me, how was the day here at home? Anything new happen?" Father looked around the kitchen.

"The little field and the biggest field are husked. We started a field on the Printz home and also the one behind the sawmill along the Pioneer Trail," Bill said while Benj nodded his head in agreement.

"*Alle drei faddeich mache mariye* [All three finished by tomorrow]." Benj was confident the small field below his house could be completed in less than a day.

"If we finish this place and your field too, Benj, then we are well on schedule. We can start the husking uptown Friday and Saturday. Monday and Tuesday, if the weather holds, we should be able to finish husking those fields, shock the fodder and get them ready for winter. We can bring the fodder in any time. We'll finish what little we have here before butchering time and Thanksgiving."

"Any news here?" Father asked. "Adelaide, how about you?" Father's blue eyes held a steady gaze on her.

Del shrugged her shoulders. "Not a whole lot to say."

Del made her way upstairs ahead of her siblings to avoid more questions. Alone in her room she did nothing but consider why no one ever saw Rachael. Hester said she never comes to this village. "Well, it surely was her I saw. What could Phillip tell me?" Del's mind raced through these thoughts and she decided she had to confirm her suspicions that it was Rachael she saw. Del's thoughts finally stopped spinning around in her head and she dropped off to sleep.

CHAPTER TWENTY

An Explanation Is Offered

Bird chatter announced the dawning of a new day and awakened Del earlier than usual. The birds were gathering to begin their flight to warmer climates. Del woke and hoped her parents would not discover she was not sharing all she knew. Maybe Phillip didn't know what happened to her outside. She stretched and tread softly across creaky floor boards. The washroom door stood ajar and she got ready for the day.

Benj was alone in the kitchen. "*Bischt frieh demariye* [You're early this morning]."

"The birds work me up. Is Mama helping to milk this morning?"

"*Wais net* [Know not]."

"Phillip?" Del questioned.

"*Schlofe. Fa sel bin ich doh* [Sleeping. For that am I here]."

"Ollie and Bill outside already?"

Benj merely nodded his head. "*Du huscht ordlich gute gadu* [You have done rather good]," Benj commented with raised eyebrows, exposing his green eyes.

Del turned quickly and stared at him. "What are you talking about?"

"*Du weescht* [You know]."

"What do I know?"

"*Du huscht epper gsehne un gekennt* [You have someone seen and understand who it was]."

"You weren't there. Why do you say that?"

"*Huscht dank ich aus gfiggert* [I think you figured it out]."

"I try not to think about it. But some things do bother me."

"*Un waz isz sel* [And what is that]?"

"You were supposed to fetch Phillip. I wasn't invited inside that house. Was Becky there?" Del looked to Benj for an answer. He made no effort to speak. "And why did Becky deliver that tea set? Adeline could have given it to me any time. Mama is suspicious and Ori is upset that I have it. Just because Ori is the oldest, she thinks everything should be hers." Del paused. "I believe I hear Phillip moving about upstairs." She was relieved that the conversation ended as Benj moved to the stairway, opened the door and told Phillip in broken English to stay there and hold on to the railing while he would come upstairs to help him down the steps.

"I can do it," Phillip said quietly.

Benj looked surprised, then motioned with his hand for Phillip to come forward. Benj leaned into the enclosed stairway. It sounded as if Phillip was taking one step at a time, probably leading with the same foot. Benj straightened as best he could while reaching with outstretched arms as Phillip reached the last two steps. Phillip stepped onto the kitchen floor. Del was amazed to see Phillip all dressed without any assistance. Maybe he got up earlier with Bill but returned to rest awhile longer.

"*Ma dunnah de shue uff* [We put the shoes on]," Benj said gruffly.

Phillip held onto Benj as he followed him to the couch. Benj reached for his shoes. Not a word was said as both worked together. "*Bischt gerischt?* [You ready]?"

Phillip nodded and Benj extended a bent elbow for Phillip to grasp as they made their way outside after stopping in the porch to grab an overall coat for Phillip to wear.

It was good to see Phillip gain strength and self-reliance. Del smiled as she flung the tablecloth across the table. Mama stepped inside.

"How did Phillip come down those stairs? Did you help him?" Mama seemed concerned.

"Phillip came down by himself. Benj opened the door and said he would help him, but Phillip wanted to come down the stairs by himself."

"How did it go?"

"He did it! I know Benj was pleased." Del continued, "I'll set the dishes on the table. Then I'll do my morning work."

"You needn't hurry. We'll have help enough coming today. Some are here already. You can take your time with the table settings and help me make breakfast. I still think one of the boys should be with him on those steps," Mama said with a glance toward the stairway. "On the other hand, it is good to see Phillip try it on his own." Mama looked at Del. "I have whole boiled potatoes in the big white dish. Get them and slice them for me. I will get the fry pan ready."

Del stood by the white table slicing cold whole boiled potatoes on a cutting board. There was no talk for a spell when Mama said, "You are unusually quiet this morning. Something on your mind you want to talk about?"

"No. Well, how is Sallie Reifinger? I haven't heard how she is doing lately."

"Becky says the gash is healing nicely. She still goes there; I don't know how often. I see Hester doesn't have any work today," Mama said as she looked out the closed porch windows and saw Hester and Ed passing by the walkway. "Ed said he would be here early to do your work and Gloria's too. Now, what's on your mind?" Mama observed how Del's expression changed upon hearing Hester's name.

"I was just thinking about something she said."

"What could that be?" Mama was interested.

"Did you ever see Rachael?" Del asked.

"Why do you ask that?" Mama was quick to inquire.

"Just because Hester said I will never see Rachael. Did you ever see her?" Del asked again.

"Yes and no. I saw pictures of her. She is some years older than I. In fact, she has a grown child. She was a fortunate young girl, Sam and Becky had the means to send her to nursing school."

"Is that why Hester says she is a second Becky?"

"I suppose you could say that."

"Is her child's name Susanna?"

"I figured you caught that name. Yes, so it is."

Del was quiet, thinking her own thoughts, when Mama asked, " What brought on the conversation about Rachael?"

Del considered the question for a moment. "Oh, Hester was telling me how she and Ed were glad Benj chose to make himself handy here. That's when I said Becky has family. She has Rachael, but I never saw her. Then Hester said, 'Rachael washed her hands of this town years ago.' I know what that means, but why would Rachael do something like that? Her mother lives here."

"It happened before your time. I know some things from hearsay, and this town was in an ugly uproar at one time. That's all I know. Go upstairs and see if Gloria is up before you go outside."

Ori was stretching when Del looked into her bedroom. "Mama asked me to see if you are awake. I'm going out to check on our chores. Time for you to get up."

"You worry too much. I always get up in time," Ori said sleepily.

Del headed for the feedhouse. She cleaned up around the corncribs. Cobs that fell off the metal chute lay on the ground. She threw the nice full cobs into the crib and the scrubs were tossed into a bucket and stored in the feedhouse. "Least that much is done," she said to herself.

Most of the children were collected around the breakfast table when Father joined them. Ori was last and set her egg bucket on the substantial safe in the closed porch. Father waited as Ori took her place at the table. Grace was offered. Mama had fried potatoes with eggs broken over them. She had sautéed onions to add if one so desired. "Eat and get yourselves off to school," she commanded.

Benj watched Phillip add onions to his plate. Ollie turned his head after he looked at Phillip's plate.

"Something the matter, Oliver?" Mama asked.

"The smell of those onions next to me is like having them on my plate," Ollie stated in a voice just above a whisper. It was well known that Ollie didn't like onions.

Benj said nothing but moved Phillip's plate closer to his own.

"I expect to get a lot of work done today," Father commented as Del cleared breakfast dishes. She knew Mama was prepared to make a late breakfast for relatives who might work during the noontime dinner meal and share supper with the whole family.

Del considered herself just plain lucky that other classmates could not answer the questions she missed during the morning session. Skipping home for the dinner hour Del saw Adeline and Phillip. Benj was approaching at the same time from farther back in the lane.

"You are going to miss dinner," Adeline said.

"I won't stay long. I just wanted to say thank you for that dolly tea set. I really like it. I will keep it always."

"I always wanted you to have it. I thought now is the time, before I grow so old and won't remember. I want to give that picture of Blackie to Phillip here, next time we decide to take it off the wall. I already told Phillip he shall have it."

Phillip displayed a smile wider than Del had seen up to now. "It looks like you will appreciate that," Del said to Phillip. She turned back to Adeline. "How is Jonathan? I hope things are better."

"He is getting better. We are still hoping the fall is the only reason for the stiffness in his side. Becky is with him right now. She'll try to exercise his arm and leg. He has to make himself use his muscles or else the stiffness will remain. It is so good to have her and caring neighbors like you."

"Walk with ya," Benj said as Del headed back to the house. He gestured to Phillip. "We'll eat later. *De Adeline hutt en schtori verzaehlt stu de memm. Alles ausgelegt. Brauche dich nimme druwwle. Ve davor, du weescht nix. Yuscht hariche* [Adeline told a story to yer Mama. Everything explained. Need yourself not trouble. Like before, ya know nothing. Only listen]." With a wave of his hand Benj said, "*Geh!* [Go]!"

Benj turned back and Del ran home, not knowing what was explained or what to expect. She entered the kitchen and immediately asked where her uncles and aunts were, as she expected they would be here.

Mama explained that the men were at Grandfather's fields above the creamery. "Did you see Adeline on your way here? What did she have to say?"

Del nodded, "Nothing much. I thanked her for the tea set and asked her about Jonathan. It's good to know he has Becky looking after him. She knows what to do."

"Was Adeline alone?"

"Phillip was with her."

"Eat, then get yourself back to school," Mama said as she opened the stairway door and headed upstairs. Del guessed she was getting materials and sewing things ready for Lillie to work on that afternoon.

Del did some serious thinking on the return walk to school. "So Mama knows something. She talked to Adeline. Benj said everything is alright because Adeline's story explained things. What was the story? Benj said I only need to listen while still keeping things to myself. That's easy to do if they no longer ask questions." Del surely hoped that was the case.

The afternoon session seemed to crawl by as Del was distracted but she came through the afternoon successfully. She noticed Mr. Strunk had a questioning look as she tried her best not to give him cause to ask if something was bothering her. She did not want him to come to her house a second time with questions about her lack of attention. Del entered the schoolhouse after recess and Mr. Strunk asked if he could help her in any way.

"Oh no. I am alright. We have lots of company at our house today. I didn't get to see them all. They will be gone by the time I get home from school is what Mama says."

"I thought there was more on your mind. I know this is a busy time and that also means extra chores."

Del shrugged, "The same thing happens every year. I should be used to it by now."

Mr. Strunk smiled. "You will fondly remember these years as you grow older." He walked away to close the door.

"Whew!" Del thought, "That was close! I really need to forget what is happening beyond school hours and concentrate on the work at hand."

Del managed the last period quite well. She skipped the school lane and then walked slowly when she reached the cement pike. She waited at the lane. Fritz was not there. The wagon rides kept him away. Anabel and Maria were the first to join her and they walked the lane together.

"When will Phillip start school?" Anabel asked.

"Goodness, I really don't know. With all the work on the farm, no one has time to think about that. I will ask Mama about that."

"How long is he staying with you?" Anabel asked.

"Since shortly after school started. Gee, that means once Thanksgiving is here, he will be with us for two months already. He will meet all our relatives then. He will have to start school before long. Teacher will have to see how much he knows and which class he will join."

Del reached home as Anabel and Maria continued on their way. Mama came in from the garden with a handful of fresh parsley, which, in its sheltered location, had pushed new tender sprigs since it's last cutting.

"Change your clothes, there is lots to do. Our relatives will be staying for supper."

Del took the stairs fast and found Lillie seated at Mama's sewing machine. "What are you making today?" Del asked.

"I am altering a winter coat for Phillip, one that I brought along. He will need something warm to wear. While you are here, I would like to see that tea set your mother told me about. I saw other dolly tea sets, but they were always china, not pewter."

"I'll get it for you after I change my clothes." Del opened her top drawer and was dumbfounded as she stepped back into her parents' room.

"What's the matter?" Lillie said, "You are pale. Did you take the stairs too fast?"

"No, no." Del managed to say.

"*Sez eppes letz* [There's something wrong]."

"I don't know Aunt Lillie, that tea set isn't in my drawer. That's where I put it, but it's not there anymore. It makes me feel sick."

Lillie got up and came over to Del. "Are you sure this is where you put it? Let's look through all the drawers, maybe you placed it in one of the other drawers. I sometimes find things where I don't remember putting them."

"I know I put that set in the top drawer, box and all," Del declared.

"Let's look anyway." Lillie leafed through all the deeper drawers after seeing it was not where Del said it should be.

"You have no other piece of furniture in the room where could it be?"

Del slowly shook her head. "I bet Ori has it. She said it should be hers."

"In that case, let's look in her room." Lillie tried the drawers in the dresser but all were locked. The door and inside drawers to the chiffonier were locked, as well as the bureau. Same thing with the dresser, which had movable wing mirrors, and its small drawers. "She can lock all the drawers to her bedroom suite. She has it. I know it. I hope she didn't destroy it!" Del almost cried.

"Let's look again, I want to make sure it isn't here." Lillie remained calm, unlike the excitable person Del had learned to know. "Rest assured. I will talk to her. You go and do your chores. No need to worry. That tea set will be returned tonight yet." Lillie put her arms around Del's shoulders and hugged her. "Go now, this will turn out alright."

Del made her way downstairs slowly and carefully. She never knew her aunt to be so calm and comforting. Del heard Benj say many times in the telling of his stories that there are many sides to every person, and their behaviors depend on different circumstances.

"What took so long?" Mama asked as Del stepped into the kitchen. "What's the matter with you, don't you feel well? Did something happen up there?" Mama waited for Del to reply.

Del shook her head from side to side and spoke very softly. "I wanted to show Lillie the pewter set Adeline gave me. It's gone. I don't have it anymore."

"Hmmm, I wonder if Gloria knows anything about this," Mama said immediately. "This will wait until our company goes home. Then we'll settle things."

Del walked slowly up the lane toward the feedhouse. *"Bischt meed* [You tired]? Too much running," Benj said as he passed her heading in the direction of the woodshed. Del responded with a faint smile. Benj turned and watched Del as she passed by.

Del went about her work very deliberately. Her thoughts were only on the missing tea set. What if Ori destroyed it? That worry made her feel sick to her stomach.

"What's the matter with you? You are always blabbering about something," Ori said as Del entered the feedhouse.

Del made no reply. She continued her work, ignoring Ori. Ori must have sensed something was wrong, because she turned and quickly left. When Del turned with the bucket and paddle to mix mash for the pigs she saw Benj standing in the open doorway.

"Waz gade au doh [What goes on here]?"

Del, with tears in her eyes, told Benj, "My tea set is missing. I think Ori took it."

Benj stood quietly for a spell. *"Es vot aulrecht* [It will be alright]."

"How could Benj be sure all will be alright?" Del wondered what Aunt Lillie and Mama were going to do once Ori entered the house. She finished her work. She did not shell corn for Ori nor place a bucket of water for her use at the henhouse door. "I'll teach her," Del thought, "I will not lift a finger to help her anymore." Del walked slowly back toward the house, stopped by the pump, and sat under the leafless grape arbor to think things over. Benj came over and sat by her side. *"Es vot aulrecht.* [It will be alright]."

"How can you say that? Ori can be real mean."

"Ya must know, ya isn't the only one that knows Gloria. Will be alright. Go help yer Mama."

Del got up to go into the house as Ori walked off the front porch and headed up the lane. Del paused and snickered.

"*Was isz letz?* [What is wrong]?" Benj said as he walked by.

"Ori must have used the front door. She didn't want to face Mama."

Del's thoughts were interrupted when she heard the Hudson coming in the lane. Del saw her Uncle Sam step off the running board on the other side of the car but he did not take time to stop and chat. She remembered Sam telling her about small and larger hurts that come one's way in a lifetime. She got the water bucket and carried fresh water in the house.

Mama immediately gave Del instructions. "Get the table ready for suppertime. We will need the extra boards for the table. Aunt Lillie came down after you left. We took care of things. That set is in your drawer again. We'll discuss this later."

"Does everybody know?" Del asked, curious to learn Ori's reaction to being foiled in her attempt to steal Del's tea set.

"Enough of us know." Mama said.

Del felt some relief, though nothing seemed to make sense. "Was Ori going to be punished?" Del had many unsettling thoughts as she silently did her work. She finished all the table settings when Ori stepped into the closed porch with her bucket of eggs. Benj, holding Carol's hand, came in at the same time. Aunt Eva arrived soon after that, and Aunt Lillie also appeared from the stairway, holding the winter coat with markings for sleeve length. There was small talk among the women in the kitchen as the men and boys completed the outside work.

Father and the others straggled in one by one. When everyone was cleaned up and seated at the table, it was Uncle Sam who offered grace. The evening meal conversation covered the day's work. The cornfields were ready for harvesting uptown. Grandfather, as always, had cut the pasture next to the dam with the scythe for the last time that year. Everyone in the township knew he could swing that scythe to cut tall grasses and leave the field looking like it was mowed with a grass-mowing machine. But with his stiff joints, it had to be a painful effort now. There was a little talk about Phillip's work shoes. Del was quiet. Most conversation came from the boys as they compared present and past years' work in the fields. Winter trapping was also discussed. Til had traps Grandfather gave to him with his name on brass tags soldered to the traps to keep anyone from stealing or claiming his trappings.

After the meal was finished, Mama said, "Adelaide, you go up stairs and bring that tea set down for everyone to see."

Del sat stunned for a second, then burst with energy as she pushed her chair back and made haste to use the stairway.

"Take your time. That set isn't going anywhere. We want everyone to see what Adeline has given for you to keep," Mama called.

There it was, right where she had put it in her top dresser drawer. She dearly wanted to know how it ended back in its rightful place. Del's heart was pounding as she placed the box on the middle of the table. She opened it and placed the pewter set neatly on its small oval tray. Everyone remarked on its well-kept appearance—many dolly tea sets were worn, damaged, or even missing pieces, but this was a complete set. Not a thing was said about its earlier disappearance. Ori had a sullen look on her face but was silent as everyone admired Adeline's gift. Del carefully wrapped each piece in the soft yellowed paper and returned them to the gray box. She took the box and headed upstairs wondering what was done to make Ori return the set. Del smiled, while holding back tears, puzzled; she was grateful for whatever the actions were that restored the set to her. She returned to the kitchen as Mama asked if there was schoolwork that needed to be done. There was none.

"My grandchildren always have work, every day and plenty over the weekend. Doesn't that happen here?" Lillie seemed concerned.

"The children have enough schoolwork. Our teacher understands the demands at harvest time. He goes easy on homework right now," Mama explained.

"When is Phillip going to start school?" Ollie was quick to ask. He would have happily done without school and figured no child could escape it.

The elders looked at each other around the room as none seemed ready to answer that question. Father finally spoke. "It will happen when the time is right."

"Girls, you may finish clearing the table. The boys can take care of the extra table boards." She gestured to the adults. "We will spend a little time in the parlor before our friends go home. Benj, you come with us," Mama said.

Benj shook his head, indicating he was going to walk home.

"Tilghman, you walk with him," Father ordered.

That suited Til just fine. He never did like kitchen duty.

Ori didn't wait too long before leaving the kitchen. "There is enough help here. I will get Carol ready for bed and myself too." Ori headed for the stairs without saying good night.

Del, Bill, Ollie, and Phillip were about to leave the kitchen as their parents and relatives returned from the parlor. Everyone said their good byes and good nights. Del made her way up stairs. Physically tired and emotionally stressed she checked her dresser drawer once more and was satisfied that the small gray box was back where it belonged.

CHAPTER TWENTY-ONE

An Uneasy Peace

Yawning and stretching Del leaned onto the deep window seat on the stair landing in her parents' bedroom. The upper half-doors under the overshoot were open, telling her the early morning work was underway in the barn. Becky walked towards the milkhouse, her aluminum milk kettle swinging from her hand. Mr. Strunk was holding a two-quart jar with wire closures over a glass lid, having a conversation with Father as Becky joined them. Mama stepped out from the milkhouse and joined the group.

Del went downstairs and took another look outside from the closed porch. Ed and Hester had joined Mama and Becky, and Del wondered what that conversation was about; perhaps this was the time decisions were made. Returning to the kitchen, she waited for Mama not knowing what was planned for breakfast.

"You are up early," Mama said as she entered the kitchen. "Set the table for you children only. I will make egg omelets this morning. I expect our relatives will be here before long. The Hoylers are expected as well." Mama grabbed a pitcher and headed outdoors.

Del considered the whereabouts of Benj and Phillip. Not seeing them, she assumed they were helping with the morning chores in the barn. Ori and Carol stepped into the kitchen. Carol was dressed and Ori was preparing to brush and braid Carol's hair. Del set the breakfast dishes on the white table.

"I will get even with you yet," Ori snapped.

"What for? I haven't done anything to you."

"I had to do your work when you were down with Adeline and talked her into giving that tea set to you. You tied my duck too. I don't care what Ed says, he's covering up for you. I was so upset I couldn't fall asleep last night. All because of you."

"I will tell you one last time. I didn't tie your duck. And you didn't do all my work either. I know others did some of my work. And besides, you STOLE my tea set."

"That's what you say. Who believes something like that!"

Del grabbed Bill's outgrown flannel-lined overall jacket for her outside chores. On her way out the door, she leaned back and said, "Everyone!"

As Del made her way to the feedhouse, Benj came up behind her. "*Alles olrecht da mariye* [Everything alright this morning]?" Benj questioned.

"Ori is on the war path. I heard enough. She took that tea set. I don't do anything mean to her. She is already saying she will get even."

"*Ich dank see hut ebbes gelannd* [I think she has learned something]."

Del shook her head. "I don't know how they got Ori to return that tea set. Ori doesn't give in easily."

"*Waise aa net. Ebbes net recht. Ich schaffe mich ouse um weg.* [Don't know. Something not right. I'll work myself out of the way]," Benj said as he headed for the house.

Del did her usual work and headed indoors.

Mama was in the kitchen. As they quietly prepared breakfast they heard Isaac's Hudson. Mama went to the small clothes closet for her pink sweater. It wasn't there. After fussing and accusing someone of misplacing her newest sweater, she grabbed her well-worn piece.

"See to it there is enough wood on the fire. Check on the omelets. Don't let them bake too dry," Mama said as she headed outside to greet the relatives.

Del headed to the side room for a clean tablecloth. She opened the buffet drawer, and then she remembered she wanted to check Mama's camera. She quickly opened the cabinet door where the camera was kept. She lifted it and immediately knew the camera didn't have film. Why was Mama concealing a camera without any film the other day? Nor did she see a new roll of film.

Both Aunts Lillie and Eva came in with Mama. Lillie removed her coat and laid it on a chair in the parlor. She came back, took Eva's coat and placed it there as well.

"How is everybody this morning? Ready for another big day? This will be my last trip before Thanksgiving, except for butchering. Sam's boss says things are looking up and they are going to get the go-ahead to start another block of houses on the other side of the street."

Mama lifted a hand. "Adelaide, go out and tell the boys to come in and eat, its time to get ready for school."

Del hurried to the door and saw they were already walking towards the house, so she returned to the kitchen as Mama continued talking.

"Do you want some breakfast?" Mama looked to Lillie and Eva and gestured to the table.

Eva said, "We didn't come for breakfast. You feed us often enough."

Mama smiled, "After the children are off to school, we can chat while having a cup of coffee."

"I won't spent any time outdoors today. I want to finish some of the sewing projects I started," Lillie said.

"What I don't finish I'll take along home and sent the finished pieces with Sam or with the Keystone Products man, when he makes his rounds your way," Lillie offered.

"I sure appreciate your help," Mama said. "I get to sit at my Majestic for an hour or two in the afternoon sometimes, but not every day. I need to be careful with it, because you can't replace the shuttle anymore."

"I sat and sewed for eight to ten hours every day in a glove factory at fourteen years of age using a machine that operated with a shuttle. It wasn't easy work. We were docked wages if we made a mistake that wasted material." Lillie recalled.

The boys came in with Benj and Phillip. Phillip smiled as he nodded to the familiar faces around the table. He didn't look scared anymore.

"Ich kendt ihm gute dricke [I could give him a good hug]." Lillie looked at Phillip pleasantly. Phillip seemed to understand something was said about him and he tried to hide his smile.

"It looks like Laura's good cooking is treating you right!" Lillie patted Phillip's shoulder. Mama smiled at the compliment.

The children left for school. Ori did not trail on behind as usual but hastened her pace to walk along side of Til. That was unusual. Til, with his long legs, walked faster than all the other children.

"She probably didn't want to be the last one in the kitchen with Aunt Lillie around," Bill said to Del with a grin.

"Lillie doesn't hold anything back. Eveyone knows what happened," Del said.

Just then a motor car turned in the lane. It was the Hoylers in their 1923 Chevrolet Coupe. They made an appearance every year to discuss butchering dates. The boys stopped walking as they looked at the passing machine, all black with yellow spoke wheels. The hood ornament had a gauge to measure the temperature of the water in the radiator. Del, looking back, saw a spare tire was positioned on the back of the two-passenger automobile.

The first session was spent as usual. At recess time some older boys were whispering and huddled behind the big rock. Ollie was disappointed they did not join in playing a game of ball and complained about that at dinnertime.

Mama simply declared, "Something is going on there. Never you mind, Oliver. Your teacher will take care of things," Mama assured Ollie.

The children entered the playground and to their surprise there was Teacher playing games with the younger children. This was most unusual. The game ended as it was time for the afternoon session to begin. Em took her seat quietly. She didn't greet Del with a smile, and was silent as she opened a book and set her eyes on that page. The whole school seemed to be in a serious mood. Del waited until recess time to ask Em what happened.

Em hesitated, then said, "Joe is in trouble."

Del looked around and noticed Em's brother was still in his seat even though his classmates were outside. "Isn't he allowed to go outside?" Del asked.

"Don't want to talk about it."

"It can't be that bad," Del countered, but didn't get any more information from Em. "Here," she said, "You might as well look through some of these other books and forget about what's bothering you."

Em looked at the library books on the window seats but never opened any of them during recess time.

The last part of the school day was spent with the usual class sessions up to dismissal time. Del noticed that Joe stood by his desk and did not line up with the rest of the children. He was the last one to get in line. Em waited outside for her brother. Del was puzzled not knowing whether she should stand by Em or start her walk home. She took slow steps looking back frequently as did some other children. Mr. Strunk finally stepped outside with Joe. He gave Joe something small as he spoke to him. Mr. Strunk returned inside the school building. Joe and Em left together, hurrying to meet the others walking down the steep hill ahead of them.

The school children, with the exception of Ori and Mae who lagged behind as usual, walked the lane as a group. The boys had plenty to say.

Abe Schultz said, "Teacher returned the pack of cigarettes but told Joe he was going to keep the matches. He warned him not to carry matches to school. He will talk to Joe's father about the cigarettes."

"Wow," Del thought, "Mr. Strunk is going to visit Em's parents."

Bekcy's brown bars and cold milk were on the table. The sewing machine was going as Del climbed the stairs to change clothes. Lillie had little to say. Carol had fallen asleep on her parents' bed. Mama had all her sewing supplies neatly arranged on the cedar chest—rick-rack, button jars, buckles, elastic, binding, hooks, loops, and clasps. Del went outside and did her evening work. She did all but feed the pigs when Mama called, "Take your wagon and fetch the empty crock before it gets dark. Be careful that you don't break it."

Ed saw Del coming. He carried the tea container from the middle of the field and set it on the wagon. She moved slowly in the lane, looking for even ground to make sure the barrel-shaped crock would not tip over and break.

"You're always somewhere else when I need you," Ori was grumpy as Del reached their work area.

"Mama sent me to fetch this crock."

"You always have some kind of excuse."

"What's your problem now?"

"Taw-Taw flew up to the highest nest and sits there. I stand on a butter box to reach into the highest nest but I can't reach him. If he'd stay put, I could get him."

"Let him be. He got up by himself, he'll come down by himself when he is ready. At least he won't get wet up there," Del countered.

"If I had a long handled wooden rake, maybe I could get him down."

"Well then go get it. I am not getting it for you. I still haven't finished my work."

"Will you carry one bucket of eggs into the house for me?"

She doesn't give up, Del thought. "Set it outside. I'll carry it in as soon as I finish."

Twilight was falling fast as Del looked around for her wagon. The tea container was no longer there. She pulled her wagon to the front of the feedhouse and propped it by the rain barrel. She headed for the house carrying the smaller egg bucket. Hermann and his wife were leaving. He had the smallest coop Del ever saw. It held two live chickens and a rooster. Father waved good-bye. Del knew Hermann would be back at butchering time.

One by one everyone gathered in the kitchen as suppertime drew near. Father sat and asked the children to say their prayer in unison.

"Oliver, did you have any ball players this afternoon?" Mama asked.

"We didn't play ball. Joe stayed inside."

"Is that all you have to say?" Mama was becoming impatient. "Tilghman, what is this all about?"

"Not all that much. Joe came to school with a pack of cigarettes and matches. Teacher caught him and some others smoking behind the big rock while we were here for dinner. Mr. Strunk gave the cigarettes back to Joe after school, but he kept the matches."

Ori wanted to talk about a different topic. "My duck climbed up on the rafters in the henhouse. I couldn't reach him, and Del won't help me. She can tie up my duck but she sure won't help me."

Mama gave Ori a warning look.

Del ignored Ori and said, "Teacher is going to visit Joe's parents."

"That doesn't surprise me at all. Your teacher has dealt with that situation more than once. One time it was chewing tobacco. Some boys got sick. He knows what to watch for when boys reach a certain age." Mama seemed amused.

"You can't fool him." Father paused. "He is right to keep the matches— the forest is close to the schoolhouse, and any flame near there is not a good idea."

There was a long pause as all the children contemplated how well their teacher knew his students.

Father looked around the table and talked about his day. "Hermann is checking on our butchering dates. That time will be here before we know it."

"If you have homework, better get it done now or Sunday," Mama ordered. "The weekend will be busy, but tomorrow you can sleep a little longer if you wish."

Del climbed the stairs slowly. Once alone in her room her mind drifted from one thought to another. Adeline, Jonathan, the tea set, Becky's daughter Rachael. "Why was she so angry with me?" she wondered. Del squeezed her eyes shut, said her prayer quietly as sleep took over for the night.

On Monday, Del entered the kitchen. "Gee, that coffee smells good. Where is everybody?"

"You are late. I was about to call you. I want to tell you something while we are alone. I have taken care of your tea set. I thought it would be better if I kept it where it will be safe from Gloria. I'll give it to you to show to your cousins when they visit on Thanksgiving Day."

"That sure makes me feel better. She says she'll get revenge because I tied her duck, which isn't so. I didn't tie her duck! She accuses me of other things, too."

"What other things?" Mama asked quickly.

"Says she did all my work the day I left to fetch Phillip. I know that isn't true. Bill did some of my work, he told me so and others helped too. She insists I begged Adeline to give me that set," Del paused.

"Go on, " Mama prompted.

"What did you or Lillie say to make Ori give that set back?"

"Doesn't matter right now. You have the set. What do you expect Emma will be talking about this morning?" Mama changed the subject.

"Plenty, that's for sure. She'll tell me what happened to Joe when her Pa and Ma found out about him taking cigarettes to school."

Mama smiled. "Do you think she'll talk about Sunday again?"

Del shrugged. "Maybe, but she always gets it wrong about when we have church and Sunday school and when it's just Sunday school. She keeps calling Phillip 'that colored boy' or 'your Black boy'."

Mama sighed. "It will take a little time for some people to accept someone of a different race. It's just good that our no-good busybody doesn't attend Sunday services regularly. I think we fixed her this time."

Del was intrigued and wanted to ask who the busybody was. Just then Ori stepped into the kitchen.

"Good morning," Mama said.

"Who's up already?" Ori grumbled.

"You can see Adelaide is here. Everyone but Carol." Mama spoke while placing split pieces of wood on the fire. "Benj and Phillip are doing some of your work today."

"I like to gather the eggs myself. That's for me to do," Ori stated.

"I know that's your job," Mama added mildly.

"Huh, Benj and Del collect the eggs sometimes," Ori snapped.

"Benj and Del have been a big help to you," Mama said and gave Ori a stern look.

"I'll go out right now. I want to collect the eggs myself!" Ori left immediately.

Mama remained quiet.

"When will Phillip start school?" Del asked.

"We need more paperwork."

"He has the paper that says he is vaccinated," Del noted.

"He needs a full name. Never you mind. We'll take care of things."

"What about Benj?" Del quickly responded. "He would give him his last name. He said Phillip Fronheiser sounds good to him."

"That's not as easy as it sounds. There is so much we need to do first. No need for you to be concerned, we are doing all we can."

"Was Benj an only child? I never heard of another Fronheiser around here."

"None other here in Rockland Township that I know of. He has a sister I never met named Mamie. She married and moved up the line. Towanda is too long a trip for either of them to manage now. That's about all I know. She may not be living anymore. I should ask Benj if he hears from her."

Del walked out thinking about Benj and Phillip.

Most of the men, including Benj and Phillip, were gathered in a circle by the barnbank. "This is what I call a businessmen's meeting, but instead of suits and ties you see blue shirts and bib overalls," Ed grinned.

"Sure looks that way," Del agreed as she greeted the men.

Del made her way to the feedhouse as Mama headed for the barn. It was quite unusual for folks to gather and talk so early in the morning when there was much to do. Edgar was there for early morning milk for Ernie. Abraham Straub was there, probably offering his help for husking. Del shelled some corn and carried buckets of water over to a capped well next to the feedhouse door.

The men dispersed in different directions. Del turned the hand-cranked wheel to the corn sheller faster than usual and set the shelled corn and bucket of water by the henhouse door where Ori could easily reach them. She gathered some corn scrubs and, along with Benj and Phillip, threw them into the pigpen.

"Finished?" Benj questioned.

"Going in for breakfast," Del replied. "You two coming?"

Benj waved his right hand motioning for her to continue moving toward the house.

After breakfast the children left for school as the Gohos approached. Anabel and Maria talked with Del and Gordon walked along with Ollie. Anabel remarked that her father thought that going to school at Funk's sparked a greater interest in learning for Gordon. To Del's surprise, Ori had been listening to their conversation and immediately asked what it was her father said.

"Boys usually talk about horses and farm implements," Anabel said. "Gordon talks about his class discussion periods. He likes to share his thoughts. He also likes those world maps rolled up above the blackboards on the front wall. We never saw big maps like that. Geography lessons are his favorite topic."

When the dinner hour came, Del and Bill walked back home together. Del turned to Bill and asked, "Do you think Phillip will be named Phillip Fronheiser? Benj once said he would give him his last name."

"I heard Benj say that too," Bill acknowledged.

"Mama told me he needs a full name before he can go to school," Del repeated the morning conversation to her twin. Bill was silent as he pondered that information. Del became impatient. "What are you thinking?"

"Maybe that's why Isaac's twin brother was here," Bill stated with a dawning look of realization.

"What?" Del was very interested in Bill's theory.

"Ira might be a policeman," Bill murmured while giving his statement serious thought.

"Why do you say that?" Del asked.

"I heard Uncle Isaac say he would talk to his brother because he knows the law. Maybe he could help find out what happened to Phillip. I didn't know what he was talking about then."

"Well!" Del was adding things up. "Maybe that's why Father and those two were husking a shock of corn all by themselves."

"Now what?" Bill was interested.

"Father and Isaac and Ira spent time together when Ira was here. Just those three husking together, apart from all the others."

Bill looked like he was doing some serious thinking as he hurried his pace to meet the Shultz boys. Del watched him go. Del's mind raced about things she heard as she skipped the dirt lane slowly and recalled Father with the two brothers. Del thought. "What can Ira do to help?"

Em was waiting. "Hurry up, you can skip faster than that. What's been keeping you?"

"Nothing much. What's up with you?" Del asked Em.

"Just thinking about home," Em admitted.

"Everybody alright? Del asked.

"I don't want to talk about it. You talk. You always have something to say," Em was abrupt.

"There's always something to talk about. We don't have many more days left for corn husking at our place. Butchering will start soon . . ."

Em blurted out, "Joe wants to quit school. Pa won't let him. Pa said Joe will graduate from Funk's school in spring with the rest of his class."

"So that's what bothers you. Is he going to do that?" Del asked.

"I guess so. Like it or not, Joe will finish school. Pa's orders."

"Don't worry Em, your parents will take care of things."

Em merely nodded her head.

Del waited for Bill by the lane as he finished conversation with the Shultz boys and they headed for home at the end of the school day. Fritz was not there to meet them.

"Do you know where Ira lives?"

"No." Bill thought a minute. "Could be anyplace."

"I thought he could live in New York. Isaac and Eva go to New York to visit his mother. When Isaac's mother was widowed she moved to New York to stay with her sister. Eva said those two do a lot of charity work. That's all I know."

"Do you suppose Ira lives in New York?" Bill asked.

"Don't know for sure. I never heard any talk about Ira but he did say something about a city. He said living there is different from living in a farming neighborhood."

"Lots to wonder about."

"Was Adeline with the huskers today?" Del asked Mama the moment she stepped inside.

"No, she is working in her own two fields of corn. Ed and Benj are helping. Ed is interested in their acreage—it's enough for a good size truck patch," Mama replied as she moved pots on the stove.

Benj came into the house and sat down on the rocker. "Ed brings my boy back."

"How was school this afternoon?" Mama asked.

"Em is bothered with Joe wanting to quit school."

"Is he going to do that?" Mama seemed surprised.

"No, his pa won't let him quit."

"He shouldn't quit so close to graduating. His father is doing the right thing," Mama said.

"Where does Ira live? I know it's a city, but I don't know which one," Del asked.

"You are full of questions," Mama hesitated. "How do you know it's a city?"

"Heard him talk about city people not being as friendly as country people."

Mama said, "It could be a city most anywhere, perhaps where his mother lives. She lives in New York with her sister."

"I'm going to do my chores," Del said, realizing she wasn't getting answers to questions from Mama.

"Check on the workers if they need something warm to drink," Mama called after Del was on the walkway.

Del walked slowly by the barn. The box camera without film—that had Del puzzled. She suspected Mama was looking after matters she was not sharing with anyone, at least not the children. Del completed her chores and returned to the house to find Phillip placing table settings while Benj slowly rocked back and forth. The evening passed by without any opportunity to get any answers to her many questions.

CHAPTER TWENTY-TWO

That Old Printz Property

Tuesday morning Del awoke and stretched lazily. Ira's recent visit was on her mind. Mama's visit to Orphelia was on her mind. And why was Rachael so angry? That question kept her awake for a spell before falling asleep last night. She couldn't share her questions about that with anyone, not even Bill. Then there was the most troubling question of all in the encounter with Rachael—did Adeline tell Mama all that happened both outside and inside her house? Mama wasn't asking questions anymore and Benj appeared unconcerned. Del needed to find out what Adeline told Mama.

"She must know what happened that evening. If so, Mama knows more than I know," Del concluded to herself. She would ask Benj what Mama was told since she no longer was drilling her for answers. At the same time Del kept trying to put two and two together, as Father would say. There were plenty of other unexplained situations, like that time when Fritz did not meet her and Bill early in the school year. She now suspected Benj could explain why Fritz didn't meet them. And why should Hester find pleasure in seeing Benj stand inside that open barn door? Del remembered the deeply concerned look on her father's face as he asked Benj if he could spend time in the barn the night Father came home with Phillip. Spending a night on the threshold floor would be very uncomfortable for anyone, especially so for someone of Benj's age. "The plank floor was uncomfortable no matter what! Loose hay or straw to sit or lay on would be as hard as a rock in a short time,' she reflected.

Father's cousin, Clint, then came to mind. He was a hobo, carrying a steel with a grooved wooden handle for a solid grip hooked onto his belt to sharpen knives as compensation for payment to sleep in someone's barn on his way to Florida for the cold winter months. It was soon time for him to make an appearance. Del wondered who could tell her more about Isaac's twin brother.

"You are rather quiet this morning," Mama observed as Del prepared the table for breakfast.

"Not much to talk about." Del spoke. "Table all set, I will tend to my morning work." Del left immediately since she wasn't interested in any more conversation.

"Good morning, Del," Matilda Moyer, a neighbor just up the road from Ed and Hester's home, called as Del left the house.

"Good morning, Matilda, you are early, I didn't see other huskers this morning."

"I want to see how much husking still needs to be done on that Printz home."

"I'd go with you, except I don't have the time this morning," Del replied. Del wondered why Matilda had to check on husking progress at the Printz farm. Ed could have told her himself. It was also curious that she wanted to help husk corn since she did house cleaning and cooking for widowers in the township like Grandfather. Del thought about the Printz house. The first floor had four-over-one windows under the front porch and paneled shutters all around. There was a shallow well, a root cellar, and a fenced-in garden that currently contained tall weeds that needed to be cut. Farm buildings included a small red barn and a large henhouse that stood farther back between the house and the barn. A weather-beaten old implement shed also stood next to the barn. Del thought someone should close the shutters over that broken pane under the porch. She completed her work and headed for the house.

The Gohos were in sight as the Heydt children started for school. Fritz was not there. Del asked Bill what was happening this day.

"Same as usual, Father is taking the milk to the creamery and Fritz is on the truck," was Bill's brief reply.

"Did you see Benj and Phillip this morning?"

"All three went down to Conrad's early this morning," Bill answered.

"Three?" Del exclaimed and quickly added, "Becky's one of them?"

"Yes, Becky took a jar of milk along."

"Goodness!" Til joined in. "Does that mean Jonathan is worse?"

"I didn't say anything like that. Just said they were out early," Bill stated.

"It could mean something else. Carrying milk, Becky might be spending the day there," Del said with a reassuring tone.

Del waited for Anabel and Maria. Gordon walked with Ollie as all headed for the school lane. Anabel commented about yesterday's chart that showed all the chambers of the heart and other organs during health class discussions for the upper grades. "Never saw anything like that before."

"I didn't like looking at that chart," Maria said.

"There are others you didn't see," Del told the girls. "We have charts that display all kinds of birds, plus wild animals from all around the world like elephants and tigers," Del advised. "There are charts with the mountain ranges and the tropics and the division of countries."

The girls separated as they met Em upon entering the school grounds.

"Hello Em," Del said, "Has your brother decided to finish school? Mama already told Ori she can decide for herself what she wants to do upon graduation and Ori wants to get a job. She will move to the city if she has to."

Ori heard Del mention her name and walked over. She nodded her head and said, "Mae is paid to wash dishes and keep counters clean in a five-and-ten cent store. I never heard of people paying for that kind of work." She added, "Teacher won't allow it, or Mae would wear lipstick and nail polish to school. I'll wear lipstick as soon as Mama lets me. You two are too young for that."

As Ori turned around, Del and Em just rolled their eyes.

Arriving home at the end of the school day the children saw Doll hitched alongside of Harry, coming in the lane with a wagon full of husked corn. Til ran into the closed porch and hurried back immediately to greet Doll.

Benj stepped to the outside of the woodshed, shock on his face. He couldn't believe his eyes as he pushed his cap back a bit and rubbed his head lightly with two fingers. *"Grosse verschtand kann des net glaawe* [This is really unbelievable]."

Bill and Del laughed, equally surprised by Til's unexpected dash indoors before greeting his beloved Doll. Anabel and Maria just listened to everyone's reactions.

"Til dropped off a package from the teacher," Bill said.

"It was under the jacket hanging over his arm," Del added.

"Bicher [Books]," Benj said.

"Yes, I believe you're right!" Del added, "I saw a brown paper package on teacher's desk tied with cord string. I never saw when Mr. Strunk give that package to Til."

Doll bobbed her head up and down and snorted. It was clear she was as happy to see Til as he was to see his horse. Mr. Straub relaxed on the wagon seat and grinned while Til and Gordon said hello. Benj, watching Til with considerable amusement, motioned with a wave of his hand for both Bill and Del to make their way into the house. Anabel and Maria were too shy to volunteer any conversation. "See you tomorrow!" Del called as she waved goodbye to the Gohos.

An assortment of snacks were on the kitchen table. Ollie helped himself to them.

"What's in the package that Til put on Father's desk?" Ollie asked.

"Is that where the package is? I know it's books," Bill said as he made his way to the table.

Del walked into the closed porch and counted the number of books as the wrapping paper exposed the top and bottom ends of the books. Four, Del said softly to herself as she went back to the kitchen, sat down and helped herself to canned pears and cottage cheese before heading for the outdoors. Benj and Phillip were walking by as Del joined them. Phillip wore the cap he liked, while resting his hand on Benj's arm as they moved at a pace that was comfortable for both. He was walking better every day.

"What are you two up to?" Del asked. "I need my wagon before long. Is it here for me?"

Benj nodded his head, indicating yes. "*Mah bleiwe doh* [We stay here]," Benj said as they seated themselves under the leafless grape arbor.

"Do you know who those books are for?" Del asked.

"*Froak mich net. Was denksch doo?* [Ask me not. What think you]?"

"You know as well as I who they are for . . ." Del cast her eyes to Phillip.

"*Huscht sel aus gfiggert* [You have that figured out]."

"They can't be for us. Our teacher would have told us," Del said firmly.

Benj looked at Phillip and patted his shoulder, "Ya gonna be a school boy, guess that's so."

Del entered the feedhouse imagining Phillip in school. She could already picture him playing ball with the boys.

The evening was spent with little chatter. As usual, Del's parents and Benj lingered over a cup of coffee as the children scattered in different directions to attend to necessary school assignments. Father and Benj left together to make sure Benj arrived safely to his home after dark. Mama finished her coffee while seated at the table with Carol and the small-and-large print alphabet book. Phillip sat close by observing them. Mama noticed Phillip's interest and his apparent understanding of the alphabet—particularly as he helped Carol learn her letters.

"Phillip, why don't you tell Carol when she is right or wrong?"

Phillip just nodded and said, "Okay."

Del thought, "If he knows the alphabet, he must have been in first grade at least."

Not much later, Mama called Ori and told her to prepare Carol for bed. One by one all the children said their goodnights.

Wednesday morning Del noticed the package of books was no longer on Father's desk and continued outside. She passed Ollie heading to the house, his early work completed. She entered the feedhouse.

"Did you see Taw-Taw?" Ori asked.

"No, I did not. He's probably getting into some kind of trouble. Maybe he found a new hiding place, you can't trust that duck," Del replied.

"You don't care!" Ori snapped.

"You're right, I really don't. But I'm the one who saved your duck from hanging himself," Del said as she opened the henhouse door to place a bucket of water there.

Ed appeared from the feed entry as Del stepped down from the feedhouse door. She ran over to him. "Taw-Taw is on the prowl somewhere. Ori can't find him," Del spoke softly.

"I know," Ed nodded his head. "He's in the feed entry, coop and all, and he can stay there awhile. I was going to be nice to that duck and release him this morning. Then he caught my little finger in his beak and pinched it something awful. The nail is getting black and blue already," Ed said as he showed Del the visible proof. "He may stay in jail awhile longer. The boys gave him grains and water. I would have left him there without food and water. That critter has lived far beyond the years for a duck."

Del smiled. "I I suppose the boys will tell her Taw-Taw is okay."

"Don't tell her how he got there," Ed said. "I don't want her to know he got the better of me."

"Oh, I won't," Del promised.

"I will be back after Hester looks at this finger." Ed hastened toward home.

Ori checked the water trough before heading to the side of the barn. Del watched briefly as she entered the walk with the bucket of eggs.

She turned slowly as she heard some commotion. First out from the feed entry was Ori and her duck. Til was close behind with the empty coop. Del could hear Til say, "Don't ask me, that duck was here—coop and all—when I stepped into the barn this morning. He got grain and water. No harm done."

Del entered the porch and set the bucket of eggs there. She entered the kitchen and washed up. Benj was seated on the rocking chair and Phillip was close by. Mama placed wood on the fire in the stove.

Del asked, "What happened to those books on Father's desk? They aren't there this morning."

"Never you mind. Finish the table settings for breakfast. Are the boys finished with the barn work? Is the milking done?" Mama spoke briskly.

"I didn't look." Del replied.

"Alles faddich" [All finished]," Benj offered.

Del finished the place settings and got ready for school. In her bedroom she thought it curious that Mama would not say a word about what happened to those books. Del could not understand this secrecy. She returned to the kitchen and heard Ori in the middle of her complaint about where she found her duck.

"I bet Del carried that coop with my duck into the feed entry."

"You were outside before me this morning. How could I do something to that duck?" Del pointed out.

"Enough! I don't want to hear anymore about your duck. You have a full day of school ahead of you, both of you. You need to place all your effort in your school studies each day. That is important. End of discussion." Mama's tone of voice indicated she would not tolerate any back talk.

The morning went well. Del managed to keep her thoughts on class topics during both forenoon sessions. Dinnertime came and Fritz was free to meet the twins. Bill was especially pleased. "A couple more days, and you will be waiting for us every day. That will be good." Bill said as he stroked Fritz's head vigorously.

Isaac's Hudson was parked by the barnbridge. Benj was not at his usual place and no one was around as Del entered the kitchen for the noon meal. Mama and Carol entered through the back door. "I have leftovers warming in the oven for you. You may choose what you want. The rest of us will eat after you go back to school," Mama stated.

"Is Isaac alone again?" Ori asked.

"Isaac didn't bring Eva along. You know she has work this week."

"I wanted Eva to look at my new stitch. I guess I need to practice more," Ori said sadly.

"I believe that's what you should do," Mama agreed.

Til got up to leave and said he would grab an apple for Doll before heading back to school.

"You know those damaged apples we keep in the washhouse will not last much longer," Mama said.

"I know." Til said as everyone left for the return walk to school. Til ran to join the rest on their way back to school. Fritz trotted with them to the end of the lane.

Em was on the see-saw placed on the falter rails across the opening to a field. Del stood by and watched as it was near time for the bell to ring.

The afternoon session seemed long. Del couldn't wait for the end of this school day. When it came, Isaac's Hudson was still parked by the barnbridge. He spent the day on the farm. Mama had red beets and endive set aside plus late ox heart and yellow tomatoes for Isaac to take along. Del set about to complete her evening detail. She moved quickly before heading back to the Printz home to clear the field of fallen cobs of corn. She started the rows farthest away, picking up full and scrub cobs of corn that were missed or fell off the wagons. She placed the full cobs of corn in buckets setting on her low wagon. She collected damaged and small pumpkins that did not grow to maturity, placing some on her wagon or on piles for later pickup. The pumpkin pieces and almost bare cobs of corn were thrown close to the stonewall surrounding the field for wildlife this winter. Del knew she would not finish the task this day, but at least she was going to the field row by row and create piles for wagonloads another day.

Bill came looking for her just as she was pulling her loaded wagon into the lane. "It's getting late. Is your other work done?" Bill asked.

"I finished everything before I came back to these fields. Need to lock up, that's all. That doesn't take long."

"Let's call it a day. We locked up for you. I'll carry one bucket of corn and shove these pumpkins over a little so they won't fall off. We can move faster."

The evening meal was filled with small talk. Father was pleased with the results of the day. He planned to get the Printz property cleaned up. He said Grandfather would take a scythe to the garden tomorrow and cut other tall grasses on the property. The property was being put up for sale.

Finishing her kitchen work, Del was among the first to climb the stairs. Her last thought before drifting off to sleep was to ponder why so much time would be spent on the abandoned Printz home if it's up for sale. There was no need for Grandfather to cut the weeds in that fenced-in garden.

CHAPTER TWENTY-THREE

The Newfangled Telephone

LOOKING DOWN FROM her bedroom window, Del saw a soft layer of frost lay on the ground. She hurriedly dressed to get ready for her morning duties. No one was present as she entered the kitchen. Stepping outside, breathing in the fresh cold air caused her to shiver. Bill's jacket was appreciated this day; she tucked it closer to her body while observing the area.

Del was startled as Ed placed a hand on her shoulder. "I didn't mean to scare you. First feel of winter is here. I don't want to forget where I lay my jacket, once the sun comes up and it warms up in an hour or two. What did your sister say about yesterday?"

"Like always she blames me for everything that happens. It doesn't matter if it's about her duck or not. How is the finger?" Del asked.

"It'll heal, but I might lose the nail. It's really sore. Hester used some of your aunt's homemade salve and bandaged it good. There's nothing better than that salve to heal anything and everything. I'll have to do what Benj did to that critter."

"What did Benj do?" Del was quick to ask.

"Benj will have to tell you."

"I'd sure like to know what happened between Benj and Taw-Taw," Del said emphatically.

"Can't tell ya."

Mama was in the kitchen when Del returned. "We'll clean up the Printz fields today," Mama said. "That tract will be finished this day and that fodder will be brought in and stacked against the back of hen-house. The stacked fodder adds warmth to the building."

"Why clean up those fields so quickly? No one lives there. I already picked the fields clean of fallen cobs of corn," Del said.

"We farm the land, and need to keep the fields in half-decent shape for the new owner. There will be a Sheriff sale to cover the taxes if something doesn't happen soon. Better to clean up now than later." Mama's abrupt tone meant that topic was closed.

After breakfast the children prepared for school. The Gohos were in the lane by the woodshed as Del entered the walkway. She ran to catch up to the girls while Gordon waited for her brothers. As they reached the pike, Del saw Ed's nextdoor neighbors, the Moyers, talking to a man wearing a gray uniform at their front door. Maybe they were getting a telephone too.

Em was waiting for Del as they reached the school grounds. They greeted each other and walked toward the school building.

"We are going to get the telephone in our house today," Ollie announced. He was most eager to share the news for all to hear. Children gathered around him as Ollie discussed the work the telephone company was doing close to their lane. He never finished all he intended to say as the bell rang for all to gather inside.

At recess time, Del asked Em to come along outside. From the school grounds Del pointed to an equipment truck and to a pole that now stood upright below Benj's house. "Look, you can easily see that tall pole. They must be going in toward my place now."

Ollie joined them. "A pole covered in what looks like black oil lies at the end of our yard and still has to be placed somewhere on our property." Ollie stood by Del's side offering his explanation to Em and other children gathered around. Em listened but made no further comments.

When dinnertime came, Ollie ran all the way home.

Til called after him, "Don't you bother with any of the workmen. You know what Mama said."

Ollie continued his run.

Arriving home, an unfamiliar reddish brown machine with a black canvas top was parked by the woodshed. Del was curious to know who the machine belonged to.

Til came in last, took his seat, and bowed his head in silent prayer. He then announced the strange machine was a Hupmobile. "Never saw one like that before—it's a different shade of red and has a spare tire on the back, and fancy tail and side lights. Maybe the top comes down on that two seater. Who put that pumpkin on the running board in front of the back fender? There's a tool box behind the front fender," Til talked excitedly about the strange car. "Whose machine is it? That owner keeps his machine in tip-top condition. I bet he doesn't use it often. Better make sure that duck isn't around. Taw-Taw could dirty the inside." Til stopped talking as he placed food on his plate.

Ori eyed Til angrily.

"Whose machine is it?" Del asked.

"It belongs to a man from the telephone company," Bill stated as he looked to Mama. "I saw that car in Moyer's driveway this morning."

Del and Bill, with Fritz between them, started back to school after lunch. Phillip slowly walked with a little help from Til. Benj followed at a slower pace without the wagon. Time passed quickly at school. Em whispered to Del that Joe was going to complete school while his class was up for recitation. Del nodded her head, acknowledging she heard Em's whisper.

After school the children were engaged in their usual chores and the suppertime talk was all about the telephone. The pole was getting placed below the garden halfway between the apple tree on the upper side and the row of sour cherry trees on the lower side, and directly behind the three currant bushes. When Del looked from her bedroom window to change into her work clothes, the pole was in direct view. She assured herself that it wouldn't interfere with her view of the surrounding area while wondering where the next pole would be placed.

At the supper table Mama announced their phone ring would be one long and two shorts. She practiced on a real phone that the telephone company man brought to the house. "You turn the crank a full circle for a long ring and half-turns for a short ring. We have to call the operator to call places other than this village."

Del considered the telephone could be handy for her grandfather, although he probably would not care to use it. All new things were considered "contraptions" not made for his use. Del thought about his changes in routine now that he sold the creamery business. He spent time each day, as always, talking to Dick and Harry, his well-groomed horses. Brownie, his fox terrier and walking companion would get more attention maybe, but Silky the cat, keeping the creamery free of mice, probably would not get a lick of cream every day. He would walk with two canes to that special corner room that was always closed except for his use. It had a comfortable chair and a bed for Silky's naps. Grandfather would now have more time for Silky to lay on his lap. Del concluded that Grandfather would surely miss not being around a host of people every day.

Saturday came. Del awakened and heard the sounds of family members getting up. Saturdays she could stretch and lay awhile longer in bed. Father and the boys were in the kitchen eating breakfast when she entered, guessing that their barn work was already completed.

"My, everybody's up real early this morning," Del said as she looked about.

Phillip, still in his stocking feet, was seated next to Benj. Til and Bill were seated on the bench behind the table. Isaac's Hudson could be heard coming in the lane. Father left the kitchen to greet him; Mama placed split wood on the fire in the kitchen stove.

The door opened; with Father were both Isaac and Sam, saying, "Nice day for outside work! We won't have many more days like this before winter sets in."

There were good mornings and hellos coming from all directions as Ollie entered the kitchen in his stocking feet and reached for his shoes under the couch. Breakfast was served, as all the children, except Ori and Carol, were present. Sam and Isaac accepted coffee and a piece of cake to dunk.

Del wondered what outside work the men were about to do. Saw lumber, perhaps. Father may have orders to fill. Maybe they'll go to the forest, cut down trees for winter's sawmill operation. After cake and coffee the men got up to leave and the boys followed. Ori entered the kitchen with Carol. Benj watched Phillip lace his shoes, then using hand motions gestured for Phillip to lift his foot. Phillip did so and Benj made a more secure tie.

"Good boy," Benj said. "We'll go watch the girls do their morning work." He patted Phillip's hand.

Del cleared the table. Phillip stepped alongside and handed dishes to her as she carried them to the sink. "I may as well go out and tend to my morning chores," Del said softly as she stepped into the closed porch.

"Be sure you dress warm enough," Mama called.

Ed came by and pointed to the Hudson, "I heard the gears shifting as that machine turned into this lane. Thought I'd wait for the milking to be finished and take it to the creamery. When I come back I will join the men on the Printz home. Lots of work there."

"But those fields are already cleaned," Del said.

"We won't be cleaning fields today. That old shed behind the barn is ready to fall over—we'll take it apart today. Save what can be used and burn the rest. It's a good day to burn scrap since it's not windy."

That news really set Del's mind to thinking. She barely noticed as Ollie rushed by Del. He was grumbling to himself that no one awakened him earlier; he ran down the lane heading for the Printz home. Del knew Mama made Ollie eat breakfast before he left for the outside.

It wasn't long before Ori, Benj, and Phillip were outside to help with the morning chores.

"My boy and I will help ya," Benj stated.

"I will collect the eggs and take care of Taw-Taw myself," Ori declared.

"We take care of other things," Benj said as he and Phillip fed the grunting pigs and shelled corn enough for another day. They left and entered the feed entry in the barn. Del thought they might do some of next morning's work for the boys to get them ready for church.

Del returned to the house, asking Mama, "What is happening at the Printz home today?"

"I saw you were talking to Ed. The men will be cleaning and clearing things on that property."

"Why there?"

"We can't just let that place fall apart. Besides it will have a new owner."

"But . . ."

"Enough said."

"I'll check whether Ori closed the feedhouse doors." No one wanted to explain anything, Del thought, and wondered what her brothers could tell her. Ollie, yes, Ollie will talk about everything he hears. Why is Mama so secretive, when the boys are there to help? After checking all outside work was completed, Del stood in the lane looking back toward the Printz home. Smoke was rising behind the barn.

She headed back to the house as Saturday was a busy day inside. There was more baking today to make a layer cake for Sunday. Since the oven was heated, some bread dough would be rising too. Cleaning all rooms upstairs and down also had to be done.

Mama was humming tunes she liked, sometimes singing song lyrics or some of her favorite hymns. She looked at Mama's opened recipe book. "This chocolate cake?" Del pointed to the open page.

Mama nodded her head. "Gather the ingredients, mix them in the order listed. I'll bake something for Jonathan and Adeline. You may take it there after it's cooled. You and Gloria can look for hickory nuts after she finishes outside. It might be a little early yet but we can't have the squirrels collect them all. I want hickory nut cakes for Thanksgiving and Christmas dinners when all the relatives come. Thanksgiving will be here before we are ready. Lillie and Eva want hickory nuts too. We needn't shell theirs. Then look for our winter garden[9] containers. Clean

---

9 Also known as a terrarium, composed of local forest plants.

them up, and get them ready for use. Lillie brings her own glass containers. Your aunts could be coming this weekend to look for moss and plants, although it may also be a little early for the partridgeberry. After a good frost is a good time for those red berries. We just had a light frost."

"We usually do that on a Sunday. Lillie shows us how to find the plants and moss to make a garden," Del said, recalling earlier years.

Mama nodded. "I like to go along and select plants for our own winter garden. Aunt Lillie fills a large round glass container for the partridgeberry alone. She has the perfect place to keep her large winter garden. It always looks so healthy and stays the year round on her front parlor window where it gets a lot of light, but no direct sun."

"Will she be here next Sunday?" Del asked.

"More likely tomorrow," Mama replied. "She'll bring some elderberry jelly along. She sells a lot of her jelly. Isaac and Sam took elderberries along more than once for Lillie."

"I didn't know she made those jellies to sell. I know she grinds horseradishes to sell."

Mama nodded. "She earns something to help her family out. She sells winter gardens to the big department store and a florist shop close by."

Mama began humming a tune. Del was fine with that, knowing Mama wasn't interested in any more conversation. Del was eager to take something down to Adeline. It would give her a chance to see Jonathan—but of greater importance, would Adeline have any explanation for the time Del stood outside their door?

The men came in for a lunch break. Del smelled the smoke odor they brought along in.

"Put those coats outside right now. I don't want that smoke smell in the house all weekend." Even Phillip seemed surprised with Mama's order.

The first baking was cooled and Mama prepared a small round basket with an AP cake on the bottom and a small cherry pie on top of that. "Here, you take this down to Adeline. I told her I would send something down today."

"Hurry up, I hear Gloria is finishing upstairs. I have work for her here."

Del grabbed her coat and walked as fast as she could while holding the basket steady. She didn't stop until she was well past the woodshed where she decided to slow down. Becky approached as Del reached the end of the lane.

"I believe you have something for the folks," Becky said glancing back towards the Conrads' homestead.

"Yes I do. I want to see both of them. I haven't spoken to them for a while."

"You will be welcome. I am sure."

"I can't stay too long though. Lots of work today."

Becky pointed to the direction of the Printz home. "It will be good to have that place cleaned up. It has good soil," Becky said as she turned toward her walkway.

Del thought, "Father must know for sure he is going to farm the land next year again. But why should he want to get rid of an old shed?"

Adeline saw Del approaching and opened the door and waved for her to come inside. "So good to see you. Yer Mama said she would send you to visit."

"I have baked goods Mama sent along."

"Yes, I know. Something smells good. I will take the goodies out of the basket and you can take the basket along home again," Adeline said turning away to store the baked goods. She turned back to Del with a serious expression. "I want to explain to you why I sent that pewter set with Becky. We had other children spending the day with us when you came for Phillip. Behavior like theirs, well, they were naughty. They pulled drawers open and went through things. They found the tea set and I was afraid they would damage it. We picked all the pieces up and put it where they couldn't reach. That was what was happening when you came for Phillip. He will probably tell you about it sometime."

"I wondered a lot about that evening."

"I didn't want you to see all the fighting that was happening over that tea set. I gave the set to Becky for her to give to you before those children come again. It is where it belongs."

"Thank you much for the set. I really appreciate it and will always keep it safe."

"You are welcome. We always enjoy having you around."

Del ran part way up the street with a light heart, wishing she could have stayed longer. Her relief at hearing Adeline's explanation disappeared when she suddenly realized Adeline never said whose children were inside. Her pace slowed. Were those Rachael's children? Del set her mind on other things as she approached the homestead.

All the menfolk came along in on the wagon with Ed handling the team. It was loaded with lots of salvaged wood that looked good enough for future use. Sam and Isaac headed immediately for the Hudson, climbed aboard and waved their goodbyes.

Del checked all the doors, turned tight a dripping spigot, and made sure enough corn was shelled for Sunday. She set things ready for Ori's Sunday chores as well. By the time Del had completed all she needed to do, Father was closing the feed entry doors. Everyone was ready to go in. Father, Til, Bill, and Del were the last to walk into the house.

The evening was quiet; the boys, especially Ollie, were very tired. He made his way upstairs after supper to take a bath and go early to bed.

Mama smiled. "He's too tired to talk about all that has taken place this day."

Del figured Ollie would have plenty to say tomorrow. Ori also made way for the upstairs after supper, taking Carol with her.

Mama placed all the dried dishes in the cabinet. "Everyone had a full day. It was hard work for the men."

"If I have time I will walk back to the Printz home tomorrow and see what kind of work they did this day," Del spoke.

"What did Jonathan and Adeline have to say?' Mama asked.

"They appreciate the baked goods." Del yawned and said, "I will head upstairs too." She didn't want Mama to ask more questions. She drifted off to sleep soon after.

Del jumped out of bed on Monday and ran to her window hoping to see people placing the pole in its spot near the garden. There was nothing to see.

Mama called, "Adelaide, time to get up."

Answering Mama's call she hurriedly dressed.

"You must have had a good sleep," Mama said as Del entered the kitchen.

"I didn't know I was late. I looked to see if the phone company was here this morning. Am I the last to get up?"

"You aren't the last. Carol is still in bed. Once she awakens she may help herself or call for help. I have hot cocoa for you this morning. It's cool outside so wear something warm. Breakfast will be ready once the morning chores are complete."

A wooden bucket with eggs was setting by the walkway as Del stepped outside. Ori must have been up earlier than usual if she completed the morning egg-gathering. Del moved quickly.

"What is the matter with you? I called you twice already," Bill said as he stepped alongside her.

"Didn't hear you," Del replied. "I can't wait to hear more about what is happening on the Printz home and why you spent most of Sunday with Grandfather. I didn't know he was going to take you along to his home after church."

That had been a stunning change of routine yesterday. Grandfather never had any of the children accompany him back to his place after Sunday church services.

"Let's go in for breakfast. Mama is ready for us," Bill replied.

She nodded but quickly ran back to the feedhouse, checking if everything was done and in its proper place. Bill was waiting.

"Is something wrong?" Del asked.

Bill shook his head no.

Benj and Phillip were several strides ahead of them and Del could hear bits of conversation as she and Bill briskly followed. In a lowered voice, she questioned Bill.

"Do those two talk a lot?"

"Yes, you know Benj."

"What do they talk about?"

"I don't know, I'm not close enough to hear." Bill shrugged his shoulders.

Phillip held onto Benj's bent elbow as they entered the porch, their slow pace perfect for both of them. Mama handed a small water bucket to Del, which meant she was to go outside and pump fresh water for the table.

Breakfast was served. Mama had oatmeal and soft-boiled eggs, although Father didn't care for eggs that way. Del paid particular attention to Phillip's actions. He quietly named the food he wanted. Phillip's progress was slow but sure. He was filling out eating Mama's farm cooking. She still wondered about the incident at the Conrad's. "I must be patient until I can talk to Phillip," she thought.

Ed came back with the truck as the children were heading for school. Fritz immediately joined them as Ed announced he would help saw logs or work some more on the Printz home. There would be no more truck or wagon rides that morning.

Bill lowered his voice as he walked with Del. "I think we will see a lot of him until he finds another job."

"For sure he needs to find work," Del admitted. "What will Ed do?" Del looked to Til, as the Gohos were stepping lively to catch up.

"He has a few options," Til answered.

"What is options?" Ollie asked.

"That means he will try one thing and if that doesn't go well, he will try something else. He knew this day was coming. He'll decide soon," Til explained.

Del told Anabel and Maria the situation for Ed now that the silk mill closed and he no longer had a job.

"He'll find work for himself, one way or another." Bill was confident.

"He is handy, he can do most anything that needs to be done," Til added.

"My father works at the coal and lumberyard wintertimes when there is little to do on the land," Anabel stated.

"Ed can always take the milk to the creamery," Del said softly.

"That won't happen much longer," Bill said sadly. It appeared Bill had something troubling him, but he was unwilling to share it.

Em was waiting for Del as she reached the school grounds. "Guess what?" Em said.

"What now?"

"Ma says Sallie's arm is healing but still painful if she tries to lift or reach for something."

"Well that's good to hear. I haven't heard any news about her for a while."

"Doesn't Becky tell you?"

"No. She's very careful to not talk about her patients. And I usually only see her come in the lane for milk in the morning."

The bell rang and school was in session.

Del waited and managed to walk with Bill once they reached the cement pike on the dinnertime trip home. Now was her chance. "I'm not around Phillip like you boys are. Does he talk to you?"

Bill responded immediately. "He laughed when Molly kicked the stool before Father had a chance to sit down to milk her. First time I heard Phillip laugh. Then he looked guilty, like he did something wrong. Father looked over toward the feed entry where we were and smiled. Father didn't yell at that cow either, like he usually would. I bet it was the first time he heard Phillip laugh too."

"That's funny. I can't wait to hear Phillip's laugh. When did that happen?"

"It only happened this morning," Bill stated.

"What I really want to know, does he talk? I mean really talk when he and Benj are walking together. I never hear more than one or two whispered words at the table."

Bill shrugged. "I don't know."

"Phillip surely doesn't understand Grandfather's Dutch talk. I bet Grandfather uses his hands to explain to Phillip what he wants done. Maybe that's why Phillip uses his hands to explain things. If grown-ups spoke only English around here, I bet things would be different."

"No one does that!" Bill scoffed. "All neighbors coming to the barn talk in Dutch to Father. Mr. Strunk does too when he's getting his milk."

"Everyone uses their hands too. You take notice." Del became quiet, thinking about Bill's comment.

"What's on your mind?" Bill looked intently at Del.

"I'm just thinking. Everyone around here, except in school, speak in Dutch most all the time. Maybe Phillip thinks you have to talk with your hands," Del said thoughtfully.

"You may be right. I watch other people, since Phillip came. Everyone has some kind of hand motions while talking, facial expressions and head movements too." Bill concluded.

"It could be that Phillip's folks spoke a different language too. Who knows for sure?" Del added.

"Well, how did the morning go?" Mama asked the children.

"Everything's the same as always. I'll be glad when school is over," Ori said and declared, "I am going to look for work in the city."

Mama frowned. "Adelaide, what do you hear?"

"Em told me she saw Sallie with her arm in a sling. Do you know how she is doing?"

"Becky is pleased with Sallie. The arm is healing nicely," Mama smiled.

"Does Becky still go there?"

"Yes, she does. Ed drove her there a couple of times on days he had no work. Ed thinks the Reifingers are suspicious of . . ." Mama never finished what she was going to say and changed the topic. "Benj and Phillip are spending time with Adeline and Jonathan this day. Ed and Hester are there too. They will clear their fields today and clean the horse stable to get ready for winter, doing things Jonathan can't do right now."

The afternoon passed quickly. Daylight was disappearing as Del came in with her last wagonload of scrub cobs gleaned from the field behind the sawmill. The pigs didn't squeal as she walked by their pen but just let out a soft grunt here and there. She checked if the work in the feedhouse was done as she unloaded her wagon. She tested all the closures before she headed for the house.

"All cleared?" Mama wondered.

"Yes, the lower field that lies wet is picked clean. The men were closing the barndoors. I'm surprised Benj and Phillip are staying out this long."

"It won't be long it will be completely dark by the time the milking is done," Mama said.

"No phone company today? Where will it be in the house?"

"We don't know yet," Mama said slowly.

Del was left with her thoughts, when she spotted a few of Grandfather's one-pound butter boxes on the window seat.

"Where do those come from?" Del asked.

"You know very well where they come from. Those are keepsakes for each of you. We also have one for Phillip."

"Is that why Bill spent some time with Grandfather on Sunday?"

"Yes, my father needs to go through things and decide what he wants to do with items no longer needed. Obsolete is what they say," Mama said with a saddened note. "I just hope this change won't be too hard on him. He worked every day in his life, except Sundays. Never took a vacation. It must be hard for him to see the creamery close and not pass on to the next generation, like he learned from generations before him. It must be a sad time. Very sad indeed."

Tuesday morning Del wished she could observe Phillip as he learned to care for the farm animals. Her brothers measured amounts of grain and hay for the animals stalls or stanchions with enough straw to maintain a clean and well-kept barn every day. Del walked barefooted on the cold linoleum floor to her bedroom window hoping to see the phone company outside this day. "Too early," she said to herself, and went to look from Mama's bedroom window on the other side of the house. To her surprise she saw Isaac's Hudson already parked by the barnbridge. She never heard it arrive. She dressed and ran the stairs and opened the door into the kitchen. Benj occupied the rocking chair, Ollie was lacing his shoes and Mama was adding splintered wood to the fire in the stove to create more heat for cooking.

"Good morning," Mama said. "You are early."

Del looked at the clock. She was downstairs earlier than usual. "Ollie is early too. I saw the Hudson by the barnbridge already. Eva isn't here, is she?"

"No, the pajama factory has a full week's work."

"Isaac wants to watch those telephone company workmen string the line from the pole to the house. The wire has to come into the house somewhere on the back wall to connect to a telephone inside."

"*Vil selwert watcha wann de zeit kummed,* [Will myself watch when the time comes]," Benj added.

"All the boys are up," Mama commented.

"Phillip too?" Del looked to Benj.

"*Kann alles selwert doo* [Can everything himself do]."

"You mean he walks by himself?"

"*Net soo schtarick. Geb ihm mehner tzeit* [Not so fast. Give him more time]."

"I'll do my morning work." Del grabbed a jacket and headed for the outdoors.

"*Ich geh mitt* [I'll go along]," Benj said as he followed Del.

Del slowed her walk for Benj to keep pace.

"*Waz druwweled dich* [What troubles you]?"

"Why do you ask that?"

"*Ich kann sel sehne. Viel dzu ruhich* [I can see that. Much too quiet]."

"I just wonder about Phillip. Our city cousins fuss and pinch close their noses when we go by the cattle stalls, and they really complain walking by the pigpen. Is Phillip bothered by things like that? He talks to you. What does he say?"

Benj just grunted, ""*Ah ha. Ich haab gwisst oss eppes dich bloughed. Ah's gute uum lanne. Du sechned osses besser gehdt de gonz zeit* [[Yes, I have known that something bothers you. He's good at learning. You see that he goes better with more time]."

"Are those books for Phillip . . . Is he getting ready for school?"

"*Bicher, Ich wais nix. De Gloria cummed. Ich verlosse.* [Books, I know nothing. Gloria comes. I leave]."

Benj had already placed shelled corn and a bucket of water by the small henhouse door for Ori.

Ori fussed a bit with Taw-Taw, then released him and put him inside the henhouse. She grabbed the water bucket and closed the door behind her.

Del went about fulfilling her morning detail.

"What were you and Benj talking about? He left when I opened the door."

"Morning greetings, that's all," Del replied.

"I don't believe you. You two were planning something."

"You aren't a mind reader. Your shelled corn and water—Benj did that for you."

Del headed for the house shaking her head with frustration at her difficult older sister. She glanced at the feed entry door as she passed by. "Good morning!" she called and waved to Isaac as he appeared at the feed entry door holding a brown paper bag. Isaac returned the wave with a big smile. Del returned to the kitchen. Carol was lying on the couch.

"She's up much too early," Del said.

"I told her to lay down awhile. Everyone is up earlier than usual," Mama said as she bustled about the kitchen.

The barn work all completed, the menfolk came in. Isaac stepped into the kitchen after handing the paper bag to Del's father. Father walked to his desk and opened the roll top. Del heard it slide down again. When Father walked into the kitchen, the paper bag was gone.

This was not Father's usual procedure. Once the roll top was opened it would remain so until the close of day.

"Good morning," Isaac said as he accepted the offer of coffee and cake. "I had breakfast this morning before I took Eva to work. I told her I would be there to pick her up.

"It is a good morning. Just perfect for this time of year. How are things with the family?" Mama asked Isaac.

"Alright. No complaints. We got a letter from Mother and Aunt Hettie, they are busy as ever. My brother has days that are productive, but setbacks too. He remains confident nevertheless."

"That's good to hear," Mama said.

Del observed Benj pull Phillip closer to himself.

"How are you children doing in school?" Isaac turned and asked the children.

"I am going to get a job as soon as I finish school," Ori announced.

"I wish you luck. There aren't too many jobs available right now and many people looking for work. Experience counts. It would be good if you could continue school," Isaac said looking to Ori.

"Mae has a job every summer in the city, she cleans lunch counters in a five-and-dime," Ori said stubbornly.

Isaac looked at Mama with raised eyebrows.

"It's not what you think. It's a relative's store. She's grown for her age and does some clean-up when the store is closed," Mama explained.

The children prepared to walk to school. Fritz boarded the truck and Father drove off to the creamery. The Gohos were walking towards them in the lane.

Del quickly asked Bill, "What was in the brown paper bag Isaac gave to Father?"

"He had some papers in that bag. Father leafed through them this morning. He never said a word but just nodded his head," Bill spoke softly.

"I bet Mama is looking in that paper bag right now."

"You're probably right," Bill said.

"There's something there they don't want us to see. Do you think we'll find out at dinnertime?" Del questioned.

"I don't know," Bill said slowly. "Father smiled when looking at the papers. Isaac looked pleased, but neither spoke a word."

The Gohos reached them just as the first phone company truck stopped at the lane. Becky approached the children, her milk kettle swinging from her hand.

"The phone company is at our house today," Ollie proudly announced as he trotted by.

Becky turned as Ollie passed her. "The day will come when Oliver will slow down and not be so hurried," she stated as she greeted the girls, Til, and Bill a good morning.

The morning couldn't go fast enough as Del was eager to get home when the dinner hour arrived. She walked faster than usual and was breathing heavily once she reached the cement pike. She started the slow walk up the hill by herself instead of waiting for Bill. Looking across the field below Benj's yard, she saw the telephone company truck parked in the field below the garden.

"I bet the wire is strung over to the house already," she thought to herself. She looked back, wondering if Adeline could see the activity from her place. Ollie raced past her and continued running on the short piece of lawn between the house and terrace and the garden below and headed to the back of the house.

Del walked into the kitchen and learned that the company was drilling a hole through the wood framing to the window in Del's bedroom. Mama appeared a bit uneasy with the sounds of a drill hitting mortar from time to time. Del thought it would have been nice if her window seat had a hinged lid. That would have meant a lot less drilling to do and she would have a little extra space to place things. The children took their places at the table and ate their dinner with little conversation. Del concluded that Mama's uneasy feelings wouldn't help her get answers about the contents of Isaac's paper bag. The drilling stopped. It was dinnertime for the telephone workers as well.

"Get yourselves back for the afternoon session, and we'll see how far the workers are by the time you come home," Mama ordered.

At the end of the school session, Fritz met the twins and danced around briskly until they arrived home. Benj wasn't there to greet them. The Hudson was gone and so was the telephone truck. Phillip and Carol were in the kitchen with Mama.

Bill immediately asked, "Where is everybody? Where are Father and Benj?"

Ollie chimed in, "Where is the telephone?"

Mama replied as she placed some snacks on the table, "Isaac went home. The phone company will be back tomorrow. There's a little inside wiring left to do."

"Where is Father?" Til repeated Bill's question.

"Benj and your father had a job to do uptown. Your father can tell us more when he comes home. I don't know enough to say anything one way or another," Mama admitted as she turned towards the stove.

Del had no idea what could cause Father to go uptown at this time of day when the afternoon chores, including milking, needed to be done.

"Behave yourselves and do your chores and schoolwork. Don't concern yourselves about anything else."

Del headed outside after changing with many questions in mind. "Why didn't Phillip go along? Benj never leaves Phillip behind," she thought.

Del saw Til and Bill and ran over to them. "Do you think something happened to Grandfather?"

Til shook his head. "If something happened to Grandfather Mama would be there and Benj would be here. I think Grandfather is okay."

"You're right," Bill said. "Mama would have gone along if anything happened to him."

Reassured, Del nodded her head and went to work on her evening chores. As Del and her brothers passed by the grape arbor later, there was Benj and to their surprise, there was Clint seated under the leafless tree, sharpening knives.

"*Zeit dafore. Wee isz dah daag gangha?* [Time for that. How did the day go]?" Benj asked while he nodded towards Clint.

Til half-raised his hand in a wave to Clint as he proceeded to the first door under the barn overshoot to talk to Doll.

Del greeted Clint and Benj. Clint lifted his eyes briefly as he tipped his cap and continued to sharpen knives. There was a growing collection of newly honed blades lying on newspaper at his feet. His clear blue eyes were very much like her father's eyes. It was easy to see the family connection, but that was the only similarity they seemed to have. Del's father was settled with a farm and a family while Clint preferred life alone and on the road.

"It doesn't often happen Father goes uptown this time of day," Del turned to Benj. "Did something happen?" She waited for a response from Benj. However, he shook his head slowly from side to side and motioned for her to head back to the house.

Phillip was placing plates and cutlery on the table as Del entered the kitchen. Mama must have carried them there for him.

Mama said, "You can fetch water after washing up. Everyone will soon be here. Supper is ready. The remainder of the high cake, bring that up. I'll cut a piece for Clint. The A.P. cake he can carry along with him."

Food was placed on the table and prayer was said. Father stood up and announced, "You saw Clint is here. He will sleep in the barn like before. I'll take food out for him and spend a little time with him."

Mama filled two plates with very generous portions. Father carried them on a large tray while Mama opened the door.

Father returned as the family was getting dessert. "He's more talkative this time. Give me some dessert and coffee to take out, and keep the coffee hot, maybe he'll have more." Father left with another tray.

The children were quiet for a spell. Del looked around the room and asked, "Who is going to tell us what happened uptown?" as she cleared the table and collected dishes. She looked at Benj.

"We will wait for your father to tell you the whole story," Mama said with a tone that put an end to further questions.

When Father returned with the tray and dishes, everyone was in the kitchen waiting for him. Father sat down and sighed, "Your grandfather's horse, Dick, was unable to get up this morning. He made no effort to try. We couldn't do anything, either, much as we tried. The vet came, looked the horse over and called him by name. He gave him an injection and after twenty minutes, Dick was able to stand. That horse saw his better days. If it happens again, the vet can no longer help that horse." Father looked at Mama sadly, "It's hard on Billy, tears ran down his cheeks."

Del felt tears cloud her eyes as she kept her face down and slowly washed dishes.

Til was affected too but managed to say, "It's always Dick he has hitched to the buggy when he goes away."

Mama murmured to Father, "It will be good to have my father closer to home. That time can't come soon enough."

"In due time, in due time," Father said softly.

After a brief period of silence, Ollie fussed about the school day including the problems with his English lesson and his dislike of spelling classes. Mama said no more but directed the children to do their schoolwork. She would help with the dishes. "Benj, Woodie will walk home with you."

The children dispersed in different directions to do schoolwork and then get ready for bed. Del was exhausted and made her way upstairs. Tucked underneath the covers, thinking about her grandfather, she remembered Father's phrase "in due time." That was her first inkling that Grandfather might be the buyer of the Printz property? Is that why Father is spending time there? As she drifted off to sleep, she realized that the paper bag never came up in conversation.

The next morning Del remembered her parents' comments about her grandfather. It was obvious that Mama wanted him living closer to her, but he was unwilling to do that. As she opened the stairway door to the kitchen she heard a truck pull up by the walkway. Maybe it was the telephone company. "I can't wait to tell Em we have a telephone in our house!" she thought.

Del made her way slowly into the house after doing her chores while keeping watch on the telephone company workers. Benj sat under the apricot tree with an open view to the back of the house.

"You're at the right place this morning."

"*Letze blatz* [Wrong place]."

"What do you mean? You can see everything from there."

"*Sie schaffe innewennich heit* [They'll work inside today]."

"Then we'll really have a phone today," Del said as they watched the Hudson pull to a stop. Isaac got out of the car, waved to Del and Benj, and hurried into the house. She continued talking with Benj. "I wonder who will make the first call."

Del entered the kitchen where Isaac stood by Father. He said something into Father's ear that Del couldn't hear and walked back outside to his Hudson again. He returned with his camera. Del suspected he wanted to take pictures as the workmen completed the wiring to put the telephone in the house. Mama came into the kitchen. "I'm glad you set the table for breakfast. Go tell the boys to come in, Gloria too. It's time to eat."

Del hadn't gone farther than the pump when she saw her brothers and Phillip leaving the barn. She ran toward the feedhouse to tell Ori. "Hurry up!" Del said. "We need to eat and go to school. Mama is waiting for us."

"I know it's time for breakfast."

Ori was surly—her usual morning mood. Del shrugged her shoulders and joined her brothers and Phillip.

Del eagerly greeted Em, ready to tell her they would finally have a telephone in the house. But before she could share her news, Em blurted out that her Aunt Ginny died. She was the city relative her family visited regularly on Sunday afternoons. Em appeared stunned by the sad news and that was the only thing she wanted to talk about. Del told Em she was sorry her aunt died. Em slowly took her seat and remained quiet. Del's thoughts drifted back to her Grandfather and the possibility that he might move to the old Printz home. "It couldn't be ready before winter comes," she mused. Del was so engrossed in her thoughts that she was late getting up as her class was making their way to the one-step platform at the head of the classroom for discussion. The teacher gave her a questioning look but said nothing.

At recess time Em talked some more about her aunt's death.

"I know you are troubled, but old people die all the time," Del attempted to console Em.

"No, she's not old! Aunt Ginny is younger than my ma. She took care of my grandmother. Now who will take care of my grandmother?"

"Oh my, I didn't know that she was younger. I know your grandmother can't manage by herself because you said that before."

"My grandmother is an invalid. She needs someone to take care of her."

"That's not for you to worry about. Your parents will take care of matters."

"Huh, there's plenty to worry about. A neighbor is staying with her until Ma and Pa can make other arrangements. I don't want to move to the city!" she cried out.

"You mean that's what your family is going to do?" Del hadn't considered that possibility.

"I don't know for sure."

"I hope you're not going to move."

Dinnertime came. Del walked slowly on the dirt lane. The excitement of receiving a telephone was diminished by Em's news. She reached the cement pike and saw Fritz and Bill waiting at their lane. She ran the rest of the way. Benj and Phillip were in the kitchen and the table was already set with the dinner meal. The phone company workers sat at their truck eating their lunches. Del took a quick peek into the side room and saw the phone in place.

"I knew you would have to look and see what things look like," Mama said with a smile.

Carol was anxious to show off the telephone. Mama stood by and admonished all the children to leave the telephone alone. "You are not allowed to answer the phone or make a call. This is for your father and I to use."

Ori was quiet for a bit and then announced as she looked around at her siblings, "I am the oldest. I may use the telephone before any of you use it."

Mama frowned, her eyes said it all as she looked at Ori but she remained quiet. Del figured Mama would talk to Ori when they were alone.

"Can we call Philadelphia and maybe find out why we have Phillip?" Ollie seemed excited about that concept of calling the big city.

"Ira, I suppose, has a telephone. All business offices do," Mama said and then stopped talking abruptly.

Del planned to ask Bill what he thought about Mama's interesting remark about Ira the first chance she had.

"Did Clint leave?" Til asked Mama.

"He left this morning. Your father gave him a ride to Boyertown. He is close to Route 100 from there. I made a couple griddlecakes for him and packed a couple to take along. He appreciated that."

"*Mehner osz sel* [More than that]," Benj said.

It was a matter of practicality. Del knew Mama would give him food that could be kept for more than one day.

All the children headed back to school. "What kind of office do you think Ira has?" Bill asked the question Del herself wondered about.

"Who cares! You can't live in a city and not have an office," Ori stated.

"Now look who thinks she's smart." It was surprising for Til to speak up and contradict his older sister. "We have relatives who live in a city but don't have an office or a telephone."

"I'm going to use that telephone, I don't care what Mama says," Ori said.

"Uh, who would you call? You don't know anybody that has a tele-phone," Ollie said with certainty.

"Mae's father has a telephone," Ori retorted.

Del and Bill looked at each other with a quick grin but neither added any further comment. They all knew that telephone was in the pack-inghouse where Mae's father worked. It didn't belong to Mae's father.

Back at school, the afternoon moved quickly. Em was mostly quiet and Del had enough work to stay busy until closing time.

"Did the phone ring?" Ollie shouted as he raced into the house.

"Of course not. You need to calm down. No one knows our phone number yet," Mama cautioned. "Get busy and do your evening work. You can look at the new phone after supper."

"Where is everybody?" Del asked. "Benj and Phillip weren't waiting for us by the woodshed after school."

"They are giving you a head start on your chores this evening."

Del entered the outside and saw their neighbor Ed. "I heard Father say you had your last day of work at the silk mill."

"True enough. I did some cleaning up and tinkering around here. I will soon be very busy."

"You have another job already?"

"Not so fast. I have a few things in mind and good neighbors willing to help," Ed paused. "Hester was given more hours in the stocking mill and that helps."

"Are you all healed from Taw-Taw's latest action?" Del asked.

"It's getting better. Time will tell if I'll have a scar and if the nail grows back."

"Gee, Taw-Taw must have really pinched you hard."

"Sure did. I fixed him, just like old Benj did."

"What did Benj do?" Del was intrigued with this reminder that Benj had some encounter with the duck that taught Taw-Taw a lesson.

Ed just laughed and said, "Benj will have to tell you."

Ed headed for the barn as Del entered the feedhouse. It was so disappointing that no one was willing to tell her what Benj did to put Taw-Taw in his place. But Ed's talk of other things to do left Del with other possibilities to ponder. She remembered that Benj offered his farm buildings for Ed to use should he have something in mind. Benj had an unused barn, henhouse and pigsty plus other small buildings in good condition. Benj has all those empty buildings and Father needs a garage to keep his truck in the dry. The Studebaker, too, could use a building to protect it from the weather. Del had much on her mind as she completed her work. She turned quickly on her heel to make sure all the buildings behind her were secured for the night. "All okay," she whispered to herself.

Everyone was ready for supper. Grace was said and plates were filled. "I want to hear the telephone ring the first time," Ollie protested.

"We can't expect much for a while. People need to know we have a phone first," Mama explained.

Mama had egg and coconut custard pies for dessert.

"Baked those today. Won't make any custard this weekend." She also had a funny cake[10] for dunking, as custard was not one of Father's favorite desserts.

"Is everyone tired this evening? I usually hear more talk. Did you play any ball today?" Father asked Ollie.

"I played outfield today. Didn't get to pitch."

---

10 Funny cake is actually a pie with a layer of chocolate along the pie crust bottom and a vanilla cake layer above.

"What did the rest of you do during recess time?"

"We played hopscotch. Anabel and Maria are really good jumpers. They must play that game a lot," Del offered.

Just then the telephone rang—one long and two short rings. Everyone, including Phillip, was surprised to hear it. "Who knows our number already?" Del wondered.

Father smiled widely. "It's Levi. I asked him to call." Father left the table and talked briefly. His face beamed when he returned. "Now you heard what our ring sounds like. Remember, only your mother and I will use the phone. This will be for business only."

Ori looked unhappy upon hearing that. Del wondered who received the first call from their new telephone. Mama gathered the dishes and the usual routine took place for the end of a day's work. Father finished his coffee and asked Benj if he was ready to call it a day. He would walk along home with him. Carol asked to stay up and wait for the phone to ring again.

Mama shook her head, "No more ringing tonight and probably not for a while."

There was no more talk about the telephone as the children scattered to do schoolwork or prepare for bed. Del was in her bedroom when she heard Father return. She looked over the new poem and the new spelling words. She worked on compound and complex sentences. She finally closed her tablet and books and slipped under the covers for a good night's rest.

CHAPTER TWENTY-FOUR

Managing a Church Service

Del used the stairs from her parents' bedroom to head downstairs the next morning so she would pass by the telephone mounted on the wall. It was a brown wooden box with black and silver attachments. She immediately thought that Father no longer needed to go uptown to check on the Boyers and be assured Grandfather and his dog Brownie had a safe walk home. The Boyers, in turn, would be able to call and let Father know if help was needed at their place or at Grandfather's home, which was within sight of their residence on the second floor of the New Jerusalem Hotel.

"Good morning," Mama said. "The boys are up and outside, Gloria too. You are later than usual."

"The washroom was in use first time I checked. I heard Father say he needed to set dates for butchering."

Mama nodded, "We always to do the first butchering for fresh pork a week before Thanksgiving. Then again in mid-December and after the New Year. Better go out, take care of your work."

"I'll do that right now." Del grabbed a jacket and left, thinking about the work involved preparing and preserving meat for the coming year. The butcher would arrive carrying a heavy canvas sack with all his equipment flung on his back. Many knives and saws were used in the process. The butcher brought his own knives for safety—being accustomed to the feel of his own knife handles prevented accidents while cutting a carcass. Clint always sharpened the knives the family would use.

"What are you smiling about?" Ori asked as Del entered the feedhouse.

"I was just thinking that Carol can soon say the sausage man is here. I heard Father say he is going to arrange this year's butchering dates."

Del thought more about the butchering routines. The women would be in charge of smoking, salting, or canning for days and weeks to come after each butchering session. Del thought about the many sausages that would be made. Ropes of sausages were hung on rods in the smokehouse over a slow burning fire for later meals. Fresh sausages were put aside for immediate use. Other sausages were cut into lengths suitable for canning in quart jars and were fried and neatly packed for later use. Whole hams were salted and hung from meat hooks in the smokehouse, along with summer sausages—ground meat blended with seasonings and stuffed into cloth bags and tied with cord string. Summer sausages, once cured and kept cold when sliced, made an appetizing sandwich. The same process would follow each time they butchered. The relatives would help with all the tasks and get meat for their own households.

Spring, summer, fall, or winter, women's work never changed: preparing and preserving food for later use meant constant canning and drying all year round. Every family had their own recipe to make scrapple. They always had fresh pork and sauerkraut the first day of butchering hogs, and liver and good gravy the first evening after butchering beef.

"What did Phillip think of all this activity? Had he ever seen an animal slaughtered? He would soon witness all the seasonal work on the farm. Would he like scrapple?" she pondered these questions as she walked towards the house.

"Did you see Ed this morning?" Del asked Bill as they met outside.

"Yes. The silk mill is closed permanently."

"What is he going to do now? He hinted at something but didn't give me any details," Del hoped Bill had more information. The twins were old enough to know that the Depression meant hard times for most everyone they knew.

"He is going to rent one of Benj's farm buildings, the henhouse. I heard him ask Benj. He also asked to borrow our brooder that we use in the spring when we get peeps."

"That means he is going to raise chicks," Del said thoughtfully.

"I suppose so."

Del and Bill entered the house, and Del could immediately sense something was wrong.

"Ed put Taw-Taw in the rain barrel this morning. He could have drowned. Why did he do that?" Ori shouted angrily. "There's not enough room for Taw-Taw to spread his wings and lift himself out of that barrel!" She was clearly distraught.

Mama said in a placating tone, "He didn't hurt your duck. And maybe that cleaned some of those dirty feathers."

"Everybody wants to hurt my duck. No wonder he flies on people's back sometimes."

"Listen to that!" Ollie said as he seated himself. "Ori knows Taw-Taw is extremely naughty." He dragged out the word extremely.

"Taw-Taw isn't naughty, he's a good duck. It's the things everybody does to him. Like Ed this morning." Mama turned her face, Father bowed his head, and Benj had a sheepish grin on his face.

"That's enough, Gloria," Mama said sharply. " I don't want to hear any more duck talk this morning."

Father changed the topic. "The School Board meeting is coming up. I need to get the tax report ready. Next month will be busy since it's the last month before penalties are levied for late payment. I'll need to spend the next two Saturdays visiting township schoolhouses for a couple hours to make it convenient for people to pay their taxes." Father paused. "I suppose those books made the rounds by now. After supper I'll call Levi to see if

Martha needs help to clean the meeting room. Maybe one of you girls can help her on Saturday. Election day will soon be here. The boys need to help with that. The voting booths need to be set up over the weekend sometime to get ready for the inspector to see that all is in order. That room should be in good shape for the Road Board meeting later in the week."

Del remembered the day she entered the voting booth with Martha, who never went to school and could not read or write. Once the curtains were closed, Del read the candidate names, and Martha then marked her selections.

The children set out for school as a group. The Gohos came breathlessly running and met them.

"We thought we were going to be late," Anabel said. "Our clock stopped this morning. We didn't realize it until we noticed that time hadn't changed."

"You're okay; we may be a little later than usual," Bill said. "But there's still time to get to school," and the children hurried to the schoolhouse.

Del reached the school grounds and saw Em. "We have a telephone and got our very first call!"

Em was quiet for a moment, and when she spoke, it was clear that her aunt's death was still uppermost on her mind. "When Joe graduates he will move to the city and live with Grandmother. One of our cousins will move there too."

"Is Joe willing to do that?"

Em nodded. "There's many more things to do in the city, he says. He is ready to move there. Father says he can go to high school since he will be living in the city."

"Is he going to do that?" Del asked with real surprise since Joe had been reluctant to continue schooling after the eighth grade.

"I don't know."

"See, I told you things will work out okay."

With that the school bell rang and there was no more talk.

Fritz pranced around as the children arrived at the lane for dinnertime and ran ahead of Del and Bill. "Something is bothering Fritz. He sure is in a hurry to get home." Bill said and Del agreed.

Once they reached the woodshed they realized why Fritz was eager to return home. The brooder was on the back of Father's truck, ready to take to Benj's henhouse for Ed's new business.

"Okay Fritz, we know why you were so anxious to get back. You don't want to miss that truck ride!" Til laughed.

Dinnertime talk was about Ed getting peeps at this late time of year. Father explained, "It isn't bitter cold yet. By then the roosters will be feathered and the brooder won't be necessary."

"Is he going to separate the chickens from the roosters?" Til asked.

"I was wondering that you waited this long to ask," Father said. "Today, you can buy peeps that are selected for laying hens or all roosters to fatten for market. Ed will try his hand at roosters."

The children were quiet. "Doesn't anyone have anything to say?' Mama asked with a smile.

"I never heard of such a thing as roosters only. I suppose there will be a lot of crowing going on each morning. That could be deafening to the ears," Del replied.

Benj laughed. "*Sie danked vannernaus* [She thinks ahead]." Most everyone laughed with Benj.

"Ed's going to give this a try. He needs to know if this will be a paying proposition," Father stated as the children considered the work and the expenses for feed and straw. He turned to Mama, "Oh, I must not forget, Ed wants my recipe for chick mash."

Mama just nodded her head. "Off to school," she told the children.

The afternoon moved quickly. Del engaged in the work before her. Em, too, was busy as Mr. Strunk kept all classes on schedule. After school, Mama had cottage cheese on the table with a variety of fruit toppings to add. There was a quart jar of canned pears with cloves. Apple butter was available plus a two quart jar of canned peaches. Del chose apple butter and cottage cheese. Carol had a new coloring book laying open on the couch. The first picture was a small and capital 'A' and a small and large animal beginning with the letter A to color.

"Where did you get that coloring book?" Ollie was first to ask.

"Mama gave it to me," Carol answered.

Del saw Father's chick mash recipe on the table. She picked the recipe up and looked it over carefully. 20 lbs. yellow corn meal: 20 lbs. wheat bran: 20 lbs. flour middlings: 20 lbs. pulverized oats: 10 pounds meat scrap: 5 lbs. dried milk: 5 lbs. alfalfa leaf meal: 2 lbs. oyster shell meal: 1 lb. cod liver oil: 1 lb. salt. Del remembered that Father and Mama saved the oyster shells after shucking oysters on those infrequent occasions Father brought a bucket full of oysters along home from the city. The oyster shells would stay in an aluminum bucket in the washhouse but she never did see what happened to them.

Mama stepped inside. "One of you boys can take that chick feed recipe out to Ed. You will find him in Benj's henhouse. He sure is ready to get started. He could have young roosters at a time not many are available, since most farmers wait until spring to raise peeps, like us."

"I will take it out to Ed. I can run," Ollie offered.

"Change your clothes first. You needn't run. I suppose Ed already knows the ingredients to feed baby chicks. He only needs to know the portions. His grandparents raised ducks, geese and turkeys for holidays."

"I need one of you girls to run an errand for me," Mama said.

"Don't ask me. I have enough to do already," Ori stated.

"Adelaide, before you change your clothes, take the path from the Printz home and go to Drumheller's store. I need two pounds of soft white sugar. Don't waste any time. Your father will pay the grocer tomorrow."

Del took the path from the Printz home, hurrying through the hilly forest, three back yards, then onto the graveled path through the cemetery, where she still hadn't taken time to look for the gravesites of Becky's husband nor the grave sites of Samuel and young Benj and Ann, their mother and Benj's wife. Now was not the time to find out. She passed through three more back yards, traveled behind Grandfather's big red barn and onto the lane between Grandfather's horse barn and creamery. Across the cement pike, there was Drumheller's store. Mr. Drumheller took his scoop and measured two pounds of sugar into a brown paper bag and tied it with string he pulled from a cone hanging overhead. Del grabbed the bag of sugar and the grocer gave her an orange sour ball to enjoy on the way home. She passed by the cemetery again, wishing she had the time to read some gravestones there.

"Change your clothes, and get started on your evening work," Mama said as soon as Del entered the kitchen with the package.

As she walked into the feedhouse, Del knew Ori would have plenty to say about her late start on her chores.

"You always coax Mama to let you do the running around. I am the oldest, so I should be doing that. I'll get even with you yet," Ori said in an accusing tone.

Del stood still while she looked at Ori. "If nothing else, Ori was predictable," she thought to herself. "Mama said she had an errand for one of us to do. You said right off, you had enough to do already," Del argued.

"She didn't tell me she wanted something from store."

"It's not my fault you never asked what kind of errand it was," Del said as she left the feedhouse to prepare sloppy mash for the pigs. Had Ori not been so quick with her response about being too busy, Mama could have sent her on that errand.

Del finished her last task feeding the pigs. She mixed their mash and poured it in the troughs. She expected more complaining from Ori once everyone was in the kitchen. But instead, the evening was spent talking about Ed making preparations to receive a shipment of peeps. The children always looked forward to the arrival of the big square cardboard carton with lots of small openings to allow enough fresh air for the baby chicks to breathe while traveling by US Mail. The cleanup on the Printz home property was also discussed.

"Who is going to live there?" Del was glad Ollie asked.

"Right now we don't know if it will be rented or if a new owner will move in. We'll have to wait and see what develops," Father said.

Benj talked about all the things Ed was doing to get his building ready for two hundred peeps and noted that Ed would need more space as the peeps grew.

"It's a good start," Father said. "This will give him something to do, especially if he keeps roosters in different stages of growth."

Til was puzzled. "But they'll all be the same size, not so?"

"Once this first shipment has grown, Ed will start another set of peeps. That way he'll always have some roosters ready for market."

"I never heard of something like that," Til was interested in these details.

"You never visited a poultry farm. I think Ed has a good plan," Father said.

Sunday morning started with preparations for Sunday school and church. "We'll have full attendance for the fall Communion." Mama looked concerned while speaking softly to Father.

"It's all okay so far. People know by now. The talk made the rounds," Father said.

"I thought we would have heard some comments by now," Mama paused and gestured with her head up towards the village.

"*Sie hut des gheert*" [She heard]," Benj offered.

"Are you sure?" Mama questioned. "One can never guess what Litzy will say or do."

"I heard said she was told," Father said.

Benj just nodded his head.

Del guessed Litzy was the vicious gossip she heard mentioned before. Dr. Schlicher had alluded to 'that busybody uptown' and Del heard about problems she created. She recalled some things Hester had said about her. 'I know lies she crafted from bits of truths to cause friction and discord between neighbors. Most folks don't talk to her. I know her a long time. She was always a troublemaker, even in school,' Hester stated in definitive terms.

Del headed upstairs dreading discord this day in church. Returning to the kitchen with her sisters, she heard Father tell the boys to walk away if anyone started ugly talk, while adding, "Litzy heard we have a new youngster. Cousin Manrow cemented a piece of walk for them and started to tell her the story. But Litzy didn't want to hear it. She said she knows all about that tramp and it 'serves Woodie right if that man is sick, he should think about his own family first.' Cousin Manny didn't say any more after that." Father paused and then smiled.

"Once she decided she knows what is what, no one can change her mind," Mama said hastily, then continued. "She didn't see Phillip at the creamery or hear from neighbors about a Black boy. Heavens to Betsy, she would have a time with that news. She never misses spring and fall communions. We'll know soon enough what she knows," Mama said with a worried look on her face. That look gave Del even more cause for concern.

The family arrived at church and waited in the packed car for Grandfather to pull up with his horse and buggy. Til struggled to get out to help Grandfather disembark. Grandfather laughed as he saw the rest of the family spill out of the Studebaker; Ollie was wedged on the front seat between Father and Mama, who was holding Carol on her lap. Til, Bill, Del, and Ori were in the back. Phillip sat on Til's lap. "Dick looks okay," Til said with a satisfied chuckle when he finally got out of the car and looked at Grandfather's horse. Til lifted the steps onto the buggy, and took the reins to lead the horse and buggy to the shelter across the dirt street.

Everyone gathered to walk into the church as a group. Edgar met the family and whispered in Father's ear. Father nodded. Edgar led the family to their pew. Del immediately saw Martin and Sally Reifinger. Del knew Mama would walk over to Sallie and chat a bit after church. Edgar pointed to the pew two rows in front of them, where Litzy, her husband George, their daughter and her husband were seated. Del's family smiled and nodded their heads.

Del was relieved that they were seated two pews behind them, but still expected some kind of disruption once that family saw Phillip. Edgar had been very careful where he seated certain people. Del figured everything would be fine until communion time. People would leave their seats, one pew at a time, walk before the altar, receive the bread, wine, and blessing, and then return to their pew. That would be the chance to see the entire congregation. Unconfirmed children remained seated. All the Heydt children would remain seated with Phillip except for Ori since she had been confirmed this past spring.

Litzy saw Phillip as she returned to her pew. Her face reddened and she reached for a fan from the hymnal rack and began fanning herself furiously. She took a backward glance; her facial expression registered shock and anger as she turned her face to her husband, staring at him. Del worried there would be some sort of confrontation after church.

Del headed toward the Sunday school room. George Bickel had a firm hold on his wife's arm, steering her toward the narthex. Del figured he was making sure his missus would not cause any disruption during departure. It was difficult to find an opening to cross the packed center aisle as neighbors moved slowly to chat as they moved on. Del's parents would go home now and the children would walk home after Sunday school.

With the Sunday school hour completed, there no time for conversation. Til fetched Grandfather's horse and buggy. Bill waited with Phillip and Carol as they would ride with Grandfather. Del, Ori, and Ollie started walking slowly so Bill and Til could catch up. Ollie hoped he could climb aboard Grandfather's buggy and ride home. The buggy passed them at the Bieber Creek Bridge, and Grandfather stopped and reached for Ollie's hand to help him climb aboard. Til and Bill caught up to Ori and Del and urged them to move at a faster pace to catch up to the Schultz boys who were also walking home from Sunday school.

"Don't any of you say anything to the boys about you-know-who when we catch up to them." Til ordered.

"I wonder what that woman is going to say now?" Del asked her siblings.

"Who knows? Who cares?" Ori replied.

"Her face turned fire red when she saw Phillip. I don't think she knew," Til replied.

"I want to hear what is said when we get home," Del spoke softly.

"Well she saw today that we have a Black boy living with us," Bill added.

"I wonder why her husband didn't tell her? He comes to the creamery every day and he's seen Phillip with Grandfather," Til said thoughtfully.

"She could have known but maybe thought we wouldn't bring him to church. Her face sure turned red," Bill murmured again.

"He probably couldn't tell her anything because she thinks she knows everything," Til paused. "I bet there will be fireworks in their shanty today," Til laughed and the others joined in. "As long as she doesn't hit him on the head with a cast iron frying pan, he'll be alright. I hear George is used to her tempers," he concluded.

"I wish Father would take him back to the big city again. It's been nothing but trouble since he came," Ori said unhappily.

"Ori, that's a terrible thing to say! He hasn't been trouble, it's other people who have problems with him," Del said quickly as they finally caught up to the Shultz boys.

The boys moved ahead, leaving Ori and Del to follow. The girls were quiet as they followed their brothers and walked together the rest of the way home.

Mama, Carol, Phillip, and Benj were in the kitchen. Mama was busy preparing a quick dinner.

"William, you may help Phillip go upstairs to change his clothes. Oliver is upstairs, I don't know what's taking him so long," Mama fussed. "Did something happen in Sunday school?" Mama looked at Del as Ori and Carol also headed upstairs.

"Not that I noticed and the boys said nothing."

"Go and change clothes." Mama made a motion with her hand.

Del was careful to hang her Sunday dress so as not to cause wrinkles for next week's wearing. When she returned to the kitchen Mama was telling Benj, "We will wait to hear what is said."

Del wished she had heard the rest of that conversation. Ori and Carol entered the kitchen.

"You all hear this—no discussion about church happenings tomorrow. Don't mention the Bickel family. Should anyone ask you, you were there. If you are asked if they were present, admit you saw them and that's all," Mama sternly ordered.

"Don't worry about me. I won't say anything more. Mae never talks about church." Ori replied.

"That's good. I don't want any gossip coming from this house. I will tell the boys too."

"*Bong es schaft net soo* [I'm afraid it doesn't work that way]," Benj grunted.

When everyone was gathered around the table for the meal Mama stressed once more not to say anything about Sunday services. "Ignore any unkind talk. Walk away. Hear me now!" Mama ordered firmly.

"That woman has to think about this first. She needs to consider what she can say that is half-believable," Father concluded.

"*Ess gebt ebbes* [It will give something]," Benj said with assurance. "*Sie muss erscht driwwerdenke* [She must first think this over]."

Father nodded his head.

It was a quiet day. There were no visits from Father's relatives. The children were engaged in schoolwork, puzzle-making and coloring books. The evening chores were completed as usual and everyone gathered for the evening meal.

"What will you talk about at school tomorrow?" Mama tested them.

"Em will surely tell me about the discussions about how they are going to take care of her grandmother. Only thing I know for sure is Em doesn't want her grandmother to come live with them."

"I would tell her to shut up. Who wants to hear that every day?" Ori said.

Mama reprimanded Ori, "That's not a nice thing to say. We have similar conversations about our friends and relatives' care too."

"I want to talk about the peeps at school. Does Ed know when the peeps are coming?" Ollie jumped into the conversation.

"I know they were ordered," Father said.

"Finish your schoolwork and then get ready for bed. Get a good night's rest. There's plenty of work these next two weeks," Mama said as she made her way to the parlor motioning for Father and Benj to follow. Del waited for the washroom to clear before making her way upstairs. A restful day, she thought as she considered Ed's new venture and wondered if Phillip ever saw baby chicks.

CHAPTER TWENTY-FIVE

Starting a Peeps Business

On Monday morning Mama advised Ori and Del that some of their morning work was already done. "Check what needs to be taken care of, but first set the table. Phillip will eat with you, your father and Benj will come back and eat later. Right now they are giving the henhouse a thorough cleaning with disinfectant. It's something we always do before hatchlings arrive. Peeps need a healthy environment."

All the outside work that needed to be done was completed in orderly routine. Mama passed pancakes and advised Phillip to take two pancakes and pass the plate to Til. She watched him help himself to butter and syrup and smiled. Del guessed that Mama was pleased to see him eat without Benj closely attending to him. The children carried their dishes to the sink as Father and Benj stepped in the door and washed up. The strong smell of disinfectant was present in their clothes.

"That's all taken care of. There's a good breeze this morning to air out the place. Ed has that building in very good condition for baby chicks," Father said.

Benj laughed as he observed the wrinkling of noses in the household. *"Dood da nix* [Does you nothing]," meaning the odor wouldn't hurt anyone, as he placed his arm around Phillip's shoulders.

"A little outside air will take care of the odor," Mama assured the children.

As the children prepared for school Mama stressed again, "Don't talk about church at school. I know this may not be easy depending on what you may hear. Be careful how you answer any questions. Your teacher hears from his neighbor about our church news. He will be attentive to all that is said. Off to school now."

Fritz followed the children leaving for school. The Gohos approached, running the short distance to join them. Fritz bounced around them. As they walked by Benj's place the odor of disinfectant spread across the lane. Ollie immediately told the Gohos about the preparations for chicks. He practically vibrated with excitement as he spoke about the anticipated arrival of the peeps. It didn't waver as he met his school friends.

"I can show you the henhouse from here," he exclaimed as he pointed in the direction of the building partly seen below the barn. "It's the red frame one story building with white trim. That building is where the peeps will grow up and become roosters to sell." Ollie emphasized once more that there would be no hens to lay eggs among the peeps. He also stressed one more time that Ed would have fattened roosters to sell, once the baby chicks were grown. Del and her siblings looked at each other and grinned. They all knew about Ollie's excitable nature. Mr. Strunk smiled too. He was fully aware of Ollie's overwhelming need to share news, any news. Del watched as Em moved over to the group gathered around Ollie as he explained how the baby chicks would arrive, how their brooder would be used and then repeating that the chicks were all roosters. The bell rang for school to begin.

As dinnertime arrived Del skipped by herself on the dirt lane towards home. Bill joined her at the cement pike. Fritz met them at the lane. He was panting. He came running from somewhere. "Where have you been?" Bill said as he stroked the dog's head.

The twins arrived home. Father and Isaac were gathering butchering equipment. The wooden tub was in place to hold boiling hot water and the three tall poles tied together to form a tripod. The scrubbing boards and tables were propped neatly against the milkhouse, and the long wooden table still glistened from its disinfection process.

"Go on in," Father said to them. "You will find eats on the table. There is something else for you to look at."

Mama wasn't around, but the table was set for the children to help themselves. Til had already picked up photos that were lying on the table.

"Where is Mama?" Ori asked, as she was the last to enter.

"Father pointed to the Printz home when I asked him," Til said. "She will be back before long."

"Why is Mama at the Printz home at this time of day? Nothing to do there," Ori asked with a puzzled look on her face.

"I didn't say she was there. She could be somewhere else," Til answered.

All the children looked at pictures Isaac had taken while the men were installing the telephone. Most showed outside work, plus a few inside pictures, which were not very clear. "I guess there wasn't enough light inside," Til said to himself.

"How do you know that?' Ollie asked.

"See those inside pictures, you don't see much more than the window," Til pointed as Ollie looked some more.

The children finished their meal, gathered the dishes and got ready to go back to school.

"We never go back this early, I am going to wait," Ori said. "Carol must be with Mama, they will be here soon."

"Suit yourself," Til said. "There's nothing to do here." Til got up to leave.

As it was, everyone followed suit. Fritz was not there but Bill's whistle brought him running.

"That's a first." Del said quietly to Bill. "We never have to call Fritz at dinnertime unless he thinks there's a possible wagon or truck ride."

It must be something very important for their loyal dog to not remain near the home while the children had dinner.

Once they reached the cement pike, Fritz ran back. Del assumed he was returning to whatever destination had his full attention earlier in the day. The group saw Ed leave Benj's henhouse as they walked by.

"No peeps yet?" Til called.

"I expect them today or tomorrow," Ed said excitedly with a smile. "I hope they come today because tomorrow is election day. I need to use my car to bring voters to the polls. I should have thought about that before I ordered the chicks. Good thing Benj is around."

"Father will be busy too," Bill answered, as he left and ran to join his brothers and the Shultz boys.

Del suddenly thought about Isaac's Hudson. "Where was it?" she thought as she skipped down the lane. Then there was the unusual absence of Mama and Carol at dinnertime. Del slowed down. "What could she and Carol be doing at the Printz home this time of day?" It was strange that Mama wasn't around at dinnertime to ask if there was any talk about Sunday. Del dropped her thoughts as she entered the school grounds looking for Em.

"You are back early. I just finished my lunch," Em said as she returned her lunch box to a shelf behind the big round stove.

"Let's go outside. We can play more games. The Goho girls said they were going to draw a play area on the dirt lane. The boys can't run through it on the way to their outhouse."

The girls had a fun time and were pleased the Goho girls thought of a new place where they could draw their hopscotch games.

At the school day's end, Fritz was there to greet the twins as usual. Del asked Bill, "Did you see Isaac's machine at dinnertime?"

Bill thought a bit. "No, I didn't. It must be on the grounds somewhere. Unless he went home already," Bill paused. "I know one thing for sure." Bill looked very pleased with himself.

"What is that?"

"Those papers Isaac was showing Father in the barn . . ." Bill paused. "The pictures on the table today were square and the backs were all white, just like the stuff in that paper bag."

"Why couldn't we see those pictures? Father placed them in his desk. I wonder where they are now?" Del questioned.

"I know what you are thinking, there is something secretive going on around here. Eva is always showing us photographs of places she and Isaac visited."

They entered the homestead. Fritz followed the twins into the house. Del was surprised to see Lillie in the kitchen with Mama. She was washing crocks, canning jars, and other butchering equipment that had been in storage since their last use. Lots of sharpened knives were laid on a white cloth to dry.

Lillie greeted the children as they entered the kitchen.

"I didn't know you were here. You never come unless Sam and Eva are here too. I saw Isaac at dinnertime. I thought he came alone," Ori said.

Lillie looked at Mama and nodded her head. "I believe we have another surprise for you."

"Bet I can guess." Ori seemed very confident. "Eva has work today, and Sam does too. Isaac brought you along to get things ready for butchering," she said triumphantly.

Lillie looked at Ori, "You are wrong. My Sam is here too."

Mama immediately interrupted.

"Eat your snack and change into your work clothes. There's lots to do this evening. Benj and Phillip will help with the evening chores."

"Are they back at the Printz home?" Ollie added.

Mama nodded her head yes.

Del did her work without any talk. There was no fussing from Ori, either. Fritz ran up and stood beside Del. She paused and stroked Fritz's head gently, before he decided to trot back down the lane to the sawmill and beyond, maybe to the Printz home.

She didn't see her small wagon in its usual place. She walked beyond the pigpen to the lane and looked back toward that Printz home. Sure enough Benj was bringing the wagon and Phillip was walking slowly alongside it with Fritz bouncing alongside.

"No wonder Fritz couldn't decide where he wanted to be!" Del thought. "What is happening back there?" Del said as she approached Benj and Phillip and pointed back in the direction they came from.

Benj shook his head. "Others may tell ya."

Phillip was silent.

Del said to Phillip, "It won't be long before you are racing Fritz down this lane."

Phillip smiled and said, "I want to run with Fritz."

Benj beamed.

It wasn't long before Father returned with the truck and entered the barn, since it was milking time. As Del finished her chores, Ori walked by with her egg buckets. Taw-Taw was in the henhouse for the night. Del heard him squawk as she checked all doors and latches. She checked the faucet by the feedhouse, making sure it was not dripping. The pigs quieted down. She heard Isaac's Hudson come down the lane. It came to a stop in front of the walk to the house and out stepped Sam and Eva as the engine idled. Grandfather was in the front seat with Brownie on his lap.

"You're surprised to see me, I can tell," Eva laughed.

"True enough, I didn't know any of you were here," Del admitted.

As usual, Grandfather refused to stay for supper. Isaac made a quick trip uptown to drop off Grandfather. Once Isaac returned, the relatives shared the evening meal. There was lots of talk about butchering and Thanksgiving and the Friday off for the city school, while the country school had the day off for Thanksgiving and no more. Nothing was said about the Printz home. Del realized with disappointment that the grownups were not going to talk about it in front of she and her siblings. She suspected that Grandfather already purchased the property. The adults instead talked about processing and canning all the butchered meat, and, after all that was completed, the yearly process for making soap.

Father ate quickly so he could get to the School Board meeting. Father always attended these meetings to report on tax collections. The relatives decided to leave when he did. Til went outside to share a moment with his Doll before heading upstairs. Ollie said he was tired and going to bed. Carol was very tired because she did a lot of walking back and forth with Mama. Ori made sure to get her prepared for bed before she would fall asleep. The uncles and aunts helped Mama clean up and also headed home after a long and busy day. Del, too, decided to call it a day.

"Before you go to your room," Mama said, "I didn't hear anything about talk at school about church services on Sunday."

"There was none," Del replied.

"Nothing at all!" Mama exclaimed.

"No, no one mentioned anything about church."

"Go to bed." Mama smiled at Del.

Del, alone in her room, felt she understood Mama's smile. That meant Mama was pleased about how the busybody was handled. Del was very curious about what Mama and her aunts did all day on the Printz home property. As she drifted off to sleep, she thought she would have to walk there when she had free time.

Tuesday morning Del completed her tasks with only Fritz to talk to as he followed her back and forth. She saw Father's Studebaker—he was ready to take people to the hotel and cast their ballot this election day. Ed was going to do the same with his coupe.

Del turned to Fritz and said, "Where do you suppose Benj and Phillip are this morning since I have you all to myself? You would surely tell me if you could talk." Fritz just wagged his tail. Del discovered her bucket of water was filled and setting inside the henhouse door for Ori. Benj did that for sure, she told Fritz. The chickens were already outside. Del reasoned that Ori wasn't up while she stood by the pigpen throwing scrub cobs of corn for them to munch on. Mama stepped out from under the barn overshoot with her milking apron and bonnet. She carefully closed the gate. That was unusual. Mama wasn't the one to secure the gate in the morning.

"Where is everybody this morning?" Del called to her.

"I'll tell you inside."

Del made her way inside as soon as she double-checked all her work was completed.

Ori passed as Del was on her way to the house. "There's not much left for you to do, I think Benj helped us out this morning. Mama did some milking this morning."

"Oh, stop your chatter. Mama told me to take care of Carol first, she said most of my work is done. They always see to it that I can never let

Taw-Taw go outside. Everybody does things against me on purpose. They don't do that to you," Ori said grumpily.

Del shrugged and left her older sister to figure out what still needed to be done.

When Del entered the house, Carol was dressed and lying on the couch. Mama added wood to the fire in the stove.

"Where are Benj and Phillip? How come you were milking this morning?"

"Ed's peeps arrived very early this morning. The mailman delivered them first thing before going back to start his mail route. He didn't want to listen to those peeps in his jalopy all day. Your father already started the milking. Ed helped while Benj did some outside work. I only finished Bessie. Phillip is with Benj. I suppose everyone is at the building by now taking care of the peeps." Mama stopped and turned to the stove. "I'm making eggs any way you like them for breakfast this morning."

Ollie entered the kitchen. Mama pointed a finger at him and said, "You stay away from Ed's peeps. We don't want that door to open more than necessary. It's important to keep the room evenly warm all the time so there's no crowding among the chicks. Ed will tell you when you can see them." Mama looked again at Ollie. "Today you can tell your friends baby chicks arrived early this morning. But you also tell them they can't see them until Ed allows it. Hear me now!" Mama looked directly at Ollie until he nodded his head that he understood.

The children had all but finished their breakfast when Father's truck was heard. Father, Phillip, and Benj entered the kitchen. All three looked pleased and Benj announced: "It's good to see the building used." He laid a hand on Phillip's shoulder. "What ya think about dem chicks?"

"They are noisy," Phillip said with a smile.

"Something new for you to watch as they grow," Father added.

"Wait until you hear all the crowing first thing in the morning. Then that place will be real noisy. Those roosters will make lots of noise. Nothing like the weird duck squawks we have around here."

Del could hardly believe that statement came from Bill. Even more unbelievable, Ori did not lash out at Bill. Father stood up from the table and walked into the closed porch to his desk. "I think you had better get ready for school," he said, "I see your friends coming in the lane."

The children scrambled outside. As they reached the school grounds they scattered to join their friends and the school bell soon rang.

Ori was quiet all the way home at dinnertime. She checked on her duck first, mumbling about who was around and why her duck was kept in his coop.

Del and her siblings continued to the house. Ori entered the kitchen asking who was visiting because Taw-Taw is still in his pen. "I didn't see a machine anywhere. I will set him free before I go back to school."

The door opened and Mama entered as Til warned, "You better wait until Mama is here. Don't disobey her and get in trouble." "Who needs to wait?" Mama asked.

Ollie pointed a finger to Ori.

Mama looked to Ori, who complained, "My duck is penned up when no one is here."

"He stays penned. We will have people going in and out of this lane today," Mama said.

"There's always some kind of excuse to keep my Taw-Taw penned up," Ori grumbled.

"You will see later," was all Mama was willing to say.

The children talked about what was going on to keep Taw-Taw penned up. "I know," Ollie impatiently said. "Some trees will be cut down along the path Grandfather takes when he comes through the forest. He doesn't like the sound of horseshoes on the cement highway."

"I think I know what is happening," Til said. "But I won't say until I know for sure."

Em waited for Del at the schoolhouse. "Ya know what, my grandmother is going to live with her widowed sister-in-law."

"I told you they would figure things out."

"They are going to sell her house and a lot of her furniture. Ma wants the library table and an old oil lamp. My aunts and uncles are dividing things they want and the rest will be sold. Ma put fresh flowers on my aunt's grave, but my Grandmother stayed in the machine." Em went on and on. Del listened, and was glad when the bell rang for the afternoon's studies to begin.

CHAPTER TWENTY-SIX

Butchering Day

Butchering was already underway on Wednesday morning when Del looked down from her parents' upstairs window. Hairless pig halves were hanging from tripods. A small truck and three machines were parked below and on the barnbank. Del quickly dressed for a very busy day. She found Lillie in the kitchen as Ori entered the porch with her bucket of eggs.

The boys, except for Phillip who wasn't in the kitchen, were eating French toast with butter and maple syrup on top. Mama didn't often make that for breakfast.

"Is Benj here this morning? And who won the election?" Del asked Lillie. She observed the large griddle pan placed over the fire, and knew Lillie would be in charge of the kitchen today, same as earlier years.

"Who cares?" Ollie said.

Lillie looked at Ollie and stated, "You'll care some day. Yes, Adelaide and the rest of you. I hear Benj stayed uptown until the results were tacked to the door. Your father brought him along home. It wasn't who

I wanted. Nevertheless Benj was up early to help Ed this morning. I want to see those peeps sometime before butchering is finished."

Benj entered alone. Del figured he was waiting for Phillip to awaken.

Lillie nodded to Benj. "I worry sometimes about Phillip, about finding out what happened to him and his parents. We all want to know what happened to that family." She turned to the children. "Your father was only three years old when our father died of appendicitis. I was ten years old at the time." Lillie paused and was interrupted by Ori.

"He was starving. They sure didn't care if he died," Ori stated firmly. "He should be glad Father brought him along home."

"Now Gloria, I'm sure he's grateful. I never said he wasn't. But everyone wants to hear stories about their elders. It's not good to be alone in this world. Your father always asks people who knew his father about him. I figure we would not have been desperately poor had he lived. He had schooling. He was an accountant and kept financial records for merchants and farmers. He carried ledgers with him as he made the rounds for all his clients."

"I thought he was a farmer," Bill said.

"Yes William, we had a small acreage, enough to feed a family, but not to make a living. I had to work in the glove factory to help make ends meet—and I wasn't more than 13 at the time. My father had been their accountant as well." Lillie sighed. "I am sure that day will come when Phillip will want to know what happened to his real parents and relatives. I'm sure he knows his name, once he's ready to tell someone. Now eat your breakfast, I think your morning detail is taken care of, but you'll feel better if you check for sure."

"Mama told us last night all our work would be taken care of this morning," Del said in agreement. "But I'll run out and make sure."

"Wear your warm coat. It's chilly this morning."

Dressed in her warm school coat Del dashed outside, saying hello and good morning to everyone she met before she entered the feedhouse. She looked around, checking if her buckets were rinsed after being used. She heard the satisfied grunting of the pigs, and the little doors to the henhouse were open and chickens were outside pecking at kernels scattered about. There was nothing left for her or Ori to do. Mama was right.

Phillip came down the stairs as Del stepped inside the kitchen.

"Ah ha, good eating this morning fer ya Phillip. Still had some of that good maple syrup at home, good time to use it," Benj greeted him.

"Did your man win the election?" Del asked Benj.

"No, 'fraid not. Just wish Pinchot had been running."

"Why do you say that?" Del asked.

"Got to be a farmer at heart. He understands ya need to respect this good earth."

"True enough!" Lillie said as she set more French toast on the table for Benj and Phillip. She waited for all the children to finish breakfast before sending them off to school.

"Lillie is Lillie," Til stressed, once they were out on the walkway.

The Gohos were within sight so the children waited for them to walk to school.

"We can see what you are doing today," Annabel said as she pointed to the butchering activity.

"That's right. We'll take care of two pigs today. It's just the start of all the work for the rest of the week." Del saw a quarter of beef now hanging from a tripod; Father and a neighbor must have traded beef for pork. "We'll make summer sausages and fresh sausage, can some and hang some in the smokehouse."

Ollie was the first to talk about the butchering work as the children reached the school grounds. "Tomorrow or the next day we will have fresh sausage for breakfast. I can't wait! Our relatives were here before I was up. I bet Phillip is seeing things he never saw before." He paused for breath and then continued, "I watched the men fold the voting booths and put them away for the next election. The peeps are here. I can't wait to see what all roosters look like." Ollie was so eager to tell everyone about all the activities at home that he couldn't stand still. Mr. Strunk smiled as he waited a few moments before grabbing the rope causing the bell to ring twice, thereby announcing the start of the school day.

At recess time, Em talked about the latest decision involving her invalid grandmother. Now she was moving to a new home. "A larger house with a sun porch and three great-grandchildren to keep her company. Joe is glad, he will move to the city once he graduates and go to some kind of job training school and spend evenings and nights at cousin Hettie's place. She's an old maid. That way she can keep her night shift job. And Joe can go to school to learn a trade. That's what Pa wants Joe to do and he seems willing." Em paused and thought a bit. "I always liked to go to the corner ice cream shop where my grandma used to live," she said wistfully.

"Could be there is another shop on the corner where your cousin lives," Del said.

"Won't be the same. Those people knew me, and they always gave me a little extra ice cream."

"You'll see once you visit your relatives at the new place. My father stops at Miller's Ice Cream shop on North Sixth St. when he goes to the city and has enough time. I'm always cold there. The heavy metal chairs make me shiver," Del said to cheer up her friend. There was no response from Em's downcast face.

Running home for dinner, the children knew from previous years that they were not to enter areas where butchered meat preparations were taking place. Lillie had food prepared for the children's lunch, and many newly washed jars, new jar lids, and clean pots and pans were ready for the canning that was going to take place for the next couple of days. Lillie made a very large dish of rice pudding. This was a favorite treat for Til, plus something that would be shared with the extra help at break times that day.

School's afternoon session seemed to drag on and on. Del wanted the afternoon session to end so she could see the progress made at home. Hurrying home after school she saw Mr. Goho waiting by the end of school lane. The Gohos had a ride home with their father and wouldn't slow her down.

Ed stood by the pump on Benj's property ready to lift the bucket he filled with water. "My chicks need fresh water," he said to the children as they passed by.

"They are all roosters. Can I see them?" Ollie quickly asked.

Ed laughed and shook his head no. "Let's give them another day or so to settle in before you see them."

Ollie was very disappointed but only mumbled, "Ok."

Lillie had the table set for the evening meal. She entered from the living room and gestured to the baking table. "Help yourselves to the snacks I have there. I will clean up later. There's plenty of noodle soup leftover from this afternoon in a pot on the stove and the ladle is resting on a saucer over by the water tank. Help yourself! Don't be messy!"

"The butcher and the help are outside in the cold most of the time. That warm soup surely is welcome," Til said with a grin.

After chores were done, Del returned to the kitchen. Benj and Phillip were seated on the couch. Carol rocked clumsily back and forth all by herself in the rocking chair where Benj usually sat. Lillie prepared a pork roast with the first sauerkraut made from the cabbages in Mama's garden. It was a very good meal for the first day of butchering and storing meat for another year. It was dark outside as the relatives said their good-byes and promised to return the next morning. Quiet set in, and the only sounds heard were from washing and drying dishes and replacing them to their rightful places.

"If you have schoolwork, get it done and off to bed. Tomorrow will be another busy day," Mama said to the children.

Phillip sat quietly on the bench next to Ollie and watched him as he worked on his arithmetic problems. Father asked Benj if he was ready to call it a day. Ori led Carol up the stairs. Del followed and once in her room she read her geography assignment, not even remembering what she read. She tried the reading a second time and did a better job. She decided she needed to read the assignment one more time in the morning as she got under the covers, yawned, said her prayer and turned over for a good night's sleep.

Thursday morning was a day very much like the day before, except most of the heavier butchering work was completed. Today pork and beef roasts would be cut in small and larger portions. They would grind meat while adding seasonings to make fresh sausages, also called rope sausages. Different seasonings were added to ground meat packed tightly into cloth bags Lillie had sewn this past summer. These summer sausages would hang in the smokehouse to cure and were used as sandwich meat throughout the year. Mama used recipes from generations past. Del knew the same recipe for summer sausage was used year after year. It took:

> 25 pounds of beef
> 1 pint of lard or five pounds of pork fat
> 1 Tablespoon black pepper
> 1 Tablespoon mace
> 1 Tablespoon cloves
> 1 Tablespoon red pepper
> ½ Tablespoon saltpeter
> ½ pound of brown sugar

This was the only recipe Del knew that used saltpeter as a preservative. Fresh sausages were also cut and fried for canning. Meat hooks were pushed through the corners of slabs of bacon, which hung in the smokehouse for curing. Other hams and bacon slabs would be salted for future use.

Ori followed Del as they both entered the kitchen. Lillie was in command of the kitchen again. Lots of green one and two quart jars were setting on deep window seats, covered with cloth, ready for canning.

"You and Mama are going to have a busy day," Del said while taking a seat at the table.

"Yes," Lillie said. "Help yourself to cereals. Your mother went outside with the milk pitcher. Toast and jelly bread is available for now until your Mama comes back with fresh milk. You will carry your dinner today and eat at school. The two of us will be canning all day."

Ori filled her bowl with cereal. "Are you going to take care of Carol again?" she questioned Aunt Lillie.

"Yes, Gloria. I'll take care of her this morning. She can sleep as long as she likes. Most morning work was done by the men folk. The eggs are collected and in the feedhouse. You can grade and pack them later today. You may take a little time with your duck."

Lillie looked to Del. "You check on your morning routine. Dress warm. It's cold enough to bring a sprinkling of snow. I hope the first snow waits till I'm ready to go looking for winter garden plants."

"I brought the glass bowls with lids down from the attic already." Del hoped she could go along when Lillie went into the forest looking for plants for her winter gardens. First gathered was plenty of moss. That was the lining for each glass bowl. Then the black forest soil went in. Then she added partridgeberry with its bright red berries and tiny lacy ferns. Rattlesnake weed and hypatica and sometimes wild violets when Lillie could find them. Wild strawberry plants with blossoms of white, and wintergreen plants, made gardens look especially nice for Christmas. Lillie sold all the winter gardens she could make. No matter where, when, or what, Lillie always made something to sell.

Del's work had been done by the adults. She returned to the house and dashed upstairs to change into her school dress. She noticed that Lillie was making sandwiches for the children to carry to school. Del spoke up. "I want to go along with you this year again, if I may, when you look for your winter garden plants. "

Before Lillie could answer, Ori interrupted, "Who took care of my work this morning? They should leave my duck alone. I like to take care of him."

Mama came from the milkhouse carrying a pitcher full of milk cooled from last evening's milking and placed it on the table. "Gloria, after you eat you can free your duck; he can roam around outside today. Most of our work is inside."

Del could picture the work that would take place in the washhouse. The low furnace had two large openings to hold two very large copper kettles. A wood fire would be built underneath the kettles. One person would heat water, and the other would cook a mixture of meat and seasonings to make scrapple. She expected she would have to take care of her evening detail after school this day. At least the corn was already shelled, and she already put a half bucket full of scrawny cobs to satisfy the squealing pigs if someone walked by their pen.

There was little conversation as all the children finished their breakfast, gathered their books and grabbed winter coats and gloves. Lillie checked everyone at the door as they walked outside. Lillie handed a basket to Til. "You know what to do with this," she said to him.

The Gohos met them in the lane as they headed for school. Ollie was so excited he grabbed Gordon's arm and began explaining why Til was carrying a basket. "I hardly ever eat dinner in school but I will today!" Ollie would have continued but he stopped abruptly as the children saw Benj, Phillip, and Ed leaving the henhouse where the peeps were kept. Ollie was quick to remark, "Look at that! Phillip sees those baby chicks before I get to see them."

"You saw peeps before. Phillip probably never saw baby chicks," Til laughed.

"It's not fair, I live here long already. I will ask to see those little roosters the minute I get home. Phillip just came and he sees those roosters before me. I just hope those sandwiches are something I like," Ollie grumbled.

Til laughed again. "Lillie doesn't make sandwiches unless there's a thin slice of onion with it."

Del knew Til was teasing Ollie, who didn't like onions. Ollie made a face and trotted along next to his oldest brother.

Em was inside as the group entered the school building. Mr. Strunk looked at the clock as he usually did since the Heydt children generally were the last to arrive. He walked with Til to the shelf behind the stove where all the lunches were kept. Til took his seat as Mr. Strunk walked slowly to the back of the vestibule, pulled the rope, and the heavy two gongs sound announced the start of the school day. The children did the Scripture reading, sang one song, recited the Pledge of Allegiance, and then took their assigned seats. Del hurriedly looked over the spelling words for this morning's session, then opened her geography book and read the lesson slowly, in case the teacher called on her to give an oral report she thought was due. But her thoughts drifted to thinking about the sausages being fried and cut into sizes to pack nicely into the canning jars. That would probably be a job for her this evening, carrying cooled jars to the cellar to store on shelves setting against the wall next to a variety of other canned meats, fruits, vegetables, and jellies. She anticipated the kitchen would have that wonderful aroma of fried fresh sausages when she got home. "We could have a fresh sausage sandwich for dinner if we would go home today," she thought.

Recess time was the first chance Em had to discuss her grandmother's situation in the city of Reading. They were going to add a hothouse enclosure to the back of her mother's relative's house. This hothouse would add warmth to the house, plus provide the proper space to raise blooming plants so her grandmother could sell cut flowers year 'round, as she had done in past years. She would be content doing her favorite pastime. All she needed was to have someone help her in the care of her plants.

"That sounds good to me," Del replied.

"Ma says my grandmother always had lots of flowers in her backyard. In a hothouse she will always have flowers to make nice bouquets. It will give my grandmother something to do."

"I thought your grandmother couldn't walk by herself?"

"Yes, that's so. The path will be wide enough and have a railing on both sides so she can hold on and help herself move forward and back again. She did that a long time already. She can tell Ma's cousin what needs to be done to help at the same time."

"That sure sounds good to me," Del responded again. She really wasn't all that interested with all the changes taking place with Em's grandmother, but Em was her friend.

Del figured she better say something to Em about their food basket this particular day. "I will be staying and eating my dinner with you today."

"You will be eating in school today? Why, for goodness sake?

"It's because Mama and my aunt will be canning meats all day. Aunt Lillie gave a basket with sandwiches to Til as we were leaving. "

Em was very surprised. "Is this the first time you eat in school with us?"

"No, when the weather is really cold or there's deep snow we stay and eat here."

The dinner hour was busy and long. Teacher ate his dinner seated at his desk. Del looked at the assortment of sandwiches Lillie had packed. There were cold scrambled egg sandwiches, jelly sandwiches and jelly/peanut butter combinations. There were chocolate cookies that Lillie must have brought along. The hour seemed long. There was more time for games, but Del was glad when the bell rang for the afternoon session to begin.

At school day's end the Goho girls wondered if they could have a look at the peeps.

Til heard their question. "Sure you can see the peeps, but we have to wait until Ed thinks its alright for us to see them. He doesn't want a lot of commotion to disturb them. I bet we can't all go at one time."

Anabel and Maria looked suitably impressed that these peeps received such special treatment.

The children arrived home and immediately changed clothes before looking for a snack and heading outdoors to attend to their evening chores.

Lillie was full of questions. "Did you eat all the sandwiches? Did I pack enough?" Lillie asked as she looked into the basket.

Ollie answered, "We emptied the basket. It was all good." He had been relieved to learn at noontime that there were no onions in the sandwiches.

"That's good to hear."

"The cookies were good. What kind of nut was in the cookies?" Ori asked.

"Did you like them?" Lillie asked.

"Yes," was said by all.

Lillie smiled. "I used my leftover hickory nuts. I will get a new supply as soon as they start dropping. That's the best nut around for cake or cookies. You all can help pick hickory nuts this year. There will be enough for all of us this winter, the trees hang full."

"How do you know that?" Del asked.

"Sam noticed when he worked in the fields."

Del headed outdoors to complete her chores. This afternoon they were there for her to do. The evening milking would soon be underway and the fires were left to burn out in the washhouse. Smoke was coming from the smokehouse, and would continue for a number of days. Most of the outside help already left.

Uncle Sam decided to offer grace as all the relatives gathered around the table. It was clear that everyone was tired from a long day of work to put away food for the year. The time after supper was spent quietly with little conversation as the relatives collected their containers of meat and equipment to head for home, saying someone would be back for scrapple and lard once the contents hardened enough to move them without spilling. Everyone looked forward to a weekend of rest with great satisfaction, knowing that much was accomplished and they already had food to last until next fall even though after Thanksgiving more butchering would take place.

Early Friday morning when Del walked into the kitchen Mama was setting filled scrapple pans, now cooled, on the windowsills in the closed porch and, wherever else she found space to place them. Her flowerpots were now on the floor. The scrapple had hardened overnight and Mama was about to pour a thin covering of melted lard on top, which, when cooled, would provide a protective cover to preserve it.

"Tend to your work, Adelaide," Mama said. "Benj is helping Ed look after his chicks. Gloria should be up too. I'll give her a few more minutes before I call her; she needs to take care of her morning work also. Ed will be here before long to help your father with whatever early barn work needs attention; the rest of the day they will be sawing firewood. We used most of our split wood just heating water these last couple of days. Your father and Ed will be busy sawing wood, enough to fill our woodshed for winter's use, and also for Benj and Ed. With all the work they've done for us, they deserve it." Mama continued on, but now she was talking very quietly. "The boys can stack today's wood in the open woodshed. I must finish cleaning up outside and return the butchering equipment to their places."

Gloria could be heard stirring upstairs.

"Where did Father go? I heard the truck," Del asked.

"I suppose he's parked it by the sawmill. The truck really comes in handy, it lets your father make a couple of wood deliveries each day. Breakfast will be ready when you return. Dress warm enough, I don't want anyone catching a cold before winter's cold really sets in; an early cold will weaken your resistance the rest of winter."

Del went about doing her work, thinking about all the work Mama and Lillie did these past couple of days. Today should be an easier day for everyone, although schoolwork had not diminished. Del assumed Phillip was with Benj and helping Ed this morning as he wasn't in the kitchen.

"Where is my bucket of corn?" Ori demanded.

"Surely you can see and hear what I am doing. There's enough shelled corn for you to scatter outside in that leaky bucket. I will shell enough for now and this evening."

"I didn't see Benj or Phillip this morning. Aren't they going help me any more?" Ori grumbled.

"Goodness she fusses when they do some of her routine, and then she fusses when they don't," Del thought to herself. She said to Ori, "I suppose Benj and Phillip are tending to the peeps. Ed is with Father sawing firewood for the winter."

"Who believes that? His baby chicks, that's where Ed is," Ori said irritably.

Ori was in one of her ornery moods. Maybe the coming Thanksgiving was a safer topic. "We'll have lots of company in less than a week. Lillie's daughters and their husbands, and all her grandchildren will be here. We'll have to lock the barn up tight to keep them from running around where Father doesn't want them to go. They would surely get into all kinds of mischief."

"Jenny will never go there, she gets hay fever the minute she is near the barn," Ori stated. Jenny, the oldest grandchild, always spent her day with Ori.

"I can't wait for Uncle Sam to take Bill and me for that long walk after Thanksgiving dinner. We always go over to the forest. When he hears a bird's call, he knows what kind of bird it is. He tells us to look for that bird by telling us to look for a particular color to find the bird. He knows all the birdcalls. I know the cardinal's call and the mocking-bird and so does Bill. We can name all the birds on our chart in school."

"Shut up. Who wants to hear bird sounds? I hear birdcalls when we are picking hickory nuts, and don't care what kind of birds are making noise overhead. Picking hickory nuts is something worth the while."

"Yes, that will happen too, if we have a light snowfall by Thanksgiving, Thanksgiving Day or shortly thereafter Lillie will go looking for winter garden plants. I like . . ."

"This is boring," Ori harshly interrupted.

"Maybe for you, but I like to be with Lillie when she looks for her plants." Del looked around and realized Ori was no longer within hearing distance. As she walked over to the henhouse door she heard Ori talking to her troublesome duck. Del just finished her work and headed for the house hoping breakfast would be ready.

"Wash up, I see Gloria is coming back, the boys too," Mama said as Del entered.

"I'm sure glad it's Friday," Ori said after fussing as to where she should set the bucket of eggs with all the cooled scrapple pans setting around in the enclosed porch. The children took turns washing hands before eating breakfast. Ollie was first to be seated.

"We have omelet this morning," Mama said as she placed the open roasting pan on a baking board on the center of the table. "I have fresh fried sausages and bread you may butter for yourselves. Add jelly if you like."

Til was especially pleased with the breakfast menu. "Father said we would have fresh sausage for breakfast."

"Yes, your father ate before you were up. He and Ed wanted to get an early start. Lots to do before winter sets in."

"Did Benj and Phillip eat already? They were up before me," Ollie inquired.

"Yes, Phillip and William came down at the same time. Benj was here early too. I suppose Benj and Phillip saw the baby chicks this morning."

"It's a rooster house," Ollie said softly.

Mama smiled.

After changing clothes the children were out the door headed for school. The Gohos were within sight, so the children moved slowly and waited for them to catch up.

Em met Del as usual. "What's new today at your house?"

"Nothing much, I didn't see the peeps yet. Phillip sees them. He doesn't say much about them, even though we ask him about them," Del replied.

"You didn't tell me he talks."

"Phillip told us the peeps are noisy."

"What else does he say?"

"Not much when all of us are there. He and Benj talk when they are alone. Mama says Phillip will have the same motions and mannerisms as Benj. He may also get our Pennsylvania Dutch accent, which will be interesting."

"He won't stay with you. He'll run away again, my Pa says."

"I don't think so. I think he likes being with us, and it's the only place he knows. Where could he go?"

"Pa says he will be a big heap of trouble for you. I hate to tell you that," Em said with a worried look.

"I hope not! I've heard that too, and so has my Father. But he said it doesn't change his feeling that he made the right decision when he held Phillip that first time."

"What does your Mama say?"

"Wait and see. That's all."

"I bet she wishes, too, she never saw that colored boy. That's what my ma says."

Del did not have time for further talk, as the bell rang for all to enter the schoolhouse. She just shook her head.

It was a big day for Ollie. When the children left school at the close of the afternoon session Benj stopped them and told Ollie to drop his books on Benj's house porch and come over to see the chicks. He motioned for Til and Bill to follow. Ollie ran so fast he almost fell. Laughing, Ed caught him as he neared the door and let him in once he gathered his breath. Ori followed as Del and Fritz continued their walk home.

"I saw baby chicks many times before. They're all the same. It's no different when we have peeps growing up to be roosters or hens," Ori said dismissively.

The boys returned, Benj and Phillip bringing up the rear. Ollie talked excitedly about the peeps and how they looked just like the ones he'd seen delivered to their home. Benj invited the girls to go back to see the peeps. "Ed is there, we only need to open the door slowly and step inside."

"I have my work to do," Ori shrugged and moved on.

Del turned and made a fast walk to the henhouse where the peeps were located.

Ed smiled as he opened the door. "What do you think?"

"They look good and healthy, and they are noisy—just like Phillip said! They don't look any different from baby chicks we get every spring."

"Phillip enjoys watching them. He gets a big grin on his face," Ed said with a quiet smile.

Del arrived home and headed upstairs to change clothes. She returned to the kitchen but no one was around. She made a peanut butter cracker sandwich and headed outdoors. Her evening chores were done quietly and quickly. Ed walked by, headed toward the sawmill. Del thought about how Ed made himself useful these days, not only helping Father but other neighbors with his skills as a handyman.

Her chores were completed without incident, and thankfully, no nasty comments from Ori. For suppertime, Mama made two beef pies with sliced creamy potatoes baked in the oven. It was a very satisfying meal that Benj really enjoyed. He explained to Phillip and everyone else that winter was the right time for such a tasty and filling meal.

Mama was very pleased with his compliments. "It takes a little more time to make, but the result is worth the while," Mama noted.

"Grandfather should be here. He would say, 'Amen to that'," Til chuckled.

The children did the dishes and clean up. Mama told them, "Tend to your schoolwork, if you don't want to do it this weekend, then bedtime after that. We accomplished a lot this day."

CHAPTER TWENTY-SEVEN

Becky's Family Story

Saturday morning meant a later rising for all except Del's parents and Til, who were always up early to do the milking. Del awakened to see a peeping sun moving slowly between gray clouds as she looked about from her parents' bedroom window. For sure, Benj would appear within the hour. Benj always made sure all was well outside before entering the house to check whether Phillip was up and about. She watched Mama walk into the milkhouse to leave her apron and bonnet on holding hooks, then, after washing her hands and arms, she returned to the kitchen to begin making a substantial breakfast. Del heard the clanging of pots and pans. She entered the kitchen, observing that Mama had started preparations for both breakfast and the evening meal later. She motioned for Del to remain quiet as she listened to Phillip taking steps one at a time on the stairway. She looked satisfied at Phillip's progress. The door opened and Phillip entered the kitchen without limping.

"Good morning, Phillip," Mama said. "Benj will be here soon. He is outside." Mama gave a look to Del to warn her not to say anything to Phillip about not limping, as Del was prone to speak up when she noticed something.

Phillip nodded his head and sat on the couch reaching for his shoes as Benj entered the kitchen. He immediately walked over to the rocking chair and greeted Phillip. "Cold outside this morning." Benj seated himself on the rocking chair and watched Phillip put on his shoes. Phillip seemed to be completely at home now, and Del sensed that Mama and Benj thought so too.

Mama sliced cold whole boiled potatoes and dropped slice after slice into a large fry pan. Fresh sausages were in another large fry pan while Benj kept watch on Phillip, ready to help him if needed. Benj said, "Have a warm coat for ya, brought it along this morning, may be a little big for right now. Left it in the porch. Will leave it here, ya can look at it later. Yer overall jacket should do for today."

Phillip was wearing Ollie's out-grown overall jacket for now.

"We'll go outside, see what kind of trouble we can get ourselves into." Benj patted Phillip on the shoulder.

Mama spoke. "There's a heavy frost out there this morning. Come back soon if Phillip isn't warm enough. You'll need to eat your fill because I won't do any more cooking until time for our evening meal. If you need a little something to hold you over until suppertime, I'll leave breakfast leftovers on my baking table. Cold sausages with buttered bread is always good, there's fruit, and other snacks you'll find in the cupboard. We'll have a full day's work." Benj and Phillip merely nodded and went outside.

Ori came downstairs, still yawning. Mama pointed to her stating, "Gloria, you keep an eye on Carol this day. Make sure you keep her close by. Check on her frequently should she take a nap mid-afternoon. I will be visiting our neighbors. I want to see for myself how Jonathan is doing."

Ori went outside while Mama was still speaking without acknowledging her instructions. Mama watched her leave.

Del noticed the roasting pan held an extra large beef roast. Mama was preparing that for the evening meal. It was big enough to warm up or possibly make cold beef sandwiches for Sunday's noon meal. Father would surely use some of Lillie's horseradish. Del watched Mama prepare a separate pot for Ollie, the sneaky eater. He didn't like turnips. Turnips in the same pot with a beef roast and potatoes always ruined the taste, according to Ollie. Although Mama always fussed, she cut a small portion of meat from the roast and placed it in the smaller pot with water and seasonings to place in the oven after the larger roast was well underway. Later she would add raw quartered potatoes when the meat was near ready to serve. The rest of the family would have potatoes and turnips with their roast.

Mama asked Del to stay close by and be available as she was about to make her last trip to the garden in final preparation for winter's rest. There wasn't much to do. Late icicle radishes were still in the ground. Turnips that were too small to harvest earlier would be harvested now, regardless of size. Del dressed warmly and headed outside to start her chores. Benj and Phillip were walking toward the feed entry. Phillip was walking on his own!

"Will open those cellar doors fer ya," Benj spoke.

"I know Mama is going to work in the garden. I'll help her after I check on my morning chores first."

"Ya tell her, Phillip."

Phillip looked up and proudly said, "We fed the pigs and I shelled some corn."

"That's great, Phillip, thank you for helping me out with my chores. I appreciate the help."

There was no further response from Phillip, except for the smile on his face. Del ran to the garden.

Mama looked at her. "Carry these few late cabbages to the cellar. Take the last of these icicle radishes and turnips too. They won't grow any larger—the ground is too cold. This horehound root, place it on top of any container. I will take care of it later. Straighten up in the cellar where necessary. Combine baskets if you see two of the same item only half full, and stack any empty baskets. We have plenty of turnips this year. We'll see if our relatives have enough to last the winter."

"Do you think Lizzie will come for Thanksgiving?"

"Perhaps, yes; my aunt and uncle are alone. Past times they always helped a local charity serve Thanksgiving dinner. But they are older now, and can't be on their feet all day anymore. Still Lizzie is just like my father, one as stubborn as the other. Come to think about it, maybe my father will come if his sister and her husband bring him along. That could work!"

Del grabbed a basket and walked by the front porch to the side entrance of the house where the outside cellar doors lay open. Benj had lifted those heavy doors for her. Someone must have taken that two by four off the brackets on the inside to unlock the doors earlier this morning. She took the steps sideways until she reached the area where other baskets stood. She saw baskets half full setting along the outside wall, which had a section built higher for lard cans and crocks. There was a potato bin on legs along another exterior wall. She slowly emptied her basket and left to fetch another from the garden, remembering she had carried many other baskets filled with garden produce into the cellar. She returned to the garden. Mama was no longer there. Del gathered up the remaining garden produce in a few trips. She knew Benj would close the cellar doors after she finished her task. She headed up to the kitchen from the cellar stairs. Heading outside, she looked around for Fritz, but didn't see him. Del decided to finish what was left of her morning chores. She set a bucket of water by the henhouse door for Ori. Although she didn't see Ori, she set a bent metal dish of shelled corn by the door for her to scatter on the henhouse floor. Next she scattered kernels of corn on the ground outside. Looking around she saw Benj and Phillip leave the feed entry and stand by the side of the barnbridge.

Del thought, "Phillip is doing better all the time. I wonder if they are doing anything about schooling him? Maybe Mr. Straub is helping him during the day when we are in school. I wish Father and Mama would tell us what's going on."

"Talking to yourself?" Ed spoke.

Del was startled. She didn't realize she was speaking what she was thinking. She smiled. "It's good to see Phillip walking, he'll be running before long. Do you know, will he be going to school soon?"

"Don't ask me about that. I don't know any more than you."

"How are your baby chicks this morning?"

"All fine. Most times you lose a chick or two, but not this time. All is good."

Del smiled, "That's good to hear," she said as she headed back to the house. Benj and Phillip were seated in the woodshed sharing the chopping block for a seat.

"*Fattich dat* [Finish there]?" Benj pointed to the open cellar doors. "Cold to sit here. Don't want that white-feathered thing going into the cellar. What a mess he could make."

Phillip smiled. He seemed to understand why Benj was concerned.

"Yes, all done. There's nothing more to carry into the cellar. It's time for breakfast."

"Yep. After me and Phillip had breakfast, we'll see what else we can do."

No more was said as Del headed down the steps and waited as Benj lowered the heavy doors so she could secure the double doors to the cellar from the inside.

Del took the cellar steps fast and returned to the kitchen.

Mama spoke quietly as Del neared. "Don't disappear. I have an errand for you."

"What kind of errand?

"I will tell you when the time comes."

Nothing more was said as Ori made her entrance. "It's cold out there! Feels good in here."

"Go upstairs, see if you can bring Carol down, I hear her moving about."

Ori moved without making a fuss.

Gradually the family gathered in the kitchen for breakfast. The family, all seated, said the children's prayer in unison.

"It's too soon to serve scrapple—that will have to set a couple more days. I have omelet with fresh fried sausage this morning. Eat your fill. I won't make dinner, but we'll have a good size beef roast for supper."

Benj looked especially pleased as he explained to Phillip that the good tasting sausages were the results of all the hard work that had taken place earlier in the week.

"Can't beat this fine breakfast. Stick-to-the-bones food," Father stated with great satisfaction.

After breakfast cleanup, Mama told Ori, "Do your Saturday cleaning upstairs. Strip the beds. Take Carol with you, have her help with the easier things."

Ori and Carol headed upstairs.

"It will take awhile for Gloria to finish that job. No one in the family is as slow as her," Mama paused, "But as long as she gets her work done, I won't say much." She turned to Del. "I'll fill the large basket setting in the porch. Put it in your wagon and pull it just beyond the woodshed. Gloria can't see it there from the upstairs windows. You take that out to Becky. She knows you are coming. We haven't given her any butchered meat as yet. You may visit a bit. Don't overstay. And don't talk or tell anyone about going there when you come back. You know how Gloria will complain if she finds out you visited there. I told Becky you could keep things you see and hear to yourself. I learned that already. Come home the back way. Pick hickory nuts and put them in the basket."

Del did what Mama said. She thought there was more to this request than taking some fresh meat to Becky. Del's mind raced with possibilities. "What on earth is going to happen when I get there? Is Becky going to tell me I saw Rachael? Or maybe, that was Susanna, her grandchild. Maybe I didn't see Rachael after all."

Becky was waiting for Del. She stepped out on the porch from her front door, which was a big surprise, as Del was headed to the side entrance that had a small side porch.

"I don't know if I can bring this up over your porch steps," Del said pointing to the full wagon

"Leave it there. No one can see it. These tall evergreens and lower shrubs hide the front and lower sides of my house. I can sit on this porch, day or night, and no one can see me. Yet I can see who is passing by. My Sam, too, could sit on this porch while anyone walking by never saw him. He liked that quiet time."

Del helped carry the sausages and scrapple inside. Becky picked up the small pot of liver pudding.

"Oh my, my favorite! There's nothing like hot liver pudding on top of mashed potatoes with cut raw onions on top of that and a piece of buttered bread."

"That's my favorite, too!" Del exclaimed.

"When you get to be as old as I, you will want that meal at noontime. Evening meals with raw onions will give you heartburn once you grow old. You'll remember Becky told you so. If you need an excuse to come over here, you can always say you came to pick hickory nuts. I picked all I need along the stonewall on the back of my lot. Picking nuts is a little hard on my back nowadays."

"The squirrels are helping themselves too. Hickory nuts make the best nut cake. I hear everybody say that. I will gather nuts for you, if you want," Del suggested, glad to have a chance to do a kindness for Becky.

"Let me put these things away. Then we will chat. Come to think of it, it would be nice if you picked more nuts for me while you are here. Your relatives are welcome to come and pick all the nuts they can find here, too. The squirrels already stored more than they need."

"I'll tell Aunt Lillie about that. She sells all kinds of things. She grows horseradish in her garden and grinds it to sell, plus other things she grows in her garden. She bakes AP cakes and ginger snaps. She makes lots of winter gardens and sells them to big department stores and flower shops. I like to go along when she gathers her plants. Maybe she can sell hickory nuts to city folk."

"Let's go inside, I have something to show you."

Del stepped into a small but tidy living room.

"This is a picture of my Sam. He is young here, a tall and slender man."

"I never saw him." Del wasn't about to mention that Benj told her Sam was a three hundred pound man.

"No. He died before you were born."

"Here are some family pictures. Do you recognize anyone?"

Del saw a photo with 4 women of ascending ages, one of a girl alone, and one miniature painting of a young woman an unusual dress that Del guessed was from some country in Europe. "I don't know. One has to be you," she said as she pointed to the photo with one girl. "You look like sisters."

"There is a likeness. This is my great-great-grandmother, Sophia. Next, my great-grandmother, Hilda. My grandmother, Annie. My mother, Olivia. I am this next one." Becky paused at the last picture on the wall. "This picture. Can you guess who this is?"

"She is younger, but favors you. Is it Rachael?" Del asked as she examined the photo, but she already knew the answer. This was the woman she encountered at the Conrad farm.

Becky nodded her head. "Yes. Six generations, my grandmother, my great-great-grandmother from the old country. Now, sadly this line comes to an end with Rachael."

"But . . . But Rachael has Susanna."

"Yes and no. She's not a new generation by blood. Do I confuse you?"

Del nodded her head. "How isn't she part of a new generation?"

"Well . . . Rachael is raising orphaned children like they are her own. You know she lives up in the coal country. Miners and their families have a hard life. She and her husband, who is a doctor, decided to raise a newborn baby when the mother died in childbirth. Another little boy was three when he lost his parents, so they adopted him. They now have four children they raise as their own because of similar circumstances. A father can't work in the coalmines and take care of young children. Nor can a mother raise a child when the father dies, if she has to earn a living. They started a small orphanage. A living parent or relative can visit their kin anytime they like. Even keep them for a few days. My good daughter will raise a child until she is a young lady or man. Grown children are free to choose to live with their own family once they can manage for themselves."

Del was astonished but puzzled too. "It's very kind of Rachael and her husband to give children a home. Why doesn't she visit you? Hester said it's her fault Rachael doesn't visit anymore."

Becky frowned. "While my daughter looks like me, she inherited the stubbornness of her father. As you grow older, you will hear of things that cause strife and friction among neighbors, yes, even within families. You will understand more as you grow older. Rachael doesn't like surprises, like what happened with the Conrads. You will meet Rachael properly when the time is right." Becky paused, and then looked intently at Del. "Things aren't always as they first appear to be. It's always later, or too late sometimes, when we learn the real truths. One day Phillip will search for the real truths about him and his family. We all do. Don't you think so?"

Del nodded her head. "But . . . but my father is trying to find out what happened to Phillip and where his people are."

"Your father is a good man. Come, let's go pick some hickory nuts."

Del and Becky went outside and walked along the stone fence until they were underneath a tall hickory tree. The ground below was littered with the small dark brown shells that contained the tasty nut inside. Del worked quietly as Becky talked about her childhood and people who lived and died before Del was born. After an hour, they had enough nuts to satisfy Becky and for Del to take along.

As Del turned back to her homestead with the wagon and its basket of hickory nuts, Becky said, "Don't feel bad about what happened when you surprised Rachael. You will meet her again, and her children. Find enjoyment in each and every day. That's what I try to do."

"Ok, I'll try," Del said as she walked outside, grabbed her wagon handle and headed for home.

Her mind swirled with emotions and scattered thoughts. Walking quickly, and nearly home, she was surprised by Benj, who was seated on the chopping block as she reached the woodshed. "Hey—is someone chasing you?"

"You scared me!"

"Was looking fer ya. Yer Mama has Ori polishing furniture. Getting ready for Thanksgiving."

"Gee, do I have to smell that polish all night?"

"Not upstairs. Downstairs parlor."

"Well I may as well stay here and get everything ready for tomorrow's chores."

Benj shook his head and pointed to the house. "Yer Mama wants to see you. Let her know you are back."

Just then the porch door opened and Mama walked her way.

"Good, you are back. How was your visit?"

"It was fine. Becky and I picked hickory nuts."

"That's good. What did Becky tell you?"

"She knows who I saw when I fetched Phillip the time Benj had hurt his eye. I don't know much more than that—like why she visits the Conrads but not Becky. Rachael looks a lot like Becky. Becky is sad."

"Why, for goodness sake?" Mama asked sharply.

"Well, she showed me pictures of her mother's side going back to a great-great grandmother. Rachael is the last one. There will be no more to follow, Becky says."

"Hmm." Mama had a puzzled face.

Del waited, but nothing more was said. Del grabbed the wagon and said, "I'll do my chores."

"Don't stay too long. I have work for you in the house and must get ready for supper," was all Mama said.

Once the outside work was finished everyone gathered for a good evening meal around the supper table. Father offered grace. Mama spooned ladles full of turnips and potatoes with broth on each plate while Father cut slices of beef and placed them on a meat platter for each to help themselves. Ollie helped himself to the special portions made for him. After the dishes were washed and leftover foods put away, the house grew quiet. Mama, Father, and Benj took their cups of coffee and spent some time in the parlor.

Saturday night was quiet time for schoolwork or playing games. Phillip and Carol played a board game. Ori and Del washed dishes and placed them in the proper locations. Til was the first one to call it a day. Father said he would walk along with Benj to his home.

"Bed time!" Mama announced. "Ed and Benj will be here early tomorrow morning to help with morning chores so we can get ready for church. Your grandfather will take a couple of children to ride with him—it all depends who is ready when he gets here. Church will be well attended tomorrow, and we need to be early if we don't want to sit in the overflow part of the church. I'll have hot oatmeal for you tomorrow morning. That's always good on a cold day. Get a good night's sleep."

As Del climbed the stairs she heard the porch door open. Father was back. Benj was at his home. Del thought about the coat Benj brought along. Surely that coat belonged to one of his boys. She wondered if Phillip had tried it on. Was it the right size? If so, she expected she would see it the next day.

Getting Ready for Thanksgiving

On Sunday morning Father, Til, and Bill were up earlier than usual to complete the barn work and milking in order to attend special Thanksgiving services. It was the day of ingathering for orphans and the needy. Ed came in to help with the work usually delegated to Ori and Del. Mama was up early and she was already dressed for Sunday services as she prepared breakfast for the family. She greeted Del and advised her to dress warmly and check whether her morning tasks, plus Ori's, were taken care of. Even though Benj and Ed were there to help with the early work, Mama still wanted confirmation.

"Come back and eat, then change into your Sunday dress."

Del was back almost immediately. Every chore was done.

"Go see if Gloria is up, tell her to dress for church, and Carol too. I will tie one of my aprons around Carol so she won't drip any food on her Sunday clothes."

Del moved quickly. She saw the winter coat Benj previously brought along laying across the arm of the rocking chair. It was a heavy brown tweed coat and a plaid scarf laid alongside. This was surely meant for Phillip to wear. She heard Phillip coming down the steps and waited at the bottom. When he stepped into the kitchen, Mama looked very pleased. "Good! Benj will be here soon. You see that nice winter coat he brought along for you to try on? If it fits, we'll keep it for Sunday wear."

Phillip seemed surprised, but was silent as he reached for his shoes. "Benj is helping with the outside chores this morning. He will be in before long to see you," Mama said to him.

As Del climbed the stairs she thought the coat was one a Fronheiser boy once wore, perhaps both of them. She was not about to ask Benj about that. She still hadn't found time to search for those graves on the cemetery in town. As Del reached the top of the stairs she saw Ori. "Mama wants you to dress yourself and Carol for church before you come down." Ori appeared to not have heard Del, so she continued, "It's cold outside today. Mama says to dress warm."

"Oh shut up! I am busy enough. You never have to help anyone in the morning. Don't tell me what to do."

Del didn't listen to any more talk as she went to her room. She closed her door and moved about quietly and quickly as she changed into her Sunday dress. She returned to the kitchen with thoughts about Ori's unpleasant demeanor.

"Adelaide, you aren't listening to me," Mama said. "I want you to go back upstairs and bring my black cloche hat along down. You know where I keep it. I should have realized before now that Tilghman outgrew his winter coat. We have to take him along to Reading and get a warm Sunday coat for him."

"What are you doing up here again?" Ori said irritably when Del re-appeared upstairs.

"Not a thing for you to worry about." Del was surprised at her own remark.

Del returned with her mother's hat plus her own winter coat and a sweater. Benj was now inside, helping Phillip with breakfast. Del watched him pin a napkin over Phillip's shirt and tie.

Father looked at Til, "You take the Studebaker today. Run the engine to warm up a bit before you put it in gear so it won't stall. I will ride with your grandfather. Our things for the ingathering will go on the back seat of the Studebaker. But wait until we are all there to take things inside." Father looked around to all the children. "I want everyone to dress warm enough this cold morning."

"Must I go to church?"

"Yes Carol, you are too young to be alone at home. Besides the fires will burn out and this house will become cold. Best you go along."

Carol said no more as a dish of oatmeal was placed before her. Grandfather pulled in with his buggy, waiting for passengers to ride with him. Father and Bill hurried outside and climbed aboard.

"This is the last year for my father to donate his 12 pound box of butter," Mama whispered softly to herself.

The church was filling fast as the Heydts arrived by car and buggy. Mama always wanted to be seated in the church where she could see the altar. They settled into a pew, Carol next to Mama and Grandfather at the end where it was easier for him to settle with his stiff joints. Councilmen were unfolding chairs to place whereever they found space. Del found her mind wandering to thoughts about Becky and Rachael, and Benj and his sons. The Reifingers were seated across the center aisle close to the choir loft. She did not see Litzy and family, who were usually seated in pews close to the front of the church. That family must be seated in the overflow area.

Del's mind drifted to thoughts of Em. She didn't mention the Reifingers anymore, except for the time she saw they had company and two boys were playing pitch and catch in the street when her family drove by one Sunday on their way to visit city relatives. Del reminded herself she was supposed to sit in prayerful thought, remembering the Lord's goodness and blessings each day. But then more questions popped into her head. What about Hester's statement about Rachael? What kind of difficulty could be so unforgiving? Del was so caught up in her questions that she was startled when the time came for the closing hymn. It was one of Del's favorites that was sung in the original German. *"Nun danket alle Gott mit Herzen, Mund und Handen* [Now thank we all our God, with hearts and hands and voices]," Del sang along with the rest of the congregation. That melody would stay with her the rest of the day. She looked around at the service end, and there wasn't anyone from the Bickel family in church. That was very unusual.

After Sunday school, Father was waiting with the Studebaker and all of the children except Bill and Ollie piled in. The two boys rode back with Grandfather in his buggy. As always he was invited to stay for dinner. And as always, Grandfather decided to go home, but he again wanted Bill to join him. Mama rushed to fill a basket of food for their dinner meal. Del still wondered why Bill spent Sunday afternoons with Grandfather. She figured it had something to do with Grandfather no longer using the second floor or preparing to move. Bill was tight-lipped about time spent there. All Bill would say was 'he was going through things, emptying the attic and make sleeping arrangements on the first floor.' Bill was taking care of the animals and sawing firewood too. Back at the house, Del and everyone else headed upstairs to change clothes and take proper care that the same Sunday clothes would be ready for the next church service.

Dinner was quickly consumed and cleaned up. Mae and her father came to visit. Del knew the men were going to discuss township business since Mae's father was a member of both the township school and road Boards. They decided to look at Father's books and discuss things in the quiet of the living room. Ori grabbed the box that held her ball and jacks and cleared the kitchen table so she and Mae could play there.

"Carol, you stay inside and watch their game," Mama said. "Adelaide, you come with me, dress warm enough to gather more hickory nuts. We need to do this before the snows come." As Mama and Del left the porch the Shultz boys arrived carrying their Parcheesi board.

With that Del and Mama began their walk by the farm buildings and the sawmill where hickory nut trees stood on both sides of a loose stonewall where a lot of nut-picking had already taken place. "We'll go beyond the Printz home and walk the stonewalls back there separating the field from the forest. Leave the trees closer by for our relatives."

"Becky said they are welcome to come over to her backyard, there's plenty of nuts there the squirrels will never pick up." Del already knew why Mama chose to go picking hickory nuts even though it was bitter cold. While enough were shelled for a Thanksgiving cake, she needed more to last through the winter months. They entered the Printz property and continued toward the forest, also surrounded by a loose stonewall collected from fields over years of plowing. Del saw the path Grandfather took when he came through the forest on horseback.

"I suppose you know what I want to ask you."

"I guess more details about what Becky talked about?"

"Yes, that's it. What was your conversation about?"

"She talked about her family, starting with her great-great-great grandmother. She showed me family pictures. Goodness, I don't remember all their names. Becky is sad that her family line ends with Rachael. I don't know why that's sad. Rachael has Susanna."

"I never saw the pictures you are talking about."

Del said to Mama, "Becky said I will meet Rachael sometime. She also said I will discover in the passing of time changes are ever constant and not always to one's liking. I thought about that. I don't know what she means. And Benj ofttimes refers to things the way they used to be and aren't so anymore. Is that because he will never be a grandfather?" Del searched her mother's face.

"Yes, that is so. I think that the passing of their sons was the onset of Ann's illness."

"How old was his wife?"

"I really don't know. Too young to die."

"It must have been a sad, sad time."

"That it was. In time Benj became the same Benj he always was. What else did Becky have to say?"

"Her favorite food is the same as mine. Liver pudding, and cut raw onion on top of mashed potatoes."

Mama just smiled at Del.

They heard a car motor. That meant Mae and her father were leaving. "We gathered plenty of nuts this cold day. Let's head home. We have a good walk ahead of us." Mama and Del walked briskly. They entered the house as Ori packed her ball and jacks in the correct places in their box.

The Parcheesi board game was still underway in the side room. Ollie was splitting time between coloring books and taking his turn with Parcheesi.

"We won't be long anymore," the boys said. "The game is almost finished."

"Twas a good day," Father said, as all the neighbors left and he returned to his desk to make a notation of the day's activities. Benj entered the kitchen and slowly moved to the rocking chair.

Just then Bill walked in the door. "Sure is cold outside."

"You were warm enough?" Mama looked at Bill with concern.

Bill shrugged, "I walked fast. My feet are cold, that's all."

"You can take a rest," Father said to Bill. "If you really feel like it, you can help with the evening chores, but Ed will be here, and we're not doing anything extra this evening." Father, Til, Ollie, Benj, and Phillip dressed to go out to help with the evening milking and barn work. Ori and Del took care of their evening chores. Bill gratefully warmed his feet near the kitchen stove.

Supper was spent talking about the activities of the day. The meal consisted of sliced beef and hot gravy for sandwiches and the leftover turnips and potatoes. Ollie, of course, spooned out potatoes only. Ori proudly stated she won more games of ball and jacks than did Mae. The boys shared their results of the Parcheesi game. Ollie was excited that he won one game, although the older boys beat him more often.

"Adelaide," Father said, "I didn't hear anything about your day."

"We picked hickory nuts enough to last the winter. They are laying full enough that we could have used a small garden shovel to scoop them up."

The boys and Father entered into farm talk and what would happen next spring when once again very busy days would start. Carol was the first to climb the stairs for bed. Ori stated she would not return after taking care of Carol.

"Have a good night's rest," Del's parents said.

Til and Phillip said their good nights and headed for the stairs.

Del was next to follow. She was dying to ask why no one saw Litzy in church. She was always at large church gatherings. She thought about Bill's afternoons with Grandfather. How much paperwork did he have to clean up? Alone in her room she wondered about Becky's line ending. She drifted off to sleep thinking about the preparations for Thanksgiving and the many relatives who would visit.

Monday morning Del woke up thinking about Thanksgiving. The whole family was full of expectations and busy with preparations for the festivities later that week. As she stretched in bed, she thought about the Thanksgiving invitation her parents had given to Benj. He had been invited before, but declined since it was considered a family holiday by most. Both Mama and Father convinced Benj he needed to spend Thanksgiving Day with the family, for Phillip's sake. Phillip would be lost without his presence when the many uncles and aunts, sisters and brothers-in law, cousins, and their offspring would arrive. It would be busy and noisy as everyone talked about work, school, and neighbors with everyone else. Phillip could be very shy meeting the host of unfamiliar relatives who would be spending Thanksgiving with them.

If Mama could do enough coaxing, Phillip would know another familiar face if Grandfather joined them, but he probably would not spend the entire day. Benj, although a bit reluctant, promised he would be present, especially since ten children neither he nor Phillip ever met could present a situation that the little boy would find overwhelming. It was decided that he could always take Phillip to his house if the situation became too much for him. They could also spend time with the Conrads, taking the holiday food that Mama always gave to them. They could enjoy the entire meal, plus pastries and hickory nut cake, and Old Black Joe cake.

Nothing was said about Becky. Maybe Rachael's family would visit her on Thanksgiving Day. Del pondered something Hester had said during corn husking time, that it may be her fault Rachael no longer visited her mother. "What possible reason could there be for Rachael not visiting her own mother? I must ask Bill again if he heard anything about an unfortunate happening between Rachael and Hester," she promised herself as she got out of bed. It probably has something to do with Ed and Hester living next door to Becky. Their house sat further back from Becky's house, giving them a full view of all activity at the Funk place.

Del entered the kitchen already dressed for school. Mama was not around. She tied her apron firmly around her waist, then grabbed a flannel-lined jacket and headed for the outdoors where she met Ed walking toward the barn.

"You took care of the peeps already."

"Yep, you know peeps, like full grown chickens, are early risers. I will check again early afternoon, then about two hours before dark until they are fully adjusted to the new surroundings."

"No word about the silk mill?"

Ed shook his head. "That won't come back. Hester says new orders are fewer dozens than they used to be. She expects longer lay-offs coming soon," he sighed, then smiled at Del. "I took care of your work. Gloria's too."

"Thank you. I won't tell Ori it's done, she'll have to see for herself." Ed grinned as he walked toward the feed entry and pointed to the finger Taw-Taw had pinched. "I will tell you today what I did to that critter when he pinched my finger. I did exactly what Benj did to him. I dropped him in the rain barrel. But I forgot about the duck and went home. Before going to bed I remembered I left that miserable duck in the rain barrel. I came back and got him out of the rain barrel. He was all but drowned after all those hours in the barrel. Only his head was above water. Now don't you tell Benj I told you what happened. Benj doesn't want anyone to know the reason Taw-Taw never bothers him anymore. He steers clear of Benj, and now me too. Surprising that ducks have some smarts too."

Del thought, "This is something Ori must never know. She already complains about Ed being around and doing some of her work."

She nodded her head as Ed admonished her again, "Now don't you tell anyone, no one at all. Keep this to yourself."

"I won't say anything, but I'll laugh every time I look at that dirty old duck!"

Mama was in the kitchen and Phillip was seated on the couch when Del returned. Fritz was there because it was too cold for the dog to stay outside waiting for the men to return from the barn.

"Good morning, Phillip. I didn't see Benj his morning. I suppose he is in the barn somewhere."

"I expect he will be here before long," Mama replied. "You better check if Oliver is awake. Check on Gloria and Carol, too. Tell Gloria to dress for school. Her work is all taken care of."

Del started up the stairs.

Mama called after her, "If Carol is awake, tell Gloria to bring her along down."

Del returned and indicated everyone was awake.

Mama said, "Mornings will be like this for a while. Ed will be here each morning until his roosters no longer require special attention. He is already considering starting another set of peeps once these are fully underway. He will be busy if things go according to plan."

Mama didn't say anymore as Benj entered the closed porch. He lifted a hand to his brow as if he was saluting Phillip. "Cold out there this morning, no winds blowing. Best to stay here for a spell, 'til I know what kind of work is out there for us to do. Mebbe a truck ride today.

Mama nodded. "Woodie and Ed will saw firewood once the morning chores are completed. Woodie has lots of orders to fill. He will be busy for many days to come."

Benj settled down in the rocker and said to Phillip, "Takes time to saw a full truck load of wood. Much less time to deliver. Need to be ready fer that big Thanksgiving day, lots of company you and me didn't see yet." Benj pointed to Del. "Yer uncles and aunts are fine people. They speak the language—even that one from Philly."

Del sat up, "Does Ira live in Philly?"

Mama eyed Benj who looked chagrined.

"Ya and they don't much look like twins. But then look at you and Bill. Bigger difference there," Benj pointed out as he tried to deflect Del's question.

"Bill's hair and eyes almost match Father's. Bill doesn't have big freckles across the nose like I do. I wish I could make them disappear."

"Growing up problems," Benj muttered.

Mama just said, "Freckles can disappear."

Del knew Ori's complexion was similar to Mama's; she had been complimented for her rosy cheeks and fair complexion many times.

"Call the men to come in," Mama said.

Del wrapped a sweater around herself, opened the door and motioned to the group already heading towards the house, "Time to eat!"

At the same time Mama walked to the stairs door, opened it and called, "Time to get down here, breakfast is ready! Dress for school. Your outside work is finished." Ollie appeared instantly.

"It's good you dressed for school right from the get go," Mama stated with a wry smile.

Father was the last to be seated. Mama fried the first scrapple of the season for breakfast. Del and most of her siblings spread molasses on their scrapple slices. Ori was the only one to spread Mama's homemade ketchup on her scrapple. There was very little conversation around the table. Carol insisted on cornflakes for herself. Mama obliged.

"That will change as you get older," was Mama's only comment. She didn't want another picky eater in the household. Books were gathered and the children headed off to school as Father finished his morning coffee.

The Heydt children quickly walked to school. They didn't see the Gohos. There wasn't much talk from Bill or anyone else. Del figured everyone was considering all the aunts and uncles, cousins and second cousins who would be present for Thanksgiving.

At the first recess, Em suggested they go outside.

"Now tell me. When is that colored boy going to start school?"

"His name is Phillip," Del said slowly. "You know his name—you met him."

"You will be in big trouble if you bring him to our school."

"We don't have problems when we take him anywhere else. There are some . . ." Del paused. "You met Phillip. He's very nice."

Em looked annoyed. "You know when he's going to start school, you just won't say, that's all."

"I said all I know." Del remembered her parents telling her brothers and sisters not to get involved in any negative talk about Phillip. She shook her head, "Believe what you will. We all like him."

Dinnertime came and Del as usual ran or skipped half the way home. She waited for Bill where their lane met the cement pike.

"Do you think we'll have any trouble if Phillip starts school?" she asked her twin.

"I sure don't know. You worry too much. Wait and see for yourself," Bill suggested.

"You really aren't worried at all?" Del looked at Bill.

"We don't have trouble on Sundays anymore since that first time. I think our Pastor and the Squire took care of things."

"Grandfather, too, would speak loud and clear if he saw something he didn't like at church, but what can he do about school?"

Bill thought a bit. "Don't know for sure."

Del wondered why some people were so upset with Phillip's appearance in their lives. "He is just a little boy who needed help. Who could be against that?" she wondered.

After school Del changed into her work clothes and went outside to do her chores. Entering the feedhouse to attend to her daily schedule she heard Ed and Benj discussing coming winter activities. She overheard Ed say to Benj. "The colder the winter the more firewood is needed. Delivering it with a truck isn't nearly as cold as riding on a wagon like I did last year when I was laid off for a couple months. I hope Hester's job lasts long enough until I know if I can make ends meet with the rooster business. Woodie's city friend is already looking for other butcher shops that want a steady supply of roosters. At any rate I have something to keep me busy for the time being. What have you heard about Ira's search for Phillip's family?"

Ed and Benj moved beyond Del's hearing. She was sorely tempted to follow them but couldn't think of a good excuse to be around them to hear more. She and Bill suspected Isaac and Eva took photos of Phillip, and now that was more likely if Ira was conducting a search in Philadelphia, where Del now knew he lived. The rest of the evening Del turned over many questions and was relieved her parents didn't notice how quiet she was as she thought about what Ira might learn.

Tuesday morning Mama was making pie dough when Del came downstairs for breakfast. Nodding at Del, she said, thinking out loud, "I will get some of the baking done early, including a double batch of bread this day, enough to last through Thanksgiving. I'll also bake my Old Black Joe cake that takes thick curdled milk. That will be nice and moist on Thanksgiving Day. Everyone likes that cake. Perhaps I can make a double batch of sour cherry pies. The hickory nut cake can be made today as well."

Del interrupted her train of thought, "Are you making mince pies?"

Mama looked at Del and smiled. "The after dinner mince pie is a must. I'll put two pies in my extra large pie tins and make some regular sized and keep them in the cooler in the milkhouse for folks to take along home. Sam can't get enough of my mince pie. This time he can take one along home. Don't let me forget the sweet cake for dunking."

Del knew that there were also scrapple pans ready for every family to take along home. There were plenty of fresh and smoked sausages to share too. She thought about Lillie's journey into the forest to find her winter garden plants. If she went with Lillie, maybe she could be persuaded to search the forest next to the cemetery, giving Del a chance to seek out a couple graves. She asked Mama, "Will Lillie let me go along with her hunt for plants?"

"I know she doesn't mind if you go along. We'll see if she takes the same regulars along to help her carry things," Mama replied.

Mama talked about baking all the while the children helped themselves to breakfast. She looked at the clock, "Time to get yourselves off to school! Did you get enough breakfast?" There was no time to say yes or no as Mama immediately turned her attention back to the Thanksgiving baking preparations.

Til was the first to speak as they went outside. "I wonder if Mama talks to herself about all the things she needs to do all the time."

Bill grinned, "She has a list she uses year after year. Always makes sure she doesn't miss a regular Thanksgiving treat. But if this happens every day, I don't know."

Taw-Taw followed Ori quacking all the way. Besides Ori being slow by nature, the duck slowed her walking pace even more. Bill talked to Fritz, telling him he would need to stay in the barn on Thanksgiving Day. "I will visit you. You will be warm in the barn, just like last winter." Bill turned to Del. "You are quiet."

"There's a lot to do for one day's company. But like Mama always says, it's good to see all the folks gathered around the Thanksgiving table." She paused, then said, "I overheard Ed ask Benj about Ira's search. Ira lives in Philly and he's searching for Phillip's family."

Bill turned to her with wide eyes and said, "That explains the pictures!"

Del nodded excitedly. They didn't have a chance for more conversation with Bill as the Schultz boys met them, nor the rest of the day.

The first thought that popped into Del's mind on Wednesday morning was when Phillip would start school. Em kept pestering her with that question. The second thought was about Ira and what he was doing to search for Phillip's family. Del figured her parents would surely let the children know when Phillip would start school. Benj might be preparing the little boy to spend weekdays at school. Getting answers to the second question would be more challenging. Del decided she would ask Mama this morning if Phillip would be going to school soon, but there was no one in the kitchen to greet her. She checked the kitchen stove; no need to add wood. Mama probably went out for milk. The preparation for Thanksgiving would continue this day with more baking. Pie tins were ready to use. Mama's big oblong basket set on the white table. That meant Mr. Link, the local huckster, might be entering the lane today. She would know for sure once she walked by the mailbox on her way to school. When an old, faded red handkerchief hung from the mailbox handle, it was the signal for the huckster to stop by.

Mama entered with a two-quart jar of milk. "Help yourself to cereal this morning. You can make jelly bread if you want more to eat. Your outside work is taken care of. Go see if Gloria is up. Tell her to take care of Carol. I won't have the time to fuss with her this morning. Lots to do today."

Del moved quickly back upstairs and saw Ori. "Oh, I see you are up. You need to take care of Carol this morning, Mama won't have time."

Once again Ori woke up on the wrong side of the bed and irritably said, "I know that much. You don't have to remind me."

Del sighed, "Our outside work is taken care of too. Get yourself ready for school."

Surprisingly, Ori did not need to get in the last word, but only made a mean face at Del. Del turned and walked to her bedroom and changed into her school clothes.

"Is Gloria up?" Mama asked upon Del's return.

"She's up and Carol's awake. Ori really gave me a mean look."

Mama just shook her head. Del walked into the closed porch, grabbed Bill's overall jacket and said, "I will check if all the outside work is done."

"That jacket will disappear one of these days. . . ."

Del didn't wait to hear what more Mama was going to say. She checked, her chores had been completed. Taw-Taw was in the feedhouse. Someone had tied him to a basket half-filled with scrub cobs of corn.

"Oh-oh," Del thought, "Ori is going to see this. Taw-Taw should not be tied to a basket that could easily tumble on top of him and maybe hurt him. Ori will surely accuse me of this." Del released the duck and placed him in a chicken coop. If that huckster was coming, Taw-Taw could not be strutting around outside. The huckster's truck had heavy canvas flaps tied down on both sides; he carried bread and an assortment of freshly baked goods including cookies all year round.

He also sold fresh fruits and vegetables. He would lift the canvas with a pull rope on the side when parked at a customer's place. There were times Mr. Link had a large container fastened to the back of his truck body, packed with crushed ice to keep fish and oysters cold when they were in season. Del walked toward the henhouse door thinking about the times they had fresh-caught fish. Porgies or shad were the favorite choices for Mama, and oysters, too, when they were in season.

All the girls' chores were done. Del grabbed the egg bucket and carried it into the closed porch where Ori would grade and pack them in the double-sided egg carton after school today. Del wondered if the crated eggs went along to market with the new firm now collecting milk. It had to be so. "Where else would we sell our eggs?" she mused. Grandfather's retired creamery was now a collection area for the new operation. 'Dairy' was the new word for milk and cheese processing plants. It was another recent change in her young life.

Ori entered the kitchen with Carol, both dressed for the day. They sat at the table. Mama placed two boxes of cereal on the table with a stack of bowls. "Help yourselves to whichever cereal you like. I sliced bread and there's elderberry or wild strawberry jelly."

Ori silently helped Carol and the rest of the children settled into their seats and poured cereal. Benj and Phillip entered the kitchen—they had been outside somewhere. Father wasn't far behind them. Mama poured a cup of coffee and set it by Father's plate. Father's folded hands let everyone know it was time to pause. Hands were folded and heads bowed as a short table prayer was said in unison.

Breakfast was a combination of small talk with bits of information coming from Father. "Ed will be helping me all day. He'll deliver that load of firewood we threw on the truck just before dark last night. We have another load cut for delivery later today."

Father paused, "What's going on at school today?"

The children looked at one another. Bill shrugged his shoulders. "I may be alone today. Lester wasn't feeling well yesterday."

"How is it with the rest of you?" Father asked as he looked around the table.

Del decided it was the right time to ask her question, "I just want to know when Phillip will start school. Will he be joining us soon or not?"

Father shook his head and said, "Once Phillip is ready for school we will let you know. The legal paperwork takes more time than I thought. Who is asking?"

"Some of my friends are asking," Bill stated, and all of his siblings nodded their heads. Phillip was a source of speculation for all of them.

Father looked around at them and said, "Hopefully we can get him enrolled before the year's end or early next year." There was a sigh of relief as all the children gathered jackets and books to walk to school.

"Good morning! Last day before Thanksgiving," Maria spoke as both girls stepped in line with Del and Bill. All the Heydt children said hello. The Gohos asked what the family plans were for Thanksgiving. Ollie launched into a detailed description of the relatives, the number of visiting children, the food, and especially the desserts Mama always prepared. Del and Bill grinned at each other. Anabel asked if they took the day off from the farm.

"Oh no," Bill said. "We have to take care of all livestock, even on holidays."

"I hate that," Ollie said emphatically and added, "Everybody should have a day off once in a while. We have to do the everyday work whether it's a holiday or not!"

"So," Til spoke softly as he turned to Ollie, "You are not going to be a farmer when you grow up." There was no response from Ollie.

As the group reached the end of the lane, Del pointed to the faded red hankie tied to the mailbox. Bill nodded his head as the boys took off to meet the Shultz boys. Del and the Goho girls walked faster than Ori. They started skipping on the dirt lane, leaving Ori behind.

At school, Del waved to Em and ran up to say, "I asked my parents and they say that Phillip can't start school yet—they need more paperwork."

Em looked at Del and said, "I can't believe that it takes all this time to get the paperwork for your colored boy. You're just afraid of what will happen if he comes to school."

"You believe what you want. My father said he will let us know when Phillip starts school. Besides, everyone met him already and will welcome him to school," Del retorted. She decided not to argue with Em. "I'm going inside. It's almost time for the bell to ring anyway."

When recess time came Em turned to Del and said, "I know why you want to keep that a secret. I would be ashamed too, if I were you with a colored boy in your house."

"We are not ashamed. We aren't making a secret of Phillip being with us. After all, we introduced him to the whole school and to our church. We just need more paperwork completed for Phillip to come to school."

When noontime arrived, Del, Bill and Til walked back to their homestead together. She told Bill that Em was trying to pick a fight. "She thinks I'm keeping it a secret when Phillip will start school. She always calls him 'that colored boy.' What do the boys say?"

"No one said anything to me." Bill turned to Til, "You and Joe carried water this morning. Did you hear anything from him?"

"Joe never talks about anything. I know he doesn't like school," Til added.

"You mean he doesn't talk about anything at all?" Bill questioned.

"Just little stuff. Like it's too hot, too cold, or raining so we have to walk faster. That's it," Til stated.

The mailbox was minus the faded red hankie. Del wanted to see what Mama bought from the huckster. Taw-Taw strutted about as Del and her siblings passed by the woodshed. Benj was not there.

"It's getting too cold to sit outside," Til told Benj seated on the rocking chair. He nodded his head in agreement. Phillip was on the couch with Carol and her coloring book. Mama made a more substantial dinner. Del already knew the evening supper would be leftovers so they could be ready for the big Thanksgiving meal with guests. Del asked Mama what she bought.

"Look in the side room and you see for yourself," Mama said.

Four thin long loaves of hard-crusted unwrapped bread were covered with a worn tablecloth.

"I want to make sure I have enough bread. My two batches of bread may not be enough for so many people. Everybody likes my homemade bread and those loaves from the huckster. There's lots of work when you come home from school today, so don't waste any time."

"Em doesn't believe me when I tell her we have more paperwork to do before Phillip joins the school. I don't think she wants him to come," Del whispered to Mama.

"She will get used to it," Mama said in a matter of fact tone. "We sent in the necessary forms. He will start school there."

Em was not talkative at all during the afternoon sessions. Mr. Strunk extended Thanksgiving holiday wishes to all the students and dismissed them for a day of feasting. Del bid Em a happy Thanksgiving with her city relatives at the end of the school day. Em wished Del a good Thanksgiving too.

Mama was right. The evening after school was busy. Mama asked Del to place a good tablecloth on the round table in the side room. "Place plates, glasses, and utensils on the center for ten people. Make sure you cover the dishes and all that bread with an old tablecloth. Make sure everything is ready to seat the younger children, same as years before." Mama continued, talking to herself as much as to Del, "Lillie wants to be seated with the children. She is bringing two large crocks of potato filling. I will make one too. Eva will bring pastries including Woodie's favorite cottage cheese custards that I never make, and most likely lemon meringue or lemon sponge, and maybe coconut custards. My hickory nut cake is baked already. I need to bake tonight after supper." As Ori walked into the kitchen Mama ordered, "Gloria, your job is to clean up in the parlor and the side room. You have time later to check on your duck. He will be in his pen all day tomorrow."

As Del expected, the evening meal consisted of leftovers. There were fried potato cakes made from leftover mashed potatoes with raw egg, onions, and parsley added—always a favorite for Del. There was also rice soup with leftover beef roast—another of Del's favorite foods with a slice of buttered bread.

Father talked about Ed, saying he could use the truck for his rooster deliveries, but didn't know his way around the city and would most likely get lost without some help. "I told him he needs to watch out for one-way streets. I'll take him along next week so he can start learning his best routes."

"If Ed is going to use your truck he'll need a different weekday from you to make regular city trips," Til observed.

"True enough," Father said. "Township residents will probably ask him to shop for items they need or even ride along and do some shopping for themselves. I already expect that once I make weekly trips, I will not be alone, but in the truck I can only take two passengers along. The Studebaker allowed more passengers, but I figure to go to the city once every week, now that I no longer make the trip to Philly."

Del hoped she could take turns with her siblings to visit Reading more often.

"What are you thinking about?" Father looked at Bill.

"Nothing much. Just wondering what Litzy will say about Ed, once she knows he drives your truck to the city," Bill replied.

"I don't want to hear any talk about that woman!" Mama meant business.

Everyone was quiet for a moment, then Father resumed talking.

"Now Loll, don't worry. We fixed her talk about things with that banking business. She still says she sees me on Wednesdays at the bank with a strange woman. She doesn't know I don't go to bank anymore. When the bank president heard the rumors she was spreading he volunteered to pick up my deposits on his way to work. Everyone knows most all she says needs to be taken with a big grain of salt," Father laughed. "

Mama looked unconvinced as she said to the children, "It's time for bed. Tomorrow is a very busy day and you'll have more chores in the morning. Off to bed with you now."

Del now had an inkling of the problems with that busybody, Litzy. Her mind raced. Was she saying Father was unfaithful!?! What else did she say? This news also brought some clarity to how her parents interacted with others at church. Litzy was often seen huddled in conversation with some folks. That conversation always stalled as Father and Mama walked by. Now Del knew why Mama referred to Litzy as that busybody who spread vicious lies. With these revelations fresh in her mind, Del tossed and turned a while before finally falling asleep.

Thanksgiving day arrived. Del stretched in bed and thought about the tradition of relatives visiting from both Father's and Mama's side of the family this special time of year. There would be Uncle Sam, Lillie, their three grown children and their families, including eight grandchildren. Uncle Isaac and Eva would be there but had no children. Many of Father's cousins and their families lived in Allentown, Emmaus, East Greenville and other villages in Lehigh County. They would stop by during the afternoon hours. Mama's relatives were located in Berks County and a shorter distance to the farm. Uncles, aunts, and cousins, most residing in the Boyertown area, would visit after the noon meal. Jeremiah and Kate, Mama's uncle and aunt, would be present for most of the day. Even though the entire day was spent with the relatives there was never enough time to talk with every visitor.

There would be plenty to eat, and homemade ice cream and an assortment of cakes or pies to choose from. Mama's Aunt Lizzie always brought her ice cream maker. It was a larger container that hooked on to a belt and a motor to churn a larger quantity of ice cream in shorter time than the smaller hand cranked ice cream maker that Del's family used. They made the best vanilla ice cream! What a day to look forward to with lots of activities for all!

Del hoped she could go with her Aunt Lillie to the forest for her plants. In addition to the plants she collected, Lillie also looked for other little items to add interest to her winter gardens. A vacated snail house, part of a bird's speckled eggshell, an interesting colored pebble or tiny stone, a nut shell, or a colored bird feather could be placed in one of her arrangements. Del decided she would wear her weekday shoes so she would be ready to accompany her aunt. Lillie could spend the entire afternoon looking for her winter garden plants.

Father's relatives always arrived early enough to help with the morning chores. The women helped Mama in the kitchen. The children paired off with their cousins as they arrived and compared school projects and experiences. The girls always mingled in the parlor and the boys accompanied the men, who walked around outside, entered the barn and sheds to see the harvest of hay and straw, the grain bins, animals, farm equipment, and the changes that took place since they last were there. Father would show his new truck and would most likely tell his relatives about hauling animals to the city for farmers in the area. The menfolk would also examine the roof over the sawmill, another new addition, built so lumber and firewood could be cut on rainy days.

Del also thought about the telephone. That was another new item to show to relatives. She went downstairs to the kitchen. Mama looked up and down at her, but said nothing. She knew full well why Del had chosen to wear work shoes and not her Sunday best. "Help yourself to breakfast. There's a big pan of egg omelet staying warm on the stove. Did you see or hear anything from Gloria and Carol?"

"I know they are awake because I heard them talking. That's all."

"I suppose I'll have to keep an eye on Carol today so Ori can spend time with Doris. We'll put the card table in the living room where it can be seen and the little ones can do some coloring and play games or other activities. There will be hickory nut pickers, I suppose. Cousins on both sides always help themselves to hickory nuts."

Del sensed Mama was doing a lot of thinking as Ori and Carol entered the kitchen. Ori reached for Carol's shoes and helped her settle in for breakfast.

"Don't give Carol too much to eat. After you have helped yourselves, clean up what's left and take care of your dirty dishes. Adelaide, help me put the extra boards in this table. You know where the boards are kept."

The first to arrive were Isaac and Eva. Bill greeted them and then came inside and grabbed Mama's large basket to carry their desserts into the cold milkhouse. Mama had already cleared an area in the closed porch where desserts would be on display while the hot foods were cleared from the table. Next to arrive were some of Lillie and Sam's family. Del greeted Lucy, who was closest to her in age and her partner for the day, while writing the names of people on a ruled tablet paper as they arrived. Lillie carried in two pots of potato filling in a well-built basket.

Mama immediately placed one large pot in the oven. "That's all the room I have right now. The goose is browning nicely. I can set my roasting pan on top of the stove before long."

Bill asked if he should carry split wood into the house.

Mama shook her head. "Oliver knows that's the only thing he needs to take care of today."

The house became noisy when the last Allentown relatives arrived. Til took the Studebaker and went uptown to pick up Mama's uncle and aunt and father. It wasn't long before the Studebaker stopped by the walkway to the house and created a commotion. Some relatives were amazed as they watched Til help Grandfather as he unbent his upper body out of the car and stepped down off the running board of the car, which was his usual way to travel by car.

Mama hastily explained, "My father is much too stiff with arthritis and rheumatism to easily get in and out of the car. He stands on the running board and just bends the top of his body through the open window and holds on to grips Woodie fastened on the inside."

Everyone laughed.

Mama shushed them, "Don't you say anything or laugh about this that my father hears. I don't want him to decide not to come in the future.

A quiet spell followed. "I don't think that would pass in the city," a cousin stated.

"I suppose you are right," Mama agreed, "But I told him he would see his sister and get some homemade ice cream. I think he'd argue with a policeman if he had to."

Sure enough, there was Mama's Uncle Jeremiah, the shoemaker, and his wife Kate. Del guessed that Kate had the measurements for arm lengths and widths for the sweaters she must already be knitting for the family's gifts this coming Christmas and birthdays. Del thought about Mama's bright pink sweater. While it was too warm to be worn inside, it needed be seen sometime. Mama made sure her Aunt Kate would see the family's sweaters worn or laying around when she visited. Carol was the only one wearing last year's Christmas gift today.

Mama walked next to Del. "Look for my sweater," she whispered, "You know, the bright pink one. I don't know where I have it, but it should be easy to see. Maybe it's folded and laying in a drawer."

Del disappeared, first checking all the closets downstairs, then going upstairs she checked Mama's closet first and then bureau drawers. Returning downstairs, Del merely shook her head indicating she did not find it. Mama looked annoyed that the sweater was not found, but she was too busy to look for herself. She most certainly was not going to wear her sweater from the previous year, which now was shabby and faded from heavy wear.

There were cousins, uncles, and aunts on Father's side who arrived, and after saying hello, set out in search of hickory nuts. They knew where hickory nut trees stood along stonewalls in the fields and wanted to gather nuts while it still was light outside.

Mama checked her oven again and again, while tending to the pots and pans on the kitchen range. The warming enclosures above the stove were filled to capacity, as were the oven and stove top. Ollie watched the wood supply so Mama to could manage the fires and control heat in different parts of the large stove.

As dinnertime drew near, the men folk stepped inside, washed their hands, and made their way into the side room and parlor. The volume of conversation in the house became even louder. Much talk and laughter was heard throughout the house. Ori and Del placed plates and glasses on the children's table; the settings were already in place for the adults' table in the kitchen. Quiet ensued only upon Mama's call announcing the meal was served. Aunt Eva and Aunt Lillie were seated at the children's table, eager to assist the smaller children. Ori and Til, and their cousins of similar age were seated at the adult table. Benj and Phillip sat there too. Phillip sat between Benj and Til to help Phillip be more at ease. Phillip was told days before that he would see many children with the Allentown folks. Everyone was very friendly to Phillip and in turn, he solemnly shook hands with everyone he met and smiled shyly at the other young children. Uncle Sam said the prayer of Thanksgiving, after which Aunt Eva offered a children's prayer.

"Everyone must have known about Phillip," Del thought as she sat at the table with Lillie, Eva, and the smaller children. She could tell that he appreciated the shelter of Benj's arm as he met new people.

Quiet set in as everyone ate roast goose, potato filling, and many side dishes. Once the main meal had been cleared away, the children's table was set with cherry pies and custards for dessert. The adult table had the same combination of pies, plus an Old Black Joe layer cake with a rich dark chocolate icing and the popular hickory nut layer cake. There was also a warm mince pie for the adults. Many of them chose a small piece of cake, plus a small slice of mince pie with rum splashed on it- a must have. The adults lingered around their table sharing conversation and laughter over an extra cup of coffee.

Del and Ori washed dishes cleared from the children's table as the elders continued to talk. Everyone said they needed to take time to visit one another more often than just one time each year. Father replied that he had a farm and animals that needed attention each day, so all the relatives were welcome to visit any time. "We are at home most all the time, except the time we all gather that first Sunday in August in the amusement park," he announced. Del and her siblings all looked forward to that day.

Most of the older folk remained in the kitchen, some still seated at the table as it was cleared and reset for ice cream and dessert for a mid–afternoon snack. Til and his older cousins were instructed to get the equipment ready to start the ice cream making process. Del monitored where Lillie was at all times so she wouldn't miss the walk in the woods.

Grandfather, Aunt Kate and Uncle Jeremiah, the oldest generation, remained in the kitchen and talked while anticipating the arrival of their Boyertown relatives. That was the moment the ice cream-making would start. Vanilla and chocolate ice cream would be made at the same time. The bigger ice cream maker was used for the vanilla, and the smaller ice cream maker that Del's family had was used to make the chocolate flavor. Del was still washing dishes when Lillie brought the last dishes from the children's table and said she would not be going into the forest. "We haven't had sufficient frost as yet. The hillside behind my parents' farm gets the early sun and has lots of partridgeberries. They haven't turned red yet. There's too much happening today anyway. I want to talk to cousins I haven't seen for awhile. I will come once we have that first light frost."

Del was and wasn't disappointed. She would now be able to help make the ice cream. The ingredients had to be mixed and poured in the metal canister. All children old enough to turn a handle were expected to grab the hand crank and turn the blades within the metal canister to make ice cream. Once the ice cream hardened to a point that it was difficult for the children to turn the hand crank, the adults would step in.

Mama's relatives and cousins arrived shortly after one o'clock. That's when the vanilla ice cream production began. Menfolk started the engine and watched that the belt stayed on the wheels turning the paddles inside the ice packed canister. Aunt Lizzie brought plenty of her homemade candies. She placed an assortment of them on the children's table and gave each child a small paper bag to select the candies they preferred. A parent accompanied the smaller children. The older children made their own selection. Lucy and Del, plus the older group, waited until the smallest children completed their selection. Then Lizzie placed more and different homemade candies, which included chocolate covered nuts, Del's favorite, plus coconut candies and cordial cherries. Mama stressed that the Heydt children should not take too much since they would receive more candy on Christmas day. A pound box of mixed chocolate candies would be given to each child with perfect attendance at Sunday school.

Father's cousins stayed until the ice cream making was completed. Everyone had a second helping of dessert, this time with the option to add ice cream to the pies and cakes that had been placed on the kitchen table for everyone to enjoy. Phillip was intrigued at the ice cream making process and thrilled with the ice cream, getting a helping of both flavors and putting a big smile on Benj's face.

The Boyertown folks were the first to leave. Families gathered, shared their hugs and thanks for spending a most enjoyable day.

"We need to think about a time during the spring or summer for a get together without one family bearing all the work. How many of us do you guess visited here today?" Lillie asked Mama.

Mama replied, "Adelaide was appointed to write the names of each person as they arrived. I hope she wrote all the names down. I'll have that information in our Christmas card."

Eva and Isaac, plus a couple of Father's uncles stayed long enough to help with the evening barn work before they gathered their belongings to head for home.

After all the visitors left, the Heydt family gathered in the kitchen and relaxed. Benj seated on the rocking chair stated, *"Ich schaff mich selvered hame* [I'll work myself home]. See ya in the morning," he said as he looked at Phillip.

"One of you boys walk along home with Benj," Father instructed.

Til and Bill both obliged.

Mama stated, "All of you help yourselves with whatever you want to eat. Help Phillip if he wants anything. I am bushed." She stood by the stairs as she looked about. She opened the stairway door and headed for bed. It was exceptionally rare for Mama to be the first one up the stairs, but everyone knew she had been busy from morning to night getting ready for Thanksgiving.

Even Phillip seemed to understand. "Good night," he called to her.

"I'll wait until the boys come back, to see if they want any more food. I had enough. Tomorrow will be a slower day. We'll do the necessary work, that's all." Father looked around the kitchen. "For now you get a needed rest."

And so another Thanksgiving day ended. After the boys returned, Father checked the barn before he retired for the night as the children trailed up the stairs to their rooms.

"What a busy day!" Del breathed a sigh of relief and barely said her nightly prayer before falling asleep.

CHAPTER TWENTY-NINE

Mama Misses Her Sweater

Del woke up and as she thought about completing her early morning tasks, she heard Mama coughing downstairs. Entering the kitchen Del saw a small red and white box containing Bromo Quinine cold tablets on the table. The price stamped on the top sliding lid read one dollar and fifty-three cents. "Leave those pills alone," Mama spoke with a raspy voice. "I knew I could catch a cold, running in and out of the house all day yesterday without my sweater. I just don't know where that pink sweater could be." Mama wouldn't wear her old sweater on a day her Aunt Kate was visiting, expecting to see the latest knitted creation in bright pink.

"I hoped that if I went to bed early, I could possibly keep myself from catching a cold. That didn't work! Hopefully I can get rid of this cold before it gets any worse. It's good we have plenty of leftovers to eat, because I want to rest as much as possible. How do you feel?"

"I'm okay," Del replied.

"What did you and your cousin Lucy talk about?"

"Lucy has different subjects in school and has inside exercise classes. They don't have an outside recess. I know more about history and geography than she does. She won't get those topics until next year. She has first year science. I never heard of that class! We don't have those kinds of books in our school at all."

"No, but you get lessons about animals and plants and about weather."

"Lucy hopes she can come along with Lillie when she comes to look for winter garden things. Lillie says someone young needs to learn where to look for the plants she hunts every year. Summertimes Lucy helps Lillie with spring plantings and weeding the backyard garden and flowerbeds. Her older sister can't do those things. She gets hay fever as soon as she spends time outside in the spring. Her hay fever is bothersome enough when the last snows melt and trees and shrubs begin to blossom. It's much worse during the summer months. Lillie says she may outgrow it."

"True enough," Mama said. "Allergies are sometimes outgrown. My sister Carrie always suffered with hay fever every time she walked by a grass field. Once she neared twenty years old she outgrew that nuisance."

Del quietly helped herself to cold milk and cereal as Ori stepped into the kitchen. "I will eat breakfast first, than I will go upstairs for Carol, she's up. She can help herself in the washroom. She just takes a little longer."

Mama coughed and said, "Your outside work is taken care of, Adelaide's too, unless you need to see your duck. Ed took care of the chores." She sniffled and continued, "I don't want any of you catching cold. At noontime, I'll have food on the table but I will rest upstairs. If you children had found that sweater for me when I asked you to get it, I wouldn't have this cold. I don't know what my Aunt Kate thought. It must be upstairs somewhere. You can't miss that color pink. . . ." Mama was still talking as she climbed the stairs and the children could no longer hear what she said.

Del was surprised that Ori sat quietly as she ate breakfast and never spoke as she went back upstairs to check on Carol's progress. As Carol and Ori appeared downstairs the boys came in, ate breakfast with little talk, and then rushed upstairs to get ready for school.

Del saw the Gohos coming in the lane as she and her siblings walked outside.

"Where is Fritz?" Gordon asked.

"Fritz is on the truck. Ed's delivering a load of firewood. Fritz won't miss a truck ride," Bill chuckled. "He knows when the men are tossing cut wood on the truck, that truck is going somewhere."

"Do you think Fritz will stay on the truck if Ed is the driver?" Gordon asked.

"Sure he will. A truck ride is a truck ride, same as a wagon ride, no matter who does the driving," Til spoke confidently.

Em was waiting by the large rock as Del approached. They exchanged good mornings and Em said that they had a very good Thanksgiving. Del said the same. Em talked a bit about Sallie Reifinger. Her family visited with them yesterday and Sallie was fully recovered from the stove explosion. The mysterious circumstances of that incident had never been learned, although Em said Mr. Reifinger had some suspicions.

The beginners class was the first class to rise and take their turn on the one-step platform and discuss their reading for this day. Del thought about how differently her city cousins' school experiences were. No single room for all ages, an indoor gym, and science classes. She wondered if they had as much time to daydream as she did.

The afternoon held a double session on geography—not much to Del's liking—although she always got a passing grade. English, spelling, reading, and poetry were her favorite topics. Mr. Strunk stepped outside during the afternoon recess, which rarely happened. He walked around the building slowly, observing the different activities. The last afternoon session passed quickly. Mr. Strunk announced geography lessons to read and instructed them to study the folded map in their books. Her grade was told to take their geography books home and read as much of the Lewis and Clark expedition as they could. "We will stay with this subject until we have the chapters completed and then I will ask you to write your own report on their experiences." Shortly thereafter school was dismissed.

The Shultz boys and Del's brothers talked a bit before they parted. Fritz was waiting as Del and the Goho girls hurried their walk to meet the big dog. Del greeted Fritz and stroked his head as she spoke to him. "No wood delivery right now." Fritz let the Goho girls pet him too, which really pleased them.

"Good dog," Maria cooed.

Bill joined the girls and roughhoused with the dog before walking with them to the woodshed where Benj was seated, keeping an eye on Ori's duck strutting about.

"Is it safe to walk by that duck?" the Goho girls asked Benj.

"Alright. Fritz is here. No problem," Benj assured the girls.

Til briefly spoke to Benj before he and Gordon made way to greet Doll. Benj remained at the woodshed just a moment longer before heading toward the house. Mama wasn't in the kitchen, but snacks were on the table. Til would be pleased. Mama had a large dish of his favorite rice pudding on the table. That meant Mama spent time in the kitchen this afternoon, and Del thought that could mean Mama was feeling better.

The children completed their chores quickly and returned to the house. Mama stood by the stove, brewing a cup of tea.

"We have one more busy time before the slow winter months," Father stated as he took his seat at the table. "We will be busy when we butcher our beef for the rest of this year and the coming year. I hope that won't be a bitter cold day."

There were plenty of Thanksgiving leftovers for the family's supper, giving Mama more time to rest. She moved through the kitchen to the stairway. "You children help yourselves to things on the table. I will get myself to bed. See you in the morning." Mama's voice was still raspy but improved from the morning.

Ori and Del were in charge of cleaning up. Ollie begrudgingly helped with the dishes. Til and Father prepared to go outside for one last check. Benj said good night to Phillip and everyone else and Father said he would walk along with him, carrying a lantern. Del headed upstairs to read about the journey and hardships of Lewis and Clark.

Saturday morning when Del came down stairs for breakfast, Mama was feeling better but decided to stay inside to continue her recuperation. Benj wanted to walk to the upper end of town to talk to neighbors, who would be outside making necessary preparation of flowerbeds and gardens to withstand the cold winter months. These would be covered with fallen leaves or straw, with burlap bags or worn materials carefully laid on top as a protective cover from cold winter winds. Heavy stones were placed along the sides and corners of the bags as anchors from the winter winds. Benj wanted to learn why the Bickels weren't in church like they usually were. Mama was suspicious that their absence meant Litzy was up to no good. While Mama welcomed the effort, she wondered if Benj was dressed warm enough to walk the distance.

He nodded and said in the Dutch dialect, "My long underwear keeps me warm. I need more chewing tobacco anyway. I'll keep company with Billy, see if he knows anything and ask how his horses are doing."

Del thought about her grandfather. It was well known how much he cared for his horses and he spent time talking to them every day. She pictured how he would open the stable door and allow the horses to enter their fenced-in area in the barnyard to romp about and breathe in the cold air while getting a drink of fresh spring water. That spring had a constant flow, spilling into a deep gutter that wound its way to a creek that ran through Rockland Township and into a connecting township. The horses would run and romp about in the brisk cold air while Grandfather cleaned the stalls, added clean straw, and placed oats and hay in the manger for the horses to nibble on throughout the day. Then he'd reopen the stable door for the horses to return to their stalls. Grandfather would spend more time currying his horses and talking to them throughout the day. Mama's conversation brought Del out of her reverie. Now she and Benj were talking about Grandfather's cat.

"True enough," Mama said. "You can be sure my father is there quite early, it's not his habit to sleep late. He will carry something for his cat. I think he will spend as many hours in his creamery building as he always did. That building is like a second home to him. However, I hope he has enough sense to stay in his house on icy or snowy days. For sure he needs to curry his horses and provide food and water for them, and see to it that they get a little exercise. It would be nice if he'd get a telephone. The line goes right by his home and the creamery. He wouldn't have to make conversation, just ring our number at a particular time, hang up and we would know he is up and about." Mama sighed and then continued, "Check if he dressed warm enough. And if you hear anything about the Bickel's, I want to know."

Benj nodded his head, indicating he would do so.

"See ya later, Phillip, too cold fer ya to walk the distance. Woodie can bring ya along when he drives his truck uptown this morning. Fritz too, enough room fer all."

"Better not walk home. It's much colder when the wind isn't on your back," Mama cautioned.

"Look fer me in Billy's creamery," Benj said as he buttoned his coat, pulled his ear flaps down and placed his scarf securely around his neck, his coat collar up for added protection around his neck from cold blowing winds.

Mama turned to Del and Phillip. "We may have a very harsh winter. The woolly caterpillars had thick coats and it's early to be this cold. Benj knows how to dress and stay warm and the exercise is good for him."

Del paused to ask, "What will Benj do when it's his birthday time? He hasn't mentioned that for a while."

"Yes, I know, and it's your birthday too. We will have a big birthday party on that Easter Sunday."

"I can hardly wait for the most important day of my life. 'Only once in a lifetime . . .' Benj says." Del reflected that there were three birthdays to celebrate, but Bill and Del counted many fewer years than Benj. He would be seventy-five years old on this upcoming birthday.

Mama smiled and said, "Dress warm enough, do your outside work."

Del left to attend to her morning chores. On her way to the feed-house, she thought about Mama's comment about the Bickels. It was a mystery why they weren't at the ingathering church service. Litzy never missed important ceremonies like that. Del saw activity in the lower part of the barn. Cows and horses would be fed and released to the outside barnyard. The watering trough had a bit of ice around its rim. It was fed by a spring that flowed freely into the trough. The spring ran constantly and that meant the trough never froze over. Cattle could always drink water from it no matter how cold it was. That trough overflow formed a little stream that flowed behind the woodshed, under the wooden bridge, and along the front of the yard by the weeping willow tree. Del's thoughts drifted again to Easter and the once in a lifetime alignment of their birthdays. "What would her and Bill's next birthday be like?" she asked herself. Mama said the Reifingers and Benj's friends and remaining relatives would be invited to their party.

Del's mind returned to the Bickels. Last Sunday was the ingathering service at church when everyone donated food for the needy. Litzy would not miss a chance to show off her basket, rounded high and covered with cloth, while looking over the tables to check if she had the largest and most attractive contribution of food for the indigent. The church was filled, yet no one saw that woman, nor any of her family. Mama would not allow any talk from her family concerning the Bickels. It was difficult for Del to get more information about them.

Their neighbor Ed was just as inquisitive about the missing Bickels. He heard talk of someone in need of help but wasn't certain if it was them. Grandfather might be in the best situation to know why the Bickel family did not attend church. He could see the Bickel home from the icehouse located behind the creamery. But Del already knew that he was not one for gossip. 'It wasn't good for business' Mama said.

Del knew Grandfather's friends liked to stop by to chat awhile and taste his latest wine. Even though Prohibition was in effect, he made wines in a windowless corner room of the creamery. She heard that a local favorite was his blackberry wine. Del remembered seeing his purple fingertips and deeper purple under his nails when he picked blackberries. All the children knew Grandfather made many wines from a variety of fruits and berries. He gave his wines to family and trusted friends as gifts, and only mentioned he would appreciate the return of the empty bottles.

At dinnertime Benj returned, and without saying a word he merely shook his head, indicating he learned nothing. "Had a good visit with Billy. No news about any happenings."

The evening meal consisted of stuffed pig stomach with diced potatoes and sausages cut to the same size as the diced potatoes, a meal that needed more time to prepare. Mama wanted to see how Phillip would react to this unusual meal when it was served. There was no need to fret. Phillip eagerly spooned food onto his plate and ate that and Mama's pepper cabbage without hesitation.

"This meal comes from all the work we did butchering and gardening this year," Father explained to Phillip. Phillip cleaned his plate, and Mama was very pleased. Benj spent a little time after supper talking about his morning visits and said he was glad to ride home with Father. When the evening was drawing to an end, Til and Bill walked along with Benj to his home to see his safe return home.

Sunday came and the children attended Sunday school. There was no snow on the ground but it was very cold outside. Father allowed Til to take his siblings to church with the Studebaker. As was the new custom, Bill left with Grandfather and spent the afternoon there. That afternoon the Shultz boys visited and everyone played board games. The youngest son, Elton, came with his older brothers to play with Phillip, who was about the same age. Phillip's shyness disappeared as he played marbles. He laughed and really seemed to enjoy the competition of sending a marble shooting from his thumb to hit other marbles scattered about on the carpeted floor. He performed better than most of his competitors and was congratulated on his wins.

Mama was feeling better, but still distanced herself from the activities taking place. There was no company for the girls. Benj and Father cracked hickory nuts on a board. Del and Ori used nut picks to separate the nutmeats from the shell. Everyone would enjoy eating hickory nut cake and cookies throughout the winter months.

Monday morning Mama was feeling better. Her voice was still a bit raspy, but she was ready to take full control of matters in the house. She greeted Del, "I have oatmeal for you this morning—it's cold outside. That will warm you up a bit before you go outside and keep you from catching a cold. You needn't bother with outside work. I also have hot sage tea. I added sugar, you may add a little butter if you like.

As Del's siblings entered the kitchen Mama turned to them. "I'll have warm food at dinnertime." She pointed at Ollie, "Wear your sweater underneath your coat. The school room could be chilly this morning." She turned to Del and Ori, "Keep your sweaters handy. Your new caps, scarves, and gloves will soon be here. Wear last year's things until Christmas. My father, Uncle Jeremiah, and Aunt Kate will spend Christmas day with us. It's only a couple of weeks away now and you will have the matching pieces to your birthday sweater for Christmas as always." She shook her head. "I still didn't find my pink sweater. I can't figure when I last wore it. I didn't leave it at a relative's house, it would have returned by now. I don't know what I will say to Aunt Kate if I don't find that pink sweater."

"Aunt Kate must be knitting all year long. She makes four pieces for each of us every year," Del added.

Mama replied, "She has more time than I to knit or crochet since they never had children. Aunt Kate also has quite an herb and root garden, She has many kinds of teas with medicinal value. People come from the city to buy her herbs and teas to ease aches and pains. Her concoctions quiet many coughs and cure bellyaches. You never see a weed in her garden."

Mama continued talking about her relatives all the while the children ate their oatmeal and got ready for school. "Off to school, behave yourselves," were her final words.

The Gohos were hurrying their pace and Del walked slowly for them to catch up. Fritz didn't like that Bill decided to walk with Til. He ran ahead and stopped in front of Bill. Bill turned and waved his arm, signaling the rest to slow a bit as the Goho children were catching up. It was too cold for much conversation, and Del met Em inside the school building. Em was quiet this day. Her family didn't visit their city relatives. All she said was that she had a boring Sunday. As usual, Del skipped by herself on the dirt lane at dinnertime. She waited with Fritz by the mailbox as Bill ran to join them.

"Fritz, this isn't the worst of the cold weather. You know times will come when we will run home on really cold days." As the children approached the homestead they saw Uncle Sam's car parked by the walkway. Del figured Lillie was here. She was sure when she walked by the pump and saw a flat box of partridgeberry plants plus another with nutshells, a few brightly colored small leaves, and some plants with tiny white flowers. Lillie also found a finely detailed small branch that resembled a tiny bare tree.

Uncle Sam walked up to Del and said, "I see you are looking at items Lillie collected today. We'll be back this weekend, if the weather is suitable, to look for more winter garden plants. She knows you want to go with her. She wants to try the forest on the Printz property, it's a new forest for her to search."

Del was very glad to hear that. She realized it was a new clue about the Printz property. As she headed indoors, she thought to herself, "Did Grandfather really buy that property or not?" It would explain why Lillie considered it permissible land to search for her plants. She had to ask Bill again just what he did at Grandfather's house on weekends and if he saw property deeds.

The family gathered around the supper table that evening. Benj said goodnight after the evening meal. He paid special attention to Phillip as he prepared to walk home. "Will see ya in the morning. My house will still be warm when I get there. Made fire in the cellar furnace this afternoon." Til and Bill both walked along with Benj to see that he got safely in his house. Del decided to take her geography book upstairs and read a bit before getting under the covers to sleep.

CHAPTER THIRTY

Til Gets His Coat

THERE WERE JUST three more weeks of school before the Christmas holiday, Del realized upon waking up. Father still had to confirm a date with the butcher for the final butchering of beef shortly after the new year. The relatives needed to be notified. Mama would address postcards to inform them. As she lay in bed, she recalled that Til still did not have a warm coat fit for Sunday wear. He would go with Father on Thursday when he made the weekly trip to the city. She wished she could take that trip too, just for the novelty of missing a day of school.

The children headed off to school after chores and breakfast. Del was intent on learning why Bill spent Sunday afternoons at Grandfather's house. He might know if Grandfather bought the old Printz home and planned to move there. "That sure would be nice," Del thought. "Grandfather would be close by and Mama wouldn't worry." The Printz house had a cellar, and maybe he could continue to make his wines there. There were so many things Del wanted to know! What could be so secretive that Bill doesn't want to talk about those Sunday afternoons? All Bill said was how spacious the attic was compared to their home attic. He carried boxes and boxes of paperwork for Grand-father to look through.

Del turned to Bill as the twins walked the lane with Fritz. "Tell me about the papers Grandfather looks at when you are at his place."

Bill was willing to talk, which surprised Del. "He chooses the papers he wants to keep and those he doesn't want. I set those on the back porch where Grandfather can easily take the paperwork he no lon-ger wants and burn them. After that I go back to the attic and bring more boxes down for him to go through," Bill said. "I saw bills for gold watches he bought for Mama and his other daughter and his wife. He wanted to keep those. Tears came to his eyes when he saw the receipt for them and a gold pocket watch for himself. You know Mama wears the gold watch she got from Grandfather only when she goes to church or visits relatives on weekends. He told me, 'My wife and old-est daughter died of diphtheria. My one remaining daughter has those gold watches. She'll know what to do with them.'"

"I know he has a long gold chain attached to his gold pocket watch. I saw that already," Del added.

There was no talk for a spell. "What is he going to do with that watch and chain? Do you think he will give it to Til?" Del asked.

Bill looked uncomfortable and just shrugged. There was no more time for talk as they reached the school grounds.

That day and the next passed by without any new answers to any of Del's many questions—nothing about Phillip's identity, why the Bickels weren't in church, confirmation of who purchased the Printz farm. It was a most unsatisfactory week so far. Thursday came. It was Father's day to go to Reading and deliver three calves and two pigs to the abattoir. Mama was finally feeling better. "I think I have this cold under control," she declared. She instructed the children, "Your father talked to your teacher and he knows Tilghman will not be in school today. Don't mention why he's not there. I don't want people thinking we don't look after our children here."

There would be no perfect attendance for Til this year, Del realized.

Mama continued talking to Del while she set the breakfast table. "When they are in Reading they can get more Bromo Quinine tablets for me. We should always have enough cold medication on hand." Mama was still bothered she hadn't located her pink sweater. "I can't think where it could be." She shook her head and looked both annoyed and puzzled.

Del wore her good sweater under the flannel-lined overall jacket Bill had outgrown as she made her way to the outside. She saw Ed leaving the feedhouse. She figured he had done most of her work this morning and probably did the same for Ori, but nevertheless she needed to check for sure. Del looked around the feedhouse. There was the empty corner where the brooder was usually stored. The brooder would return once spring arrived for that was when Father would need the brooder for the baby chicks he always received—a mix of roosters and egg-laying hens. Glass eggs rested on a corner shelf. A floor scraper hung between two nails; it was used every spring and fall to scrape the cemented henhouse floor clean of all the hardened grit that accumulated between those times. That was a dirty and smelly chore. Ed had completed all the work that Del and Ori did in the morning. Del gratefully returned to the house to change into her school clothes and eat breakfast.

The children left for school. Em waited outside and noticed that Til wasn't with his siblings. She immediately asked, "Is Til fetching water this morning already?"

"Goodness, no one fetches water before school starts. Til will miss school today. He is going to the city with my father. Teacher knows that."

"Did he say that was alright?"

"I guess so, Father talked to our teacher about this."

"Is he allowed to do that?"

"I guess so," Del replied. "If not, my parents wouldn't take him out of school."

The morning sessions went well for Del. She correctly answered the geography questions and had time to listen to a higher grade's recitation of a poem. She could have accurately recited it too after hearing it repeated several times. The walk home for dinner was uneventful. Fritz was mournful that the truck took off without him—no truck rides that day for him. Bill and Del tried to console the dog as best they could and gave him extra attention while they ate their noon meal.

Em looked to see if Til was with the Heydt children once they returned after the dinner hour.

"The whole day gone!" Em exclaimed as Del returned.

Del merely nodded her head.

"Will your brother be back on Friday?" she wanted to know.

"Of course," Del replied as she walked over to the chart with all the organs of the human body on display and studied it.

"Why do you stand right in front of that chart and look at it? It's scary to look at."

"We need to know about all our body organs and their functions. Ori's class is studying them right now, she complains about that too," Del replied.

"Why?"

"I don't know. I don't ask her."

At the end of the school day, Del and Fritz waited for Bill as he came running to meet them and walked the lane together. They called out and waved when they saw Til dressed in his work clothes as he walked by the pigpen toward the sawmill.

"I can't wait to see his new winter coat," Del spoke.

"Me too," Bill agreed with a grin. "I'll probably wear the one he outgrew sometime soon."

"True enough," Del agreed.

"That doesn't happen to you. You never wear Ori's things."

"That's because her clothes never fit me. She is chubby. Mama doesn't allow me to say she is fat. Aunt Lillie calls me the skinny rail."

"I'm the same as you."

"Do you wear all of Til's outgrown clothes? I never really took notice of that," Del remarked.

"No. Some clothes come from our Allentown cousins. My trousers and overalls are usually new."

"How was school today?" Father asked as the children stepped into the kitchen.

"Ok. Where is Til's new coat?" was the common refrain from all the children as they stepped into the kitchen.

"We found a coat, but it needs to be altered. The sleeves aren't long enough. I'll pick it up next week when I go to the city again, and then you can see it," Father promised.

Mama was glad a warm coat was selected for Til, but fussed that Til would miss another week of church. She thought Father should have looked for another shop that might have had a coat that didn't require alterations. Father only went to one men's clothing shop.

Til described the county courthouse to his siblings, "The inside has a lot of shiny marble, really fancy. It's big too. There were lots of folks all dressed up like they were going to church." Del could tell she wasn't the only one a little bit jealous that Til had the first trip with Father to Reading. She could only imagine how that fact infuriated their older sister, Ori, who always insisted that as the oldest, she should be the first in everything.

Til said it was interesting to see the abbatoir where Father delivered the animals for slaughter and watch his usual city routine. After hosing off the truck they went to the County courthouse to take care of errands for his own business and for neighbors. After that they shopped for his coat on Penn Street and then drove to a large warehouse to pick up merchandise for Drumheller's store and neighbors. Til said "Father had a list that Drumheller gave him. It took a while to get everything on that list, but once we had it all loaded in the truck, we headed back. It took some time unloading it at the store too."

Del knew that Father was glad that the local grocers heard about his truck. They always waited for a once-a-month delivery to their grocery store, but now they could receive the ordered merchandise on a weekly basis. Father accepted that business immediately. It was one more opportunity to make extra income on the city trips—coming and going.

All the children wanted to go to Reading with Father. Mama had said to them, "By late April or early May, depending on how many snow days we have this winter, you will be able to take turns and ride with your father. You'll have chances to do that all summer long too."

The weekend came. Because of the cold temperature, Father took the children to church in the Studebaker, except for Til. Phillip also stayed at home. Grandfather was too stubborn to accept Father's invitation to pick him up and take him along with the children to services. Mama suspected he didn't want his church friends to see his unique way of traveling with the Studebaker, and it would have been very cold on his arthritic joints. Bill was assigned to watch for Grandfather from the church vestibule. After the service Bill would get the horse and buggy and offer a helping hand for Grandfather to climb aboard. Afterwards he rode along with Grandfather to his place. Del was still puzzled about the Sundays Bill spent at Grandfather's house. Til, being the oldest boy, would have been the logical choice for this duty. Why Grandfather requested Bill was a mystery to her. He must have collected a lot of business records for all the years he operated his creamery to need Bill's help every Sunday.

The day grew colder with strong winds blowing constantly. The weather kept visitors away and the day was quietly spent playing games and catching up on schoolwork. The children took turns playing checkers with Father. He usually won, although he'd let the youngest children win. Jigsaw puzzles were made on two separate tables. The smaller table in the side room and the folding card table were used for schoolwork and poem memorization. Mama worked with Carol and Phillip on letters and numbers. It was obvious that Phillip had some schooling as he was familiar with the alphabet and recognized a number of basic words. Father took the truck to go to Grandfather's house and bring Bill home. Bill was wearing his Sunday best and would have to walk home against strong blowing winds. His Sunday clothes weren't made for such bitter cold winter days.

When Bill returned with Father, he said to Del, "I'm really glad I didn't have to walk back when it's this cold."

Del asked, "What did you do today at Grandfather's house?"

Bill shrugged and said, "Nothing different than before. There are a lot of boxes in that attic full of ledgers, receipts, and other papers. Most of it goes out the door on the porch to burn."

Monday morning Del met Ed on her way to the feedhouse.

He greeted her, "Mighty cold for these early days of wintertime. We need to get used to colder temperatures all over again."

"Do you think we will have lots of snow this winter?" Del asked.

Ed shrugged and said, "I can't tell. For you young ones though, it really doesn't matter. More snow means more sledding. You can stay at home, don't need to go anywhere or do anything. It's no fun at all for us older folk. Us men have to shovel open lanes where people live. Those snow plows only clear the main roads."

"But," Del said, "I still didn't go with my Aunt Lillie to make winter gardens with all kinds of things we find in forests."

"You mean those things they call sweat jars?"

Del thought for a moment and said, "I suppose you are right. People have different names for them. Some call them terrariums. My aunt makes lots of them."

"You have to show me one after all the work is done, so I can see if it's what I think it is," Ed replied.

"Oh, I will. Aunt Lillie always gives Mama one for letting her search our woods too."

"It's time you come in to eat. Soon time to go to school. Where are the boys and Gloria?" Mama called.

Del ran back inside. All the children converged in the kitchen at the same time. Mama was ready. She had scrapple ready to serve and hot tea to drink.

"Eat, then change into your school clothes. It's cold out there, but may warm up a bit by dinnertime. Behave yourselves!" With that said, she went upstairs and Del heard her working on her sewing machine.

Del and Bill, with Fritz between, walked the lane together. Ori followed slowly, although the cold temperatures prodded her to move faster. Anabel, Maria, and Gordon ran to catch up to them. Bill and Del kept walking, but slowed down for them to catch up, each resting a hand on Fritz. The Gohos started talking about Christmas. They wanted to know what happened at the Y Farm. Del and Bill exchanged glances. Some things were always the same, but there was always a surprise or two.

Del answered, "We always get matching sweaters, gloves, scarfs, and hats that our Aunt Kate knits. Grandfather gives each of us a silver dollar and an orange. But the rest is a surprise. We also have a big dinner with roast goose or duck, depending on how many relatives come."

The Gohos shared their plans for Christmas festivities and what they hoped to receive for Christmas. That conversation kept them going all the way to school. During the school day, Del was bored. She not only knew her class's material, but since she heard the work Ori and Til's classes did plus their work at home, she was very familiar with that too. She thought about a conversation she had on Sunday with Mama about Bill's visits with Grandfather. Mama didn't know exactly what Bill was doing for her father either, and was very interested to learn what Del knew.

When Del relayed her news, Mama nodded and said, "He doesn't climb steps, so that makes sense. His bedroom furniture was moved downstairs to the living room several years ago." Mama knew the attic held quite a collection of boxes filled with paperwork when she still lived there. She said her father saved every slip of paper his hands touched, including every carbon copy of all the milk receipts with recorded amounts and the names of the farmers. There were boxes and boxes of paper. She said, "It must be boring to go through all of that, I'm certain William sees receipts for farmers who are long gone and buried. Does William say anything else?" Mama looked closely at Del.

Del just shook her head no. "No, I had to beg him just to tell me what I told you."

Del sat at her desk and thought about another comment Mama made to Father. She overheard Mama say, 'It's better for Til to carry all those boxes from the attic for my father to look through.' He was older, but Bill was strong enough to carry boxes. The more Del thought about it, the more puzzling this recent Sunday routine was. Even if Grandfather had bought the Printz property and planned to move there, Til could have helped him reduce his paper files. It also bothered Mama, and that meant Grandfather hadn't explained his reasons why Bill was the one there.

The week proceeded quietly, and then Thursday came, Father's day to go to Reading. This time he had three pigs and a young heifer to take to the abattoir. He had to pick up grocery items for Heimbach's store. But most importantly, Father would pick up the much-needed Sunday coat for Til.

Mama was still focused on that winter coat. "It's my fault," Mama said, "I knew Tilghman was growing like a weed this summer and outgrowing his summer clothes. I should have realized his winter coat would be too small. I bought bigger work overalls and shirts, but never gave a thought to a coat for him."

The children ran home at dinnertime. Mama had prepared a hot beef and noodle soup for dinner. "That's the last piece of beef until we butcher. Since this is a run-around day, your Father will see if he can find the butcher and make arrangements for that."

"I just can't wait to see the color of Til's new winter coat!" Ollie said excitedly. "I am wearing his old brown coat now. I like it, it is really warm."

"Yes, that was Til's coat, but it was too long for you. Lillie did the alterations and she did a fine job. It looks nice on you."

"My Sunday gloves match my coat. Were those Til's too?"

"No. Lillie used the extra material she cut from the bottom of that coat to make a pair of lined mittens. Not many boys your age have fancy lined mittens for cold winter days to wear. You should be proud to be wearing tailor-made clothing." She continued, "Your Aunt Lillie worked in a glove factory and then a coat factory. She can make or alter most anything as long as she has a good sewing machine." Mama paused and looked sad. She said, "I used to sit on the floor and move the treadle with my hands for my mother to sew when I was still quite small while she was recovering from an operation. She died when I was sixteen." She dabbed a tear at her eye. "My older sister also died then—both had diptheria. She had a two-month old baby who also died from it, along with her husband, and all within two weeks. Only your Grandfather, my brother Homer, and I survived that dreadful disease."

Bill asked, "Why don't we see Uncle Homer and his family?"

Mama said, "My brother has a family and a large farm, so just like us, he has animals that require daily care. That's why we rarely see them."

Ollie interrupted, "Are we going to die from diphtheria?"

Mama smiled and said, "No, there's a new vaccine and we made sure you all received it when you were old enough. Now it's time for you to get back to school."

On the walk back to school, Del thought about how one disease affected her Mama's family. That must have been quite a shock to Mama to lose her mother, sister, brother-in-law and their young baby. Del didn't even know if it was a boy or a girl. Was the baby buried with Mama's sister? She remembered Bill talking about how Grandfather had tears in his eyes when he saw the receipt for those gold watches. It must have hit him hard too.

All of these questions, and not enough information about them, Del thought.

The school day ended and the Heydt children hurried home to complete their chores. Del fed the pigs, just a couple fewer after the butchering, and set water out by the henhouse for Ori. She headed back to the house and found Mama in the kitchen. Mama was in a reflective mood as she prepared the supper meal. Del suspected she was still worried about what Grandfather would do now that he sold the creamery. She talked about Grandfather, which suited Del just fine because she had just been thinking of him. "My father is living to a good age. I think he developed his arthritis and rheumatism from those trips to Philadelphia during the cold winter months with horses and sleigh to deliver his butter. He got a better price there. He had near frozen feet and hands many times on those trips. It was a two-day trip back then. But that was a good decision. He accepted all the milk local farmers could produce. The creamery was the township's main business. His butter was prized in Philly for its quality." She sighed, "It's been a good life for him, but he suffered heartache enough during his lifetime." She started humming one of her favorite hymns, a signal to Del that she was finished talking.

That evening the family was eager to see Til's new coat. He brought it out of the closet. It was navy blue with brass buttons. It was a bit large, but everyone was sure he was still growing and would fill it out in no time.

"That coat is just dandy," Benj said. "Would like one like that fer myself. Ya could be a Navy man. Girls will turn around and take a good look at ya," he teased. Til just blushed.

The remainder of the evening was spent quietly completing school assignments. Del helped Ollie with his spelling tests. Phillip and Carol worked on a puzzle. Bill was the first to say he was going to bed. One by one the other children headed upstairs.

Arriving home from school for dinner on Friday, Del learned that a postcard had arrived stating Sam and Lillie would be there early Saturday. Mama gave the card to Del to read. *Hope things are fine and running smoothly all around the farm. Sam will help my brother with anything he has in mind this day. Will try the forest I never visited before. Adelaide and William are welcome to go along. Sam had a cold and cough. All that is gone now, but needs to take it easy. Hope your family is well. Did Tilghman get a new coat? See you Sat. A.M.—Lillie*

Mama said to Del, "You can go tomorrow, but don't make the buckets heavier than you can handle. Take your wagon along. Leave it as close to the forest as you can." Mama spoke hurriedly, while Ori was outside visiting her duck before coming back for breakfast. "Take this postcard and slip it under the embroidered bureau cover in my bedroom. Don't let Gloria see it. Don't tell anyone else. Not even William."

Del said "OK," but wondered why Bill couldn't know about this invitation to join Lillie on her hunt for plants.

The children gathered for dinnertime. Mama had set out cold sausages with butter or jelly bread and canned pears with whole cloves. Mama had a large dish of rice pudding ready to place in the oven. Til saw this and smiled. Rice pudding was his favorite snack anytime of day.

CHAPTER THIRTY-ONE

A Walk in the Woods

Awaking Saturday morning Del moved quickly and walked to her parents' bedroom window to see if her aunt and uncle had arrived. No car was parked outside or near the barnbridge where Sam usually parked. Though early, she decided to get ready to spend time outdoors. She needed to dress warm for this day. She went downstairs. Mama was bustling about and turned to her to ask, "Did you tell Gloria we are expecting company this day?"

Del shook her head. "Not a word. She never tells me anything, unless it's something that isn't nice. I couldn't fall asleep thinking about all the moss and other things we need to find. How many gardens do you think Lillie makes every year?"

"I don't know. My family never made them. I never saw a partridge-berry plant before I met your father's relatives. My roses, tulips, pansies, and peonies around the house and in the garden are enough for me to look after."

Del was impatient to take care of her morning work. She had already shelled extra corn for weekend use for the chickens. Benj and Phillip were out and about, spending time in the barn with her father and brothers. The chickens were penned inside, which meant Ori hadn't tended to them yet. She heard them cackle as she continued her work. Del was leaving the feedhouse as Ori approached to do her chores. They both heard the sound of a machine coming in the lane at the same time.

"Who is coming this early in the morning?" Ori spoke, while turning around to see the approaching machine. It was Sam and Lillie's car, and there was a third passenger Del did not recognize.

Lillie practically jumped from the car and waited for the other lady to get out of the back seat. Sam got out and asked Del, "Where are the menfolk this morning?"

"Still in the barn, I suppose. I bet they heard your car and will be out here in a minute."

Sure enough, Benj, Phillip, and Til stepped out from the feed entry of the barn and walked towards them. Next Father and Bill came walking down the barnbridge. Ollie came running from the house. Ori, watching, stood in the doorway of the feedhouse as Mama came from the house holding Carol's hand, both properly dressed for the cold breezes sweeping by. Just then Ed came walking in the lane and approached the group now gathered. Ori finally stepped away from the feedhouse door and stood by Del's side to greet the visitors.

Lillie grabbed the passenger's hand and brought her closer to the group. "This is Sam's sister, Verna. She's a nurse from Philadelphia and works in a big hospital there. We don't get to see her very often and she'll join us gathering plants in the forest today."

Verna greeted everyone and said, "I haven't hunted for glass house plants since I was a child. I wonder if I still know where to look for them."

Del was surprised. " I never heard 'glass house plants' before now."

"Me either," Ori spoke.

Verna smiled at Del and Ori. "I went with my mom, but I didn't like going in the forest. There were eerie sounds, especially on a windy day."

Father said, "There's not much doing this day, so Tilghman and William can go with you to carry your buckets. Adelaide also. We expect you will find plenty today, since the Printz woodland wasn't trampled on by people for a long time. You never know what you'll find."

"I have a list with me. The new woods should be a good place to find nice things. I expect there's lots of fallen trees and rotted tree stumps in there. We'll have to be careful. Wild mushrooms may be plentiful, and could be poisonous, too! One touch, and the mushroom bursts apart and spreads powder all around. If you inhale it, it could kill you." Lillie looked closely at Del, Bill, and Til. "Avoid all mushrooms always. Stay close to me all the time. We must be very careful with what we touch or pick up. Don't pick anything up if you don't know what it is. And don't walk ahead of me," she admonished.

Ori looked exceedingly angry that she wasn't chosen to go along, but Del figured she knew better than to contradict their father's order. She turned and stormed off to the feedhouse. Lillie showed Del and her brothers the list of things. They read out loud, "Buckets full of moss, scarlet berries of wintergreen, red partridgeberry, rattlesnake weed, wild strawberry, tiny ferns, hypatica, and wild violets."

Lillie said once more, "Stay behind and with me all the time."

Del grabbed her wagon. Til and Bill carried the empty buckets and trailed the women to the forest. They walked along the most level land so the wagon moved easily. Lillie found an opening in the woods that looked promising. There was a little stream trickling there. Leaving Del's little wagon parked there, they followed Lillie as she stepped on rocks to cross the narrow stream. Once across Lillie stood still and looked all around. "Let's walk in this direction. Just follow me until I know it's safe to spread out a bit." She produced some hand cultivators and small trowels from her bucket. "Use a forked stick or one of these tools to brush leaf litter aside to see what lies underneath. If you see any blooms of any color, let me know. I will show you how to get some of that plant so that it will continue to grow for next year. We never take everything so there's growth for next year."

They moved to an area that wasn't heavily wooded. It was Bill who first said, "I think I found something here." Del looked and saw a small patch that looked like pasture grass with tiny white flowers.

Lillie exclaimed, "Oh yes, indeed! You found wild violets! They will only be good for one year. We'll pick a small patch, and leave the rest for next year's gathering. Put them in this small cardboard box all by itself."

"I found a patch of the partridgeberry. Lots of them!" Verna said excitedly.

Lillie ran over to Verna and glanced down. "That's the largest patch I saw for a long time! I can make a container of partridgeberry alone and have enough to add to other arrangements. We'll leave some to grow for future years."

It was a successful morning spent plant hunting. Del was surprised but grateful when it was time for lunch, and even more surprised when Lillie produced sandwiches for everyone. They all found fallen logs or rocks to serve as seats and enjoyed a welcome break.

Their work continued after their meal. They filled their buckets with dainty ferns. They found more wild violets with white and blue flowers. Del found small, umbrella-like trees that were only about 4 inches tall that Lillie admired. Lillie had an eye to find the interesting nutshells, bird feathers and bark that she called accent pieces. The boys hauled out buckets filled to the brim with different mosses, including some that looked like grass. Lillie surely had plenty of winter garden supplies to keep her busy for a while. When they returned to the car in the late afternoon, Sam decided it was time to go home. He was still getting over a cold. Lillie also said she was too tired to stay for a visit and would probably sleep going home. Verna laughed and said she was used to being on her feet a livelong day, but this plant hunting had the best of her. She, too, was ready to call it a day. Del was quite tired from all the time spent in the cold outdoors. Her brothers had worked even harder carrying those buckets which could be very heavy weighted down with mosses and other plants. They still had their strenuous evening barn work to do.

They loaded all the boxes and buckets in a manner to support them from tipping over. Sam stepped on the running board and got in. The car motor started and everyone called out goodbyes. Del decided to get an early start on her evening work. Benj and Phillip had already taken care of the pigs. Ollie was helping Ori with her evening chores, which was very unusual. Del figured Sam helped Father with some of Ollie's usual chores. She helped Ollie round up all the chickens and coax them to climb their ladders and enter their house for the night.

After supper, Del thought she'd go upstairs to her bedroom and read a new book she found in the school library. She hadn't finished more than a couple pages when she drifted off to sleep.

"Winter is at the door!" Benj said as he entered the closed porch early Sunday morning. He placed his heavy winter coat across a chair in the porch and stepped into the kitchen. "Cold outside this morning," he said as he stepped inside, eyes directed toward the far end in the kitchen where Phillip was seated on the couch. Benj made his way to the rocking chair in the corner. He pointed a finger at Del and Ori, seated at the table. "Yer work is done. Ed took care of it.

"I'll bring your coat inside," Mama said to Benj. "The porch is cold. You'll be shivering all the way home wearing a cold coat." Mama took it into the side room warmed by a coal-fired furnace in the cellar. An open grate in the floor kept the whole house warm. Benj shook his head, indicating the closed porch is where his bulky winter coat belonged. Mama returned to the kitchen and said, "I can't stand this cold weather so early in the season. Thanksgiving was chilly enough. Tilghman will surprise the folks once they see the new coat he is wearing, after missing a couple weeks of services. It's not good for his attendance record. But I didn't want him to catch a cold, before winter really sets in. Weakens your resistance, if you catch a cold early on."

"Phillip," Benj said, as he watched Phillip sit at the table, "what do you think about Christmas candy?"

Phillip gave Benj a big smile and said, "I like candy!"

Benj leaned over and gave him a hug. Mama just smiled as she fried scrapple.

Del looked forward to spreading a little molasses on her scrapple. That and a piece of buttered bread would do just fine for her breakfast.

She went upstairs to dress for Sunday school. She told Ollie to get up as she passed his room and advised him that he didn't have to put on his work clothes to do his outside morning chores.

Del heard Ori talking to Carol in their bedroom. "The boys will soon be in to eat and get ready for church. We can hardly wait to see Til wearing his new coat, can we?" Del smiled as she heard Carol ask if she would get a new coat. Del knew that the youngest children almost always had hand-me-downs the older children wore in their extended family. Del took the steps down slowly as she opened the stair door.

Mama talked to Benj. "I hope I don't see a horse and buggy this day. My father should stay home. He won't like letting his horse stand outside, this cold, cold day. He should do the same for himself. Best to stay where it is warm."

"Is Bill going up to Grandfather this Sunday again?" Del asked.

"Probably not if my father doesn't show up for church."

"I still wonder why Grandfather has Bill helping him," Del muttered.

"It will come out in the wash," was Ollie's silly answer to all questions he heard as he entered the kitchen, dressed for Sunday school.

Benj and Phillip heard Ollie's answer and looked at one another. Phillip giggled.

"I have scrapple ready and can make more for those of you who are here."

"I had enough for breakfast," Del immediately stated.

"Enough here," Benj said as he placed a hand on Phillip's head. He had Phillip's warm coat and gloves lying on the couch.

Father, Til, and Bill entered at the same time. Mama quickly cut more pieces of scrapple and placed them in the fry pan, saying, "You boys go upstairs, wash up, and get dressed for Sunday school. By then, your scrapple will be ready."

"Will Til come down wearing his new coat?" Ollie asked.

"Probably not. No reason to do so until he is ready to go to Sunday school."

Til reappeared with his coat hanging over his arm and a red, white, and blue scarf. Everyone in the kitchen said nothing for a minute.

Ollie was the first to burst out with the question, "Is that a new scarf too?"

Mama glanced back at Til's scarf and said, "The scarf is not new. That once was your father's scarf. It goes well with his new overcoat."

The kitchen was quiet as the boys and Father completed their breakfast and Ori and Carol came downstairs.

"All aboard," Father said, "time to get going to our church."

The children gathered quickly. Del watched as Til put on his new coat. He really did look very sharp in it.

Benj got Phillip dressed for the cold weather. "Ya will stay warm bundled up like this," he said as he turned Phillip towards the door.

All the children piled into the Studebaker, which Father had started earlier to warm up the car. There would be no shivering this cold morning. When they arrived at church Father told them he would return to pick them up after their Sunday school hour.

The service opened with greetings to everyone present this very cold wintry day. Hymn number 346 was sung. "Oh For a Thousand Tongues to Sing." The classes scattered to their areas for the day's lessons. The lesson time was shorter than usual as the classes were shown several Christmas programs they needed to look through and decide which one each class would perform on Christmas Eve. The class settled on a pantomime of the angels announcing the birth of baby Jesus. There were no speaking parts to remember and everyone would wear white gowns with angel wings attached on the back. The pantomime was easy to do, the teacher said. She would show everyone the movements so they could practice alone and together. For Del and Bill, there was only one problem to this plan. The class was expected to meet several times the week before Christmas to practice the pantomime. Del raised her hand and said with some concern in her voice, "We might not be able to come for practice."

The teacher smiled and said, "I understand. Children living on farms are excused. I grew up on a farm and know that it's not easy to get away from your farmwork, even in the winter." Del and Bill exchanged a glance of relief. They still had a chance for perfect attendance and their reward of a pound of chocolate candy for each of them.

Father was parked along the dirt road to pick them up after Sunday school. Til reported there were no problems from any students or teachers with Phillip. Whatever had been said to the initial troublemakers had worked. Father looked very pleased to hear that. The rest of Sunday was spent quietly. Bill stayed home because it was too cold to walk to Grandfather's house and back again. For that reason they also didn't have visitors. They entertained themselves with games, puzzles, and schoolwork. Phillip showed Carol how to play marbles. Mama, even though it was Sunday, did some hand mending. She said, "A woman's work is never done," and was busy replacing buttons, hand-stitching and darning socks. She tried to undo knotted links on a chain. Til said he was complimented by his teacher on his nice coat. "I told her it was worth missing two Sundays to get that coat—it's a good warm one."

Mama looked at Til and said, "I hope you don't grow so fast that this one doesn't last you the rest of this winter! I think you will be as tall as my father."

Til looked very pleased at that remark. Del wondered who she resembled most in the family. She didn't look like her mother, but had more the shape of her father's face. She was definitely a more slender build than her older and younger sisters—everyone said so. She and Bill didn't have much in common in their appearance either being they were fraternal twins and not identical twins. He was taller although also slender. He looked more like Mama, she decided. She thought about how that would be to have someone that looked like your mirror image. Ori noticed Del wasn't paying attention to their game and took that opportunity to scold Del. That brought her back to reality and made her determined to win the game of Chinese checkers, which she did.

CHAPTER THIRTY-TWO

Snow Days

Monday brought snowfall that caused school to be delayed. The cement road was plowed open, but side lanes and roads were not open due to the six inches of snow that fell overnight. Men in the neighborhood got together to open the school lane, shoveling snow by hand. Even so, many children were snow bound, living down roads and private lanes that weren't cleared. Long private lanes could remain closed for quite a while. Rockland Township was hilly and full of creeks. That meant many lanes were steep or had icy bridges and curves to navigate. This snow delay could be the first of many that would impact the completion of school days, and possibly farmers' plans for spring planting.

Fritz was getting older, and Father did not want him to walk with the twins on the coldest days nor snowy days like today. Fritz stayed in the barn at night with a well-worn comforter that served as a bed to keep him warm. Del could see that the cold air caused Fritz to shiver, something he hadn't done in past winters. Father explained that if the daytime temperatures warmed up a bit, Fritz might meet them at the cement pike. "If Fritz is not there and you don't see the truck, you know Fritz is getting a truck ride. Ed and I will be delivering lots of firewood, so he'll be with us."

With extra time on her hands while waiting for the school lane to open, Del thought about what her Grandfather did when there was snow on the ground like today. How did he get about with his canes? His joints were stiff enough without winter weather—was he still able to get out to care for his horses every day? The storekeeper across the street or the people in the hotel were close enough to look in on him, but they were busy with their own work and couldn't be counted on to provide daily care for two horses and his mouser in the old creamery building.

After two days with all the children able to get to school, Thursday presented the same problems with another snowfall. Paths and roads had to be opened all over again. This storm brought strong winds that blew all night, leaving some areas with deep banks of snow, while exposed land was scoured clean to the bare ground. Father could get about anywhere on the property but not beyond the sawmill. The lane was closed beyond it. Del thought Father would open the lane beyond the sawmill sometime soon. Yet she knew it was hard work to open a pathway by lifting a shovelful of snow and throwing it on snow banks that grew higher with each shovelful. It had to be very tiring work for the men for sure. Those snow banks could remain all winter long. Fierce winds could pick up that snow and create drifts that would close an opened path more than once.

Like the previous snowday, Benj and Phillip walked to his house to tend Benj's fires and play games until suppertime. Del was happy to stay inside on Thursday. She never liked the cold air and blowing winds. Mama announced, "Good time to do some sewing. I can get things done since there is nothing else that needs immediate attention. Winter is the best time for it." Del was eager to help her. Mama's first project was an apron. She also had a pattern and material to make a dress for spring and summer, saying her summer Sunday clothes needed replacement. She would then wear retired Sunday dresses around the house and her new dress for Sunday services, and for visiting relatives and friends.

Del was looking out from an upstairs window when Mama said, "You can pin those pattern pieces to the material now. Follow the folds of material and you will do alright."

Del liked to pin pattern pieces to cloth. She never cut the material. Mama always did that.

"When I have a straight line to sew, I may let you use my sewing machine. Or maybe sew a piece that needs mending. That would be better for your first try," Mama said half to herself. Del wanted to try her hand at sewing. She thought she would like it. Then she could perhaps make her own clothes.

After a fair amount of time spent quietly working upstairs, they heard Father and the boys entering the house.

Mama stopped sewing. "I must lay this aside for now. Time your father and the boys take a rest. They should warm up before doing the barn work." Ollie came out to the kitchen to join his older brothers. He worked on jigsaw puzzles all day. He knew better than to bother Mama when she was sewing.

Father spoke, "We're finished shoveling snow today, not much left for tomorrow. Our pine trees did a good job sheltering the lane from the winds." Benj and Phillip entered the kitchen as he concluded. "Cold outside," Benj said swinging his arms.

"There's enough wood on the fire til I go home." Benj turned to Phillip. "We played lots of games, didn't we?"

Phillip said, "Yes, and I won all of them!"

Everyone laughed and Benj beamed with pride. Phillip suddenly turned shy again and pressed his face against Benj's arm. Benj put his arm around Phillip and said, "The radio says all schools closed, even in the city," Benj said, and Phillip nodded in agreement.

Mama said, "I have a good size piece of roast pork and sauerkraut in the oven for dinner. The girls will set the table."

"I knew something really smelled good," Ollie said.

"We could tell when we walked in. Right, Phillip?"

Phillip nodded his head and said, "My favorite!"

Mama smiled and said, "Well, now that I know that, I will make it for you again."

Father looked at Ollie, "Oliver, what did you do all day?"

Ollie looked like he couldn't decide if he should be happy or unhappy about his situation. On the one hand, he always wanted to be where his big brothers were, but on the other hand, they were doing hard work outside in cold and windy weather. Ollie knew he couldn't really help at shoveling snow at his age. He said, "I stayed inside. Mama didn't want me to go out. I made puzzles all by myself."

Father said, "Well, don't you worry. When you get older and bigger you'll be out there shoveling snow too." Bill and Til just grinned as they stretched their sore arms and legs.

A large platter filled with pork, mashed potatoes, and sauerkraut was placed on the table. Mama slid an oblong glass dish of apples with sugar and cinnamon sprinkled on top into the oven. Apple crisp was one of Del's and Bill's favorite desserts.

"Always good eats here," Benj said as he looked to Phillip, who smiled as Benj filled his plate to eat.

"If you want to stay in your house tomorrow, we can bring Phillip to your place and bring sandwiches along for you to eat," Father offered. "Fritz will stay in the barn or in the house. You don't have to walk here and back to your house to fetch him."

"Nah, the walk is good fer me. Good for this feller, too." Benj patted Phillip on the shoulder.

It got dark early, and after supper when it was time to walk Benj home Til grabbed a flashlight while Benj carried a lantern. Father said, "Oliver, you grab a coat. You need to breathe a little colder air. Til will have company to walk back. You wait until Benj is safely in the door before you head for home." Ollie did not fuss. He looked pleased to walk along as part of Benj's escort.

Friday morning came. Del heard someone in the washroom so she debated if she should stay in her warm bed or look out her parents' bedroom window at the activity in the barnyard. Curiosity won out. While waiting her turn, she was grateful that her parents had installed a wash-room with an inside toilet. Grandfather's was the only other house in the area with an indoor flush toilet. She was happy she did not have to sit on the ice-cold wooden seats as they did in their school's outhouses.

She looked outside from her parents' bedroom window. Til and Bill were out there, helping Father with the morning milking, and releasing the cows into the barnyard to get a fresh drink of water. The walled-in barnyard and the barn itself kept the barnyard pen free of deep snows. The cold weather even affected the cattle. The cows did not have to be called to enter the barn after their fill of the very cold spring water. As soon as the stable doors opened the cows lined up to re-enter the barn.

Del saw Ed, who probably first took care of his peeps. It looked like Ed was doing Ori's chores. Del thought this would be one of the rare times that Ori wouldn't complain about someone doing her work. She always was the first to complain about cold hands in the winter. Her gloves were never warm enough for her. Del entertained herself with different ideas of how Ed was dealing with Taw-Taw since that old duck spent the night in the henhouse.

"Finally!" Del said to Ollie as he appeared in the hallway, "The wash-room is free!" Ollie gave her a look, shrugged his shoulders, and made his way downstairs. After Del was back in her room, she heard Ori talking to Carol.

When the barn work was completed, all the menfolk except Ed came into the kitchen for breakfast. Even though Ed was always invited, he went to his home for meals. Father waited outside for Benj as he saw him coming in the lane. Mama had scrapple frying as Del, Ori, and Carol entered the kitchen. Phillip was already dressed and seated on the rocking chair. Del was really surprised. "You taking Benj's place now?" Del smiled as she spoke to Phillip.

He responded, " I will warm the seat for Benj."

Del laughed along with the other children.

"I told him to say that." Mama smiled. "Let's see what Benj has to say."

Del was happy Phillip was opening up more around her family. He still seemed to do most of his talking with Benj, because she often saw them talking when they were outside. She tried to imagine what they talked about but gave up. Del waited to see what would happen when the door opened. Father and Benj were talking as they stepped inside the porch. Mama called out, "Bring those coats inside here to keep them warm for the time being."

Benj stood motionless when he saw Phillip seated on the rocking chair and then grinned. "That's my boy."

"I warmed your seat for you," Phillip proudly said and then giggled.

Benj immediately walked over to hug Phillip. He said, "You make living worthwhile."

Everyone was quiet for a moment, then Mama ordered, "Sit down and eat," as she took a platter full of fried scrapple from a warm oven and placed it on the table for everyone to enjoy. Mama had enough scrapple fried for everyone, although she was still frying more.

"First time in a while that the whole family is here for breakfast," Father said.

"Everyone has time today," Mama observed.

"You could almost think this is suppertime. That's the time all the family is usually here," Father said as he helped himself to scrapple slices and molasses. "We will take it easier today. There is a little shoveling left to do but the wind lifted a lot of snow in the lane by the sawmill. I need to see what Edgar's lane looks like in case he needs help to get out."

Mama looked at Benj and said, "I suppose you are going home again today?"Benj merely nodded his head.

"I have some dinner things in a basket for you to take along for you and Phillip."

"I would not be here exceptin' fer you and Becky. Yep, I could cook fer myself when younger, but . . ." Benj sighed. "It's different when yer alone." Benj hugged Phillip again. "Yep, life is worth living again."

Tears welled in Del's eyes. She thought about her unanswered questions about what happened to Benj's two sons. It was clear that Benj considered Phillip his own flesh and blood.

After breakfast, Father and the boys went outside to clear wind-blown snow that had settled in the paths they previously cleared. Benj and Phillip left to go back to his house for the day. Benj thought it was time for him to check his fire. Benj had Phillip bundle up.

Mama looked at Phillip and said, "I'm glad we found good warm clothes for you in our hand-me-downs."

Phillip smiled and said, "I like my hat."

Mama and Benj exchanged a long look but said nothing. When they were gone, Del asked, "Why did you and Benj look at each other like that?"

Mama replied, "Oh, that was a hat one of his boys wore."

Del was just about to ask what happened to Benj's sons when Mr. Strunk appeared at the closed porch. He walked inside, stomping off snow and exclaiming at the cold temperature. He said school would resume on Monday. "All the lanes will be cleared by then. The School Board doesn't want me to open until all seven schools are accessible. That's wasting a lot of time, but they want all schools to finish the term on the same day. This snow delay has gone long enough."

Mama agreed. She wanted the family at home when it was time to plant and sow grain. More snow days wouldn't help them be ready for planting if they had an early spring. That could mean the middle of April.

Late that afternoon Del and her sisters were in the kitchen helping Mama with supper preparation when Becky came into the house with a piece of mail that was dropped in her mailbox by mistake. "It's the first time I had mail since we had this last snow, and it's not even mine! I hope you don't mind. I read this postcard. Maybe you will have questions answered," she said as she handed it to Mama.

Mama read the card, speaking softly. "Ira located the section of town Phillip lived in. He has a name. He's contacted his folks. Depending on weather conditions, he might be here this Saturday with more news."

Becky said, "I don't know if I should be happy or sad. While this could be wonderful news for Phillip and his kin, Benj will not like this news at all. This could break his heart all over again."

"I can believe that," Mama answered. "And at Christmas time!"

Mama sent Del and Ori upstairs to clean the bedrooms. That meant she wanted to talk to Becky alone. Ori took Carol along too, grabbing a coloring book and crayons as they headed up the steps.

Del went to her room. She wondered what the conversation downstairs was all about. Becky knew Benj better than any other person in the neighborhood. This was a most unusual situation. Del already had tears in her eyes considering what this would do to Benj if Phillip left. Thoughts raced through her head. "Would his family see how well Phillip is provided for and cared for? Other families left children with relatives and orphanages when they couldn't take care of them. Ed and Hester left their their boy with his grandparent since they couldn't afford to keep him without steady work. Would Phillip's parents be willing to allow him to stay with us?" She shook her head no. Del already heard people say, 'No one leaves their child behind if there's anyway they can take care of them.' Del heard Becky say goodbye and heard the porch door close.

Mama came upstairs and called Del and Ori to her. "You keep this to yourselves—you say nothing to no one," Mama said sternly. "I will show this postcard to your father when we are alone. We must do as my father always says, 'Take things one day at a time.'" Mama stopped talking for a moment with her head bowed. Del could see she was trying not to cry. Then Mama lifted her head and said, "I warn you—not a word to anyone! Go do your outside chores quickly now and return." She went slowly down the stairs.

Ori and Del looked at each other. For as many times as Ori had complained about Phillip and all the commotion he caused, she was now teary-eyed and quiet. Del guessed that in spite of her declarations to the contrary, Ori really did care. Del walked around with a heavy heart as she finished straightening her room then prepared to go outdoors.

Benj and Phillip returned at suppertime. Mama kept herself busy with meal preparations. Benj talked about the day he and Phillip spent indoors. Phillip described the puzzles they made and how he helped

Benj stoke the fire. It was clear the young boy was becoming more and more comfortable with his surroundings.

That evening it was difficult for Del to keep the news and her feelings to herself. She had to be especially careful that Bill didn't sense something was wrong. Ori solved her dilemma by announcing she was going to her room to read and did not want to be disturbed until it was time to take Carol to bed. Del decided to do the same, but she could not concentrate on one paragraph as she struggled to read her schoolbook. Mama and Father stayed in the kitchen after all the children went to bed. Del didn't hear when they came up the stairs to their bedroom.

Saturday came. Del anxiously waited to see if her Uncle Isaac and his brother Ira would appear. She wasn't hungry for breakfast. Ori had even been kind to her that morning instead of her usual grumpy self. She also noticed that Mama and Father were quieter than usual. Del now had an inkling of how Phillip's family must have been sick with worry not knowing where he was. "What would happen now?" she thought to herself. Father always said he would return Phillip to his family if they were found. But no one realized how attached Benj would become to the young boy, or how he was like a member of their family now. She wondered what it would feel like if she was lost and taken in by strangers.

Noontime came and Isaac and his brother Ira weren't there. They weren't there by mid-afternoon. It was then Father said to Mama, "I expected Isaac would be here by now if they were coming today. We'll look for them tomorrow."

Suppertime was quiet. Everyone was subdued and sensed that something was not quite right. Bill asked Del what was happening, but she just shook her head. If Bill could be evasive about his Sundays with Grandfather, then she could hold back some information too. Even Fritz, lying under the table and soaking up the warmth of the kitchen, seemed to sense the tension in the household and looked for consolation from Bill and Del. Father talked to Benj about the Printz property and the repairs continuing on the old home. Del was all ears. Maybe now she'd learn the full plan for that homestead.

Father laughed and said in the dialect, "Billy bought the property for the birch trees. That's all he burns in his stove."

Benj nodded in agreement.

Mama spoke up, "I tried to convince him to move in there so he would be closer to us, but he's not budging from his home. He says he will die in that house. He is fixing up the Printz home to rent it out."

Del and Bill and the other children all nudged each other. This was news to them. They were going to get neighbors sometime when the house was repaired.

Ollie immediately asked, "Who is going to rent it?"

Mama just shook her head and said, "You are so much like your aunt Lillie—you must know everything going on. We don't know because it hasn't even been advertised as available yet."

Undeterred, Ollie said, "Well I hope there are some boys I can play with."

Ori rolled her eyes and said, "I don't care who moves there."

Del and Bill just grinned at Ollie. He was always looking for someone to play catch with him. The rest of the evening was quiet—Del could tell her parents were trying hard to not alert Benj that they were awaiting news about Phillip's family, now found.

On Sunday morning when Del woke up she stretched as she remembered it was a special day—today all the children would have their attendance records checked for the year. Perfect attendance would result in a pound box of chocolates. All the Heydt children eagerly did their chores and then put on their Sunday clothes. They didn't need any reminders from Mama to step lively. The cold weather kept Grandfather at home, no bone-chilling horse and buggy ride for him that morning. Father drove the children to church and reminded them he'd return in an hour.

Til, as usual, took Phillip along with him to class. Del wondered what Phillip would think about the chocolates going to other children but not to him or Til. After classes all the children gathered upstairs to receive their reward. They divided in lines according to age groups. Del watched as Til was nudged by his teacher to join his class's line. The teacher also guided Phillip into line with Til. Del was close by enough to hear him say quietly in protest, "But I was absent." His teacher put a finger to his lips meaning Til should be quiet. Til looked perplexed, but moved on with Phillip behind him. He was handed a brown paper bag, and Til and Phillip quickly walked out to join the other Heydt children as they struggled to get into their coats, hats, and mittens without dropping their precious boxes of chocolate. Father was waiting for them, idling the car to keep it warm. Once in the car, Til immediately said to Father, "I missed two Sundays. But I got three boxes of candy."

Father said, "That's not just for you and Phillip. You should have one for your Grandfather too."

Til nodded and said, "There are three boxes. But I thought it was only children and teachers with perfect attendance that got candy."

Father chuckled, "The only reason anyone gets candy is because your grandfather buys it every year. He knows it's a good reason for folks to bring their children to Sunday school every Sunday. They aren't going to short Billy Henry's grandchildren when you had good reasons to miss two Sundays."

Del was pleasantly surprised to learn that. Her Grandfather was a regular church-goer when his rheumatism allowed, although he didn't seem more pious than anyone else in her family. She had heard some adults say that he had the most colorful Dutch language they ever heard. She suspected that wasn't good.

Mama served a dinner of sausage and refried potatoes that had eggs broken into them. Everyone, including Benj, ate while the children chattered about their favorite chocolates and negotiated trading amongst each other to get their favorites. Ollie counted his to figure out how many he could eat each day. Mama put her foot down and said, "You are each limited to two pieces of chocolate each day. I don't want to see any chocolate stains on your bed sheets or pajamas—you leave your candy downstairs."

Father chuckled and added, "You'll get more candy as Christmas gifts, too." He motioned to Bill and said, "Get yourself ready to go see your Grandfather. I'll pick you up late afternoon."

Christmas was always a quieter holiday than Thanksgiving, and the preparations weren't as elaborate. They wouldn't have as much family visiting, as all the Allentown and Boyertown relatives celebrated the holiday with their immediate families. Mama planned to roast a goose for Christmas dinner. That's what Grandfather preferred for his Christmas dinner. It was the once-in-a-year time that Mama could convince her father to spend an entire day with the family. Her Aunt Kate and Uncle Jeremiah would join them too.

Del believed that Grandfather must feel rather lonely. She didn't even know if he had a radio to keep him company. Maybe that was the reason Bill spent most of the Sundays at his house. "Although Til did a lot for Grandfather too," she thought to herself as her siblings chattered around her. Til walked Grandfather's horses to the blacksmith shop when they needed new shoes. She also recalled that Til told her once that Grandfather would stand by a field when Til plowed it with a ruler in hand. He'd lean over and measure the depth of the furrow to ensure that Til plowed deeply and evenly enough to turn the soil for good growth. She shrugged. It was still a mystery to her why Bill was singled out by Grandfather for Sunday visits.

In the meantime she couldn't wait to hear what was discovered about Phillip's family. What a time! Would Ira come visiting today with Isaac and Eva? The day passed slowly without any visitors—not the Schultz boys or any of the other regular company. Father retrieved Bill from Grandfather's house, and as usual, Bill was silent on the subject of what they did together.

Monday morning was another bitterly cold day. Mama had hot oatmeal with raisins. Mama told Phillip and Carol that Benj would keep an eye on them. She said, "I need to see Aunt Kate this morning, and this is a good time to see if Fritz wants to spend a little time in the house with you too. That dog is beginning to show signs of age and he'll appreciate the warmth."

Mama looked around at the children as they ate. "Eat your oatmeal and there's more here so you can help yourself. Dress warm, then off to school." Mama checked that everyone had a scarf correctly placed and coats buttoned. As the children walked past the barnyard, they saw Father and Ed carry the full milk cans in the milkhouse. The new dairy would come by and pick the milk cans up from now on. Father no longer had to take his milk to the creamery.

For once, Em and her brother arrived after the Heydt children made it to school. Del and Em immediately compared notes about how high snow had drifted in their lanes and roads. They shared talk about Christmas day, what they would eat, and what gifts would be received. New clothes were the usual gifts, especially gloves and hats. Del knew better than to mention the oranges and silver dollars to Em. Del's parents told the children many times to not make much talk about their Grandfather's gifts. In hard times, it did no one any good to point out when they had it better than someone else.

Christmas day was another cold day, but the house was warm and filled with lively chatter as the children admired the Christmas tree that mysteriously appeared overnight and opened their presents. Del was very happy to get two books. She admired the new knitted mittens and hat that matched the sweater Aunt Kate made for her, although she still wished for a better color than the rust color her aunt had chosen. Carol was thrilled with the new doll she received—as the youngest she was accustomed to also getting the hand-me-down toys from her older sisters and cousins. Something brand new was an unusual event for her. Til received a hunting rifle, to the immediate envy of Bill and Ollie. He wanted to try some target practice.

Father and Mama looked at each other, and then Father said, "Alright, but you know well enough to set up targets that aren't in the direction of anyone's home or any of the roads. Be sure to come back when your Grandfather gets here." Til needed no further encouragement, and was pulling on his coat, hat and gloves as Bill and Ollie pleaded to come along and try shooting too. They raced outside. Phillip didn't seem very interested in the new gun. He admired the coloring book and crayons he received. Benj arrived with presents for everyone. Perhaps it was because Phillip spent the most time with Benj, or because Benj considered him family, but Benj had a baseball and bat, plus a worn, boy-sized baseball glove that he gave to Phillip. "Come spring-time, we can play catch," he said as Phillip jumped up and down with excitement.

Mama eyed the gift and said to Phillip and Benj, "No swinging that bat or tossing that ball in the house, you understand?" They both solemnly nodded their heads yes.

Grandfather arrived in his horse and buggy and Til ran to stable Harry in their barn while Bill helped Grandfather down the buggy steps. As predicted, Grandfather had an orange for everyone, including Father and Mama. He also produced the silver dollars for each child, and admonished them to put their money in their bank accounts.

Mama had been busy all the previous day preparing the Christmas feast. She set the roast goose on the table, followed by potato filling, bread filling, rich gravy, chow-chow, dried corn, and a number of vegetables from their garden that had been canned earlier that year. Unlike Thanksgiving, she limited the desserts to mince pie, a hickory nut cake, and cherry pies made from cherries they picked that summer.

Phillip exclaimed at the size of the goose. "That's a giant bird!" he said over and over. Bill laughed and said, "It sure is, and it tastes good too!"

The day ended with everyone well-fed and the children exhausted from the day's happenings. Del reflected that night as she laid her head on her pillow that she hadn't thought much about the anticipated visit from Isaac and Eva and the information they would bring. She drifted off to sleep wondering if Phillip would celebrate another Christmas with them.

Isaac and Eva arrived on the following Sunday shortly after dinner. Del never heard an explanation why they delayed their visit by a week, but she guessed something important caused them to postpone their trip. Benj had already taken Phillip along to his house for the afternoon. Bill also left right before dinner to spend the afternoon with Grandfather. Mama had packed a basket with plenty of food for her father and Bill to share for dinner, with enough leftovers for her father's supper, too, while grumbling that if he wasn't so stubborn, he could have as many meals as he wanted with the family.

Del's parents asked all the children to find something to do while the grown-ups talked. They moved into the parlor for more privacy. Til, Ollie, and Del decided to play jacks at the kitchen table, while Ori and Carol went upstairs where Ori read a book to Carol. Del was keenly interested in hearing what her parents and uncle and aunt were discussing, but she could not make out more than a few words like 'So relieved,' and 'Benj will be heartbroken.' She couldn't concentrate on the game as her mind raced with questions. "Did Ira obtain more information that caused Isaac to wait another week? What had he learned?" she thought. Ollie and Til were surprised that they beat her every round.

After an hour, or a bit more, the adults returned to the kitchen. Mama called upstairs and told Ori and Carol to come downstairs and say hello to their uncle and aunt. Aunt Eva handed out Christmas cards and candies to the children. She held on to the cards for Bill and Phillip, and that told Del that maybe they would stay for supper. Mama made a pot of coffee and again the adults headed for the parlor, but not before Father told Til to take the Studebaker and fetch Bill. Til immediately grabbed his coat. Ollie asked to ride along.

Til said, "Come on, get your cap and coat. Hurry because Bill and I have to start our evening chores as soon as we get back."

Del found excuses to remain in the kitchen, helping Carol with a puzzle while Ori read a book in the rocking chair. Just 10 minutes later Til and Ollie returned with Bill, plus Benj and Phillip, who were picked up as they were walking to the Heydt house. "Had a short ride," Benj said as they entered the kitchen.

Benj looked around and saw the parlor door was closed.

"*Waz gade au* [What is happening]?" Benj asked.

"Don't know." Del shook her head. "They want to talk about something we are not supposed to hear. Told us to stay in the kitchen and be quiet."

Just then Father, Mama, Uncle Isaac, and Aunt Eva entered the kitchen. Eva handed Christmas cards and more candy to Phillip and Bill.

Phillip shyly said, "Thank you," without any prompting.

Benj just beamed and said "*Mi bui* [My boy]!"

Mama had a fleeting expression on her face that Del had never seen before—a deep and resigned sadness.

"You should stay for supper," Father suggested to Isaac and Eva.

Mama instantly agreed although she said apologetically, "It's warmed up leftovers tonight. I have goose and gravy and will make potato cakes."

Del could see that Benj was not his usual talkative self. Perhaps Becky told Benj about the card that was dropped in her mailbox. She already felt sorry for both Benj and Phillip. She still had many more questions than answers, but the bits of news she did have left her feeling there would be many more hurts coming soon to people she loved.

Father and Isaac along with Til and Bill bundled up to head to the barn for the evening milking. Ori and Del did the same to take care of their work. When supper was ready, Ollie ran out to tell them to come in and eat. After supper, Father invited Benj and Isaac to come and take a seat in the parlor. Aunt Eva stayed in the kitchen to help Mama clean up after their meal. Ori and Del were told to wash the dishes.

"Oliver and Phillip, you do your best to dry those dishes. Set them on my white porcelain table. I will put them away," Mama ordered.

Both boys grabbed a towel and immediately set each dish dried on that table. Carol worked on one of the new Christmas puzzles at the kitchen table and Ori helped her once the dishwashing duty was done. Del opened one of her new books to read once she completed her chores, sitting in the rocking chair. She wanted to be close by to hear what was going on in the parlor.

The evening turned into night quickly. Mama and Aunt Eva had joined the men in the parlor, where Del guessed they were discussing the news with Benj. She had almost finished a chapter when Isaac and Eva entered the kitchen, followed by Benj, who looked pale and tired. Eva announced it was time to go home. Father and Benj rode along with Isaac and Eva, who would drop them off at Benj's house. It was quite a while before Father returned home.

The week started uneventfully as the family prepared for a new year. Del sensed that some plans were underway, but her parents were not telling the children what was going on. Mama and Father asked Benj to watch Carol and Phillip at home on Wednesday as the older children put their coats to go to school. That was a most unusual event.

As they walked to school, Del asked Bill if he knew where they were going. Bill shook his head no. Til was the one who spoke up.

"I heard them talk about seeing Grandfather today and something to do with the Printz home," he said.

"Maybe they are renting out the house," Bill suggested.

Del thought that was a good guess, but that only triggered thoughts about who would be their neighbors. She asked, "Are all the repairs done to the place?"

Til and Bill both nodded, and Bill said, "As far as I know—yep."

Ollie repeated his wish that he'd have someone his age to play with. He liked Phillip, but definitely considered Phillip too young to play with him. Del thought that Phillip's recent gift of baseball gear might make Ollie reconsider.

New Year's Eve was spent quietly at home. Some of the men in the area liked to gather at the New Jerusalem Hotel and shoot off their guns at midnight. Mama didn't want the children near anything like that, because the men were often drunk, and she was very certain that they shouldn't be handling guns.

New Year's Day was bitter cold and very clear—not a cloud in the sky. They had the traditional meal of pork and sauerkraut with mashed potatoes for good luck in the coming year. Mama made coconut custards, one of Father's favorite pies, in addition to mince pies. Phillip declared coconut custard was his favorite pie. He seemed completely comfortable with the family now.

"He no longer hides his face, he no longer limps, and he no longer looks scared," Del thought with pride. But the next question that popped in her head just filled her with a mixture of happiness and dread. "What would happen now that his family had been located?"

The situation changed the second Saturday in the new year. Del was the one who retrieved the mail that day, and she hurriedly read the postcard before reaching the house. Ira sent it to her Father, writing: *Father will make a trip to Phila. I'll bring him to you. Wants to thank you in person. Have not mentioned your ideas—best to do that when you meet him. Ira."*

Del ran inside and handed the card to Mama. Mama read it, and then looked at Del, "I suppose you read this already?"

Del nodded yes, it would do her no good to fib to Mama.

Mama said, "Keep this to yourself—not a word to anyone. I know you can do that. Now tend to your chores."

Del turned and again went outside to do her afternoon chores. She was very surprised to see the feedhouse was rearranged and swept clean. She suspected that Ed took it upon himself to organize the crates with scrub cobs and food scraps for the pigs.

Del finished her work and checked on Ori. As she opened the feedhouse entrance to the henhouse, she was again surprised. Ori was whistling a Christmas carol. She might have actually been happy. Del shut the door quietly and headed back to the house.

"What are things like out there? Mama asked.

"Someone rearranged the feedhouse. I could never manage to move the cornsheller. The water hoppers that aren't in use are in a crate on the floor. They are easy to get to and they won't tip over like they could when they were on the shelf above. I suppose Ed did that."

Mama nodded, "I suppose Ed did too. He probably learned to do those things from his grandfather. He had a poultry farm."

"I don't know what Ori will say. If it was her idea, she would brag about that. But since it wasn't she might complain and say, 'Nothing is where it belongs.'

Mama gave Del a long look, and finally acknowledged, "You are probably right. I don't know where that attitude comes from. It certainly doesn't come from my side of the family. We're particular about how things get done, but we accept improvements and new ideas." With that she turned back to the stove and started humming a hymn.

CHAPTER THIRTY-THREE

A Mystery Is Resolved

It was a cold January, and the third week was set for the final butchering of beef. Mama had a pile of postcards that advised the relatives of the times their help would be needed, and, as always, they would receive a supply of meat for their own use. Only heavy snow and blizzard conditions could delay this day from happening.

"Monday," Til groaned as he stretched and looked at the calendar in the kitchen. "Wish I didn't have to go to school. Could have slept a while longer. It's still dark outside."

Del just nodded and shivered as she thought about going outside to do her morning chores. She heard Bill come down the steps.

"It's cold this morning," Bill stated. "The windows are coated with frost."

"Wear your warm jacket when you go out. Drink this cocoa to warm you up a bit before you go outside," Mama said as she handed a cup to Bill. "I hope Phillip stays in bed a little longer. I'll be glad when this last butchering is done so we can put all the knives and grinder equipment back in the right places. I'll have to set the dull knives aside for our hobo to sharpen when he comes by again." Mama turned to Del. "Set the table," she said. "We'll be ready when the barn work is completed, so everyone can eat at the same time. Benj should be here before you head for school." Mama paused as Phillip and Ollie came down the stairs at the same time. "I hope the fires didn't burn out for Benj during the night. I think he gets up in the middle of the night and adds more wood to the fire in the stove. A bit inconvenient, but better than waking up in an ice-cold house." Mama shook her head. "He never mentions coal. It would last longer."

Del nodded in agreement. She knew her parents were glad they had a coal furnace in the basement to heat their farmhouse. They often talked about how convenient it was compared to a wood fire. Ori and Carol opened the stair door and entered the kitchen at the same time the men returned from the early barn chores. They brought Fritz along in. Father worried that it was too cold for Fritz even if he stayed in the threshold with his old blanket. Mama looked at Father with a quizzical look.

Father just nodded and said, "He's acting like his old self again. I think he's recovered."

The children prepared for the school day. Til carried the postcards with the butchering dates to the mailbox. He laid the cards inside, closed the lid and lifted the red metal flag to an upright position. Del saw light inside Benj's house and figured he was getting ready to come see Phillip. As Del walked with her brothers and sister to school, she thought about what news Isaac's brother Ira might have for them about Phillip's family. What would happen to Phillip? Del knew worrying about that wouldn't help the situation. She decided to ask Bill about Fritz.

"Why was Fritz penned up in the barn?"

"Father will tell us when he knows everything is all right again," Bill replied.

"What was wrong?

"Fritz was sick. He didn't do anything but sleep most of the day, and he didn't want to go outside. Father had the vet come in and look at him."

"What was the problem? Will he be all right again?" Del pleaded. She didn't want anything bad to happen to Fritz.

"I don't know what the problem was, but the vet said he's all right," Bill said with a reassuring tone. "He just needs more rest until he's completely recovered."

They arrived at the school grounds. Em was not waiting outside—it was too cold. Del and her siblings entered the schoolhouse. The Goho children were already there. Em was standing close to the big round stove, the warmest place in the school building. Mr. Strunk walked to the vestibule, and pulled the rope attached to the bell. It rang but once sounding like a gong. All was quiet. School was now in session.

"It's so cold today," Em whispered as they took their seats.

Del merely nodded her head.

Teacher announced, "Everyone is present today. I suggest you stay inside at recess times today. I will have inside games for you."

During the first, second, and third graders class presentations, Del couldn't focus on the history lesson before her. Her thoughts strayed to the news about Phillip's family. She overheard her parents talk about Phillip's father, who delivered ice for home iceboxes. What did he do to earn a living in the cold winter months when the icebox wasn't necessary?

Mr. Strunk called on the class as Del and Bill took their places on the one-step platform to discuss and answer questions on the harsh winter when Washington crossed the Delaware River. But the uppermost concern for Del was thinking about what would happen to Phillip. Things had been going so well until the news came from Ira. Del knew she should be happy for Phillip that he would eventually be reunited with his mama and daddy, but she was old enough to realize that losing Phillip would be very hard on Benj, who was obviously very attached to the boy. And Phillip seemed just as happy to be with Benj.

However, she didn't have all the details. She figured her parents and Benj talked about the situation with Phillip when the children were in school. Fortunately for Del, the teacher didn't notice her lack of attention to the class and didn't call on her to answer any questions.

A couple weeks passed as the family prepared for their last butchering for that winter. Salting, smoking, and canning conversations dominated mealtimes. One school day the Heydt children walked by themselves back to their homestead without the usual presence of the Shultz boys, who had packed lunches for that day. Del thought it was a good time to ask Bill what he heard about who would rent the Printz home.

Bill shrugged. "I know something is happening, but nothing more than you."

"Doesn't Grandfather talk about things happening there?"

"He doesn't say anything about that. He talks about how he doesn't like all the free time he now has." Bill hesitated, then continued. "Sometimes he talks like I am his boy."

"Why do you say that?" Del was very surprised.

"I don't know. You know I've been helping him go through boxes and boxes of papers on Sundays."

Del nodded her head.

"He points out papers that he thinks I should pay attention to, things like deeds and court records."

Del pondered that. That was very puzzling. It was unusual that Grandfather had Bill, rather than Til attend to his paperwork chores. Til was the oldest boy among his grandchildren, and typically the first to be called on for such tasks. Bill was more talkative about spending Sundays at Grandfather's place than usual. Something about this work was bothering him, she could tell. She remained quiet, hoping he would continue talking.

Bill blurted out, "He even said I'm going to inherit property from him, but I don't think he's doing that for Til or anyone else."

Del was stunned. The usual way for property and goods to be inherited was from one generation to the next. But why would Grandfather favor one grandchild over the others when he was equal in his treatment in so many other ways? Shouldn't Mama get his property? There was no more time for conversation as the twins entered the homestead and met the relatives who were on hand to help with butchering.

Lillie was waiting for them. She, as always, had prepared a dinner-time meal for the children to eat. She was talking a mile a minute, just like her husband, Sam, at times described her.

"How is the school day going? Are you hungry? It's good to see you—did you dress warm enough this morning? Tomorrow there's no need for you to come home at dinnertime. We don't want any interruptions tomorrow so we can finish the necessary cleanup work here. We'll get all the knives, grinding equipment, and large kettles all cleaned up, and the washhouse ready for your mama to do her weekly laundry."

Ori found a moment to ask a question as Lillie paused to take a breath. "Are you finished making terrariums? Next year I want to go along to help collect plants and those red berries."

Lillie shook her head. "They are all made. But I don't know about you with your hands that get so cold in the winter. Your need to wear gloves as soon as it's cold means it's not easy to handle the delicate plants I use."

Ori looked disappointed. Del hadn't known that Ori's sensitivity to cold was the reason she hadn't gone on previous plant collecting trips. If Ori got too cold, her fingers could go numb and turn white, and only return to warmth when she plunged them in warm water.

After a meal of canned sausages and twice-fried potatoes, the children left for the afternoon session of school. Del thought about Bill as she and Fritz walked with him. It was clear that those Sunday visits bothered Bill, and he had been puzzling over the situation for a while before telling Del. It saddened Del that he kept this from her, but then she remembered that she had secrets too, like the news that Phillip's family was found. They used to tell each other everything, and it wasn't easy to deliberately hide information, at least for Del.

Thursday, as the children came home from school at day's end, folks were still cleaning up all the butchering gear. Nothing was said about Ira being in touch with Phillip's father. The evening meal was one of Del's favorites—liver pudding. As they ate, Father revealed that someone had slipped some kind of poison to Fritz, probably on one of their firewood delivery trips. Father kept this quiet so that the children would not talk about this in school or bother Fritz while he wasn't feeling well.

"He needed quiet time. The vet came three times to see Fritz. His medicine did the healing. Fritz will be alright. Just give him time to get his strength back."

Del and her siblings were very upset. Del just couldn't imagine anyone doing something so mean to a dog. Ollie demanded to know who it was.

Father just shook his head and said, "It's impossible to know who did it for sure. We'll be very careful to keep him in the truck from now on when we go on firewood deliveries."

All the children leaned under the table to pet Fritz. Mama kept a close eye on them to see that they didn't slip him a morsel of food from their plates.

February was the short month, that's what people said. It did not appear that way as far as Del was concerned. School days were filled with more homework and preparing for tests as each child would learn whether they would proceed to the next grade. Ori had been held back once to repeat a grade. Now Mr. Strunk devoted time especially to her during the eighth grade lessons. Del thought about what work was underway to prepare Phillip for school. She suspected that Benj and her parents were teaching him letters and numbers at home when they were in school. Mama was helping him with the same coloring books and worn early primers like she did for Carol, who would start first grade in September. Mr. Straub, a retired teacher, might have those school books Mr. Strunk sent home a couple of months ago. Her parents might know what grade Phillip would join once he enrolled in school—if he stayed there.

Del overheard her parents talk about Phillip's father. He had to save up some money to travel to Philadelphia and meet Ira. Just what would happen when Phillip's father saved enough money to make the trip to Philadelphia? How would he be reunited with Phillip? Would they have to take Phillip back to Philadelphia or would his father travel to New Jerusalem?

Del squeezed her eyes closed just giving that a thought. Del couldn't see any way around a heartbreak for Benj and her family. As much as she might wish that Phillip's father would let him stay with them, she knew that wasn't realistic. She heard her parents talk about what a difficult decision it had been for Ed and Hester to send their son to the grand-parents who were financially able to care for him when their jobs were unreliable. "That was family, not strangers like we are to Phillip's kin", Del thought. Del already noticed Benj's eyes often had tears after walk-ing to their home to be with Phillip for breakfast and the rest of the day.

Mama observed that too, muttering, "Those tears weren't from the cold blowing winds."

Del also noticed that Benj wasn't talking about that special birthday celebration like he did before Ira's news. He had been looking forward to celebrating his birthday on Easter Sunday for many years.

"Like tears of happiness and sadness at the same time," said Becky, when she brought that postcard in for Mama to read.

Mama was planning the big birthday celebration on March 24. Aunt Eva was going to bring a birthday cake along from a bakery in Emmaus. The cake and all the other food would be on the kitchen table. People would serve themselves and carry their plates to the side room, where many could be seated at the round table or at card tables. Grandfather, of course, needed to be seated in a chair with arms to help himself get up. Mama was going to take care of that.

Isaac and Ira arrived at the house on the first Saturday of March after supper. Mama and Father were expecting them.

Mama looked at Til, "You will be in charge, we will be at Benj's if you need us. You look after things. We'll be back before long."

The adults went up to Benj's home for conversation. Del knew they would be discussing Phillip, and was sorely disappointed that she wouldn't have a chance to overhear the conversation.

After an hour Mama was back saying, "Your father is talking with Benj a while longer." She turned to Phillip. "Benj will see you in the morning, it's too late for him to come back over here and then head for home again."

Phillip just said, "Good night."

Mama smiled. "Yes, he said 'good night' to you too."

Father came back a short time later. He and Mama just looked at each other for a long moment. Del sensed that something had changed, but she couldn't tell what that was. Nothing was said, but the children did their schoolwork and quietly made their ways upstairs. Del tossed and turned, bothered with what had happened that day. What decisions had been discussed about Phillip? She was awake quite awhile.

Monday morning came. Mama had fried scrapple for breakfast. With a little molasses on top and buttered bread, it was a good meal for a cold day after completing chores. Everyone except Carol was up and about. Benj had his usual place in the rocking chair. Although the weather had warmed up a bit, it was still very cold. Mama made hot cocoa for everyone to drink. "Warm you up inside before you head for school."

The children returned at the noontime break for their dinner. As they reached the cement pike, a large truck was turning into the lane.

"Whose truck is that?" Til exclaimed. "Father isn't getting another truck. Not a closed truck like that."

The children were very curious to see what it was doing at their place, but there was no truck parked there as the children reached the homestead.

Til stepped up his pace, not only to see his precious Doll, but to find out where the truck was and who drove it. Til strode down the lane past the sawmill and then turned around. "That truck," he pointed a finger back as he joined the group, "it stopped in front the Printz house. I think someone is moving in." Til looked to Bill. "Did Grandfather rent that house to somebody? He didn't sell it and I know he doesn't want to move there. Father is going to farm that land." Til continued, "I thought I saw Ira's car there too. What is he doing there?"

Bill just shook his head no and added, "I didn't hear anything about him renting out the Printz home."

Just then Mama called, "Come in and eat. You can look at that some more when you come home from school. Get out of the cold!"

Til was full of questions as he stepped inside, along with the other children.

Mama raised her hands to quiet them down. "Yes, people are moving in. We will tell you all about this when you come home from school this afternoon. It the meantime, you know nothing to talk about with your classmates. My father is renting out the property."

The children could all read Mama well enough to know that this discussion was at an end and ate their meal quietly and then left for school. As soon as they were out the door, they commenced to talking again.

"Do any of you know what is happening?" Ori asked the big question. Everyone looked at each other and all shook their heads.

As they moved on to the schoolhouse, Del looked at Bill and said in a whisper, "I bet you know something about this."

"I overheard a little, not much. I only heard someone was moving into that house. Grandfather is tired of people gossiping that he is fixing that house for himself. He said it's not good for a house to be empty a long time."

The afternoon session crawled by as all the Heydt children were eager to rush home and learn the news about the Printz home. Del observed the particular agonies for Ollie, who always wanted to be in the know on everything. He was twice scolded by Teacher for not sitting still.

As the children gathered around the supper table, Father spoke. "We have a family moving into the Printz home. You will meet them soon. Phillip and Benj will meet them tomorrow. Your mother, your grandfather and I will meet them later while you are in school."

The children were excited about getting new neighbors. There were many questions as they considered this news.

Father just chuckled and said, "Now, now, that's enough. I only met Mr. . . ."

Mama hurriedy interrupted him asking, "Would you like some more potatoes?" which seemed to serve as a warning to Father.

He nodded at Mama and continued, "There will be plenty of time to get to know our new neighbors."

Ollie again expressed hope of finding a boy his age who could play catch with him. Carol decided a girl her age would suit her just fine. Del puzzled over Mama interrupting Father, as well as something Father said. Why would Benj and Phillip meet them first? She would not get any answers that evening. Because she had not slept well the night before, she was one of the first to head upstairs. That drew a questioning look from Mama, who knew her children well enough to note this change in routine.

The next day Del and her brothers and sisters did not need reminding to do their morning chores or get ready for school. They worked on the assumption that the sooner they got school over with, the sooner they'd have answers to all their questions about the new family in the Printz home. When school was dismissed, they raced home, even Ori, the slowest runner in the group.

Mama spoke as they burst into the kitchen, "Before you change into your work clothes, I will go with you to meet our new neighbors. Just leave your school books here and let's go."

As the children and Mama approached the home, Benj and Phillip came out of the house and stood on the porch. Benj waved and motioned them to go inside to meet their new neighbors. Phillip had a big smile on his face as Benj said, "Come in and meet Phillip's family."

Del and Bill looked at each other in astonishment, and then at their siblings, who also looked amazed or stunned. They quietly trailed their mother into the home. Inside Del saw her father with two adults and two girls that might have been her age or a bit older. Father spoke, "Children, this is Mr. Solomon Fisher and Mrs. Nancy Fisher, Phillip's father and mother. These are his sisters, Mattie and Arlene. I want you to introduce yourselves to our new neighbors." Til quickly stepped forward and was followed by Bill. Ori was so overcome with surprise at this turn of events that Mama had to nudge her to go up and introduce herself and shake their hands. All the children, even Carol, shook hands with the Fishers. Carol seemed very delighted to do such a grownup thing.

Mr. Fisher looked at the Heydt children and said, "I already said this to your mother and father, but we can never thank you enough for your kindness in taking in my son. You'll never know how much this means to us."

Mrs. Fisher started to cry, and Mama took her hand and cried too. That also astonished Del, who hadn't seen her own mother display many signs of tenderness towards her own family. Once the two women dried their tears, Mama wanted to know if Mrs. Fisher needed any supplies that may not have survived the move, and offered to introduce her to the local grocer and suppliers.

Del asked, "How old is Phillip and what's his real name?"

Mrs. Fisher laughed and said, "We named him Solomon Junior, but he told us he likes Phillip better, so we're going to call him Phillip Solomon Fisher from now on. He's 6 years old."

Ollie was ready to pipe up with a question when Mama shushed him. "Our neighbors must unpack and get settled into their new home," she declared. "We'll have plenty more time to talk."

Father laughed in agreement. "Yes, we have a big birthday party celebration planned in less than two weeks. Bill, Del, and Benj all share the same birthday on Easter Sunday. Come and meet the neighbors and the rest of our families."

As the Heydt family prepared to leave, Phillip tugged on Benj's hand and said, "You stay."

Benj, with tears in his eyes, said, "Ya Phillip, I stay."

The family said their goodbyes and walked home. Phillip and Benj remained behind with the Fishers.

Del was bursting with questions, as were her siblings. Bill, who shared a bed with Phillip, was very interested to learn if he'd now be back to sharing with Ollie. For Bill, Phillip was a much better choice, since Ollie thrashed about in his sleep.

Father said, "For the time being, Phillip will stay with us but I expect he'll want to spend more time with his family once he fully understands what happened to him."

While that answer pleased Bill, it left Del wondering about the circumstances that led to Phillip being found. The Fishers seemed like very nice people. How did their child get into the situation her Father found him in? She asked that very question.

Mama and Father looked at each other. Father said, "We'll tell you the full story at supper tonight," as everyone entered the house.

Mama nodded and ordered the children to hurry into their work clothes and do their chores. The children hustled through their chores, anxious to learn the story that led to Phillip's rescue months earlier.

That evening, after a satisfying meal of beef stew and mashed potatoes, Father related Phillip's story. "The Fisher family planned to move from Philadelphia to Baltimore, where Mr. Fisher had lined up steady work instead of the part-time job he had as an ice hauler. They sent their furniture on ahead, and bought bus tickets to get the family to their new home. Phillip, being under 6 at the time, was going to ride on the laps of his parents. However, the bus driver refused to believe that Phillip was that young, and wouldn't let him on without a ticket. They didn't have money for another ticket." Father paused and looked around at the children. "You know we live in hard times. People don't have lots of money, and especially when jobs are not easy to find. You know how it is for our neighbors. Mr. Fisher couldn't stay behind because he had a job waiting in Baltimore. Mrs. Fisher had to go because she also had a new job. Their two girls were already registered for school." Father shook his head. "It was a difficult situation, and the bus driver only made it worse by calling the police. You remember how Phillip reacted when he heard us mention police?"

Del and her silblings looked around and nodded at each other. Phillip had been very upset.

Father continued talking, "He certainly was affected by his memories of the scene at the bus station. Now Phillip's grandfather had gone with them to say goodbye to his family at the bus station, and said he would keep Phillip until the Fishers could save enough money for bus tickets to bring Mr. Fisher back to get Phillip. Mrs. Fisher said he said would be good to spend more time with his only grandson. While it was very upsetting for everyone, it was the best solution at that time."

Father sighed. "What happened next couldn't have been predicted by anyone. The grandfather wasn't in the best of health, and just a few hours after the rest of the family started their journey, he suffered a seizure and was taken to a hospital by his neighbors. They didn't know he had brought his grandson home with him, and Phillip hadn't spent much time at his grandfather's house, so he didn't know any of the neighbors. We can only guess that Phillip was taking a nap when this happened, because no one realized he was there. To make matters worse, his grandfather was not successfully revived and died at the hospital a day later."

Del gasped and saw that her brothers and sisters had looks of sympathy and concern on their faces.

Ollie couldn't resist asking a question. "But why didn't the neighbors contact Phillip's parents?"

Father smiled and said, "Oliver, you have a logical mind. The Baltimore address was written on a scrap of paper, and by the time responsible neighbors knew what happened to the grandfather and looked to find family, Phillip had wandered away from home, probably looking for anyone he knew." He paused again, with tears in his eyes. "I put myself in the position of the Fishers. They received news from those neighbors about the grandfather, but there was no mention of their son. The police showed up at the grandfather's neighborhood to search for Phillip too, but we suspect that he was afraid of men in uniforms given what he witnessed at the bus station and probably hid from them. The Fishers were frantic with worry about what happened to their boy, but lacked the resources to learn more. Mr. Fisher did make one trip back as soon as they got the bad news to look for his son, but he wasn't able to find him. They prayed that he was safe."

Mama looked each child in the face, and said, "Your Uncle Isaac's brother Ira is a police detective in Philadelphia. He made many inquiries. It took some time, but he finally found a neighbor who recognized Phillip from photographs we took after he had recovered and gained some weight. From there he was able to locate the Fishers in Baltimore. Once he made contact with them, he was able to determine the full story your father just told you. It was important for us to know that Phillip had a loving family that wanted him back, even though we all knew it would be hard to lose him."

The children were silent as they thought about what their parents told them. Del thought about how Carol, at practically the same young age, would have coped in a similar situation. "What would Carol think about her parents if it happened to her, or if it happened to me?" she wondered. "Would I blame them for what happened?" She also realized that some of the questions that had been nagging at her, like why her aunt Eva brought a camera along, and why Ira suddenly appeared in their lives now had answers.

Til asked, "Does Phillip know the full story? He never said anything about what happened, and I bet he didn't know why it happened."

"We asked him to tell us what he could, but he never said much," Mama said. "The doctor said it was probably such a terrible series of events that he wants to forget it. He said that is what happens sometimes when you experience a trauma."

"A what?" Ollie asked in bewilderment at this new word.

"Trauma," Mama replied. "Phillip may remember more details as time goes by. He definitely remembers his parents, but he also seems to consider Benj as family too." Mama and Father looked at each other for a moment, then Mama nodded.

Father said, "We talked it over with the Fishers, and we're all willing to give Phillip time to readjust to having his family around. We'll just be a second family for him, and Benj wants to be a grandfather to the entire Fisher family."

Del thought this was the perfect time to get more information about Benj as her parents were in a talkative mood. She took her chance. "What happened to Benj's family? Why is he so attached to Phillip?"

Ori rolled her eyes in disgust. "You're such a busybody!"

Father turned to Ori and said, "Gloria, it's an important question, and it's time you children hear what happened."

Ori turned bright red, but didn't say anything.

Father scanned the faces of all the children sitting at the table. They were all quiet, waiting to learn what happened to their neighbor's family. "Benj and his wife had two boys, Benjamin and Samuel. When the boys were alive, and long before I bought this farm, it used to belong to Becky and her husband, but they leased the land to other farmers. The barn wasn't used like it is now—it was empty except for some farm implements." He took a breath, and then continued talking. "You know that your mother and I have a rule that you cannot be on the barn threshold floor, but do you know why?"

All the children shook their heads no.

Father nodded. "It's because Benj's two boys were playing one day and saw that the barn door was open. They ran inside and while chasing each other around, fell through one of the trap doors that we use to shove hay and straw down to the cement floor below."

The children gasped and looked at each other. Bill and Til exchanged a glance, and Del suspected that they may have figured out the truth before hearing it from their father.

Father shook his head as he looked around at everyone at the kitchen table and said, "I heard that one boy died instantly from a broken neck. The other one lingered for a couple of hours before passing away. You see, there was no doctor around to help tend to him."

Mama broke in, "I heard it was something awful to see how Benj and Ann grieved over the loss of both children. She wasn't able to have any more, and she never recovered from the shock of losing her two sons in one day. She was ill for several years. People said that she just wanted to join her sons. Poor Benj took care of her until she passed away, and then just rattled around in his home by himself all those years. It wasn't until Adelaide and Bill came along that he showed any real interest in living again."

"Is that because we share the same birthday?" Del interrupted.

Mama nodded, "Yes, and that's one reason why we're making a big celebration for this year because of the rarity of the date also being Easter Sunday."

Del's head was spinning with all this news. Now she understood why Father had asked Benj, on that eventful night months ago if he was willing to go onto that threshold to stay with Phillip. Benj did it, even though it had to bring back the worst memories of his life.

All the children were quiet, each with their own thoughts. This information gave Del much to consider, and she realized that it explained so much about Benj's interactions with Phillip.

Finally Til asked, "How old were his boys?"

Mama said, "They were eight and ten years old when the accident took them." She looked at Father, and another unspoken moment occurred between them. She then closely looked into each child's eyes and sternly said, "Now don't you pester Benj with questions about this! You know, but you keep it to yourselves. He doesn't need to be reminded about it!"

Everyone nodded solemnly that they would not talk about it. Just then, Benj and Phillip entered the porch—it was time for Phillip, and the rest of the children, to get ready for bed. Del and Ori helped Mama wash dishes while Ollie and Phillip helped dry and put away dishes and utensils. As Del climbed the stairs to her bedroom, she heard Father say he would walk back to Benj's home with him, carrying an extra lantern to be sure that the old man arrived safely.

Del had answers to some of her questions, but many still remained. She wondered if God's hand had been at work to bring together Phillip and Benj, since she heard her parents often say that God works in mysterious ways. "There was so much to ponder on," she thought as she drifted off to sleep.

CHAPTER THIRTY-FOUR

Family Secrets

Del and her sisters plus Benj and Phillip were in the kitchen the next morning when Mr. Fisher knocked on the porch door. Mama walked out there and invited Mr. Fisher in, saying, "You don't have to knock—all our neighbors know they can just open the door and call out hello to let us know who is here."

Mr. Fisher thanked her and said hello to Phillip first, and then to all the other children.

Phillip said "Hello, daddy," and smiled at him.

Del noticed that Mr. Fisher looked pleased that his son called him that. Benj looked happy too, and patted Phillip on the back. She wondered if the trauma Mama had mentioned the previous evening was mending in Phillip.

Mr. Fisher asked Mama if Father was at home. He wanted to learn when they would go up to Mr. Henry's place.

Mama smiled and pointed to the barn. "Woodie and the boys are finishing up the morning chores. Why don't you join us for breakfast while you wait for him? I'm making bacon and eggs."

Mr. Fisher said, "No thanks, I already had breakfast but your cooking does smell good! I'll take a cup of coffee if you have that."

Mama quickly poured a cup and handed it to him. She said, "You won't need to call my father 'Mr. Henry'. Everyone calls him Billy Henry. You'll need to learn a little Pennsylvania Dutch to keep up with him."

Mr. Fisher laughed and said, "I'm not sure I can learn a different language."

Benj chuckled and said, "I'll teach ya, just like Phillip."

Mr. Fisher looked at Phillip and asked, "Son, will you help teach me some Dutch?"

Phillip giggled and nodded his head yes.

Father and the boys came in and exchanged greetings with Mr. Fisher. Del was very interested to learn why Father and Mr. Fisher were meeting with her grandfather. Her curiosity was soon satisfied. Grandfather wanted to hire Mr. Fisher as his handyman and take care of his horses and property until Mr. Fisher found another job more to his liking. Not only that, but he also wanted to hire Mrs. Fisher to cook and clean for him—similar to the work she had lined up in Baltimore before they moved.

Mama looked especially happy about that arrangement, and Del realized that Mama had worried more than she let on about Grandfather all alone in that big house of his. This would also mean more people were around him every day now that he was retired and he wouldn't be lonely.

Mr. Fisher was eager to get started. While he had some experience with horses, Grandfather was very particular about how his horses were treated.

Father said, "If everyone hears that you satisfied Billy Henry with your handling of his horses, you'll find more work because people will know you are capable."

Mr. Fisher said, "I'll do my best."

Benj nodded in agreement. The talk then turned to taking a walk around the Printz property to learn the boundaries. The men agreed to wait until it was a bit warmer for that.

Mama asked, "How are your wife and daughters settling in? Do you need anything?"

"Everything is going as good as can be expected," Mr. Fisher replied. "We still need to get the girls in school, but since this is the middle of the week, I'd like them to start next week so they can help Nancy get things organized at home." He turned to Phillip and said, "How do you feel about going to school again? I hear you've been getting lessons from a neighbor."

Phillip shyly said, "Ok, I want to go."

Del was now sure Mr. Straub had been giving lessons to Phillip while the other children were at the schoolhouse. That would explain those schoolbooks Til brought home. But before she could ask, Ollie did.

"Who was giving Phillip lessons?" he asked with a bit of suspicion. He wasn't too keen on spending time with a neighbor who could be another teacher in addition to the one he already had.

Mama wasn't happy that Ollie interrupted the adults' conversation. She gave him a look of warning and said, "Mr. Straub is a retired teacher. He worked with Phillip since we need time to complete the necessary paperwork—all easier now that he's back with his family." She turned to Mr. Fisher and said, "Your son will be well prepared to start school with his grade in September."

Mr. Fisher nodded. "I'll have to think of some way to pay Mr. Straub for his time."

Father said, "I think he enjoyed spending time with Phillip and teaching him his letters. I could be wrong, but I think he's happy to know that he did a good deed. We can go visit him today after talking with Billy."

Del and Ori helped Mama clean up breakfast once everyone had their fill and them Mama said, "You get to school today. You let your teacher tell the school that there will be new students joining next week. You don't talk about it until he announces it."

Del wondered when her parents had talked with Mr. Strunk to arrange for the two Fisher girls to start school. So many things happened outside of her observation that it was becoming difficult to keep up with all the changes. The children hurried off to school and were met by the Gohos as they walked up the lane. Ollie of course was the first to share the news about their new neighbors. He proudly informed them about being Phillip's family and how they had moved into the old Printz home.

Del chimed in, "We found Phillip's parents! Now we know the story about how Phillip came to be separated from them."

All the Heydt children supplied key pieces of information as the Gohos gasped and sighed in turn. The story wasn't fully told as they entered the schoolhouse yard, so Del and her siblings promised to complete the news at recess time. Mr. Strunk noticed the group of children and asked Til to go with him to fetch some water for the class-room, which he usually did when he wanted to have a word with Til. Del was curious what they talked about but had no chance to ask Til as Teacher rang the bell as soon as they returned with fresh water.

At recess time, Del told Em all the news about the new family in the Printz home.

Em was dumbfounded. "You mean you found Phillip's parents! Didn't they abandon him?"

Del emphatically shook her head. "Oh no! The bus driver didn't believe that Phillip didn't need a ticket. He wouldn't let him get on the bus."

In a puzzled tone, Em said, "Why wouldn't he believe Phillip's parents?"

Del shrugged. "I don't know, he just didn't."

Em had a very thoughtful look on her face, but then asked about the sisters. "What grades will they be in?" "Goodness, I don't know," Del admitted. "I never thought to ask. I'll have to ask Mama."

The Heydt children walked home for dinner and met Mrs. Fisher in the kitchen with Mama, Benj, and Phillip. Mrs. Fisher brought over a cookie that was Phillip's favorite before their accidental separation. It was clear to Del that he still liked them as he had one in his mouth and another cookie in his hand. Benj was eating one too, and said, "Never had a cookie like this. *Schmeckt gut* [Tastes good]!"

Mama allowed each of the children to have one cookie before eating their noon meal.

Del looked at hers, which looked like a sugar cookie but had chocolate chunks in it. She bit into it and said, "Yum!" So did her siblings.

Bill exclaimed, "What do you call this cookie?"

Mrs. Fisher said, "It's called the chocolate chip cookie. I got the recipe last year from a home where I did the cooking and cleaning."

Mama laughed and said, "I can tell from the children's faces that they really like this cookie. Will you give me the recipe?"

Mrs. Fisher said, "I sure will—as long as you give me the recipe for that hickory nut cake you mentioned."

Del asked Mrs. Fisher what grades Mattie and Arlee would be in when they started school.

She replied, "Well, Mattie is the oldest, and she's twelve. Arlene is two grades behind her and will be ten in a couple of months. We want to have your teacher test them to see what grades they should be in."

Mrs. Fisher turned to Mama. "We had another child, a boy, before Phillip, but he only lived a few hours," she said sadly. "When we lost Phillip, I thought I'd lose my mind."

Mama reached out a hand to Mrs. Fisher. "It's the most difficult situation a mother can face—losing a child," she said with real sympathy. Mama turned business-like very quickly and said, "Eat up everyone— it's just leftovers today, but there's plenty to find to eat."

The children ate quickly and returned to school, where Del satisfied Em's curiosity as best she could about the two new girls joining the school.

The rest of the week passed quickly, with Benj and Phillip splitting their time between the Heydt home and the Fisher home. There was even some talk Del overheard between her parents about 'easing Phillip into a new routine' although she wasn't quite sure what they meant.

Sunday started off as a typical day of rest. Del and her siblings attended church services and Sunday school after that, and Father picked them up, with Bill joining Grandfather to go directly to his place. Phillip and Benj were with the Fishers. But that early afternoon, things took an unusual turn. Bill came running home. It looked to Del like he had been crying when he burst into the house. He shouted at Mama and Father, "How could you lie to me?" turned, and ran out of the house. Father and Mama looked shocked, then Father asked Til to chase him down, and Til grabbed his jacket and flew out the door. Del and the rest of the children turned to each other in hopes of an explanation, but everyone was silent. Before Mama could even get any words out, Del heard Grandfather's horse and buggy pull to a stop by the house. Father rushed outside to help him down.

Grandfather was weeping as Father led him into the house, saying "I just couldn't keep the secret any longer. I told him the truth."

Del and Ori just looked at each other in total shock. What secret? What could he be talking about?

It was clear to her that Father and Mama were stunned, but not surprised. Del had never seen Mama turn so pale before, not even when she had been sick.

Mama just said over and over again, "How could you tell him without warning us first?" She finally realized that all the children were watching in worried silence, and Carol was beginning to cry. She ordered Ori to take Carol upstairs, and told Del and Ollie to run over to Becky's house and tell her she was needed.

Del and Ollie numbly obeyed her order. As they trotted out the doorway, Del looked back. Father had a stricken look on his face that she hadn't ever seen before. It frightened her.

Ollie turned to Del and pleaded, "What is going on???"

Del just shook her head and said, "I have no idea—but it's not good, whatever it is."

As they headed to Becky's house, they could hear Bill shouting, "Let me go, let me go!"

Both Del and Ollie turned in the direction of his shouting and saw Til, the older and bigger boy, holding Bill in a bear hug, hanging on as Bill flailed away at him. Father came running out and together they half carried, half dragged Bill into the house.

Del and Ollie ran up to Becky's door and knocked. When she opened the door, she scanned their faces and said, "What happened?"

Del and Ollie both tried to speak at once. Becky held up her hands and said, "Calm down—come inside and Del—you tell me what happened. Take a deep breath—both of you."

Del took a ragged breath, and then said, "Bill is really upset—he came into the house and yelled at my parents about lying, and then ran out. Grandfather came down to our house and said he couldn't keep the secret anymore. What secret?"

Ollie jumped in and said, "Mama told us to come and get you."

Becky stepped back and put a hand to her heart. "Ahh," she said. "*Nichts recht.* [Not right]." She gestured for them to stay there in the warm kitchen. "I must gather a couple things. Wait for me," she commanded.

Del and Ollie were unable to stand still. Del swayed back and forth and Ollie impatiently tapped his foot on the floor, and then started pacing until Becky returned with a wicker basket that contained several herb bundles and a couple of jars.

"Let's go," she said as she pulled on her coat and hat.

The three of them entered a house in an uproar. In the kitchen, Grandfather and Father were trying to calm down Bill, who sat at the table and had his head on his folded arms. He was sobbing. Til, frowning, tensely stood aside Mama, who focused her worried gaze from Bill to Grandfather and back again. Becky signaled to Mama that she had the fixings for a tea that would calm Bill down, and Mama set a pot of water on the stove.

Becky told Grandfather and Father to step aside and she seated herself on the bench next to Bill. She asked Bill to take a deep breath. Del felt herself doing the same. Bill gulped in some air and looked at Becky accusingly, "You were in on this secret too, weren't you?"

Becky simply nodded her head and said, "Yes."

Bill shuddered as he struggled for breath and composure. "Why?"

Grandfather started to say something but Becky silenced him with one raised hand. "Do you remember how some people reacted to Phillip coming here?"

Bill said, "Sure, but what does that have to do with me?"

Becky replied, "Some people look for anything negative to say or think. Maybe they just want to create problems. That was what we thought would happen if the truth was known back then."

Grandfather couldn't be silent any longer. "We didn't want you known as my bastard child."

Del, Til, and Ollie's mouths dropped open—all the adults had forgotten they were right there. Del stumbled backwards as the realization hit her—Bill was not her twin brother. If he was Grandfather's son, then he was her uncle! Ollie caught Del as she fell to the floor, crying.

Mama quickly seized control of the kitchen. "You and you," she said pointing to Til and Ollie, "put Del on the couch." She took a washcloth and ran cold water on it to place on Del's forehead. "Stay," she said to Del. She poured hot water over Becky's herbal mixture to steep.

Bill and Grandfather had eyes locked on each other. "Why did you wait until now to tell me?" Bill demanded.

Grandfather sighed, and said, "You needed to be old enough to handle the news, and I've watched you become a responsible young man who can do that. I'm very proud of you. You deserve the truth." He looked around at his grandchildren. "You all deserve the truth. Call Ori and Carol downstairs."

Ollie raced up the stairs to get them as Becky handed a cup of her tea to Bill and Mama handed one to Del.

When Ori and Carol were seated on the rocking chair and everyone else was at the kitchen table or on the couch with Del, Grandfather said in Dutch, "My wife died of diphtheria twenty years ago, along with my eldest daughter, her husband and their baby—my first grandchild. I regularly went to Philadelphia with my butter and eggs and stayed as a lodger overnight on those trips rather than return home to a cold and empty house. The landlady and I became very friendly, and then she was pregnant. I was prepared to marry her, but she died in childbirth. I brought you," Grandfather pointed to Bill, "along home. You were born on the 22nd. Adelaide was born on the twenty-fourth. It was not easy for me to ask my daughter if she would raise my son for me, because I was ashamed of my behavior. But my daughter and son-in-law have been very kind. Becky had to know since she was there for Adelaide's birth, but agreed to the story we told about twins. Benj also knew the truth from the very beginning—there's not much that gets past that man. It's not easy for me to say this, but I'm sorry for what I did. I am not sorry to have you as my son."

The room was silent. Tears slid down Del's face. She felt like something was ripped out of her body. She had heard adults talk about heartache, and suspected that's what she felt now.

Bill listened to his real father's explanation in silence. He turned to Father and Mama. "When did you plan to tell me the truth?" he demanded.

Father and Mama looked at each other, then Father said, "We wanted you to be old enough to understand, and make sure people knew you for who you are, not for any label that could be put on you. There are people in this township who are on the lookout to make trouble. No child needs that. But it was his," Father nodded to Grandfather "decision to declare himself as your real father."

"What happens now?" Bill pressed on with questions and in a challenging tone he wouldn't have presumed to use with adults just a few hours earlier.

Del's grandfather answered, "You may live here or live with me—it's up to you. You will be my heir and I will give you my last name if you want it. You have my first name already."

"I need to think about this," Bill said.

"Take as much time as you need, son," Grandfather said. He slowly left the room, put on his coat, and headed outside. Father followed him.

Mama turned to Del and asked, "Are you alright?"

Del shook her head no. She felt miserable. More than anything else she wanted to talk with Bill, but he wouldn't even look her way.

Bill finally stood up and said, "I am going to take a walk, alone."

Mama nodded, but said, "You come back now, you hear?" She held Del's hand, an unusual gesture from a woman who generally didn't have time for any acts of tenderness. Even Ori looked at Del with sympathy, while Carol, not fully understanding the situation, stroked Del's hair.

CHAPTER THIRTY-FIVE

That Once-in-a-Lifetime Birthday

Two weeks passed. In that time, the family agreed that they would not tell the community yet about Bill's real father. Mama was very stern in warning everyone to not share the news about Bill, with extra emphasis placed on Ollie. He knew he'd be the first one suspected of spilling the beans, and promised solemnly that he would not say a word. It was agreed that the news would be spread once school ended. That way, all talk would die down by the time the children returned to school.

For Del, it was very hard to continue on as if nothing had happened. Neither she nor Bill went to school the Monday after Grandfather's revelations. Mama decided they needed extra time to adjust to the news. Em knew something was different when Del returned, and the teacher asked her what kept her and Bill from school. She just said they were both kept at home because Mama was fearful they were coming down with something.

The big day—Easter Sunday—finally arrived. Del awoke, stretched, and reluctantly rolled out of bed to get ready for the early Easter sunrise service. Maybe this day would be a happy day. The whole family attended, all in their Sunday best. Many women, like Mama, sewed new outfits especially for Easter Sunday with new hats too. Del was intrigued to see that busybody, Litzy, and her family seated in the very front pew. She wondered where they had been for those months of absence from church. Even more curious, the family seated up there never arose to sing, and they received communion seated in that front pew instead of walking up to the altar rail like everyone else. It wasn't until later at the birthday party that the family learned the reason why.

Mama and Father left after the church service. They needed to get home to prepare for the big birthday party. Bill had decided he would keep the 24th as his birthday, and no one would be the wiser at the party about him actually being two days older than Del.

Grandfather was at the church services too. Til stayed with him and went back to his house after services. Bill was still struggling to accept the news about his real father, and didn't want to spend time with him. It was a sad situation, but Del heard Mama and Father say that everyone needed time for this to be resolved. She wondered if her heartache would heal over time.

Father had brought one of Grandfather's heavy wooden chairs on his truck the day before so he had a comfortable seat for himself for the birthday celebration. Grandfather was seated on his chair in the side room where most of the activity was going to take place. Eva and Isaac were the first guests to come. They brought a large cake made by a bakery in their town. It was the first time Del had seen Happy Birthday written in colored icing. There were frosting flowers of all colors. Benj and Bill's names were in bright blue icing and Del's was in deep pink. Ed and Hester arrived, but did not bring their son. He preferred to stay with his grandparents on weekends, and go to a park for pony rides. Lillie and Sam came. They brought a good quantity of blue mint tea that they placed in the milkhouse to stay cold. They brought a large dish of chocolate pudding also, knowing it was Del's favorite. Becky came with sticky popcorn balls on sticks. The Fisher family arrived with Benj. Nancy made her chocolate chip cookies and brought a large batch to share. The whole neighborhood crowded into the house. For many of the outlying neighbors, it was their first chance to meet the Fishers. Del overheard many greetings and expressions of welcome and gratitude that the family was reunited. It seemed to her that that was one very serious situation with a happy ending.

Del was standing next to Bill when Phillip walked up to Bill. "You," he said as he put a finger up to Bill's chest, "you have a good home." The little boy just held Bill's gaze until Bill nodded in agreement, and then Phillip walked away. Del wondered if he heard about her Grandfather's story.

Becky came, and, to Del's surprise, Rachael was with her. She was accompanied by a teenaged Black girl, a Chinese boy with coal-black hair, and a younger boy with curly blonde hair. She introduced her children. "This is Susanna, my daughter, and these are my sons Adam and Newton. For the sake of the Fishers who were trying to sort out how Rachael could have children of such different backgrounds, Becky explained, "Rachael runs an orphanage for a few children who lost their parents. She brought Susanna and some other children down to meet Phillip over the past few months."

Del observed that Phillip did hold Susanna's hand and seemed to know the other children too. She suddenly remembered Phillip saying, 'Like me, like me' that memorable day when she surprised Rachael at the Conrad farm. He must have been talking about Susanna being the first person he'd seen with his same skin color since he arrived in New Jerusalem.

Rachael walked over to Del and said, "I am sorry I yelled at you, but I was so surprised to see you and reacted badly. There are lots of rumors in this town when people see me with children. She looked over at Susanna and said, "She wants to be a nurse too, but she only wants to work with children."

Susanna heard Rachael speak and walked over to them. She nodded and said, "Since I lost my parents when I was young, I know how a young child understands what happened. These changes need lots of time to adjust to. We all understood Phillip suffered terribly when he was separated from all the kin he ever knew, so we thought it would help for him to see and talk to others who had similar experiences."

Del nodded her head, and thought Susanna would be a good person to talk to about the situation with her and Bill. But not today.

Hester sheepishly walked up to Rachael. "When I saw you, you were pregnant. The next time I saw you, you had a Black baby." Hester paused. "Well, I immediately thought she was your child. I'm so very sorry I jumped to the wrong conclusion and started a rumor about you. I should know better. I'm not surprised that you have the same kindness and generosity that your mama, Becky, has." Rachael only hesitated for a moment before reaching out to take Hester's hand.

During the festivities, Ed was busy all day taking the children, two at a time, to walk out the lane to Benj's property and show them the feathered young roosters. The roosters were beginning to crow in the mornings. They would soon be big enough to sell at the market. The neighbors exchanged a little gossip at the party, which included news about why the busybody and her family were seated at church services. Litzy fell down the stairs, and since her husband was ahead of her, he tumbled down them too. She broke a hip and might never walk correctly again. Her husband broke an arm. They stayed away from church while they were healing up. It was basic pride that wouldn't allow her to let people know she couldn't walk without help.

Mama just said, "That's terrible news, and I wish her well."

Del thought maybe this was just desserts for the trouble she caused to everyone in the area with her deliberate rumors and outright lies. She knew that wasn't kind of her to think that, but she couldn't help but wonder how differently her life would have been if her Grandfather hadn't been concerned about malicious gossip.

Benj introduced the neighbors to the Fishers and called them his new family. When it was time to blow out candles and cut the cake, he said his wishes had come true because he now had a new family to care for. Everyone applauded, and Del could see a couple of women dabbing their eyes with handkerchiefs. Everyone congratulated Del and

Bill on their eleventh birthdays, but the wishes rang hollow to Del, and she suspected Bill felt the same.

The party started winding down as the day turned to dusk. People again congratulated Benj on reaching his seventy-fifth birthday and wished the same for Del and Bill. There were still the evening chores to do, but Eva and Isaac pitched in and Del's chores were done quickly. Father and the boys entered the house. They had finished the evening farm chores. Ori took Carol upstairs; after running around with all the smaller children she was ready for bed. Even though, or maybe in spite of, this being a special day for Del, Ori had been busy all day reminding people again and again that she suggested the name Phillip, and he wanted to keep it. She had plenty of opportunities to do that since her job was to keep refilling empty glasses with tea from the pitcher.

As Del settled into her bed, she thought about all the changes that had occurred in the past few months. Her special day seemed a lot less special given recent events, but she was very happy for Phillip and how things were working out with his family and with Benj.

The first week of April came. School was now over until the day after Labor Day. The snow was all melted, except for the very high snow banks in shady areas. Father decided that since the snows were all but gone, he would ask Mr. Fisher, Sol, as he preferred to be called, to walk along the boundary lines to the Printz home property. That following Sunday afternoon Father, Sol, Til, and Bill walked the property lines. Father explained that Sol could shoot rabbits and pheasants on the Printz home property without a hunting license, if he wanted to. Til, an excellent hunter, offered to take him along to share some of his knowledge. They walked the acreage and then along the lines of the Heydt fields and property. While walking along the areas of Father's land along a raspberry row and then the strawberry patch, it was Til who saw something pink under a thin layer of snow. He pointed to it. "I never before saw snow that color when it's melting."

Father looked, and then looked closer. Then he and the boys started laughing, explaining to Sol, that here was the pink sweater Mama had been accusing all of them of having hidden somewhere!

Bill told Del what happened later. Father decided to put it in the washhouse where Mama would find it on Monday morning. They all had a good laugh about it, and the boys could hardly keep a sober face that evening at the supper table. Mama knew something was amiss, but they weren't telling—it seemed everyone was good at times at keeping a secret.

On Monday morning, Mama wanted to get an early start on the washing. She almost immediately returned to the kitchen. "Okay," Mama said, "Who found my sweater?"

Father, Til, and Bill burst out laughing. "You left it in the strawberry patch to keep the plants warm all winter. We'll have big, bright red strawberries this year," Father teased.

Spring, summer, and fall were busy times for farmers. Sowing garden vegetable seed, planting corn, and cultivating between corn and garden rows to keep weeds from growing faster than the young plants was hard work. Then would come harvesting wheat and oats and grass fields to feed immediately to the cattle or to dry for hay. Then September would come and the start of another school year. And so Del and her family, now forever changed, continued on.

Years later, when Del was a grown woman, she would reflect back on the year she turned eleven and the months and weeks leading up to it. Times were hard, but people took care of each other. Neighbor helped neighbor and families supported each other. It was a time when what had been lost was found, and what had been thought to be true was false. Circumstances shook her family and herself to the core, changing hearts, changing minds, and changing plans.

Bill eventually moved in with his real father, Del's grandfather, until Grandfather passed away. That happened when Bill was eighteen. He had never really forgiven any of the adults for the secret they shared, and he left the area after that funeral. Del rarely heard from him, and she was the only one he ever contacted. There was an occasional postcard, always from a different state, that just said he was well and hoped she was too.

The Fishers became an established and respected family in the small community, and they eventually bought the orchard when the Wolfgangs retired but remained in what was still called the 'old Printz home.' Del figured that name would never change. Phillip grew strong and tall, and remained devoted to Benj until his final days. Benj left everything to Phillip and his sisters, who he informally adopted as his new family, and the Fishers likewise treated him as one of their own. With the money Benj left them, all three Fisher children went off to college and found success, but none of them continued the orchard when their parents retired. Phillip never missed a Heydt birthday or holiday celebration, and even when he moved away to California with his engineering job, he remained in regular contact with all of them.

Del's parents continued to farm and did well, eventually adding another farm to their holdings. They had many grandchildren running around on their farms, playing mostly, not responsible for the daily chores their parents had to complete.

Til was drafted for World War 2 and thankfully survived the most combat days of any US soldier in the European theater. He said it was due to being a Pennsylvania Dutch country boy—he had hunted his entire life and knew how to live off the land. He also understood the German language. Those skills served him well from North Africa to Germany and every battleground in between. The men who served with him said they wouldn't have survived the war without him. When he came back he never picked up a gun again. He took over the family farm when Father retired.

Ori longed to get a city job, and she did land a factory job when she graduated from the eighth grade. She was done with hard farm work and with country life. She moved to a nearby town and was content to have a little garden, but no more. She eventually married a man who had an orchard, but she refused to do more than sell apples at their roadside stand. She and Del never really got along when they were young, and that didn't change as they grew older. Del was happy that their paths didn't cross very often.

Ollie also wanted to get away from the farming life, so he learned the welding trade in high school. When they were still children, he used to ask Del if he was really her brother or if he was like Bill. Del didn't know how to answer him other than say he was too much like Aunt Lillie, Father's half sister, to be from anyone other than Father. He stayed in the area, met and married a nice girl from the Boyertown area, and ended up building a home on a parcel of land from Father's farm.

Carol, as the youngest child, had the fewest memories of the year Phillip arrived or the following revelations about Bill. Maybe that was why she seemed to have the least cares of any of the Heydt children, and she was always laughing. But farm life was not for her either, and she had a long career working in progressively more senior managerial positions for a nearby factory even as she married and raised a family. Del remained close with her and her children.

As for Del, she finished high school and wanted to go to college, but her parents couldn't afford to send her. She joined the Army to start a career in computers, but had promised her parents she would come home once her enlistment was up. They had lost Bill, and they didn't want to lose her too. And she did come home, where local employers refused to believe a woman could do the technical work she did. She took care of both Father and Mama until their deaths, and was the one in the family that everyone turned to for advice. She often wondered how differently things would have worked out if Grandfather had kept his secret to his grave, because it seemed to her that her parents were committed to doing that. They often told her how they regretted the way things turned out with Bill, and hoped to their dying days to see him again, but they never did. All Del could do was hope that one day she'd be able to tell that to the man she still considered her brother.

RECIPES

These old family recipes were handwritten and being old, don't always have the detailed instructions modern recipes have. An oven temperature was rarely provided, and quantities of some items were judgment calls. For these recipes, use an oven temperature of 350 degrees Fahrenheit and use your best judgment on when things are completely baked.

A.P. Cakes

1 C granulated sugar
1 C shortening
1 C milk
1 ½ t baking powder
½ t baking soda
Flour to stiffen the dough

Arrange dough in a ball on a greased pie tin. Flatten with your palm to spread over the base of the tin. Sprinkle the top with granulated sugar and bake at 350 degrees Fahrenheit until the top is lightly browned.

Funny Cakes

MIXTURE I
2 C granulated sugar
¾ C shortening
2 eggs
1 C milk
2 C flour
2 t baking powder

MIXTURE 2
1 C granulated sugar
½ C cocoa
1 C hot water
1 t vanilla
Four 7 or 8 inch pie tins
with raw pie shells.

Mix each batter in a separate bowl. Pour the chocolate mixture into the pie shells. Pour Mixture 1 on top. Bake at 400 degrees Fahrenheit for 15 minutes then reduce to 350 degrees for 30 minutes.

Shoo Fly Pie

1 C light brown sugar
¼ C shortening
1 ½ C flour
1 C molasses
1 C hot water
1 t baking soda

Cream sugar and shortening. Add flour. Scoop ¾ C of this crumb mixture aside.

Combine molasses, hot water and baking soda in separate bowl. Add liquid to main portion of crumb mixture and stir. Batter will be lumpy. Pour into two raw pie shells. Spread reserved crumb mixture on top of batter. Bake at 400 degrees Fahrenheit for 15 minutes, and reduce temperature to 350 degrees for 30 minutes.

Hickory Nut Cake

½ C shortening
1 ½ C granulated sugar
2 C flour
2 t baking powder
1 t salt
¾ C milk
1 C ground hickory nuts
1 t vanilla
4 eggs (separate whites from yolks)

Cream shortening and sugar. Add in egg yolks and mix well. Combine flour, baking powder and salt, mix into the sugar and eggs. Stir in milk and vanilla. Stir in ground nuts. Whip egg whites to soft peaks and fold into the batter.

Pour into two greased and floured 8 inch round cake pans. Bake at 350 degrees for 40 minutes or until done. Cool the two layers on cake racks and then ice the layer cake with Hickory Nut icing.

HICKORY NUT ICING

1 C granulated sugar
1 C ground hickory nuts
1 C milk
2 T butter
½ T flour

While the cake is baking, combine all ingredients into a saucepan and slowly heat to boiling, then keep on low heat, stirring frequently, until the liquid thickens. Allow to cool and then carefully spread on cooled cake layers.

Crumb Cake

2 C granulated sugar
½ C shortening
2 eggs
1 C milk
1 t baking powder
1 t cream of tartar
2 ½ C flour
pinch of salt

Cream sugar and shortening. Beat in the eggs, and alternate adding the remaining dry ingredients with the milk. If you like, you can add in 1 t vanilla or almond flavoring to the batter. Pour into layer cake pans or an angel food cake pan.

CRUMB TOPPING

2 T sugar
1T butter
½ C flour

Combine these ingredients—use your hand if necessary to create a crumbled consistency. Spread on top of the cake batter and bake at 350 degrees Fahrenheit for 30-40 minutes or until done.

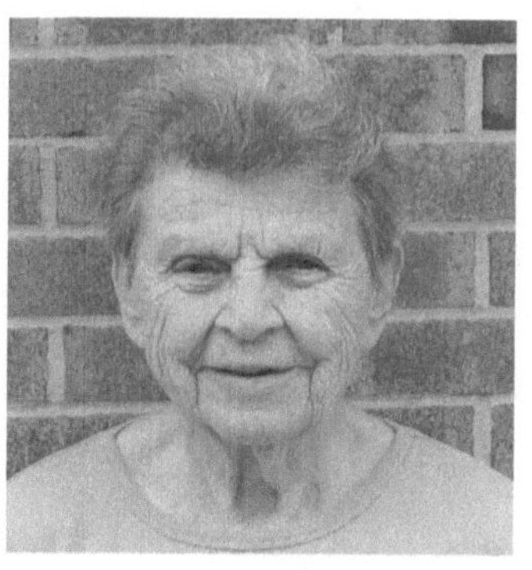

ABOUT THE AUTHOR

Ruth Hertzog was born and raised on a farm in New Jerusalem, Pennsylvania on March 24, 1926. She attended a one-room schoolhouse through 8th grade and then went to high school nearby. She joined the war effort and became a code girl working as a civilian in the Army on the early computers used to decrypt enemy communications. After the war ended, she returned home and worked an office job in the local hosiery mills until getting married and raising two children. She has been the caregiver for her family her entire life, including nursing care for her mother and father, child care for siblings, more nursing care for her husband, and rescuing a sibling from elder abuse (while in her 80s). She's been a pillar of her church, becoming the first woman to sit on her church council and teaching the adult Sunday school class for decades. She managed volunteers every summer making chow-chow as a popular fundraiser for her church. Countless quarts and pints of that chow-chow traveled coast to coast as she negotiated with suppliers. She was the tax collector for her township for a number of years and then focused her energies on organizing trips for a nearby senior citizens center. She did all this while being a homemaker.

It was only after taking care of everyone and everything else that she could focus on her own intense desire to write. This story has been a long time coming. She now resides in a retirement community in Topton, PA where her children, grandchildren, and great-grandchild plus her siblings and their children know they can count on birthday and Christmas cards from her.